RASPUTIN'S BASTARDS

DAVID NICKLE

ChiZine Publications

FIRST EDITION

Library and Archives Canada Cataloguing in Publication

Nickle, David, 1964-
Rasputin's bastards / David Nickle.

Also issued in electronic format.
ISBN 978-1-926851-59-4

I. Title.

PS8577.I33R38 2012 C813'.54 C2012-900397-2

CHIZINE PUBLICATIONS
Toronto, Canada
www.chizinepub.com
info@chizinepub.com

Edited and copyedited by Sandra Kasturi
Proofread by Samantha Beiko

Canada Council for the Arts Conseil des Arts du Canada

We acknowledge the support of the Canada Council for the Arts which last year invested $20.1 million in writing and publishing throughout Canada.

ONTARIO ARTS COUNCIL
CONSEIL DES ARTS DE L'ONTARIO

Published with the generous assistance of the Ontario Arts Council.

Printed in Canada

RASPUTIN'S BASTARDS

незаконнорождённые
дети Распутина

to Olga Nickle
who dreams better dreams than anyone within these covers

Dramatis Personae
Главные герои

The Spies

Alexei Kilodovich—A spy who remembered
Fyodor Kolyokov—A spy who loved too much
Lena—A spy who adored life
Babushka—A spy who disdained death
Jean Kontos-Wu—A diligent spy
Vasili Borovich—A spy who dreamed badly
The Koldun—A spy who slept quietly
Richard [REDACTED]—A spy who broke
Miles Shute—A spy repurposed
Ilyich Chenko—A spy who made his fortune in real estate
Tanya Pitovovich—An associate of Chenko's; a spy who is good at it

The Americans

Stephen Haber—A talentless orphan
Holden Gibson—A terrible father
Heather [REDACTED]—A rebellious daughter
James [REDACTED]—A recalcitrant son
Leo Montassini—A man in who fell into mystery
Gepetto Bucci—His boss

Dramatis Personae
Главные герои

The Turks

Amar Shadak—A purveyor of arms and collector of submarines
Konstantine Uzimeri—A "submarine guy"

The Children

Vladimir—A baby, filled with too much wisdom
Zhanna—A girl, filled with too much love

The Villagers of New Pokrovskoye

Darya Orlovsky—A shopkeeper of surpassing beauty
Pavel Orlovsky—Her father, who stopped killing without regret
Nikolay Trolynka—A fisherman
Makar Trolynka—His son

"A particle of the Supreme being is incarnated in me. Only through me can you hope to be saved; and the manner of your salvation is this: you must be united with me in soul and body."

—**Grigori Yefimovich Rasputin**

"All happy families are alike."

—**Leo Tolstoy**

PROLOGUE

пролог

The steam carried the smell of Babushka's death like a soaked sponge. It leaked between the wooden slats of the bath house's door, and whipped and whirled from there in thin, hot tendrils to mingle with the ice fog that had enshrouded the village of New Pokrovskoye since the early days of March.

March was an important month. It was the month that Babushka had first set down a schedule for her own death; the month the giant squid came to the harbour and presaged it all, by dying there itself.

The squid arrived sometime in the night. It thrashed and twisted underneath the translucent grey ice for hours before it died, its tentacles braiding and spreading—a woman's long dark hair in a suicide bath.

Suicide seemed the best explanation. The squid could have dived—gone back south, and deep, into the cool dark ocean where its brethren dwelled in unguessable numbers. But something stopped it; or it knew, somehow, that its time was up. Whatever the reason, it stayed there beneath the harbour ice of New Pokrovskoye, thrashing and twisting until finally it slowed—its giant form stretching under the grey-green sheet for fifteen metres, like a great, dark stroke of watercolour.

Babushka wheeled herself out onto the ice in the predawn, breath making a contrail behind her as she huffed along to the squid's remains. The ice creaked as she leaned forward in her wheelchair, propped on her walking stick, and glared down at the creature.

The walking stick was old. It was said that it had been carried to St. Petersburg by a holy man a hundred years ago, and was cut many years before that—and it was hard as iron. She leaned over, hacking at the ice, eventually tumbling out of her chair and falling to her knees with the effort. By this time, someone had called the Koldun—the fishing village's lodge wizard and healer, second only to Babushka herself in esteem and influence.

He went out and joined her for a time. A growing crowd of villagers watched at the bank as he wheedled and cajoled and finally took hold of her arm. But she shook off his attempt angrily, and that was all it took. The Koldun had known Babushka for many years. But neither he nor anyone else dared confront her when she became like this.

She glared down into the squid's eye for a full minute—then finally, drew back, barked a harsh laugh, and spat in it.

She turned to the Koldun and the rest, and that was when she said it, loud enough to carry through the whole, ice-bound village:

"When this kraken is gone—I go too."

The Koldun and the others laughed, uncomfortably at first—and then, as she joined them, with more assurance.

And because of that, the people of New Pokrovskoye concluded:

Everything is fine. It's just another of Babushka's jokes.

But it was no joke.

Babushka knew the lay of her years the same as she knew the lay of this foreign and rocky earth, the hearts of the men and women who believed they controlled it, and the movements of the long, dreaming war that had long ago faded to mere skirmishes. As the ice from the waters in the north mingled with the waters to the south, so would Babushka mingle with the air.

And so Babushka reached from the bath house, and quit of her flesh, she joined the icy air swirling in the breaths of her grandchildren.

To each one, Babushka's scent was different. Darya Orlovsky, who had suckled at the Babushka's teat and loved her more dearly than her own mother, smelled breast milk and coffee and sausage. "Oh," she said, as she lifted a crate of caviar from the back of the truck and turned to carry it into the store. "Babushka."

Old Nikolay Trolynka, who was in his fishing boat as it crossed the part of the harbour where candle wax chunks of the iceberg had still floated just a day before, smelled ginger and garlic. "Ah," he said, nodding to himself. "'The kraken goes, and so do I.' That explains it."

"Heh?" said Makar, Nikolay's oldest son. His nostrils flared around a sharper smell—of sulphur and mint—as he wheeled the fishing boat.

"Babushka," said his younger brother Oleg, smelling old sweat not his own. "She has gone, and drawn the fish with her."

"Makes as much sense as anything." Makar ran his arm across his nose and snorted. It did no good; the smell remained.

It remained, and it spread—through the town store, in hues of blueberry and whiskey and pine needle; in shades of clove and musk and olive, through the rambling Museum of Family History that was the Koldun's gift many years past; and across the fishery, where the flatulent stench of rotting cod guts was replaced by a mélange of odours—each one better or worse than fish death, depending upon the predisposition of the particular grandchild's nose that it touched.

Babushka's body lay still on the top bench of the bathhouse. Babushka herself rested somewhat higher, suspended above her great, still breasts, in a concentrated cloud of vapours.

The Koldun removed his coat and set it on the peg in the dressing chamber, before he pulled the door shut behind him.

So you did it, said the Koldun. His eye moved up and down, from the Babushka's body to her essence and back again. *I confess, my dear, I am puzzled. You had obviously been planning this. Yet why?*

The essence of Babushka whirled and twisted, as the air from the closing door swept to the rafters. The Koldun understood it as a shrug.

Why now? You should have to ask. Look at the world, my dearest. It is past ten years ago that our masters are fallen. Yet we still live for their dying will.

Not so, said the Koldun. *When was the last time that any of us were called in the night? When was the last time we even heard them in Discourse? And really—you never lived for them. We all live for ourselves. For our children.*

The essence of Babushka loosened itself, and spread across the cedar ceiling planks like a pool of liquid, inverted.

For our children. Her voice was a whispering in the Discourse. *The ones we know of, perhaps . . .*

What are you talking about? 'The ones we know of.' The Koldun rocked back and forth on his heels uneasily. He looked again at the Babushka's body—heavy and naked, its flesh was yellow as an old bruise. He looked up again at the steam at the ceiling. It was dissipating; the Babushka's voice was fading.

The Koldun stepped over to the water barrel, and dipped the ladle in to pull out a cup of rainwater. Eyeing the ceiling, he flung the water onto the rocks by the fire. Hot steam stung his eyes and burned down his throat.

What do you mean? said the Koldun again. *'The ones we know of?'*

The Babushka was angry now, though; she roiled and burned across the ceiling, and crept toward the crack above the door.

Enough, she said. *I will go see my grandchildren now.*

You already have, said the Koldun. *Your passing is known across the village.*

Across the village perhaps it is, she said, *but I must yet visit my grandchildren. All of them. Across the world. They must all know.*

The Koldun raised an eyebrow at that. *The world?* he wondered, but he didn't pass that thought on to Babushka.

That's a great many grandchildren, he said, *if you mean the whole of City 512 and—*

City 512—pah! The cloud rolled back from the door now. It thickened, and began to descend. *You have no idea, my love. You could not have had an idea, until a time such as now.*

A time such as now?

A time of gathering, my love. The cloud crept further down the walls of the sauna. Its belly fattened. *A great gathering, here in the harbour—here in New Pokrovskoye. A gathering of the children we've loved and dreamed. And more. Of children whose fine luck was to never know their fathers. Who never knew us.*

What are you planning?

You know, said Babushka, and drew in upon him.

They cremated the body a day later, in a pyre near the lighthouse. There was no shortage of ceremony to go with the burning. The town gathered first in the greenhouse, where they sang and drank and wept in accordance with their understanding of the Babushka's final wishes. Then they moved, with the body, up the hill to the pyre of driftwood. It took five men to lift the Babushka's litter onto that pyre. All stood and watched as the wood lit, and breathed deeply of the scent, as the fire grew to consume her ancient flesh.

Everyone in the village attended—everyone but for one, and he was excused for obvious reasons. For the past day, the Koldun had lain wrapped and snoring in the Babushka's blankets at the bathhouse. When he was finished dreaming on her behalf, no doubt he would join the village to remember their matriarch in fitting form.

Or such was the word around the village. In truth, the Koldun would have no trouble remembering Babushka, whom he had loved and served in life.

And now, in death, whom he was preparing to betray.

In his dreams, the Koldun found himself drawing back to Babushka's whispered answer to his question.

What am I planning?

Many things: to be loved; to be remembered; to be worshiped, maybe; to set things right, perhaps.

But one thing for certain.

Not, my love, to ever die.

THE IDIOT
Идиот

The face looming over his own could have belonged to God: an old, tired, and infinitely pissed-off God.

Well, thought Alexei Kilodovich as he gazed up into His heavenly glare, *He has every right to be*. God must have better places to be than here out in the rain on the deck of a boat in the middle of an Atlantic night, pulling an undeserving wretch like Alexei Kilodovich out of the drink. One small eye squinted as a rivulet of water ran into a tiny pink tear duct from the broad slope of His forehead.

"What the fuck happened to you?" He demanded.

Alexei looked back at the face and considered the question, and the unspoken questions that cascaded from that one.

How did you get that bruise on your own forehead, all yellow and blue and soft? How did you wind up in that little dingy, here in the Atlantic? How could you let Mrs. Kontos-Wu down? Leave her to the Romanians?

How could you be so stupid?

Alexei opened his mouth to answer. But the truth stuck in his throat like a bone.

"I remember nothing," he lied, and with that lie he settled into a new role: the amnesiac castaway, confused and grateful and frightened—but most of all confused—as much a mystery to himself as he is to his benefactors.

"Ah," said God, "should have let you drown." And He pulled away and vanished in the dark.

"Did your boat sink?" It was a new face this time—a long one, with a little van Dyke beard and a head shaved bald. His breath smelled funny—like burning sugar, and something beyond. The smell came and went as a sea breeze.

"I do not—" Alexei paused, to frown and think on the question, or at least give the appearance of honest thought "—I do not remember."

"What about its name?" asked a young woman who sounded American—possibly from the southern States, maybe Georgia. "Your boat's name."

"It was—" Alexei made a show of snapping his fingers, as if the noise alone would summon up the name like a well-trained dog.

"No," he said. "I am sorry."

"What are you doing off Maine?" said the bald man. "You sound Russian or something."

"Maine?" said Alexei. The woman was pulling up the rope ladder from their own boat. This one was at least as large as the Romanians' big cabin cruiser—from the brief glimpse of it he'd gotten as it approached his raft, he'd guessed it might be even larger, and more opulent. From inside the main cabin, Alexei could hear faint music—although he couldn't tell what kind, against the noise of the ocean. Yellow light shone warm as a fire through the curtains of a nearby porthole. It all should have conspired to give him comfort. . . .

Comfort is the torturer's first tool. Succumb to that, and you've failed already. Who had said that? Alexei frowned, and shivered. Maybe the amnesia trick wasn't such a lie after all.

"You can't not know where Maine is," said the woman. She had the hood of her raincoat up, so he couldn't see much of her. But the skin on her face shone like a seal pelt in the misting rain, and her eyes, small and suspicious, flashed at him. "You can't," she repeated.

"It is in the United States," replied Alexei. He let a sliver of uncertainty creep into the trailing sentence for effect. "Sure."

"So you haven't forgotten *everything*," said the woman. "What year is it? You know that?"

"1997," he said, and she said, "See?"

She threw her hood back, damp hair falling to her shoulders in faux-Rasta Medusa-snakes. She was younger than he'd thought—not more than twenty-five, certainly, with an oval face, scorched eyebrows and small dark eyes—and in the act of pulling back the hood, the accusation in her eyes had changed to a kind of triumph.

Alexei let his hand flutter up to the cut on his forehead. "Ah," he said, and loosened his knees. *Take me to a bunk*, he willed, as he let his eyes turn up into his skull and relaxed his shoulders before he hit the hard wood slats of the deck. *Take me inside, make me warm and well, and save your questions for the morning.*

"Take him inside," shouted the bald man. "Get him warmed up, and lay off the questions—plenty of time for that later. Okay, Heather?"

Alexei had to fight to keep his mouth slack, suppress the smile. His mother would have said he'd had the power. The strength of a Koldun, a lodge wizard, going through him. She had believed in that kind of thing.

Heather grunted something and took hold of an arm. Another crewmember took Alexei's other arm, and together they hefted him off the deck. Alexei was a big man—no fat on him, but like they used to say back at school, he had lead in his muscles. He let them drag him under the canopy and inside, down some stairs to the warm lower deck where the cabins were. Long before the crew selected a bunk for him, gotten him out of his sodden clothes and wrapped him in thick woolen blankets, Alexei slipped into genuine unconsciousness—a blank, dreamless oblivion that erased Mrs. Kontos-Wu, the Romanians, and the kids. Especially them: the little bastard kids that put him in this predicament to begin with.

"Did they try to kill you? Is that it?"

Alexei blinked awake. There was a bandage wrapped around his head, and from the prickly aching underneath, he thought that someone might have sutured up the gash in his scalp. Although it wasn't bright, the white fluorescent light in the cabin hurt his eyes and for a moment he couldn't focus.

"Hey. I'm talking to you." Alexei felt a hand on his shoulder, saw a blurry shadow intersect the light. It was another American, and his breath stank of garlic or something, and all told he made Alexei want to puke. But he held it down.

"Who are you?" asked Alexei. "I can't see well right now."

The hand moved off his shoulder, and the shadow settled back to resolve itself into the shape of a round-shouldered hulk of a man. He could have been the one from the deck—probably he was—but he reminded Alexei more of some of his former colleagues. It was something in the heaviness he projected; a weight that went beyond his wide jaw, his blunted nose, or even the expanding gut that crept an inch too far over his belt-line. Even starvation couldn't do much about the kind of mass this guy carried, Alexei thought. It was a weight of the soul.

"I'm Holden." The man leaned back further, so the chair legs creaked and the few remaining shadows from the overhead light vanished. "Got a good look?"

"Thank you," said Alexei.

"Don't fucking thank me. Picking you up wasn't my idea. But you better thank me for not tossing you back when my kids told me what they did. You'd be dead out there, last night. On a raft in the middle of fucking nowhere. This isn't even a shipping lane. Nobody comes out here, except to fish and you don't look like a fucking fisherman. Now start talking. Somebody try to kill you? Or what? How'd you get that cut?"

Alexei tried to sit up. Yes, he knew this kind of guy. "I fell—or something. Don't remember."

"Bullshit."

"Maybe . . ." Alexei felt a nauseating wave of dizziness as he propped the pillow behind him. "Maybe it's going to come back to me later. What's this place?"

Holden regarded him levelly. "Mine," he said. "This place is mine."

"What do you do here?"

Holden laughed. "Sell Avon," he said. Then he twisted his larynx into a creepy falsetto: "*Ding dong, Avon calling*. You remember that commercial?"

"Okay." Alexei had no idea what he was talking about.

"Like that."

Alexei nodded politely.

"That's not what you wanted to know, though—is it?"

Alexei didn't answer, and Holden clearly didn't expect him to. "Well I'm not hearing what I want to know, either," said Holden.

"I'm sorry. I don't remember."

"You don't remember." Holden crossed his arms. "Sometimes," he said, "I get instincts. About people. About things. About what to do. And you want to know something?"

"Sure," said Alexei.

"I got an instinct about you."

"I see."

"Yeah, see that's the thing," said Holden. "I don't fuckin' see. I got no idea what that instinct says. It's just screaming at me. Fuckin' *screaming*. So you see—" he leaned forward, making the chair legs creak dangerously "—I gotta know your story."

"I don't know it myself," said Alexei. "I'm trying."

"Well good for you." Holden kicked the chair out from behind him and stood. "When you've got a story for me, we'll talk again. Right now—" he opened the door to the cabin and stepped out "—I've got a schedule to keep."

The door swung shut again. It made a rubbery sound as it bounced off the doorframe, and finally settled, closed but unlatched.

Alexei rolled onto his side. His legs drew up toward his chest. He felt himself begin to shake. His eyes closed.

Alexei's instincts were screaming too: they made a high, wailing sound in his brain like feedback, a microphone held too near a speaker. If he had any piss in him, he'd put it in the bed sheets now.

This was maybe not instinct at all, thought Alexei.

It felt more like terror. A formless, directionless terror—such as he had never felt.

It's the Romanians, he told himself. *The fuck-up on their boat. You are feeling bad about the fuck-up. You are feeling bad about where you are. Worried. This is, after all, hardly a U.S. coastguard rescue. Present circumstances are naturally upsetting.*

It has nothing to do with . . .

. . . with the snow-covered tarmac outside a low cement block barracks building, beneath a clear sub-arctic sky and the rivers of dust at the base of a cave in Afghanistan and lights that flashed and Czernochov and trigonometry and . . .

. . . that game of floor hockey.

The thoughts slipped away as fast as they came, into a storm of memories—and Alexei opened his eyes.

He was looking at the little bedside table. It was cheap—made out of pressed board covered in dirty white laminate. It looked to have been originally in a child's room, because the laminate was covered in stickers that someone had tried to scrape off with a pallet knife. The only two that were left was a brilliant green one of a cartoonish frog, next to a bright blue hairy monster with goggly eyes and three thick fingers on each hand, that did not look threatening at all.

Alexei smiled. He liked the blue thing. It reminded him of more innocent times, of childhood.

"Cute monster," he whispered, and reached out to touch the sticker with his thumb.

Finally, Alexei pulled the blankets from his bare legs and swung his feet onto the deck. The dizziness came again, but it wasn't as bad this time, so Alexei rode it out. Whoever it was had put him to bed had taken his briefs as well as his pants, and the cold cabin air actually seemed to help. He put his weight onto the balls of his feet, and holding onto the top bunk for support pulled himself upright. And stood there, facing the bunk, leaning forward on both arms like an athlete warming up for a race. A shaky athlete, after a bad night of too much vodka and maybe one too many rounds with an over-energetic whore—but still, Alexei thought, an athlete.

"Not so bad," he said aloud.

"Depends on where you're standing."

Alexei started and turned—hands instinctively leaping down to cover himself.

It was the woman—Heather, he remembered, the one who had hauled him downstairs. He recognized her mainly by the dreadlocks and the eyes. The shapeless raincoat was gone, replaced by a snug-fitting pair of tights and a matched black sweater.

Her eyes flickered down Alexei's torso. They finally settled on his hands.

"You're hiding something," she said, shutting the door behind her.

"I—beg your pardon?" Alexei stumbled a bit, and finally managed to duck his head and sit down—knees together, hands still clasped on his lap. *Like a nervous schoolboy*, Alexei thought.

Heather smiled, and when she blinked her eyes had left his groin. She met his eye steadily.

"This amnesia game of yours," she said, "is what I'm talking about." She lowered her voice, to just above a whisper: "I overheard your talk with Mr. Gibson."

"Mr. Gibson?"

"Holden."

"Ah." Alexei crossed his legs, and reached over with one hand to draw a blanket over his lap.

"Holden can be a prick," she said, crossing the tiny room so that she stood directly over him. Now her tone went playful. "But you're used to dealing with pricks, I bet."

"You meet all kinds," said Alexei.

"—in your business," she finished for him.

Now Alexei was quiet. He looked up at Heather with raised eyebrows, and for that instant her face was a mirror, throwing back his whatever-can-you-mean expression with one of her own.

"You can't remember how you hit your head," she said finally. "Or so you say. But maybe you remember how you got this." Her hand fell onto his shoulder, and the long string of scar tissue that went nearly as far as the base of his neck.

"Or the one on your ass," she said. "Left cheek. Looks like a piece of shrapnel hit you."

Actually, it had been a knife, and the scar was a lot uglier than the wound that had made it. But Alexei merely sighed, reached up and put his hand on top of hers. "You," he said, "have been peeking."

"Not just at your ass," she said, and reached under her sweater. "I found this in your pants pocket." She pulled out what looked like an oversized black pen, but Alexei recognized it immediately. He had been in pretty bad shape in the dingy, so he could excuse himself for not noticing—but he was sure they had taken it, along with the Glock and the butterfly knife, before setting him adrift. Alexei grabbed for it, but she stepped away too quickly, and lifted the weapon above her head.

"Give that to me!"

Any chance they give you—take it. Escape is your duty.

He jumped to his feet, the blanket falling away as he did so, and—the old instincts kicking in—he dove at her. She tried to twist out of his way, but he anticipated her action and caught her under an arm. She reached for the door with her free hand, but Alexei spun them both around so that his own body blocked her. In the same move, he reached up with his free hand and twisted Heather's wrist. She gave a little cry, and the weapon fell to the deck.

"Wow," she said, gasping for breath. The two of them were locked in a bizarre parody of a tango clinch—he with one arm locked under her arm and around her waist, his other hand holding hers high above their heads.

As they stood panting, Alexei realized with a blush just how close they were.

"What are you?" she murmured. "Russian mafia? KGB?"

"Not these days," he whispered, before he could think. "No," he said at volume. "There is no Russian mafia. I'm not KGB."

She smiled at that. "All right," she said. "It's coming back to you."

Alexei blinked. He heard a noise in his ears, like tinnitus. Like a radio, swooping up a blank stretch on the AM dial.

Some of them will try sex. It is the next thing after comfort, but it is much more difficult to combat.

Ah ha! It was Kolyokov! Alexei remembered now. Old Fyodor Kolyokov, talking in the upper lecture hall while the autumn wind whipped up a new snow from the shipyards. "I will tell you about sex now," said Kolyokov, who had dimmed the classroom lights and switched on the overhead projector. "There will be a time when you are on your own, in a weakened state—perhaps a prisoner, perhaps simply drunk. Old Kolyokov will not be there to advise you. So you must understand about sex."

"Hey! I'm talking to you."

Heather pulled herself away just enough to get her free hand in the space between them, and took him into her sweat-slick palm. Alexei shut his eyes, let her draw a low, grateful moan from him as she worked him harder still. He let her other hand go, and wrapped both his arms around her middle, so that his hands moved up and underneath her sweater, then crept again beneath the elastic of the tights. She didn't seem to mind—she gave a pleased-sounding little moan—but she squirmed anyway, so that before Alexei knew it, his hands were back outside, and empty. He opened his eyes, to find himself looking directly into hers, and when he moved forward to kiss her, she pulled back too quickly. In the same motion, she released him.

"Lie down," she commanded.

"All right." Alexei returned to his bunk—first scooping up the weapon, which he tucked against his wrist. Heather came over and sat on the bunk beside him.

"I'm not going to fuck you," she said matter-of-factly.

"All right," said Alexei. "What are you going to do? Torture me?"

"Depends."

"On what?"

"On how forthcoming you are. What's your name?"

Alexei shrugged. "I can't remember."

"Bullshit."

Alexei looked at her levelly. "Are you having instincts too?" he asked.

"Funny guy," she sneered. "And you say you're not KGB anymore."

"I don't work for the KGB," said Alexei. "I'm pretty sure about that."

"That wasn't what I asked," she said, and motioned to the weapon in his hand. "What's that thing?"

Alexei smiled at her. No harm there.

"Would you like me to demonstrate?"

"If you need to."

"It is called an asp." With a flick of his wrist, Alexei extended the asp to its full eighteen inches. The black steel ball at the end of it gleamed in the light, and made an ethereal line of reflection as Alexei flicked it back and forth on its steel-spring shaft. "You can buy it at the shopping mall," he said. "Legal in your country, and pretty dangerous in the hands of someone who knows how to use it."

Heather nodded, apparently satisfied. "Good. Now we'll try again—if you don't work for the KGB, who do you work for?"

Alexei sighed.

"I am," he said finally, "between employers."

"Recently so, I take it."

"Yes."

"Bullshit," she said. "You're here for Holden. From Time-Warner, right?"

"Think what you like." Alexei could feel himself starting to get pissed off. "What the hell do you mean, Time-Warner? The television people?"

"The magazine people." Heather nodded as she spoke, raised her eyebrows and lowered her voice—as though she were revealing some sinister truth. It only pissed Alexei off more.

"Whatever you say," he mumbled.

"He's a real prick, you know." Heather's voice dropped, and she leaned toward him as she spoke. Her hand fell casually on his hip, and her forefinger inscribed an arc on the flesh there. "If you're not here for him—you should be. You should see what he does to people. To little *kids*."

"Little kids," repeated Alexei, and thought about that.

"And—he's getting *worse*," said Heather. The nail dug in—not quite painfully.

"I'm not in the mood," he said, and lifted her hand away.

She stood up, face blank.

"Understandable," she said, before she turned to the door, "I guess. I guess

I'm not in the mood either, then."

When she left, closing the door firmly, Alexei put a hand behind his head and regarded the asp, which she'd thoughtfully left him. Why did he still have it? The Romanians should have found it on him—they were professionals in every other respect, and a professional didn't leave his enemy with a weapon in his pocket. Even an innocuous little weapon such as this.

He took hold of the ball at the asp's tip, and pushed it back into the shaft, so it became like a pen again. He bounced it once in his palm, and tucked it under his pillow.

It scarcely mattered now, of course; there were other, more immediate things to worry about.

But he still couldn't stop asking himself: *What the hell was their angle? Crazy damn Romanians. They had to have an angle.*

Упущенная A LOST OPPORTUNITY возможность

Alexei had been working with Mrs. Kontos-Wu for nearly three months when they boarded the Romanians' cabin cruiser outside Boston, and nearly all of that time was spent in travel. Mrs. Kontos-Wu was an associate with Wolfe-Jordan, which had meant nothing to Alexei when he came to New York following an extended stay in Belarus. His work there hadn't left much time for reading newspapers—particularly the financial sections where Wolfe-Jordan might have rated mention.

Because of that, her executive assistant Stephen Haber had been resolutely unimpressed with Alexei. He peered over his resume with undisguised disdain, the day they'd sat across from one another in a little hotel conference room in mid-town Manhattan.

"You worked with the KGB," said Stephen, "until 1992. Am I wasting my time asking your duties?"

Alexei shrugged. "No," he said. "I worked in Moscow in an office for two years in the early 1990s. It was not dramatic work. Before that—I was in foreign work. That is harder to talk about."

"We're all friends here," said Stephen, in a tone that suggested that they weren't friends at all.

"Okay," said Alexei. "I spent time in Pakistan. East Germany. Czechoslovakia. Little bit in Poland."

"What about Chechnya?"

"After my time."

"Afghanistan?"

Alexei didn't answer that one.

"Well." Stephen was just a kid. He was probably twenty-five, but if Alexei ran into him on the street he wouldn't have guessed him any older than twenty. Here, it was clear he'd managed to acquire the unpleasant confidence of many more years. Stephen tilted his head back and looked at Alexei hard—like he was trying to read his mind. "You won't be doing much business in Afghanistan."

"Okay."

"But you may be working in a lot of other countries. Any problems with that?"

"I like to travel."

"Good. You ever kill someone?"

Quiet for a moment. Alexei looked at the presentation board behind Stephen. There was a smear of blue ink across the bottom—Alexei thought he could make out the letters D and L in it.

"You ever kill someone?" asked Stephen again.

"Sure. Everyone in KGB killed someone."

Stephen rolled his eyes and made a note on a yellow tablet.

"You were in Belarus most recently I hear."

Alexei nodded. "Sure."

Stephen eyed him. "You found good work with the *Mafiya*."

"Sure," said Alexei. "That's all the work there is for KGB people in Belarus. Only killing people who piss off *Mafiya*." He held up his hands and wiggled his fingers. "That and washing the blood from our hands. Two hours a night."

Stephen smiled thinly. "Funny," he said.

Alexei smiled back. "Anyway," he said, "there is no Russian mafia."

Stephen looked at him. "You talk like someone who doesn't want this job."

"Oh," said Alexei, "that's not true."

Stephen shook his head. "You poor bastard," he said.

Alexei took it to mean that he'd blown the interview. Stephen Haber wouldn't be calling again—not after a self-sabotaging interview like that. Thinking about it later, he had to wonder if maybe something inside him simply warned him away—was doing its best to keep him clear of this American workplace with its nursery school management.

But he'd been wrong. The next day, Alexei got a call and they met in the hotel bar—empty even of staff in the early afternoon. Alexei sipped a ginger ale. Stephen fiddled with an unlit cigarette and seemed nervous.

"You really don't need to know this," he'd explained, "but you're working with one of the best. Mrs. Kontos-Wu is very hands-on. She doesn't just pick companies out of the air. She doesn't just sit in the office. She looks. That's why we brought you in—Mrs. Kontos-Wu needs discreet protection; these companies are in pretty unstable places, some of them—*politically* unstable, you get what I mean."

"That is what makes her so good, yes?" Alexei said, trying to at least belatedly pick up some of Stephen's enthusiasm for his new boss.

"Not good," said Stephen. "The *best*. Like you're going to be."

And so they had travelled: to tour diamond mines in South Africa; a computer chip factory in Taiwan; a biotech company in Calcutta and a half-built hotel complex in Borneo. On all of these, it was Alexei's job to see that Mrs. Kontos-Wu came to no harm—that neither terrorists nor industrial spies nor, for that matter, common thieves even got near Mrs. Kontos-Wu and her entourage. Alexei carried a little arsenal of weapons—from the asp to the butterfly knife, to an electric stun-wand and a Glock semi-automatic handgun—and if pressed he knew he could kill with any one of them. But if he were ever so pressed, Alexei also knew it would have meant he'd already failed.

Seen in such terms, his first three months had been an unqualified success. Alexei swept their hotel rooms, hung back watchfully during Mrs. Kontos-Wu's many meetings, scanned the crowds as they passed among them and generally enjoyed the sights and sounds of the new cities.

And Mrs. Kontos-Wu seemed to do well too. Everyone she met with seemed to be very agreeable—gave her all the information she needed—and even, sometimes, gave her more. Stephen Haber had been right: Mrs. Kontos-Wu evidently was the best.

Perhaps it was a combination of that—the sight of so many unfamiliar places, the chaos of so many smells and tastes, so many voices speaking in so many unintelligible languages, his boss's uncanny ability to close a deal—that had made him careless in the banality of Boston Harbour.

Perhaps it was just stupidity.

"I have some people to talk to in Boston," she told Stephen, the previous afternoon. "You can stay behind."

Alexei was sitting on a wing-backed chair in the outer office, flipping through the back pages of the Post, counting time until his boss needed him. He folded the paper and looked out through the open doorway. Alexei could see Stephen, but Mrs. Kontos-Wu was hidden by a filing cabinet. As for Stephen—he didn't look pleased at the news.

"You'll still take your protection," said Stephen—barely glancing at Alexei, who by this time had stood up and was leaning in the doorframe.

Mrs. Kontos-Wu glanced over the filing cabinet at Alexei. She was a small, slender woman, with long black hair and a faint Asian cast to her eyes. Now all he could see were those eyes. They were crinkled in a smile. "I don't know that I'll need him," she said. "What do you think, Alexei?"

Alexei shrugged. "Never good to travel alone," he said.

"But it's up to me." Mrs. Kontos-Wu leaned back in her chair, and disappeared behind the cabinet again. "That's what I like about you, Alexei," she said, a little sharply. "You leave it up to *me*."

Stephen made his fingers into a steeple and stared ahead, blank-faced. Alexei stepped into the room, his own hands folded, in what was for him a gesture of servitude. Mrs. Kontos-Wu was still smiling at him. "All right, Stephen." She didn't look at her assistant. "Alexei comes—although I don't think he'll be needed. The sea air will do us both good."

"Where are we going?" said Alexei. "If I may ask."

"We are going to Boston," said Mrs. Kontos-Wu. "And from there—who knows?"

Later, in the car from the airport, Mrs. Kontos-Wu had told him a little more. "I'm meeting with a broker," she said. "He's a Turk. His name's Shadak."

"That is interesting," said Alexei. He remembered he used to know a Shadak once. Back in Pakistan. Nice guy. Had a pretty girlfriend. But he didn't say anything.

"He's—an old friend," said Mrs. Kontos-Wu. "He has some associates he wants me to meet. I want you to keep an eye on them—they're Romanian."

"And?"

"Just keep an eye on them."

Keeping an eye on the Romanians wasn't, as it turned out, all that difficult—because when they got to the club where Mr. Shadak's motor yacht, *Ming Lei 3*, was moored, Mr. Shadak was nowhere to be seen. So far as Alexei could tell, the yacht was filled with Romanians, stem to stern, and he could have looked anywhere and counted on seeing at least one. Altogether, Alexei counted a dozen of them by the time they disembarked—five men, ranging in age from maybe twenty-five to fifty; two women, both in their late twenties, and—incongruously—five children, none older than fourteen, the youngest one surely not more than eight. So far as Alexei could tell, the children were engaged as help on the yacht. They moved the baggage, opened doors and even offered to serve a selection of spirits once he and his employer had settled in.

Mrs. Kontos-Wu seemed unperturbed at the arrangement. One of the Romanians, a balding stork of a man who introduced himself as Mr. Hzekul, told them that Mr. Shadak would be joining them tomorrow, and when Alexei quietly voiced his skepticism at just how Mr. Shadak would do this if they were to be at sea, Mrs. Kontos-Wu waved his suspicions away.

"This isn't unusual," she said. "Not *that* unusual, not for Mr. Shadak."

"I will keep an eye on them," said Alexei, "all the same."

Ming Lei 3 debarked from Boston Harbour late in the afternoon, and it was warm enough for Mrs. Kontos-Wu to change into a shorts and a light cotton shirt, to bid the land adieu. Alexei wished he could do the same—the afternoon sun was hot, particularly as it beat down on his dark suit jacket. But he was worried about the Romanians. He'd worked alongside some of them in the old days, and from everything he'd heard, Romanians in general and their *Securitat* in particular were still among the shiftiest bastards in the Eastern Bloc. And given that—and the little premonitory crawl that moved up and down Alexei's back like a line of feeding ants—there just weren't enough places to hide what he deemed to be the necessary arsenal in a pair of swimming trunks.

So Alexei sweated the afternoon out, sipping on ginger ale and watching the Boston skyline shrink on the horizon behind them. A little girl, maybe eleven, with wide black eyes set in a gaunt and serious face, hovered around him like a mayfly, forever tempting him with food and hard liquor in horribly broken English: "Cawiar?" "Meester want wodka?" "Shreemp?" "Hawe weeskie now?"

"No," he would say, "nothing for me." But she would persist—much to Mrs. Kontos-Wu's amusement, if not Alexei's.

"She's a little professional," she drawled to Mr. Hzekul as she sipped at her own martini, just mixed by a fourteen-year-old boy with a little s-shaped scar on his chin, and hair, like the rest of them, jet black.

"As is your man, I see," said Mr. Hzekul, leaning close to Mrs. Kontos-Wu. His fingers brushed the bare flesh of her arm in a way that made Alexei tense, and Mr. Hzekul must have sensed this. He turned to Alexei, smiling broadly. "Good! Do not drink on duty! Always on guard. Good policeman, yes?"

"As you say, sir." Alexei smiled and bent slightly at the waist. Mr. Hzekul leaned back against the seat cushion, and sipped at his own drink: a Canadian beer, which he drank straight from the can.

Behind them, the line of land vanished and the sea air sent an evening chill across the deck. Before Mrs. Kontos-Wu could even comment, another child came scurrying from the cabin with a blanket. Mrs. Kontos-Wu accepted it readily, and smiled her thanks as she wrapped it around her shoulders. This child was the smallest yet, so young and dressed so androgynously that Alexei couldn't even tell whether it was a boy or girl. The child vanished inside, and Alexei, his professional attention fixed on the lecherous Mr. Hzekul just then, didn't give it much thought.

I should have, he thought a day later, lying in a bunk on board Holden Gibson's boat and fingering his bandaged scalp.

That night, for instance, every instinct had told him to be out on deck. Mrs. Kontos-Wu had again dismissed his concerns for her well-being where Mr. Hzekul was concerned; even suggested playfully that Alexei might have been a bit jealous. "But you have nothing to fear," she said, and shuddered theatrically. "He's *not* my type."

Alexei had blushed, and Mrs. Kontos-Wu had laughed and winked and sent him out the door. "Go be a guard," she said. "But leave Mr. Hzekul alone. This business will all be done soon enough."

"What is this business?" asked Alexei—realizing even as he said it that he had stumbled across an invisible line of decorum. It was a line he'd managed to avoid for three months—that one between employee and associate—but tonight . . .

"I am sorry—" he began.

"Go guard," said Mrs. Kontos-Wu firmly, and shut the door.

Ah shit, he'd thought. *That's why you never made the Party. No sense of politics . . . or the politic.*

So Alexei went up on deck. He didn't know what he expected to see, but he didn't feel at all right about things as they stood, and he'd done everything he could below: swept Mrs. Kontos-Wu's cabin for listening devices, put a contact alarm on her door-frame, checked the battery in her panic button. All that was left, he supposed, was for a crew of Romanian assassins to come aboard clandestinely. And anyway, here was where his gut told him to be.

The weather had shifted mightily since sunset. By midnight, when Alexei emerged from below, the calm clear summer sky was replaced by rolling black clouds and the air was filled with sharp, cold rain. He fished a Maglite from his jacket pocket and played the beam across the water-splashed deck. There was a faint light up in the cabin, where one of the Romanian adults held the wheel, but it wasn't much brighter than Alexei's own flashlight, and otherwise the boat was entirely dark. Which struck him as odd—wasn't there some kind of maritime law requiring ships to run lights through the night?

A scuffling sound brought him to attention. It came from the gangway around the main cabin, toward the foredeck, but when he shone his light in the sound's direction, there was nothing there but the misting rain.

Alexei shifted the Maglite to his left hand and drew his Glock from its shoulder holster. He shut the light off, and when he judged his eyes had adjusted well enough to the darkness he started to make his way along the edge of the boat.

The bow was as dark as the rest of the vessel. He nearly tripped over the dingy as he moved from the gunwale towards the middle of the boat, and when he righted himself he kept down on one knee—the deck here was curved, and his stomach twisted as he realized it wouldn't take much for him to slide off it and end up freezing to death in *Ming Lei 3*'s wake—or perhaps more mercifully, chopped into shark chum in its propeller.

Somewhere in the dark, he heard a wet thud, and another slapping sound. Maybe something moved in front of him, maybe to his side—it was too dark to tell.

He raised the gun, and turned on the flashlight.

And God help him, he nearly fired.

It was the little girl—the "wheeskie?" girl, with the dark eyes and the underfed demeanor. She was standing not four feet in front of him, and she blinked in the light, held up her hand to ward it off. He put the safety back on the Glock and returned it to its shoulder holster, but kept the light on her face.

"What are *you* doing here?" he demanded.

"*Cee tee five twelf*," she said.

"What?"

"Cee tee five twelf," she repeated. "*You are de one.*"

The girl stepped backwards, and Alexei started to follow.

He heard a thumping sound from below, followed by a *crack!*, and a shouting man. Alexei redrew the Glock, and jumped onto the deck below the wheelhouse. There, he caught a glimpse of one of the Romanians—the woman—but she didn't see him. At that, a buzz moved up his back—almost like the vibration that Mrs. Kontos-Wu's pager would set off, if the pager had been set directly at the base of his spine. The sensation was a look-out-behind-you kind of prickling, that his mother might have named precognition.

He spun around, nearly losing his footing, as a quick shadow moved in his peripheral.

But Alexei was quick too. Just quick enough to see the smallest child—the boy-girl one, who'd been so fast with the blanket—swinging a boat-hook in a blurred arc through the rain. It cracked hard against his forehead—and before he could even react, the kid brought it down again.

There was a hollow thumping sound, and the little . . . girl? . . . jumped down next to Alexei. She moved with a steady care, and her eyes didn't leave his.

"Baba Yaga," she said. "Manka. Vasilissa."

The back of Alexei's head hit hard against the deck, and the world went dark as his Maglite skittered across the deck and into the sea.

Ah God, he thought with a horrible certainty. *They got her. Lured me away, and they got Mrs. Kontos-Wu.*

The girl stood over him now, and repeated the words: "Baba Yaga. Manka. Vasilissa."

And then: "For your own good, cousin."

And before the full humiliation of the moment could hit, the real blackness crept up to take him away.

THE IDIOT
Идиот

The bald man with the van Dyke beard visited Alexei next, but he was only there to bring a mug of chicken soup and a bundle of clothes, and didn't stay to chat half as long as the last two visitors had. He asked if Alexei remembered anything yet—which suggested that Heather hadn't spoken of their earlier encounter—and when Alexei said no, he shrugged. "We cleaned your clothes, but there's still a pretty bad bloodstain on the shirt. So I loaned you one of my sweaters. Take a walk around when you feel like it—the weather's cleared up so it's not too bad, and we've got a few hours yet."

Alexei wrapped his blanket over his shoulders and sat up, cradling the soup mug in his hands. It was instant soup from a powder, but still quite hot, and when he swallowed the first mouthful it felt remarkable going down.

A few hours until what, precisely? he wanted to ask.

"It is like coming back from the dead," he said with some relish—but the bald man didn't appear to get the joke. He gave Alexei a funny look.

"My name's James," he said, on his way out. "Take a walk when you feel up to it."

The soup gave him a kind of strength, but he still took a moment before reaching over to the stack of clothes and dressing himself. Really, this amnesia game would have to end sometime—if he was a true professional, he would never have attempted it in the first place. Just told the people here what had happened, radioed to the coast guard and told them about the possible homicide on the Romanians' ship. He finished the soup, slurping back the noodles at the bottom of the cup and swallowing them whole, and set it down on the floor at his ankles. The game was childish, he knew. Pointless, too.

Sooner or later, he would have to stop remaking himself like this.

Alexei unfolded the clothes. The trousers were a mess—they were dress pants, and really should have been dry-cleaned. At least they hadn't shrunk. The bald man's sweater was really a bright red sweatshirt, and it had a big logo with the dark blue words SUBSCRIBE! underneath an arch of pale blue laminate. The whole thing looked to Alexei like a monochrome rainbow. When he put it on, he noted with distaste it was also a size too small for him. It stretched across his shoulders, the sleeves rode up his forearms, and the collar grabbed around his neck like a noose. He reached under the pillow and slipped the asp into his pants-pocket. He slipped his bare feet into his shoes and made his way outside.

Sooner or later, Alexei would have to tell someone—besides the woman Heather, who seemed altogether too willing to keep his secret for him—what had happened on the Romanians' yacht. Mrs. Kontos-Wu might be dead. He might have failed, the drama might be over. But she might have simply been wounded, or still be alive on the boat, on her way to God knows where. If that were the case, his little game was his real failure.

Comfort is the torturer's first tool.

And sex is the second, and ill-fitting sweatshirts is the third, and a misguided appeal to duty is the fourth, thought Alexei. Score one for Kolyokov.

The cabin opened onto a narrow corridor that was lit only dimly. It felt as though the boat's motor was directly underneath this spot, because the corridor hummed and vibrated in a way that tickled up through Alexei's shinbones—like the feather of unease that tickled up through his middle. That made him behave as though he were a prisoner. Or an infiltrator.

Alexei passed by a steep, narrow set of stairs, and he started to climb them. But he abruptly changed his mind. He wasn't a prisoner here, and he wasn't an infiltrator—at least not yet. He was still Gibson's guest.

But Gibson . . .

Like Heather said, he was a prick.

And he did things to little kids.

When they'd fished Alexei out of the ocean, an instinct had told him to keep his mouth shut. Now, that same instinct kept him from climbing the stairs onto the main deck.

The corridor bent here, and Alexei continued along it. It seemed to bend back in a U shape, so that Alexei was looking at another row of cabins. At the end of it, a door stood ajar.

Alexei started down the hallway. It wasn't until he made it to the edge of the door, and began to peer around it, that he realized he'd been rolling his feet so as to make no noise and had extended the asp so that it hid ready behind his thigh. *Training never leaves us*, he thought, as he looked into the empty closet. He was about to turn away, when that training nudged him back, and he noticed the faint light coming from cracks around the edge of the closet's far wall.

Alexei went forward, and pushed open the hidden door.

"Shit," he mouthed, looking into the room.

It was a cabin, maybe three times as big as the one they'd put Alexei in. But its portholes had been blacked out, and it was lined with white pine bunk beds and plain foam mattresses. At the far end, there was a little chemical toilet, and a watercooler just like the one outside Mrs. Kontos-Wu's office in New York. It made a belching sound as an enormous air bubble shot to the top of the tank. Alexei looked at the bunk beds—he counted fifteen, and he wouldn't have been able to stretch out comfortably on any one of them. They were far too short for a grown man.

But the size was perfect for little kids.

"Shit," Alexei whispered.

This room was a smuggler's hideaway.

For smuggling children.

Before anyone could show up to make trouble for him, Alexei returned the door to the slightly-ajar position he'd found it in, and made his way back to the stairs. When he got there, the asp was back in his pocket. From above, he could smell the salt and rot of the sea air. Still putting it all together in his head, he climbed. Feigning amnesia, Alexei thought, was the smartest thing he had done in recent memory.

"You speak Russian?"

Alexei stood on the yacht's prow, watching Holden Gibson approach. He had been standing alone there for a few minutes, watching the waves break against the hull, occasionally looking back across the deck, or glancing out to the horizon, which was grey and featureless under the thick cloud. He was thinking about what to do next—find a radio, try and contact the coast guard, call in the Marines on this fucking child smuggler, and let them know about Mrs. Kontos-Wu at the same time—when he spotted Holden Gibson. Alexei waited for the big man to make his way across the mist-washed deck.

"Of course you speak Russian," said Holden. He was wearing a raincoat like Heather had worn last night, and he stopped not a foot away from Alexei. "I think I understand where my instinct is taking me now," he continued. "It could be either way—telling me I should just kill you and dump the body in the drink. Or that you might be useful. I think maybe I shouldn't kill you. I think it's telling me to offer you some work."

"What kind of work?"

Holden threw up his hands and rolled his eyes. "Christ's sake, boy—what is with all the questions? Look, just tell me—do you or don't you want to work? Because we are going to be there soon and I want to hedge my bets, all right?

Now are you remembering things any better?"

"No," said Alexei.

"Good. Do you remember your Russian?"

"*Da*," said Alexei.

"What the fuck's that?"

"Russian for Yes."

"Russian. Good." Holden's hands came together and he rubbed them, as though warming them in the spray. "Now here's the job. I'm meeting some people—we're meeting real soon—and I think some of them will be speaking Russian. That is the sense I get. But I don't speak Russian, and they know I don't speak Russian. Got that?"

"Yes," said Alexei.

"Good. Now. These Russians, they don't know about you, and they don't know you speak Russian. So the thing I want you to do is listen—keep your mouth shut, but listen—and when they're talking Russian, remember what they say and tell me that. Can you do that? Or does your fucking head hurt too bad? Because I don't have to tell you—you're dead weight on this boat right now." He looked at Alexei. "You're ballast. You know what ballast is?"

"Yes," said Alexei. "I know what ballast is."

"And?" Holden Gibson's hands made fists, and he jammed them into the pockets of his raincoat. "And?"

"I can do this for you."

"Good." Holden grinned at Alexei, his teeth improbably white. They were the teeth of a healthy young man, stolen in the night and hammered into the gums of a sick old monster's head. "Good. This is a good idea I've come up with, isn't it?"

Alexei pushed his own hands into his pockets, and felt the asp in one of them. He gripped it, and smiled back. "You're the boss," he said.

"Yeah," said Holden. "I am the boss. And you should get inside, you stupid fuck. I don't want you fainting with pneumonia." He squinted at Alexei's sweatshirt. "Where did you get that?"

"Borrowed it," he said. "From one of your people, I think."

"Looks like a hand-me-down," said Holden, and shook his head. "My kids haven't worn one of those since, what?—'91."

"A significant year," said Alexei.

"Yeah." Holden's eyes brightened at that, and he snapped his fingers. "Yeah! That's when you guys threw out the commies—Yeltsin in the tank and knocking over Lenin and all that shit. You there for that?"

"I can't remember," said Alexei.

"Right—amnesia." He said it quietly. "Of all the luck . . ." And at volume:

"You're going to do okay here, pal."

Pal. Outwardly, Alexei kept up his smile. But he couldn't stop thinking about the children's room below and the padlock on the outside of it. "I will go inside," he said, and broke away from Holden.

Alexei went back inside, but he didn't return to his cabin. First he wandered up to the bridge. There was only one crewmember on duty there, holding the wheel and staring at the horizon over the bow. The radio was within reach of the guy. If Alexei wanted it, he'd have to take him down. Alexei clutched the asp in his pocket. But the moment was lost. "You're welcome to stay, just don't touch anything," said the crewman, before Alexei could even introduce himself. Alexei made a show of looking over the controls here, then wandered over to the big map table. A chart of a coastline had been pressed down under a sheet of heavy glass. Maybe it was Maine, but Alexei couldn't say exactly where—the chart was navigational, and awash in numbers.

He asked where they were right now, and the crewman tapped the glass with his fingertip, over open sea: "Right about here." Alexei didn't see any scale to the map, but he noted with some interest that they were about an inch to the east of the dotted line that indicated the 200-mile limit.

When Alexei asked where they were headed, the crewman just shrugged. "Okay," said Alexei, and didn't ask again.

If he wanted to use the radio, and have any hope of surviving to wait, he'd have to pick another time.

So Alexei climbed down to the main deck, and made his way into the yacht's lounge. On the Turk Shadak's yacht, the equivalent room had been lined with cushioned benches and was decorated with a kind of faux-nautical kitsch that included a fishing net overtop the small bar and a half-scale lobster trap dangling from the ceiling.

Holden Gibson's boat was considerably larger, and so it was with the lounge. But by comparison, this one was stripped down. A small part of the room had been sectioned off as an office area—Alexei saw a fax machine, as well as two laptop computers hooked up to a printer. The rest of the room was set up like a theatre—or, more appropriately, a lecture hall. Folding chairs had been arranged in rows along the length of it, facing a projection-screen TV next to a wooden podium. There were some long tables along the sides of the room, stacked with cardboard stationery boxes. Alexei went to a table, and opened a box. He picked up one of the pieces inside—printed on thick red paper stock.

He read:

SELLING IS YOUR LIFE!

And underneath, in slightly smaller type:

FIVE SURE-FIRE TIPS TO HELP YOU BEAT THAT QUOTA!

1 - Tell the customer that you are RAISING FUNDS for CHILDREN! Think about it—that is JUST EXACTLY WHAT YOU ARE DOING! RAISING FUNDS for CHILDREN! This is NOT A LIE!

2 - Show the customer your CHARITABLE CARD! Remember, DO NOT say you are from a REGISTERED CHARITY! That is a lie! Just showing the CHARITABLE CARD is not a lie! And that alone will CLINCH more than ONE-HALF of your sales!

3 - If the CUSTOMER says NO, ask her what YOU have DONE WRONG! If what she tells you makes you want to CRY, then GO AHEAD AND CRY! It will make the CUSTOMER feel SORRY—almost as SORRY as you will feel if you do not make QUOTA!

4 - DO NOT let the CUSTOMER think about the sale and CALL YOU later! DO NOT ever give out our TELEPHONE NUMBER! If the CUSTOMER insists, TELL THE CUSTOMER that she can CANCEL her subscription within TEN DAYS if she changes her mind! That is NOT A LIE! Just DO NOT tell her that her MONEY WILL BE REFUNDED!

5 - START filling out the SUBSCRIPTION FORM before the CUSTOMER has even agreed to PURCHASE a SUBSCRIPTION! She will SEE YOU WRITING and think she has ALREADY AGREED! Or she will FEEL SORRY FOR YOU—particularly if you tell her that you will be PUNISHED for any PART-WAY FINISHED SUBSCRIPTION FORMS IN YOUR BOOK AT THE END OF A SHIFT! This is NOT A LIE! You can CLINCH up to ONE-THIRD of your potential SALES this way!

6 - (Okay, we lied! There are really 6 tips!) Smile! Because remember—NOBODY likes a SAD SELLER!

"A sad seller," Alexei repeated under his breath. It was marginally better than what he'd suspected of Holden and his crew. More than marginally, actually. But Alexei reminded himself that it still didn't preclude his worst suspicions being true.

He put the paper back down and looked over some of the other sheets. They all had similarly themed titles: SELL THAT MAGAZINE! And DON'T TAKE NO FOR AN ANSWER! And WHO SAYS YOU CAN'T SELL THIS PRODUCT! Further down the row, the titles varied intriguingly: HELLO

MR. POLICEMAN! And CHILD WELFARE WORKERS—ANYTHING BUT! And THE YOUNG OFFENDERS ACT: CANADA'S GIFT TO YOU!

"Canada?" Alexei muttered. What do these people have to do with Canada?

"We used to spend a lot of time in Canada."

He looked up to see Heather, standing in the doorway leading astern. She was back in her raincoat, and a cigarette dangled between her fingers. She closed the door with her shoulder and sashayed across the lounge. Her brow crinkled in a little, remembering to frown. Her eyes took a faraway cast as she continued:

"Toronto, Mississauga, London—yeah, they've got a London up there. I remember we spent about a week in Ottawa—that's the Canadian Washington—back in '88. Kept the vans in a trailer park outside at night, and through the day, it was just like scooping money off the ground. Ottawa was *good* to us."

"1988?" Alexei tried to remember what he was doing that long ago. Afghanistan? No. Afghanistan was finished for him. He wondered about Heather. "You must have been a little girl," he said.

But she appeared not to hear him. "*Time*, *Newsweek* . . . I remember *Popular Mechanics* did *real* well in Ottawa in '88. Housekeeping magazines, though . . ." She stopped in front of him, put her hand on his shoulder so the ember of the cigarette warmed his earlobe and looked up at him with lazy, laughing eyes. "They never did go in for *Good Housekeeping* much in Ottawa."

Alexei frowned. "How old are you, Heather?"

"Are you going to do something?"

She leaned close to him, so that if he wanted—if he leaned just so—their lips could brush and kiss and it could have seemed like an accident. But all he could think about were the tiny bunk beds in the brig below, and the children on the Romanians' yacht, that served Mrs. Kontos-Wu drinks and had him pegged as KGB—and literally pegged him, across the forehead, before dumping him into the ocean.

"And when did you start working for Mr. Gibson?" He took hold of Heather's wrist and pulled her hand from his shoulder.

"A long time ago. All right?" Now the languor was gone, and all that was left in her eyes was a suspicious resentment. "You want to play brave social worker and rescue me? You know what you got to do."

Alexei smiled coldly. "Take care of Mr. Gibson?"

"That's right."

"Why don't you tell me some things first."

"What do you need to know?"

"First: what is this place? What is with the magazines?"

"Magazines." If she'd been angry a second ago, she'd forgotten it now. She said "magazine" like it was some exotic sex act, and she tried to sidle close to Alexei again as she went on. "Magazines are everything. They bought this boat, they bought our house down in Florida, they bought . . . hell, they'll buy anything. Magazines are our business. Can't you see?" She swept her arm over the bank of flyers and pamphlets. "It's almost all profit!"

Alexei didn't see how that could be—unless, of course, you never delivered any magazines—but he kept that question to himself.

"How old were you when you started with this wonderful business?" asked Alexei. "Twelve? Thirteen?"

That stopped her short. "I was old enough," she said quietly.

She glared at him—and he could tell that this time, it wasn't just pique. He knew he'd touched a nerve in Heather.

"He's a prick," she said. "Back when I started, it was just magazines. Lately, though—it's been getting weird."

"Weird? In what way?"

"He's fucking nuts," she said. "You know why we're here?"

Alexei raised his eyebrows in a question.

"A fucking dream—that's what he says whenever we ask."

"So you want me to kill you a crazy dreamer," said Alexei. "Why don't you just do it yourself?"

Heather shut her eyes. She pinched her cigarette hard between her lips and drew a lungful.

"Did he by any chance do something to you?" asked Alexei.

Heather's cigarette crumpled in her fist, and the tip of it burned the side of her finger. "Fuck!" she shouted, and from upstairs, someone yelled: "Everything okay?"

"Fine," she shouted back—her voice just about twisting back on itself to be cheerful. "Just stubbed my toe!"

"Sorry," said Alexei, meaning it. He knew about bad memories.

She glared at him. "So what about it?"

"I don't think so," said Alexei. "Here we are, in international waters, well off any of the main shipping routes I am told. Right now, I am very curious about where it is that we are going to dock next. Perhaps after I find that out . . ."

"You're a fucking traitor," she said. "That's what you are. I protected *you*, you know. You could at least—"

She stopped in her tirade, and looked out over Alexei's shoulder, out one of the windows. "Shit," she said. "They're early."

Alexei followed Heather onto the deck, where various other crew were already gathered. Everyone's attention was focused on the trio of Zodiacs bearing down on them. When Alexei wondered aloud whether it was Greenpeace, he got a big laugh.

"Then who?" he asked Heather.

"Russians," she said. "Or something. That's all he tells us."

"That's right," said the bald one, whose shirt Alexei was still wearing. "That's all we need to know."

Beneath them, the engine noise changed and Alexei could feel the deck pitch slightly as the yacht started to turn towards the Zodiacs. After a few minutes of manoeuvring, the three little boats had managed to pull up parallel to the yacht, and the crew moved to lower rope ladders. Alexei peered over the edge of the railing. Each of the Zodiacs carried three men, wearing dark green rain gear. The only clue as to their Russian origins were the AKMs slung over the shoulders of—Alexei made a quick count—seven of the men. The Zodiacs were otherwise unmarked, and their crew all wore their hoods up. It would be funny, Alexei thought, if he wound up recognizing one of the men here from the old days.

Depending, of course, on who it was.

Just to be safe, Alexei moved from the railing and sidled back into the lounge. There, he busied himself sorting stacks of paper, pretending to read through the TIME IS MONEY! pamphlet—all the while watching through the window, scoping the company.

In all, four of the men came up, and when the last one passed the window and made his way up to the bridge, Alexei let out a breath that he hadn't realized he'd been holding. *No trouble*, he told himself. No trouble.

Shortly afterward, the crewman he'd met on the bridge came into the lounge, along with two others.

"Finished your watch?" asked Alexei conversationally.

"I've been relieved," he said. "They're taking us the rest of the way."

"Ah." Alexei nodded. "Like a harbour pilot."

"Yeah," he said, and shivered a little. "But with no harbour."

Alexei was about to ask something else when Holden burst into the room and fingered him. "You!" he shouted. "Get up to the bridge! It's time to start work!"

"Okay," said Alexei, and started toward the door. "See you later," he said to the yacht's former pilot.

"Screw the good-byes," snapped Holden. "*Vite*, Russkie, *vite*!"

As soon as Alexei got close enough, Holden grabbed his arm and all but hauled him up the stairs.

"These fucking Russians," he muttered to Alexei, "are taking over my ship. Listen to what they say, and tell me after."

"I will listen," promised Alexei. "And keep my mouth shut, yes?"

"*Da*," said Holden. "You'll do fine."

Less than ten seconds on the bridge, and Alexei wasn't so sure.

"Hey!" shouted one of them as Alexei and Holden climbed up into the room. The men were all lean and athletic—they looked to Alexei like commandos more than anything. But they seemed completely at home on the bridge of an American motor yacht. "No one here but us!"

He was speaking English, but even so—he didn't sound Russian at all. Alexei looked at Holden with a question in his eye, but Holden's face was granite. Alexei felt his own stomach twist, even as one of the others muttered something in his native tongue.

No, it was not Russian—not even close to Russian.

He was speaking Romanian.

And Holden Gibson—Heather's prick, who'd taken over this child labour ring and come here on the urging of a dream—this American couldn't tell the difference between Russian and Romanian.

Alexei should have let on to Holden; the same way, he supposed, he should have worked a little harder to radio in some kind of a distress call over Mrs. Kontos-Wu's disappearance. He could barely even speak Romanian—he remembered a couple of words, from a language course more than a decade ago, but languages had never been his strong suit.

"Get off! Or deal is done!" shouted the Romanian. He actually lifted his AKM from where he'd leaned it against a cabinet, and waved it at the two of them. Holden recoiled at that.

"Hey!" said Holden. "This is my ship! And—" he paused "—and Jimmy here doesn't know jack shit about navigating boats! Do you, Jimmy?" He nudged Alexei hard in the ribs.

Alexei shook his head.

"So he's staying up here! Like a guard!"

"Like a guard," said the Romanian, and turned to his two compatriots. They whispered among themselves in Romanian, and Alexei struggled to listen. "Deal," and "injury," and possibly "water." These Alexei could make out. Otherwise, he didn't have a clue.

"No," said the Romanian finally. "Don't want to let us alone to drive boat, you turn around, go home. Deal off."

Angry colour stained the capillaries of Holden's face, and he stepped forward—unmindful, for the moment, of the assault rifle between him and the Romanian. "Fuck you!" he screamed. "Fuck—" and he jabbed his finger at the Romanian's chest "—you!"

Alexei put his hand on Holden's shoulder, and gently pulled him back.

"Maybe you don't go home," snarled the Romanian. "Off the bridge!"

Holden raised up his hands and backed down the steps, and when another of the Romanians motioned to Alexei, he followed. At the bottom of the steps, there waited two other Romanians. Holden didn't argue when they ordered him back to the lounge, where the rest of the crew had been marshalled. It was there, explained one of the Romanians, that they would just have to wait.

"They said that you should stop meddling," Alexei told Holden. "They said that you were a fat ugly fuck who could as easily be drowned. The one guy said, 'Why doesn't he do as he's told?' The other guy said, 'Why don't you just shoot him. He is a real prick.' Then the guy with the rifle said, 'Let me deal with this.'"

Of course, not having understood more than a couple of words of the Romanian's conversation, Alexei had made it all up—but Holden seemed to swallow it as word-for-word Russian-to-American translation. And Alexei had read Holden correctly—the invective seemed to convince him more than anger him. Holden's eyes wrinkled distastefully, but he nodded.

"All right," said Holden. "All right, I was half-expecting some shit like this. These are the kind of people we're dealing with. Right, Russkie? Hey Russkie, what kind of guns were those fucks waving?"

"AKMs," said Alexei. "Like the AK-47, but a little better."

"Hah!" Holden grinned broadly, and slapping Alexei's shoulder. "You're remembering shit! You remember where you come from any better?" He dug his fingers savagely into Alexei's shoulder, and his grin turned feral. "Like maybe you recognized some people? Your comrades up there? For instance? Is this a fucking double-cross, Russkie?"

"Hey!"

Holden grunted as Heather grabbed his arm, and pulled it away from Alexei. "Leave him alone!" she hissed.

Holden turned to her, and for a second Alexei was afraid he was going to hit her. But he didn't—instead, he reached around her with his other hand and patted her ass. She glared up at him, and he laughed.

"Relax," he said. "I'm just yanking his chain. We'll be done with this whole thing in a couple hours." She let go, and glared at him as he made his way up to the podium. The rest watched him too, but without the same rancour; their heads swivelled like sunflowers marking the passing of hours. "Don't worry," he said to the group. "This is part of the plan—these guys are just super-cautious, all right? We'll be ready to load up in a couple hours, tops." And he raised his hands slightly, like a maestro at the ballet.

As if Holden had cued it, the motor yacht's deck shifted to port.

He'd grabbed her ass. Alexei thought about the empty barracks down below with their tiny beds, and the slim likelihood that fraudulent magazine subscriptions were as far as this apparently highly profitable racket went. As they began the long, lazy turn, Alexei looked at Heather, then at Holden Gibson, and then something turned in his stomach. And he made his decision.

THE GAMBLER
Игрок

Fyodor Kolyokov hadn't needed the isolation tank for a long time: not since the early days when all needs Physick were safely defined by the razor-wire fences of City 512. But need and desire often mingle to the same effect, and so as soon as he found a way, Kolyokov moved the tank from Russia to America. The tank was as much a part of his life as his eyes and his lungs and his heart.

The tank was an early prototype, baffled against sound with a set of casings pressed inside one another like nested Russian dolls—dolls made of iron and steel, concrete and horsehair, ceramic and lead. Sealed inside the tiniest doll, it wasn't hard to imagine weathering a nearby nuclear detonation.

The Cyrillic notations stamped on the outermost doll indicated expectations falling just short of that. Kolyokov had at various times tried to fill those letters with different types of cement—but the cold steel of the tank sucked moisture from the air like a thirsty whore, and Kolyokov's attempts at camouflage crumbled within days of their application. There was no making it into anything beyond what it was: an old KGB sensory isolation tank, that to anyone but Kolyokov would stink like an open sewer.

To Kolyokov, who had first swum in its briny middle three decades ago, it merely smelled . . . comfortable.

For the last of those decades, the isolation tank had gathered dust in a large storage locker in New Jersey. During that time, Kolyokov never visited—not in person. But he kept a watch on it all the same and once a year, he would send a sleeper to see to matters of cleaning and maintenance in person. There would come a day, he was sure, when such things as this tank did not matter to the intelligence community and its existence would no longer need be secret.

In 1997, with the Soviet Union half a decade in the grave, Kolyokov deemed that day to have arrived.

So now, the tank occupied most of the en suite bath to Kolyokov's rooms on the Emissary's 19th floor. The bath had at one time contained an immense Jacuzzi tub set in pink marble. But that luxury had been sacrificed to make room, so the tank had only to share the space with a low-flow toilet and a shower stall.

The floor was a thick slab of concrete underneath the tile, but Kolyokov had wished to take no chances and so had constructed a second floor, just inches above the original. It was more of a platform, really, made to distribute the tank's immense weight beyond its own dimensions.

The platform creaked as he placed a bare foot upon it now. Kolyokov was still groggy from shattered REM sleep, but he had to piss something fierce. The pissing, he thought, was why the dream had gone so badly. The reason that it had turned nightmare on him, and driven him awake.

This wouldn't have happened in the old days. The tank had been fitted with an assembly from the old Soyuz spacecraft—but the pump had failed years ago.

So Kolyokov hopped on one foot and the other, bladder twisting and wringing as he moved. He splashed brine all over the bathroom's two floors, as he made his way around the tank to the toilet. A thick stream of urine made a roar in the bowl that was deafening to Kolyokov's silence-calmed ear.

The door to the bathroom slid open as Kolyokov was finishing. He looked over a shoulder.

It was of course Stephen—his helper, his prize, and his great secret, Stephen Haber—who had been attending in the sitting room since the operation began. When was it? Kolyokov glanced at the wall clock. Thirteen hours ago. Just thirteen hours.

"Sir? Everything all right?"

Kolyokov sneered. "If everything were all right," he spat, "I would be still inside. I would know what was happening to my people. I would not be pissing in a toilet when there was work to be done."

"A bad dream," said Stephen with a little grin.

"Hah." Kolyokov shook himself off and moved back to the open hatch of the tank. He sat down on its rim and regarded Stephen. "Have you received any word?"

Stephen frowned. "Me? Oh. You don't mean over the phone?"

"Yes. By telephone, by fax, some e-mail. Anything?"

Stephen's eyes widened. "Shit," he said. "You *did* have a bad dream. You lost the scent, didn't you?"

What a little shit, thought Kolyokov. *That's what a lifetime in America does for you—a couple of decades of MTV and situation comedies and rap music turns you into a smart-assed little shit like Stephen. Not even good, purebred parents make a difference.*

Kolyokov had only found Stephen two years ago after looking up those parents. The two of them had been on the lam for nearly three decades, after the Weather Underground cell they'd infiltrated had broken up in '72. His search had ended not with them—they'd died in '91, in an unfortunate police standoff at a rented house in Michigan—but with Stephen, their only son, who had been living on the streets and turning tricks in Manhattan since he was twelve.

The parents had done their job, he supposed. Kolyokov could use Stephen and even trust him—despite the matter of his obstinate mind. But there was enough of America in him—including a dangerous amount of heroin that was easily expunged, and a percolating dose of HIV that wasn't—to make the young man something of an annoyance; much more so, certainly, than the farm-bred boys and girls he'd worked with over the years in City 512.

"Dogs pick up a scent," said Kolyokov. "Are you calling me a dog?"

"No," said Stephen. "You're not a dog. You lost the scent all the same, though." He smirked. "Have to show me your tricks some time. Before it's too late."

Kolyokov ducked back into the tank. "You spend enough time sleeping," he said. "Check the fax machine."

Stephen came over to the hatch. He leaned on it. "Something happened," he said. "I can see it in you. Tell me what it is. Did the ocean get you?"

"No. I know better." Kolyokov squinted at the circle of light as he sloshed back into the brine. "I lost the Goddamn scent," he said. "I had to piss. Don't you ever have to piss, boy?"

Stephen shrugged, and lifted the hatch cover over the light. And it was dark again. Kolyokov took a breath of the dank air in the tank. And he began to sleep.

For someone else with Kolyokov's problem, falling asleep would be a problem; restlessness would intervene and the night would stretch from minutes into an eternity. But as a rule, Kolyokov didn't fall asleep. Sleep was his avocation—and the word "fall" implied a clumsiness, a lack of forethought—an amateur mistake. Kolyokov approached sleep methodically. "Red," he whispered. "And orange and yellow. And green, and blue . . ."

And with the words, his eyelids fluttered shut, his breathing slowed, the spectrum flashed through his mind. The water numbed his flesh, and then all other sensation in his body was gone. There was a familiar rushing feeling, as of a body moving swiftly through a tunnel of chilled air. At the end of it, Kolyokov looked upon a brilliant, stratospheric light.

A less experienced dream-walker might have imagined himself dead—staring at the brilliance of his Creator, waiting to welcome him into the glories of the afterlife. But Kolyokov had been around long enough to tell the difference between Heaven and seven thousand feet. He rotated his gaze from the sun, and looked down through thinning clouds, at the grey-green waves of the Atlantic.

The fogbank was the last thing he'd seen before being driven out of his dream.

It was still there. It had grown in fact—now it squatted on the ocean like a pus-whitened sore, miles across.

It was not a real fog, though. Kolyokov could see through a real fog, at least well enough to find his people and move in them. This one was as impervious as lead.

Kolyokov took a breath, and let himself descend to its crown. The last time he had tried to penetrate the dome, he had done so without preparation—he had underestimated its strength.

And so it had thrown him from sleep, left him bug-eyed and shaking in his tank, clenching his bladder and gasping like an old man at the top of a stairway.

This time, he would prepare himself for the descent. He would not underestimate his opponents again.

So Kolyokov began to study the fog. As he did so, he began to apprehend certain flaws in its camouflage. It was white, but it was a white too pure—it bore no shadow, even though the cloud overhead was beginning to break and yellow sun was punching through. While wisps of vapour came off the fog, as Kolyokov studied it more closely he saw that by and large the vapour clung to it, as though made from a solid dome of dry ice. He fell slowly towards it, thinking that this was what the form of the fog must in fact be: a solidified dome—solidified to beings such as himself, that is—covering an area of the Atlantic of perhaps a dozen square miles.

Kolyokov laughed to himself. An old trick, that. It was the same thing he used on the hotel; the same thing the others had used on Petroska Station, to hide when hiding was needed, all those decades ago. But this one—this was the true thing that the Party had hoped for: a dome of psychic energy that would cover Moscow, so powerful that spy satellites would be confounded by its opacity and ICBMs would bounce off its hardy surface.

This artefact was still not such an encompassing defence—as Kolyokov contemplated it, he saw a flock of sea birds disappear within its folds to the south, penetrating the fog as easily as a cloud bank. To the world of Physick, it was nothing but a blind.

But it was enough, to convince him that the trade they were arranging was a good one. And it had been more than enough to drive him from his one remaining sleeper's mind.

Kontos-Wu had been dozing in her cabin on board the motor yacht when it began—in that semi-dreaming state when the two of them might confer directly, without the impediments of the conscious cover to intervene. As with all his sleepers, the conversation occurred in a metaphorical classroom. Kontos-Wu's was in a boarding school that she understood to be located in Connecticut.

Kolyokov was there to discuss a crisis. Alexei Kilodovich had gone missing just a few minutes before. Kolyokov didn't think he'd been killed—he'd have been able to tell that through other means. But the signal was lost all the same—and that was serious. Kolyokov had gone to great trouble to bring Kilodovich back into the fold. His presence in the upcoming exchange was crucial. His disappearance needed to be investigated.

Kontos-Wu sat at her little desk in the middle of the empty classroom. Outside the window, snow swirled and darkened the east coast American sky. The fluorescent tubes overhead flickered. She had a notebook in front of her and a thick pencil in her hand.

"In a moment," said Kolyokov, standing at the front of the classroom in front of a chalkboard, "you will awaken and step out of your cabin. You will proceed first to Kilodovich's cabin, and determine if he is there, and his state of well-being. If you are satisfied that all is well, you will return to your cabin. If you do not find him, you will search the ship. You will do so under the guise of a walk on deck to get some air. If anyone challenges you during this search, you will immediately become seasick, and vomit over the side of the ship."

Kontos-Wu raised her hand.

"Yes?"

"Sir, what if the vomit fails to convince?" The metaphor that Kontos-Wu constructed for herself here—a plump, short-haired child—took on an expression that Kolyokov recalled from the hand-to-hand combat exercises. "May I—"

"No killing," said Kolyokov, before she could finish. "We wish to retain Shadak's goodwill for now. And there is the matter of your cover. You are an investor—engaged in unseemly business, with unseemly people, yes. But not a killer. If vomiting doesn't work—maintain your cover. Which, as far as you understand, is the unvarnished truth. You are even less a liar than you are a killer. And if the truth doesn't work—get out of there. Any way you—"

The fog had begun as a singularity, an atom of Mind, then exploded, driving him away as if it were the edge of a shockwave. It may not have been impervious to Physick; but to the probing of a dream-walker, it was solid as neutronium. Kolyokov was worried that the instruction might not have taken—but in the end, he was glad to have given instruction rather than risked dream-walking her himself. Because the fog would have made a perfect block—and had he been dream-walking her, she would have fallen.

Now—assuming she interpreted the instructions—assuming there were no completely unforeseen hitches in the coming hours—at least she had a chance.

Kolyokov skimmed across its surface, ran his hands along it as he flew. It felt rough to the touch—if the hand had been Physick, the fog would have torn away flesh like it was the skin of a shark. As it was, Kolyokov could only maintain the contact for a few moments before he pulled away, and paused, just a few feet above the immense dome. It was unlikely, he thought, that he would find a way in from here. He sighed.

There would be no easy way.

So Kolyokov dove. Not at the dome—the impact of such a manoeuvre attempted so soon after the last one would no doubt shock his sleeping body into cardiac arrest—but at the waves that lapped about its perimeter. He slid through them as easily as did the sea birds, through the mind-fog above.

Kolyokov took a moment to orient himself in the cacophonic din of the ocean. There was too much life here—more to the point, too much life that communicated in the alpha range where Kolyokov walked. The salt water conducted the Discourse of that life like a giant single brain. A dream-walker could lose himself in such a place; fall into the rhythm of whale and squid and plankton, and let that replace his own, more disciplined cadence. The dream-walker thus ensorcelled would live and sleep and eventually die in the deep green song of the sea—unless a comrade knew where he had fallen, and had the wit and skill and inclination to come and pull him free. There were no such comrades these days, though, so Kolyokov had to rely upon himself.

Fortunately, Kolyokov also had his training, and even a little experience—once in the North Sea in 1973, and three times off Cuba, when he was helping hide the Petroska Station project. He dreamed himself a great, Mind-baffling sphere, and the din of the ocean quieted. The thing descended through the deepening green like a bathyscaphe.

"Byup," said Kolyokov. "Byup. Byup."

Byup was a mnemonic that Kolyokov's masters in City 512 had impressed upon him early—an onomatopoeic metaphor for the sound that a Soviet submarine's sonar made circa 1962. In an agent trained as Kolyokov was, the mnemonic would trigger a heightened awareness in the dream state, allowing the agent to discern details in dark or clouded conditions that would otherwise seem impenetrable.

Of course, nothing was truly impenetrable in the dream-walk—the "body" which Kolyokov occupied was a mnemonically constructed mirage of its own, and so were its eyes. At the core, Kolyokov knew he didn't need light and visibility. Dream-walking, he could see anything he damn well wanted to.

But like the bathyscaphe buffer Kolyokov used to dive safe undersea, the sonar was a necessary metaphor for Kolyokov to access his own innate talent—without completely disconnecting himself from his own identity.

So, "Byup," said Kolyokov again, and the mental sonar map of the sea around the cloud bank became marginally clearer.

The first thing he noted was that the cloud was a sphere and not merely a dome upon the water. No doubt it was as impenetrable underwater as it was above. He'd expected this, so was only a little pissed off. "Byup," he said.

The ocean floor was not far below the sphere's south pole—maybe fifty metres in parts. Kolyokov used a second and third "Byup" to determine that the sphere was no longer expanding—the distance between the two points remained the same through all three "byups."

Metaphors like the "byup" were useful for things like that kind of work. Still, this was a part of his dream-walking Kolyokov didn't relish. It showed just how long a time it had been since the art was practised by Italian peasants who wandered from their bodies each night armed only with metaphorical axes and spears, to fight the devils that threatened their crops. As with too much of the 20th century, it seemed that mechanization had overtaken the metaphors of dream-walking.

"Byup," said Kolyokov. "Byup. Byu—"

He stopped abruptly, and hung silent a moment in the waters. The sonar had struck something hard—a great metal thing. "Byup." Thirty metres long. "Byup byup." Seventy-five metres beneath the surface. "Byup." It was moving toward the cloud sphere. "Byup byup byup byup," said Kolyokov, then listened as the picture assembled itself: the sleek metal form of the conning tower; the propellers churning sea water behind it; the byup-byup-byup of its own sonar, probing the Physick of the sea around it.

Kolyokov drew a breath. *So*, he said to himself.

So. Can this be them? Can this be how they come?

Kolyokov stopped himself. There were no more answers to be had here in his bathyscaphe, uttering "byups" into the deep ocean. There was only one place to go—one thing to do now.

Kolyokov charted the old Soviet attack submarine's course, and set his own course to intercept it.

The cloud sphere may have been impenetrable to him—but Kolyokov passed through the concentric hulls of the submarine like the ghost that he effectively was.

He emerged into a hallway barely wide enough for two men to pass each other, narrowed to nearly a crawlspace by barnacle clusters of unidentifiable electronic equipment bolted at irregular intervals along its walls and ceiling. The lights in the corridor were dim, widely spaced, and vaguely reddish. More light came from the cathode ray tubes and blinking green and red jewel-lights attached to the equipment.

When Kolyokov allowed himself to listen, he found there was conversation everywhere. He smiled to himself as that conversation resolved itself into the Discourse—a mental shorthand that he recognized immediately from his earliest days. In City 512.

They are *here—this is the shipment!* he thought triumphantly—even as another part of him wondered at Shadak's reckless decision to use a decommissioned Soviet submarine to deliver them. It wasn't like Shadak to take this kind of risk; the Cold War may have been over for closing onto a decade, but that didn't mean the Americans would have switched off their satellites and ended their surveillance of the waters off their east coast. Why not use a fishing trawler? A cruise ship? A zeppelin for that matter? Even that would have been less conspicuous.

Kolyokov settled himself against the bulkhead, and listened to the Discourse. It was difficult to tell immediately what was being said—these children were, after all, the product of a much later generation than Kolyokov. Their breeding would have honed them on every level. Their training would have too—except, of course, that their training would not have progressed very far, in the ruins that were left after Rodionov's thugs shut down the program and left them all for dead.

Given such circumstances, Kolyokov was filled with a kind of familial pride, at the speed with which the Discourse played out. Why, it proceeded so quickly that he couldn't even tell for sure how many participants were engaged.

If only he could figure out what it was they were all saying to one another. Kolyokov pushed his pride down and listened—still feeling for all the world like a doddering retiree, trying to keep up with his toddler grandchildren during an afternoon at the beach.

Discourse would confound even a young man, of course. In its purest form, the conversation between properly attuned minds was like the chatter between computer modems—the 1s and 0s in the memory of a computer. But the computers—the processors—were minds. The talk of those minds would be nonsensical to anyone—but tremendously quick, an immensely powerful way to communicate.

The only way to access that communication—the images and thoughts and sensations that it communicated—was through a filter.

A metaphor—like the bathyscaphe. But in this matter, Kolyokov had long ago found that a simpler idea did the job.

The metaphorical pen Kolyokov had placed in his hand scratched across the metaphorical pad he had placed on his lap. He divided the page into columns. In the first column was a list of all the names he could derive from context of the Discourse. In the second column, a record of that context. So when one of the participants referred to Vladimir in the midst of a long string of images—of numbers and instrument panels and a thin-faced man in a navy blue jersey—Kolyokov would write down *Vladimir*. In the column next to it, he would record those images and ideas: numbers and instrument panels and the face of the man, with a kind of photographic accuracy only possible in the field of metaphor. He would do the same for Vanya and Olga and Doonya—and more numbers and ideas and faces, waiting until he had enough information to form a picture, discern the meaning of this accelerated dialect of Discourse. . . .

And then, abruptly, he stopped.

Next to Olga, he had written only one thing. A face that he recognized all too well. Black hair, one thick eyebrow crossing two small, squinting eyes; a wide-jawed, vaguely handsome face marred mainly by those dull eyes, the unimaginative cast of his mouth.

It was Kilodovich. Alexei Kilodovich. Kolyokov's lost sleeper. The *prize* in this whole sordid exchange.

What are you doing here? he said to himself.

"What are you doing here?"

Kolyokov started at the words, and the metaphor of notebook and pen vanished. He turned, and stared wonderingly at the child who stepped through the hatchway behind him.

She was tiny—not much more than two feet tall. Her black hair was short and baby-fine, and her fingers were small and weak—an infant's. When she walked, it was with the halting, uncertain clomping of a baby, still mastering the balance of her inner ear. She even wore a baby's red sleeper.

God, thought Kolyokov. She was so tiny, in so many ways so like an infant . . . and yet not at all like one. Not with those eyes.

"Well?" said the girl.

Kolyokov drifted toward her. "Which one are you?" he asked, wonder in his voice. "Little Olga? Doonya?"

The girl stepped back from him, as though she feared his touch. "Say what you're doing here," she said to him.

"I have come—" Kolyokov considered, assembled his thoughts to go with his words "—I have come to take you to a very good place. Where you will have all the wonderful food you can eat, and play wonderful games all of the time. No one will be cross with you ever again."

"Oh," said the girl. She stopped, her back against a black box twice as tall as she. "You are Fyodor Kolyokov, yes?"

"Yes," he said.

Kolyokov drifted closer to her still. He could see her eyes now—they were brown, but so dark a brown as to be almost black. It was a marker for them, those black eyes.

Incredible, he thought. *This one must be among the youngest to come from City 512; untrained, but so very, very potent.* Had she been the one who made the cloud sphere? He wondered. He wouldn't have doubted it.

"Vladimir," said the girl. It was the first time she spoke—all her other words had been thought. Her mouth opened wide around the word—wide as a great, red cavern, with nubs of new baby teeth sticking from the damp floor and ceiling. "Vladimir says Fyodor Kolyokov is a big bastard who I should not hesitate to eat if he is stupid enough to return."

"Eat?"

The little girl didn't answer. Her cavernous mouth simply closed tight around him, and the submarine—and everything else in the physical world—vanished for Fyodor Kolyokov.

The isolation tank was too well insulated for the sound of his sloshing and pounding and screaming to be heard beyond its confines. The sound baffling would quiet a bomb; it would be nothing for it to silence the death throes of a weak old man.

Desperately, he fumbled for the handle of the hatchway to let himself out. It should have been right above his head. Kolyokov's hand grasped about for it, but at every turn, he found himself holding empty air. Although he knew it would do him no good, Kolyokov screamed again: "Get me out! Stephen! Get me out of here! It's gone to hell! Everything's screwed!"

Kolyokov turned himself over, lowered his knees to touch the bottom of the tank so he could at least orient himself. But his legs kept going, and when they eventually straightened there was still no bottom for even his toes to touch; only the warm brine that smelled so distinctly of Kolyokov. Swearing to himself, Kolyokov began to tread that water.

"Those bastards," he said. "Those clever, vicious little bastards."

He meant it as a compliment. For trapped in what he was now sure was the baby girl's metaphorical belly, his body inert in a dark tank hundreds of miles to the west, Fyodor Kolyokov found that he wanted all the children with him, more than he ever had.

THE IDIOT
Идиот

While the yacht followed its escort of Romanian-piloted Zodiacs, Alexei ran through what seemed like dozens of schemes for killing Holden Gibson. A push, a squeeze, with his Asp, a sharp *tap!*, in any one of five places on Holden's body. Or more simply, a bullet.

None of them satisfied him. There were too many witnesses about, and too many of those witnesses were carrying guns.

And in any case, he had more to think about than Gibson's impending doom. The presence of Romanians, for instance. Were these the same Romanians with whom Mrs. Kontos-Wu was planning her rendezvous? It seemed at once the most likely and unthinkable prospect.

Which led to another obligation—one that would almost certainly override his pledge to kill Holden Gibson. If these were the same Romanians as had abducted Mrs. Kontos-Wu, Alexei would have to deal with them too, and extricate Mrs. Kontos-Wu from whatever trouble she'd found with them.

And then there were the children on board *Ming Lei 3*—were they the ones that Gibson intended to lock in his children's brig? Was he buying them from the Romanians in some kind of child slavery deal? They knew how to mix a drink and bring a blanket when it was cold—that was certainly a selling point—but, fingering his tender scalp, Alexei wondered if Gibson knew what he was getting into.

Some of the others in the lounge had gotten up and were milling around, so Alexei joined them. He stepped around the projection TV, and squinted out the windscreen. There was something up ahead—the yacht's prow obscured any direct view, but Alexei could make out peripheral activity on the water—a distant churning. Nearer, he saw their escort was beginning to fan out on either side of the yacht, and he felt the motor throttling down under his feet. The deck lurched as the motor yacht slowed down.

Holden strode across the room and stopped beside Alexei, near enough to strangle. "So what are we meeting here? Where's their Goddamn boat?"

Alexei peered ahead at the water, which was boiling like a soup. He'd seen water like that before.

"Underwater," said Alexei softly.

Holden didn't seem to have heard Alexei. His face began to redden. "This is not good," he hissed, and he glared down at Alexei. "You watch my back, Russkie."

"Do not worry," said Alexei, and meant it: Holden's worrying just made him a more difficult target. "But tell me who it is you are meeting?"

Holden snorted. "None of your business," he said.

Alexei stood and walked to the fore section of the lounge. Ahead, the churning water boiled and broke as the conning tower surfaced.

Alexei leaned against the railing below the windscreen. "Shit," he whispered.

"That's a submarine!" said Holden.

"Yes," said Alexei. It was a Soviet Project 641 Attack Submarine. Diesel-electric powered, and too noisy by half, which was why the Soviet navy had decommissioned the last of them in the late 1980s. He didn't see any point in sharing that insight with Holden just now though.

"A submarine!" Holden cupped his hands together and shook them like he was rolling dice. "Shit and hell, shit and hell."

The sky overhead was a flat grey, and the light it threw added not a hint of colour to the black gleam of the submarine's hull as it followed the tower into the air. Water fell from it in sheets, making froth that festered like infection along the length of its hull. The motor yacht pitched noticeably on the displaced ocean, and Alexei noticed with a chill that there were no markings on the submarine—at least none above the water line. Holden's crew lined the edge of the lounge, gaping. Evidently they weren't expecting this any more than Alexei was.

Or Holden. He grabbed Alexei's shoulder. "You better tell me what's going on," he said.

Alexei shrugged—in so doing extricating himself from Holden's grip.

"How should I know?" he said. "You won't even tell me what you're up to."

"I'm going to buy some children," he said. "Haven't you worked that out for yourself?"

Alexei opened his mouth and closed it again. Did Holden know that he'd found the smuggler's hold? He dismissed the thought quickly, though. Holden was on a different tack.

"Even if they own a submarine, which I wouldn't have thought possible, why have they got it doing this kind of work?" Holden's face was reddening again. "It's like putting up a fucking flag—look at us, Mister U.S. spy satellite! We're selling children off the shore of the fuckin' United States! They could kick off a fuckin' nuclear war!"

Much more of this, and my troubles are over, thought Alexei. *He'll give himself a coronary.*

"You are purchasing children?" he asked innocently. "Do you buy them for fucking, or just to change your linen when you jerk yourself off?"

Alexei had hoped to push Holden that little bit farther—if not to a heart attack, then at least toward some further indiscretion. But the words had the opposite effect. Holden's face drained of red and he regarded Alexei calmly.

"I'll kill you, you keep talking like that—you know that?" he said. "Remember whose boat you're on."

Holden jammed his hands into the pockets of his windbreaker and turned away from Alexei, watching the submarine rise. Which was good. Alexei wasn't sure how the old man would have interpreted his smile if he'd seen it.

The Zodiacs were wheeling back around now, making sharp smacks as they crossed the waves made by the surfacing submarine. Behind them, the door to the lounge swung open. Alexei turned and saw two of the Romanians from the bridge. Both had their AKMs slung over their shoulders. One of them caught Alexei's eye and motioned him over. Holden, preoccupied an instant longer than Alexei by the spectacle of the unanticipated submarine, hurried to catch up.

"You come with us," said one of the Romanians. He pointed at Holden, and then at Alexei. "You also, heh?"

"And her," said Holden. He pointed to Heather. "And him." He pointed to James. "And—"

"Enough," said the other Romanian. "She may come also. But no more than that."

"Fine." Holden patted Heather—on the shoulder this time, but it might as well have been her ass to Alexei—and moved to follow the Romanians. Alexei gripped the asp in his pocket and followed them all onto the deck.

The submarine's captain was a slight woman, with black hair cropped short and eyes wide as a fawn's. Alexei thought two things about the captain: first, he recognized her from somewhere—where, he couldn't say, but familiarity stuck in him nonetheless. And second, to his eye, she was no older than twenty. She would not have been born when this submarine was taken from service.

Alexei shivered. The submarine was growing nearer the bow as the Zodiac turned once more towards it. The young woman who behaved like the submarine's commander was looking out at the Zodiac now, her arms crossed, black hair blowing in the ocean wind while her crewmen stood still around her.

God, he recognized her from somewhere. But where? The memory was locked from Alexei.

The Zodiac's outboard throttled back, and Holden sat back, folded his hands conspicuously on his gut. Alexei met Heather's eye, and he shrugged. *What do you want me to do*?

Alexei had been a great many places in the service of the People, and arrived in those places by many conveyances; but none of those involved spending any time at all on a 641 Attack Submarine. Standing on the deck now as it pitched in the gentle ocean swells, the first thing that struck him about it was its narrowness. Two wrong steps to either side and Alexei would be sliding down the submarine's slick black hull and into the ice-water sea.

The same, he realized sickly, could be said for Holden Gibson, who wandered dangerously near both edges of the deck in the space of just a single step. Alexei added the possibility to his growing archive of M.O.s.

But it was not to be. The young captain had disappeared below for the moment. But a pair of the Nike-wearing crewmen stood in too-easy reach, and three more watched them from the conning tower. One of those held a submachine gun, its barrel balanced against the bulkhead. Even Heather knew enough to stop sending her *kill-him-kill-him-now* looks Alexei's way.

"Now I don't want either of you to say anything to fuck this up," said Holden under his breath. "This is very fucking delicate work coming up and I want you to remember that."

Alexei opened his mouth to say that he would be sure to remember that, but Holden held up his hand to shut him up.

"Not *anything*," he repeated.

Heather nodded obediently, and Alexei did the same. For that instant, he was sure the two shared the same thought: *If there is a fuck-up here, it will be Holden's—not ours*.

Alexei looked back at Holden's motor yacht. It was distant enough to appear quite small, but even with the crappy visibility, Alexei could make out details: the dingy on the aft-deck, the bridge, the steel cable railings. He could see some figures against that railing.

"Hey!"

All three of them turned to the voice at the top of the conning tower. It was high-pitched enough to come from a girl, and first Alexei thought it was the young girl they'd seen before. But it wasn't. It was a little black-haired boy—or rather his head, sticking up over the top of the tower like he was standing on his toes. He couldn't have been more than six years old. He was waving at them.

Holden squinted up at him, shading his eyes as though it were a sunny day, and waved back. His mouth twisted into something that it only took Alexei a second to recognize as a warm smile.

"Hey there yourself, big guy!" he shouted back. "Watchya doin' way up there?"

The boy giggled, and Alexei shivered. It was as though, with the boy's arrival, a different man came to inhabit Holden Gibson's skin: a happy grandfather who always brought the best presents for birthdays, and delivered funny bedtime stories on cue. Alexei shouldn't have been surprised—Holden had done well by his junior kindergarten magazine cult, and he couldn't have done it being thick-thumbed with the kids. Alexei half-expected Holden to offer the boy a candy bar next.

It wasn't necessary, though. The boy was in Holden's spell. "Funny man!" he shouted in Russian, and disappeared. But he was only gone for a moment, while he scrambled down the ladder rungs at the back of the conning tower. He reemerged at the tower's base, running full tilt along the narrow deck towards them. He was going so fast that Alexei worried the kid would slip off the side of the submarine. Of course, he didn't slip or fall or even falter—even when he tangled his way through the crowd of adult crewmen and nearly knocked one of them off as a result.

Kids never get enough credit, Alexei thought. *They're smarter and faster and stronger than any of us are willing to admit.*

Which, he supposed, *is why adults like Holden Gibson find them so very useful.*

Holden bent to his knees and threw his arms open to catch the kid just an instant before collision. The kid fell against Holden's chest and Holden's arms dropped around him in an enthusiastic bear hug. "Funny man," said the kid again.

Holden picked the kid up and turned to face Alexei and Heather. Alexei expected to see a glint of calculation in Holden's eye, but there was none of that—there was only the dumb cheer that new grandfathers get in the maternity ward. Just to look at him, Alexei couldn't imagine Holden Gibson ever having presided over a gang of whipped boys and girls scamming their way across North America. He would have blown his bankroll buying them all presents.

Heather elbowed Alexei—at first, he thought, to bring him back to reality. But she was pointing, past Holden and back to the conning tower.

"Shit," said Alexei.

The tower base was surrounded by children.

Alexei hadn't even looked away from it when Holden turned; he'd just focused on Holden. For an instant. His peripheral vision should have spotted movement on the ladder; he should have seen these kids coming down.

And they should still be coming down. It *had* only been an instant.

"Hey!"

Alexei started. He was slumped, Heather's shoulder jammed into his armpit holding him upright. His feet were tangled underneath him, barely supporting his weight. Heather repeated herself, *sotto voce*: "Hey. Are you okay?"

Alexei shook his head, straightened his feet and stood up. He didn't let go of Heather, though. He'd blacked out—and couldn't even remember having done so. It was a miracle he hadn't slid off the submarine and drowned in the ocean.

"Fine," he said. "I'm fine."

"I think you got a concussion," said Heather.

"Maybe," said Alexei. He was distracted, though. The children had moved again since he'd last looked. They were crowded around Holden, who had by now adopted the combined mannerisms of a department store Santa Claus and a rock star. He beamed across the upturned faces of the children—taking each in individually, his smile broadening progressively until his gaze rose to meet Heather's.

"Yup," he shouted, "Thirteen of them. Just like she promised. Now let's get the fuck off this tin can and back to civilization!"

They returned to the motor yacht in a convoy of two Zodiacs—one with Heather and eight of the children, and a second with Holden and the remaining five kids. Once again, Alexei found that he had an opportunity to fulfill the bargain he'd made with Heather, and kill Holden Gibson.

All right, thought Alexei. *This is it.* Even with less than half the kids on board, the Zodiac was overcrowded. And for that, there was only one Romanian on board with them, and he was operating the outboard. The children sat in moon-faced silence around him, and Holden and Alexei were at the front.

He gripped the asp in his pocket and sidled close to Holden. He would take the asp in his right fist so that only an inch of the metal would extend out. With his left hand, he would encircle Holden's immense head, and with sudden force smash the asp into his temple. Holden would die quickly—more quickly than he deserved—and with luck, Alexei could guide his body over the side before the murder had even registered. If necessary, he'd deal with the Romanian afterwards. And the children, thought Alexei, should only thank him.

Alexei glanced at Holden—intending to meet his eye, draw the old man close enough to kill. But Holden wasn't biting. He was frowning, and looking at the horizon.

"What now?" he said.

Alexei looked—and his heart leaped.

A second motor yacht was bearing down on them. It must have been occluded by the conning tower of the submarine as it approached, because it was quite near—not more than 200 metres off, sending up white water as it rode across the Atlantic swells. It throttled back and turned as they watched, and as it turned, Alexei could read the words on its stern:

Ming Lei 3.

Amar Shadak's yacht.

Crawling with Romanians.

Where Mrs. Kontos-Wu was presumably still being held.

Alexei let go of the asp. The plan for killing Holden Gibson would have to be put on hold once more. Alexei needed to figure out a way back to the yacht. And there was only one way for that. He took his hands out of his pockets, rubbed them together for one last grasp at warmth before plunging, and prepared to roll off the side of the Zodiac himself.

He was stopped by a tiny hand on his arm. He looked down—it was one of the smaller ones, a little oval-faced girl of maybe three. She stared solemnly at him and shook her head.

"Don't go there," she said in perfect Russian. "She's gone."

It was no more than a second later that the plume of water arose in front of the submarine, and a second after that, that Alexei understood what that plume signified.

He put his left arm—the one that seconds ago would have helped kill Holden Gibson—over the old man's shoulder, and pulled him to the floor of the Zodiac along with the little girl. The other children were already down.

"What the fuck?" said Gibson again.

Ming Lei 3 exploded as the torpedo struck home. The explosion was, by any definition, spectacular: it sent a jet of water into the sky and a fireball flecked with debris across the water. There was even a shockwave that roared past the Zodiac like a gale and nearly flipped it over. When it passed, there were only fragments of *Ming Lei 3*—visible for seconds, before they vanished beneath the waves.

A moment later, the submarine followed.

Alexei slumped against the rubber gunwale of the Zodiac and screwed his eyes shut. His misery grew by an order of magnitude. For he had failed at two things today: killing Holden Gibson—and protecting Mrs. Kontos-Wu.

THERE ARE NO GUILTY PEOPLE

Виноватых людей нет

Mrs. Kontos-Wu spent her formative years at Bishop's Hall, a girl's boarding school in the hills of northern Connecticut carved out of the rambling summer home of Emmanuel Bishop. As she would explain to anyone who asked, Emmanuel Bishop was of the textile Bishops, a clan who during the Second World War became better known as the Parachute Bishops and in the post-war boom of the 1950s and beyond became more infamous as the Cuban, the Costa Rican, and finally the Atlantic City Bishops.

The tuition was steep, but her guardians were willing to pay the price. Bishop's Hall had a reputation in certain circles. Ask a Bishop's Hall Girl what she'd learned at Bishop's, and without even having to even consider the question, she'd answer:

Everything.

Mrs. Kontos-Wu was a Bishop's Hall Girl now and forever. It seemed as though every morning, she would wake up recalling a new morsel of information or advice gleaned during her years walking those oak-panelled halls—advice that had direct and frequently devastating application in the course of her day. Even the bad days—the worst days, the days such as this one—were improved by the memory of her education.

This morning, for instance, she'd remembered something about the truth.

You are even less a liar than you are a killer, Mr. Bishop had told her, towering over her in the drawing room math class at Bishop's Hall, as the wind whipped snow across the leaded-glass windows over the bookshelves. *Tell the unvarnished truth.*

The unvarnished truth.

She recalled this kernel of advice once more in the afternoon, as a very nice couple named Jerri and Elmer Bergensen hauled her out of the ocean and onto their motorboat.

No matter how awkward it might be to do so, she would answer all of their questions with only that—the truth. Unvarnished.

"Are you all right?" asked Jerri.

Mrs. Kontos-Wu said that she was. She had simply felt it necessary to leave the company of the disgusting Romanians on a motor yacht called *Ming Lei 3*, whom she had joined on the pretext of discussing a business deal. Jerri made a sympathetic noise.

"Should we radio the coast guard?" asked Elmer. "Is this a—a criminal thing?"

"In international waters, maybe," said Mrs. Kontos-Wu. But she didn't think the coast guard would carry any jurisdictional power there, so she said it didn't make sense to call them.

"I only want to get home," she said.

The next roster of questions concerned Mrs. Kontos-Wu's life raft, which as they watched, Mrs. Kontos-Wu deflated and folded back into a satchel no bigger than a seat cushion. Mrs. Kontos-Wu explained that she'd bought the thing last year at Trekker's Outfitting Co-Op in Manhattan. This made Jerri instantly curious. Jerri and Elmer were wearing matching TOC windbreakers and drank their tea from a stainless steel thermos with the TOC logo stamped prominently on the side. According to Elmer, Jerri bought her underwear there. TOC's home page was book marked on both their web browsers. And neither of them recalled seeing a TOC self-inflating life raft that fit in a seat cushion. They would have bought two if they had. What gives? they both asked.

Mrs. Kontos-Wu explained that as she had a special relationship with a founding member of the co-op, she'd been given a lifetime subscription to the Iron Curtain Catalogue, which was delivered quarterly by encrypted email. The catalogue included a whole range of interesting equipment and weaponry decommissioned from the Soviet arsenal that the co-op deemed unsuitable for the Western market. Jerri and Elmer both laughed. They thought Mrs. Kontos-Wu was kidding.

The questions stopped for the moment, and Elmer went to the wheel, to guide the motorboat back to their club in Long Island. Jerri reached into the cooler to offer Mrs. Kontos-Wu a beer. She accepted it gratefully, and leaned back, watching the horizon grow from a blur to a line to the jagged hint of a skyline. Jerri offered her a second beer when she was finished, and when Mrs. Kontos-Wu declined, she shrugged and opened another for herself. Halfway through that beer, Jerri could no longer contain her curiosity. What kind of business, she asked, did Mrs. Kontos-Wu have with a bunch of filthy Romanians on a yacht called *Ming Lei 3* anyway?

Mrs. Kontos-Wu leaned over the side of the boat, heaved once or twice and vomited a spray of thin yellow foam into the boat's frothing wake.

Jerri helped her clean herself up, but wasn't to be dissuaded, and asked again:

What kind of business did Mrs. Kontos-Wu have with the Turks?

So Mrs. Kontos-Wu answered her truthfully.

This led to a lot of activity.

"Holy shit," said Jerri, "you're not kidding are you?"

"No," said Mrs. Kontos-Wu.

"You fucking *monster*," said Jerri. She started to get up, and opened her mouth to yell. Mrs. Kontos-Wu stopped her by stuffing the neck of her empty beer bottle into Jerri's mouth. She grabbed her hair for leverage to push the thing down Jerri's throat. Elmer, at the boat's controls the whole time, hadn't even heard their conversation, which itself was far noisier and more animated than Jerri's death throes. When Mrs. Kontos-Wu joined him at the controls, he asked her how Jerri was doing back there.

More truth. Elmer yelled and jumped out of his seat, and as he did so Mrs. Kontos-Wu took hold of his leg. Elmer sprawled to the deck, right next to Mrs. Kontos-Wu's TOC rubber-raft seat cushion. Before he could get up, she took hold of the cushion, straddled Elmer with both knees on his arms, and held it over his face until he, too, was dead.

Mrs. Kontos-Wu gave herself a breather then, and squinted over the bow to the skyline and smiled. This was not just any skyline, but a Manhattan skyline in perfect twilight, the windows of its skyscrapers ignited with that come-hither glow that had first mesmerized her three decades ago. She knew them by name—the Chrysler building, the Empire State; Trump's magnificent golden towers. The World Trade.

And of course, the Emissary. The Home. The Hall. Though its windows were dark, it gleamed with inner light amid its taller siblings.

Mrs. Kontos-Wu was near now. But was she near enough to paddle ashore? She would have to take the chance. She rummaged under the gunwale, where a small oar had been stowed, then rummaged again in the TOC cushion-raft for the spare CO_2 cartridge. It only took a minute to hook it up to the raft's valve. As the raft began to inflate, Mrs. Kontos-Wu felt a pang of guilt. She wasn't a killer, Mr. Bishop had said.

The half-inflated raft slapped against the waves like the palm of an angry giant's hand. Maybe, thought Mrs. Kontos-Wu, old Mr. Bishop had been wrong about her not being a killer. The dead Bergensens certainly made for compelling evidence to the contrary. So maybe—maybe there was a part of her that Mr. Bishop had not been able to apprehend so well during her years at Bishop Hall. Maybe that part was a killer.

Maybe the voice that spoke to her now—the one that was congratulating her for her quick and smooth reactions, her ability to make difficult and necessary decisions—maybe that voice was a truer one than Mr. Bishop's ever was.

THE HOUSE OF THE DEAD
Дом мёртвых

The brochures didn't lie when they said the Emissary Hotel had a view of Central Park. Not technically. It was true for nine rooms, stacked on top of one another on the 11th through 19th floors. If you knelt on the corner of the king-sized beds, pulled yourself up on the headboard and craned your neck just so, you could make out the tufts of greenery through the twenty-metre space between the water tanks that crowned two ancient apartment blocks.

There was a better view, of course, but it took some work to see it. You had to slow down your breathing, empty your mind of worldly worry, reach into yourself and unleash your imagination. Then you could expand the greenery here and here, there and over there, transform the buildings and water towers into transparencies until the deep green splendour of the heart of Manhattan was spread before you.

For guests of discipline and vision, these nine rooms were a deal. The rooms cost no more than the other thirty-seven similar-sized rooms at the Emissary that looked out on the roof of the parking garage next door.

Stephen Haber sucked his cigarette dead and climbed down off the corner of the bed in the topmost of those rooms. The vision of Central Park shrank back to its unimpressive line of green.

The telephone was ringing. Stephen lifted it from its cradle and readied himself for the worst.

"Good afternoon Amar," said Stephen.

"M-m-mister Haber?"

Stephen relaxed. It wasn't Shadak, or Shadak's people. As per Kolyokov's instructions, Stephen had put the call in for the Turkish gangster—but he wasn't looking forward to having it returned. Amar Shadak liked to fuck with him on the phone, play the big-time power broker to Stephen's meagre executive assistant, and Stephen did not like that at all.

This was just Richard, the day guy at the front desk. Richard used to be one of their professors at MIT, before they'd retired him in '95. Kolyokov had locked up the old identity as tight as he could, but nothing was airtight, and the procedure had left poor old Richard with a quavering voice, a tic in his lower lip, and an unshakable sense he should be off inventing something instead of here, waiting for reservations that seldom came. Stephen liked talking to Richard a lot more than he did Shadak.

"Hello Richard," said Stephen.

"The-e-ere is a young woman here to see you, sir."

"Yeah? Don't move, buddy." Richard gripped the phone tight against his head and shut his eyes.

Kolyokov wasn't teaching him shit about dream-walking, so Stephen had done a little work on his own. Last month, he went down to the psychic fair in Jersey while the old bastard was sleeping.

There, he'd met Lorelei Jones, a middle-aged lady with wide raccoon eyes and a constant smile, who claimed to be able to use telephone lines to read people's feelings. She'd sold Stephen some tapes that promised to help him do it too. The tapes turned out to be a pretty basic alpha-state inducement loop, but she had some handy visualization metaphors and Stephen had incorporated a couple of them into his repertoire.

So, eyes closed, Stephen imagined himself climbing a set of spiral stairs that went up the twisty wire of the telephone receiver. He opened the big iron door behind Richard's ear that led into his head. And he sat down at the big control panel behind the old engineering prof's eye sockets. He flipped the on-switch to fire up the twin security monitors that would tap into Richard's visual cortex, so he could get a look at this woman who knew he was staying at the Emissary.

"Mr. Haber?"

The metaphor dissolved and Stephen's own eyes snapped open. "Fuck!" He bashed the telephone receiver against the night table. "I said sit still!"

The outburst had left Richard flummoxed. He cleared his throat for a few seconds before asking: "Mr. Ha-a-aber? She say-ays she works with you? At Wo-olf-Jordan? Shall I send her u-u-u-up?"

"Wolfe-Jordan." Stephen calmed down: he wouldn't need to get a look at Richard's "young woman" if she was from Wolfe-Jordan. He knew who she was. The only other person in the world who worked at Wolfe-Jordan was a piece of thick-necked ex-KGB muscle named Kilodovich—whom they'd hired just a couple of months ago over Stephen's objections.

It would have to be Kontos-Wu. And neither she nor Kilodovich should have any reason—any means—to be showing up at the Emissary tonight. Unless—unless she was coming back with some resolution to the snafu with the pickup this morning.

"Send her up," said Stephen. "Just have Miles follow her. Make sure she's not being followed by anyone else."

"I-I-I'll call him, sir."

Miles Shute was the Emissary's Convention and Conference Liaison. Being as the Emissary didn't generally attract too many of either, it didn't matter that Miles' true skill set lay elsewhere. If there was any trickery in this unannounced visit, Miles would ferret it out and eliminate it before the elevator had made it between the 12th and 14th floors. Stephen hung up, satisfied that he'd covered everything. He thought briefly about going and rousing Kolyokov, and thought better of it. The old man had been in a rotten enough mood the last time he'd woken—and that was only because he had to pee. Stephen didn't want to think about what kind of wrath a deliberate interruption would bring down on him.

And frankly, it was only Kontos-Wu. Stephen didn't need Kolyokov awake to deal with her.

So Stephen shucked his bathrobe, pulled on a pair of pants and a T-shirt, lit another cigarette and waited for the knock at the door. Kontos-Wu would be easy. It was Shadak he was worried about, and that call might not come for a while.

There were no elevators at Bishop's Hall—if a young lady wanted to change floors she used the sweeping mahogany-banistered staircases with plush violet-patterned carpets, thank you very much—so Mrs. Kontos-Wu didn't even think about using the ones here. There was a staircase around the corner, under the creamy white EXIT light, and there she went.

The stairs immediately disappointed her—The Emissary was no Bishop's Hall, not by any means. The banisters were metal, for one thing, and the steps weren't carpeted but covered in a knobby black plastic deal.

Mrs. Kontos-Wu ran the first nine floors before the cumulative fatigue of the day caught up with her and she had to rest. It was then, as she stood bent over, gasping for breath, that she heard her pursuer—just for an instant, clattering up the stairs as she had been. Then the noise stopped. Mrs. Kontos-Wu gulped one more lungful of air and pulled back against the wall. She slowed her breathing, willed her thundering heartbeat back, and as she did so, she could almost trick herself into believing she was standing on a landing in the west wing of the Hall—evening sun casting shafts of light through the leaded glass windows behind her. She could almost imagine the other there with her: not Mr. Bishop this time, but a student—her best friend Lois? Yes! Lois! Thick black hair and the palest of skin, Mrs. Kontos-Wu had thought she was the most beautiful girl in the world. She'd wanted desperately to be like Lois, and missed her fiercely when she'd graduated.

Now, Lois stood in the shadows beneath the window, visible only by the faint ember of the cigarette she was smoking. The smoke curled over her head and joined the dust motes in the sunlight. *Don't let them catch me*, she said. *Whatever you do*.

"Don't worry," said Mrs. Kontos-Wu. *Shh*, said Lois, so Mrs. Kontos-Wu repeated: *Don't worry*.

The footsteps were still coming up the stairs, but more slowly. Over the banister, Mrs. Kontos-Wu could see the pink curve of a bald man's scalp—she could hear his own laboured breathing as he climbed.

In the shadows, Lois lit another cigarette. Lois took a brief puff, and gestured impatiently to Mrs. Kontos-Wu.

Well?

The bald man's eyes were well over the top of the banister by then, but he didn't get a chance to see Lois or anything else before Mrs. Kontos-Wu was upon him.

"Jesus," said Stephen a minute and a half later, "you look like hell."

Most of the time, Stephen would have found something more diplomatic to say—but looking at Mrs. Kontos-Wu standing in the hallway, Stephen thought that if anything he'd understated the case. More than anything, she resembled a street person. The kind of street person who'd gone off their medication a month ago, been rolled for their coat and last bathed in an East River garbage scow's wake. It was a long way from the sleek, predatory Wall Street maven she was programmed to play. Her long black hair was tangled like dry branches—her face was smudged with dirt and maybe blood—and the walking shorts and tank top she was wearing were grey and torn.

Her eyes were the deadest thing about her—they stared blankly at him and through him, hooded as they were beneath slightly swollen lids.

"Well, get inside," said Stephen. He stood aside and beckoned. Mrs. Kontos-Wu nodded and stepped across the threshold. He shut the door behind her as she continued across the floor toward the suite's modified bathroom.

"Hey!" said Stephen, following after her. "What're you doing?"

"*I have to pee*."

"What?" Stephen frowned. She'd said it in Russian—idiomatic Russian, which so far as Stephen understood, Mrs. Kontos-Wu was not programmed to speak. And she was heading to the bathroom.

Where Kolyokov's tank was set up.

Evil premonition lanced through Stephen.

Someone was dream-walking in Mrs. Kontos-Wu, and it wasn't Kolyokov. Stephen had seen the master at work in Mrs. Kontos-Wu, and this dream-walker was an amateur by comparison.

It wasn't Kolyokov. But she was going to see Kolyokov. And when she saw him, Stephen was sure, she was going to kill him.

Stephen launched himself across the room. He connected with Mrs. Kontos-Wu in the small of her back, and his momentum carried both of them into one of the armchairs flanking the bathroom entrance. Stephen locked his arms around her waist.

Mrs. Kontos-Wu shrieked. She twisted and bucked in his grip, but Stephen held tight. She managed to get hold of his left ear and twisted hard. The pain was incredible, but Stephen didn't let go. He had, after all, been through this before. He'd been through worse than this, in fact—with his parents, no less, when he was eleven.

They were hosting a dinner party in Wisconsin when the call came. Stephen didn't have any idea who it was at the time—although later, with Kolyokov's help, he would learn that it was from a New York-based embassy official named Gregor Ivchyn. When Stephen caught up with him much later, the old ex-Commie had stutteringly explained he was doing the KGB equivalent of cleaning up his office on the way out.

Like shredding documents, da?

At the time, all Stephen had known was that a shadow had drawn across his mother's eyes as she handed the phone to his father, and when he took it he nodded and that same look fell upon him. *What is it*? said Mrs. Stewart from the dining room. *Is everything all right*? Dad strode across the room like a marching soldier and strangled her before she could say anything else. Mr. Stewart tried to stop him, but Mom brained him with the cast iron frying pan and he collapsed into the mashed potatoes. Their son, Ted—an athletic 13-year-old whom Stephen had developed something of a thing for—was upstairs in the bathroom at the time. The fact that he wasn't in the room—and that Stephen had such an overpowering thing for him—was probably what saved Stephen's life. Before his Dad had even released Mrs. Stewart's neck, and his Mom had recovered her balance from the second fry-pan swing, Stephen was on the staircase. He burst into the bathroom, found Ted was just buckling his trousers, and somehow managed to convince him to follow him to the back bedroom where there was a window that opened and a small porch roof. Ted was halfway out the window when Stephen's Mom appeared in the door, framed against the hall light. She held the pan like the weapon it had become.

But she dropped it as she saw Ted making his escape, and lunged across the room. Stephen's Mom grabbed his foot with both hands and yanked hard. Stephen can still remember the cry that Ted let loose—a surprisingly girlish sob as his middle hit against the windowsill. Stephen's Mom braced her foot against the wall beneath the window and prepared to yank again. But Stephen didn't let her. He jumped on her back, pulling at the long, greying hair around her temples like reins on a horse, and digging his knees hard into her side. She shrieked and let go of Ted, who scrambled outside.

Mom! Stop it! Stephen screamed, but Mom wouldn't. She threw herself backwards so hard he could hear plaster sprinkling loose from the ceiling below them. Stephen let go, the wind knocked out of him, and as he lay there gasping his Mom rolled over and got to her knees. She straddled him, and placed her left hand over his mouth. Without so much as blinking—so much as blinking!—she pinched his nose shut with her right hand. Stephen could feel his lungs closing off and his breathing diminish almost immediately.

He would have died but for Ted, who shouted through tears: *Hey! Stop it, Mrs. Haber! Where's my Mom! MOM*! Stephen's Mom let her only son go to finish the job on his best friend—and Stephen took the only chance he had. He grabbed the frying pan from where it had fallen and swung it the same way he'd seen his Mom swing it at Mr. Stewart. He wasn't tall enough to have the same devastating effect—he just managed to reach the middle of her back—but it sent her to the floor twitching if not dead. Stephen yelled at Ted to run and call the police before heading out the window—followed by the pounding footsteps of his father running up the stairs.

When the police got there, they found four corpses. Which, as Ivchyn explained later, had all been according to their programming. A catastrophic termination was how he put it. *Like the paper shredder, da?* Ivchyn had smiled—still not understanding the depths of his predicament so far as Stephen was concerned. *I am glad they did not finish you too, boy. You are a treasure of the state—a true treasure*. And then his eyes had widened, and taken a quite sinister cast. He leaned forward, and spoke the words:

Baba Yaga. Manka. Vasilissa.

The old man had thought those words would shut Stephen's own programming down—make him docile, knock any thoughts of murder from his mind; and then make him pliant to whatever new programming Ivchyn wanted to install. Baba Yaga. Manka. Vasilissa. That's what the words were for: every sleeper in the *Komitet* could be switched off, their programming accessed with the little mnemonic. Had Stephen known the words the night of his parents' death, everyone would have been spared a lot of grief. Of course, at the time they would have had a similar effect on him—his parents had been programming him since he was old enough to see straight.

It was comical, actually, watching the brief triumph in the Ivchyn's eye turn into terror as Stephen raised the little revolver and shot him through the heart.

Thanks to Kolyokov, Stephen wasn't programmed for anything these days.

But Mrs. Kontos-Wu was. "Baba Yaga. Manka. Vasilissa," said Stephen as the cartilage in his ear made a cracking noise. "Baba Yaga—"

"—Manka. Vasilissa," said the boy at the top of the book-ladder.

"Sh-sh!" said Mrs. Kontos-Wu. The boy was making her angry. Mrs. Kontos-Wu had found what she thought to be a refuge in the library; just her and the books, the wonderful smell of the old leather and house dust, cooked to a sharp intensity by the afternoon sunlight.

Lois had sent her here for a while, to relax; catch up on some reading; maybe get a little shut-eye curled up in one of the high-backed leather chairs by the windows. Let the setting sun do its work on her. *You're putting yourself under too much pressure*, Lois had said, and Mrs. Kontos-Wu had to agree.

So the boy at the top of the ladder did nothing but tick her off. She closed the pink and blue covers of the Becky Barker book she'd picked for the afternoon, and set it down on the end table beside her.

"Just what do you think you're doing here?" she snapped. "This isn't the gym! Get off that ladder now!"

"Ow!" said the boy. He appeared to be on some pain. "Listen—Manka! Ow! I mean—Baba Yaga—Manka! Vasilissa!"

What a hateful, curious boy. Mrs. Kontos-Wu got up and crossed the library floor. She stood at the base of the ladder and gave it a good shake. "What kind of talk is that?" she demanded.

"Hey! Let go!" The boy's face scrunched into a mask of pain and he swatted at his groin—as though an invisible hand were grabbing and twisting there. "Jesus! Mrs. Kontos-Wu! Wake up!"

Mrs. Kontos-Wu shook her head. "I came here for a nap you—you fucking little weasel," she said. "Talk to Lois."

"Who?"

"Just go—fuck yourself! How about that, smart boy?"

And then the boy did the most peculiar thing. He let go of the ladder with both hands, raised a fist, and brought it down in a swift punching motion. As he did so, a stray cloud passed over the setting sun behind Mrs. Kontos-Wu, and the library was for just a few seconds plunged into the deepest darkness. When the cloud passed, Mrs. Kontos-Wu blinked and searched the library. The boy was gone. Without a trace.

Mrs. Kontos-Wu shrugged and returned to her chair. She must, she assumed, have nodded off after all—and the hateful, curious boy had been nothing more than a dream. An unusually intense one, to be sure—it wasn't every night that Mrs. Kontos-Wu found herself sleepwalking through the library—but a dream nonetheless.

Stephen winced as the disinfectant settled into the twin gashes across his cheek and started to fizz. The fizzing stung, but Stephen had expected as much; the disinfectant would have plenty of work to do there. Mrs. Kontos-Wu's nails were filthy, and probably they were home to more harmful bacteria than a crack-house toothbrush. Stephen hoped the disinfectant would be enough; Stephen's immune system wasn't up to dealing with stragglers.

It could have been worse, of course. The gashes across his cheek were the only part of Stephen's skin that Mrs. Kontos-Wu had broken. The other injuries she'd inflicted were the kind that didn't come with a mark; she'd twisted his ear hard enough to leave an ache that seemed to reach all the way down to his tonsils, and she'd twisted his balls hard enough to send another tree-root of pain up as high as his tonsils. But that was as far as it went. She'd missed his eyes, left him his teeth, and hadn't pulled out more than a few strands of hair or broken even a single bone.

Indeed, it could have been much worse. In her weakened state, Mrs. Kontos-Wu succumbed with little fuss when Stephen had brought his fist hard against the side of her head. She hadn't even made it through the bathroom door to where Kolyokov slept.

And overall—cut for cut, injury for injury—taking down Mrs. Kontos-Wu had been a piece of cake.

So why was Stephen shaking?

It might, he thought, have something to do with the mnemonic. It should have worked. Hell, nine times out of ten it would work—if Kolyokov was the dream-walker, and Kolyokov was the master. The mnemonic was a serious enough trump card that Stephen was on standing orders to kill anyone who heard it in the context of use. It was tangible mojo.

And yet here, he'd used the mnemonic four times, and the dream-walker hadn't budged.

Who the hell was it in there? Stephen stuck his head out the bathroom door to check, make sure the restraints were holding. They were: he'd strapped Mrs. Kontos-Wu to the bed with thick leather belts that Kolyokov had brought over from Russia along with the tank. He hoped they'd be enough to hold the dream-walker when Mrs. Kontos-Wu came to.

Stephen was more worried about what would happen to him when Kolyokov came to. The old man's mood wouldn't be improved by the sight of Mrs. Kontos-Wu tied up in bed. It would only be improved slightly if Stephen could convince him that in tying her up, he had been doing nothing more than saving Kolyokov's life.

On the whole, Stephen would have rather let the old bastard sleep, and figure this situation out on his own. But that, he knew, would be the worst mistake of all. Kolyokov trusted Stephen to a point—but he didn't trust him enough to teach him the dream-walking tricks. If Stephen left Kolyokov out of the loop in a situation such as this? Kolyokov's rage would be limitless.

So Stephen propped open the door and turned back to the sensory deprivation tank that dominated the room.

"Now or never," he said, and gave the locking wheel a quick turn. The door opened easily.

Worries of Kolyokov's anger evaporated in the stink that wafted out. Stephen's image of Kolyokov the master dream-walker was instantly replaced by that of Fyodor the incontinent old man. Stephen took his hand from his nose and sniffed again to confirm it: the old man had done it. Pissed himself, and—yes, and shat himself too. Probably a couple of hours ago. In the enclosed space of the tank, the smell had thickened—notably foul even among the catalogue of stenches Stephen had learned to recognize from his years on the streets.

"Sir?" Stephen stepped back to the opening, and peered inside. Kolyokov kept the bathroom lighting low—so as to not shock his eyes when he woke. The light level meant that Stephen couldn't see much of Kolyokov in the tank, however. All he could make out was a fan of hair spreading in thick grey tentacles through the swamp made by Kolyokov's bladder and bowel. Stephen leaned closer, tried not to choke, and whispered: "Sir. You must—wake up."

Nothing. Stephen cursed. He wished there was a mnemonic to wake the master as well as *Baba Yaga, Manka, Vasilissa* woke his underlings. Grimacing, Stephen reached into the tank and touched Kolyokov's forehead. He recoiled as quickly. It felt waxy and cool to the touch. Kolyokov didn't stir.

"Shit." Maybe the dream-walker's visit had been redundant. Was Kolyokov dead in his tank?

Stephen reached in further, found Kolyokov's wattled throat. He searched for a pulse. Nothing.

"Shit shit shit." Dead. Fucking dead in the tank. What the fuck had happened? A stroke? Heart attack?

Stephen wouldn't be surprised if it was. Kolyokov was only getting older, and more to the point refusing to accept the fact that he was getting older. He ate badly and drank too much and got all his exercise dream-walking in young people's bodies. Sooner or later, something would happen. Today, something had.

Stephen returned to the main phone and picked up the telephone. It rang twice at the main desk before Richard answered.

"Ye-e-es sir?"

"Richard," said Stephen, "we've got a situation here. Send up Miles immediately."

"Muh-iles? Isn't he-e up there a-lready?"

"No," said Stephen, "he's not. He didn't—"

—didn't make it.

Stephen mentally kicked himself. Of course he didn't make it. Miles had been shadowing Mrs. Kontos-Wu. Mrs. Kontos-Wu had a dream-walker in her. A dream-walker who was no doubt expecting a shadow.

Stephen glared over at the bed. Mrs. Kontos-Wu's eyes were open, and whoever it was behind them glared back.

"All right Richard," said Stephen, "you're going to have to come up here yourself. It's an emergency."

"Sir—I-I ca-an't leave—"

"An *emergency*," Stephen repeated. "I need you up here—now!"

He hung up the phone without waiting for a reply. "Shit shit shit shit shit." Stephen crossed the room to the bedside. "What the fuck did you do with Miles!" Stephen shouted. "You fucking killed him, didn't you?"

Mrs. Kontos-Wu blinked and smiled a little.

"Well fuck you, whoever you are!" Stephen could feel his eyes heating up. Tears were starting. "Fuck you! Get the fuck out of her! You got nothing to do here, all right? Get out!"

Stephen wanted to punch her again, but as he raised his hand to do so, he saw the smile broaden.

"Go ahead," said Mrs. Kontos-Wu in thickly accented English. Stephen lowered his hand. He would only be hitting Mrs. Kontos-Wu, he knew. Whoever it was that was dream-walking her wouldn't even feel a sting.

"Baba Yaga," he said. "Manka."

"Vasil-issa," finished Mrs. Kontos-Wu. Her mouth enveloped the word like it was melting chocolate. "Baba Yaga. Manka. Vasilissa. Funny words."

Stephen moved to the foot of the bed. He felt like that guy in The Exorcist—the priest with faith problems facing down the devil in the little girl, with the Exorcist himself dead in the other room. Stephen wasn't in the same situation exactly—he was no doubter where dream-walking was concerned, and Fyodor Kolyokov was no Exorcist.

He also had more to worry about than driving the Devil out of Mrs. Kontos-Wu. There was the matter of Kolyokov in the bathroom—

—and the ringing telephone.

Stephen snatched it from its cradle. "Richard!" he snapped. "What the fuck did I tell you? Upstairs!"

"What is upstairs?"

Stephen's blood turned to ice. It wasn't Richard on the other end of the line. It was the call he'd been dreading most of the day.

Amar Shadak.

"Stephen? Have I caught you at a bad time?"

Stephen took a breath and forced his voice to modulate. The world may be collapsing, but Stephen couldn't afford to let Shadak in on that little morsel of information. Just because he was across an ocean and a third of a continent further didn't make Amar Shadak any less dangerous.

"No. Things are fine, Amar." The line was secure, but Shadak insisted on keeping things on a first-name basis anyway.

"I am pleased to hear that things are fine, Stephen. Very pleased." Shadak cleared his throat. "I was wondering if I might speak with Fyodor? Is he available just now?"

Shit. Stephen glanced at the bathroom door, took a breath.

"Unfortunately, no. He's not available just now."

"In a meeting is he?" Shadak laughed mirthlessly. "I think he can speak with me. We've an urgent matter to discuss."

Stephen took a breath. *Shit shit shit*. "I don't, ah—"

"Why Stephen," said Shadak, his voice taking on a tone, at once edged like a butterfly knife and soft as honey. "You're hiding something from me. Something's got you so scared, you're hiding something from me. Fyodor's not in a meeting, is he?"

Stephen didn't answer. Something was up—something that included Mrs. Kontos-Wu, Kolyokov's death, the thing that Kolyokov was investigating—the anomaly at the yacht. It was something that also evidently included Shadak. What was it? Stephen still had no idea—so kept his mouth shut.

"I think," said Shadak after a second, "that there are two possibilities here. Either he is dead, or he is fucking me."

When it was clear that Stephen wasn't going to bite, Shadak continued. He was rolling now, relishing his big-time-player-versus-nervous-executive-assistant gambit. "Either possibility explains this nervous little bum-boy I'm talking to now. He's got a corpse in the hotel room, and he doesn't have a fucking idea how to tell this to Fyodor's honest business associates and not fuck things up. If that's what's happened, I understand.

"But I'm afraid it's not that at all. I'm afraid that Fyodor is fucking me. And I'm afraid that you are in on it, little bum-boy."

Until now, Shadak's voice had been the deep, confidence-inspiring rumble that Stephen had come to recognize in their telephone sparring matches over the years. But as he continued, his voice grew louder and more shrill. And as this happened, a peculiar calm came over Stephen.

So what if Mrs. Kontos-Wu was tied up on the bed making like Linda Blair? So what if Fyodor Kolyokov was dead in the isolation tank, which was so full of piss and shit it would take a Home Depot full of cleaning products to make it right again? So what if Miles was bleeding in some corner of the hotel and Stephen's only prospect for some help was a 63-year-old computer engineer good for nothing but manning the front desk at Kolyokov's hotel? And yeah, so what if Amar Shadak—the cool fucker from eastern Turkey who normally played Stephen like a mandolin—was so freaked out about something he was ready to scream?

In this sea of calamity, Stephen would be the one signpost of serenity and control. He thought back to the tapes he'd purchased from the psychic fair. The telephone mind-reading trick.

Stephen cleared his throat.

"Amar," he said, "would you stop talking for a moment?"

As he said the words, Stephen imagined himself climbing the spiral staircase inside the wire of Amar Shadak's telephone. He got to the metaphorical door to his brain, and metaphorically booted it in. He turned on the two TV screens behind Shadak's eyes.

"Fuck you, you little piece of shit!"

Stephen opened his eyes. This really worked best with a cooperative subject—

"—the fuck did you do with my boat? And my 641! You used your fucking tricks to send a fucking torpedo! My people are killed!"

—but a cooperative subject isn't always available. Sometimes, you have to learn to make do with what's at hand. He shut his eyes, and willed the words away.

It seemed to work. He ran up the spiral stairs, pushed open the door once more, turned on the television screens and looked—

At mountains. Shadak was operating out of an old caravansary he'd remodelled near Silifke these days. It was older than Jesus, as Kolyokov liked to say. Now it had electricity and running water and floors redone in fine Italian tile, and an army of Romanian mercenaries who ran the thing like Castle Dracula.

It's working.

In the background, he could hear the muffled noise of a diesel engine, and a voice. Stephen leaned forward, to better hear. "—Hzekul's dead? I think you fucking KILLED HIM YOU FUCKING LITTLE—"

The voice quickly mutated into a high-pitched yowl, and as the pitch rose higher, the television screens exploded into prismatic fire.

Whoa. Feedback.

Stephen blinked and sat up. The phone was on the floor beside him. The back of his head was sore, but not from any impact.

"Feedback," he said wonderingly. The combination of his words over the telephone and the words coming from Amar Shadak's head had created a feedback loop that had blown Stephen's empathic link like a cheap pair of bookshelf speakers.

Stephen picked up the phone. Shadak had hung up. Stephen wondered if the feedback had hit him in the same way.

And what, Stephen wondered, *did he mean by torpedo?*

Before Stephen could wonder any more, the hotel room door swung open. Richard stepped in. To Stephen's relief, Miles followed. He was limping, with a bright red handkerchief pressed against his forehead, the handkerchief matching the bloody red blotches on his shirt. From the cast of his eye, he was pissed off beyond belief. But he wasn't dead.

"That's the bitch," he said as soon as he stepped in the room. He limped menacingly toward Mrs. Kontos-Wu. "Let me go to work on her."

"No," said Stephen. "That's not why you're here."

Richard gave Stephen a helpless look. He brushed a long white strand of hair from his eyes. "You-ou said the-ere was an emergency, sir?"

"Right," said Stephen. "Mr. Kolyokov has . . . taken ill. I need the two of you to help me remove him from the tank and get him to the infirmary."

Richard sniffed the air—no doubt he was smelling the stink of the tank, which had now wafted out from the bathroom.

"Shou-ouldn't we perhaps call an ambulance?"

Miles and Stephen shared a look. Poor, brainwashed Richard—he really did think he was a desk clerk in a Manhattan hotel, and that the reasonable thing to do when Fyodor Kolyokov fell ill was to ship him off to the Sisters of Mercy in a city-run ambulance.

"Ah, no Richard," said Stephen. "The infirmary will be fine."

Miles gestured to Mrs. Kontos-Wu, who was grinning malevolently at him. "You want me to call housekeeping then?" he said.

"Not housekeeping," said Stephen. When a death was involved, the Emissary's housekeeping crew consisted of a tightly knit Croat family, with a cart full of sulphuric acid and a bone saw. "But you might want to call a maid up here once we've got Mr. Kolyokov downstairs."

Miles raised his eyebrows in a question.

"The tank," said Stephen. "I'm not getting in that thing until somebody gives it a good cleaning."

THE IDIOT

ИДИОТ

As far as Holden Gibson was concerned, Alexei Kilodovich was a big hero. He was, Holden said, the kind of guy Holden wished he had twenty of: "A guy who sees a bullet coming and gets in the way of it. No ifs ands or buts: he doesn't waste time figuring the percentages, sussing the odds. Just steps right in the way. Without even thinking."

Alexei, of course, had done nothing so heroic as taking a bullet for Holden Gibson. He had simply pushed Holden Gibson over, an instant after deciding to postpone his murder—while not far off an old Russian torpedo hit a yacht and blew it up.

But to Holden Gibson's way of thinking, that was enough. So far as he was concerned, the torpedo explosion was immense—just shy of thermonuclear in scope, sending tons of razor sharp debris whizzing through the air at about neck height, aiming for Holden Gibson. When Alexei tackled him, he had saved him from untold mayhem. So Holden Gibson imprinted on Alexei, in the manner of an orphan duckling imprinting on a passing turkey vulture. Alexei had never felt so complete a piece of shit as he did the moment he climbed on board Holden's motor yacht.

"You could take a lesson from Mister Fuckin' KGB here," Holden told Heather as she climbed up the ladder from her own raft.

Heather rolled her eyes to indicate the half-dozen small children in the raft below her. *Language*, she mouthed.

"Oh. Right." Holden nodded. "But you get what I mean."

"Oh yes," she said. When Holden turned away from her, she shot Alexei a look more venomous than all previous looks combined.

Five of the crew-members had gathered around the rope ladders to help hoist the children on board. There were a few children too small to use the rungs and they had to be passed up by hand. And the ones who were big enough were slow and timid as children can be. Finally, the last of them were on board and the

Romanians cast off.

"Good riddance," muttered Holden. "Those fuckers gave me the creeps."

Alexei shrugged.

"Well—" Holden turned to Heather "—the sooner we get these little darlins locked up below decks, the sooner we can go home."

"Right," said Heather. Out of Holden's sight, Alexei nodded glumly.

Of course. The children would be locked below in Holden Gibson's smuggler's hold, and they would all return to the United States where Holden would put the children into what amounted to criminal slavery, playing out some elaborate magazine sales scam in the far-off lands of Ottawa and Mississauga.

That's right—*that* was why Alexei had decided to kill Holden Gibson. Because he was an evil son-of-a-bitch bastard who exploited little children. In the pit of self-flagellating misery he'd made for himself, Alexei spotted a darker corner still and headed for it.

Meanwhile, Heather had put on her game face—a vapidly happy grin topped with wide, sparkling eyes that was probably her idea of how a kindergarten teacher looked.

"All right children," she said, "who wants to have a little nap?"

"No time for napping," chirped a little voice from their midst. A chorus of other voices murmured assent.

"Well," said Heather, "we're going to have to go downstairs anyway. So come on—" she clapped her hands merrily "—let's all go!"

She started for the door into the lounge, but stopped when the children didn't follow. They stared at her wordlessly.

A silence had fallen onto the ship—the only sound was the blustering sea wind and the low thrum of the engines under their feet.

Heather's game face started to crack.

"Come on." She said it in the kind of voice that would send a kindergarten class into spasms of tears. "Let's move it, gang!"

"No," chirped the little voice. "Let's not."

The children looked down to their feet then, and slowly moved apart to make way for the speaker.

Alexei's eyes widened. "Holy fuck," whispered someone nearby.

The speaker was an infant—not much more than five months outside the womb, if Alexei were any judge. It wore a little blue jumper—so Alexei guessed it to be male—and had a gossamer-thin curl of black hair, the same colour as the rest.

He crawled forward on his hands and knees, and stopped in front of Heather.

"We are not going downstairs. I have had my nap already today. The rest of the brothers and sisters are likewise well rested. I think instead we will go up to visit your pilot. We have more brothers and sisters to collect before we do anything else."

Holden's crew stared slack-jawed at the marvel of the baby's impossible speech. Holden himself lumbered over and lowered himself to his haunches.

"Well look at you," he said. "She wasn't kidding when she said you were special."

"P-pretty fucking special," said Heather. "This is impossible. Somebody's playing a trick. Babies can't talk—their mouths . . . aren't well enough developed."

Holden's eyes narrowed. "Good point," he said.

"It is," said the baby. "Do you see me using my mouth?"

The baby's lips were pursed shut as he spoke.

Holden grinned then. "Of course not. Because one of you other kids is doing a ventriloquist trick, isn't that right?" He laughed and stood up. "Which one? Let me see you. We can always use someone who can throw their voice. Which one's lucky?"

"Me," said the baby. "My name is Vladimir. I am throwing my voice. Into your heads. Now how about I throw something else into your heads?"

Alexei clutched at his forehead. He felt as though he'd just swallowed too much ice cream on a hot day. His forehead and sinuses screamed in pain and he felt himself slipping.

And he shook his head. The pain was gone. Everyone around him—the adults at any rate—seemed to have experienced something similar.

"Now," said the infant Vladimir. "Who will take me to the pilot?

"You?"

Vladimir looked up at Alexei.

"Yes," he said. "Kilodovich. Pick me up—gently, with your thumbs hooked in my underarms."

Alexei did as he was told.

"No need to support my head," said Vladimir. "I'm not some newborn mewler. Now hurry—my brothers and sisters won't last forever on this changeable sea. Hurry!"

Heather spotted the rafts. There were two of them—yellow dinghies, crowded with little passengers. Vladimir ordered the yacht brought about to intercept them, and Holden didn't argue. Alexei didn't think it would have taken much to obtain his co-operation—Vladimir could have foregone the whole ice cream headache stunt and simply promised more children. Holden would have gone along with it happily.

But, Alexei supposed, Vladimir was young: chock it up to the impetuousness of infancy.

"You think I'm impetuous, Kilodovich?"

Vladimir reached up and grasped Alexei's nostril with his thumb. The nail was tiny, but razor-sharp against the inside of his nose.

"I didn't say—"

Vladimir's thumb dug into Alexei's flesh. "Don't talk—just think. I want this conversation to remain private."

Okay, thought Alexei. *How is this*?

"Good," said Vladimir—still apparently speaking aloud for all Alexei could tell. "Now we are talking privately."

And now that we are talking privately—how do you know my name?

"I think you know the answer to that one."

I don't think I do.

"Where do you think those rafts came from? Jolly old England?" Vladimir waved a chubby arm to the fore, where the little flotilla now lay waiting. "They came from the same place you did. They're the ones who sent you here."

The kids . . . from the yacht?

Vladimir nodded solemnly. "*Ming Lei 3*."

This will raise uncomfortable questions, thought Alexei.

"About your amnesia, you mean? If you want my advice, just keep up the act. The old man has his own amnesia problems to contend with, and he's already ready to adopt you. He'll believe anything you say. And the lady—she won't fuck you no matter what you do, so just forget about killing anybody."

Alexei blinked. *What does a five-month-old know about fucking and killing*?

"It's all anybody ever thinks about," said Vladimir. "You would be surprised."

Hmm. So you are a mind reader?

"Isn't it obvious?"

It's pretty obvious. I assume also that you are a mind speaker.

Vladimir's little mouth opened and he let loose a baby giggle. "Mind speaker. Yes. That is good. At City 512, they use the word 'telepath,' and they call what we are doing 'Discourse.' But I like your word better."

Alexei frowned. *City 512. Where have I heard that before?*

"You tell me."

Probably not important. But you tell me, Vladimir—why are we on this boat together?

Alexei was starting to enjoy this exchange. The little bastard might have inflicted a blinding headache on him a moment earlier, but in conversation Vladimir had a refreshing bluntness about him.

"The bluntness of infancy," said Vladimir. "So why are we on this boat together? Because it will take us to a better place than *Ming Lei 3* would have. Because Holden Gibson has reason to join us, and we have need of him. And for

. . . other reasons that are none of your business right now, Kilodovich. Now. If you will excuse me—" and with that, the quality of Vladimir's voice changed and amplified, and he addressed the group. "Okay. You see the rafts? Help my brothers and sisters from them. When they're up, pull the rafts on board, slice them open and fill them with ballast. Then throw them overboard. Bring the brothers and sisters to the lounge, and leave us all alone there until I say. And Andrea—" he waved at a little girl no more than five "—kindly direct the pilot on his new course."

"New course?" Holden stepped forward angrily. "What the fuck do you mean, new—"

He bent over then and grabbed his skull in both hands. "Fuck!" he screamed.

"Take me downstairs, Kilodovich," said Vladimir in his private voice. "I'm tired of this shit. And I'm getting hungry. See if you can find me a tit."

It didn't take long for the truth of their predicament to settle in: effectively, the child-traders' ship had been taken over by pirates. That the pirates were a gang of orphaned Eastern Bloc children and their victims were a band of criminals themselves was a complicating factor, and a source of some amusement to Alexei. But he kept his amusement to himself. The rest of the crew didn't find anything funny about their situation.

Most of them were locked in the former children's brig below decks: only adults deemed necessary for the operation of the ship were allowed to roam. And those were under the ever-watchful eye of the children, who now numbered twenty-two.

Alexei was among those kept below decks—but it had been made clear to him that he wasn't a prisoner the same way the others were. Vladimir had placed him in the brig as a guard. "Anybody tries anything, and you know what to do." Vladimir ran a tiny finger across his chubby throat.

Why do you trust me? thought Alexei.

"Let us just say—I know that you of all people on this boat won't fail me."

Well okay. That makes as much sense as anything else you've said.

So Alexei spent his time with the prisoners, in a situation uncomfortable for more than the obvious reasons. The brig was fine for twenty little kids, but it was cramped when you stuffed half as many adults inside. The bunks were too short, the ceiling was too low to stand straight, and the watercooler ran out in an hour. And, as it turned out, a dozen adults locked in a confined space together got on one another's nerves much more quickly than twice as many frightened children would have.

Alexei broke up no less than four fights in the first eight hours of their stay there. The first fight was between James and a fat little guy named Simon.

Apparently they had history, and some incident over the past couple of hours had dug it up. Alexei never found out what it was—the feud had devolved so that now they were only communicating through a proto-language of glares and snorts. Heather's repeated admonitions to "knock it off" only made matters worse and within a half-hour Simon brushed past James a hair too close.

James' nostrils flared and his eyes widened into a churlish, schoolyard glare. Simon pretended not to notice—or maybe he really didn't notice, because he seemed completely surprised when James' foot shot out and tripped him. Simon went down and in a flash, James was on top of him, fists flailing.

Alexei groaned inwardly—*this loser is the guy who brought me soup*—and got up from his bunk. "Let him go," he said in as reasonable a tone as he could muster.

"Fuck off." James punctuated with a sharp jab at Simon's ribs, and Simon yelled.

Alexei didn't let the conversation continue. He stepped over to the fight, bent over, and grabbed James' left ear between thumb and forefinger.

James started to turn to grab at Alexei, so he twisted, and James yelled instead. "That hurts, eh?" said Alexei. "It can hurt more."

Simon had rolled over and was crab-walking away. James' eyes were screwed shut in pain. "All right," he said through clenched teeth. "Let go."

Alexei let go. He stood straight and looked around. Holden's pirate crew were staring at him. "Any trouble?" he said to the group.

"Fuckin' right, no trouble." Holden stood up from the bunk where he'd stretched out. "Everybody—you listen to the Russkie. This isn't the time to settle old scores. We want to get out of this, we got to stick together—isn't that right?"

It was a good speech—Holden showed some real leadership, thought Alexei. The group nodded and mumbled assent. James and Simon shook hands. And Holden led the group in a sing-along of old U2 songs that Alexei thought must have been a carryover from the days when these people were all children in Holden's junior high school thieves' guild.

But even as a seedling of grudging respect for Holden Gibson started to blossom, it withered again when the old bastard got into it himself. Alexei had to hold down Holden Gibson for nearly five minutes to prevent him from "strangulating" James—who had made the mistake of looking at Holden wrong during the second chorus of "Where the Streets Have No Name." Every time the old man relaxed, Alexei would let go and Holden would lunge. After a couple of these attempts, Alexei thought it might be a good time for the killing thing—there was certainly enough confusion to make it seem like an accident—but he couldn't really bring himself to do it. Only a couple of hours ago, Holden Gibson had proclaimed his fast friendship and admiration for Alexei. And here, pinned to the mattress, grinning ingratiatingly up at him while making unconvincing noises that things were fine now, he'd gotten it under control—now, Gibson was less a figure of evil than ever before.

The only way Holden would get it would be if he tried to escape, decided Alexei. Those were Vladimir's instructions. Right now, Alexei trusted the kid's judgement.

The question remained, however—why on Earth did Vladimir trust Alexei?

Just past the ninth hour, Alexei found out. The latch opened and the door swung open, and two little girls who might have been twins stood there.

"You," said one, pointing at Alexei.

"Come with us," said her sister.

Alexei nodded, and turned to wave his finger at the prisoners. "No fucking around while I'm gone," he said, and left them to themselves in the children's brig.

"Change me," said Vladimir. "We will talk as you wipe."

Vladimir was squirming on the folding table next to all the pamphlets in the lounge. Someone had laid out a blanket, a roll of toilet paper, and a fresh Pampers diaper.

I have never changed a baby before, worried Alexei.

"Neither have I," said Vladimir. "It's not difficult. Just pull off the dirty diaper, give me a good wiping and put on the clean one. Oh—and don't forget the baby powder. It helps with the itching."

Alexei sighed and started to work. *What did you want to talk to me about*?

Vladimir was quiet for a moment. His eyes wandered from Alexei to the ceiling. He grunted as Alexei unfastened the diaper and lifted his feet.

Did you want to talk at all, Vladimir? Alexei struggled to get the old diaper clear without smearing shit on everything.

"Kilodovich," said Vladimir finally, "I want to apologize."

Alexei made a big cloud of baby powder. Vladimir sneezed. "Hey! Easy!"

I told you I've never done this before. What are you sorry about?

"I can't let you go on the way you're going."

What do you mean?

"Killing Holden Gibson. This mission you've set for yourself. Or that you've let be set."

Alexei set his mouth.

"You think he's evil. You think you're—blameless. Well things are not always as they seem."

Alexei set down the baby powder and rested both his hands on the table.

Do you know what he does to children?

"Oh yes. I know about Holden Gibson. I also know about you." Vladimir gave a little baby shrug. "You are going to have to guard them for a little while longer. But I am sorry—I cannot let you do that yourself. Understand that doing things this way is not my preference—just because you've been misused this way in the past gives me no right to do it now."

Alexei held up the dirty diaper. *Where does this go*?

"There's a bucket under the table."

So what are you saying?

"You can't go ahead and kill Holden Gibson. I can't trust you not to do it. But—there is something else. Maybe I can make it up to you in another way"

What way?

"Finish with this," said Vladimir. "Then you'll see."

Alexei blinked in yellow winter light. He took a breath. Smelled the petrochemical tang of the heating oil, the spring frost tugging delicately at the cilia in his nostrils. He flexed his hands that an instant before had been pulling velcroed diapers across Vladimir's tiny baby ass. Now it was Alexei's hands that were tiny. He started to ask himself where he was, then stopped. He knew where he was. He was in the old exercise yard. At school. In Murmansk. It was a place he had not been since he was a boy; a place that no longer existed, except in memory.

"Alexei!"

Alexei turned. He was facing Ilyich Chenko. When he was older and marginally larger, Ilyich would die in the belly of a tank in Afghanistan. Now, he was grinning across the yard and beckoning Alexei to join him.

Alexei shrugged and followed. Ilyich was heading toward the back of the yard, amid a low copse of pine trees where the older boys would sometimes gather to shout and gamble and settle old scores. From there, you could see the low outline of the school—a nearly windowless cinderblock structure with narrow red-brick chimneys at either end—but that was all.

"Let's play cards," said Ilyich. He produced a thumb-worn deck and set it on the ground between them. "It will pass the time."

"What is going on, Ilyich?" said Alexei. "Why are we here? Like this?"

Ilyich looked at Alexei. "We are passing the time in your safe place," he said. "You don't remember coming here before, do you?"

"Well yes—but a very long time ago." *When I really was this small.*

Ilyich nodded. "You have blocked your memories of more recent visits. That's sensible."

"Stop talking in riddles!" Alexei felt heat rising in his face—he was getting frustrated, so frustrated as to make his small, child's body start to cry. He willed the tears back into their ducts. "What do you mean, calling this a safe place?"

"All the sleepers have one," said Ilyich. "You were last in this one just a day ago. You remembered playing hockey, and the smell of the shipyards, and then you remembered some things that your old teacher Fyodor Kolyokov told you—about sex and torture—and that helped you to keep your mouth shut with Holden Gibson and more importantly Heather. She still will not sleep with you."

Alexei leaned forward, and studied his old friend Ilyich Chenko in the details. The mole was there, and the red hair. But the eyes were an imperfect copy. They resembled someone else's.

"That is you, Vladimir, isn't it?"

Ilyich nodded. "Yes. I am inhabiting the metaphor with you whilst you acclimatize yourself."

"Why should I need to acclimatize myself? If I have been here as often as I apparently have, I should think I would be more accustomed to this than my own skin."

"That is true," said the Vladimir/Ilyich hybrid. "Just like your own skin, you are so accustomed to it that you do not even know when you are in it. And that is why you must acclimatize yourself. So that you may take control of matters and defeat your programming."

Alexei frowned. "My programming? What is my programming? I don't have any programming. Do I?"

"What did you spend the last few months doing?"

"I was working with Wolfe-Jordan," said Alexei. "A bodyguard for Mrs. Kontos-Wu, who is an investment banker for one of the company's mutual funds. We travelled the world. I—I failed to protect her."

"Tragic. Also a lie. You travelled around the world all right—but not protecting Mrs. Kontos-Wu, which is not her real name. You were—you were there for another purpose."

Alexei swallowed and thought about that.

"What about before that?" demanded Vladimir.

"I was in Belarus," said Alexei. "I—worked for a guy."

"Worked for a guy. " Vladimir smirked. "Great. What before that?"

Alexei smiled back. "I worked for the KGB as an agent. In—" Alexei thought about it. All he could conjure at first were names of places—Berlin and Paris and Kowloon. But they didn't seem right, quite. Finally, he settled on a memory—a convoy of trucks, pushing through mountainous desert while the sound of mortar fire thumped in the distance. "Afghanistan? Is that a lie too?"

"I'm not going to tell you everything," said Vladimir. "That would only be more programming layered on other programming, and in such a way you would never regain your senses."

Alexei's boy mouth opened and closed and opened again. He'd been spun around enough times that he couldn't even frame the next question.

"Okay," said Vladimir/Ilyich. "Just one more thing to help you along the way." He made a beckoning motion with his forefinger. Alexei leaned forward.

"Ilyich here did not die in Afghanistan."

"That is what I remember."

"Well he is very well. I saw him just the other day."

"Funny joke," said Alexei, but Vladimir/Ilyich didn't so much as smile.

"Your understanding of your entire life until now is an immense tapestry of a lie—sewn from many small truths," said Vladimir/Ilyich. "You must spend the rest of your life tearing this lie to pieces and putting it back together. Only then will you find the truth. Play cards until you're ready to start work."

When he was finished, Vladimir/Ilyich looked away for an instant. When he looked back, his eyes had changed—they were returned to a perfect copy of Alexei's memory of Ilyich Chenko, in the smallest of details. Ilyich fanned the deck of cards in his hands.

"So are we playing, Kilodovich? Or are you going to just sit there mooning at me all morning like some queer boy?"

Alexei started to reach for the cards, then withdrew his hands.

"No cards today, Ilyich," he said. "I remembered something inside. I'll see you later."

And with that, Alexei turned and headed to the low buildings to the south.

THE GAMBLER
Игрок

Fyodor Kolyokov had never met his real father but he had over the years found a surrogate: Ari Krieghoff, an old Nazi physician who showed up at City 512 after the War, on the lam from the Allied prosecutors and his own betrayed comrades.

Krieghoff was a rotten surrogate—he was a cold bastard when sober—and when he drank too much, he was prone to catastrophic tantrums.

And drunk or sober, Krieghoff liked little boys altogether too much. He had kept trying to feel Kolyokov up in the guise of examinations, and in the dark corners of his mind he plotted far worse intrusions. Eventually Kolyokov would decide enough was enough and orchestrate the old man's death.

Really, Kolyokov's years with Doctor Krieghoff were nothing to get misty about. But, Kolyokov mused, one should never underestimate the power of nostalgia. For Ari Krieghoff sat across the table from him now, in a metaphor he had apparently constructed for himself to resemble the old City 512 testing room where the two of them had spent so much time.

Kolyokov was little again—or littler, anyway—and Krieghoff was his old self; whitening hair combed back from a broad forehead, his congenital harelip hidden from the eugenics-mad Reich by a long, bristled moustache.

Krieghoff had a stack of cards in front of him, and he sent a pale, narrow tongue across his malformed lips as he drew one. He looked at it briefly, then looked at Kolyokov. "Well, boy?"

Kolyokov sighed, and turned his attention to the old man's forehead. "Circle," said Kolyokov. "Underneath it, a wavy line."

Krieghoff smiled slightly and shook his head. He scratched a notation on the clipboard by his other hand, and drew another card.

Kolyokov concentrated.

"Square. Circle underneath this time."

Krieghoff raised an eyebrow. "*Nein*," he said and made another mark on the paper.

Kolyokov frowned: this metaphor didn't jibe with what he knew to be true. He'd scored perfect on the card tests from the first day he began working with Herr Doktor Krieghoff. Nazi draws a circle, little Fyodor says circle; Nazi pulls out a triangle, little Fyodor sees a triangle in his mind. And even the tricky ones: Nazi draws a wavy line, thinks "Circle! Circle!" Little Fyodor Kolyokov says, "You're thinking circle, but you're looking at a wavy line."

"Bullshit," said Kolyokov now. "There's a square with a circle underneath it."

Krieghoff let the trace of a grin emerge from beneath his moustache. "Bullshit yourself," he said, and turned over the card. It was a star, unmistakably. "Are you feeling well today, little Fyodor?"

"I'm fine," said Kolyokov stiffly. If he remembered the tests going differently, there was nothing changed in the look of the old man's eyes today that was any more or less than the lecherous evil he'd spied sixty years ago. "Let's continue," said Kolyokov.

Herr Doktor Krieghoff nodded—a little disappointed? Kolyokov couldn't tell for sure. "Another card, then," said Krieghoff, and drew from the deck.

Kolyokov redoubled his concentration. The last couple of attempts, he had been confusing imagination with true sight: a common early mistake, he supposed—although not one that he ever recalled making.

But who could say where memory was concerned?

So when his imagination conjured up a square, Kolyokov pushed it aside and continued his push. He felt sweat gather in his armpits, bead at the end of his nose. He screwed his eyes shut, and his breath was forced and ragged in his throat.

"Fyodor," said Krieghoff pleasantly, "are you trying to read my mind, or take a shit?"

Kolyokov opened his eyes and glared across the table. The extent of the old Nazi's harelip was revealed grotesquely in his broadening grin.

"It is a square," said Krieghoff. He drew another line on his chart, and pushed his chair back. "That is enough for today, I think," he said as he stood.

"Fuck," said Kolyokov. "This isn't right."

Herr Doktor Krieghoff walked around the table behind Kolyokov, and leaned against the door.

"The test is over," said Krieghoff. "Now, you know what it's time for."

Kolyokov felt a premonitory sinking in his stomach. He turned around, to see Krieghoff fiddling with his belt.

Kolyokov got up, and rushed around to the far side of the table. This, precisely, had never happened—Kolyokov was as sure of that as he was of anything. Krieghoff had thought about it enough—Krieghoff's fantasies about Kolyokov and some of the other boys were an open book to little mind-reading

Fyodor Kolyokov—but the Nazi understood too well what would have happened to him had he dallied with any of City 512's young subjects directly, and had accordingly limited himself to only marginally limited "examinations." The fear of Stalin and his minions that had kept him at bay had only started to dissolve later on. Kolyokov had taken care of Ari Krieghoff before there was a real danger of him doing any serious damage.

But here—the old bastard was unbuttoning his fly now!

"This isn't right," said Kolyokov. Krieghoff's grin went wide.

"No one will know," he whispered, and started across the room.

Kolyokov felt a calm come over him. When he destroyed the real Krieghoff, he'd done so using his abilities—the old man's mind had become supple enough that he could penetrate it like a syringe and fill it with psychic poison enough to wipe the slate clean. Here in the metaphor, however, he didn't seem to have any abilities. He would have to rely on such objects and circumstances as he could find.

Kolyokov looked at the table. It still contained the cards and the clipboard. But Krieghoff had taken his pencil. Of course it was gone: the only obvious weapon in the room, and Krieghoff had taken it for himself.

"This," said Kolyokov, the realization dawning upon him as he spoke, "is not my metaphor. It is my prison, yes?"

Krieghoff took hold of Kolyokov, and started to spin him around. But Kolyokov ducked between his legs and rolled under the table.

"You are talking nonsense, boy," said Krieghoff.

"Funny you should call me boy," said Kolyokov. He made for the other side of the table, where the door was. "You're just a boy yourself, aren't you?"

Kolyokov came out from under the table just as Krieghoff was starting around it. He kicked out and managed to snag his chair. He sent it skittering across Krieghoff's path. The Nazi stumbled—long enough for Kolyokov to reach the door. He yanked down on the handle—half-expecting to find it locked—and allowed himself a grin when it opened. Without turning to look, he stepped out the door and shut it behind him.

"Ah, shit."

He was in the same room as before—but a mirror image of the first. Krieghoff stood at the far end, his grin wide and hungry as a fairy story wolf's as he beckoned Kolyokov to join him.

The little bastards. They'd used the metaphor to make a prison for him—in one of the little rooms in City 512 that he remembered so well, but folded in on itself so that any attempt to escape the room brought it back.

Only it was more than a prison. They'd fashioned City 512 into a torture chamber—a place where he would suffer the horror that he had feared so greatly that he had killed an old man for merely contemplating the act.

He shouldn't have been surprised: *Children are nature's sadists*, he reminded himself.

But they are also unschooled. Kolyokov laughed to himself.

To a six-year-old prodigy, the spectre of a Nazi child molester might be the worst thing imaginable. Take away his psychic abilities, and my goodness! It was enough to make a fellow pee in his pants!

But Fyodor Kolyokov wasn't six. He was seventy-two, and he'd faced down the real Ari Krieghoff a long time ago. He was the first of many adversaries, and far from the worst. Krieghoff's resurrection now marked more annoyance than trauma revisited. And damned if Kolyokov was going to keep running away from an annoyance.

"Okay, Ari," said Kolyokov. "My test is over. Now let's see about you."

Herr Doktor Ari Krieghoff threw back his head and laughed with monstrous lechery.

Clearly, thought Kolyokov, he had not a clue as to what was about to happen to him.

"Take off your pants," said Kolyokov.

From the depths of Bishop's Hall came a scream, high-pitched and garbled by shocked and dismayed sobs. Mrs. Kontos-Wu put down her Becky Barker book. "Now what on earth . . . ?"

She said it to no one in particular. She had been alone in the library since the peculiar boy had appeared and vanished again from the book-ladder, and that must have been—what?—hours ago. The sun had fallen below the line of trees to the west, and thereby shifted light from the library's high windows brilliant gold to a deep purple. Mrs. Kontos-Wu was now reading about Becky's adventures in France by the greenish-yellow light of the table lamp. She set the novel down so as to save her place, and got up. She walked over to the mahogany pocket doors, turned the brass latch, and slid them open. The hallway outside stretched away from her, long and empty.

"What do you think you are doing?"

Mrs. Kontos-Wu started and turned around. Lois was standing behind her. Her arms were folded over her chest, and she tapped one toe on the carpeted floor. She seemed very cross.

"I heard a scream," said Mrs. Kontos-Wu. "So I went to—"

Lois shook her head no. "You didn't hear a scream. There was no screaming. Go back, read your fucking book and relax!"

"Lois!" Mrs. Kontos-Wu felt her face flush. "I can't believe you said that word!"

Lois blinked and smiled. "I'm sorry," she said. "I don't know what came over me. Look—just go back and finish the book. Everything will be fine."

Mrs. Kontos-Wu frowned. "How did you get in here?" she said.

"I was back in the stacks," said Lois. "You must have been concentrating very hard not to have heard me. What are you reading?"

"Becky Barker." Mrs. Kontos-Wu went back to her chair and picked up the book. "*The Adventure of the Scarlet Arrow*."

"Let me borrow it when you're finished," said Lois. "I've got to get back to work."

"Work?" Mrs. Kontos-Wu smiled to herself. "That's not like you."

But there was no answer. Lois was gone—vanished into the stacks. Mrs. Kontos-Wu shrugged and turned over her book.

It *was* a good book. Becky and her friends were in France—the foreign exchange program they were on all but forgotten after three men wearing fezzes had kidnapped Antoine, the irritating little Parisian brat whose parents were playing host to the three of them. One thing had led to another, and now Becky was tied up in the mail car at the back of the Orient Express, racing through a thunderstorm towards Istanbul and a rendezvous with the mysterious Scarlet Arrow. She had read all the Becky Barker books a long time ago, but Mrs. Kontos-Wu couldn't for the life of her remember how this one turned out. Was the Scarlet Arrow a person? An actual arrow from a bow-and-arrow set? Or something entirely different, like an airplane or a gem or a necklace or a decoding machine for the Russians—something just called the Scarlet Arrow so as to throw Becky off the scent? The cover didn't tell her anything—it was just a picture of a big swarthy man with a fez on his head and a curved dagger in his fist, threatening Becky in front of the Eiffel Tower. There was nothing for it but to finish the thing. Mrs. Kontos-Wu curled up in the chair and started to read.

"Shh."

Mrs. Kontos-Wu rolled her eyes. "I was being quiet, Loi—"

She stopped. It wasn't Lois. It was a boy—not the one she'd seen earlier, either. This one was taller, a little older than the other one, with badly clipped brown hair and wide, hungry eyes that she was sure she recognized from somewhere. He wore ill-fitting green trousers and a white T-shirt, and he had a bright red gasoline can in one hand. The other hand was at his mouth, forefinger extended across his lips. "Shh!"

Mrs. Kontos-Wu didn't know why—a strange boy shows up at Bishop's Hall with a can of gasoline, a girl should really say something—but she did as she was told. The boy smiled and nodded. He unscrewed the top of the can and began sloshing gasoline in a line around the edge of the room. When he came to a bookshelf, he made sure to slosh the gasoline up the spines of the books, but he didn't bother splashing too high. Mrs. Kontos-Wu supposed that made sense—

the paper would burn well enough by itself, after all.

Wait a minute. Mrs. Kontos-Wu set the book down and got up again. *Burn*?

"Hey!" she ran across the room to where the boy was working. "What do you think you're doing! This is a library! You can't burn down a library!"

The boy turned and glared at her. "Shhh!" he said.

"I will not!" Mrs. Kontos-Wu took a deep breath and let out a scream. It was a good scream—better than the one she'd imagined hearing a few moments ago—all high-pitched spooky-movie shrill. She took a breath and screamed again—louder this time.

"Ah, shit, Kontos-Wu," said the boy, reaching into his pocket. "Do we have to go through this?" He pulled out a book of matches, and before Mrs. Kontos-Wu could recover herself, lit one and dropped it to the floor.

The flame spread fast as sunlight along the trail of gasoline, only at first it was a line of blue, not gold. The gold came an instant later, in an explosion of flame and smoke that engulfed the boy all at once. Mrs. Kontos-Wu felt the ground fall from beneath her feet as the force of the fire threw her back. Roaring flame and the crackling combustion of wood and paper filled her ears as her back hit the floor and the air heaved from her chest. Mrs. Kontos-Wu gasped a lungful of black, evil-tasting smoke, and coughed it back out again. She felt as though she were suffocating—she couldn't get a breath past her throat.

She felt a hand on her back, and another on her arm. The hands were large, and their grips firm. She looked up through the thickening smoke, and felt a moment of comforting reassurance.

It was Mr. Bishop! Her schoolmaster! He was wearing one of his familiar tweed jackets, the wire-rimmed glasses perched on the end of his nose. And behind them, his eyes—

Mrs. Kontos-Wu gasped—and took in a little air this time. She blinked the stinging smoke away and looked more closely. She'd been right.

His eyes were the same as the boy's. Older, stuck into a different face. But they were the same.

"Come on," said Mr. Bishop. "We must leave this place—before they get back."

With Mr. Bishop's help, Mrs. Kontos-Wu got to her feet. The fire was spreading quickly. Flames licked across the shelves at the far side of the library in little blue streaks. The wall by the entrance where the fire had started was consumed in a terrible mix of roiling flame and black smoke. The tall windows had shattered, and now the oxygen-rich night air blew in past the billowing, flaming curtains to feed the conflagration.

Mr. Bishop dragged her toward the flaming wall. Mrs. Kontos-Wu pulled against him. She was not going anywhere near that fire.

"Quickly!" he shouted. "We've got to get out of here—before they come back!"

"We'll die if we go there, Mr. Bishop!" shouted Mrs. Kontos-Wu. She squirmed free of Mr. Bishop's grip and ran toward the far end of the library.

"We won't!" shouted Mr. Bishop. He started to run after her—and might have caught her all other things being equal.

But at that moment, an immense gust of wind knocked both of them to the floor. The curtains flew nearly straight out from their rods and the flames blew back an instant before returning, brighter and hotter in the fresh outside air.

Lois stood at the window. Her arms were folded across her chest and she appeared very cross indeed. Strange light flickered behind her—green like the reading lamp, but moving across her shoulders like a thick liquid.

"You," she said. "You bastard."

"I'm a—" Mrs. Kontos-Wu stopped herself. Lois wasn't calling *her* a big bastard—she was looking straight at Mr. Bishop, who had climbed to his feet. He towered over them both—his head seemed to reach as high as the ceiling.

"We are all bastards," he said. "Rasputin's bastards, they used to call us? That is our common bond."

"Vladimir wanted to destroy you outright," said Lois. The flames behind her diminished as she spoke—out and out vanishing in spots. And where they vanished, the wallpaper and bookshelves and hangings reappeared unblemished. The liquid green light grew brighter. "Maybe he was right."

"Vladimir is merciful, then. I presume it wasn't he who devised my reunion with old Krieghoff."

Mrs. Kontos-Wu gaped. As Mr. Bishop spoke, the flames started up again—consuming the fresh wallpaper and bookshelves and hanging as fast as they'd been made. *Becky Barker and the Adventure of the Scarlet Arrow* was forgotten in the face of this new mystery.

"That was me," said Lois. "You had it coming."

"I see. I have been very wicked—of course. And who are you, little girl, who judges an old man so harshly for a lifetime of sin?"

There was a series of loud pops then, as a row of lights on the far side of the library blew out. New flames climbed up the rails of the staircase to the library's second level in brilliant lines of blue and yellow.

And as that happened, another thing occurred, which gave Mrs. Kontos-Wu even more pause. Mr. Bishop—a tall, fit man of about fifty-five, with sandy grey hair and a tweed single-breasted sports jacket—began to melt and change. He grew shorter and his hair receded; his sports jacket melded and extended down to near his ankles, and transformed into a thick, terrycloth bathrobe that had once been a deep, luxurious purple but had faded with washings to a threadbare pink. His belly swelled and his feet grew, and his chin darkened with late morning stubble.

"Fyodor Kolyokov," she said, nodding. This wasn't Mr. Bishop. She was not a schoolgirl at Bishop's Hall. She was Mrs. Kontos-Wu, who worked for Wolfe-Jordan, where she managed offshore mutual funds. Except that there really was no Wolfe-Jordan—Wolfe-Jordan was a cover, a money laundering front, and her real master was Fyodor Kolyokov, who ran his own kind of financial empire out of a hotel at Broadway and 95th, which was called . . .

"The Emissary," she said aloud, looking down at her hands. The fingers, which had been small and pink and a little pudgy, narrowed and lengthened and dried out into what seemed by comparison a mummy's claw but in fact was only the more weather-worn hand of a thirty-six-year-old woman who had not been at Bishop's Hall for a quarter century.

She looked at Kolyokov, and he nodded to her: *Good*, he mouthed—and then he spoke some other words to her—not with his mouth, but in her head. They flashed across her mind like quicksilver. And then he mouthed again: *Now*.

Lois screamed at her to stop, but it was too late. Mrs. Kontos-Wu flung herself into the flames—felt them lick and tear at her clothes and her flesh—felt the illusion of the metaphor burn and bubble away like the skin on her arms and face and thighs—felt the pain of burning nerves and searing flesh—and then felt its absence, as death came to her sure and final, in the crumbling metaphor that was Bishop's Hall.

It was dark enough, but that was it as far as sensory deprivation went in Fyodor Kolyokov's tank. In spite of the buckets of cleaning products that had been flushed through the thing over the past several hours, the air inside was filled with old man stink. If anything, the antiseptic made it worse: it made it smell like a geriatric ward. And it wasn't completely silent, either. Stephen heard the scream from the living room with both hatches closed.

"Piece of shit Soviet junk."

Stephen muttered it under his breath, but in the tomb of Fyodor Kolyokov's isolation tank it echoed like the voice of God. He sighed—which sounded to his sense-starved ears like a hurricane hitting a Florida beach—and opened the two hatches. The scream had come three more times before he was out.

"Shut the fuck up!" he yelled. "I'm fucking trying to fucking concentrate!" He kicked his feet into his slippers. "Fuckwad!"

"Ste-Stephen? That you?"

Stephen shrugged on a bathrobe and opened the bathroom door. Mrs. Kontos-Wu looked at him from the bed. Her eyes were wide and wet with tears. Terrified. Which was interesting: it was the first spark of humanity in her that Stephen had detected since she'd returned. And the accent was gone.

Maybe, he thought, *the dream-walker's gone too.*

Or it could be a trick—like those scenes *in The Exorcist* where Linda Blair seems okay for a second, to trick the priests to come in close enough so the devil can let loose another green puke whammy and knock them out the window to their deaths.

"It's me," he said carefully. "Yeah."

Mrs. Kontos-Wu glanced down at the straps. "What's with these things?" she said. "Can you undo them?"

"I don't think so," said Stephen—*Can you undo them*? being one of the first things a tricky dream-walker would ask once he'd gotten the knack of humanizing his host.

The door to the suite opened then, and Miles stepped in. He was carrying a Glock at chest height. He gave Stephen a pissed-off look; Stephen had sent him from the suite an hour ago, on the theory that security man's aura was what was fucking up his dream-walking. Miles had argued—he didn't trust the straps where Mrs. Kontos-Wu was concerned, and thought Stephen was taking a foolish risk leaving her unguarded while he "sloshed around in Mr. Kolyokov's tank."

Stephen had a hard time looking Miles in the eye now. He'd responded by pointing out that he was the dream-walker, Miles was the goon, and while Miles might have nothing better to do in a tank than "slosh around," Stephen had the capacity to use the tank to its full advantage.

Except that it hadn't exactly turned out that way. Stephen had spent the last three hours using every trick in the book, several on tape and even a couple he'd picked up off the Internet. And try as he might, he hadn't been able to invoke even a hint of the dream-walking state that Kolyokov entered so effortlessly in the tank.

"Is everything under control, sir?" said Miles, in a tone that made Stephen want to hit him.

"The straps are holding," said Stephen. "If that's what you mean."

Miles lowered his handgun. He regarded Mrs. Kontos-Wu, and she frowned back at him.

"Miles—Shute. Right?"

Miles nodded warily. Her eyes tracked him as he stepped around the bed, and settled on the bandage on his scalp. "What happened to your head?" she asked.

"Is this for real?" said Miles to Stephen.

"Not sure. She's doing a good impression of herself. But who knows?"

"Why," said Miles, "don't you just get back in the tank and check for yourself? Dream-walk into her. That's your knack—right, Stephen?"

Stephen looked away, out the window. It was late afternoon in New York City. Central Park was a long vertical sliver of gold-hazed greenery. Stephen couldn't imagine what the park was like to either side of the sliver. All he saw now was two ugly old water towers, and below that, deep red brick, drawn curtains and the black cross-hatch of fire escapes. It was a shitty view, and there wasn't anything he could do to change that.

"Who knows?" said Stephen.

"How is Mr. Kolyokov?" asked Mrs. Kontos-Wu. "He said he might be injured—maybe in a coma?"

Miles raised both eyebrows and scrunched his lips. Stephen looked over to Mrs. Kontos-Wu. "'He said'? You've been talking with Fyodor?"

"Look—Stephen. Cut the shit. Undo the straps." Mrs. Kontos-Wu threw him a full-teeth smile. "What am I going to do? Kill ya with my hands?"

"Wouldn't put it past you," said Miles. "Don't untie her."

"You don't have to tell me that," Stephen answered. He turned back to Mrs. Kontos-Wu. "If our positions were reversed, you wouldn't untie me either. Don't ask again."

Mrs. Kontos-Wu's eyes narrowed. "Something happened," she said. "I pulled some stuff, didn't I? What did I do?"

Stephen kept his mouth shut, and motioned to Miles to do the same. There was no point in giving Mrs. Kontos-Wu, if that's who she was, any more information than she already had.

But she was working it out for herself. "I did that to you—didn't I, Miles? Your head?" Miles stared at her, stone-faced. "Shit, I'm sorry if that's what happened. Did I—" Mrs. Kontos-Wu's eyelids fluttered, which Stephen knew to be one of the few signs of real distress that his comrade would show "—did I kill anyone?"

"Save the questions," said Stephen. "Right now, it's important *you* tell *me*—what did Fyodor—Mr. Kolyokov—say to you?"

Mrs. Kontos-Wu considered the question. "All right. I guess holding out won't go far in convincing you I'm of sound mind and body. Here goes." She shut her eyes and licked her lips. When she spoke again, it wasn't her voice—it was Fyodor Kolyokov, speaking as it were, from beyond the grave.

"Stephen my love. If you get this message (said Kolyokov through Mrs. Kontos-Wu) then my ruse has worked and I have succeeded in returning our operative to herself. You may have encountered her in her previous state—she was inhabited by a powerful dream-walker, up to no good—but if that happened, I doubt both of you would be alive—and therefore I doubt you would be hearing this.

"Assuming the best, then, I also assume you have encountered certain truths already. You will—I hope—have found me by now, in a coma or unconscious, in my tank. You will have taken the appropriate steps—yes?—and had me moved to the infirmary on the fifth floor. If you have not done so yet, in hopes that I may return to my corporeal self—abandon that hope for the moment, and put my body in a doctor's care immediately. I will wait here until you're finished."

Mrs. Kontos-Wu's eyes blinked open. "Oh," she said, in her own voice. "I'm supposed to stop and wait until you've taken care of Mr. Kolyokov—unless you already have?"

Stephen felt himself flush. "He's taken care of," he said. "Keep going."

Mrs. Kontos-Wu shut her eyes again.

"All done? Good. A couple of other things have no doubt come to pass in my absence. Unless I miss my guess, Shadak will have telephoned you by now. He will have been very angry, I'm willing to bet, but it's his own fault. He sent a submarine with our cargo—a submarine!—and the cargo we were meant to collect escaped, and took it over. I don't know what's happened beyond that. I have been—compromised for the time being.

"I trust you have revealed nothing of my state to Mr. Shadak. That is good—always play your cards close to the vest as the Americans say. But it is time to contact Mr. Shadak again. We need to find out everything he knows about the cargo—where it came from, how many children are in fact involved, who else has had contact with them, and so on.

"And there is one other thing that we must discuss now. This one is . . . difficult. Our operative Alexei Kilodovich is missing. I know you are saying: so what? Kilodovich is nothing, just more sleeper muscle, new in the organization in any case—cannon fodder in the event things became ugly. That is what I led you to believe, and I must apologize for that, because I misled you, Stephen. In fact, Kilodovich's disappearance is a very serious problem indeed.

"I know you were suspicious when we brought Kilodovich on board. And you were right. We didn't go to all that trouble to recruit him as muscle. In fact, Mrs. Kontos-Wu is more than capable of taking care of herself. Kilodovich was a part of the exchange. Mr. Shadak was very interested in meeting our Alexei Kilodovich. He believes that there is advantage in having that one. In a way he is right. But whatever the matter—without Kilodovich, there is no exchange.

"To make matters worse, I believe that our . . . cargo . . . has taken possession of Kilodovich. They are clever children, Stephen, smarter than we ever had imagined, and stronger too. Who knows what they will do with him . . . how they will use him. I think it will not be to our benefit, however it goes.

"So. When I'm recovered, and out of this prison they've made for me, I will take up the search for Kilodovich. In the meantime, you must lay groundwork. Contact Shadak. Apologize to him on my behalf. Find out from him exactly what happened so far as he knows. Allow Mrs. Kontos-Wu to assist—Shadak likes her—but take the lead yourself. You have worked for me now for five years. There is more in you than you know. And I know that you are ready for this new responsibility."

Stephen stood a little straighter at that. He *was* ready.

"But Stephen (said Kolyokov through Mrs. Kontos-Wu)—that doesn't mean you're ready for the tank. Under no circumstances are you to go in there. The tank is still my dominion.

"And the children—our cargo—are too dangerous to deal with on their own terms. Particularly for you. And particularly now that they've got Kilodovich. Goodbye for now, Stephen. Remember what I've told you."

And with that, the voice of Fyodor Kolyokov was gone from Mrs. Kontos-Wu's lips. Her eyes blinked open. "Stephen?"

"Stephen's gone to the can," said Miles.

THE INSULTED AND THE INJURED

Оскорблённые и униженные

It was almost a day before the doors to the children's brig opened again. The little room stank of sweat and blood and shit and the stink seemed to leave too little room for oxygen. It all reminded Heather of a *60 Minutes* segment she'd seen on life in Russian prisons—which, she supposed, was not far from the truth. The Russians were running the show here, and sure as day turns to night, they'd turned Holden Gibson's yacht into a prison after the old Soviet ways.

And shit—but didn't those Soviets stick together when it came to the crunch? Alexei the KGB agent stood in the open door. He was carrying Holden's Glock in one hand, aiming it in the general direction of the crowd. His mouth was cast firm, and his eyes had a cool, empty determination to them that Heather barely recognized.

Christ, she thought. *Where was he yesterday, when* I *needed him*?

"Get up," he snarled.

"Jesus fuck," said Gibson, who had been snoring contentedly on the bottom bunk for about an hour. "I am going to tear you another asshole, you fuckin' traitorous mutinous Russkie."

Heather smiled in spite of herself. It so often amazed her how Holden Gibson managed to stay alive at all, the way he behaved with the most dangerous of people. Alexei, for instance. He pointed the gun at Holden now—lined him up in its sights. "Get up," he repeated.

"Je-sus." Holden squinted at Alexei—and evidently saw the same thing Heather had in his eyes: an absence. Alexei would shoot him if he didn't get up. Heather felt a quickening of her pulse, a faint hope that Holden would defy her KGB killer.

But Holden saved himself, and stood up with the rest of them. Seeing everyone on their feet, Alexei backed out of the door. "Come," he said. "All of you. Follow me to the deck."

"Who died and made him Captain?" muttered James as he passed close by Heather. She gave his ass a tweak and followed close behind as they pushed into the corridor.

"No one yet," she whispered in his ear, and he smiled a little back.

The two of them had been planning a move on Holden since Dallas. He had been behaving more and more strangely since then—following this "dream" of his; pulling his kids off the routes, and finally, piecing together this bizarre operation. Heather had confided in James from early on, and at the best of times they agreed their boss was abusive, incompetent, self-destructive, had poor communications skills. And sooner or later, needed killing. The Russian Alexei Kilodovich, with his little ballpoint pen brain-smacker and his shady secret agent background had seemed like a godsend. Until, that is, Alexei turned out to be a chickenshit when it came to killing evil old men who had it coming.

It was true that the freak show kids Holden had managed to pick up here on the ocean were a complication. But shit—it wasn't like she and James weren't giving him opportunities. Heather could count at least four missed opportunities since Alexei arrived, and a couple more since they got back with the kids. Hell, for one of them she even got James to pick a fight with Simon in here, to give Alexei a distraction. How hard could it be to kill a smelly old bastard like Holden Gibson? Heather'd do it herself—if she thought for a second she could get away with it around this crew. Too many of them still paid lip service to Holden's insistence on absolute loyalty to hand over the reins of power to an obvious assassin. Heather knew that—and as she'd found out early on in their association, when she approached *him* to do the deed for her, James had worked it out as well. James was a bright boy, all right.

And looking over his shoulder at Alexei, who was now beckoning them all forward with one hand while he levelled the Glock at them with the other, Heather was beginning to worry that her Russian stooge was a bright one too.

Alexei led them upstairs to the lounge. It was four in the morning, so the sky and sea were still dark beyond the windows. And it wasn't much brighter inside. In the dimness, Heather could see that the chairs had been arranged facing aft, as for a seminar. Normally, Holden Gibson would hold court from behind the table they faced. Now, three of the children sat behind it. Their faces and forms were in shadow, and they were still as statues. Heather shivered. Even outnumbered, they were scary little fuckers.

"Take seats," commanded Alexei. "Keep silent."

The crew did as they were told. Gibson motioned for Heather to join him, but she pretended not to see and sat by James at the back.

"All right." It was the baby's voice, preposterously deep and serious. "We are nearly at our destination. I must apologize for your incarceration. It was a necessary thing until we completed the journey. We didn't want to risk—a premature awakening until we were near the safe harbour. I hope that we can put that behind us and become friends in the days and months ahead of us—for there will be much reason to, I think."

"What the fuck are you talking about, 'friends'?" demanded Holden, standing up. "And what's this 'days and months ahead of us' bullshit? And—"

Holden yelled and grabbed his head, and the baby continued. "You are all a part of something—the same thing, in a way, as we children. As Alexei. It will become clearer to you in the next few hours, as we make our way to land, and finally meet the Koldun face to face."

Gibson rubbed his eyes, and gasped: "What the fuck is a Koldun, kid? Why the fuck are we even up here, anyway?"

This time, to Heather's disappointment, Gibson didn't double over in pain.

"To prepare ourselves," said the baby. "We children have been doing so for years—but you Americans . . . you've forgotten the ways. So in the hours before we make landfall, I have decided that we shall meditate together. Close your eyes now. It is time to begin."

"Fuck this," said Gibson, and turned on a heel. No one stopped him as he stepped out onto the deck.

"Close your eyes," said the baby again.

You can't be serious, thought Heather.

But she shut her eyes like everyone else. She wasn't about to fuck with this kid—if he could talk in her mind like that, who knew what else he could do? If he wanted her to sit and meditate, that was fine with her. It wasn't like she hadn't done weirder shit at Holden's behest.

In fact, there was a time when they'd done stuff just as weird. It was the late '80s, maybe three months since she'd joined up with his little team. She'd run away from the stuffy-assed upstate New York boarding school her parents had shoved her into six months earlier because she didn't like the structure.

And before she knew it, there she was, at a Transcendental Meditation retreat at a rundown summer camp in Northern California, learning her mantra from an old hippie named Pete and watching Holden and Shara, his girlfriend at the time, try their hands at yogic flying. Or more accurately, try their asses at it. Even though she was just eleven years old and fairly gullible, it seemed to Heather that yogic flying was basically jumping with your ass. Which struck her as bullshit. So Heather took her personal secret mantra, which as she told anyone who asked was *mi*, watched the old videotapes of the Maharishi and meditated for ten minutes twice a day for two weeks—until Holden got tired of Shara and jumping with his ass, and hauled them all off to New Mexico for three years of much more lucrative magazine subscription scamming.

What was the camp like? asked a quiet voice.

It was pretty low-rent, compared with the sort of thing that Heather had been used to growing up. There were a couple of big clapboard buildings in the middle that smelled of flypaper and mould, and surrounding that a dozen little cabins. There was a lake a five minute hike down a trail, but Heather wasn't allowed there and so she'd never been.

Hippie Pete said—

"Sometimes there are snakes that come from the lake and meeting them can cause stress and discord."

He was smiling down at her as he spoke, his eyes taking that faraway slightly stoned look that came from spending your days and nights meditating with incense sticks burning at your feet. His breath smelled of oatmeal and herb tea, which was not surprising; that was all they ate and drank there, three times a day.

"We eliminate stress with meditation. Playing with snakes does not aid us in eliminating stress. So we do not go to the lake, where sometimes the snakes come from. This will cause stress, which we eliminate through meditation."

Heather's eyes shot open. "Fuck a duck!" she exclaimed. She had forgotten how creepy and irritating Hippie Pete had been. That sing-song voice; that take-you-around-in-a-circle-until-you're-so-dizzy-it-makes-sense approach to selling things that fundamentally made no sense; that vacant smile that Heather assumed came from not having enough stress or too much meditating or both.

And there he'd been—right in front of her. A guy she hadn't seen for fifteen years. Clear as day. She shut her eyes again, and took another look.

Yup—there he was. Smiling and nodding, holding his fingers and thumbs together with hands upturned in way that would make him look like a Buddha—if he were sitting cross-legged in a monastery and not standing out in front of the old Arts and Crafts Lodge giving her gentle, meditative shit for wanting to go down to the lake and take a swim.

And shit, but he towered over her. At first, she thought he was some kind of giant—it seemed like he was eight feet tall. But she quickly realized that it wasn't him that was big—she was small. As small as an eleven-year-old girl from New York would be. She looked at her hands—they were soft and tiny. From the look of things, Holden hadn't gotten around to starting the aversion therapy that would eventually stop her from biting her nails, because they were gnawed down to nubs and a couple of fingertips were pretty scabby. She was wearing a My Pretty Pony T-shirt, cheap stonewashed jeans and a pair of even cheaper rubber sandals.

"Fuck a duck," she said again.

"Consider the rose," said Hippie Pete. "How it has many petals which grow from a stem. Though the petals grow from the stem, it is the stem which also grows, and the petals which grow from—"

"Oh no," she said. "We're not getting into the rose thing."

The Maharishi used to talk about roses all the time. There was a whole EP video about roses, in fact, six hours of the Maharishi sitting on a cushion in a studio in Calcutta or somewhere, dishing the dirt on roses and consciousness and how one was like the petals of the other. The last thing she needed now was to hear Hippie Pete recite the director's cut.

"—and the stem," said Hippie Pete, as oblivious as ever to Heather's blossoming boredom, "constitute the consciousness which we—"

Fuck it, she thought. *It's now or never*.

"I am out of here!" Heather yelled, and with that, she spun around on her little sandaled feet and took off along the path to the lake.

"—seek to expand!" hollered Hippie Pete behind her. "Hey! We do not go to the lake, where sometimes snakes come from! Stress, Heather! *Stress!*"

She ignored him and ran faster. This was too weird, and she needed the space to work out what it meant.

Heather spread out the sequence in her head: she closes her eyes for a couple of seconds in the lounge of the yacht, and suddenly here she is—back fifteen years ago, at a Transcendental Meditation camp where she spent two lousy, boring weeks before embarking on her more engaging career as a junior subscription scammer. It's not just remembering—it's reliving. Like she'd been transported back into her memories to relive that tedious, repetitive and ultimately short-lived phase of her life. The baby had said they needed to be prepared for something. What exactly did he mean by preparation?

Was it preparation for action? For this partnership and life-long friendship the baby had been prattling on about? Or just a neat way to keep her out of the way?

If that was the plan, it seemed to be working. As Heather ran she tried to will her eyes open. But all that happened was her eyes opened wider here, in the past. She saw the old growth cedar and pine trees more clearly, the sunlight as it sent shafts down between their branches, the bed of brown needles on the forest floor. This world was getting more and more real every step she took. Even though it wasn't real—except in memory, and maybe the odd post-pizza dream.

That's what they were doing—putting her people into these dream worlds, locking them up safe and sound, so the little bastards could do God only knew what when they got to God only knew where.

Heather slowed down. As an adult, she could make the run—Holden made sure they were all in fighting trim once he got going on the magazine biz—but she was using her untrained little kid legs. And when she was a little kid, she wasn't much of a runner. Or an athlete at all. In fact, she couldn't do much of anything well—not even—

"S-swim," she said aloud.

Heather thought about this.

She couldn't swim at that age.

She remembered bad dreams—of falling; of drowning; of being chased by the man with a hook for a hand. You didn't always win in those dreams. Sometimes the water would get in your lungs, or the ground would come up to meet you—or the hook would catch you through a rib.

But you didn't die. You thought you were going to die—but exactly the opposite happened. Your heart sped up—your breath caught—your eyelids twitched . . .

You woke up.

She put a hand on her side, where she was developing a stitch, and took off again. For the lake, with all the snakes. The stressful, stressful snakes.

But in spite of what Hippie Pete said, Heather didn't think that the snakes would cause nearly as much stress as would death by drowning.

Heather came out of the forest at the top of a low cliff, which she could scale via a rickety wooden staircase that led down to a dock, on the edge of a smallish lake that was rimmed by rock and evergreen. Heather ignored the stairs, figuring she'd chicken out if she had to slow down to climb down twenty-five steps to a dock. She set her jaw, took a deep breath and ran full tilt over the edge of the cliff.

What followed was a brief moment of transcendent joy as Heather became airborne. Just as briefly, she worried that this weird dream-memory might turn into a flying dream—which would be bad, because she'd probably enjoy that too much to go down into the lake and drown herself properly.

But the moment passed quickly, and Heather's feet struck the ice cold surface of the lake. The rest of her followed shortly, and before she knew it her head was underwater.

The stress was unbelievable. Every nerve in her body screamed at her to get out of the water: *Get back on shore! Don't let the air out of your lungs! Find the bottom! Put your feet down! Get Your Head Out Of The Water!*

Heather felt herself struggling, heard her heart thundering in her ears. She concentrated and force d herself to open her mouth, and watched as the quicksilver bubbles of lung-air fled past her eyes. The lake water poured into her mouth, her sinuses, and filled her lungs and chest in an instant.

She struggled to cough, push it out, as her limbs flailed and her nerves shrieked:

GET OUT! GET OUT! FOR CHRIST'S SAKE YOU SUICIDAL FUCKWIT, GET OUT!

Heather blinked. She was back in the lounge on board Holden's yacht. The sky outside the portholes was a deep azure streaked by deep red clouds.

Inside, everyone was where they had been, straight and still in their chairs. The yacht's engines thrummed beneath them, but there was another noise—softer, more insistent—that it took Heather a moment to recognize as breathing. Slow, synchronized breathing. Heather looked to the front of the room. The three children and the baby were sitting there now. Or rather, they were slumping there. The baby was on the table, back propped against the arm of one of the older children. His head lolled. The four of them seemed to be asleep.

Gingerly, Heather stood up. She braced herself—half-expecting the baby to send one of his punishing ice cream headaches her way. But nothing came. They were too busy, probably, keeping the rest of the people in a dream state. Heather sidestepped around the edge of the chair in front of her, bent to pull off her deck shoes. She laid them neatly on the floor underneath Holden Gibson's chair. Barefoot now, she padded her way behind the table and then to the hatch that led to the aft deck and the bridge. Just in case anyone was listening in, Heather recalled her top secret personal mantra—which they would have probably expected her to be saying in her dream retreat about now. It would block them, maybe.

Mi, she thought as she crept along the narrow corridor to the stairs, *mi, mi, mi, mi, mi*.

Alexei the KGB agent was alone on the bridge. He was manning the helm of the boat. There was no end to this guy's skills.

Heather squinted. Alexei was the only person she'd seen so far that wasn't a) a kid, or b) stuck in meditation.

Mimimimimimimimimimimimi, thought Heather, and summoned a picture of the Maharishi from her memory. It wasn't, unfortunately, from TM camp. It was the one with John Lennon and Paul McCartney from when The Beatles went all mystical the '60s. It would have to do.

The yacht lurched then, as Kilodovich throttled back on the engine. He turned the wheel, and as he did so Heather felt another lurch, as the boat started to come about. Where in hell were they going?

As stealthily as she could, Heather climbed the rest of the way out of the hatch and crept to edge of the bridge. She poked her head up, and looked out over Alexei's shoulder.

She suppressed a gasp. There was a coastline ahead of them—a wall of high black rock caught fire in the sunrise, waves breaking in a golden froth over the shallows. Nearer, she could see a great swarm of large birds, circling over their path like a funnel cloud. Further, thin lines of smoke rose from beyond the jagged edge of the rock-face. And approaching them was the oddest collection of boats that Heather had ever seen.

"*Mimimimimimi*," she whispered, trying to drive the wonder from her mind. Alexei turned then, and for an instant their eyes met.

"Hey," she said softly, and made a little smile. "KGB."

Alexei's eyes were still and lifeless for but an instant. Then they seemed to come alive—with a kind of light, borne from the back of his skull. Heather tried to look away—but she couldn't now.

"*Mi*," she said. "*Mi mi mi mi*."

But it was too late. She felt herself slipping, falling toward the light in his eyes—smelled the scent of pine and tar and lake breeze that told her TM camp was not far away. She felt a falling sensation in the middle of her gut—and for an instant, she thought she heard a voice:

"What the fuck are they?" it said.

"What the fuck are they?"

Holden Gibson counted ten boats coming to greet his yacht and bring it back to the Koldun's home. Two of those boats were narrow wooden sailboats painted red and green, big enough to hold a cabin but only just. They belonged to Nikolay Trolynka, and were piloted by his sons Oleg and Makar. Three of them were long canoes, fitted with outboard motors and run by the Stol sisters. There was a cabin cruiser—less than half the size of Holden Gibson's yacht—painted red and green, same as Trolynka's boats but belonging to his second cousin Orlovsky—the most dangerous man in New Pokrovskoye.

Darya Orlovsky, his daughter, stood at the bow, holding an unlit storm lantern ahead of her as though lighting the flotilla's way as it headed into the sunrise, her long purple gown trailing her narrow shoulders and hips in the onrushing ocean breeze. The remaining three boats were licensed fishing boats owned by the Koldun himself, their nets gathered high at their sterns and set out like strands of gold in peacocks' plumage, in the light of the rising sun.

There were more boats in the Koldun's harbour that might have come to greet the children for the rejoining, but these ten were deemed to be the finest and fastest—and only the finest would be appropriate for so historic an occasion as this.

The boats slowed as they approached the yacht, and for a moment, it seemed as though sound was swept from the sea. The motors died, and the wind slowed, and even the cries of the birds overhead stilled.

Holden Gibson gasped deeply as he suddenly found his feet firm on the deck of his yacht. He clutched the lapels of his untucked shirt as though he were trying to tear them away, or maybe reassure himself of their reality. He drew a breath in quiet wonder at the sight.

He stood like that for an instant more—until the silence was broken, by a man's shout: "No! Not again! I'm sorry! Oh—thank God it's you." It was followed again by the scampering of feet across deck, another shout, and a woman's surprised yelp. This last was followed by a muffled thump.

Gibson blinked, and turned away from the flotilla—this crowd of boats whose pilots and passengers he seemed to know by name. Holden Gibson was a large man, but he moved with a child's lightness as he turned to see about the noise.

Words and ideas and memories cascaded through him as he stepped back inside, and climbed the steps to the bridge. He blinked slowly, as he stood before the tableau. He was on the bridge of his boat. His pilot was nowhere to be seen. The girl—Heather! Yes, dear little Heather—was sprawled face-down, her Rasta locks fanning across the deck like the head of a discarded mop.

Standing over her was a tall, black-haired monster; a faceless thing that would kill without remorse.

"Nah," said Holden, as he put the new memory in its place with more recent recollections. "You're not a thing. You're the fuckin' Russkie."

Holden let go of his shirttails, leaving sweaty handprints on them. The Russian, Alexei, was looking at him—or if not exactly at him, then in his general direction.

Holden knew he should know what was going on here with the thousand-yard stare—there was a kind of familiarity to it—but he couldn't quite put it together. He was thinking about some time in a farmhouse—a long time ago, when he was very, very young and very bad things had happened to him. It was very far away.

He had lost part of himself back then, and for some reason . . .

For some reason, it made him think about this Russian.

The murderous sense of déjà vu slipped away again before he could put it all in order.

The Russian stepped toward him now—and for an instant, Holden thought he was coming for him; there was a faraway look in his eye that Holden had seen in men bent on killing. That, Holden was sure, was what the Russian meant to do right now. Kill Holden Gibson. He'd never been more certain of anything in his life. Desperately, Holden balled his fist, raised it, and as the Russian got into range—

—Holden swung at the air.

He was looking forward now: at Heather, who moaned and stirred on the deck; and the slate grey sky, over a dark sea that was suddenly quiet with the approach of the Koldun.

Holden whirled around. The Russian was climbing down the steps that led to the lounge. He seemed unperturbed. As though he had walked through Holden.

Fascinated, Holden followed the Russian.

The Russian ducked under the top of the doorway and stepped into the lounge. Holden followed, and peered around. It looked like nobody had moved—nobody but Heather, who'd had the misfortune to make her way to the bridge—since he'd come there. The kids were even there. Including that talking baby that they all worshipped like their fucking father.

Someone had propped him upright on his pillow like a little Buddha statue. He was the only one with his eyes open, and he looked back over his shoulder as the Russian came up behind him. The baby grinned as the Russian picked him up. Together, the two hustled back through a narrow path between the chairs.

The other kids stood, and filed along behind them. Nobody seemed to take any note of Holden Gibson, and that was fine by him. He waited until they'd all stepped out the back. He cleared his throat.

"All right, crew," he said, in his most commanding voice. "Now's our chance!"

And all at once, the entire crew's eyes snapped open, and each stood.

"*Now's our chance*!"

Holden reeled back.

The crew reeled back.

"What the fuck?"

"*What the fuck*?"

He stared at them. They were repeating his every word—in a creepy kind of unison. He lifted his hand.

Two dozen hands raised.

He raised his middle finger.

The crew returned the gesture.

Holden suppressed a chuckle.

Well fuck, Holden thought, looking out the glass door at the assembly of children, watching the flotilla arrive to collect them. *I'm the same as you little freaks!*

Holden moved forward, among his crew—or not his crew, but his sleepers—careful not to manipulate them this time. He had to go—talk to Vladimir—see the flotilla for himself—

Rejoin his family.

He hurried now, stepping through his crew like they were ghosts, his feet slipping in the substance of the deck. Through Neil and Jude and Allan—

Until finally, he came upon one he'd nearly forgotten.

Holden.

Holden Gibson stood face to face with himself. He studied the minute lines on his face, the dark sag of skin beneath his eyes, the spots that were starting to grow on his forehead. He looked embalmed. Like a corpse. A walking corpse. *Holden Gibson*.

Holden Gibson took a sharp breath. *Holden Gibson* sucked air too, but more violently. He must have looked that way last year, when they'd had to take the defibrillator to him. Maybe they'd have to again. Holden Gibson felt his heart racing—he could feel his breath on his cheek—and a sharp tugging, like the line was going taut on fish-hooks embedded in his stomach, his thighs.

The room shifted then, as those hooks yanked him around so he was facing backwards. The fishhooks were gone, and he couldn't see himself anymore. Weight returned to him. And with it, a terrible weakness.

But he knew it wasn't a heart attack. Not this time.

It was . . . there was a word for it.

The Returning. That's what they'd called it at Kiwichiching.

The Returning.

Sometimes, they warned, it could be very traumatic indeed.

By the time Holden Gibson hit the floor, the trauma was coming at him full tilt. The world grew dark. He barely heard the tumbling clatter of his crew falling to the floor beside him, their strings cut as consciousness fled from Holden Gibson's re-inhabited skull.

Великий THE GRAND INQUISITOR инквизитор

Amar Shadak was just getting started with his submarine guy when Kolyokov's boy finally called him back. "You wait," he said, pointing a finger from inside the coil of leather belt he'd just finished wrapping around his fist. He grabbed the cell phone with his free hand and let the belt trail behind him, its buckle clicking a gentle staccato on the floor tiles as he walked back along the corridor into the great room of the caravansary. The submarine guy's whimpering faded to a moist echo as he thumbed the cell phone on.

"Hello, Stephen," he said pleasantly. Shadak always adopted a pleasant phone manner—even when he said things like, "What the fuck is going on over there that you hang up and don't call me back, you little piece of asswipe? And who the fuck do you think you are not to take my calls?" he would say it in such a pleasant and solicitous tone that no one, he was sure, not even his gravest enemies, could ever think ill of him for it.

"We've had some problems here too," said Stephen. "That's why I'm calling you back. We've both got problems, and we both need answers. I propose we share information."

Shadak smiled warmly. It was the kind of smile that conveyed itself through the voice—no matter that his words were more to the effect of, "Fuck you, Stephen. Put Kolyokov on the line before I cut your liver out and feed it to crows."

"Mr. Kolyokov can't come to the phone just now," said Stephen. "He personally asked me to take the lead in dealing with—our problem."

Shadak considered this as he settled into a wide leather chair. Kolyokov told Stephen to take the lead? On *this*? Everything else being equal, how likely was that? The last time that Shadak had spoken to Kolyokov—when they were negotiating the delivery of the children—the old man had done nothing but complain about the boy. Since Afghanistan, since the dark time, Shadak had had plenty of dealings with Kolyokov. He knew him well, and on many occasions got along with him just fine. But he knew him well enough to know the old bastard wasn't one to give so much as an inch of responsibility to his underlings. That was one of Fyodor Kolyokov's most reliable weaknesses.

Why would he change his ways now?

Of course, the answer to that question was easy: he wouldn't. Stephen was pulling some kind of a coup, a subterfuge—fucking over the old man and Amar Shadak all at once.

The only question was: how, precisely, was he fucking them? What did it have to do with this fuckup with the submarine? Even at this early stage of the interrogation, Shadak was pretty sure his submarine guy didn't have any clue. He'd work him over a little longer to make certain, but so far as Shadak was concerned the answer to the riddle lay elsewhere.

Perhaps within himself—in the dark place, the Black Villa where the better part of his soul rested; in the things the Children had done to him, their scratching in his head, their dubious promises of Paradise . . . of Rapture.

Amar Shadak took the phone away from his ear and shook his head. He had to focus. Perhaps, he said to himself, the answer to the riddle lay in another place.

With Stephen perhaps? Why not? He liked that better. He returned the cell phone to his ear, and let his smile broaden a little, the better to transmit his goodwill across the ocean.

"Tell me what you know, then," he said, glancing back the way that he'd come. "But be quick about it—I'm in the middle of . . . a meeting and I'm anxious to get back to it."

Mrs. Kontos-Wu's wrists hurt from being tied, but overall she was feeling better. Stephen had let her take a shower and clean up in one of the adjoining suites, and ordered her a plate of pasta and seafood from room service. So she was clean and bandaged and well-fed. She would have liked a drink. But she knew better than to get one now.

Across the room, Stephen was dealing with Shadak. Veins stood out on his neck as he spoke into the telephone receiver, and dark bands of sweat were painted across his back.

He should be sweating. Stephen was trying to explain to Amar Shadak that both sets of cargo had gone missing: the children that he was supposed to be supplying to them, and the individual that they were to be supplying to Shadak. It was a task made more difficult because Stephen was under instructions to keep much of Kolyokov's activities—in particular, his death—a secret from the Turkish gangster. Yet he had to convey enough useful information to entice Shadak to give up a list of people who were involved in the transaction.

Kolyokov's death. Mrs. Kontos-Wu was still trying to get her head around *that* one. Fyodor Kolyokov had been with her longer and more completely than her own subconscious mind. All the lies that made her life bearable . . . and there were many . . . he had been at the core of them, making them live and breathe.

When Stephen had told her the truth about what had happened to Kolyokov, it was as though he'd yanked the foundation from beneath those lies. She'd closed her eyes, trying to will herself back into the metaphor of Bishop's Hall that she now knew to be nothing more than a metaphor. In reality, she'd taken her early education in the Urals. Kolyokov had been her master since before she'd graduated, and everything about her had been dictated by his presence: her likes and dislikes, her daily habits; and ultimately, her own personal morality.

In the end, Mrs. Kontos-Wu took Stephen's account of Fyodor Kolyokov's death as more of a theological problem than one of grief and acceptance. So she opened her eyes again and, according to her training, put it all aside. There were more important things to worry about.

Like this phone call with Amar Shadak. At this point, Stephen was down to one-and-two-word answers, interspersed among the long silences as Shadak presumably berated him: "No . . . That's what . . . Right . . . No . . ."

Finally, Stephen held the phone away from his ear so Mrs. Kontos-Wu could hear Shadak's deep Count Dracula voice made into a tiny squawk by the phone receiver. Mrs. Kontos-Wu mouthed: *Do you want me to try*?

Stephen nodded resignedly, and handed her the phone.

"—bullshit a bullshitter," Shadak was saying. "I'll rip you—"

"Amar," said Mrs. Kontos-Wu. "Slow down."

Shadak stopped talking, and Mrs. Kontos-Wu heard a sharp intake of breath.

"It's me," said Mrs. Kontos-Wu. "Remember—from Istanbul?"

Shadak chuckled over the phone. "Why hello," he said. "What happened to that little dancing monkey Kolyokov keeps? Not that I want him back on the line, mind you . . ."

"He's taking a break," she said.

Shadak's voice was all wounded innocence. "From what?" he asked. "We were simply going over some details. I trust I did not upset him?"

Mrs. Kontos-Wu gave a flirtatious laugh. "I can't imagine you upsetting anyone, Amar. Now tell me: how can we fix this?"

"Ah, my beautiful Flower of Manhattan, I fear that matters are damaged beyond repair. The monkey-boy will reveal to me no clue as to what has happened to my ship—my submarine—my people in America . . . my cargo, and yours also. They have vanished without a trace, all of them. Little Stephen is, as ever, no help at all."

"Well really, Amar," said Mrs. Kontos-Wu. "How can you expect him to be? He's been here in Manhattan all this time. He knows nothing of what happened to us at sea."

"That is right. You were at sea. With Kilodovich, yes?"

"Oh yes," said Mrs. Kontos-Wu. "Until very nearly the end."

"Ha!" There came the sound of a clap, or perhaps a snap, from the other end of the line. "Most excellent! Oh my Beauty! Then you can tell me what precisely happened to my ship and submarine and all of it!"

"Well," said Mrs. Kontos-Wu, smiling a little, "I can. But . . ."

"Yes?"

"You first, Amar," she said, and mouthed to Stephen: *Get out*. She pointed at the door. Stephen threw up his arms, turned around and left.

Good boy, she thought. If she were going to work Amar Shadak properly, she'd need a little privacy.

Stephen headed down to the lobby for a smoke. *Take the lead*, Kolyokov had told him. What a fucking joke. There was nothing he could do to intimidate that fucker Shadak. That had been clear from the moment he picked up the phone and Shadak had started cussing him out. The fundamental problem was one of respect: Shadak just didn't respect Stephen. As far as Shadak was concerned, Stephen was just a little harem-boy for old Kolyokov, who took the old man's phone messages when he wasn't sucking his dick. Never mind that that wasn't the case—sexual preferences aside, Kolyokov wouldn't touch Stephen for fear of catching his AIDS cooties—that was how Shadak saw things, so that was how it was.

The elevator door opened on the lobby—which was, as usual, nearly empty. Stephen strode out and went to one of the threadbare sofas near the front desk. He sat down, yanked a cigarette from his pack with his teeth, and lit up. Behind the counter, poor old Richard fussed over some file cards. He looked up and smiled tentatively.

"Goo-ood afternoon, si-ir," said Richard.

"Fuck off." Stephen lit his cigarette with one of the 2,500 Emissary disposable lighters Kolyokov had made him order a couple of years ago. He took a deep drag.

"Ri-ight, sir," said Richard.

Stephen let the smoke curl out his nostrils and up into his eyes, and he regarded Richard through the stinging blue haze. The guy was a wreck—he could barely sign his name, he had so little confidence in himself. It was what made him such a good whipping boy, which is how Stephen used him most days. Stephen would tell him to fuck off and order him around. He would let the shit he took from Kolyokov flow downhill onto Richard. He would try to mind-read him, and maybe even succeed once in a while. And every time he did one of those things, Stephen would feel like a pretty effective guy.

But the fact was, all this time Stephen had been sparring with a crip. There might have been a time when it was different—Richard had been Kolyokov's main sleeper at M.I.T., and he must have been some use there all those years, stealing technology secrets and sabotaging research.

But now? The only thing Richard was good for was taking reservations for the hotel, and giving Stephen an inflated sense of his own importance.

In the real world—where Amar Shadak moved millions of dollars of merchandise across Europe with a word, and Fyodor Kolyokov moved an army of sleepers with his dreams—Stephen was less than an insect.

And yet . . .

You take the lead, Kolyokov had said. It seemed like a joke now, but the fact was that Kolyokov had ordered it. Not, as it turned out, in the tank—he'd gone back and given it another try after Kolyokov's little ghost-message, but as the first time, he got nowhere in the smelly old tank. And he'd done terribly with Amar Shadak outside the tank; it was true that Shadak didn't respect him. So he couldn't deal with him as an equal.

Richard glanced up sheepishly, saw Stephen staring and looked away again as quickly. He started to fiddle with something before the countertop.

What a fucking write-off, thought Stephen.

As he thought it, an image came into his mind: of Richard fiddling below the countertop for a moment longer, looking back at him, and raising a small automatic pistol with a silencer on the end. He aims it carefully, one eye shut while the other sights along the barrel, and pulls the trigger three times. The bullets hit Stephen in a small triangle over his heart, and Stephen slumps over dead—before he's been able to even process the fact that poor stupid Richard knows how to put a silencer on a gun, never mind shoot him with it.

In such a scenario, Stephen's contempt for Richard would work against him. Richard could take him out in a second, and Stephen, in his utter confidence that Richard couldn't even wipe his own ass without help, would be defenceless.

In the same way that Amar Shadak would be without defence, if Stephen ever took the right kind of initiative.

"Si-ir?"

Stephen set down his cigarette and looked back at Richard.

"Mi-issus Kontos-Wu is ready for you," Richard said.

Stephen smiled. "Thank you, Richard." Stephen stood up and stretched so his back cracked. "You've been a big help today."

"Here goes," said Mrs. Kontos-Wu when Stephen returned from his smoke break.

"Shadak first heard about the children through a lawyer friend of his named Tanya Pitovovich in St. Petersburg. She specializes in seeing through foreign adoptions—which in St. Petersburg makes her a bribery and blackmail specialist as much as a lawyer. According to Shadak, the baby trade is huge in St. Petersburg. There are more than 600,000 orphaned and abandoned kids in Russia—and they all live in these orphanages, where, if you know the right people, you can pluck 'em like fruit.

"Anyway—that's what Pitovovich does, and when the market was right, Shadak would sometimes act as a middleman for families in America and elsewhere who wanted a kid."

"Do you know where Pitovovich is now?"

"Yes. I got an email address, a mailing address, and a cell phone number. We'll want to talk to her eventually, I'm sure. But shut up and let me finish."

"Sorry."

"About six months ago, Pitovovich contacted Shadak to tip him off to a possibly lucrative shipment. An associate of hers—Shadak thinks they were fucking, but we'll call him an associate—named Ilyich Chenko had recently taken possession of an old dormitory facility near Odessa. He let slip that he was gathering a number of very 'special' children there, for his own orphanage. Pitovovich thought this strange—Chenko's G.R.U., and dabbles in the same business as she; and there was no percentage in keeping children yourself. So she took a plane there for a visit. And that was where she saw . . . the shipment."

"Do we have an address for that warehouse?"

"Yes, yes! I have all the addresses and names and other shit written down. Do you want to know what he said or don't you?"

Stephen said nothing.

"Fine. When she got there, she saw that the 'dormitory' was in fact an old apartment block, and a nice one. There were maybe two dozen children there, all living like kings and queens. And they seemed like siblings; they all had the same black hair. There was something about their eyes. They seemed . . . aristocratic, she said.

"She asked Chenko a price for them—and he explained they were not for sale. They were too valuable here. But before she left, one of the children—a young girl—came to her and quietly whispered: 'We do not like it here. See us to America.'

"'How can I do that?' asked Pitovovich.

"'Through Amar Shadak,' replied the girl.

Stephen threw up his hands. "And how the fuck did she know about Shadak? He's bullshitting you."

Mrs. Kontos-Wu shrugged. "Maybe, maybe not. I'm just telling you what he told me."

"Fine. Go on."

"So that's when she contacts Shadak—lets him know about this opportunity for these children that Chenko finds so valuable he won't even talk about selling them. Shadak is intrigued, but not convinced. If Chenko's not willing to sell then it might be more trouble than it's worth if he's got to snatch them.

"But Pitovovich goes on describing the kids, Shadak remembers a conversation he had with Kolyokov—about this bunch of kids that he'd pay top dollar for. Black hair and funny eyes were two of the characteristics he pointed to—but there were other things too. So Shadak said, 'Okay, I'm intrigued. Let's go have a look.'

"And that's when he gets convinced. Because a day later, he takes a trip over to Odessa, meets up with Pitovovich and together they go to the apartment block to meet with Chenko. And it's like night and day. Chenko sits Shadak down, gives him a drink, and tells Shadak that he's heard a lot about him and thinks he'll be a perfect guardian for these beautiful children. Chenko has gone so far as to arrange the papers for their passage across the border into Romania and then to Turkey. Shadak's kind of amused at first; but when he asks what the price is going to be and Chenko says 'Don't worry about it,' he starts to get suspicious.

"But then—then he meets the kids, and it's a completely different story. They charm him, in a way that none of his own children have over the years. They say to him, 'Mister Shadak, take us to Turkey! Take us away!' And he says: 'Okay kids.'"

"Doesn't sound like the Amar Shadak I know."

"It doesn't sound like the Amar Shadak that Amar Shadak knows either," said Mrs. Kontos-Wu. "Shadak wondered if he mightn't have been drugged. Because two days later, Shadak's got the first shipment of five kids at his house in Belgrade, and Pitovovich has made arrangements for him to transfer them to Hzekul and his people in the United States, which he then does, without giving it so much as a thought—until, that is, they're gone. By the time the next batch of kids has showed up in Belgrade, Shadak has come to his senses. He's contacted Kolyokov, told him what's happened—and that's where we all came in. Kolyokov agreed to a pretty steep purchase price—Shadak let that much slip—and made arrangements for the shipment, once all the kids were present and accounted for in Belgrade.

"Shadak never saw the next bunch of kids, though—that was when the earthquake hit in Turkey. So he left the details to iron out with his people in the U.S. and Belgrade while he went to Ankara. He seemed a little fuzzy on what happened after that: he told me he was 'studying the fuckup' on the delivery now. But he'd get back to me once he'd nailed down the details."

"Good of him."

"No," said Mrs. Kontos-Wu. "Not really."

"What do you mean, 'not really'?"

"Nailing down details means a direct conversation with Fyodor Kolyokov."

"What did you tell him?"

"Same as you told him: that Fyodor's not available right now. But he didn't seem satisfied."

Stephen snorted. "He wouldn't be . . . *I* wouldn't be, frankly. So how did it leave off?"

"Shadak said he wanted to hear from Kolyokov by the end of the day, said that he meant it, and hung up the phone."

"Well," said Stephen, smiling, "Mr. Shadak's going to be disappointed. In the meantime, it sounds like we've got enough information to get a start on tracking this thing down. Nice work."

"Thank—"

Mrs. Kontos-Wu sat down on the bed. Her hands flopped on the bedclothes at her side, and her gaze fell to her lap. For an instant, she looked as though she were a marionette, whose strings had been cut.

"Hello?" Stephen leaned over her, and cupped her chin in his hand. He raised her face to look at him.

"Nice work," he repeated.

Mrs. Kontos-Wu blinked and smiled at him.

"I'm gratified you think so," she said. "Now prove you're pleased, and get me a drink."

Uzimeri stared at the mountains longingly. Amar Shadak's caravansary was perched on the face of one of the smaller mountains of the Toros. The mountain's larger cousins were spread within the scope of Uzimeri's view. Uzimeri picked the nearest one, and as a kind of game he set out to figure a way to the top of it, on foot and with only minimal climbing gear. He imagined what kind of gun it would take to shoot a man who'd made it to the snowy peak, from this spot here in the caravansary. He imagined himself as that hypothetical man, standing there, looking back at the caravansary with its great stone walls and its broad timber deck, the helicopter sitting idle on its steel-reinforced roof, Amar Shadak firing off round after round from his hunting rifle in a vain attempt to kill him. Tears streamed down Uzimeri's cheek as he struggled to hold onto the image. A few weeks ago, had he imagined such a thing he would have been able to make it as real with little effort; he would have, in the barest second, found himself on that peak, his ankles deep in the snow, the thin air clutching at the hairs in his nostrils. He would have been free of this chair in the blink of an eye. The plastic bonds that were cutting off circulation to his hands would be gone, the deep cut across his cheek where the belt buckle had struck him would be healed and he would be free—free in a place where men like Amar Shadak could never find him.

He could have done that a few weeks ago—indeed, he had done so many times in the company of the Blessed children. But since they had boarded the submarine in the pen at Istanbul, and taken his men there, Uzimeri had lost the ability. In truth, he now realized, it had never been his ability—it was the workings of Zhanna, and her siblings the Children; their powers. And when they had left him, they had taken those powers with them.

Uzimeri had been a moderately religious man before the children came and went. Since they left him, in one of the Foxtrot submarines he kept and maintained on behalf of Amar Shadak and accompanied by his finest crew, he had become positively fanatical. Every day, he prayed for the return of the Blessed Children—so that they might again return him to the glimpse of paradise he'd been afforded in their brief acquaintance.

He began to pray now.

"Oh Blessed Children," he begged, "hear me now, and deliver me from this evil place again, as you had from the sadness and despair of my life before You. I will serve you with all the fire of my soul, though it be the tiniest spark as compared to Your Greatness—"

Uzimeri's prayers were interrupted by the sharp smack of leather across his face. Trembling, he turned to face his torturer again.

"Thank you for waiting," said Amar Shadak. Thick hair tumbled in curls across his broad shoulders. His features were hard enough that he could get away with it without looking effeminate. Indeed, many in his organization found him simply awe-inspiring.

There was a time when Shadak inspired that kind of awe in Uzimeri. But now . . . Now, Uzimeri was sworn to another master. He looked Amar Shadak in the eye, and although his voice trembled in anticipation of the tortures to come, his words were clear.

"I have nothing to say to you," said Uzimeri, "that I have not already said."

"I'll see about that, you traitorous little bastard."

Shadak said it in that pleasant, lilting voice of his, as he pulled the belt tight so the buckle gleamed silver against his fist. There was only a little blood on it, a faint pinkish smear across its edge.

"Babushka deliver me," begged Uzimeri one last time, before the beating resumed.

THE IDIOT
Идиот

Alexei Kilodovich set out on his quest to unravel the lie of his life with enthusiasm. It didn't last. Adults who wish they could return to the pleasures and vitality of their youth, he decided, would do well to amend those wishes, lest someone like Vladimir be within earshot.

Because facts were facts: even in the most generous interpretation, Alexei's youth was nothing more than a kind of prison. He had not seen his mother since he was tiny, and he lived and learned in a boy's school in a frozen wasteland. At night, he slept in the upper bunk in a drafty wooden barracks heated by a coal stove. In the day, he attended classes and performed exercises and studied texts in a low complex of grey classrooms and gymnasiums. Life would undoubtedly have been more brutal in an actual Soviet prison—but that was cold comfort for Alexei. Life was a drudge, an institutional routine—and what was more depressing, as the days progressed he slipped into it as easily as a tractor wheel falls into a well-worn rut.

He thought it would be so different on that first day, when he returned to the buildings from the exercise yard where he and Chenko had been playing cards, his mission from Vladimir fresh in his mind: *You must spend the rest of your life tearing this lie to pieces and putting it back together. Only then will you find the truth.*

"Let's get tearing, then," Alexei said optimistically.

He pushed open the doors to the main hall and looked around for some clue as to where to begin. So far, it was the same as he remembered it: a long hallway with lockers on either side, a poured-cement floor with a worn green rug running up the centre of it. On the right, there were doors to classrooms: on the left, washrooms and a little down-sloping hallway that led to the machinery rooms, where lay the generators and heating system.

Where to begin?

First, Alexei kicked hard at one of the lockers—willing it to vanish in an orange puff of rusty sheet metal. It made a loud clanging noise that echoed from the cement floors and steel-clad walls and when Alexei looked at it all he could see was a foot-shaped dent near the bottom. It did not vanish.

So Alexei moved on to the nearest classroom door. He threw himself against it, as though trying to break it down. It didn't vanish either—but it did swing open, sending Alexei sprawling across the classroom floor. A dozen boys looked back at him from their desks, while at the front of the class, a teacher who Alexei recognized as the sadistic Czernochov speared him with a look of shock and anger.

Czernochov strode across the room to Alexei and demanded to know what the meaning of this intrusion. Alexei bit him on the ankle—all the while thinking, *Vanish, Czernochov, like the pestilent lie that you are*. Czernochov didn't vanish any better than the door or the locker. He kicked Alexei hard in the stomach, grabbed his hair and used it to pull him, still doubled around the pain, to his feet.

Czernochov sneered and pushed Alexei away, so that he stumbled against one of the desks. Several of the boys snickered. Alexei couldn't get at any of them for the purposes of hitting, and when he willed them gone they only laughed harder.

"You are on drugs," said Czernochov quietly to Alexei, then turned to the classroom and said more loudly: "Young Kilodovich here is addled by drugs. See, it makes him crazy enough to think that he can best me here in my own classroom. But can he? No—he bites at my ankle and crumples at the first touch of my boot. Let this be a lesson to you all: drugs make you too confident even as they weaken you against your enemies. A terrible combination, as Kilodovich here is about to learn firsthand."

Later, in the infirmary, Alexei found cause to reassess many things. He wondered if perhaps Czernochov had been right, and he was simply coming down from a crazy LSD trip. Perhaps it had all been an elaborate hallucination—his career with the KGB, his time in Belarus, his job with Wolfe-Jordan, the two yachts, the submarine; Heather, Holden Gibson . . . The talking baby Vladimir. All those things certainly seemed less real than the two broken ribs in his chest and the bandage over his left eye.

The only trouble with that was that while Alexei had many, many memories from his adulthood, he couldn't recall even considering taking drugs here at school. They weren't, as far as he could remember, even very widely available here. A couple of boys had been caught once smoking marijuana, and there was a lot of contraband vodka that made its way through the dormitories. But acid? Alexei couldn't recall it—and he couldn't bring himself to believe that one or two doses of the stuff would so completely erase his memory of even considering taking it in the first place.

So for the time being, he decided he would maintain his initial premise: that he was thirty-five years old and not twelve, and that his experience here was an elaborate brainwashing metaphorical prison, whose code he would have to crack if he were to ever learn the truth about himself.

They kept Alexei in the infirmary overnight, and he spent most of it awake, thinking it through. By morning, he had concluded that his brute-strength approach to the metaphor had been his undoing. Of course, if he flings himself against a door, kicks a locker, bites an ankle, the metaphor will not falter: the simple fact of those actions imply acceptance of the metaphor's rules—and acceptance conveys strength.

By the time Alexei hobbled back to his dormitory to get ready for the day's classes, he had begun to assemble his second strategy for destroying the foundations of this particularly well-made metaphor.

This time, Alexei had decided, he would test the metaphor's philosophical boundaries. There were a few kids in the metaphor's dormitory when he got there. He singled out little Ivan Tovich—who he recalled as being one of the brighter bulbs in the bunch. Ivan was bundling his books together in preparation for his chemistry class when Alexei tapped him on the shoulder. He started and looked around at Alexei with wide and fearful eyes.

"Are you going to hit me?" He raised his binder and textbook in front of his chest like a shield.

Alexei smiled. "Of course not," he said. "Why would you think I would hit you?"

Ivan tried to smile back. "Well, there was the drug thing yester—"

Alexei waved his hand. "The drug thing was bullshit. I never did—that is, I don't do drugs. I was trying something out."

"Ah." Ivan nodded. "Did it work?"

Alexei stepped back and indicated his face and ribcage with a hand. "Does it look like it did?"

Ivan frowned now. "What do you want with me, Kilodovich?"

"I want you to tell me something," said Alexei. "How do you know that you exist?"

"How do I—" Ivan stepped back, looking around the room for allies. "You *are* on drugs," he said. "Go . . . get some rest, Kilodovich."

"No," said Alexei. "I'm fine. I'm asking you a serious question. How can you be sure of your own existence?"

"Okay," said Ivan, "here's how: *I think, therefore I am*. René Descartes gave that answer, and it's good enough for me too."

Alexei put his finger to his chin and frowned. "Hmm," he said. "So thinking confirms your existence. That's all you've got?"

"Look, I've got to get to class," said Ivan. "Can we pick this up later?"

"I will accompany you to class," said Alexei. "We can talk as we walk."

Ivan gritted his teeth. "All right," he said.

"So where," said Alexei as they stepped outside to cross the sports field to the main building, "does that leave the ground underneath our feet? The rocks? Those little trees over there?"

"I don't follow."

"I don't believe that *they* think," said Alexei.

"You didn't ask me about the rocks and trees and the earth," said Ivan. "I don't know that I can be sure about the reality of those things. Certainly, Descartes' test fails them."

"And yet they exist for you—day after day, you step outside and see the same trees, the same rocks, your feet touch the same earth. How can you explain that?"

Ivan didn't answer right away. He stopped walking, looked down at the dirt around his feet. It was strewn with fist-sized rocks. He looked at Alexei, then bent down and picked up a rock. Hefted it in his hand, studied it a moment. Looked back at Alexei.

Finally, Ivan swung the rock in an arch over his head. He cracked it on the side of Alexei's head. Alexei felt his legs buckle, and watched as a dark curtain crossed his vision. The next thing he knew he was on the ground staring up at little Ivan, who still brandished the rock.

"Seems real enough for my purposes," said Ivan. "Now fuck off, Kilodovich. Next time, I kill you."

After this second beating, Alexei Kilodovich slipped into a kind of dormancy. He attended classes; ate and shat and pissed and slept and studied and so on. In the background, a part of him remembered who he was: Alexei Kilodovich the adult, trying to unravel the mystery of himself. But each day, that part grew smaller, faded deeper into the weave of this supposed lie.

And yet, even while the greater part of Alexei sleepwalked through his childhood, that smaller part did make progress. The metaphor was good, but not perfect—there were differences between this place and Alexei's recollections.

For instance: Alexei remembered a broad plaza fenced in by barbed wire to the south of the compound, where sometimes helicopters would land with supplies. Here, the plaza was a gravel lot, where a couple of old trucks and a dark green school bus often parked.

He also remembered a room: tiny but tall, with frosted-glass windows near the ceiling, and nothing but a simple table with two chairs in the middle of it. He remembered doing some kind of test here—not with pencil or paper, but with words and pictures and a single person administering it. There were no such rooms here.

And he distinctly remembered a teacher named Fyodor Kolyokov.

Indeed, whenever he thought of his childhood, the memory nearly always involved Kolyokov—delivering some lesson, some advice . . . or, more often than not, some very specific instruction.

Yet here? There was no sign of Fyodor Kolyokov. Sometimes Alexei's fellow students spoke of him, but always with a kind of distance: *Kolyokov used to say* . . . or *Reminds me of Kolyokov* . . . or *Kolyokov will find out* . . . And the few times that Alexei tried to continue the conversation, it seemed as though the subject would always change to something else—or the conversation would simply end and Alexei would find himself standing alone in the yard as his schoolmates wandered off in separate directions.

The tiny, inquisitive spark in Alexei Kilodovich rejoiced at this apparent dissolution of the metaphor, even as his larger part shrugged it off and threw his young body into another game of floor hockey in the gymnasium, or a fitful sleep in the dormitory, or a shit, or a meal, or the delicious intensity of a pubescent jack-off in the privy.

Alexei might have gone on for many years in such a state, through his metaphorical teens and into his metaphorical adulthood, his inquisitive thirty-five-year-old diminished to nothing more than a pinprick and then vanishing—were it not for the appearance of the apparition in the pines, and the things that its mere existence implied.

Alexei was to meet Ilyich Chenko amid the evergreens for a game of cards at the end of class. It was heading towards winter now; the sun was beginning to set and the snow was thick and golden on the ground; it hung from the pine boughs like buttery baker's dough. The secret card games would have to move indoors soon—if they could continue at all in the closeness of the long winter night. Alexei had arrived a little early in his eagerness to make the game stretch as long as he could.

So he settled himself against the trunk of one of the larger pines, his mittened hands stuffed between his legs for warmth—a chill wind was building from the west—and waited.

As he sat there, the wind began to grow. It stirred up eddies in the snow, that danced in golden swirls by his feet. Further south, the wind was more decisive; it scoured the surface grains of snow and drew them in a gossamer sheet between Alexei and the school buildings, Alexei and the sun. The gold seeped from the snow around him, leaving the faintest pink. And then the wind came to him. The snow stung at Alexei's cheeks, and he shut his eyes against it. A shiver travelled up his back.

"*Kilodovich*." The voice was a whispering in his right ear.

Alexei started, opened his eyes and turned to see who spoke. There were only trees and swirling snow.

"Who is there?" he said.

The voice resumed in his left ear.

"*They are tricking you, Kilodovich. Like they tried to trick me.*"

Alexei scrambled to his feet, his back pressed against the tree trunk. He looked from side to side in a panic. The snow squall had surrounded him in a bubble of white.

"Show yourself!" he shouted.

"*All right, Kilodovich. But not for long.*"

And in the snow to the south, a shadow of a man resolved itself. He was tall and barrel-chested, with long hair that whipped to one side in the wind. He seemed to be completely naked. Alexei squinted, and a part of him that had been quiet for too long stepped forward to speak.

"Fyodor—Kolyokov?"

The apparition raised its immense hands and clapped them together twice. "*Very good*," it said. "*Now we do not have much time, Kilodovich. You have been trapped in here by our cargo, and it is time for you to escape—to return to the true world. You have work to do on my behalf, and I want you to listen to my instructions very carefully.*"

"Return—to the true world?" said Alexei. "No. Not before I've laid the metaphor bare, and unravelled the lie of my life I don't."

"*What are you talking about*?" The apparition shuffled. "*No?* You disobey me? *Fuck. All right, listen carefully*: Manka, Vasilissa, Baba Yaga. *Now do as you're told.*"

Alexei felt a tugging at his middle, but the pressure was slight enough that he could ignore it. "What are you talking about?" he said. "I've got business here now."

The apparition Kolyokov raised its fists and strode forward. Now Alexei could make out more details—and those details confused him more than ever. This was not the Fyodor Kolyokov he remembered: he was at least twenty years older and thirty pounds heavier for one thing—his hairline had peeled back from his forehead and now rested near the crown of his skull, catching its breath for the final ascent to the top—and in all Alexei's memories of his old instructor, never had his eyes blazed with such raw fury as they did now.

"I *have business here*!" he bellowed. "*And you, Kilodovich, are a part of that business*! Manka! Vasilissa! Baba Yaga! *Obey me! You are my tool! Step from the metaphor! Return to the Physick*!"

"Ah," said Alexei. "So it *is* a metaphor."

"*Kilodovich!*"

"I remember you being here," said Alexei. "Very distinctly. And not as an old ghost. But as a young man. Where are you?"

"*It is too much to explain,*" said the ghost, which was becoming flustered and dissolute. "*It—look—*"

"I have to unravel this before I leave," said Alexei. "You have convinced me of this."

And with that, the winds died down, and the apparition of Fyodor Kolyokov fell into the cold ground along with the thin flakes of arctic snow. The school resolved itself in the distance. Nearer, little Ilyich Chenko ran towards him, his deck of cards clutched in a bare hand, the setting sun painting a bright halo around his shoulders. Alexei smiled.

"So Ilyich," he said as his old friend came closer. "You are not dead after all."

Ilyich grinned, breath puffing a vapourous beard across his young chin. "Not today," he said. "I've still got to win back those rubles, eh, Kilodovich?"

"One last chance," said Alexei, and sat down to enjoy the card game.

Two days later, midway through his trigonometry examination, Alexei made up his mind: enough was enough.

He put down his pencil and stood up. Czernochov was presiding over the exam, and he glared at Alexei, motioned for him to sit.

"No," said Alexei. "Vladimir did not have trigonometry in mind when he sent me to this place."

"Are you back on drugs, Kilodovich?" Not taking his eyes off Alexei, Czernochov reached behind him and grasped hold of his yardstick. It was of limited use for drawing lines or measuring, as Czernochov had long ago cracked it—beating suspected drug addicts who interrupted his lessons.

"I was never on drugs," said Alexei. "You were never my instructor. It was always Fyodor Kolyokov. Why is he not here? Because this is not true."

Czernochov sneered, and opened his mouth to speak. But nothing came out. The windows grew lighter and the shadows shifted as the sun began, impossibly, to move higher into the sky.

And with that, the world of Alexei's trigonometry exam began to fragment and fade.

Alexei now stood in a setting that was more familiar—even though he had not truly recalled being there for twenty years. This was an examination room, but it was a real examination room: a small room with shiny painted cinderblock walls with high, frosted-glass windows and a single flickering fluorescent tube providing all the light. He was alone.

"What are the colours I am thinking of?"

The voice came from a speaker somewhere near the ceiling.

"Red. Black. A sort of green."

"'A sort of green.' Can you be more specific, Kilodovich?"

"There is blue in it. So it's not completely green." Alexei concentrated on the colour he was seeing behind his eyes. It reminded him of the surface of the ocean, near a port; on a grey day, with seagulls crying in the air, and bobbing in the water, a nautical buoy—shaped like an oilcan, with a black metal latticework supporting a blinking red light. The buoy was numbered, and something was written on the side. In Spanish?

"We are near Cuba."

The speaker was silent. Alexei concentrated.

"Okay. I see a boat approaching. It's a motor launch, pretty small, with what looks like three American college students in it. In fact, though, none of them go to college. The pilot is a man named Harvey Abelson. He's CIA. He's thirty-two but looks eighteen, He has two others with him who are also operatives: a woman named Ruth Etterby and a man, Fred Winslow. They're watching for a particular boat, coming from Cuba."

"I see. And who—who is in *that* boat?"

Alexei thought about that. Abelson knew a name—Emilio Torres—and he knew a face—a thin, bald man with a long black beard and a patch of nearly white skin in front of his left ear, where a burn had healed badly.

But Alexei didn't think that was right. He concentrated further, and finally said: "One of ours. Abelson doesn't know it, though."

There was a staticky shuffling at the microphone, and a woman's voice spoke next.

"How do *you* know it, then, Kilodovich?"

"He is nervous, our man. His thoughts are like a horn across the water."

"Spare us the similes. Keep watching. Tell us when he arrives."

Alexei waited. He cast his eye across the water, dwelled on a growing mass of thunderheads to the east, white and grey against a stratospheric blue. The ocean had a smell to it, too—one that he, who had never been near a large body of water, had no words for. An alien smell. Alexei let his attention return to the Americans.

Although he didn't let on to his team members, Abelson had seen more than a picture of Emilio Torres. The two had known one another years ago, at school in Southern California. They'd been good friends—shared beer and crib notes and even, for one intense month, a girlfriend named Sue Denson, who'd eventually left them both for a kid in pre-med. These days, the "kid" ran a successful private practice in San Francisco—which helped him keep up with the staggeringly high alimony payments that Sue won in their divorce.

Abelson kept track of his ex and her ex's fortunes out of a vaguely malicious curiosity. He kept track of Torres' comings-and-goings in the course of his job. Torres had been working in deep cover in Havana for the past eleven years—working as a cleaner at the house of Pyotr Oprinchuk, one of Castro's foreign policy advisors from the Kremlin. He had been reporting for several months now on the movement of ships and submarines from Havana Bay, to a point in the mid-Atlantic—all having to do with something called Petroska Station. He'd also managed to photograph a group of very high-level Russians, who visited Oprinchuk for dinner a week ago. Among them: Vasili Mishin—who'd taken the fall for the failure of the Soviet lunar program—and General Karim Karimov, who was also engaged in the cosmonaut program. Were they building a launch facility in Cuba then? The Russian plans for Petroska Station were a most tantalizing mystery.

But it would be someone else's mystery to solve. Torres had been compromised. One of Oprinchuk's maids had begun to suspect, and two nights ago let on to Torres that if he didn't come up with some money, she'd spill it all.

After disposing of her body, Torres had made a fast radio transmission, headed for a cove at the north end of the island where he kept a boat, and from there, debarked for a rescue rendezvous.

What he hadn't figured, of course, was that the maid wasn't just a maid; she was part of a KGB counter-intelligence team on a spy hunt—making sure the top secret Petroska Project stayed secret. She was only fishing when she approached Torres.

With her murder, Torres gave himself away. The KGB team intercepted his transmission, and shortly thereafter, intercepted him, on his way to the boat. Torres was now on his way to an interrogation camp in Russia. And one Jorge Alvarez, a KGB recruit from Havana who bore a passing good resemblance to Torres, was on his way to the rendezvous to try and find out how much the Americans knew.

The motor launch was in sight now—the whine of its engine on the edge of audibility.

"Fred," said Abelson quietly, "start the motors. Torres is coming in."

Fred nodded and climbed up to the bridge. Ruth slipped below decks. Abelson lifted a pair of binoculars to his eyes, and focused them on the launch.

"He's put on weight," said Abelson as Ruth handed him the rifle. He set down the binoculars, lifted the gun to his shoulders, and peered through the scope. He drew it slow across the horizon, until it lit on the prow of the boat. From there, he pulled it up and onto Jorge's worried face.

"Oh no," said Alexei aloud.

"What is it?" said the woman behind the wall. "Say what you see, boy."

Alexei ignored the question. He'd misapprehended the situation! Abelson was there as part of a hit squad—not to pull in an agent. Jorge was a second away from death.

He had to act quickly!

Frantically, he pulled out of Abelson's sphere, out of his mind. He had to get to Jorge—to warn him. With all his energy, Alexei flew across the water—fast as a bullet would travel, maybe even a little faster—to warn the unsuspecting agent that things were not as they seemed . . .

That he should duck.

"Duck!" screamed Alexei, as he set a metaphorical foot into the doomed man's mind.

He was doomed. Because as fast as Alexei travelled, he only arrived a scant two seconds in advance of the bullet bound for the middle of Jorge's skull. That was enough time to speak the warning—for Jorge to start at the thought, wonder where it came from—for Alexei to apprehend the texture of a life (childhood in Havana, spent helping his mama clean toilets in a hotel owned by a Miami-based mobster known to him only as Brother Jules; a revelation like a touch from God, when he met the lean, handsome Che Guevara for the first time and swore himself to the Revolution; and years, moving into decades, spent in service of that Revolution, filled with loves and slights, triumphs and humiliations).

And then, a bullet—which tore through Jorge and Alexei and the universe all at once and forever.

But it only seemed forever. Alexei blinked awake, bullet-free and alive, in Bed 4 at City 512's infirmary. Unlike the examination room, which had small, frosted glass windows near the ceiling, the infirmary was completely subterranean. The only light came from wire-caged lamps set into the painted cinderblock walls. There were a dozen of these, two lights for each bed, with additional lamps on long goose-necks attached to the headboards.

"Sorry, Kilodovich. You failed."

Alexei didn't recognize the voice or the man who was using it at the foot of his bed. He had black hair, a long thick beard and two thick eyebrows, conjoined into one. He wore an expensive-looking leather coat, and his hands rested in its pockets.

"What do you mean?"

"Failed. You messed up. Got the signals wrong. Took the wrong course of action. You're out of the program. Do you understand what I mean now?"

Whoever this guy was, he was pissing Alexei off. He'd never seen him before, never even heard his voice through the intercom during a test. And here he was, delivering the news that Alexei had failed.

"I don't believe you," said Alexei. "This is still a part of the test. Where are the others?"

"They don't care about you any more. Like I said—you're out of the program. Finished. You got no talent as far as they're concerned. They've already wasted enough of the People's valuable time and resources on you."

"May I ask," said Alexei, "what caused me to fail?"

The bearded guy nodded, as though something had just been confirmed in Alexei's question.

"You fabricated," he said. "You sensed energies. But they were random, meaningless energies—and you used your mind and imagination to transform them into a narrative. A few simple suggestions from the box, and there you are—floating over the waters off the coast of Florida, imagining something out of a James Bond novel in your head."

Alexei looked more closely at this man: the cast of his brow, the way his chin bent beneath its beard. He was younger—in better shape—but . . .

"Fyodor Kolyokov," Alexei murmured.

"You know my name." The man frowned. "That's not talent," he said. "You've been snooping. Trying to trick me into giving you a second chance. That's not a wise course."

Alexei shook his head, as though clearing hangover cobwebs. He blinked up at Kolyokov—the real Kolyokov; not the one he remembered, teaching him spy tricks from the classroom. And not the strange ghost that had accosted him in the schoolyard.

The real Kolyokov. The bastard.

"You were never my teacher," he said. "Were you now? You took me from the program here, after they'd written me off. And instead, you put me in—"

Alexei snapped his fingers—the words wouldn't quite come. Lies and certainties shifted and melded as his understanding grew.

"There was never a spy school. Not the one I'm remembering. Spy school—school—was—" *a tiny room, where lights flashed and food came infrequently and when it did come, was infused with narcotics; a place of needles and repetitions and ultimately, emptiness . . . a terrible emptiness, with the power to draw away the soul—*

"Shit."

Alexei jumped off the bed. Kolyokov stepped back, hands still in his pockets.

"Think what you like," he said. "It doesn't matter. You'll come with me in the end."

"I will," said Alexei. For the path with this man—this younger incarnation of Fyodor Kolyokov—was the path to the truth of his childhood. And it was, Alexei began to realize, a more terrible truth than he'd ever dared imagine.

THE GAMBLER
Игрок

The dream-haunted corridors of the Murmansk spy school faded and bent under the grass, and in the distance past the apartment blocks and razor-wire fences and machinegun posts, a great, dark cloud began to form. Old Fyodor Kolyokov squinted at its dissolution. It had been a good try, he thought, entering Alexei Kilodovich's metaphor to pull him back awake.

A good try. But there was only so much he could do.

Kolyokov was beginning to understand his predicament: he wasn't just having a very long sleep in his tank. He was, in body at any rate, deader than the proverbial doornail. Whatever lived now, whatever his thoughts inhabited, was his ghost. The world he inhabited? A metaphor, true—but not his own.

Briefly, it had been Kilodovich's. He knew it to be so, because he had been central in constructing it. He recognized the work of his own hand—and he knew it well enough to contact young Alexei, and try and get a warning across.

But Kilodovich had had other ideas—put in him, perhaps, by the Children? Who knew. The important thing was that Kolyokov began to dismantle the metaphor too quickly—and that dismantling threw Kolyokov out. Kilodovich had moved on—to another place; a metaphor no longer of his making, perhaps closer to true memory.

There would be no communication with him here, in this ruin.

Soon, there would be no *here*.

Kolyokov started to walk across the ruins. The metaphor was losing its form with each step—the ground shifting between gravel and asphalt and mud depending upon how he lowered his heel. The air was neither cool nor warm. In spite of the growing cloud on the horizon, neither did that air move.

The world was coming undone with stillness.

Stillness everywhere, but in that terrible cloud. Kolyokov watched it for a moment. The cloud spread across the horizon most menacingly: black at its base, but topped by a range of purple and golden thunderheads that stretched over the curve of this world like distant mountains. Would there be tornadoes underneath that cloud? Kolyokov wondered. Lightning strikes? He heard no thunder, felt no wind, but he knew somehow that it would come. The cloud tops churned and twisted discernibly. Weather would accompany them.

But it would not. Kolyokov's chest hitched at the realization:

I am dying.

Kolyokov had denied it for as long as he might: but when they'd pulled him from his tank and ingested him into the chaos of their Discourse—of course, they were killing him in the world of Physick. Of course, his body would not survive the ordeal.

Of course—

He was dying.

In the silence of the crumbling metaphor, Fyodor Kolyokov fell to his knees. He knew better than to pray for absolution—for entry into Heaven. Because if ever there was a God to give it, Kolyokov would not find favour with Him.

All he could hope was that the message he planted in Kontos-Wu had arrived—and Stephen had the wit to follow his advice. He hoped Mrs. Kontos-Wu had the strength to break her programming. Even if he died now, Kolyokov thought bitterly, he might still leave some legacy for his kind.

Kolyokov reached down to touch the crackling dry grass at his knees. He could feel it beneath his fingertips—but through a veil of numbness. Soon, that sensation too would be lost to him. His body—or the metaphor of his body—would crumble and blow away like this poor construct he'd made for Alexei Kilodovich all those years ago.

"Oh, Alexei." Fyodor Kolyokov shut his eyes and wept unsalted tears. "Oh me."

The storm cloud must have grown nearer as he wept. Because after a time, Kolyokov became aware of a breeze against his cheek, wafting through the long hairs that remained on his skull. A smell, unfiltered by numbness, excited his senses.

"Strawberries," he said, and opened his eyes.

The storm was not only nearer—now it roiled about him, in dust devils eighteen feet tall and tiny lightning flashes from the belly of the deep ochre cloud that now made his ceiling. Kolyokov wiped the dampness from his eyes even as the rain began to fall.

"Garlic," he said, sniffing the air like a hound tracing a scent. "And—what is that under-scent?"

Peat.

The sensation brought about by that word in Kolyokov's skull was more novel than even the breeze and smells in this place. He had not, he realized, heard a voice speak in his skull like that since . . . since the Soviet. When he had controllers of his own to deal with.

Kolyokov smiled.

"Children?" He pushed himself to his feet, and stared into the wall of cloud and dust that now surrounded him in a vortex just fifty feet across. "Vladimir? Doonya? Which one of my beauties is this?"

The cloud rumbled a deep laugh.

No children here.

"Ah," said Kolyokov, "there is no need to dissemble, my children. I am quite at your mercy. For I am nearly dead, now, is that not so?"

That, said the cloud, *is the only thing that is so. Understand, Fyodor Kolyokov, that the Children you have been seeking are quite beyond your reach now.*

"I see."

There is only Me.

"Only you. I mean, forgive me—You."

The cloud was silent, but for the lashing of its winds and the rumbles of thunder in its belly.

"So what is my predicament. Am I talking with God now?"

Only Me.

"Yes. Upper case 'Me.' You're claiming to be God, am I right?"

Not—quite.

"Well, let me tell you something, not-quite God," said Kolyokov. "I never bowed to you in my life—and I won't now."

A moment ago, you were weeping.

"Yes. You're omniscient, so you can tell that poor little Kolyokov is weeping from thirty kilometres south of the metaphor. Forgive me if I'm not impressed."

There is no reason you should be. We both know, Fyodor, that the metaphor is but our own construct—and the powers of a God can be fashioned there as readily as can a convincing bowl of soup. But I repeat: a moment ago you were weeping.

Kolyokov shifted and wiped a strand of hair that was tickling his eye. He coughed; the cloud now stank of strawberry and garlic and peat.

"A man faces his death as best he is able," said Kolyokov.

You think you are dying?

"Did you not say as much yourself?"

Yes. For dying was how I found you. But Fyodor—you must know that dying is not dead. You may yet be saved.

Fyodor threw back his head and laughed.

"Saved? Ha! So You *are* God! A very Orthodox God, yes? Do You want me to confess my sins before we depart unto Heaven? I warn You, terrible cloud, it could take some time—for I have been a very wicked Kolyokov and I have not been to confession in seventy-two years! Ha!"

The cloud rumbled and quaked, and the vortex for a moment drew closer to him. Kolyokov could see a blur of rocks and branches in its substance. When it spoke again, its voice was as a thunderclap in Kolyokov's head.

You have not changed, you bastard.

It took Kolyokov a moment to regain his senses. The intensity of the cloud's voice was bad enough—if such a shout had entered his Physick brain, it might have caused him a stroke. But that intensity was nothing compared to the shock of recognition.

"You," he said as he sat up and dusted himself off.

Yes.

Kolyokov felt that ball-tightening anxiety all wicked men feel at one time or another in their lives—the day they enter the interview for a coveted new position, only to discover the interviewer is a former lover with whom things ended poorly; the night they come home to find their wife and mistress sipping tea together in the kitchen. And most of all on that day very near the end, when they sit alone on a vast plain beneath a cloud that could be God, and at once recognize by Her voice that not only is God a woman . . .

. . . but . . .

It is I.

"Shit," said Kolyokov.

You don't seem pleased to see me.

"Well," said Kolyokov carefully, "I'm not really seeing you—am I?"

The cloud rumbled with deep laughter. *This is me now, Fyodor. Me. No dissembling, as you put it.*

Kolyokov had to think quickly; this was a worrying development, this thing above him.

"And how—how does that come to pass?" he said, smiling ingratiatingly. "The last I recall, you had . . . you had the fine features of a Romanov, my dear—the delicate form of—"

He was cut off by an angry thunderclap.

Spare me! I am beyond the flesh, Fyodor, and so are you! That is why I am here!

Kolyokov swallowed nervously.

Ha! You are more fearful of an old friend than you are the Creator. You truly haven't changed.

"Am I—" Kolyokov licked his lips. "Am I facing your wrath, then?"

Far from it. I am come here to offer you a bargain.

"What bargain?"

Very simple. You are dying: your body is crumbled, and your mind only lives now in the substance of the Discourse. Before long, you will have vanished, but for your presence in the imperfect memories of others. Do you wish this for yourself?

"Of—" Kolyokov felt himself tremble at the thought of it. "Of course not."

Then, she said, *here is your escape. Join me, Fyodor Kolyokov—in the cloud. Together we'll live forever—in more than memory. Far more.*

Kolyokov squinted up the moving walls of the vortex, to the ochre cloud ceiling, what seemed like hundreds of metres above. A glow descended from it now—like a light from Heaven. Or, thought Kolyokov ruefully, like the special effects glow they used on television when showing a flying saucer abducting FBI agents who should know better.

"Bullshit," said Kolyokov. "I don't know how you've done it, but you've done it. You've spirited the Children away from me and you've hidden them somewhere. You just want me out of the way so you can do what you want with them."

The vortex tightened so close that Kolyokov had to hop quickly to avoid being pulled up in it.

You are going to die if you don't come with me, Fyodor!

"Ha! That's what you want me to think! You've constructed this metaphor most carefully, my dear! As I look around, it has all the signatures of the metaphors you'd make for us in the old days, yes? Those great romantically constructed clouds and thunderstorms were your favourite, weren't they? All that's missing is the Ivan Rebroff music in the background and the warm firelight, and that cheap, sweet wine you thought so highly of! Clever witch, you've done nothing but made a metaphor to trick me into mourning my own passing!"

Fyodor, Fyodor. Your paranoia that weakened you in the war will prove your undoing now! Accept my bargain and join me!

"My paranoia," said Kolyokov quietly as the vortex narrowed to tug at his shoulders and whip his shoelaces against his ankles, "is what kept me alive."

It's not helping you now, said the cloud. And with that, she snatched Kolyokov from his feet and high into the whirling chaos of her vortex.

THE STRANGER-WOMAN

Незнакомка

The feeling was not dissimilar to the course their affair had taken those many decades ago.

They had met while dreaming an interrogation. The KGB had pulled in what they believed to be an American sleeper in Berlin, and City 512 had its orders to confirm this supposition.

Kolyokov remembered the day the orders had come in. He was just a month shy of his nineteenth birthday, but had already participated in three successful operations. A regular little Hero of the Workers—although most of his involvement had been in manipulating those workers that had been implanted as sleepers: strictly internal work. Foreign espionage remained his dream.

"Your dream is about to come true, Comrade Kolyokov," said Vasili Borovich, his titular commander, as he revealed the mission over tea that morning. The two were sitting in an office in one of the lower sub-levels of City 512—an area baffled with the new e-generators that were supposed to keep eavesdroppers out. "We are engaged in serious work. We think that our friends in the KGB have uncovered an agent who is—I would not say our equal. But formidable."

"Well," said Kolyokov.

"This agent is American—he has been active in North Africa—and he's got contacts all through Germany and Czechoslovakia." Vasili smiled and opened the spigot on the little brass samovar, refilled his tea. "So you see? Finally, young Fyodor Kolyokov gets to see the world."

Kolyokov laughed at that. Kolyokov was only young compared to Vasili, by the fine measure that children bring to the lay of their youth. Vasili was in fact only a year ahead of Kolyokov—and not, in truth, much more experienced. At that, he was still one of the eldest in City 512 at that time and he lorded it over the rest of them, like an upperclassman.

"So how's this going to work?" said Kolyokov. "I'm happy as ever to serve the Party and the People—but I don't think I've ever even heard of anyone doing an interrogation like this before, with a hostile mind, who might be trained."

Vasili nodded. "It's tricky. That's why it won't just be you. I'll be working it too. And there's one more. From Canada."

Fyodor raised his eyebrows. "We're working with Canadians now?"

"Idiot. No. I said *from Canada*. Not a Canadian. One of our operatives there."

Fyodor set his teacup down and squirmed. He had to pee something awful—even then, he had a bladder that wouldn't keep quiet for very long. Vasili could hear it too: you didn't carry many secrets from each other at City 512. He let a little smirk cross his lips.

"So he's coming all the way from Canada for this," said Kolyokov impatiently. "It seems wasteful."

Vasili's smirk broadened and he laughed. "Not he, my friend—she. And yes—all the way from Canada, where she's been—"

But Kolyokov didn't wait for the rest. He rushed to the lavatory—where he would, in a moment, void his bladder, and scrub his hands and face to wash away the terrible premonition that stained him as Vasili spoke the words:

Not he, my friend—she.

Kolyokov's isolation tank was shiny as a new car in those days, and it didn't smell at all. It was situated in a room nearer the surface—insulated from the thrumming e-generators that would make dream-walking impossible, and just deep enough that the roar of the trucks and the airfield over-top didn't likewise disturb the dreamers' sleep. Its Soyuz urinal even worked—so the fullness of Kolyokov's twitchy bladder was neither here nor there when it came to dream-walking.

They would be dream-walking to the subject. The location of City 512 was a secret kept from all but the most senior members of the KGB—and bringing a prisoner who could well be from America's counterpart into City 512 would represent an insane breach in security. An old farmstead in East Germany, surrounded by black cars, was the subject's prison. Comrades Kolyokov and Borovich would meet the Canadian operative there. Together, they would dream-walk into the American spy's mind, in a process not dissimilar to the one they used to operate trained sleepers. But they wouldn't operate this one's mind. They'd crack it, and toss it like a dissident's flat.

"Red," said Kolyokov as the technician turned the latch on his tank. "And orange, and yellow . . ." *And green . . .*

Oh, how Kolyokov loved dream-walking in those days. To step from his imperfect flesh and into the crafted, beautiful form of his metaphorical body. They were all Gods—terrible and beautiful in the guise of their dreams. Vasili might erase his thin face and pale, too-long fingers—extend the jawline that in reality receded beneath a slight overbite. Kolyokov could trim away the roll of fat that even then spread over his belt, and replace it with the sharp-lined torso that only seemed to appear in sculptures.

In such an idealized form, Kolyokov rose over top his tank—up past the gantries, over the rows of fluorescents that hung in a row on thick black wires.

"Hey—Fyodor! Wait for your leader!"

Kolyokov stopped, and hovering there waiting, glanced down at the tanks. He marvelled at the luminescent thing that rose out of the tank marked BOROVICH.

"Look at you," said Kolyokov as Vasili Borovich's newly tuned metaphor rose to join him.

Vasili had pulled out all the stops. His chin was sculpted heroically, to social-realist proportions, as was his newly minted chest. His hair, clipped short to keep out the lice, here hung to his shoulders in a wild black mane. At first, Kolyokov thought he might be wearing robes, but as Vasili rose Kolyokov saw they were no such thing.

Vasili had given himself wings—white angelic wings, over a slim, naked form that would have fit snugly on an Olympic swimmer.

In spite of himself, Kolyokov laughed.

"Comrade Commander," he said, "don't tell me you've taken up religion? Or is it a woman?"

To his surprise, two pink spots appeared on Vasili's magnificently sharp cheekbones, and his perfect blue eyes glanced downward.

Kolyokov laughed again and gave one of Vasili's immense wings a tug with one hand.

"She must be a wonder," he said.

"You have no idea," said Vasili, still not meeting Kolyokov's eye. "Now let's go—it's almost time for the rendezvous."

And with a single flap of his wings, Vasili Borovich led the way to Germany, and the interrogation.

A thin layer of snow enshrouded the farmstead. The little cluster of buildings was surrounded by a web of tire tracks, spreading out from a smaller circle of vehicles tucked close into the house. Yellow light came from one window, stretching across the mucky white for what looked like twenty metres before it faded. In that light, Kolyokov could see the shadows of the KGB men as they paced to and fro—waiting for the interrogation to begin.

Kolyokov and Vasili settled to the ground outside that window and peered inside.

There were three KGB men in a large room that had at one time been a family room. One tended a coal fire in a little pot-bellied stove in one corner. Another was walking back and forth, his eyes darting nervously about the room. A third smoked a cigarette in a chair, beside a bed where their subject, a heavy-set young man with curly blond hair, was strapped naked.

"Look at them," said Vasili with a grin. "They're scared out of their minds."

"Why shouldn't they be? They're alone in the winter, waiting for interrogators that are invisible and can read their very thoughts." Kolyokov reached inside, and idly entered the mind of the pacing man.

"You see? That one—I can't make much sense of it, but he's thinking about a sum of rubles—a sum I'm pretty sure he shouldn't have on his salary." Kolyokov smiled thinly. "I'll make a note of it."

"Is this what we've come to at City 512? Peeping into the minds of our brave Comrades?"

Both Vasili and Kolyokov started. The voice was a woman's—and Kolyokov thought it was the sweetest thing that he had ever heard. He and Vasili turned to see her.

She stood in a long, hooded robe, lined with mink, that covered all but her mouth, which was pulled now into a mischievous smile. Kolyokov's hand slipped from the KGB man's mind.

"Lena," said Vasili. Almost of their own accord, his wings extended outward and over his head.

The woman—Lena—laughed. "Vasili Borovich? Is that you in the folds of that outrageous metaphor?"

The wings faltered, but Vasili kept his composure. "None other, my dear," he said, and stepped forward—surely, thought Kolyokov, as though he were expecting an embrace. Kolyokov had to suppress a smirk, as this woman Lena stepped passed him, ducked underneath his extended left wing-tip, and brushed past Kolyokov to peer into the window.

"My name is Lena," she said.

"Fyodor," said Kolyokov.

"Well, Fyodor," she said as she stepped through the glass and wall and into the room, "I'm glad to see *someone* didn't overdress for the occasion."

The interrogation took only a few hours—but in those hours, Kolyokov learned more about his gift and its application than he had in his entire lifetime spent studying at City 512. Lena had done this before—and she knew the tricks of a dream-walker's defences as a locksmith knows the tumblers of a well-made safe.

Their subject turned out to be a formidable lock indeed. As they stepped into the metaphor of his defences, they found themselves standing upon a great plain. The ground was cracked like a dried sea bed—the sky the colour of fire and smoke. Kolyokov was confused—there appeared to be no entry point here at all.

Perhaps they should dig? Vasili swore and flapped his angel wings in frustration. Lena held up a hand, and slowly began to turn, her eyes narrowed to observant slits. Finally she pointed.

"That horizon," she said, "is closer than the others. We go there."

It took what seemed like an hour to get there, but finally they found what the closer horizon signified: a cliff, dropping treacherously into a deep canyon. It might be scalable—looking down, Kolyokov could see things nested in crooks and ledges; and they would have had to have gotten there somehow. But if this were a defence system, he didn't think the route would be easy.

"Hell," said Lena, looking further.

"Don't despair, my dear," said Vasili, putting a hand on her shoulder. Lena shrugged it off.

"I'm not despairing," she said. "Just observing. This place—it's a Christian Hell. Look." She pointed into the yellow mist that clung to the floor of the great canyon. Kolyokov peered.

"I see what you mean," he said. "There are circles—tiers, going down in ever smaller circles. Think there's an ice field in the middle?"

Lena spared Kolyokov a dazzling smile. "You've read your Dante," she said, and made a scolding noise. "Careful, Fyodor. *The Divine Comedy* cannot be on the approved reading list at City 512."

Kolyokov shrugged. Had he been there in Physick, she might have seen him blush.

"Well," she said, "this is no doubt a terrifying metaphor for the weak Christian bourgeoisie in the West. Here, though, we are made of sterner stuff, hey Comrades? There is no Hell for we Soviets, but the chains and wheels of unchecked Capital."

"You are very wise, my dear," said Vasili.

"Actually," she said, "I am very funny. That was a joke, my little Comrade Angel. Now why don't you flap your wings. Perhaps it will break your fall." And with no more than the tiniest of nudges, she sent Vasili Borovich cartwheeling over the edge of the abyss.

She laughed sweetly, as he plummeted and rolled and finally, when he was no more than a distant speck—began to spin and glide into the yellow sulfur of Hell's ground mist.

Breaking the American's shield was a complicated business. At the bottom of the cliff, there waited an army of red Imps, carrying pitchforks, breathing flame and uttering unsettling commentaries concerning Vasili's parentage. Kolyokov was inclined to dive down and help out, but Lena held him back. While Vasili kept the American occupied, she meant to outflank him. If this metaphor was anything like the defensive metaphors that she was familiar with, there was only so much of it the American could control at once.

So they moved along the ridge, until Vasili's cries and the clanging of pitchforks blended in with the droning laments of the damned. Lena stopped, and looked down at the rock. Sure enough, it was smoother here—the cracks in the clay had a blurred quality to them. When Kolyokov put his hand against the firmament of Hell, it yielded like foam rubber before solidifying under his touch.

Lena knelt beside him—put her hand on his. She smiled at him. He smiled back. And as they touched, the ground shifted and bent, and the edge of the cliff extended. Lena took her hand away, stood, and stepped on the new ground they had made. It was the top landing of a long set of stairs cut into the cliffside, extending step by step down to the next circle of Hell.

"Abandon hope, ye who enter," said Kolyokov.

"Stop showing off," said Lena, "or I'll report you. Now come on. This is our way in."

There was a great fat demon waiting for them at the bottom—but he remained lethargic and indistinct while the American put his full attention on the defeat of the angelic Vasili. Lena and Kolyokov were able to sneak past him without incident.

Kolyokov was beginning to think the whole thing would be a piece of cake when, in the midst of a stony plaza approaching the blasted out archway of a bone white cathedral, he stepped into a puddle of flaming pitch. The pain was so intense that it was all he could do not to sit up in his tank back at City 512 and shriek like a baby. Lena hauled him back, and told him not to blame himself: the puddle had literally appeared as he stepped into it. They had apparently wandered into a psychic minefield. They both concentrated, and the pain vanished as his metaphorical foot reconstituted itself.

They took greater care as they resumed their march—and for that, still trod on sudden spikes and razors and lengths of barbed wire that popped up unavoidably as they made their way along.

They met Vasili again at the edge of the next circle, and for the next phase of their journey, faced the defences of the American head-on: clouds of flesh-stripping locusts and great black tentacles, sudden gouts of red-hot magma that leapt at them from fresh-cut fissures in the rock.

They battled an immense two-headed serpent and played a riddle game with a hunchback, and cut their way through a great rose bush that grew thorns long as fingers.

Finally, on a basalt mountain in the midst of the ice field that encrusted the firmament of Hell's centre, they met the American himself: a giant, black-skinned demon with wings pulled from a bat and thick-lidded eyes that glowed like headlamps.

"'Night on Bald Mountain.' How unoriginal," said Lena.

The American Satan let out a terrible roar.

"But what do you expect from Americans?" she continued. "They drop a little LSD on their tongues or chew on the peyote, and think they can control the world. You're better than most—I'll give you that. But still—the best you can come up with for your defence is an image you stole from a Walt Disney film."

Lucifer the American shrieked, swelled his immense chest and spread his wings so they blacked out the sky.

"Oh, that and I suppose your vaunted faith. But really. *Fantasia*? Why don't you just have the mouse send broomsticks after us? That is every bit as terrifying as this scribble of a demon you've made of yourself."

Kolyokov could see the metaphor beginning to dissolve, as Lena's words cut through the Yank Beelzebub's belief. That was always key to defeating these things—destroy the belief in the metaphor, and it begins to crumble. Keep playing by its rules—and it grows stronger.

"Or what," she continued, "about that funny dog? What is his name—"

The demon's wings began to show light through them, like thinning fabric—

"Pluto?"

The creature opened its mouth and closed it again. The light in its eyes began to dim. And so it began: the American's metaphor of Hell began to fragment and collapse upon itself.

She'd made it look easy. But afterward, Lena told them that she'd only encountered stronger defences in the best of the younger generations—younger even than Kolyokov's. This one—John Kaye was his true name; they'd managed to extract that from the mewling remains of the American agent—must have been an aberration to have built up such a fortress around his mind, and Lena suggested they keep him alive for his genetic material if nothing else.

"You *are* still breeding at City 512, aren't you?" she said, looking directly at Kolyokov as she spoke.

"That is the main of our work there," said Vasili, his wings drooping forlornly by this point.

"Ah, yes," said Kolyokov. "Mostly that is what we do there now." At their feet, Kaye had mostly finished twitching, and the KGB men had come back into the room. Lena got up from the creaky old rocking chair just as one of the agents moved to sit down on it.

At this point, she'd shed her robe to reveal a pair of dark slacks and a baggy grey turtleneck sweater. It would have been a complete contrast to Vasili's outlandish seraphim getup but for her face; her eyes in particular, which she had crafted into a sum of what was to Kolyokov at any rate, womanly perfection. He couldn't stop staring at her—even, he found, when she stared levelly back, as she was doing now.

"Well," she said, "I think we are finished here. Vasili, my dear?"

"Yes!" Vasili's wings perked and spread, and his face flushed red. "I mean—yes . . . my dear?"

"Why don't you use those magnificent wings to fly back to City 512 with our report?"

"But—" poor Vasili's face took on a puzzled mask "—I thought I'd send Comrade Kolyokov back. So we might—"

Lena raised a finger. "We might not," she said. "Comrade Kolyokov can wait here a minute. I've some questions for him before he departs."

"But—"

Lena's finger pointed to the window. "Go," she commanded.

Although he clearly was not pleased about it, Vasili had no choice but to obey. No one did, Kolyokov would later reflect bitterly, when Lena commanded.

The farmstead soon emptied after Vasili returned to his tank, and City 512 sent back a radio message that the interrogation was finished. The agents all but bolted from what to them must have been a haunted building. Kolyokov wondered if it was their laughter that drove the agents so quickly. Lena wiped a crystalline tear from a perfect eye and settled back into the rocking chair.

"So tell me now honestly," she said. "Did you enjoy your first time outside City 512?"

Fyodor sat on the edge of the bed, and shrugged in what he hoped was a worldly way. "It was not my first time," he said. "I have performed many successful operations in Leningrad and Moscow."

"Yes," she said. "Playing the sleepers, isn't that right? Making them check up on their traitorous neighbours, rounding up the dissidents. That's good—but it's not the same thing as dream-walking here, is it?"

Now Fyodor felt himself blushing. "No," he said. "Not really."

"Well, I've enjoyed my trip here to Germany too," said Lena. "I'll tell you—there's one place in the world that's worse than City 512: Toronto. In January."

Fyodor laughed at that, and looked up. "Toronto. That's right. Vasili said you were the Canadian."

Lena shook her head. "Not Canadian," she said. "Russian. In Canada, true, but Russian."

"Are there many of you there?" Fyodor tried to imagine an operation the size of City 512 in hostile territory.

"No," she said. "Just me for now. But—" she smiled in a way that gave Fyodor a chill "—that won't be for long. I'm making friends."

Lena leaned back in the chair and crossed her legs. Her smile broadened as she regarded Fyodor.

"You said—you said you wanted to ask me some questions?"

"Do you make friends?" she asked.

"Not many," he said. "There are only so many people at City 512, and—"

"That's not what I meant."

"What did you mean?"

Lena stood and reached into a shadow for her cloak. "Better," she said, throwing it over her shoulders and pulling the clasp tight around her neck, "that I show you."

Lena took Fyodor to the sky first—and then, from a height where the world curved at the edge—pointed at a line of coast that Fyodor took a moment to recognize:

"Africa," he said.

"Tunisia," she replied. "Some of my friends are there now."

Fyodor followed Lena back down again into the thickening air. They travelled quickly, but the sun was quicker, and its rise had hit the low, ancient buildings of Tunis by the time they'd arrived, making it a golden desert world out of a boy's adventure novel. Lena led him overtop telephone wires and antennae; past a railway station; over a tall iron fence; and into the diplomatic residence of the Canadian Embassy. They finally stopped in a bedchamber—where a striking dark-haired woman who appeared to be in her early thirties slept alone, beneath a slowly whirling fan.

Lena leaned over and stroked her cheek.

"Fyodor," she said, "I would like you to meet my dear friend, Mrs. Elizabeth Dunn."

"Pleased to make your acquaintance," said Kolyokov.

"Wife," continued Lena, "to Montgomery Dunn—the Canadian Ambassador to the Republic of Tunisia. She and he have been stationed here for three years now—since the French pulled out, and the ancient lands of Tunisia have become once more ripe for the picking."

"She is a sleeper?" Fyodor bent over and studied the woman's face. In waking, the aristocratic lines to her jaw and nose might seem harsher—but now, in the early morning light, Mrs. Dunn's face held an innocence. She might have been a child.

"Yes," said Lena. "We're not making too much use of her these days, unfortunately—we'd hoped that things might have progressed differently when the French handed over power to the locals. But it's always good to have friends in warm places, hmm?"

Mrs. Dunn's eyes blinked open.

"Well hello there," she said—looking straight at Kolyokov.

"Shit!" Kolyokov leapt back. "She can see me! Lena! Get out of here!"

But Lena didn't answer: and as Kolyokov looked around the room for her, he quickly realized that she was gone.

"Shh, shh," said Mrs. Dunn as she sat up in bed. She was wearing a light, gauzy nightdress suitable to the tropical climate. In the morning light, it left little to the imagination. But her eyes—her eyes had a perfection, a clarity to them, that was unmistakable.

"Lena?"

Mrs. Dunn cocked her head and smiled. "One and the same," she said.

"What—what are you doing?"

"The same thing," she said, "as you have done so many times with your Leningrad sleepers. I'm dream-walking her."

Mrs. Dunn ran her hands down her sides, lifted one well-formed leg in front of her. She looked at it appraisingly, turning it slightly to admire the ligature of the calf. "She is still looking after herself, I see."

"I don't think," said Kolyokov as Mrs. Dunn's hand then crept up under her nightgown and towards her middle, "that you are doing the same things with your sleepers, that I do with mine."

At that, Mrs. Dunn threw her head back and laughed. "Oh Fyodor," she said, "you *have* been missing out—haven't you? Come on—" Mrs. Dunn extended a hand "—let me introduce you to some of my other friends. This is going to be a wonderful holiday!"

Lena made her sleeper bathe and dress and eat—so it was mid-morning before she ordered a car to take them to Dan Knowling's apartment in *La Goulette*.

Knowling was a stringer for the Toronto Telegram, who Lena had placed here at the same time as she had Mrs. Dunn. He was meant to be Mrs. Dunn's backup, said Lena, in the event that dream-walking proved impossible. "Old fashioned mnemonic programming," said Lena, "should never be discounted. We can only be so many places at once."

Lena made Mrs. Dunn knock twice on the door to Knowling's apartment. Mid-morning was evidently still early for a journalist in Tunisia; Mr. Knowling answered the door in a pair of grimy pajama bottoms, with bleary eyes and a dusting of blond stubble on his chin.

"Um . . . hello," he said. "Can I help you, ma'am?"

Lena gave Kolyokov a fast sidelong glance.

"Quickly," she said. "*Inside*."

"Um, pardon me?" said Knowles.

"What?" said Kolyokov.

"Walk him!" said Lena. "Before he sees too much!"

"Before—?"

"Before—?"

"Now!"

At first, controlling Dan Knowling was a bit of trick—like driving an unfamiliar automobile. Kolyokov was used to stout little bureaucrats and underfed military personnel: Knowling was tall and athletic, with an assassin's reflexes and 20/20 vision. It was the difference between driving a broken-down delivery van and an American sports car.

"You took too long, my sweet," said Lena as she made Mrs. Dunn step into the apartment and shut the door. "He saw."

"I'm—sorry," said Kolyokov, through Mr. Knowling. "You should have warned me."

"Well, then—consider yourself warned."

As she spoke, Mrs. Dunn's hand reached to the drawstrings of Mr. Knowling's pajama bottoms and pulled them undone. With the other hand, she reached down and took hold of Mr. Knowling. Kolyokov gasped.

"Exquisite, isn't it?" she said, pulling close so that Mrs. Dunn's breasts pressed against hard against Mr. Knowling. "All the sensations are there for you to enjoy—but they do not possess you, as they might in ordinary lovemaking. You remain your own, Fyodor."

Kolyokov didn't know about that: in both ordinary lovemaking, and this game that Lena had devised with the sleepers, he was a complete virgin until this moment.

Not that he was about to let on about that: he guided Mr. Knowling's hand to the back of Mrs. Dunn's thigh, hiking up her skirt and sliding his fingertips down the tops of her panties with what he hoped was the assurance of an experienced lover. Mrs. Dunn let out an appreciative growl as his hand slid further down. Meanwhile, her fingers had wrapped tighter around Mr. Knowling's member, and she pulled it free of his pants. With flattened palm, she pressed it against the trembling flesh of her stomach.

"The bed," said Mrs. Dunn.

"Yes," said Mr. Knowling.

And together, in a slow dance of marionettes, they crossed the tiny flat to the old iron bed, and fell there in a tangle of limbs.

They stayed in bed the day—putting the two sleepers through what must have been an exhausting array of gymnastics for their mutual pleasure. Lena was the more experienced of the two—but Kolyokov made up for his inexperience with enthusiasm, and Lena voiced no complaints.

By late in the afternoon, however, Lena announced that they were finished.

It produced a premonitory pang in Kolyokov: he remembered suddenly how she'd dismissed Vasili so easily, and was filled with an unreasoning fear that she should do the same to him now that she'd taken her pleasure.

"Don't worry," said Lena, "we shall meet again. Not here perhaps—but I am not finished with you, young Fyodor. And you—you still have much to learn at my knee."

"I am glad," said Fyodor. He nestled Mr. Knowling's face into the crook of Mrs. Dunn's shoulder.

Mrs. Dunn patted Mr. Knowling on the cheek. "Good. Now it's time for you to leave Mr. Knowling," she said.

"Now? While you—I mean, while Mrs. Dunn is still here? Won't that compromise security?"

Mrs. Dunn smiled for Lena. "Oh my dear—we are well past that. Now step out."

Not quite knowing what to expect, Kolyokov did as he was told. As he watched, Mr. Knowling blinked twice, and looked up at Mrs. Dunn, eyes wide in confusion.

"You—but . . ."

Lena made Mrs. Dunn smile down at him—and Kolyokov's heart fell as he finally understood what was to happen. "Sorry, Danny," she said, wrapping her fingers around his throat as she straddled him one last time. "Fyodor was a second too slow—and you saw too much."

Although Kolyokov did not end the affair at that precise moment, it was that moment—its reverberations and implications; what it said about him, about Lena, and most important, about the two of them together—that finally caused him to quit.

He might have been better off to end it sooner. Things were never the same between himself and Vasili afterward. Vasili stopped inviting Kolyokov for tea and vodka, and after a while would not even acknowledge his presence when the two found themselves alone in a room. Within a year, Vasili had had himself moved out of City 512 to do fieldwork in the European theatre—and after that, he and Kolyokov never had cause to speak again.

Kolyokov, meanwhile, turned away from the foreign work with which he had once busied himself, and spent his days working with the next generation of City

512 students. During those years, he did much commendable work—developing among other things the internal metaphors for new sleeper agents and the three-word mnemonic that could break a program like a stretch of magnetic tape; and, like so many of his colleagues there, building his own network of sleepers that spanned the globe.

Kolyokov and Lena met as often as they could, given the demands of their work. Through the course of their affair, they made love in Rome and London; New York and Nairobi; Gdansk, and Berlin; and Hong Kong, where Kolyokov finally ended it.

"We are craven together," he said as Lena dressed Wei Yu, a little Taiwanese prostitute who normally did this sort of thing for a clientele of bankers, government and military officials. "Like a couple of unclean puppeteers."

Wei Yu shrugged for Lena. "So? I do not see why this is a revelation. You just don't like your body today."

Kolyokov patted his host's ample gut. He was in another newspaper man—they seemed to use a lot of journalists for sleepers—but this one was no Dan Knowling. At fifty-three years old, Archibald Lonsdale was a glutton and a drunk and probably wouldn't survive to see his fifty-fourth birthday the shape he kept himself in.

"That's not it," said Kolyokov. "It's just—look at this fellow. He's had a life, with a wife and children. And here we take him away from that to fuck a little hooker young enough to be his granddaughter."

"It's only flesh, Fyodor."

Kolyokov shook Mr. Lonsdale's head. "I make these sleepers, you know."

"So do I."

"Granted. But I watch them come up, some of them, from little children. From the cradle. And I can't help wondering—are we going to take possession of these children someday, to slake our lusts?"

"We don't have to do anything you don't want to," said Wei Yu.

"And what about our superiors? We're squandering the sleepers, Lena! Don't you imagine there will be an accounting?"

"Fyodor," said Wei Li in a quiet, reasonable tone. "Which superiors are you referring to? I'm not aware of anyone superior to you or I, in the whole world."

Kolyokov set Mr. Lonsdale's lips in a thin, hard line.

"We have to end it," he said.

Wei Yu put a small hand on Lonsdale's thick, hairy forearm.

"Don't leave me, Fyodor," she said for Lena. "You don't know how alone I am."

On Kolyokov's behalf, Lonsdale took hold of Wei Yu's hand and kissed it delicately. Wei Yu's face was a mask—Lena had pulled back from it already, and would soon depart altogether.

"Goodbye," said Lonsdale.

"Fuck off," said Wei Yu, and as her eyes changed and Lena receded altogether, Kolyokov cursed.

The little prostitute was back in herself now. Lena—in a fit of spite—had pulled out before they could separate the sleepers. Which meant that Wei Yu had seen Lonsdale. And if Kolyokov were to play by the rules, she would have to die.

She had certainly gotten a good look at Lonsdale by now—her eyes were locked on him as she snatched her hand back.

Kolyokov looked down at Lonsdale's thick-fingered hands. It would be easy—and it would be according to procedure.

But he didn't. Instead, he moved the hands to his wallet and pulled out a ten-pound note. He had no idea if that was the going rate—and Lonsdale was no help. He liked his fine food and liquor, but it turned out the old boy drew the line when it came to paying for sex.

"I'm sorry," he said in his rudimentary Mandarin. "Here." And Lonsdale put the money down on the bed between them. "Good?"

Wei Yu calmed down at the sight of the money, and looked between him and the cash. Kolyokov didn't need to read her mind to see what she was doing: piecing together her lost afternoon from the best evidence—that she'd at some point met up with this fat old man, come to this room here, and blacked out, somehow managing to forget the whole exchange.

She nodded. "Good," she said.

"Goodbye then," said Lonsdale again.

And at Kolyokov's direction, he pushed himself to his feet, gathered his jacket and stepped out the door. He wobbled down the stairs to the muggy heat of the Hong Kong afternoon and started back to the press club. Kolyokov stayed with him for several blocks—then left the poor man where he stood, confused and disoriented, ten pounds poorer but none the wiser—and still, blessedly, alive.

THE GAMBLER

ИГРОК

Now, his own life slipping away, Kolyokov spun through the vortex and did his best to deafen himself to her increasingly hysterical entreaties.

Fyodor! cried the cloud. *You're dying! If you don't join me now, you'll vanish.*

Fyodor snorted. "Maybe. Maybe not. Who knows what lies beyond the lay of our lives?"

Nothing! Nothing but dark and quiet.

"You speak as though you know. Are you alive or are you dead, Lena?"

What are you—a Goddamn philosopher? The cloud roared around him, tossing him higher and higher until he breached its top and saw stars spread above him. *Look—the only life after death is in the Discourse!*

"In the Discourse," said Kolyokov, spinning around so he faced the vortex once more. "Interesting: you *do* know. Because you've died in body too. And the Discourse—is that where you live now? In the lines of chatter between the sleepers and their masters?"

You'll die without me.

"Let me tell you something. I've been living in the Discourse, quite comfortably, for quite a while now. How do I know I'll die?"

Trust your senses.

He laughed. "My senses are the one thing I know that I cannot trust here. One minute I'm in a metaphor of an old spy school I made—then I'm in the desert talking to Yahweh—the next I'm here in the sky, tossed about like a rag doll. And now—and now—" he squinted down "—there you are."

Join with me, Fyodor.

The voice came from beneath him—she had coalesced now into her old metaphor; the beautiful Lena, draped in a hooded cloak. Her face uncovered, she was an ice-queen—as beautiful as the face of a glacier. She rose to meet him.

"If I join with you," he said, "I'll have surrendered to you. You're too powerful in this place. And my Children—my beautiful Children—will finally be lost to me. They'll become your playthings."

Ours, said Lena.

"*Our* playthings, then? See? You admit it. But that is not why I risked so much to bring them to me."

Fyodor, she said, her eyes ablaze with cold blue fire, *you risked too much for a thing you may never have*.

A rumbling came over the world then, and he realised with a horrible twist in his gut that here in the clouds, he'd misjudged the scale of things. He'd thought Lena was no more than a dozen metres off as she spoke with him. But no—she was much farther than that. She *was* a mountain face; a continent.

When one of her perfect hands finally reached him, fingers thick and long as rockets spread about him, and closed around him like a cage. The giant hand brought him closer to her eye, which stared at him through the spaces between those monstrous digits.

"Impressive," said Kolyokov. "But if what you said is true—that we're here in the Discourse, and this is just a metaphor you've made for me: then I've got nothing to fear from you. Everything—my dissolution, this—storm that you are. Just a metaphor. Just a dream. So what am I risking now, truly?"

My displeasure, she said simply.

And with that, the Goddess Lena lifted Fyodor Kolyokov over her head, to an altitude that would be in low orbit were this more than a metaphor, and with a snap of her wrist, flung him down through the clouds . . . down and down, until he plunged into the very deepest part of this metaphor's ocean.

"*Je-sus*."

The word echoed and boomed through the sky where Kolyokov floated. He peered up into the darkness and shouted: "Hello! Who's up there?"

"*This thing's got nothing to do with us*."

Kolyokov frowned. The voice sounded, what? Italian? No. Not quite Italian though near to it. Italian-American, maybe.

An accent from an Italian-American twenty storeys high. Kolyokov treaded water and called out again. "Hey! Down here!"

"*What about the old man*?" Similar accent from a different speaker. Kolyokov shouted again, but he couldn't compete.

"*The old man's not here. Maybe he's dead. But we got two out of three and that ain't too bad. C'mon*."

Kolyokov stopped shouting then—because the next thing he heard was a clang that was unmistakable: the sound of the hatch on his isolation tank, swinging shut for one last time.

"Oh no," he said to himself, looking around at the dark waves that danced around him. "Oh not this."

It wasn't long after that that those waves pulled him under, and the darkness of the ocean became complete.

THE HOUSE OF THE DEAD

Дом мёртвых

When he lived, Fyodor Kolyokov did not preside over an organization so much as he did a distributed network. It was his great strength; in the final accounting, it became a paralyzing weakness.

The trouble was that most of the people who worked for Kolyokov had no idea they were doing so. They were stockbrokers and government officials and engineers—men and women who'd been placed here decades ago by the former Soviet intelligence machine, to infiltrate Western business and government. They had no idea who they were serving when the Soviet Union was extant—and now that it was gone, they had no clue they worked for Kolyokov.

But work they did. Or rather, they paid him a considerable tithe—pieces of the paycheques and dividends they'd amassed in their all-too-successful infiltration of the American establishment. That tithe was the firmament of Kolyokov's wealth.

In Kolyokov's absence, that firmament crumbled. The off-shore bank accounts, which rose and fell like a well-managed system of river locks, began to drain.

But that wasn't as bad as it got.

Kolyokov's distributed network was also a shield for him. Should the I.R.S. look too closely at one of his tax returns, his operatives there would see that the inquiry was ended before it had significantly begun. Should the City of New York begin to ask questions about some of the modifications and additions he'd built on the Emissary over the years—again, the matter would be closed.

And as for Kolyokov's active enemies—well. Kolyokov himself saw to it that he and his material assets were covered in a cloak of invisibility, a great bank of fog that guaranteed inattention.

And yet—should an enemy arrive in the lobby of the Emissary—one who smelled weakness like a pheromone, and would pounce upon it like a ravaging Cossack—well, Kolyokov's distributed network would converge upon that enemy in a heart's beat, and if need be tear him limb from limb to protect Kolyokov and the network.

But Kolyokov was dead. The cloud was dissipating. And his distributed network of an organization was crumbling into ruin.

Leo Montassini stepped up to the threshold of the ruin, and squeezed the end of his cigarette between finger and thumb. Like everywhere else in Manhattan, the Emissary posted a "No Smoking" sign at the entrance to its front lobby. Montassini and his crew, Nino and Jack, would have enough to worry about with the hotel security later; there was no point in drawing attention at this early juncture. Smoke curled over his blunt fingertips like water, and he dropped the butt into an ashtray thoughtfully provided by the doors.

"Hey," said Nino, squishing his own cigarette under his heel, "where's the fuckin' doorman? What hotel doesn't have a doorman?"

Montassini shrugged. "What an interesting question."

"I'm just saying."

"What the fuck is this place anyway?" Jack was hanging back, looking at the sign that hung out over the sidewalk. "How come I never seen this fuckin' hotel before?"

"Questions, questions." Montassini rolled his eyes, to show his crew he didn't want to hear questions right now. Particularly not good questions, like the ones Jack was raising. Yeah, Montassini wondered too: How come he'd never seen this place before either? This was Montassini's territory—midtown east side. He knew all the businesses here. Montassini had a list in his head and he kept it up to date.

But when Gepetto Bucci got the call from the Turk, telling him to go over and see about snatching a couple three people—go to the Emissary Hotel at Broadway and 94th—all he could think was the stupid foreigners must have got the name wrong. There was no Emissary Hotel at Broadway and 94th.

Yet here he was. In the front lobby of the Emissary Hotel.

A hotel had sprung up between Sal's Wine and Liquor Store and the Lucky Variety overnight. Right in front of his eyes.

"C'mon," said Montassini. "We got a long day ahead of us."

He pushed the door open with his shoulder, and led his crew through the lobby.

"Hey," whispered Nino, "how come the desk clerk's cryin' like that?"

"How the fuck should I know?" said Montassini. He strode up to the desk. "Hey!"

The desk man looked up. He wiped tears from his eyes.

"C-c-c-can I help?"

"Fuck yeah. I got to see—" Montassini reached into his pocket and produced a list. "Alexei Kilo-do-vich. He got a room here?"

The desk man looked at him. Tapped something on his computer.

"H-he's not in," said the man.

Montassini hefted himself up on the desk and looked at the computer screen. Wrote down the room number. The old man started to object, but sniffled instead.

"Fyodor Kolyokov."

The old man backed away. Montassini leaned over and typed the name himself. Another number came up.

"Stephen Haber. Jean Kontos-Wu."

"No rooms here," said the desk man. He was clearly terrified. "P-please. D-don't."

Montassini looked in the old man's eye. There was something there at the back—a hard thing, a powerful will. Montassini felt his breath hitch. He slid down off the table.

"Fuck this," he said. "We got what we need. Fifth floor. Thanks."

The four of them hurried to the elevator. They jostled each other to get inside, and waited there uncomfortably as the doors slid shut.

Mrs. Kontos-Wu had been sleeping for the better part of the afternoon—ever since she'd downed the vodka-lemonade Stephen had brought her. At first, he'd supposed that she needed the sleep—after everything she'd been through. But there was something about the particulars of this sleep that made Stephen uneasy. Her breathing was too shallow—she didn't stir or move at all.

In truth, however, he didn't mind that old Kolyokov's chief sleeper operative was, well, asleep. At least not for a while. While she slept, Stephen had been busy. He'd called the number for Pitovovich; fired off an email to the address; even checked airline schedules to Odessa. Mrs. Kontos-Wu may have been Kolyokov's main field operative. But he was the one who was really best-equipped to get them out of this mess.

And even if he wasn't best equipped—even if he wasn't sure exactly what to do next: Stephen was rightfully Kolyokov's heir; Kolyokov had said so.

And that counted for something.

Stephen was standing over Mrs. Kontos-Wu's sleeping and possibly comatose form, pondering this truth, when the phone rang. It was flashing the security extension. Stephen lifted it from its cradle.

"Miles?" he said crisply. "What is it?"

The phone was quiet on the other end. Quiet but for a slow, raspy breathing. Stephen tapped on the earpiece.

"Hello?"

Nothing.

"Miles," said Stephen—his own breath catching in his chest, "what's going on? You okay?"

"I haven't been paid."

It *was* Miles. But his voice sounded oddly flat.

"What?"

"I've been living in this little shit-box of a hotel room for what—five years now?"

"You all right?"

"And it's just occurred to me—I haven't been paid," said Miles.

"Miles, what's—"

"Not ever," said Miles. "I left a paying job . . . my family . . . to come here to work for you and Mr. Kolyokov. But you never got around to paying me. It only just occurred to me—isn't that funny?"

Stephen swallowed. He looked over at Mrs. Kontos-Wu. He looked at the phone, and put it back to his ear. Miles was breathing again, waiting for an answer.

And Stephen knew at that point, that he didn't have a good answer, other than the obvious.

Kolyokov was gone.

And the work he'd done, to amass his network of people and assets and cash—it was gone too, or nearly so.

It explained Mrs. Kontos-Wu's coma-sleep. And it was why Miles suddenly woke up to the fact that he didn't have a house in New Jersey or a job at the United Nations building any more.

"Go lie down," said Stephen—concentrating. "You need some rest."

"Fuck you," said Miles. "What did you do with my house?"

Stephen looked over his shoulder at the bathroom door, and found a simmering resentment of his own. If Kolyokov had had an ounce of trust for him—if he'd really treated Stephen as an heir—he would have shown him how to use that thing; how to manage the network to which only he had access. Miles wouldn't be going through this now; Mrs. Kontos-Wu would be up and running; and Stephen would be able to do something other than sit here and wait for a phone call.

"Well?" said Miles. "What? It was a good place! I had a gym in the basement! I had satellite TV! What did you do—sell it?"

Stephen took a breath. No—they hadn't sold it. The old bomb shelter in Miles' back garden contained a cache of weapons big enough to overthrow a state legislature—a cache that had been purpose-assembled for that eventuality.

Where in New Jersey are we going to find a hideaway half the size, and a quarter as safe? Kolyokov had wondered, when the question of listing Miles' bungalow came up during a cash crunch. *Find me a blind man for a tenant and I'll be happy.*

"We didn't sell it," said Stephen.

"Well I want it back," said Miles. "I want it—ah, fuck it. What am I talking to you for anyway?"

The line disconnected.

Stephen's hand was shaking as he put the telephone back in its cradle. He stepped to Mrs. Kontos-Wu's bedside.

"Hey!" he snapped. "Wake up!"

He lightly slapped her cheeks, and repeated. "Up! Come on!"

At that, Mrs. Kontos-Wu's eyelids fluttered. The pink end of her tongue darted out between her teeth and over dry lips. She made a sound like a moan.

"Good!" Stephen slapped again, harder. "Upsy-daisy. Come on."

Now her lips were moving. She was whispering something.

"What?" Stephen leaned closer.

". . . *Vasilissa*," said Mrs. Kontos-Wu. "*Baba Yaga*."

Stephen pulled back. He saw that tears were welling in the corners of Mrs. Kontos-Wu's eyes as she stared sightlessly toward the ceiling. She coughed, and repeated:

"*Manka. Vasilissa. Baba Yaga*."

Stephen felt a sympathetic ache in his middle as Mrs. Kontos-Wu's fingers bent into claws. The cords on her neck stood out, as though she were having a seizure.

"*Manka*!" She was shouting now. "*Vasilissa! Baba Yaga*!"

As though she were O.D.'ing, Stephen thought. Watching her, he was drawn back to that time five years ago, bottoming out in the crack-house in Queens. He was going through some bad times, then—the heroin flowed free in his veins; he fucked anything with a dick and a wallet. And there in the night, came the ghost of the old man, stepping over the sleeping bodies, ducking underneath intestinal droops of wiring and insulation. Those three words had entered Stephen's mind like a torrent of spring water, opening and cleansing him at once. When they'd passed, the old man was in his face, close enough to kiss him on the mouth.

You are not alone, he'd said.

Here in the hotel room, Mrs. Kontos-Wu was coming to the understanding that she *was* alone—possibly, for the first time in her life.

Stephen leaned close to her again, and awkwardly at first, wrapped his arms around her shoulders. He could feel the breath ratchet in Mrs. Kontos-Wu's chest.

"It's okay," he said. "You're not alone."

Mrs. Kontos-Wu's shoulders twitched again, and her arms came up around Stephen's shoulders. When her face buried itself in his chest, he felt the heat of her tears like steam from an iron.

The elevator door opened on the 14th floor, but Montassini and his crew did not emerge from it immediately. Jack was ready to bolt, but Montassini put a finger to his lips and motioned to wait a second. He reached into his coat and pulled out his Glock. Nino gave him a look—*the gun so soon*?—and Montassini gave him a look back. *Questions, questions* . . .

Truth was, Montassini didn't like the idea of getting out on the 14th floor of a hotel that he hadn't known existed until he stepped through its door three minutes ago. He didn't like the crying guy behind the front desk. He didn't like the quiet of this place—like it was cut off from the world, in a little Manhattan snow globe all its own.

With one hand on the elevator door to keep it from closing on his neck, Montassini stuck his head out to take a look.

The hallway was empty—both sides. It was the kind of hotel with just one hallway going up the middle. It was the kind of hallway about which Montassini had mixed feelings. The hallway was good for reconnoitering—he could tell immediately that the hallway was clear. At the same time, some guy with a gun comes out of either of the two end stairwells, that clear view would work against him. There was nowhere to hide.

But there was nothing to be done about it. He turned back and nodded at his crew. Both Jack and Nino had followed his lead, and pulled out their own guns.

"Room 1402," said Montassini. That was where Kolyokov was holed up. Or so he hoped. The room where Kilodovich was—503—had been empty. Hopefully they'd do better here.

Nino stared at the little room number sign outside the elevator for a second, and pointed to their left. Montassini nodded. He lowered his gun to his side and walked down the hall.

1400, 1401, 1402 . . .

The three of them stopped outside 1402.

Nino squinted, put his ear near the door.

"More fuckin' tears," he said. "What the fuck—someone die?"

"That's what we're here to find out," said Montassini. With his free hand, he pulled down on the door handle. It wasn't locked.

"Here goes," said Montassini. He pushed the door open with his foot and took the gun in both hands.

Stephen closed his eyes and prepared for death. He prayed that Miles would make it a quick one—but knowing what he did about Miles' professional background, it really could go either way. If Miles felt good about him—it'd be over before he knew it. If Miles was as pissed off as he'd sounded on the phone—Stephen shivered—it could take days.

"You can have your house back," he said, face buried in Mrs. Kontos-Wu's hair. "Anything—"

"Shut the fuck up!"

Stephen lifted his head to look.

That wasn't Miles talking. It was a little swarthy guy in a maroon sports jacket and an open-necked shirt. Flanking him were two taller guys—one kind of skinny, with black shoulder-length hair yanked back over his forehead; the other, a little older and starting to lose his greying hair—but thick around the shoulders and still tight in the hips.

Stephen pulled Mrs. Kontos-Wu's arms from around his shoulders. She curled into a ball on the bed as he stood, keeping both hands visible.

"Okay," said the little one with the gun. "Now I got some questions I'm supposed to ask you."

"On whose behalf?" said Stephen.

"On whose—?" the little guy raised his gun. "I'm asking the questions."

Stephen looked at the big guy—and nodded in slow recognition. Stephen was sure of it; this was Jack Devisi. The guy was known among the boys that Stephen used to run with. He was a big spender, and made no bones about where that money came from: Gepetto Bucci, who ran the Upper East Side. Devisi must have recognized him too; he blinked twice, then looked away.

"What are you fuckin' starin' at?" he said.

Stephen shrugged—letting him off the hook in front of his buddies. Stephen maintained his outward cool, but inside he was starting to sweat. Jack Devisi in the Emissary was not a good sign. Kolyokov had gone to great lengths to shield this place from the local mob—sent out what he called psychic ablative, the substance of which he'd never properly explained to Stephen. But the effect of it was to keep this place off the map for certain key New Yorkers, Gepetto Bucci's bunch among them.

"First question." It was the little guy. "I'm told there is an old man here. Fyodor. Also a younger guy—but big. Not like you. Alex he's called. But I don't see either of them." He motioned with the barrel of his gun to the washroom. "They in the can?"

Stephen shook his head.

"Yeah, fuckin' right they're not." The little guy motioned to his long-haired friend. "Nino—go in and get the geriatric case off the throne."

Nino nodded and stepped over to the door. Back against the wall, he reached across, turned the handle and pushed it open. From across the room, Jack aimed his gun inside so as to cover him. Meanwhile, Stephen noticed the little guy was developing a new skin of sweat on his forehead.

"What the fuck you lookin' at?" The little guy pointed the gun at Stephen's face. Stephen noticed the hands were shaking and the knuckles were white. There was a very real possibility, thought Stephen, that this guy could pull the trigger without even knowing it.

"Easy," said Stephen. "You said you had some questions?"

The guy calmed down a bit. "In a second," he said. "Nino! You find the guy?"

There was a shuffling sound in the bathroom. "No," said Nino. "But you ain't gonna believe what's in here."

"What?"

"Looks like a fuckin' UFO!"

Montassini took a deep breath. A UFO? Why the fuck not? He was here in an invisible ghost hotel, talking to a kid who looked like he'd been just about to go down on some broad when they came in. An *X-Files* flying saucer in the toilet of a hotel room he'd never known existed until now was not such a strange thing.

"Cover them," Montassini said to Jack. He stepped over to the washroom to see what Nino was talking about.

"Holy shit."

The thing wasn't saucer shaped exactly, but Montassini could see where Nino had made the comparison. It filled up most of what was a pretty big bathroom. It was shaped sort of like a pill, and about the size of a Volkswagen. There was a hatch on the closest end of it—it had one of those submarine-door latches on it. And there were tubes and hoses sticking out of the far side, trailing on the floor and hooked up to the plumbing under the sink. The thing's surface was white, and smooth like an eggshell.

"I don't mind tellin' you, Leo, I'm fuckin' starting to freak out here," whispered Nino.

"Don't be a pussy," said Montassini. "We got a couple of things to do here and we're gonna do them. Just try and stay focused on that. Now—you take a look inside of there yet?"

Nino shook his head. His eyes were wide.

"Well open it!" Leo's voice was going high—like on helium. Or panic. He cleared his throat. "Open it," he rumbled.

Nino gave the wheel one turn, and then another. He sobbed a curse, then with shaking hands pulled the hatch open—like he was opening Dracula's crypt, thought Montassini. *Way* too much like he was opening Dracula's crypt.

Montassini held his breath as Nino peered inside.

"There's water in there," he said. "Smells like fuckin' Javex. I don't see no old man though."

Montassini bit down on his lower lip. *You wouldn't see him*, he thought, *if he was a fuckin' shade*.

Nino pulled his head away from the hatch.

"Look for yourself," he said, shrugging. "Empty."

Montassini swallowed, and bent over. He couldn't go all chickenshit in front of his crew. *Nothing to do but look in the fuckin' coffin or whatever it is*. On his knees, he slid his head in through the hatch.

"Je-sus." It did stink of Javex in here. And it was full of water, about a third of the way up. That was all he could tell, though; in the blackness, Montassini could see neither top nor end to the interior chamber. It could go on forever, he thought: up and out, its own fucking ocean in here under a sky with no stars or moon or daylight ever. Who the fuck knew what swam under these waters?

A voice tickled at the back of his head, high and desperate:

Down here!

Montassini clutched the edges of the hatch, and pulled his head out.

"This thing's got nothing to do with us," he said, struggling to keep the shaking out of his voice.

"What about the old man?" said Nino.

"The old man's not here. Maybe he's dead. But we got two out of three and that ain't too bad. C'mon."

Montassini stood up. It had sounded good. Firm. Leaderly.

Almost as though he'd believed it himself.

Jack Devisi motioned with his gun at Mrs. Kontos-Wu.

"She's some looker," he said. "Don't you think?"

Stephen rolled his eyes. "Whatever," he said.

"I mean to say that she's got a nice ass," said Jack. "C'mon kid—I saw you two goin' at it."

Stephen wouldn't even dignify that one with a response.

"All right," said Jack. "Up to you, kiddo."

The other two Bucci boys chose that moment to step out of the bathroom. Both of them, Stephen noted, looked a little pale—like they'd stepped in something.

Or seen something.

"Okay," said the little guy. "Here's how it's gonna go. You two are coming with us. You're going to go down with us in the freight elevator and you're going to come with us to see a mutual friend."

"Mutual friend? Who might that be?"

The little guy gave him a look. "I think you know," he said. "Listen—" he motioned to Mrs. Kontos-Wu. "She okay to walk?"

"She's a fuckin' vegetable there, Leo," said Jack. "She won't be able to walk."

"I'm not—a vegetable."

The four of them looked as one at Mrs. Kontos-Wu. She rolled over.

"You're taking us to Shadak—right?"

The little guy, Leo, hesitated for a second, as Mrs. Kontos-Wu sat up. She looked him in the eye.

"Come on," she said. "Right?"

Leo nodded.

"Good. That's what I thought. Now if you're bringing us to Shadak, he obviously didn't want you to shoot us first—right?"

Leo made a show of glaring at her and raised his gun. "That don't necessarily follow—"

"—Right?"

"Right."

"Good," she said. "Then put the guns down—they just make you look foolish. Do you have a conveyance?"

"A what?" said Jack.

"A car?"

"A truck," said Leo. "Yeah. Should be out back by now."

Nino leaned over to Leo. "This is bullshit," he said. "We got a whole fuckin' hotel this guy could be in. We gotta—"

Leo held up his hand. "Shut the fuck up," he said. He blinked and rubbed his temple. "He's not here. We got a plan. Take 'em to the fuckin' plane."

Mrs. Kontos-Wu pushed herself out of bed. "Excellent. Then let's get to it." She looked at Stephen. "You packed?" she said.

"Packed?" said Stephen.

"I'm assuming that Shadak's not in town," she said. "You'll want one of the passports and an overnight bag, I'm willing to bet."

Stephen and Jack shared a look. *What's with the broad?* Jack mouthed. Stephen gave a little shrug.

"Let me pack some shit," said Stephen.

Behind him, Leo Montassini swatted Nino's arm away from his shoulder. He dug a finger into his ear, like he was trying to scratch a very deep itch.

The laundry truck pulled out of the Emissary's loading bay and rumbled into crosstown traffic—where it sat for a moment waiting for the flow to resume.

Miles regarded the truck from the coffee shop across Broadway. It was white, with a stylized picture of sheets drying on a line. Not from the usual service.

Miles knew he should be on his cell phone right now; taking steps to learn the identity of the mysterious laundry truck. Find out how badly security was breached.

Or just as likely, he'd be seeing those steps taken for him, feeling his eyes flutter and a curious sapping of his will; watching as though on a closed-circuit television, as his arms moved to his cell phone, and listening as his lips made strange words into it.

But this fine New York evening, Miles did neither thing. He watched as the truck crested the small rise in the street, and vanished among the cascade of brake lights and cab signs. A scent of lavender tickled his nose, and he felt a smile creep up his face.

Miles raised his coffee mug to them in a farewell salute.

"*Nazdorovya*," he said, following as he did the lavender's course across the street—and from there, inexorably to the north.

Великий
THE GRAND INQUISITOR
инквизитор

Amar Shadak equivocated through the night. He needed, he knew, to strike a delicate balance. There was warmth: the geniality of a good host. And there was terror. He wouldn't get anywhere, he knew, without a solid weight of terror at hand. He posed in front of a tall mirror in his bedchamber as he thought about it; pulled his lips taut into a thin smile and raised his dark brows in the middle, as though asking a polite question. He slackened his shoulders, rolling them quickly back and forth like a dancer or an athlete, then abruptly stood straight and threw them back. Warmth and terror—terror and warmth. Somewhere, he thought, looking for himself in the reflection of his eyes. Somewhere in spaces between . . .

In the space between the fountain and the kitchen where blood dripped from the draining goat, where the Devil Kilodovich tore Amar in two . . .

"Ah," he said to no one, "this is shit." And he relaxed his shoulders and flung his arms into the air, and fell back onto the rumpled sheets of his unmade bed. He would just have to play it by ear, when they arrived. Try and piece the mystery of the missing submarine and Alexei Kilodovich together as best he could.

Shadak's head hurt. He felt, these days, as though a thousand tiny hands were pulling the anatomy of his brain to and fro, scratching at it with nail-point fingertips. It reminded him of that month—the month that the devil Kilodovich had taken him into the caves in Afghanistan—tried to work his sorcery on him, took him to the Black Villa, and left a piece of Shadak's soul there. When the bastard children had fucked with him, pulling him to bits all over again. Same kind of thing—fingers in his brain, pulling the neurons apart, looking for gold.

Fucking Rapture.

Shadak thought of it more as brain rape.

Ah, what to say—what to say?

When he'd called Gepetto and asked him to fetch the people from the Emissary, he'd really hoped that he might find Kilodovich there. The widow

Kontos-Wu's presence in the hotel when he called suggested that this might be so, that Kolyokov had engineered a double sting, stolen the children through some third party, and had pulled all his people back to the home base.

If that had happened, then Kilodovich would be on his way here now. The terrible losses he'd suffered—his American organization, a yacht, and the usefulness of his submarine guy . . . the trouble with the children, their demonic influence . . . all that would have been balanced by the possession of Kilodovich.

But it was not to be. Kolyokov was gone—dead? Or simply on the move? Somewhere with his treasure, the devil Kilodovich, perhaps?—and there was no one to bring but the useless piece of shit of a boy Kolyokov kept—and Kontos-Wu.

Ah, Kontos-Wu. There was something else. When he'd known her, she'd been a raven-haired beauty in the blossom of her twenties—the bride of old Tom Wu, a Taiwanese banker who ran some ships out of Hong Kong and sometimes did drug business with Shadak. He hadn't really seen her since those years—but when they spoke on the phone, it was the beauty of those years past that he remembered. He'd held some information back—in particular, that horrible scrabbling of claws inside his head, the Black Villa, and what he thought Kilodovich and the children meant to it—but still, he'd spoken too freely with her; told her far too much about the children and their devilish powers.

In the morning, they would have another conversation face to face. Shadak hoped that she'd gotten fat—or stringy—or developed a skin condition. Anything to give him the edge in their interview.

"Pah," he said aloud, forcing himself to sit up in his bed, "you are a shallow creature, Amar. Moved by lust and sentiment before sense."

Shadak stood again—threw back his shoulders and tightened his smile—and strode across the room, through a curtain and into the hallway. To his left, tall leaded-glass windows cut into the stonework admitted silvered moonlight, painting themselves across the stonework of the narrow corridor. A man with an Uzi dangling from a strap on his shoulder nodded deferentially as Shadak strode past. Shadak barely acknowledged him.

Lust and sentiment. Jean Kontos-Wu had played to those two vulnerabilities well in the early years: an agonizingly beautiful girl, trapped by a wicked husband. He might have killed him for her—he would have, if congestive heart failure hadn't taken the old man first.

He stepped around a corner and out onto a low balcony, facing west. He regarded the darkened, jagged horizon. Far beyond it, over the ocean, the two of them—Jean Kontos-Wu and Stephen—flew toward him. They would talk in the morning. Settle things. Find answers together, in a pit beneath the caravansary's mosque. Shadak regarded the night a moment longer, then turned back to his bedchamber.

In the morning, Jean Kontos-Wu would open up to him. Amar Shadak would, he vowed, be the one in control—not her. Not this time.

Маленький THE LITTLE HERO герой

Up until they got on the plane, Mrs. Kontos-Wu was in control. No question about it—she was so much in control that Stephen had all but forgotten Kolyokov's message to him: *Allow Mrs. Kontos-Wu to assist, but take the lead yourself.*

He should have remembered that—never mind that Mrs. Kontos-Wu had managed to take charge of the mobsters like a kindergarten teacher with a busload of preschoolers. The fact was, in the process of ordering them around, she effectively surrendered to them. She'd done it with such confidence that Stephen was sure she had something up her sleeve—but by the time they got to the little airfield up in Connecticut, clambered out of the back of the laundry truck and stomped across the tarmac to the waiting Lear jet, Stephen was starting to suspect that maybe this was not so.

The jet was not Shadak's; it appeared to belong to a woman named Ming Lei, if the monogrammed toiletries in the washroom were any indication. The same Ming Lei as the boat that Shadak's people lost? He would have asked her, but Ming Lei was not on board—just a thickset pilot who sounded like he was from Louisiana and a bald-headed gentleman in a dark suit who introduced himself as Mr. Beg.

"We are all old friends," he said when Stephen started to ask a question about Shadak. "Old *comrades*. That's all."

He collected their passports, then in a barely perceptible accent explained what would happen at the first sign of trouble.

"The Atlantic is very deep," said Mr. Beg. "You can be above it, or below it."

Mrs. Kontos-Wu smiled sweetly and thanked him for the information, and Stephen banished his suspicions about Mrs. Kontos-Wu's competence. She *had* to have a plan. She was too cool—her expression too utterly unrevealing of any doubts in this enterprise. Not like Stephen—who felt like he was betraying every anxiety—every terror—with each blink of an eyelid or intake of breath.

She'd seemed cool. But hours later, once the plane landed, and they descended the three steps to the rougher tarmac outside this *castle* of Shadak's, he revised his opinion.

"This doesn't look like Bishop's Hall," she said as she looked at the square stone towers crawling up the mountainside. Then she looked at Stephen. "Do you suppose the library's still intact?"

"This isn't Bishop's Hall," said Stephen nervously.

Mr. Beg merely chuckled.

"It is a mad time, yes?" he said, and laughed. "Like Afghanistan."

Stephen looked at him with another question. Beg held up a finger and ducked back into the plane.

Mrs. Kontos-Wu regressed quickly. As they climbed a great curving set of stairs to a wide grated gateway, she was chattering on about a book she'd apparently been reading—about some girl called Becky, and how she'd finally wound up in London after being chased by men with funny hats from one end of the Orient Express to the other. "London's safe," said Mrs. Kontos-Wu as they were led by four machinegun-toting Romanians along the base of the wall to a tower. "No foreigners."

"Really? When was the last time you were in London?" said Stephen, grasping at a final, desperate hope that Mrs. Kontos-Wu was just having him on.

"Mummy's taking me this summer," said Mrs. Kontos-Wu and the last of Stephen's hope slipped away.

He swore under his breath. *Should have killed the fucking wops when I had the chance.*

Killing the three mobsters wouldn't have been easy without Miles' help, but Stephen thought he could have done it. And he would have had the Emissary's housekeeping services, with their gloves and bone saws and acid bottles, to help him clean up the mess.

But no—Stephen had somehow managed to misread Mrs. Kontos-Wu's mental capacities. Just as he'd misread everything else that had happened since Fyodor Kolyokov had departed. And that included Kolyokov's parting words: *Take the lead yourself.*

It was a bit late for any lead-taking now. The four Romanians were big, and their guns were out. There was a moment of confusion, when they seemed to be discussing where to take their prisoners. Two of them seemed to think they should go straight to the main manor building in the middle—the other two pointed insistently at a tower.

It was confusion, yes—but not enough confusion to override the inherent advantage of the four big Romanians with guns. When they finally took them to the tower, and into a little triangular room half-way up, Stephen's options for lead-taking diminished to nothing.

Almost nothing.

No sooner had they settled down into the dark of the tower room than a voice, cracked from thirst and injury, came from the shadow beneath the chamber's single narrow window.

"You—you are here from the Children . . . yes?"

Stephen pushed himself up on his haunches.

"Who are you?"

The voice snorted. "Uzimeri," it said.

The name meant nothing to Stephen. "You—you okay there?"

"Do I sound 'okay'?"

Stephen squinted through the dark. He could make out what looked like a pile of rags, propped up here and there by what looked like broken broom handles and straw. It could have been that—or it could be an injured old man called Uzimeri.

"What do you mean about, 'the Children'?"

"Hah." The pile of rags might have shifted as a rat scuttled out from underneath—or this Uzimeri character might have waved a hand dismissively. "You have to ask, you don't know. I made a mistake."

"What'd you do to piss Amar Shadak off?"

The rag pile chuckled. "I know your game," it said. "You two are coming in here to make me give a jailhouse confession—aren't you? Shadak thinks I'll tell you about what happened to the submarine, things I wouldn't tell him at the end of his belt."

Stephen's ears pricked at that.

His submarine?

The same submarine, perhaps, that allegedly sank *Ming Lei 3*?

Stephen got up and walked across the straw-covered floor. He settled down again next to this rag pile of a man. The smell was awful nearby—of piss and shit and something worse.

"Tell me what happened to the submarine," said Stephen.

"Ah," said Uzimeri, "go fuck yourself. The Children will protect me."

"Whatever." Stephen wasn't going to play this game. He crossed his arms and stared ahead.

"Boy," said Mrs. Kontos-Wu from across the room. "What are you doing here in the library? This is for girls only. Can't you read?"

"Out of her fucking mind," said Stephen under his breath.

But Uzimeri seemed to take note. He pushed himself up, shuffling his feet in the straw on the floor.

"Heh. You think you are in a library?"

"Who said that?" Mrs. Kontos-Wu's voice sounded small and distant—and oddly frightened.

Uzimeri hunched forward—both hands falling to the straw below him to support his weight as he did so. "It seems very real, does it not?"

"I'm not talking to you." Now Mrs. Kontos-Wu sounded more pissed than frightened. "Leave at once, or I shall call for help."

"Hah." Uzimeri leaned back again. A stick-like hand fell on Stephen's shoulder. Stephen looked at him with dark-quickened eyes. He saw a thin-faced man with an eye swelled shut, and lips swollen nearly as bad grinning at him. "I was wrong about you. You are here from the Children. Not from Shadak." With his other hand he motioned across the room. "You see? Your woman there is in their Rapture."

"What do you mean—their Rapture?"

"Rapture. The thing that happens to so many of us, yes? When one of the Children touches you, Childhood grows before you again. You become—reminded—of the wonder of the time." Uzimeri's eye-and-a-half met Stephen's, and shone. "The *innocence*."

Stephen didn't think of his childhood that way. To him, childhood was an elaborate lie that ended in flight, squalor and disease. He was constantly amazed to find out that others thought well enough of theirs to be susceptible to nostalgia.

"But of course that is only the beginning," said Uzimeri. "Returning to childhood, it is like . . . drawing back to leap. The breadth of the leap is farther when one makes it so, yes?"

"I suppose." Stephen squinted at the damaged old man and thought about that. "What do you mean by leaping?"

"*You* know," said Uzimeri. "I've lost the means lately but I'm no fool. You know what it is to leap. You do it in your dreams, yes?"

"Holy fuck," said Stephen.

Unless he was mistaken—and that was not outside the realms of possibilities, Stephen had to admit—then this guy was talking about dream-walking.

And he seemed to be saying that these children—these Blessed Children—were the key to it.

No wonder Holden had wanted them so badly.

"But her now," said Uzimeri. "She's still drawing back. She is unready to leap, yes? Or perhaps she is like me."

At that, Uzimeri fell forward onto his hands and knees and began to crawl across the floor to Mrs. Kontos-Wu. He clutched her face, as though he were about to kiss her. "You are, aren't you now?"

"Hey!" Stephen followed him. He tried to pull Uzimeri away, but the rag-man held on like a lamprey.

"You are in ruins now, aren't you?" Uzimeri's voice was low and sharp. "This . . . library . . . is not what you remember, is it?"

"I'm sure they're just fixing it up," said Mrs. Kontos-Wu.

"But no one is there—isn't that right?"

"Not—not that I can see."

"Not at all. You are alone in your memories. They have abandoned you, yes?"

Mrs. Kontos-Wu was quiet.

"Yes?"

Stephen pulled at Uzimeri's shoulder again, and this time it was enough. Uzimeri slumped back. "She will not listen," he said.

"She was—" Stephen swallowed. "She was fine earlier. A day ago. She seemed right in control."

Uzimeri nodded. "It is always possible," he said, "to turn one's back on enlightenment for a short while."

"Okay," said Stephen, "why don't you tell me about enlightenment."

Uzimeri went back to his spot beneath the arrow slit and settled down.

"What do you want to know?"

"I want to know," said Stephen slowly, "how it got you."

Uzimeri chuckled at that. "You want to know about enlightenment, boy? All right. Listen. I will testify to you."

AWAKENING
Пробуждение

"Allah," Uzimeri began, as the stars still glimmered in the arrow-slit over his head, "is a distant master. This is what I always believed. Fools keep religion alive, but the deity—neglectful. In face of catastrophe, He looks the other way.

"It has been a useful belief in my business. All my life, I have worked for men like Amar Shadak—watching their mistresses, exacting their revenges.

"If I cared for Allah's opinions—well. The truth is that men like Shadak are Allah in their own eyes. And they do not like other gods.

"This changed for me when the Children came to see me at the pen.

"What," said Stephen, "does a pen have to do with anything?"

"It is one of Shadak's great secrets. There is a cove on the Black Sea. Shadak owns land all around it. He's dug in that land—made a city like the ones dug centuries ago to south. Tunnels and chambers. All the way down to the sea. I don't know how many centuries it will last.

"But for now, this city has become a treasury; a museum of the Twentieth Century. He has there submarines and gunboats—rooms and rooms filled with small arms and explosives; corridors lined with ammunition and uniforms and deep lockers. He has even got some plutonium and parts of a nuclear device, which we store in a room deeper than the others, awaiting the day . . .

"This has been my place and my work for the past ten years—keeping and building Shadak's little arsenal.

"I think when Shadak was younger, he thought he could be a warlord. With the Soviets gone, maybe he could have a private army his own. But no. Who wants to make war with Soviets gone? Some, maybe. But not Shadak. Business is too good for war. So he does his business in Russia and Europe and America. And the armoury is a collection. Not an arsenal.

"That has been fine by me. My men and I have lived well in Shadak's hidden city. And keeping it secret against the efforts of Shadak's enemies has proved to be a good challenge. A diversion, yes?

"But I know now that it was never more than a diversion. Oh, how many nights did I walk the deep corridors of the armoury—sit alone in front of the banks of television screens, staring into the caverns full of rockets and firearms and explosives—and ask myself: is this what you have come to, Konstantine? Ah, I was ripe. We all were in Shadak's armoury. It was no wonder that the Children found us there first.

"I will not forget the night that the first one came to us. For it was I, Konstantine Uzimeri, that she found first. We met on one of those nights, when I was finished with the labyrinth, and had taken myself to the cliffs overlooking the sea. I'd driven a jeep to this point, as I often did, to listen to the waves and breathe the air that was so different from that in the deep tunnels under my feet.

"And so it was that Zhanna, the first child, came to me. Although this one, I will tell you, was barely a child: Zhanna was fully grown—long black hair, eyes black as the midnight sky. Were I younger . . .

"But I am not younger, and not a fool either—and when a woman, no matter how beautiful, appears unannounced on Amar Shadak's lands, I don't think of those things.

"She appeared behind me at the cliff's edge, so suddenly I nearly shot her. She laughed.

"'Konstantine Uzimeri,' she said, 'what a dull life you lead here in this magnificent treasure-house.'

"'Identify yourself,' I said, and when she answered, 'Zhanna,' I asked, 'How do you know me?'

"'I know you through and through,' she said. 'I know your longings and your fears. And of course I know your crimes too.'

"'You are a friend of Mr. Shadak's?' That seemed likely: that this girl was some new mistress of my master's, out for a tour of his magnificent arsenal. She was not dressed as Amar Shadak likes—no tight designer clothes and thick makeup for this one. She wore the loose coveralls and heavy boots of a worker, her hair tied tight at the back of her skull. Yet he might have broadened his tastes. As I said, he did not visit his collection as much as he used to.

"But Zhanna shook her head no. 'I have never met Amar Shadak face to face,' she said.

"'Did one of the men here bring you on-site?' I demanded, thinking I had a different sort of problem then. 'Name him and you might live!'

"'You know,' she said, 'that it's not so simple.'

"And I had to admit that she was right. I did know that, in the wordless way we come by true knowledge. No one had willingly let her in here.

"'What do you want?' I asked.

"'You have submarines here,' she said. 'Isn't that so?'

"I nodded. It was funny—after a decade of maintaining a cordial lie with the local government officials about the contents of the property here, ten years of hiding Shadak's treasures from his enemies, all that it took was this black-haired girl Zhanna to ask about the submarines. And I told everything.

"Later, I'd learn lying was pointless with Zhanna in any event. She'd only pluck the information from my mind as easy as a grape from the vine. But I didn't wish to lie to this girl anyway, no matter her questions.

"Zhanna stepped up to me, took my hand in hers, and together we walked to the elevator house, and descended to the pens.

"Oh, she was delighted with everything she saw: the wide corridors that circled the main armoury; the massive security room, adjoining to the little recreation centre that Shadak let us construct back in 1994; and of course, the pens themselves. She marvelled at the birds that swooped over the conning towers—laughed when I pointed to the high cracks, where a legion of bats slept during daylight.

"'This is everything I dreamed,' she said as we looked down at the three bays, lit by floodlights. 'Though seeing it with my eyes . . .'

"She grasped the lapel of my coat—her fingers working it, as though feeling its texture as a new thing. '. . . touching with my own fingers. What a magnificent world you have made here, Konstantine!'"

"I shuffled my feet and protested that I had made nothing here.

"'Say what you will,' she said. 'I'm in awe.'

"Here I have a confession to make—one that does not come easily. At that moment, had circumstances not intervened, I think I should have kissed young Zhanna. It was—how shall I say? A great bubbling joy in my middle, mingled with a terrible yearning. I might have kissed her and touched her and—"

"Get on with it," said Stephen irritably.

"You understand, though—that this was no mere lust I was feeling. It was a *Rapture*, well and true. And I knew this, soon enough, when I heard the footsteps clanging along the gantry and saw Nochi, who watches the night guard, running toward me. 'Who is she?' he demanded angrily as he drew up. And then, as Zhanna turned to him, that anger vanished. And his eyes—which had never been troubled by expression or even a sign of life from the time I'd known him—softened and focused on her.

"'Who is she?' he breathed.

"'Zhanna,' I said, as though it explained everything.

"She turned back to me as though he wasn't there. 'Thank you,' she said, 'for showing me the world you made. Let me return the favour, Konstantine—and show you mine.'

"And then—then my young friend—my world changed forever.

"A holiness—not what you think—a holiness came over me then. The fullness of the Rapture that is the Children's gift to us. The world brightened for a moment, as though God were coming to me through the firmament of the earth. I felt—a sense of belonging—a sense of rightness, can you understand that?"

"No," said Stephen.

"Then I weep for you, my boy. You have never experienced joy. Can you even dream of it, I wonder?"

Stephen stared at him. "Go on," he said.

"Very well. The important thing is that over this moment, I saw my life spread before me. I inhabited a space of time in it that I can only describe as perfection. To begin with, it was frightening; a dull tingling in my limbs, as though they'd rested still too long. Sensation abandoned me, as I felt my soul suck back to a needle along my spine. And then—are you listening, boy?—then that needle fired out of me, through the top of my skull. And for an instant, I hovered there, in the steel rafters of the submarine pen. It was a sensation of weightlessness—swimming, shall we say? The fear vanished, as the lightness overcame me. And at once—at once I shot upward again, through the rock and earth, and into the starry night sky over the Black Sea."

"You were dream-walking, you fucker," whispered Stephen. But Uzimeri didn't seem to hear him. He was lost in his own tale.

"She beckoned me, and we rose together—through thinning air and into the hard vacuum of space, yes? I saw the world spread below me—the moon at my shoulder, a great grey stone in the sky—and stars all around me. And so it was that I saw enlightenment. And the Rapture overtook me."

"Dream-walking," said Stephen, shaking his head. "You."

"Dream-walking, Rapture. You call it as you will. All that matters is that it brought me to a realization., I knew that now, whatever Shadak might do, this pen and the men within it, and yes—me—belonged to Zhanna. It was her wishes—no longer those of Amar Shadak—that I would die to fulfill.

"I blinked and coughed, and said something or other. Zhanna placed her hand on my arm, and with her other hand pointed down into the bay.

"'Show me that one,' she said. I followed her finger down to the middle bay. That is where the Project Cobra submarine rests. It is an ancient diesel-powered 641 Attack Submarine. You Americans called them Foxtrots."

"I know shit about submarines," yawned Stephen.

"A Foxtrot," said Uzimeri. "Shadak spends a fortune keeping his Foxtrot running. You know, if I were ever more objective about it, I'd have told him years ago to scuttle the thing. The *Soviets* stopped using them they were so old. But there was something honest about them—in their simplicity. Like keeping an old U-boat.

"Zhanna—Zhanna saw it too.

"'We're going to Heaven in this,' she said as we climbed onto its deck for the first time."

You sure she didn't mean we're gonna die in it? Stephen pursed his lips and let Uzimeri continue. The sick old bastard's voice was thickening more with religion with every word. That was how this story was going to go, and if Stephen wanted to hear how it came out, he'd just have to put up with it.

"You don't know *shit* about submarines—that's what you say, right? So I'll tell you then: the Foxtrot submarine is very small. Inside, it's not much wider than a bus. And the walls and ceilings are all lined with cement, and pipes, and valves. It's noisy. Runs off diesel fuel when it's going near the surface and great banks of batteries when it goes deep. If I were a kid, I'd run screaming from the place once I got inside. I don't think you would last more than a few minutes there before you went crazy. But when Zhanna climbed down into the control room, she just nodded.

"'This is in good running order, yes?' she asked as she ran her fingers along the cool iron piping. We had just painted the valves—Soviet Navy standard red and blue—and the place still smelled of it.

"'Of course,' I replied. "She is always kept ready to run.'

"'Does your rescue hatch function?' she asked.

"'For what good it would do,' I replied. You see, Foxtrots are equipped with a special hatch that allows the submarine to dock underwater. All well and good—if there were anything else still in service that used the same couplings. There is not, alas. The Foxtrot went out of service nearly twenty years ago. I explained this to Zhanna, but she waved it away before I could finish.

"'It functions, though?'

"'Yes,' I said. 'We take good care of her.'

"We spent hours touring the inside of the submarine. She did not speak—for the most part, she simply looked. Very closely, as though she were taking photographs with her eyes. With my assistance, she climbed into one of the torpedo-room bunks, and lay on the thin mattress for nearly a half-hour, before climbing down.

"'This is familiar,' she said finally. 'And good for us. I'm finished for now.'

"We climbed back up through the conning tower, as we had entered. But when we had entered, the pen was all but deserted. Now, it was filled. Every man in Shadak's armoury was there, standing as though at attention along the edge of the dock. That would have been enough—but it was also the water at the mouth of the cave. Someone had opened the sea gate, and let a half-dozen small boats inside. There were old fishing boats; a little sailboat; a small inboard motor boat. These were filled too—with one or two adults; but for the most part, with children.

"This strangeness snapped me briefly out of my reverie. I demanded to know what was what.

"'These,' she said, 'are some of my family. Not all. There are many, many more, who are to be with Amar Shadak in Belgrade. And we must take this beautiful submarine, to fetch still more. But these are many.'"

Великий THE GRAND INQUISITOR инквизитор

As dawn came to the caravansary, Amar Shadak found himself puzzled. He'd expected to see at least one guard at the edge of the pit he'd reserved for Kontos-Wu and that little bastard Stephen. But here he was, standing outside the wide chamber beneath the caravansary's mosque, and the lights weren't even on. Someone would be fucking dead in an hour, he thought. Shadak found the switch, rolled his shoulders, and stepped through the archway and down the steps to the oubliette.

"Good morning, my dears," he said in a pleasant tone, and waited for the satisfying cries from below. He took a breath. Licked his lips. Took another breath.

"Good morning," he repeated. "Wake up. Amar has come to chat with you."

Shadak's pleasant smile faltered. He strode over to the edge of the pit and leaned over. He licked his lips, and his mouth went slack. There was no one there.

He thought back to the twisting sands on the floor of a cave, and to the dance in the dust, when the world had betrayed him, his comrades had risen up as with one mind, and he'd fallen into the Black Villa for good.

He turned away.

Rapture, he thought, *fucking Rapture all over again.*

He turned and stepped out through the crumbled arches of the mosque. The world was dangerous now—ghosts walked here. No, he reminded himself. Not ghosts—the Children.

Across the room, Mrs. Kontos-Wu stirred.

"It's time," she said, in a thick Russian accent.

"Zhanna?" said Uzimeri.

"What?" said Stephen.

There was no time for an answer. The door crashed open then, and Mrs. Kontos-Wu was on the move.

"Take no chances," Shadak had said, a moment before, to the three fidgeting guards outside the tower room. "The Rapture has begun again, and it won't be long before it comes upon us."

The Rapture. That was what Uzimeri had kept calling it. Shadak knew it by a different name—he'd been fucked by it before. He didn't know if he could beat it this time. But he took what steps he could.

He gathered his men together in the courtyard, and in the morning glow looked each one in the eye. Sure enough, one in four was not himself. As Shadak spotted one such man, he separated him out—and again and again, until he had determined which one was which.

Then, the en-Raptured ones placed in the midst of a circle, he set the others upon them to first beat them senseless and chain them together behind the main house. It would likely take a short time for the devil children to regain their senses and take possession of someone else.

Or so Shadak hoped. He had not attempted this before.

Once the en-Raptured were safely chained up, Shadak set about interrogating the remainder of his men. What had happened when Ming Lei's jet had landed on the strip? They had debarked, yes—and the men who were now tied and beaten senseless had taken the prisoners to the mosque. Shadak did not care for that answer, however; his men gave it too quickly and confidently—as though they had not had to think about the question for a second. Shadak swore to himself. The bastard children hadn't just ensorcelled the men he'd taken care of; they'd buggered with the memories of the rest of them too. They might have even fiddled with Shadak's mind. Who knew?

Swearing aloud, Shadak then marched his men up to the security room, where a bank of a dozen television monitors gave a view of all parts of the courtyard and many of the rooms. The man on duty there through the night claimed that nothing had happened. But Shadak made him rewind the tapes anyway, to the time of the plane's arrival.

Ah, he'd said when the time came, *here we are*.

And the seven of them watched, slack-jawed, as the prisoners moved through the front barbican, first towards the oubliette, and then to the tower—the place where Shadak was keeping Uzimeri. The submarine guy.

Shadak would have liked to head there straight away. But he had dallied a moment too long in the security room, and the little demons had the time to refocus their energies. It pissed Shadak off; he was so absorbed in the video footage that one of them had nearly managed to slip a knife between his ribs before he knew what was happening. Shooting first that one and then the other two was a reaction more in anger than self-defence. And that pissed Shadak off more.

"Okay," he said, outside the tower room, "now."

And with that, one of his men swung the great iron bar from the door, while another slammed his boot against the door.

It was amazing, thought Stephen, as Mrs. Kontos-Wu snapped the knee of the first one through the door, the difference between watching the woman at work and being on the receiving end of her peculiar skill-set.

She really *was* good.

No sooner had the first one fallen down than Mrs. Kontos-Wu rolled over and kicked the door closed against the second and third. As fast as that happened, Stephen rolled over to the fallen rent-a-cop, who was clutching his thigh and whimpering. He had a small Ingram submachine gun on a strap, and Stephen yanked it away from him. He rolled to the side and levelled it at the entryway. The door pushed open again, and as it did, Stephen fired. The sound was deafening—the light from the muzzle flash blinding—and two rent-a-cops fell backwards down the stairs.

Sometimes he had to remind himself: Mrs. Kontos-Wu wasn't the only one who knew what they were doing. Stephen was no slouch himself.

"Shit!" Uzimeri scrambled back, and pointed at the feet of the now-screaming rent-a-cop who'd been left behind. Stephen looked, and instinctively held his breath.

One of the rent-a-cops had managed to drop something before they'd left: a small cylindrical canister, that was spewing what Stephen hoped was only tear gas.

Stephen lunged for it. Smoke was pouring out of the thing like a burst steam pipe, and as he put his hands around it, Stephen felt his eyes begin to tear and sting.

"The window!" said Uzimeri. "Ah! It hurts!"

It did hurt. Stephen could barely see, but he could still make out the glowing rectangle of the open window here in the tower. He flung the canister toward it.

And swore, as he heard the *tink! tink! thunk*!, of the metal impacting too low, and landing on the wooden floor of the tower room.

Uzimeri screamed and coughed as the gas welled up around him. Stephen found himself doubled over. His lungs demanded that he inhale, but he knew better than to give in. They'd be completely at Shadak's mercy if he did.

If they weren't already. The rent-a-cop who'd survived was making strangled bubbling noises now; who knew what had happened to Mrs. Kontos-Wu; and he and Uzimeri were blind and choking in this room. The next round of rent-a-cops, on the other hand, would have gas masks. And he didn't think they'd be gentle.

"I'm going to fucking skin that bitch," said Shadak, standing outside at the tower's base and watching the tear gas drift northward in the morning light. He was standing alongside just three of his men now.

Three were in the tower. Maybe they were dead. Maybe they were en-Raptured. Either way, it was a problem. The three men beside him were scared shitless; he could hear them muttering among themselves, about sieges and traps and ghosts that walked here among the living. Superstitious cowards, he thought. Even given the comforting plume of tear gas coming out of the arrow-slit, the likelihood that Kontos-Wu and the boy were clutching their throats like a pair of G-8 protesters—storming the room would be out of the question with these cowards at his side.

There was only one thing to do.

"Watch here," said Shadak, and pointed at the tower. The three men nodded gratefully. After having seen what they'd seen inside the tower, watching from a safe distance was about their speed. "I'll be back with reinforcements."

And with that, keys jingling in his pocket, Shadak circled around the house to where he'd chained up the en-Raptured guards. They were still there, of course; Shadak's chains were well-made and his locks first rate. He knelt down, and looked into one man's eye after another. Finally, he stood, and addressed them all:

"Does anyone know why they are here?" he bellowed. They stared back like beaten dogs. "No? Good. I will unchain you now. We have work to do in the north tower."

"The north tower?" said one. "What's there?"

"What have we done to anger you?" said another.

"We thought you had been invaded," said a third.

"I am sorry!" shouted a fourth, thumping his chest as a chain came loose. "Whatever it is we have done, I for one am sorry for it and shall not do it again!"

Shadak smiled as he worked the locks. They had no idea, of course. Their puppet-masters had fled, and these men were fresh to the day. Reborn.

And that was what Shadak needed now—fresh troops, with no idea what they were getting themselves into.

Stephen coughed as the poison air finally made its way into his lungs. He felt like he wanted to throw up, or to die, or to throw up and then die. He let the Ingram down into his lap. He didn't want his finger anywhere near the trigger with the way the gas was working on him.

Stupid, stupid. He should have thrown the canister out the door and down the stairs. It was a bigger target and it was closer. If he'd been thinking—not letting this Uzimeri character make his decisions for him—that's what he would have done.

Why the hell had Kolyokov trusted anything to him? Stephen was mystified. The only thing Stephen had managed to do was set them all up for a slow and painful death at the hands of a psychotic Turkish gangster.

Stephen coughed, and bent closer around the Ingram. When he felt the hand on his shoulder, he shook it off.

"F-F-F—" He coughed. "f-uck off."

The hand returned. This time it held tight on his upper arm, and pulled.

"Up."

It was Mrs. Kontos-Wu.

Stephen stumbled upright. He held the Ingram by the stock. He was all but blind. Mrs. Kontos-Wu dragged him a few steps toward the window. He could feel her bending down to Uzimeri.

"And you," she said. "Get up."

How the hell could she even move in this miasma, let alone speak? Stephen could barely keep his balance. From the sounds of his protests, Uzimeri was in no better shape.

Yet within a few seconds, they were all shuffling across the room to the still-open door. Mrs. Kontos-Wu paused over the corpses of the two rent-a-cops outside to retrieve their weapons, then led the three of them down the stairs.

"Careful," she said. "The stairs here are old and they are not too regular. Don't want to fall."

"N-no," said Stephen. The air was clearing as they made their way down, and he was starting to feel better. Not better to the point where he could see straight and the rivers of snot running out of his nose had slowed any. Not better to the point where he could breathe without coughing.

But he was feeling well enough to realize that Mrs. Kontos-Wu wasn't speaking in her normal voice. It was that heavily accented Russian voice.

The one he'd first heard her use at the Emissary, where she'd returned after apparently having been drowned by Amar Shadak's smelly, diesel-powered Foxtrot submarine. The one that Konstantine Uzimeri had appeared to recognize just now, as belonging to—

"Z-Zhanna?" said Stephen.

"That is right, little one," said Mrs. Kontos-Wu. "The very Zhanna that poor Konstantine here has been telling you about all night. It was a good telling, Konstantine."

"Praise—" a cough "—praise to Zhanna," said Uzimeri.

"Stop it," said Zhanna/Mrs. Kontos-Wu. "This religion of yours is very foolish, Konstantine."

"Forgive me," said Uzimeri.

They reached a landing near the bottom. Stephen was able to stand straight on his own now, and he could even see a little, enough to judge the round chamber at the tower's base to be empty.

"Where are they?" said Stephen.

"Outside," replied Zhanna/Mrs. Kontos-Wu, a little contempt sneaking into her voice. "They won't come in again soon. They're getting to be like Konstantine here—superstitious."

"Forgive me," said Uzimeri.

"But—" Mrs. Kontos-Wu's grip on Stephen's arm slackened for an instant "—but they're not above shooting us as we come out the door. Stay here. I won't be long."

"Where are you going?"

Mrs. Kontos-Wu's hand slipped from his arm. Reflexively, Stephen grabbed at her and it was a good thing he did. Mrs. Kontos-Wu's knees had buckled, and in another instant she would have tumbled down the stairs. As he held her in his arms, she began to cough.

Outside, Stephen could hear another kind of coughing: of small-arms fire. Taking Mrs. Kontos-Wu's slack form in his arms, he pressed back against the wall, and waited for it to end.

"I will fucking skin her alive," Shadak vowed under his breath.

He was pressed against the wall of the caravansary's main house as he said it. He and four others had pulled back just in time to avoid the hail of bullets that had mowed down the remaining three of his makeshift squad. But it wasn't too late to see that the ones firing were his other three men, whom he'd left to watch the tower.

Shadak knew what had happened as fast as the firing had begun; those dream-walking little bastards had gotten into his men, and driven the cowardice right out of them.

"Bastards." There was nothing for it but to shoot them. Shadak raised the little Skorpion machine pistol he kept at his belt and fired a couple of rounds all but blindly around the corner. Then he spared a glance—only to see one man down, and two others with their hands raised.

"Sir!" shouted one. "What have we done wrong?"

"You have wounded Hugo!" shouted a second. "Do not fire please!"

"Ah!" yelled the third, whose name Shadak took to be Hugo. "I am bleeding!"

Shadak's instincts kicked in, and he whirled just in time to see the three men behind him shake their heads, and begin to raise their weapons—training them on him. Shadak was quicker, and emptied the rest of the Skorpion's clip into their bellies. Their weapons fired off harmlessly in the air as they tumbled backwards with looks of wounded incomprehension on their newly liberated faces.

Shadak swore. Those little bastards would have him kill everyone in this caravansary before they were done with him. No one could be trusted—there was no one that Amar Shadak was not better off shooting, given the manner of the attack that he was now certain had been mounted against his stronghold here.

"Well, so be it," he said, and stooped over the bodies of his men to gather their weapons and ammunition. "I will slay them to a man, if that is how the fight is going to go. If—"

Shadak stopped dead, dropping a green satchel of ammunition, as an all too familiar pain—the infernal scratching at his grey matter—began to blossom in his skull.

"No," said a girl's voice. One that, like the pain, was both familiar and well inside his cranium. "No more shooting."

Shadak felt his fingers slacken, and his waist straighten—

—ah?—

—and then he was there, in the place again: a place of intolerable joy and peace, where fingers clutched and pulled at the substance of his brain like masseurs, and his mind spread across a field of light in a relaxed and delighted puddle. Peace was short-lived, however. Transcendence coalesced into the broad stones of a plaza, in the great courtyard of the Villa. The sky was bright and his hands clenched into small, soft fists.

"I'll skin her," he squeaked.

Mrs. Kontos-Wu was near the end of the book and she had to say that it was a strange one. Usually, at this point, Becky and her friends would be closing in on the thief, or the kidnappers, or the smugglers. Things might look pretty perilous. But Mrs. Kontos-Wu was sure she'd never read a Becky Barker book where Becky had had to leave her best friend Bunny Miller in an abandoned warehouse bleeding from a gunshot wound, in order to save Jim from the fez-capped terrorists who'd shown they meant business by sending Jim's severed left hand to Becky in the post. Mrs. Kontos-Wu wondered if the series had found itself a new author.

"Hey."

Mrs. Kontos-Wu looked up from the book and smiled. Lois was back! She was there, framed in the doorway to her dormitory room. Mrs. Kontos-Wu had to shield her eyes from the light—it was certainly bright out in the hallway! Brighter than daylight. Brighter than the sun, Mrs. Kontos-Wu was willing to bet.

"Hello Lois," she said.

"Hello," said Lois. "Are you enjoying the book?"

"Yes. Hey—how come you're talking like that?" Lois was speaking with a funny accent today. Or a funnier accent than her usual Bostonian drawl, anyway. She sounded like Mrs. Kontos-Wu imagined that foreign secret agent talked in Chapter Nine, before Honey had taken her out with the ice pick.

"You know why I'm talking this way," said Lois. "You know who I am."

Mrs. Kontos-Wu felt a wiggle in her stomach. She drew her knees up, and tried to focus back on the book. "Chapter Fourteen," she read aloud. "'A Necessary Evil.'"

"Snap out of it," said Lois. "You know that this is all make-believe. It was shattered by that Kolyokov bastard. You shouldn't come back here anymore."

"Fuck off." Mrs. Kontos-Wu said it before she knew what she was doing. Eyes wide, she put a hand to her mouth and drew a shocked breath. She couldn't believe she'd just said that!

"You fuck off," said Lois. "I was hoping to be able to count on you as a conscious operative—not have to dream-walk you through your manoeuvres. There are other things for me to be doing."

Mrs. Kontos-Wu closed the book. She could barely make out the words anyway; the light from the hallway was literally blinding her.

"Stop it!" bawled Mrs. Kontos-Wu. "I don't want to be a conscious operative or whatever it is you say I should be! I'm busy reading! And I happen to like it here!"

Lois stepped into the room, and reached down to take Mrs. Kontos-Wu's hand. "Of course you like it here," said Lois sadly. "It was made for you to like it here. But if you stay here, you'll die."

As Lois spoke, the light from behind her grew—tearing into the substance of the wallpaper and the rug and the little study desk in the corner, like hot flame across newspapers. Mrs. Kontos-Wu tried to cover her eyes with the book, but it was no good. The light passed through like it was made of glass.

Lois tugged at her arm. "Come on!"

Mrs. Kontos-Wu had no choice. She stood up in a dizzying rush, and stumbled forward. Lois caught her in both arms, and helped her steady herself on a floor that seemed maddeningly insubstantial.

"Now," she said, "pay attention. We've been holding Shadak and his men off as best we can, pitting them against one another. But there are more than we can deal with at any one time. So you've got to move quickly. You're at the base of the tower now. When I say, you'll lead your two friends in a run out the main door. You will run to your left, where you'll see a large gatehouse. Run through the main gate, and wait. There's a truck that's making its way up from Silifke. It should be here in a few minutes. When it shows up at the gate, you'll have a minute clear where you can get into the back. Do you understand?"

Mrs. Kontos-Wu let the programming sink in. "Yes, sir," she said.

Lois slapped her. "No! Don't run a program through your head! That's not how it's going to be anymore! Do you *understand*?"

"I understand," she said.

"Then good. Now listen carefully," said Lois. "Manka," she said. "Vasilissa. Baba Yaga."

Mrs. Kontos-Wu blinked. The light was gone. She was in a room at the base of the tower. There were bodies everywhere. Her eyes stung and her mouth and nose were wet.

And apparently she was propped on poor little Stephen Haber's shoulder.

"Zhanna?" said Stephen. "You're back?"

"Who the hell is Zhanna?" said Mrs. Kontos-Wu. "Come on, kid." She looked from Stephen to an old man, who was staring up at her with an altogether creepy awe. "You too. We've just got a few minutes, if we want to get out of here alive."

The old man grinned. "Ah," he said. "Your friend is back in herself. See?"

Stephen squinted at her. "Are you?" he asked. "No bullshit this time?"

Mrs. Kontos-Wu thought about that—about exactly where she was; whether this was herself really; and whether the bullshit was finished or not—but immediately pushed it down again.

"No bullshit." She said it uncertainly, but Stephen's relieved smile showed he hadn't picked up on it. That kid could be dense some days, no doubt about it.

Together, the three of them climbed down the rest of the stairs and made a break for the arched doorway at the tower's base.

Shadak awoke with a mouthful of brackish spit and a sharp lump travelling down his throat. The lump was, Shadak knew with doomed certainty, the key to the padlock that held the chains in place around his shoulders and wrists and ankles. He let out a volatile stream of curses. The two men who stood over him looked down at him apologetically.

"We are sorry, Mr. Shadak," said one.

"We do not know how this came to be," said the second. "We found you like this. And—"

"You see, we cannot find the key," said the first.

Shadak swallowed, and felt the key slide another few inches down his gullet. Christ—it was going to cut his insides to ribbons if he didn't get to a doctor soon.

"That is because," said Shadak, "I have swallowed the key."

"One of the devils has made you do that," said the first. "Just as one made me shoot poor Tomas, and caused Pyotr here try to shoot you although you were not looking."

The second—Pyotr—gave Tomas a look.

"Where—" Shadak winced, as the key tore past a sphincter. "Where are the prisoners?" he finished.

"Escaped, sir," said Tomas. "In a truck. Viktor tried to pursue on a motorcycle, but I am afraid that I threw a chain into his spokes before he could get going."

"He is all right," said Pyotr.

Shadak couldn't have cared less whether Viktor was all right or not. But he didn't want to antagonize his men at this point. It was a small blessing they were still apologizing and not just leaving him to die.

"That is fine," said Shadak. He forced himself to ignore the pain. He modulated the tone of his voice to the familiar, pleasant lilting. He forced his mouth from a grimace, to pleasant repose. He looked first Victor and then Pyotr in the eye. "We will catch up to them later. For now, I want you to get to work on these chains. And contact our surgeon in Silifke. I believe that I will have need of him presently."

"Of course, sir," said Viktor, moving off to the tool shed to fetch metal-cutters.

"I will find the phone," said Pyotr, stepping around the corner of the main house.

And so Amar Shadak sat alone for a space beneath the brightening sky. He leaned back, and stared into it—the still deep blue, marred here and there by a light pasting of sun-painted cloud.

Men could lose themselves in such a vista. Too many men strove to do so. And that, thought Shadak as the key cut sharply into his innards, was the thing.

That was the thing.

"I'll—" Shadak coughed, and felt the hated key hitch higher in his chest. He tasted salt in a mouthful of phlegm.

"I'll skin her," he said, and lowered his head against his shoulder, as the old love for her sunk like a spill of acid through the little cuts the key made down the middle of his chest. Alone beneath the lightening sky, Amar Shadak began to weep.

THE IDIOT
ИДИОТ

"You are a KGB agent. Elite. You know all sorts of tricks for killing a fellow. You can make yourself unseen should you need to. You have other tricks to get people to tell you things they'd rather not, and more tricks still to make sure that they can't get that kind of information out of you. Where do you think you learned these tricks? On the street?"

Alexei shook his head. The lights were flashing more rapidly—in a way that caused his testicles to pull close to his abdomen and his fingers to grip painfully into the plastic arm rests.

"Of course not on the street. You learned them in this place. Outside Murmansk. In the cold. It is a terrible place. But also a safe place. A place where you return when your eyes are shut—yes?"

Alexei shut his eyes. He did this every day at City 512. He sat in the chair, arcane cocktails of narcotics coursing through his veins, and shut his eyes when the flashing became too much, and retreated—retreated to the windswept field behind the low buildings of the Murmansk spy school, where eventually he would play cards with Ilyich Chenko; or to the classroom, where he would learn Trigonometry from psychotic old Czernochov, who'd beat him senseless at the slightest sign of inattention.

The spy school was a metaphor—a metaphor that his new master Fyodor Kolyokov used to train him in the ways of his cover. Alexei was barely twelve years old when this happened. Alexei could think of nothing more depressing than to relive it now. He was not sure that the baby Vladimir was doing him any favour by revealing the truth to him.

Still—truth is truth and there's not much to be gained in its denial.

And he had to admit—it was fascinating to see the construction of his delusions in such vivid detail. Kolyokov and his team were only beginning to implant the details of his metaphor. So when Alexei, in his new metaphor, walked the field behind the school, it was more a sheet of white cloth over a soft mattress than thin snow over permafrost. Czernochov looked like the Western film actor Vincent Price. The washrooms were still in black and white. The door to the gymnasium opened onto a deep, whistling void. Dormitory B, where Alexei's friend Chenko ostensibly slept, was simply dark—a gateway to the Id, where things chittered and floorboards creaked and cold drafts tickled the neck—but no light ever shone.

Alexei shut his eyes.

"Good," said the voice over the speaker system. "Now. Describe to me what you see."

"I'm on the ocean," said Alexei. "There's Cuba over there. Spies are everywhere."

"Don't joke," said the voice. "You are not helping. Describe what you see."

Alexei looked. He was standing at the front of the building. There was a long landing strip. The sky was a crown of brilliant blue, combed over with the thinnest wisps of cloud. Alexei squinted.

"An aircraft," he said. "An Antonov. One of the new ones. An AN-72, it looks like. It is approaching from the west. It is filled with important men. One of them is a General with the KGB. He has business with you. One of them is a writer. A dissident, I think. Both the General and the writer are unhappy. Not for the same reasons. Their names are—are—"

"Enough!" said the voice. "Stop joking, Kilodovich! There is no aircraft. No general. You are in school. Yes? Your teacher Fyodor Kolyokov has something to tell you."

"Of course," said Alexei. He turned away from the approaching Antonov. He turned back to the building, peering vainly into windows and doorways for his spy teacher Fyodor Kolyokov.

No sign of him. Alexei sighed and ran up to the school's front doorstep. He'd have to be somewhere inside.

Of course, Alexei found the old man quickly enough. Fyodor Kolyokov was the most believable thing in the metaphor—because, at this early point, he was the only thing here based in reality. So if Alexei was in one of his bare, unformed classrooms, sitting amongst classmates that looked to have been made by an air brush, he could tell Fyodor Kolyokov instantly, by the pockmarks on his left cheek and the web of lines at the corner of his eyes; the colour of his eyes. Kolyokov drew attention here by his anomalous solidity.

It gave his proclamations more solidity too. When Kolyokov told Alexei that he was a KGB agent—a skilled assassin—that he was able to do this, and this, and that with his hands—why, when Alexei awoke and they led him from the little room, he was able to repeat the tasks as though he had trained since a boy. Once, Kolyokov had told him to put out a lit match with the tip of his tongue—

to not cry out from the pain, or even flinch—and he'd done it, just like that.

Today, Kolyokov was alone in the classroom. He was wearing a blue turtleneck sweater and khaki trousers and big, black military boots that laced up to his calves. He smoked a cigarette that he'd rolled himself. He sucked deep on it, expelling the smoke through his nostrils, as he regarded Alexei.

"You," he said, "are a KGB agent. Isn't that right?"

"That's right, sir," said Alexei.

"You," he continued, "don't fool around with that other stuff—that dream-walking. You never did. Did you?"

"No, never," said Alexei.

Kolyokov didn't take his eyes off Alexei. He moved across the perfect grey floor of the proto-classroom. "You never did," he said in a low, grim voice.

Alexei nodded. "Right."

"Good. Answer questions truthfully. Don't volunteer anything. Don't look away from your interrogator. Wash your face thoroughly. Behind the ears."

"Behind the ears," said Alexei. "I've got it."

"Good boy. Now," said Kolyokov, taking the cigarette from his mouth and dropping it to the floor, "wake."

Alexei found he was far less constrained when he was locked in the metaphor than during his waking time at City 512. In metaphor, he was free to explore. More and more, he found he was simply responding to programming while awake. A small part of him was able to watch him go through the motions—but it was as though he were watching the progress of a marionette, through a tiny camera mounted on the top of his head.

So he watched, as the marionette Alexei Kilodovich scrubbed his hands and face with abrasive soap—took extra time around his ears—then dressed himself in the coveralls that had been laid out for him in his little room. He pulled on his boots and laced them up, and ran a hand over his close-cropped scalp. Then he stood and waited until the door opened, and he was able to join the procession of his classmates to the mess hall.

They wore identical coveralls, and all had hair shaved to stubble on their scalps. But that was where the similarities ended. Alexei's classmates were of all ages—the youngest one was a girl of about six years old—and there were two or three that looked to be in their seventies. There were blacks and Indians, Arabs and Asians—lots of Asians—and even a few Caucasians like Alexei. As they started to walk, the group sorted itself by ethnicity. Alexei found himself walking next to an old, balding man who wore little wire-rimmed spectacles, and a girl only a few years older than himself.

They moved along a corridor with walls of poured cement, lit by flickering fluorescent tubes set behind wire cages. They finally gathered on the platform of a large freight elevator, and once they were safely away from the edges, the old man pressed the green button on the controls. The elevator began its ascent. In short order, the old man smiled, cocked his ear like he'd heard something and pressed the red button. They continued into a large room, like a hangar. There were trucks with grey canvas covers over their loads parked along one wall. A long black car was stopped at an angle in the middle of the chamber. Its back door was propped open. A group of men dressed for the cold stood around it—conferring with someone seated inside.

Alexei and the others stopped, and shuffled themselves into a line. The group—there were five of them—continued an animated discussion with the one seated in the car. The acoustics of the huge room were poor enough that at first Alexei could only make out a few words—could only surmise what was said.

But as he listened, the words became clearer. It was as though he were standing in their midst.

"They should not be all together like this."

"It is true. In Moscow, the ones we trained were kept separate from one another. Groups of three who knew each other by face were as large as we dared."

"City 512 is not Moscow, Comrade General."

"It certainly is not. It is a colossal waste here. This sort of game will bankrupt us. Worse than Petroska Station."

"Hear hear."

"City 512 is not *Moscow. And it is not Petroska Station."*

"You said that, Comrade Kolyokov."

Ah! Thought Alexei. Fyodor Kolyokov! He looked similar to the Kolyokov of his metaphor—but a little older. A little fatter. Less confident, perhaps? Kolyokov pushed his fists into his jacket pockets. One of the other men clapped him on the shoulder.

"Why don't we let you show us how different this place is. Let's go see your pupils."

The men stepped away from the car. And as they did so, the seventh man appeared. He was a tall man, with dark hair and a lean look about his face. But his body appeared incongruously heavy under the military greatcoat. He carried a dark fur cap in one hand, and as he strode across the floor to the group, he pulled it down over his head.

There were stars sewn into the hat. Four of them. He stopped, facing the assembly, and ran a gloved hand across his chin.

"That is quite a crowd," he said. "I count fifty of them. Are they all agents?"

"Yes, Comrade General Rodionov," said Kolyokov. "There are seventy-two."

"I was at our sleeper training facility in Moscow—along with Pyorovich here. It only carries a class of—how many, Comrade Pyorovich?"

"Twelve," said a stocky man who must have been Pyorovich. "That is as many as is practical."

"Hmm." General Rodionov squinted as he regarded the class. "This must be a very impractical project indeed, then," he said. "Seventy-two! That is exactly six times what you are doing for us, Pyorovich."

Pyorovich bristled, but said nothing. The barest sprinkling of smile touched the corners of Rodionov's mouth.

"Of course," he said, "none of it has really proven itself to me. To the Party. Not your twelve, Comrade Pyorovich. Nor your seventy-two, Comrade Kolyokov."

Kolyokov and Pyorovich looked at one another. General Rodionov's smile broadened.

"Make them dance for me," he whispered.

And Alexei was back in his classroom. He was alone this time—no Kolyokov, no fellow students. But the place seemed to have gathered some solidity. He scuffed his shoe across the floor and it made a sandpapery sound. He looked down and saw the bare grey had been given the substance of concrete. And the desk where he sat was more than a wire frame now. The top of it was a light wood veneer. There were nicks at the corners. The seat was uncomfortable and too small for him, in a most convincing way. And the chalkboard was covered with smears of chalk dust. There was a tiny line up the middle, where two pieces of slate joined. Across the line, Alexei saw three words, written in a firm, teacherly hand. He leaned forward, and read them aloud:

"Manka. Vasilissa. Baba Yaga."

He read them again, just to be sure.

"Now what the hell does that mean?" he wondered aloud. And then it came to him in a great rush.

"Vladimir," he said.

The world spread apart—and Alexei found himself now in dark. He felt as though he were falling. But he was not, for the air around him was still, and stale, and without odour.

"How is it going here, Alexei? Are you any nearer the truth of your life?"

"Well, let me see. I know that my life learning to be a spy at the hands of Fyodor Kolyokov was a big lie. I find that all I ever was, was a sleeper agent. A stupid sleeper agent in the KGB. Fyodor Kolyokov was not my instructor. He was the man who controlled me, and tricked me into thinking that I was a sleeper agent. I know that I am talentless when it comes to the dream-walking and psychic powers that you and the others enjoy. I know that everything I remember is a lie. Did I say that already?"

"Yes."

"Did I remember to thank you for the opportunity to come to this truth?"

"You did not."

"Well *thank you*, little Vladimir. Remind me to wipe the shit from your ass again when I come back to the world. That is one thing I am apparently good for."

"You are not very good at that, actually."

"Well I'll take a course. Or maybe you can just walk me through it. I'm good at being *walked* through it."

"You think that, do you?"

"Why shouldn't I? What are you getting at?"

"I cannot stay long here. The others will begin to suspect. Things are not as fine as we thought they were, my cousin. Not as fine. This place—it was a trap for us."

"A trap?"

"I cannot stay."

"No. Don't drop that on me without more explanation."

"But you. You stick it out a little longer, Kilodovich. You're not at the end of things yet."

"Vladimir! Vladimir! I have a question yet."

"What did you mean by cousin?"

Alexei came to in a little room that was not his school. He was there with the Caucasian girl, the general and two of his assistants. And Kolyokov, who stood by Alexei. They stared at him.

"Is this one of the 'artefacts' you were talking about?" asked the General.

Kolyokov looked down at Alexei. "I confess I don't know. I haven't seen that before."

The General gave Kolyokov an approving look. "That is a good answer, Comrade. I find that too many of the men I deal with will try to conceal a problem—brush it over—when I ask about it. It is good, Comrade, that you are so honest about your project's shortcomings. It makes all of our tasks so much easier."

"I don't know that it is a shortcoming. But we are on the edge of discovery in this place. Each new class going through here reveals a new vista."

The General smiled and looked sidelong at one of his aides, who marked something down on a clipboard. "Quite right, Comrade Kolyokov. It is like your other class—the dream-walkers, yes? They become more powerful with each passing year. Each passing generation. Soon—soon, they will win us the West. The Motherland will be triumphant."

Kolyokov was silent.

"Dreams," said the General. "I leave dreaming to others. Let us see what these ones here can do. With their hands."

"Very good, sir," said Kolyokov. There was an odd resignation in his voice. It was the voice a man bound for the gallows, thought Alexei. He thought General Rodionov might have detected it also, the way his smile broadened.

A door opened behind Alexei. Two men in dark uniforms came in, leading a third—an old man whose whitening beard reached his collarbone. Dressed in dark brown prison clothes. He looked warily around the room as they led him to its middle.

The General and he met gazes.

"Comrade," said General Rodionov.

"Rodionov." The old man spat as he said it.

"I trust your journey was comfortable."

"Fuck yourself, Rodionov."

General Rodionov smiled and shook his head. The old man looked around him once more. He seemed to be counting. Finally, he spoke:

"This is to be my execution, then?" he said. "Here, in this little room? With these people present? This old man? This girl? This—" he motioned to Alexei contemptuously "—this *boy?*"

"You prefer a bullet in your head?"

Alexei felt his palms beginning to sweat. He could not look at the old man, he found.

Kolyokov was also clearly uncomfortable. But he knew what he had to do. "Tanya," he said to the other Caucasian girl.

She didn't even look at Kolyokov. Her eyes, already dim lights, clouded and darkened, and she began to move forward. Alexei saw her hands make a claw—the frame of her shoulder tense—the old man, seeing what was to happen, suddenly lose his composure the way that men do when faced with their deaths—and the General, still smiling, and now nodding to himself with a terrible knowledge.

Alexei lurched forward. The girl was older than he—maybe seventeen—twenty centimetres taller and at least as strong. But he caught her in the small of the back, and in the thrall of her programming—and it was enough to cancel her natural advantages. She fell forward onto the concrete floor, Alexei on top of her. She twisted underneath him, swung a clawed hand toward his eyes. Alexei managed to deflect the blow, so her nails simply scored sharp red lines across her forehead. Before she could attack again, he reared back and flung himself, elbow first, into her chest. She made an odd whooshing sound, went briefly limp, and began to cough. Alexei grabbed first one hand and then the other, and pressed both hard against the concrete. She made a strangling noise and glared up at him with eyes that seemed not her own.

Breathless, Alexei looked up. Kolyokov was glaring at him, his mouth working speechlessly. The old man was looking at him too—with gratitude and relief. He was nodding at him: *Good lad*, he was thinking. *Good, good lad. Fuck them, hey? Fuck their benighted Party. We will drink vodka in gulag together, hey lad? Good lad.*

General Rodionov had crossed his arms, and forefinger and thumb cradling his chin. He wasn't looking at Alexei, or the old man, or any of the other pupils here. Just Kolyokov. After a silence that seemed eternal, Comrade General Rodionov cleared his throat.

"I go to a Gypsy fortune teller," he said quietly. "Ask her to tell me the future. She says, I will do so, Comrade. Give me two hundred rubles. Very good, I say. I reach into my coat. She looks at my hand expectantly—for surely I am reaching for my purse, where all those rubles are waiting for her. Instead—I take out a pistol. I hold it up to her forehead and fire twice. And she is dead. Brains spread across the back of her tent.

"It is no great waste. Those brains, it seems, had little knack for the telling of fortunes. Had they, they would have told her of the gun days ago, and she might have seen her own sad fate. She might have taken precautions.

"You are like that fortune teller, Fyodor Kolyokov. But in a different way. I bring my old friend here and give you every indication he is to be killed. I give him every indication this is so. And so naturally, you set your girl about to kill him.

"But I do not wish him killed. Why should we kill him? This—" he motioned to the old man "—this is my long-time Comrade. I have read all his novels. His poetry is a delight to the senses. We have so many more conversations to have before either of us is permitted to die. So there is no good reason. I don't wish him dead. This is topmost in my mind. And do you have the wit to stop the killing? Do you read my mind, and stop it yourself? No. It is left up to this—" he motioned toward Alexei "—this one, who so far as any of us know simply disapproves of killing old men for no good reason, to stop the execution. What am I to make of this?"

Kolyokov's face was reddening. He opened his mouth and shut it again.

"Did you perhaps *dream-walk* this one—" he pointed again at Alexei "—that is the term you use, isn't it? Did you dream-walk him to prevent the needless killing? No. You are wide awake the whole time—not in your little piss tank. I watch you."

"Speechless, Kolyokov?" smirked one of the aides.

"You must know, Comrade General Rodionov," said Kolyokov finally, "that the City 512 dreamers do not work that way."

"Oh, but my Comrade. I do know that. That is why I am here." He looked back at Alexei, who was still trying to restrain the girl. "Why don't you take these pupils of yours back to their cells? We have a great deal to discuss before we leave here, and there is no point in involving more *innocents*."

As if on cue, the old man began to weep softly. Alexei let go of the girl. She stood and brushed herself off. Kolyokov nodded, and under his orders, the three of them left the room. By the time he had stepped out the door, Alexei was already gone from City 512, and back at school.

In his brief absence, the classroom of his metaphor had become more real again. The ceiling was now criss-crossed with tiles and the buzzing, clicking fluorescent lights that Alexei remembered so well. The windows looked out on a frozen wasteland of tundra and snowflakes. He had classmates, too. At the front of the classroom, seated behind his desk, the evil math instructor Czernochov made notations in a great ledger.

What a place, thought Alexei, a metaphor of the lie of his childhood, embedded within another metaphor that was the truth of it. Or he supposed it to be the truth. Alexei began to wonder just what the nature of truth might be in this place. He ran his thumb across the wood-grain of his desk. Could not, he wondered, any recollection be constructed with detail as convincing—so that he could not be certain, truly, of anything in his past? Could not the recollection—now distant—of Holden Gibson and the boat and Heather; of Mrs. Kontos-Wu and the Romanians; of New York City, the world itself, his own name, his own identity—all of it—couldn't it all be a fabrication, just as cunningly wrought as this desk? If that too were a fabrication . . . if the firmament of his life truly were a lie—then what good was anything?

The direction of his thoughts made Alexei queasy. Trying to talk it out, he recalled, had led to a metaphorical rock in his metaphorical head from the little bastard Ivan. So rather than seeking some equilibrium in further dialogue, he stood up and asked if he might be excused.

"Bladder too small, Kilodovich?" asked Czernochov mildly.

"I'm not feeling well," said Alexei. "Think I'm going to sick up." He put his fingers to his lips and inflated his cheeks like they were filling up with bile.

"Well then. Better go deal with it." Czernochov sneered as he spoke it. Several of his metaphorical classmates snickered. Alexei got up and made his way to the door. The hallway was still a work in progress—if he squinted, he could see through walls as though they were simple strips of canvas, into washrooms and meeting rooms, and, as he passed it, the great void of the gymnasium. He went straight to the north doors, pushed them open, and stepped outside into the freezing cold of the afternoon.

The sky was perfect blue today. Maybe, thought Alexei bitterly, by tomorrow Kolyokov would have thought to add some attractive cloud. He'd obviously spent his time up to now on the snow and the rock. Alexei trudged across it, his freezing hands jammed into the pockets of his trousers.

When he was far enough away from the building, Alexei shouted, “You are a bastard fuck, Comrade Kolyokov!”

The wind howled in answer. Fyodor Kolyokov did not appear. Alexei found himself suddenly hoping that he might.

Not, of course, the Kolyokov who was probably now playing Party politics with Comrade General Rodionov—trying to secure the survival of his precious City 512. Not him—but the ghost Kolyokov who'd appeared to Alexei what seemed like months ago: a geriatric specter in wind-blown snow; aged and ominous and fleeting. That one, Alexei decided, was the real man—the Fyodor Kolyokov who drew his rage; this one, here in memory, hadn't yet begun to exact the indignities upon him that had led him into this terrible spiral of memory—this unhinging of truth.

Alexei came to the very back of the exercise yard. Here, the snow was not nearly so distinct—it clotted on his heels like half-frozen cream. The air was cold, but it was more an idea of cold than the thing itself: a Platonic chill.

And so it was with the fence. Eventually, the fence would be eight feet high and capped with razor-wire. Now, it was a flat, vertical plane, etched with just the blurry indication of chain link. Alexei reached out to touch it. It felt like metal, but was yielding like a skin of rubber. Alexei pulled at it until he'd made a space wide enough to step through.

“Bastard fuck,” he said, looking back at the low buildings, the icy fields—all of it, the evil and manipulative lie of his childhood. Then he turned from it, and bending only slightly, stepped through the fence.

Маленький THE LITTLE HERO герой

The last time Stephen had seen sky was the dawn outside Silifke, just a day ago. It had been something: fluted streamers of cloud pasted against a slate of a sky that ran tones between purple and orange and deep, deep blue. A contrail of some high-flying jet transected it like a filament of gold. There were smells, too—the faintly sweet, faintly corrupt odour of the port, mingled with turpentine-fresh gasoline from the inboard motor of the fishing boat that was taking them out the mouth of the Goksu River to the Mediterranean Sea.

Eyes shut and fists clenched in the tiny midshipman's cabin they'd given him, Stephen tried to summon that sky. It might just banish the sweating metal pipes and red-painted valves that hovered just three feet over his hard, narrow bunk. But seeing sky through the roof of a submarine was more difficult than discovering Central Park behind Manhattan water towers from the 14th floor of the Emissary. They had been running deep since the fishing boat had unloaded them on the sub's deck. And the distractions in this place—the thrumming of the engines; the *stink* of the engines; and the clattering of footsteps and hatches and the occasional words of spoken conversation—made Stephen's carefully studied exercises all but useless.

If, that was, Zhanna hadn't been right—and those exercises hadn't been useless from the beginning.

Stephen opened his eyes and rolled off the bunk. There was just enough room for him to stand up. If he turned to the left a little, there was a little table. If he turned to the right a little, there was the hatch to the submarine's spinal corridor. If he took one step in any direction, he'd bash his head on a valve or a pipe or one of the dozens of little lozenge-shaped light fixtures that buzzed and clicked through the day.

Stephen cleared his throat.

"Shh!"

A red-fingered, bandaged hand shot out from the bottom bunk. Uzimeri glared up at Stephen. He clasped his hands together as in prayer and rested his head on them, and mouthed: *Sleeping.*

Fuck off, mouthed Stephen. But he kept quiet. Glancing out into the corridor, he saw that the lights had indeed been turned down. Most of the submarine's cargo was asleep—and that meant that those who were awake had to keep quiet, because a sudden loud noise to wake one or two of them could spell disaster.

The first time the crew went to sleep, it very nearly did. Uzimeri was in a tiny galley no bigger than a men's room stall, boiling water for a porridge, and Mrs. Kontos-Wu, Stephen, and two other guests—a thirtyish red-haired woman and a round little man with a thumbprint-sized mole on his cheek—were settled in the cramped mess hall. They'd been in the submarine just a few hours.

Mrs. Kontos-Wu had tried to convince Uzimeri to take it easy—he'd been damn near dead when they'd found him, after all.

"Stephen can cook," said Mrs. Kontos-Wu, taking Uzimeri's stick-thin arm and guiding him to a seat.

But Uzimeri had refused.

"I am restored," he said. "I am back amongst my people now. Let me feed you this simple breakfast, yes?"

Mrs. Kontos-Wu gave up after that—and Stephen was less worried about making sure Uzimeri was steady on his feet than he was about Mrs. Kontos-Wu's own interior stability.

After all—she'd *seemed* fine back in the Emissary, when she'd basically given them up to the mob. She seemed fine now, too. But like a junkie, she could be back into her never-never land of metaphor in a second. Stephen didn't take his eyes off her as she conversed with the two Russians.

"I am Ilyich," said the man, in Russian. "This is Tanya."

"We have been on board since Odessa," said Tanya. "How was Silifke? Did you happen to visit the Tekir Ambar?"

"The—?" Mrs. Kontos-Wu frowned, her lips turned up in a question.

"No," said Tanya. "You would know what that was if you had seen it. It is a great cistern, next to Silifke Castle. There are stairs climbing down the side of it. You can walk to the bottom. It was made by Romans. You can feel their presence in the stones. Ghosts." Tanya beamed. "Silifke is a wonderful town. The Romans, the Christians—everyone had a hand there. And the people—so friendly!"

"We really didn't spend much time in the town," said Mrs. Kontos-Wu. Stephen put a hand on Mrs. Kontos-Wu's arm—he was afraid that she'd start to explain to them how it was hard to take the Silifke walking tour when you were locked up in Amar Shadak's fucking caravansary and sucking back lungsful of tear gas. How you couldn't get much of a view of the beautiful Roman architecture when you were hiding under a blanket in the back of a delivery truck while it bombed down a mountain road. And how the guy who ran the fishing boat seemed friendly enough in a dream-walked zombie kind of way, but by and large you didn't get to spend too much quality time with the happy friendly people of Silifke when you were on the run from a psychotic Turkish gangster like Amar Shadak.

But Mrs. Kontos-Wu was all right. She patted Stephen's hand and gently pushed it from her arm.

"Tell me all about Odessa," she said. "That's one place that I've never been."

Ilyich smiled. "Well then that is one place you must visit. Odessa is every—"

His smile vanished then, and he tilted his head as though listening for something. Stephen didn't hear anything. But the little Russian frowned, and put his finger to his lips.

"Shh," he said.

Both he and Tanya sat straight in their little seats.

And that was it for their little dining car conversation. Tanya and Ilyich sat up with their hands folded. Mrs. Kontos-Wu did the same. Stephen followed their cue.

It all would have gone swimmingly—were it not for Uzimeri, and his porridge. Stephen later kicked himself for not paying more attention to the frail old Turk, who had insisted on boiling a brimming pot-full of water by himself. When Ilyich has said "shh," Uzimeri had taken it as Word from the lips of Jesus. So standing not six inches from the edge of the tiny cooking range, Uzimeri had simply stood straight, taken a deep breath—and, after less than a minute, fallen into a dead faint.

There was a clattering and a splashing sound—and when Stephen looked, the first thing he saw was the pot of not-quite-boiling water hissing over the stove element and streaming down onto Konstantine Uzimeri's right side.

Stephen leapt up from his chair and pushed his way into the galley, just as Uzimeri opened his mouth to scream. Slipping in the puddle on the floor as he did so, Stephen pulled Uzimeri away.

Except that the scream didn't come. Uzimeri had been scalded—not as badly as if the water had been at a complete boil, but badly enough. His mouth stretched open for an instant, and the tiniest squeak came out. Then it closed and a look of peace came over him.

"What—"

"Shh," said Uzimeri, then whispered, in a thick Russian accent that Stephen had last heard from Mrs. Kontos-Wu: "Konstantine will be fine. He is in a safe place. Sit here quietly now, Stephen. Until we are all in a safer place. Past Cyprus."

Later, the young woman to whom the voice belonged would come and meet Stephen and Mrs. Kontos-Wu. Stephen didn't swing that way, but he could see how this Zhanna girl had managed to charm Uzimeri and the other men guarding Shadak's warehouse museum. And how they might have thought that it was lust that drove them at first to worship at the feet of the slim-figured, black-haired Russian girl. She was still blinking the sleep-sand out of her eye and had a bad case of bed-head. But with her wide, dark eyes and delicate, half-smiling lips—she could have been a film star.

"Everything is all right now," she said. "There are a lot of people on Cyprus who have an interest in watching the comings and goings of submarines. But we fooled them."

"Fooled them? How?" Stephen was intensely curious. Zhanna—and, he supposed, the boy who shushed them—the two of them were the first of Kolyokov's children that he'd met face to face. When they'd come to the submarine, it was just the small crew of scowling Romanian men who greeted them. And Ilyich and Tanya after that. Zhanna and her family had remained hidden elsewhere on the submarine until Cyprus.

"There is not just one way," said Zhanna. She spoke quickly, not meeting Stephen's eye. "Some ways are very old. There is a way of placing a field around a submarine, like a great cloud. It obscures the eye of dream-walkers, and sends the eyes of others looking elsewhere when it passes before them. That works for the people who look on the feeds from spy satellites, and on radar operators if there are not too many of them. If there are too many of them—in places like the base on Cyprus—and they are watching too attentively . . . we must plan ahead. It is good to have a sleeper on the site. Lucky us—we have three still at Cyprus. So—first we distract—then, sabotage of records. Lots of work for everyone. That is why it is so important to be quiet. None of us can afford to be awakened."

"Sorry," said Stephen.

"No harm done." She smiled shyly. "We got to you through Konstantine, and now we are safe."

"Lucky for us," said Stephen. Then he frowned, as he thought of something. "But tell me: Why didn't you just dream-walk inside of me—shut me up that way?"

"I might have." She looked at Stephen hard. "But you are very special boy."

Stephen felt his heart racing at those words. He was special—even if Kolyokov hadn't recognized it; hadn't let him develop his special talents. Screw him. Stephen had the dream-walker moves—Zhanna said so.

"Really?" Stephen put his fingers into his belt-loop and leaned back. "Special—in what way?"

"You," she said, "are a complete cipher to us. So far as we can tell, you have no senses beyond the Physick whatsoever. You alone, Stephen, are entirely safe from we dream-walkers."

Stephen stood quietly in his quarters for nearly an hour before the alert was over.

"We were passing through the Strait of Gibraltar," said Uzimeri as he sat up in his bunk. "Very tricky. The British guard that passage jealously. And it is shallow. It is only by the grace of the Most Holy Children that we have been able to pass through it as often as we have."

Stephen slumped against the bulkhead and glared at Uzimeri. "Stop talking about them like they're fucking Jesus," he said.

Uzimeri raised his eyebrows. "This," he said, "coming from a man who is deaf to the words of the Divine. I think I shall keep my own counsel."

I'm not deaf to anything! Stephen clenched a fist behind his back and pressed his lips together. What the fuck did Zhanna know anyway? Stephen wasn't deaf—he was just having a bad patch. Stephen remembered Kolyokov coming to him—in dream, using Discourse. Hadn't he? Fyodor Kolyokov wouldn't have taken him on in the first place, if he was completely untalented—would he?

Ah, he could drive himself in circles thinking about this. He turned himself to the matter at hand.

"We're passing Gibraltar," he said. "So what—are they taking us home?"

Uzimeri shrugged. "That would depend," he said, "on what you regard as home."

"Well aren't you a cryptic man today." Looking down at Uzimeri, all hunched around his scalded arm and staring back like some crazed zealot, Stephen found himself missing old Richard. At least Richard had the good sense to be fucked up by all the messing that went on with his head. Uzimeri had turned his servitude to advantage. And Stephen—Stephen just didn't know what to make of it.

"I'm going for a walk," he said and turned on his heel.

"Good idea, boy," said Uzimeri. "Why don't you go on the deck and get yourself some air?"

"Funny Turk," said Stephen and stepped out into the narrow corridor.

It was maddeningly narrow. And the single deck that was fit for human habitation was crammed with equipment. He couldn't take more than two steps without having to duck or bend to get around some protuberance. There were, Uzimeri had told him, fifty people on board this submarine. He'd have to take the old man's word for it. Because there was nowhere on board where you could put all those fifty at once.

It was, thought Stephen, just a bad patch. He couldn't be completely tone deaf to dream-walkers—because he was, or had been, working an apprenticeship with Fyodor Kolyokov. He'd been to psychic fairs and bought the tapes, and practiced his remote viewing like a kid doing piano scales. Maybe he wasn't a Chopin—but Stephen wasn't a failure, either. He walked into poor old Richard's mind again and again—and Christ! He'd walked into the formidable skull of Amar Shadak, using the telephone lines as a gateway, and seen the ruins of Ankara through his eyes. Over the years he'd had premonitions and visions and on one embarrassing occasion an actual seizure, which old Kolyokov hadn't completely dismissed as merely an attention-getting device.

Stephen stepped out onto the cramped bridge. There were a half-dozen of Shadak's Romanian guard here, working the valves and controls like monks at a wine press. These guys weren't deaf to the words of the Divine. They were so attentive that one touch from Zhanna was all it took to turn them into her slave boys.

Stephen stepped around the periscope, ducking beneath another low-hanging valve. A short, bearded Romanian stepped around Stephen to refer to a chart on the table. Stephen glanced down at it.

"That Gibraltar?" he asked. The Romanian answered with a blandly polite nod. Stephen stared at him—tried to push his way inside his head. For an instant, he thought he might have done so—felt a flow of language, a lifetime of large regrets and little triumphs. But staring into the Romanian's blinking eyes, Stephen realized that that wasn't the case. He was just fooling himself. As he always had been, maybe.

"Good then," said Stephen. He stalked off the bridge.

What if he *had* always been fooling himself, thought Stephen. If he were to go through his psychic history systematically, he'd be hard-pressed to find an actual event where he had unequivocally managed to subvert one of his subjects. He could get into Richard's head—or so he thought—and he could seem to affect Richard's actions. But if Stephen were honest about it, he'd have to admit that most of Richard's actions were entirely predictable. That was one of the offshoots of the psychic damage that brainwashing had inflicted on him.

And as for Shadak?

Stephen hadn't done anything but piss the Turkish gangster off. And while he'd used the telephone to do that, Stephen had to admit that he hadn't really needed any psychic powers to do so.

Maybe Zhanna was right—and Stephen didn't have any psychic powers at all.

Maybe Fyodor Kolyokov was just stringing him along—just to keep him loyal. As Stephen thought about it, an unswervingly loyal psychic deadhead would be a valuable commodity for a man like Kolyokov. None of the old man's enemies could dream-walk into the little deaf-brained executive assistant and tell him to stick a letter opener in the Fyodor's eye. They'd have to bring someone like Mrs. Kontos-Wu across the ocean to do it.

Stephen bent down through a circular hatch. Crawled past some more bunks, underneath another hatch, and from there into the forward torpedo room. It was almost as big as the bridge—mostly because two of the six torpedoes that would store here had been fired. Stephen hoisted himself onto one of the empty bays and stretched out. Craning his neck, he could see most of the way down the narrow tube that led to the ocean.

He shut his eyes, and tried to imagine what might lie beyond that tube now. Tried to picture the ocean, the sunken wrecks—the trio of ship-sized squid that accompanied the submarine like an escort of jet fighters as it made its way out into the Atlantic.

"Ah, fuck." Stephen's voice buzzed and hummed off the metal walls that confined him here. *Giant squid. How rich. How fucking Captain Nemo.*

He really was a fuckup when it came to dream-walking.

Mrs. Kontos-Wu was radiant. She looked, thought Stephen uncharitably, like she'd just been laid.

"Get out of the fucking torpedo tube, Haber," she said. "We've got lots to talk about."

"This isn't the tube," said Stephen as he rolled off the empty torpedo bay and clanged noisily onto the grated decking. He pointed to the fore. "That's the tube."

"Whatever." Mrs. Kontos-Wu leaned against the opposite bank of torpedoes. "Lots has been happening since we got on board this submarine, and we've decided that it's not fair you shouldn't be in the loop."

"We?"

"I'll get to that. But first, let's deal with what we came here for."

Stephen gave her a look.

"The mystery of the children," said Mrs. Kontos-Wu. "What happened to them, why we were hijacked at sea, all that."

"Ah. For a second there I thought you meant why we gave ourselves up to the Mafia and let ourselves be gassed in Amar Shadak's fucking headquarters."

"You're angry about that, are you?"

Stephen sighed. "What about the children?" he said.

"Well. First off—did you make the connection with Ilyich and Tanya?"

"The connection?"

Mrs. Kontos-Wu rolled her eyes. "Here's a hint: their last names are Chenko and Pitovovich."

Stephen thought a moment. "Weren't they the ones involved—" he snapped his fingers. "They were! Pitovovich is the lawyer from St. Petersburg, and Chenko is her—her man in Odessa. The one who found the kids and set them up in a dormitory. Right?"

Mrs. Kontos-Wu nodded. "True as far as it goes."

"I guess those email addresses are pretty redundant." Stephen frowned, working it out. "But what are they doing here?"

"They've been with the children for many days now," said Mrs. Kontos-Wu. "The children—they look after their own." Her eyes batted then, and her face took on an expression that Stephen had never seen before.

"You okay?" Stephen was worried she was slipping back into her metaphor again while a dream-walker stepped inside. He looked around for a weapon.

But Mrs. Kontos-Wu wasn't going into metaphor. There was no dream-walker. She sniffed, and dabbed her eye with her sleeve.

"Shit," said Stephen. "Are you *crying*?"

"Fu-fu-fu-fuck off."

"You *are* crying," said Stephen wonderingly. "Shit, Kontos-Wu. *Shit*. I didn't think your tear ducts even worked anymore."

"Fuck off. All right?" Mrs. Kontos-Wu looked up, sniffed noisily, and cleared her throat. "Pitovovich and Chenko are both sleepers from way back. For most of their lives, they'd been deactivated. Both were apparent GRU operatives. Pitovovich maintained a secondary cover in St. Petersburg as a lawyer, and Chenko was more open—he was a Colonel, and operated a station in Odessa and dealt with informants and so forth."

"So wait a second. Chenko was a sleeper agent in the GRU? Isn't that redundant?"

Mrs. Kontos-Wu shrugged and dabbed her eyes. "Our missing colleague Alexei Kilodovich was a sleeper in its predecessor the KGB. You don't think the bureau felt the need to spy on itself from time to time?"

Stephen always marvelled at the layers of paranoia that formed the strata of this organization that had abused and murdered his parents.

"How could I have been so naïve?" he said.

Mrs. Kontos-Wu chuckled. Stephen was amazed: first tears, now laughter.

"Chenko first met the kids eight months ago. It wasn't exactly as Shadak understood it. A brood of them showed up in an old school bus—at an apartment block that Chenko found himself owning. Chenko had, unbeknownst to himself, taken a sizeable chunk of the station's slush fund and thrown it into real estate. He'd put a half-dozen of his local muscle to work, clearing the place out and doing what minor repairs were required. Chenko met the kids—there were fifteen of them at that point—out front, and hurried them upstairs to the special suite he'd prepared."

"Special?"

Mrs. Kontos-Wu nodded. "It was sterilized. Had to be. It was going to be a birthing room."

"What?"

"That was one of the things Chenko didn't tell Shadak," said Mrs. Kontos-

Wu. "Zhanna arrived in Odessa pregnant. She gave birth just a day after they arrived."

"Pregnant." Stephen crossed the narrow torpedo room and leaned beside her. "What—*who* did she give birth to?"

"They named him Vladimir," said Mrs. Kontos-Wu. "He's a very special baby."

"Who are these kids?" said Stephen. "They're like Fyodor Kolyokov is—was. Are they relatives of his? What? Why did he want them?"

"You ever hear," said Mrs. Kontos-Wu, "of City 512?"

"No."

"Me either. At least not—not at first."

Ah fuck, thought Stephen. *She's tearing up again*.

"What is with you?" he said. "You've never been this—this close to the surface before."

Mrs. Kontos-Wu smiled weakly. "That's so true," she said.

"So what is it? What is it about this City 512?"

Mrs. Kontos-Wu took a breath. "Well—as it turns out—it's the place where I was made."

"Where is it?"

"I don't know. Somewhere in Russia. The place is mostly underground—very secret, obviously—and it's where Kolyokov—where he worked before he came to the United States."

Stephen nodded. "Okay. That's where he learned how to dream-walk. Where the sleepers like you came from. It's also where these kids came from. That makes sense. They can dream-walk like Kolyokov could. So why're you all misty?"

"Because," said Mrs. Kontos-Wu, taking a deep breath, "I've known all that. All my life I've known all that. If I really concentrated—really pushed it—I could remember that I spent my childhood in a bunker in the Soviet Union. I could remember that these—these men from City 512—took me and turned me into their puppet. But every time I would do that—it'd slip away. And I'd think about Bishop's Hall. Where I went to finishing school to be a proper fucking young lady."

"But you don't have that problem now," said Stephen. "So what's the problem?"

Mrs. Kontos-Wu looked at Stephen. "Do you ever think back to the night your parents tried to kill you?"

"All the time," said Stephen.

"Is it getting better?"

He thought about that for a second. "You mean less painful? Sure. I guess. Time heals, you know?"

"Well," said Mrs. Kontos-Wu, "I haven't had the luxury of time. This shit is fresh pain for me, because I haven't been able to look at it squarely until now. So—so—please—*fucking—excuse me—if I'm—a little—*"

Stephen tried to duck out of the way as Mrs. Kontos-Wu lunged at him. She wrapped both arms around his neck, and Stephen prepared for the inevitable *crack!* as she snapped it. The unmerciful end. But all he felt was hot tears soaking through his shirt.

"*—if I'm a little emotional*!" Mrs. Kontos-Wu wailed.

"Oh." Belatedly, Stephen raised a hand and patted Mrs. Kontos-Wu's sobbing shoulder. He felt like it was the creepiest thing he'd ever done—but he kept at it, this *comforting* thing, until she closed her eyes and drifted to sleep.

Mrs. Kontos-Wu cleaned herself up for dinner. But she kept to herself as the five of them—her, Tanya, Ilyich, Stephen, and Uzimeri—sat around the little galley table eating their poached fish and rice. The engines thrummed and made the cutlery rattle where it sat. The mess smelled of fish and oil and battery acid.

"She is going through another phase in her recovery," said Uzimeri. "Do not worry about her."

Ilyich Chenko nodded. "We all went through this," he said. "These children—they're not like other dream-walkers we may have encountered. They need our help, but they don't want to keep us tied up and in their unthinking thrall. So they release us. That is good—for it is always better to be a free man than a puppet. But it is also painful at first. Memory comes upon you in a torrent. Quite distressing. I am still sorting mine out."

Tanya Pitovovich smiled and laughed. "I'll take the pain of memory any day," she said around a forkful of fish, "over oblivion."

Chenko clapped and laughed. "Good," he said. "We must all be so brave."

Tanya reached across the table and held Ilyich's hand. Stephen had to fight to keep from rolling his eyes.

Stephen cleared his throat.

"Tell me about the children," he said. "Tell me about Vladimir."

Ilyich disengaged from Tanya's hand. "Vladimir," he said. "The baby. You've heard about him?"

"Mrs. Kontos-Wu said he was born—in Odessa was it?"

"That's right. We made a special room for it, in the top floor apartment. Whitewashed the walls and ceiling, tore up the carpets and scrubbed the floors down to the boards. The children brought two midwives with them. Pretty German girls. One had tattoos all up her arms and hair shaved short to her skull. The other one was a yellow-haired girl who couldn't have been more than twenty years old. I wouldn't have taken them for midwives. But they knew their stuff. They put me to work soon enough. 'Boil the water, Chenko!' 'Bring the cloth, Chenko!' 'Stand here!' 'Out of the way!' I did as I was told. It was good to have work to do, because it's an incredible, terrible thing when a child is born. A woman comes apart for the occasion—split up the middle—and for a long time, it's all blood and screaming. The pain is—indescribable."

"How would you know?"

"I was assigned to be her coach," said Ilyich. "That meant that I shared the pain of it with her—because of what she is, I shared it quite literally."

"That's a pisser," said Stephen.

"No," said Ilyich, "really it's not. It was an agony—but when the baby Vladimir finally emerged—well, it was like looking upon the sun after spending a decade in *gulag*. Don't wince. You asked about Vladimir and I'm telling you. The baby was special. When he looked at you, he was really looking at you: not like most babies, who just point their unformed little eyeballs in your direction and blink for two weeks. Vladimir could see. And he had—he had a voice."

"A voice. What did he say to you?"

"'Hello Ilyich Chenko. I am sorry.'"

"Fuck off."

"No. That is what he said. 'Hello Ilyich Chenko. I am sorry.' I remember it like I remember my name. It seemed as though I could hear it with my ears. But it was not with my ears. He was speaking in my head. Using the immense powers of his mind."

"Fuck. Off." Stephen didn't like being jerked around. "You're telling me that a newborn baby called you by name and apologized."

"I don't blame you for being skeptical. I did not believe it myself when it happened. 'Which one of you said that?' I demanded. The midwives had no idea what I was talking about. Zhanna, who held her bloody little baby crooked in her arm, just ignored me. I didn't repeat the question, because it was then that it dawned upon me that none of those three girls could have said what I heard. For the baby spoke in a voice that was deep and melodious. The voice of a grown man. And there were no men in the room but I."

"All right," said Stephen, "so the newborn baby got a good look at you, figured out your name, and then he spoke inside your head. And his first words were, 'I'm sorry.' What was he sorry for?"

"As it turned out, pretty much everything," said Ilyich. "But immediately, he was sorry for having used me to establish this base of operations; for siphoning Zhanna's pain of childbirth; for robbing me of my time and my money. Plenty to apologize for."

"But he didn't let you free."

"Oh yes—that was to be the bargain. As he suckled at his mother, he told me I could leave any time I wanted to. But he asked me if I would stay and help him and the others finish their work."

"And you agreed."

"Yes," said Uzimeri. "We all agreed, boy. Because we saw the light of Vladimir. We—"

Ilyich raised his hand, and Uzimeri nodded. He shut his mouth, and Ilyich continued.

"There were eighteen children with Zhanna and Vladimir. They were siblings. They ranged from three years old to eighteen. The closest thing they had to a parent was Zhanna—and she was their sister. It was hard at first to learn much about them. They rarely spoke, although they didn't seem to have much trouble communicating with one another. Mostly I spoke with Zhanna and Vladimir—and that was mainly to take instruction: 'Bring us groceries, Chenko' 'We require medicine, Chenko' 'What can you do about some new clothes, Chenko?' That kind of thing. The rest of the children kept to their rooms—staring at one another and occasionally nodding or shaking a head."

Stephen nodded himself now. "Discourse," he said.

"Yes. They were engaged in what you call Discourse. It was two months before they introduced me to it. It was an icy November night, and I was frustrated. My superiors in Moscow were raising questions about the apartment block and some other unauthorized purchases I'd made. There was talk of replacing me in Odessa, with someone more reliable. I'd just received news of this, through a contact of mine in the Kremlin. The children, when I arrived, were sitting in a tight circle underneath a frosted skylight—hands joined and eyes shut. Vladimir was in the middle, apparently asleep. Zhanna met me at the door and pulled me aside.

"'This is private business, Ilyich,' she said. 'Go away.'

"I am afraid that I became very angry. I said all kinds of things, all of which boiled down to this: that I may indeed go away, to someplace where none of them would see me anymore, because of the resources that the group of them demanded.

"'You use me like a bank,' I said. 'And what do you give in return? I've a mind to leave right now. Make my way in America, perhaps.'

"For the first time since I'd met her, Zhanna looked genuinely alarmed. She pulled me to a side bedroom and sat me down on the bed. 'You cannot mean that,' she said.

"Of course, I did not mean that—I couldn't. The children exerted a force on me even then. But I was angry and Zhanna saw that, and she decided then to appease me.

"'Lie down,' she commanded. 'Loosen your belt. Unbutton your shirt collar. Remove your shoes. And close your eyes.'

"I did as I was told—although I had no idea what to expect. I admit, the idea that Zhanna might make love to me crossed my mind. But I knew in my heart that this was not in her plans. She wanted to show me something else. Something—greater."

Uzimeri set his cutlery down and looked heavenward. Tanya and Stephen shared a glance.

"Discourse," said Ilyich. "Zhanna set about to show me the raw magnificence of Discourse."

Stephen sighed. Of course she was. "What was it like?" he asked.

Ilyich was ready with a description. "Like a drug," he said. "Like a drug that lets you listen to a stadium full of chattering grandmothers—and hear what each of them is saying."

"No," said Uzimeri. "That's not entirely right. You are not hearing what they are saying—you are feeling it. In your soul!" He thumped his chest. "Discourse is the language of the Soul!"

"Konstantine," Tanya said, "the children do not even admit the existence of a soul. You only feel what you imagine you feel. The Discourse is entirely physical—"

"—and yet," said Ilyich, "it brings such a great sense of peace to us when we are permitted to enter it. And the visions—I haven't even begun with the visions yet."

"You see?" said Uzimeri to Tanya. "Visions. Visions! A thing of the soul."

"A thing of the optic nerve," said Tanya.

"Why does this always have to get theological with you two?" said Ilyich. "Cannot we accept the truth and value of inner peace without attaching a religious connotation to the experience?"

"Who said anything about religion?" said Uzimeri.

"Oh, come on," began Tanya. "You haven't said anything else since—"

Mrs. Kontos-Wu started to rise. "E-excuse me," she said.

"Of course." Uzimeri slid out from his seat to let Mrs. Kontos-Wu pass. She hurried away to aft, down the corridor. The sounds of her sobs echoed off the bulkheads.

It was finally Tanya who broke the silence around the table.

"It is difficult," she said, "for all of us at first."

Whatever their intentions may have been at the beginning of the day, after dinner, none of them—not Mrs. Kontos-Wu, not Uzimeri nor Chenko nor Pitovovich—seemed inclined to bring Stephen any more up to speed. So that night, Stephen decided to take the matter into his own hands. He went to see the Children.

They were holed up in the officer's section. It wasn't far—nothing was far on the antique Russian submarine—but it felt to Stephen as though he were passing through a time zone when he stepped through the round hatchway and into the wood-panelled corridor leading to the Captain's suite. They'd placed one of their Romanian monks there as a guard, and Stephen half-expected trouble from him. But he just looked at Stephen, nodded, and said in imperfect Russian: "Go on through. Zhanna is expecting you. Third hatch on left."

Stephen passed four rooms before Zhanna's, each one open—each with a small form swaddled in thick wool blankets on the narrow bed. They weren't really that small. Zhanna's crew of "children" were mostly in their teens. Over the course of his stay, he'd seen two of them—but understood there were seven that had stayed behind on the submarine after the encounter with Shadak's boat in the Atlantic. The children all seemed to be sleeping now—one, a heavyset boy with his hair cut very short, lay on his back snoring softly as Stephen tiptoed past.

He had no trouble finding Zhanna's cabin. Light from it painted a sickly yellow square on the opposite side of the corridor. Zhanna was sitting up at the room's little desk. She smiled at Stephen when he appeared in the doorway.

"Not a step further," she said.

"All right." He raised his hands palm outward. "I'll stay here."

"Good. Because you know, if you think you can pull anything—I've got a man in the cabin behind you and to fore with a gun aimed at your back. Go ahead—look."

"A gun in a submarine?" Stephen turned around and peered into the cabin across the hall. A man peered back at him with glassy, determined eyes. He held an old Russian automatic pistol, aimed straight at Stephen's chest. "You sure that's wise?"

"I don't expect to have to use it," said the man, his deep voice taking on the accent and cadence of Zhanna's. "Just don't get any ideas."

"Why would I get any ideas?"

The Romanian meat puppet continued: "You're the right hand of the evil bastard Fyodor Kolyokov; you've received instructions from him, from the lips of his operative Mrs. Kontos-Wu, to deal with us and bring us home to him; you are a young man—and I, I am told, am a beautiful woman who many men desire. And I cannot see your thoughts to put my mind at ease on any of these things. So I am taking a precaution."

"Okay, well first off—you don't have to worry about me ravaging—" he stopped himself, then turned back to Zhanna, whose eyelids were fluttering with the effort of controlling her commandeered bodyguard. "Could you please stop that? I came to talk to *you*. Not some—some surrogate mouthpiece."

Zhanna blinked and looked at Stephen. She took a deep breath, and patted her chest and shoulders. "Just so we understand one another," she said.

"Perfectly."

"You may sit down," She motioned toward her narrow bunk. Stephen sat so that he had a good view of both Zhanna and the Romanian guard outside.

"I have some questions," he said.

Zhanna turned around to face him. She crossed one leg over the other and smiled. "I like questions."

"Um. Okay. First, I want to know about your son."

"My son?" She frowned. "Oh! Vladimir! Yes—he is my son. You must excuse me. I don't usually think of him that way."

"Why's that? You gave birth to him."

"Yes. And I carried him for nine months. But he was not given me in the regular way. No husband—no sex. Just a long needle and a doctor. Do you know that technically, I am still a virgin?"

"Um, right. No. I didn't."

"It is true. For I have lived only among brothers and sisters. And the few technicians and scientists that maintained City 512 after the Revolution. Now some of those desired me, and I might have—but they were filthy old men who—"

Stephen interrupted. "Vladimir?" he said.

"Oh yes—of course. Forgive me, Stephen." Spots of red appeared in Zhanna's pale cheeks, and she looked down at her hands. "I don't talk to people—I mean, *just* talk to people—without knowing their thoughts also. It is unusual, this—talk. Having to guess what you are thinking of me as we talk." Zhanna looked back up and met Stephen's eyes. "Ask your questions."

"What is Vladimir?" said Stephen. "Ilyich Chenko claimed the baby could speak when he was born."

"Vladimir could speak long before he was born," said Zhanna. "We had many conversations as I carried him. That is how we were able to leave—to make it all the way to this submarine without being caught or killed. Vladimir guided us all. I think he spoke his first words—" she squinted one eye and looked away, as though trying to remember "—after four months. 'We must rejoin the others,' he said to me. 'It is nearly time.' You asked me what Vladimir is—not who. That is a good way to phrase the question."

Stephen waited. "And the answer is—?"

"I don't know," said Zhanna. "I don't think that Vladimir knows. He is something that they had been planning for a very long time. But I do not think they know what he is either."

"You mean *they*," said Stephen, "as in City 512."

"At least," said Zhanna. "Yes. They at City 512, at the very least of it. We were all a part of a grand experiment there. Each generation, would be better and brighter and more nimble than the last. Do you know that our grandparents could barely manage to dream-walk if they were locked in an isolation tank? That the slightest breath of air would send them scurrying back into their bodies? That they could only communicate properly with poor wretches—who had been conditioned for years to open their thoughts to a dream-walker? They could barely stand the sea. And now—look at us! Look at . . . Hey. What is happening with your face?"

Stephen started, sat up. "What do you mean?"

Zhanna leaned forward and squinted. "Colour is draining from it. Your eyes are looking down at your hands. And you were shaking your head. What does that mean?"

"You can't read my mind," he said, "so you have no idea—do you?"

There was a shuffling in the hallway as the Romanian crossed it and stepped into the room. He brought the barrel of the gun up to Stephen's face. "You are playing with me," he said in a voice like Zhanna's. "You think that because I cannot read your mind that you have the upper hand in this."

"I don't think I have the upper hand in this," said Stephen carefully. "I don't think I have *any* hand in this."

The Romanian jerked the gun away, and raised it over his head, as if to strike. Stephen took a breath. But he didn't flinch away.

"Would you like to fuck him?" said the Romanian.

"What?"

The Romanian stared at him matter-of-factly. "You like to lie with men, and not women. That is what Kontos-Wu knows for a fact. So there is no hope for you and I. But perhaps—I thought with this one . . ."

Stephen turned to Zhanna and stared at her. He had no idea what to say.

Zhanna opened her eyes. The Romanian shook his head, looked at the gun in his hand, at Zhanna, at Stephen. He muttered something in a reverent tone and stepped away. Stephen wondered if this guy had had any idea that he'd just been offered up as a sex toy by his high priestess.

Zhanna put a hand to her forehead and scrunched her eyes shut. Her mouth tightened.

"Hey," said Stephen. He reached across and patted Zhanna's knee. *More fucking tears*, he thought with an unkindness that made him ashamed. "Don't cry," he said.

Zhanna stopped. She put her hand on Stephen's, pulled it further up the fabric of her pants. She rolled her chair towards him. "Can it be—?" she said, eyes widening with a creepy kind of optimism.

Stephen yanked his hand away. Zhanna took it like a slap on the face.

"I'm sorry!" she bawled, pulling her hands to her chest, raising her knees to her chin. "I'm sorry! I'm no good at this, Stephen! No good!"

Stephen was jolted by a sudden spark of empathy. It was not unlike the times when he thought he'd gotten into Richard's skull, or walked behind Amar Shadak's eyelids. This poor girl had lived her life in this City 512. Everyone she spoke to, she did through the stark honesty of Discourse. Those who didn't have the talent or training to speak back were open books to her. If a man wanted to sleep with her, he'd broadcast his intentions clearly—even though his eyes might be discreetly averted and his hands busied with paperwork or at a computer keyboard. Zhanna had lived a life without guesswork. She was about as intuitive as Stephen was psychic.

Stephen reached out again. He put his hand on Zhanna's trembling shoulder.

"I'm sorry," he said. "Look. Don't—don't cry. But I'll lay it out for you. Your intelligence is good on one thing: I'm queer. Here's another fact Mrs. Kontos-Wu might not know: I'm HIV positive. You know what that means?"

"Y-yes," said Zhanna. She nuzzled Stephen's hand with her chin. "You've got the AIDS. I am sorry."

"It's shitty," Stephen agreed. "But I'm not exactly sick with AIDS yet. I've just got the virus—and I'm not going to go spreading it around here."

Zhanna opened her eyes and looked at him with fierce determination. "One day, we will cure the AIDS."

"That's what they say," said Stephen.

"No," she said, firmly, "one day *we* will cure the AIDS. That will be a part of the new world that we design."

Stephen smiled.

"New world. It's no wonder that they're making a religion out of you with ambitions like that."

Zhanna lifted her head and snorted derisively. "The religion. That's foolishness. Like the Babushka nonsense."

"Babushka." Stephen sighed with inward relief; it looked as though Zhanna was as anxious to steer the conversation back to normalcy as he was. "There's that word again. Who is Babushka?"

"Ask me questions I can answer," said Zhanna. "I'm not sure who Babushka is. She contacted Vladimir when he was two months old. She convinced him that he could come to North America—arrange passage there—and together, they could bring everyone together. End the oppression. Now that Vladimir is there, however—he's not so sure. Babushka—whatever, whoever she is—she's the one who turned this into a religion. And that wasn't what any of us wanted."

"That's right," said Stephen. "Vladimir wanted to do the Spartacus thing." Zhanna gave him a quizzical look. "Free the slaves," he explained. "That's what he told Ilyich Chenko. And now—now he's with this Babushka, against his will?"

Zhanna nodded.

"Is that where we're going then? To Babushka?"

"Not right away," said Zhanna, "and when we do, we'll not go by ourselves."

"Then when—and with who?"

"After we go deep," said Zhanna, "to Petroska Station. We need the help of the Mystics. And we have to go deep to find them."

"Mystics?" said Stephen. "Petroska Station? Who are—?"

Zhanna stopped him. "Stephen," she said, "I am sorry. But no more questions. I must—I must talk with my brothers and sisters for a while. This communication in the Physick is exhausting. And there will just be more pain if we keep it up longer."

"I'll go." He pushed himself up and slid into the dark corridor. The guard was gone when he got to the hatchway back to the part of the submarine reserved for mortals. Stephen ducked through it and slunk his way back to his cabin.

Stephen lay in his bunk with his eyes shut. Below him, Konstantine Uzimeri kept up a regular, wheezing snore that mingled with the irregular drone of the engines, and the clanking of the pipes over their heads. Occasionally, Stephen could hear the clattering and clanking as the Romanian crew went about their business operating the old Foxtrot submarine. Stephen watched the multicoloured patterns of retinal ghosts crawl across the inside of his eyelids. They could be anything, he thought, as he drifted off to sleep. They could be squids—seven of them now, submarinal giants with deep eyes and tentacles as long as a ship—following in the frothing wake of the Foxtrot, as it dove ever deeper to its rendezvous with the Mystics in Petroska Station.

They could be squids. They could be anything.

THE IDIOT
ИДИОТ

Alexei gasped and blinked in eye-stinging heat. His spit felt cold on his tongue as he sucked steam over it. He coughed as the steam hit his lungs. He sniffed at a strange and familiar scent, of rising bread and boiling cabbage and pine and struggled to focus his eyes on something in the hazy darkness.

"Aie, shit," he said. Alexei was surprised, pleased even, to hear his own deep man-voice. He ran his hand over his steam-slicked shoulders, the thick hair on his chest. "I'm back."

In the darkness, another voice chuckled. "Back, are you?"

"Who is there?"

Alexei came more to himself each passing second. He knew he was sitting on a wooden bench; his feet dangled to touch what felt like bare stone, cold as ice in the heat of this room. He blinked again, and now he saw a shape—a lean figure of a man, lolling naked on another bench across this strange, log-hewn room.

"Hello, Alexei," said the man. "I am Vasili Borovich. They call me the *Koldun* here. Welcome to the bathhouse, my cousin. And welcome home."

Alexei squinted. "Home?"

"For all purposes—yes. You have slept a long time. Nearly two days. I know that seems a terribly long time, but there you are."

Actually, it didn't seem that long at all. As far as he was concerned, he'd spent literally months in the strange metaphor of his recollections. But he just nodded.

The Koldun, Vasili Borovich, smiled at him. "What did you dream?" he asked.

Alexei started to answer—to talk about the onionskins of his memories, the spy school and the psychic stuff and the sleeper school which were all lies or so he thought—and then a familiar reflex took over.

"I don't remember," he said.

The Koldun leaned forward and peered at him—as though trying to read something in his eye, spot the object of the truth and pull it out of him. Evidently he couldn't find it, because he finally blinked and just shrugged.

"It will come to you," he said. "That is fine."

"I am sure," said Alexei. He looked skeptically around the log-hewn room. "So this is home. Where exactly, Mister Koldun, is home?"

"You don't remember your dream—it's not likely you'll remember this place."

Alexei shrugged now. The Koldun smiled, and raised his hands, looked around.

"The village," he said, "of New Pokrovskoye. It is home for us all."

"If you say so," said Alexei.

The Koldun's smile faltered and his eyes narrowed, and Alexei found his hands going to cover his privates.

"You don't remember it as home. But the Babushka has prepared it for you. You and your cousins. You should be very grateful."

"The Village of New Pokrovskoye." Alexei rolled the word around in his mouth. It did come easily—more easily, say, than City 512—or Murmansk. "You should thank Babushka for me."

"I will—pass it along."

"So I have been asleep for two days?"

The Koldun nodded.

"Are you in charge of this place?"

The Koldun hesitated. "No," he finally said. "Well, that is not true. I am—transitionally in charge. But I will not be for very long."

"And this place is my home."

"You are coming back to yourself. Good."

"I'm only repeating," said Alexei.

"You know, we are not going to accomplish anything sitting here in the bathhouse." The Koldun slid down off the bench and drifted through the steam to the door. He turned back to Alexei and beckoned.

"Come," he said. "It is time to go outside."

Alexei followed the Koldun through the door, into a small antechamber. It was colder here, and small. The two had to shuffle and dodge to keep out of contact with one another. The floor was bare rock and Alexei curled his toes against the cool. He felt gooseflesh run up and down his arms, the backs of his thighs. There was a little window that was frosted with condensation. It admitted a cool, blue light to the tiny room. Beside the window was a door of wooden planks.

"Ready, Alexei?" The Koldun smiled over his shoulder as he pulled on a wrought iron handle and pushed the door open.

The sky held the consistency of fine marble—little lines of white transgressing a perfect blue dome that covered the world like the ceiling of a cathedral. Alexei drew a lungful of the cool, maritime air as he stepped naked out of the bathhouse. The sweat and steam cooled on him and ran down his flanks in little rivulets. If this one was a trick, he thought to himself, it was a good one.

"Name the smells," said the Koldun.

Alexei frowned—crinkled his nose.

"Pine needles," he said. "Mushrooms. A lady's perfume."

"Interesting," said the Koldun. "Myself, I smell the city. Engine oil. Exhaust fumes. You, I think, are more in the Babushka's favour than I today."

"Babushka?" Alexei squinted down the hill. There was supposed to be a village there, but all he could see was the tops of thin scrub, and farther off, the ocean. "You mentioned her inside. Who is she?"

The Koldun laughed. "You wouldn't know her by name—but you will have felt her in your dreams. You might have even dreamed of her. If you did, you smelled her, most likely. One day when you smelled a peculiar smell, a short time ago perhaps—did it not change your destiny?"

"My *destiny*?" Alexei frowned. "Burnt sugar," he said. "I smelled it on a man's breath, who pulled me from the ocean. It caused me to lie to him."

The Koldun nodded. "The Babushka favours you," he said. "As to who she is? She is the one who made this place—her and some others whose names and bones are lost."

"Is that so?"

"Yes. She was one of the first to come here—one of a small group of agents like yourself. Sent here to establish a base of operations for the dreaming army."

"And where," said Alexei, "is here? Don't say New Pokrovskoye."

The Koldun laughed. "We're in Labrador, which is a part of Canada no one much goes to. We established it to keep a close eye on the NATO base at Goose Bay. We keep it now—well, let me just say that it suits our purposes, past and present."

Alexei stomped his bare feet on the rock. He took another breath. This time, the smells were gone.

"We are in New Pokrovskoye, and Labrador. And you call yourself a Koldun."

Borovich smiled and nodded.

"That's an old name," said Alexei. "It means that you are a village wizard." He waggled his fingers. "Casting charms on people and such."

The Koldun shrugged. He gestured to the log building behind them. "There is my sauna," he said. A village Koldun, Alexei knew, spent a lot of time in saunas. "A good place to meditate. I do not cast many charms, though."

"Except metaphorically," said Alexei. "Tell me—did you preside over the awakening of all the newcomers to—" he snapped his fingers.

"New Pokrovskoye."

"Right."

"No."

"Another question, and I won't trouble you. You talked about a 'dreaming army.'"

"I did," said the Koldun.

"Am I dreaming now?" said Alexei.

The Koldun laughed. "Truly," he said, "that is a question I cannot reliably answer. Come over here—" he gestured around the side of the structure. "We should put some clothes on you. Your balls are as small as pebbles in the cold."

A few minutes later, Alexei was dressed in a pair of cotton trousers and a thick woollen sweater—clothing he'd never seen before but which nevertheless fit him perfectly—and walking down the hill with the Koldun.

He regarded the smaller man. The Koldun was old. Maybe he was old as Kolyokov was these days. But he was in much better shape. His hair was all there, and still mostly black, combed back into a thick ponytail. His beard had borne the years more vividly—it was streaked with grey and white where it drooped below his chin. Alexei felt as though he ought to like this Koldun character, and in many ways he did. A Koldun, at least as far as Alexei remembered from his mother's stories, was a wizard true enough—but force of good in a community. And this one seemed to be that. He had, after all, pulled Alexei from the pits of dream; helped him back into himself; answered his questions as best he could; and given Alexei clothes and a bath.

But Alexei could have said the same things about Holden Gibson—and he didn't like or trust that old bastard at all.

And on the subject of Gibson . . .

"I came here with some people," said Alexei. "In a big boat. A yacht. I don't see them here."

The Koldun put up his hand to hush him.

"In time," he said, "you'll see them all."

Alexei frowned. Something was in the Koldun's tone he didn't like.

"What about the children?"

The Koldun looked at Alexei sidelong, and smiled.

"In time, Kilodovich," he said. "In time."

They had been walking down a broad, rocky pathway between planted rows of small conifer trees. The path was ending now, intersecting another at a wooden platform from which a long, precarious stair descended down a cliffside. For the first time, Alexei got a proper view of the village.

He made an appreciative noise.

The village spread below them to the left and right, hugging the crescent of a wide and stony harbour like lichen. It seemed to Alexei that it was snatched not out of time, but memory. The houses were all of dark log, neatly cut with bright window trims and great red and green beams along the spines of their wood-shingled roofs. Did a village such as this ever truly exist a century ago? Probably not. But its sight filled Alexei with an almost painful nostalgia—far from his just-relived memories of City 512, this was the place he wished to have come from.

Past the water's edge, it seemed as though another village began—this one stretching up long docks and out to the harbour's middle. It was a village of boats—and a strange, incongruous collection of boats. There were fishing boats, with netting gathered at their sterns like dark peacock plumage; narrow wooden sailboats, painted outrageously in brilliant primary colours; long canoes with outboard motors dangling off their backs; a little cabin cruiser, painted like the sailboats; and at the end of the longest pier, a plainer motor yacht that dwarfed the rest. Alexei recognized it immediately as Holden Gibson's.

"This is a forward base?" Alexei frowned. "Pretty conspicuous, I'd think, for that kind of work."

The Koldun laughed. "Not at all. No one knows about it who doesn't live here."

"Of course not."

It occurred to Alexei then that the Koldun's words might have meant something else—that the place didn't exist but for those who lived here—that it was nothing more than a dream. *Nothing is real*. Alexei was beginning to think this was a more and more reasonable proposition.

The Koldun leaned on the railing of the strange staircase. He spared Alexei a brief but penetrating glance.

"Tonight," he said, "there will be a dance in the town. You should come to that; we'll maybe talk some more. But I don't think a lot of talking is what you need now. You don't remember anything. So what you need is a lot of thinking—yes?"

"If you say so," said Alexei.

"Don't come down to the town straight away," said the Koldun. "No point in seeing too much at once. Go to the lighthouse for now. When more people come, they'll be billeted there. But for now, no one but you."

"You have a lighthouse here? Is there shipping?"

The Koldun laughed. "No shipping. Just what you see here. The lighthouse was here when I came. There's a story behind that. But for later."

Alexei was puzzled—he had half a mind to protest, to go down the stairs to the town. But he had to admit, the idea of food and rest was tempting.

"All right," said Alexei. "Which way?"

The Koldun waved a hand to his right. "That path," he said, "takes you straight there. I've got some business to attend to in town—more new arrivals to greet, I'm afraid. So if it's all right, you just go off on your own—take it easy for a couple of hours? Yes?"

"Sure," said Alexei. He waited until the Koldun had disappeared over the edge of the staircase—listened as the older man's footfalls diminished down the rock side—before he set off down his own path.

The path led Alexei along a high ridge of sea-weathered rock, over the town and toward the lighthouse. The path was lined with brilliant yellow wildflowers here, their shoots encroaching on Alexei's stride. The nearer he came to the lighthouse, the narrower the ridge became. Alexei could barely maintain his footing. How the hell did they get the trucks and machinery out here they'd need to build the thing?

It was the least of the mysteries that this strange hamlet presented. Quite aside from the peculiar tug on memory that the place presented to him—the discomforting aura of comfort—it was difficult to imagine how the people here had managed to keep it hidden; particularly given the Koldun's explanation that this village was nothing less than a forward base for old Soviet espionage activities.

No, Alexei decided. This Koldun character was lying—or at the very least, not telling the whole of the truth.

Alexei stepped up to the door of the lighthouse, and paused to examine the stonework. This building was no Cold War relic—even to Alexei's untrained eye, it was clear it was no younger than a century. It looked like it was made out of hand-cut limestone, in the fashion of a fortification. What had been in this isolated harbour before the Koldun and his crew had come here?

He shrugged, and smiled to himself. The Koldun had been right about one thing: Alexei needed some time to think things through more than he needed to ask questions. He pulled the heavy wooden door open and stepped into the cool dimness of the lighthouse's base.

Alexei let the door swing shut behind him as he stepped into the middle of the lighthouse's deep silo. Planks creaked as he shifted his weight. The floor here was dark, but the glow of the afternoon leaked past the wooden stairs that crawled up the inside of the tower to the light room. And the Koldun wasn't lying about other things: there were cots lined against the curving walls, with clean white linen and yellow wool blankets folded at their feet. A card table was set up in the middle, and atop that a cloth-covered dish bulging in ways suggestive of bread and meats. A metal jug held water, and Alexei poured some of it into one of the cups beside it. Under the table, Alexei spotted a bottle of Smirnoff vodka—but he felt it best to leave it alone for now.

So was this a dream then? The water was cold on Alexei's lips and it made a very convincing line of coolness down his middle as he swallowed it. But the water he'd dreamed drinking the past two months was just as convincing—less sweet, more brackish, but very realistic nonetheless. So sure—he could be dreaming. He could be a sleeping child now in the depths of City 512, recasting his future into the life of a former secret agent who'd somehow wound up in this lighthouse drinking a cup of nice sweet water. That might have been the dream. He might have another dream ahead of him. . . .

Alexei pulled the cloth off the food. The bread was thick and white and looked as though it had been freshly baked. Beside it were slices of a dark sausage, infused with garlic and thick clots of fat. Alexei took some meat and some bread and made himself an open-faced sandwich. He bit into it. Tasted good.

"Not a bad dream, if that's what it is," he said to no one. "No point in spoiling it by sleeping."

Sandwich in hand, Alexei made his way past the cots with their convincingly fresh linen, to the base of the stairs. He wanted to see what the view was like from the top—before the daylight spent itself back to darkness.

Alexei could see a fair distance from the aerie. He found one road leading inland, but it ended at the gleaming roofs of what Alexei took to be a long, low set of greenhouses, maybe a kilometre off. They formed a cruciform around a tin-roofed structure that climbed two storeys more. Just beyond that, Alexei could make out what looked like concrete pads—and some long, low buildings with flat roofs and low chimneys. Thin gravel roads crawled between them. But beyond that, the land was barren. Alexei shook his head. What kind of a village these days doesn't even have a concession road coming in to service it?

Someplace like City 512, perhaps? Alexei settled back into the canvas chair next to the lamp assembly. It could follow. If that was real—if this was real—if the things that Alexei had learned about himself were anything approaching the truth.

The Koldun may have been lying about everything else—but one thing he had gotten right. Alexei needed some time to think this through.

First point. It was clear to him that the Russians—his masters—were operating a sleeper agent program. Alexei had gone through a raft of programming to become one of these sleeper agents—men and women who were operated remotely by psychics who could, at the drop of a hat, fly through the air or pass through walls like ghosts. He had gone to a training school called City 512 to learn how to be a sleeper. And the memories he carried could not be trusted.

"Fine," said Alexei aloud. The false memories included potentially several layers: one, of his education as a KGB assassin somewhere near Murmansk. Alexei was unclear as to why, however, such a false memory would be implanted in a sleeper agent who was meant to spy on the Americans. Unless he was meant to spy on someone else. Someone . . . nearer.

"Aha," said Alexei aloud. That could be it. Alexei Kilodovich was a manufactured KGB assassin—made, perhaps, by one of the many factions of politicians in the Kremlin who wished to have an ace up their sleeve for this purpose. Why not have one of their assassins empowered to turn on his Comrades if necessary? He was an insurance policy for some ambitious Communist.

"But," said Alexei as he chewed on his sandwich. What of the dream-walking? He had assuredly, at least in the early stages of his life, been vetted to become one of the puppet-masters. Fyodor Kolyokov had indicated he was a complete failure at dream-walking.

And yet, had he not prevented the old poet's execution—based on his own sudden intuition? Had he not predicted the arrival of General Rodionov?

Why, if Alexei were enough of a psychic to do that, had Fyodor Kolyokov cast him down into the company of untalented sleeper agents?

Alexei crossed his arms and looked out the glass. There was, of course, one easy answer.

This all might have been a dream. All, nothing but shit.

Alexei had been sulking over the view for nearly an hour when he spotted the lone figure making his way along the path to the lighthouse. "Aha," he said aloud. It was James, the shaven-headed fellow who'd pulled him from the sea on Holden Gibson's yacht. Alexei leaned on the railing around the circumference of the light room as James approached the lighthouse—then made his way down the stairs as the door opened.

Alexei watched from the stairs as James came in. He looked to the left and the right. Alexei was about to shout hello, when a glint of metal in James' hand caught his eye. The shout caught in his throat, and Alexei pulled back on the stairs and stilled his breath.

The glint was from the barrel of a gun.

No dream, thought Alexei.

James squinted up to where Alexei had hidden himself. James moved to the base of the stairs and raised the gun.

It looked like Holden Gibson's Glock semiautomatic. James held it in both hands, one elbow crooked so he could sight along it. He'd aimed it along the curve of the wall—if it fired now, the bullet might hit Alexei in a ricochet. But if James saw Alexei—it would be nothing to adjust the aim a degree up and another to the left, and shoot him there.

James started up the stairs. He blinked, as his eyes adjusted—and the barrel of the gun moved up and to the left and trained on Alexei's chest.

"Russkie," he said—in a voice that seemed not his own. "I got you, Russkie. Don't fuckin' move."

"I am not moving," said Alexei.

"Good." James wasn't moving either. He stood in what seemed an impossibly uncomfortable position, aiming the gun at Alexei's chest, while he spoke in that strange, incongruous voice.

"Now, I want you to tell me simple. How the fuck come you've been thinkin' about nothing but killing me?"

"Ah—don't be upset, James. But I've barely thought about you at all."

James stood as a statue. "I meant Gibson. Not—not me. How the fuck come you been thinking about nothing but killing fucking Holden Gibson?"

Alexei squinted. He thought about City 512; about what he'd learned from his childhood; about the dream-walking and Fyodor Kolyokov, and the horrifying dance for General Rodionov, and everything else. He looked closely at James.

"Holden Gibson?" he said. "Is that you?"

"Hold the fuck still!" The statue of James was screaming at the top of its lungs. "Hold still or I'll fuckin' kill you! Now why the fuck do you want to kill me?"

Alexei was amazed. It *was* Holden Gibson standing there—holding his own gun on Alexei. He somehow inhabited the body of his worker James. Gibson was to James—what Fyodor Kolyokov had been to Alexei all those years: his puppet-master.

"Get out," said Alexei. He willed it.

James/Gibson's composure began to waver. The hands trembled—and suddenly, it was as though James' strings had been cut. James stumbled back, the gun went down, and it slipped from his numb fingers and clattered down the stairs.

"Jesus." James leaned against the wall staring at his empty hands, then up at the golden light now trickling down from aerie. By the time he looked down the stairs to the lighthouse's main room, Alexei had already jumped down, retrieved the gun, and trained it on James' chest.

"He's gone from you now, isn't he?"

James blinked down at him. "You." He raised his hands over his head, and flinched.

"Relax," said Alexei. "I'm not likely to shoot you if you keep still."

James did relax a little.

"S-so," he said. "You look . . . well. You get your memory back?"

"My memory—?" Alexei stopped himself. Of course—for him, it was months ago that he'd told that peculiar lie on the deck of Gibson's ship: A knock on the head had knocked memory out his ear like pool water after a swim. "I think I'm doing better now, thank you." He paused, and stepped closer to the base of the stairs. "How about you?"

"Me?"

"Yes. How's your memory doing, James?"

"Well . . ." The stairs creaked as James shifted his weight. "Do you—do you mind if I sit down? I'm kind of stiff for some reason."

Alexei nodded. "Sure." The poor kid was probably cramping, what with the amount of time Holden Gibson had kept him standing still. "Just keep your hands in sight."

James lowered himself to the steps. Once he was seated, he extended first one leg and then the other. His joints cracked like an old man's.

"You didn't answer my question," said Alexei. "How's your memory? Do you remember, for instance, how you got here?"

James settled his left leg back to the steps. "I do not," he said.

"You showed up here with this gun and a mind to shoot me."

James shook his head in bafflement. "The last thing I remember was dreaming. I was back at school—Kindergarten. In Illinois. I was so small . . ."

Is that how it goes? Alexei wondered. When one of the bastards comes in and takes over your body, they send you back to school? Some memory like that? Alexei recalled many dreams such as that through his career—and (here, he shuddered) hadn't he just spent the past two months or so remembering his school days in a vivid, unending nightmare?

James was still dwelling on his own. "—and at play time, the Barker twins took my Big Wheel and—"

"That's bullshit," said Alexei , and James' eyes went wide.

"Don't shoot me!"

Alexei noticed that at some point he'd raised the gun for emphasis, training it between James' rounded eyes. He lowered it now.

"Sorry," he said. "I've had enough grade school reminiscences to last me a while. Tell me the last thing you remember. Before coming here?"

"Well—I went to sleep last night. I was really tired—they've got us working in the scaling house most days . . . I just washed up and went to bed."

"They have you scaling fish?"

"That's my new job," said James. "Part of my—re-education."

"Too bad," said Alexei. "So you went to bed. And the next thing you know—"

"Here I am."

"Here you are."

"Right."

They regarded one another quietly for a moment.

"What's Holden up to lately?"

James shrugged. "Don't know, really. He seems to sleep a lot."

"Of course he does."

James must have read something into Alexei's expression, because he squirmed uncomfortably. "Hey—you're—you're not going to beat me up again, are you?"

"Beat you up again?"

James gave him a worried look.

"I have no recollection of ever beating you up," said Alexei. "Just," he added, thinking it through, "as you have no recollection of coming here with a gun belonging to Holden Gibson to shoot me." Alexei lowered the gun to his side. There really was no need—the puppet masters were gone for now. It was just Alexei and James. Alexei felt a tugging in his chest. He flipped on the safety and stuffed the gun barrel-first into the back of his pants.

"No, James. I'm not going to beat you up. Come on down. There's some food here. Let's eat and talk."

James looked relieved. "Thanks," he said. He winced as his cramping muscles pulled him to his feet.

When one has suffered a very bad trauma—a rape, a beating, a terrible childhood spent with cruel and demanding parents—there always comes a point at which it is good to talk about it. And not just with a psychotherapist, who can at best understand the trauma intellectually. The point comes where one must speak with someone who has gone through the same thing—or one so similar as to be indistinguishable. Even among men who are otherwise complete strangers. Such a conversation can lead all sorts of places—not the least of which is simple insight.

So it went with Alexei and James as they tore through the rest of the cold cuts, and got into the vodka. The talk they had ranged on for hours, until the light from the top of the tower dimmed and diminished into a cool blue, and the base became dark and cold.

James did most of the talking. The mind control stuff was new to him—or so he claimed. But the abuse he underwent at Holden Gibson's hand was a lifetime's worth. He'd been with Gibson since he was eight or so—he at this point only had vague memories of his life before that, and most of those memories centred on school, not his parents. Gibson, he said bitterly, had no doubt done a thorough job of erasing those memories, so he could use James for his own purposes.

"Did he—"

"Feel me up? What do you think?" James swallowed his vodka too quickly and coughed.

"Since you brought it up . . ."

"No. At least—I can't remember."

"So what did he do?"

"*Used* us."

Gibson had a succession of houses and ranches—or at least the use of them—dotted across the U.S. and Canada. Some of the places were quite nice—big estate homes on the edges of nice little college towns, or near defence contractors. There were a couple of farms—and boats. Gibson would move his "family" around for weeks at a time. Once there, he'd set up shop and start the business. The magazine sales racket that Alexei had stumbled across on board the yacht was just one enterprise of many, and they covered the whole range. One month, they'd be selling chocolates for fictitious school fundraisers; the next, running dope for one of Holden's contacts in Seattle; three months later, picking pockets in train stations.

"There has to be an easier way for someone like Gibson to make a buck," said Alexei.

"What do you mean?"

Alexei poured himself another mug of vodka. "I'm just saying—he can . . . get into your head, make you do what he wants. . . . Why make you pick pockets?"

"No no no," said James, his voice slurring with the vodka. "I like pickin' pockets. I don' think he did that mind stuff too much—until lately."

Alexei patted James' arm. "Sure he didn't."

"But he was always a prick," said James. "I remember he locked me in the trunk of his car—well, not his car—this stockbroker guy whose house we were using. . . ."

"That's terrible," said Alexei.

At length, Alexei began to talk about his own pain.

"The worst," he said, "is not being able to remember anything."

"Oh yeah—the amn- amen—amnesia." James tapped his forehead.

"No. That was bullshit. I'm talking about not being able to remember anything at all . . . reliably. I have memories—but they're not full. For instance—I can recall being in Moscow in 1986—I remember that: Alexei was in Moscow. But do you know what comes to mind when I think of it?"

James shook his head.

"Nothing! That's what. Just words: *Alexei worked for a guy in Belarus until last year*. If I think hard I can remember an address where I lived; a part of a telephone number, maybe some street names. But nothing—nothing of the senses. I don't think I was ever in Belarus—do you know that?"

"That's fucked up," said James.

"Yes," said Alexei, "it is. But," he added, not wanting to make James feel badly having been outdone, "your story is fucked up too."

"Thank you."

They clinked their mugs together.

Fyodor Kolyokov's afterlife had become like the ocean he feared so much as a dream-walker—a great, chattering place where the language of the mind became a drowning medium; a metaphoric sea all its own.

A sea of Discourse.

It was useful to think of it in such a way, at any rate; metaphor had always been Kolyokov's lifeline in life—and here in death, it helped.

It helped a great deal in fact: for although a state might in some forms be inescapable, a metaphor sometimes pointed to an otherwise invisible exit.

And this sea—well, no matter how deep their bottoms, didn't all seas also have a surface?

Kolyokov apprehended that surface now—by pinpricks of light, wavering down through the tumult.

So Fyodor Kolyokov swam up to them. His metaphorical lungs strained, and the sea bottom called to him, but Kolyokov strove upwards. As he drew closer, he saw what those pinpricks were—they resolved into binocular pairs looking out upon a thousand vistas. They were, Kolyokov realized, the eyes of sleepers. A thousand sleepers, maybe more.

Many of the vistas were meaningless to Kolyokov; the back of a bus seat; a magazine article; a highway ahead, white dotted line strobing beneath the hood of a car.

But one—one caught Kolyokov's eye.

Kilodovich.

Kolyokov's penultimate hope.

With his last strength, Kolyokov swam towards the vision of Alexei Kilodovich—closer and closer, until the sleeper's vision became his own.

As he emerged into the young man's vodka-soaked consciousness, Kolyokov felt like a man who'd traded one drowning for another. Alcohol was one thing that made dream-walking difficult—if he had it himself, it would send him straight to a dreamless stupor; and in another . . . well, it was like trying to make sense to a drunk at a party. An exercise in frustration.

Nonetheless, this time he had to try. The young man was talking to Kilodovich—and before it was too late . . . before he had diminished too much to even make a peep—he had to take over that conversation himself.

But first—he listened, and watched. This was the first time he'd seen Kilodovich in weeks. The man looked good—healthy. He had a discolouration on his forehead, some kind of a bruise, but that looked to be healing now. If Kolyokov had still had lips, they would have pulled into a smile. *The boy looks good*, he thought.

The phantom smile vanished, however, as Kolyokov listened to what

Kilodovich was saying.

"The old bastard jerked me around like a puppet from the time I was a boy—just like you, James. He made me do God knows what—replaced my memories. Worked me like a Goddamn marionette. It would have been better"—Kilodovich paused to sip his drink—"it would have been better, you know, if he'd just sent me to a work camp. That, at least . . . That might have left me my soul."

"Hear hear!" said Kolyokov's host.

"Fuck Fyodor Kolyokov," said Alexei, raising his glass. "Fuck him, wherever he is!"

Kolyokov reached out, to take hold of his host's drunken lips and tongue and larynx. He grasped at them, but they slipped from his fingers again and again. Finally, Kolyokov let them be.

I wouldn't know what to say with them anyway, he thought miserably, as he sank back into the murk. He opened his throat, and let the metaphor of water, the spreading Discourse, flood into his lungs. *Drown me*, willed Kolyokov. *I'm done here. I am past done.*

THE INSULTED AND THE INJURED

Оскорблённые и униженные

Mi, thought Heather. *Mi mi mi mi*.

"Have some more tea," said the big bald man who had introduced himself as Miles. His friend, Richard, who looked about a hundred years old, wiped tears from his eye. Across the dining room of the little café, a table of fishermen avoided looking at them. The big bald man picked up the little steel teapot and started to pour it into Heather's mug. She put her hand over it. *Any more tea, and I'm going to be peeing a whole ocean*, she thought, then, as the tendrils of her master tickled behind her ear, remembered to stop thinking.

Mi! Mi mi mi mi!

"Okay," he said. "No tea for you. Richard?"

"Y-yes. P-please. Oh God."

Miles poured more into weeping Richard's cup. Hands trembling, the old man lifted it to his lips and slurped it noisily, like soup.

"You're wondering why my friend's crying?"

Mi, thought Heather.

"Well I'll tell you. Richard's a scientist. He spent—how long, Richard?"

"Oh God—thirty years! *Thirty years*!"

"Thirty years, at MIT. He was a full professor there for a while. Isn't that right, Richard?"

"Oh God!"

"Actually, Richard, you know God's got nothing to do with it. You were robbed of your life by a Devil, weren't you now?"

The old man shook his head and lowered it over his teacup. His sobbing intensified. *Mi*, thought Heather, and put her hand on his shoulder. *Mi mi mi mi*.

"O-one d-day," said Richard, "I-I just . . . left."

"And where did you end up?"

"E-E-E-E-"

"The *Emissary*," said Miles. "Say it, Richard."

"E-Emissary."

"Good man." Miles reached over and gingerly pulled Heather's hand off Richard's shoulder. "I know you think you're comforting him. But human contact—well. Old Richard's had enough of that."

You can fucking say that again, she thought.

Hey—bitch—go kill the fuckin' Russkie, said Gibson, from a corner of her mind.

Mi! Mi mi mi mi!

Miles smiled coolly. "Yeah. You had enough of that too, haven't you? Everybody here's like us, aren't they?"

Not—mi mi mi mi—not everybody. Heather glanced out the front window of the café, up the slope, to the greenhouse. The place where they all slept—all the ones that ran things around here. It was a sprawling thing like a giant cut diamond. At one end squatted a little outbuilding, fashioned out of cut logs, with little windows painted brightly. Its roof was highly peaked, and wood smoke billowed out of the top of it. How hot was it in there? she wondered. As hot as that bathhouse up the hill?

Okay, baby. I'm not gonna hurt you. Let me in.

She shut her eyes and summoned the mantra. Every time, it seemed more difficult to do. But she still could—the idea of Holden Gibson walking around in her brain—making her do stuff, like he was doing to everyone else on the crew . . .

Mi. Mi. Mi. Mi.

"So how'd you come here, little girl?" Miles gingerly set her hand back on the table in front of her. "Was it a smell? That was how we got the call—wasn't it, Richard?"

Richard nodded, still not looking up.

"I'm sitting in the donut shop across from the hotel. And I'm talking a donut shop in New York City. Manhattan. Nothing smells good in that donut shop. Closest thing is the stale dough they use to make their crullers. Otherwise it's piss and cigarettes and old coffee. But this smell—" Miles looked up at the ceiling, snapped his fingers "—what a smell—a—"

"—a-a m-mélange?"

"Yeah, Richard. A *mélange*. Good. You cheering up, buddy?"

In fact, Richard seemed to be doing just that. His old lips were still quivering, but they'd pulled back in a kind of a smile. He started to look up. "Pipe smoke," he said. "Baking bread. Rosewater."

"See? Richard smelled it too. Only not the same smells—just good smells. The stuff you smelled when you were a kid that let you know you were safe. I can't speak for Richard here, but when I caught my whiff I was pretty much bottomed out. I'd just remembered—well, never mind what I just remembered. I was bottomed out. But I caught that whiff, I knew what I had to do."

Richard nodded vigorously.

"I went back into the hotel lobby—isn't that right, buddy? Walked up to Richard here—and said to him: *Babushka*."

"Babushka." Richard repeated it like a line of liturgy at a prayer meeting.

"Yeah." Miles spared Richard a sidewise grin. "He said it back to me because he'd smelled the same smells. Or the same kind of smells. And he knew like me that it was time to go. So we went!"

Richard gulped down the rest of his tea, and nodded. "G-g-g-got bus tickets up to H-H-Halifax," he said. "The b-bus was pretty crowded."

Miles nodded. "A lot of people. But we got there early, hey bud? Found ourselves some seats near the back."

"Near the b-b-back."

"See, before—before I came here, I used to work in security. At the Emissary. So if I'm on a bus, or a plane, or whatever, I like to see what everybody's doing. I like to have my back to a wall."

"T-t-t-tell about the others."

"I'm getting there. So we get on the bus. Sit down. We didn't pack too much to bring with us."

"W-w-w-e knew we-we would be provided for."

"Right. Anyway—the bus is pretty empty at first. But after we stop in a few towns up the east coast, the bus starts to fill up. And it's like a family reunion.

"But you probably know all this. You probably got on a bus too—saw all these people you recognized, or thought you recognized."

It wasn't a bus. It was a boat. And yeah—that's what I thought.

Heather's hand twitched, as dreaming fingers reached around her momentarily forgotten mantra, tugged on the tendons in her wrist. *Good girl,* said the voice of Holden Gibson in her head. *That's how it goes . . . Now give it up, and rela—*

"Mi!"

Heads turned and the tearoom went quiet for a moment. Heather blinked, flexed her fingers, and smiled weakly at the fishermen who stared at her from their table by the window. *Mi mi mi mi mi,* she thought.

Miles gave her a funny look. "You're like Richard here, aren't you? All fucked up inside because of what those bastards did to you?"

Heather found herself nodding quickly—this time of her own accord, but not, still, because she completely agreed with Miles. She didn't want to go too deep on the question. Formulating a more complete answer would take thought. And thought would let Gibson back inside her, and then before you knew it, she'd be gone and Gibson . . .

Mi mi mi mi. The mantra—*mi*—was her only—*mi*—shield.

"It's amazing all the people they got over the years, isn't it?" said Miles. "Remember when we stopped in Boston? That's where Richard used to teach," he said in an aside to Heather, then turned back to Richard. "There were people who got on that bus that you hadn't seen in what—twenty years?"

"M-Mike B-Berry," said Richard.

"Right. He was one of your grad students."

Richard shook his head sadly and looked down again. "N-n-no," he said. "H-he o-only p-p-pretended to be."

Miles' face fell a bit. "True," he said. "We were all just pretending—weren't we?"

Heather started to get up. The last—*mi*—thing—*mi mi*—she needed was another—*mi mi mi mi*—morose conversation with another of the growing crowd of fucked-up freaks that were dropping into this town like mayflies.

Miles put his hand on her arm. His eyes held a sad desperation.

"Wait!" he said. "Don't leave us alone!"

Ah, fuck it, she thought. *How long can a girl keep this up?*

"Don't worry," she said, feeling herself slipping back into her own memories, the world fading in front of her, "you're never alone for long, here in the fuckin' village."

"Fuck," said Heather, sitting on the long porch outside the old Arts and Crafts building of the Transcendental Meditation camp. "Fuck!"

Hippie Pete crouched down beside her. "Swearing," he said, "can cause stress, and stress can take us further from the centre. Seek the centre, Heather."

Heather turned around and glared at him. "I'm pretty much *in* the fucking centre right now, aren't I Pete?"

The big man shrugged. "The centre is not an 'in,'" he said.

"Oh fuck—off," she said, and stood up. "I'm going for a walk."

Hippie Pete let her go. The first few times Heather had found herself back in this recollection since coming to the village, he'd been just about impossible to shake. Now, she could get rid of him any time she wanted. It seemed like mental holograms made of a boatload of false memories were no different than other men: given enough time and patience, you could train them one the same as the other.

Train them just like Holden had trained her and everyone else on the yacht. Maybe, the way someone had trained everyone else in this evil little village. Heather stomped down the crude stairway and along a green roadway between rows of man-planted cedars high enough to scratch cloud.

Now who the fuck, wondered Heather, *had trained Miles and Richard?*

She put that question at the end of the growing list she'd been making since she'd first seen the weird fairy tale fleet of boats, chugging and sailing and humming and rowing down on them through the sunrise, over the bow of the yacht.

Heather's head was swimming—that bastard Alexei had just brained her after all—and she thought she might have been hallucinating.

It wasn't just the weird colours they painted their boats, or the Halloween costumes they wore. Heather picked it up immediately, as the canoes bumped up against the side of the yacht and those strange brothers climbed on board to guide them into the harbour: the people here were strange—and not *Star Trek* fan strange, but really different-planet strange. They never quite looked at her when they were looking at her. They seemed to look through her and past her, and when they talked they talked to that space, and not Heather.

It freaked her out pretty significantly at first. When she came to on the bridge of Gibson's yacht, and looked out the windscreens, the first things she'd seen had been those strange banners, all red and green and orange. . . .

It was as though they were doing the Santa Claus Parade in boats.

Of course, the children caught her before she could make a fool out of herself.

"Don't worry lady," said one. "They're just celebrating—because we are home and united at last."

When she went out onto the aft deck, little Vladimir beamed at her from that bastard Alexei's arms. "We are delivered from our shackles," he said. "Ha! This is a great day, lady."

"Put him down," she'd hissed at Alexei. "You fucking monster."

Alexei didn't appear to hear her, but Vladimir giggled. "Alexei," he said, "is not here right now. He will join us later."

Heather nodded. It made the most sense of anything she'd seen or heard in the past few minutes. Maybe Alexei had gone to someplace like her Transcendental Meditation camp, and this guy who'd whacked her on the head was somebody completely different. Somebody else calling the shots.

"Good," said Vladimir. "You're not as stupid as you pretend to be."

Heather told him to fuck off and had gone back inside—where the rest of the crew were shaking their heads groggily amid fallen down chairs, and babbling to one another. James, for instance, was going on about kindergarten and some kind of tricycle. Sheri couldn't stop talking about a cabin her family had in Wisconsin—which didn't make any sense, because Heather remembered they'd picked up Sheri in Florida and her parents were dirt poor drunks who lived in a trailer park. Even stranger, Leonard was going on about elves and hobbits like he'd grown up in the freaking Shire.

Heather finally had to clap her hands and shout: "Hey! Reality check!"

Everyone stopped and stared at her.

"Where's Holden?" she said.

The crew parted, and looked down as if for the first time, to see Holden Gibson lying splayed on the floor, eyes open and staring sightlessly at the ceiling. Heather had to suppress a monstrously inappropriate laugh.

He appeared to be dead.

"Holy fuck," she whispered, wrestling back a smile.

"Shit," said James. "How'd I miss *that*?"

"Someone fucking killed him," said Sheri. She looked at Heather accusingly. Heather put her hands out in front of her, shook her head and widened her eyes in innocent denial.

"He's not dead," said Leonard, kneeling down and touching his throat. "Pulse."

"No," said a commanding voice from behind them. "He is not dead at all. Step away from him, sleepers."

Heather turned. Standing in the doorway was a tall man, fit, with a greying beard and long hair tied behind in a ponytail. He wore a long oilskin raincoat, and he was old enough to be Heather's grandfather. But that didn't seem to matter: he made her weak in the knees like he was a high school jock. And when he spoke, she obeyed the same as everyone else and stepped back.

"Well if it isn't old John Kaye," he said, looking down at her sleeping boss. "This might be the first time we meet in person, and still you can't see me. Well. What would she be bringing you here for?"

Gibson snorted in his sleep.

"Can't talk now, hmm? That's fine. But soon enough we'll meet again. And then we can speak a great deal."

John Kaye? Who the fuck is John Kaye? Heather wondered.

She would have asked the question—maybe even pointed out helpfully that this wasn't John Kaye but Holden Gibson and he was such an evil bastard that they'd do best to toss him into the ocean and have done with him before he came to. But she couldn't seem to make her mouth work.

"Until then," said the tall man, "we're going to have to find a better place for you to rest." He clapped his hands. "Sleepers! Take care of your dream-walker!"

Dream-walker?

And along with the rest of them, Heather had lurched to work. They hefted Holden onto one of the tables, and lifted it like a litter between six of them, to carry him out onto the deck. The children were gone when they got there. Heather thought she could see them out of the corner of her eye, crowded onto the deck of a fishing boat that was motoring away.

Alexei hadn't gone, though. He stood beside the old man—staring ahead with those creepy unseeing eyes of his. Heather wondered if he was in the same kind of thrall as the rest of them. And if he was, why wasn't he fucking well helping? The table weighed a ton.

But there were no answers that day—not from Alexei, who boarded the sailboat with Holden and the children and the old man—and not from any of the other crew, who all worked together, to steer the yacht alongside the flotilla of boats, first toward the coast and then through the rocky teeth of an inlet, and finally into a fantastical village's harbour.

Heather hadn't seen Alexei since. Indeed, it was only when she remembered to use the mantra that she was able to see much of anything. Once they came close to the docks, Heather had felt the world growing grey, her breathing slowing down—and there she was, back in the Transcendental Meditation camp, being stalked by that terrible giant Hippie Pete and completely oblivious to what was going on with her body.

And try as she might, she couldn't find another way out of the camp than drowning herself once more in the lake. Since she'd come to this creepy place, Heather figured she'd killed herself some nine times. Every time she forgot to say her mantra, it wouldn't take more than a few seconds—somebody would be there to come in and take over her mind.

Lately, that somebody appeared to be Holden Gibson. Or John Kaye, or whoever the fuck he really was.

That was something that Heather would have dearly loved to have been able to figure out: just who was Holden Gibson; and how, even though he hadn't woken up once from his little coma, so powerful and all of a sudden?

As she emerged at the top of that old familiar cliff overlooking the same old fucking lake, and readied herself to take another Goddamn plunge to yet another fucking watery death, Heather hoped she'd be able to find at least some small clue about what it all meant this time through.

She had almost made it to the end of the cliff, when she pulled herself up short. Looked at the thing that was floating in the water, like a fat white jellyfish. A jellyfish with rounded shoulders and grey hair that washed out in tendrils around its wrinkled head. A jellyfish that floated face-down in the lake.

"Now who the fuck," she said out loud, "is that?"

Suicide could wait, Heather thought as she plunged headfirst into the water. This time, rather than diving down and sucking all the lake her lungs could hold, Heather did a fast crawl across the water towards the body. From a distance, she couldn't tell who it was—but she had a faint and irrational hope that it might be Holden Gibson, finally sucked into his own little Transcendental Meditation hell.

If that was the case, there was no way she was going to let him drown and escape this place. *What's good for the goose is good for the fuckin' gander*, she thought as she came up to the floater and hooked an arm to him. She paddled back to shore, and gasping for breath herself now, dragged the body onto the beach.

She crawled further up, shook out her hair and flipped over onto her haunches. She swore. It wasn't Holden Gibson at all. It was some old guy—older than Holden by about a decade, she figured. What hair he had left was long and almost as grey as his flesh. He was completely naked, and he looked like he'd been dead about a day.

"Fine." Obviously, someone had figured out Heather's escape route and was planting distractions to keep her inside. "*Mi mi mi,*" she said, tromping back up the steps to her original launch point and preparing herself for a proper death once more.

She'd almost made it to the top when a voice stopped her.

"*Hey! Leetle gorl!*"

A part of her told her not to look, to just go through with the death scene and get back to the village where she could actually do something. But Heather stopped all the same, and looked back down the stairs to the beach.

The corpse was sitting up—like a big German tourist, vainly trying to sun away the pallor at a Club Med beach.

Except he didn't sound German.

He sounded Russian.

And while there were plenty of Russians in the village, and Heather figured she must have seen them all by now—she didn't ever recall seeing this one.

"Who the fuck are you?" she demanded.

"I should ask the same, yes?" The corpse stood up, primly moving one hand over its private parts while it beckoned her with the other. "Come down. I don't bite."

"Fuck off," she said, taking a step backwards. "I'm going to kill myself and you can't stop me!"

"Why would I stop you?" said the corpse. "Aren't we both dead already?"

Heather squinted down the steps at him. "Do I know you?"

The corpse squinted back. "I don't know," he said. "You are—one of the children, yes? Maybe you know me as an 'old bastard'? Ha!" The corpse threw both hands into the air in a sudden revelation. His lake-shrunk member bobbed grotesquely between his legs. "That is it, yes? You have come to see horrible old Kolyokov off, before his spirit dissolves into the nothingness of the ether."

"Kol-yokov?" Heather started back down the stairs. If this was a trick to get her to stay a while longer at summer camp—well what could she say? It was just intriguing enough to work. "Sounds Russian. You another KGB guy?"

The corpse was pacing in circles now, hands waving in the air with extravagant sarcasm. "Yes, yes, mock poor Fyodor Kolyokov as he vanishes into the Godless void. For what is he, but a pestilent bastard who would only harm his young prodigies? A foolish old monster! Well—we will see if you like your benighted Babushka any better!"

And with that, the corpse Fyodor Kolyokov whirled on a pale, rotting heel and headed back for the water. "I should have known better!" he spat as the lake water lapped higher and higher on his thick calves.

"Wait!" Heather started to run down the little stretch of beach.

Fyodor Kolyokov waved a hand dismissively and stepped in up to his waist. "What does it matter?" he muttered. "I am long enough dead that I should have the good grace to die properly. Fuck, this is cold on my balls! For a warm brine again . . ."

Heather was running full tilt when she hit the water, and her momentum sent a silvery wave of it smack into Kolyokov's pale dead ass. He squealed, clutched at his sagging butt and stumbled—but before he could fall into the water, Heather had him by the arm. His flesh felt like loose rubber, but she didn't let go, and step by step pulled him cursing and thrashing back to the shore.

"You are not going anywhere," she said through gritted teeth as they stumbled back through the wet silt at the water's edge.

"How true," he spat. "Trapped in incessant metaphor . . . I am fixed. Denied even a clean passing."

"Oh fuck off and get over yourself." Heather gave him a two-handed push in his middle, and sent Kolyokov sprawling on his ass in the shallow water. "Now. What do you know about this Babushka? It's all I ever hear around this fucking village."

Kolyokov smiled down at her and shook his head. "What a mouth on you, little girl," he said. "Babushka? That is what they call her now, yes. This woman you have tried so hard to rejoin. And she's trapped you here, hasn't she? Like a moth in a jar."

"I wasn't trying to rejoin anyone," said Heather. "But you're right about one thing: I am a moth in a jar. Every time I let slip."

Kolyokov narrowed his eyes and his smile faltered. "I see." He stopped, ankle-deep in water, and pulled his hand back. He regarded her appraisingly. "Your American accent is very good, little girl. Vladimir taught you that, did he?"

"That little shit?" Heather laughed. "No way. And I don't have an accent. You're the one with the accent."

Kolyokov nodded, and slowly, his smile reasserted itself.

"I see," he said again.

"See what? What the fuck is going on?"

But Heather was shouting it at the old zombie's back, as he climbed up the rocky beach to the stairs. As he climbed, it seemed as though the colour returned to his flesh, in tiny patches on his back and his ass—like watery ink drops, spreading themselves over age-mottled parchment.

They settled at the top of the stairs, where they had a view of the lake. Kolyokov said he wanted to be somewhere where he could watch the horizon, and once they sat down he never took his eyes off it. It was as though he thought he was a sailor, watching for signs of a coming storm.

"Now," said Kolyokov, "tell me how old you are."

"Twenty-seven."

"Very good." He laughed. "You say it like a little girl still: 'How old are you my dear?' 'I am almost SIX!'"

"Fuck off. My voice isn't that high."

"No," said Kolyokov. "It isn't. Because this is all bullshit now, isn't it? Your voice, your size. You're living in something like a memory. You're really a grown woman. But just now someone's stuffed you into yourself as a child. Do you know why that would be?"

"Tell me."

"It makes you feel weaker," said Kolyokov.

They sat quietly for a moment. Heather glared at Kolyokov. "I'm not weak," she said. "If I wanted to, I could make you do anything in the world."

Kolyokov looked down at her from the corner of his still putrefied eye. "By beating me up? Or maybe by seducing me? Maybe out in the real world of Physick. But here? You're too little to do either." Now he looked away, casting his eye back to the lake. He squinted at it—like he was appraising a painting. "This is a very pleasant metaphor," he said. "What does it signify?"

"Metaphor?"

"I'm sorry. You're confused in here, and I am not helping any. Just tell me—what does this place signify? It seems familiar."

"I'm not confused. This place is *bullshit*. It signifies complete *bullshit*. It's a *bullshit* summer camp in *bullshit* California that Holden took us to when I was little—it was run by the Transcendental Meditation people and they—"

"Ah! Of course! CIA."

"Are you going to let me finish?" Heather stood up. Her fists were angry balls at her sides. "What do you mean, CIA?"

"The camp was a CIA camp," said Kolyokov, "if it's the one I'm thinking of. And yes . . . yes, I think it is. I think I have been here."

"What?"

"It was before you were here. It was probably before you were born. The CIA was using this lakeside camp to train sleepers. Quite a few of them passed under the gates of Kamp Kiwichiching before they shut it down." He stood up. "Yes! I remember it now! That is why it was so familiar! The lake I only saw by moonlight, as we swooped in. We were very nearly captured here—they had placed their dream-walking sentries about the camp. But the Americans were amateurs at this sort of thing in those days. They had barely mastered what they called 'remote viewing' then."

"No," said Heather. She didn't like where this was going. She took a deep breath and went on. "This is a Transcendental Meditation camp. *Transcendental Meditation*. Hippie Pete runs this camp. Not the CIA."

"This," said Kolyokov, "is an imaginary place. And the place it was modelled after? It was never a Transcendental Meditation camp. It was a place for making sleepers. People who would do their master's bidding, without even knowing it were so. Sleepers would spend years here. That's how long it took in those days, to lay in the metaphors. No simple business."

Heather swatted at Kolyokov's flank. "Fuck off!" she yelled. "*Mi mi mi mi!*"

"Ah. You are attempting a mnemonic block. Clever girl." Kolyokov smiled sadly. "But that won't work here. And it won't work out there for long, either, once the people who are controlling you figure out a way around it."

Heather felt herself beginning to cry. A part of her wondered why this was so. What had she really to be sad or upset about, talking to this old zombie about two groups of people—one who walked in their dreams, the other who just seemed to sleep all the time? It was obviously bullshit.

Wasn't it?

Kolyokov put a hand on her shoulder. "You're working it out now, aren't you? The fact that you may not be the person you thought you were. It is common to cry out when such a realization comes upon you."

"What do you mean, 'such a realization'?"

Kolyokov knelt in front of her.

"Such a realization," he said softly, "that you are a sleeper and not a dream-walker. And because of that, you are even more powerless than this metaphoric little girl they've stuffed you inside.

"You are as powerless," he said, in a tone like he was intending the words to be kind, "as a sock puppet."

The sun never set at the Transcendental Meditation camp. It was always afternoon here—sometimes cloudy, sometimes bright and sunny—but the sun always sat above the tree line on the far side of the lake. Heather lay curled on the dock with her eyes shut against it. Kolyokov sat beside her.

"We could do this forever, you know," he said.

"Forever?"

"This place seems safe," he said. "We have been here for ten hours by my accounting—and no one has come for me."

"Would someone come for you?"

"The creature you call Babushka. I think. If she knew that I lived—yes."

Heather opened her eyes. Squinted up at the zombie. His flesh was getting some of its colour back now, and the lake-water bloat was melting from him. White hair tufted up from his shoulder blades like wisps of lake mist. He squinted at the sun.

"Who's Babushka, anyway?"

"Her name," said Kolyokov, "is not important. It used to be Lena. But I don't think she uses it any more. She's past that—or she believes that she is which is the same thing here. But she's very powerful. And she wants to become more so. That is why she seized the children. That is why she put you here."

"Oh no," said Heather. "Babushka didn't put me here."

"Really, now?" said Kolyokov. "Then who did put you here, if not her?"

That one was easy. "Holden Gibson," she said. "The old fucking bastard."

Kolyokov frowned. "Holden Gibson," he said, then shook his head. "No. Doesn't ring a bell."

Heather lay quietly for a moment. She thought about Babushka—and how according to old Kolyokov, she'd used to be called Lena. An idea came to her.

"He might have had a different name," she said. "Before."

Kolyokov looked at her with raised eyebrows. His face was almost living now.

"What was the name?" he said.

"Kaye," said Heather. "The Koldun guy—he called him John Kaye."

Colour flushed back into Fyodor Kolyokov's face, and he leaped to his feet with uncharacteristic agility. "Kaye?" he said, hauling Heather up too. "Are you certain?"

Heather nodded—flinching back at the zombie's sudden intensity. "Um—pretty certain," she said.

Kolyokov said something in Russian, and started up the dock. "John Kaye," he said. "After all these years. He should be dead—we thought he was dead. . . . But . . . It begins to make sense now. Yes . . ."

"Hey!" shouted Heather. "Where are you going?"

"You'd better join me," he said. "We've got dark work ahead of us."

"*Dark* work?" Heather rolled her eyes.

"Yes." Kolyokov turned. He seemed to have grown a little bigger—and the sunlight, the way it reflected in his eyes, made it seem as though they burned inside with their own light. "We have to get out of this metaphor of ours once and for all."

"Oh great," said Heather. She started up the cliff. "Okay. I'll kill myself first, and you follow."

"No. It's not ourselves who must die. Tonight," he said, stomping up the hill, "we must murder this Hippie Pete of yours. That is the thing that will break this place's hold on you."

Murdering Hippie Pete. It was, of course, a brilliant idea. Something that Heather was a little disgusted with herself for not having considered before.

Kolyokov stopped. "You are not squeamish—are you my dear?"

"Squeamish?" Heather ran to catch up with the old zombie. "Fuck no! How're we gonna do it? There's no guns here, but I know where the power tools are! Can I help? Can I?"

Kolyokov laughed and patted Heather on the top of the head.

"You are," he said, glancing back at the horizon as he spoke, "a delightful child. Truly. I wish I had ten thousand of you."

Thunder rumbled in the distance, and Heather could see flashes of what looked like lightning in the gathering clouds beyond the far treetops. That was fine with her. Whatever storm the sky could let loose on their heads would be nothing compared to the shitstorm of trouble she and her zombie pal Fyodor Kolyokov would let loose on Hippie Pete when they found him.

THE GRAND INQUISITOR IN THE HOUSE OF THE DEAD

Великий инквизитор в доме мёртвых

There were five guys in the Emissary's lobby when Amar Shadak arrived. They wore track pants and jackets and expensive running shoes with squishy balloons in the heels that were supposed to make high-impact athletics easier on the ankles. The balloons were wasted on these guys. For one thing, there were at least twice as many chins as guys here. For another, when they talked, they made a wheezing fat man sound. And finally, two of them were smoking, in defiance of what Shadak understood to be a rigidly enforced anti-smoking law in the new mayor's New York City.

But smoking and morbid obesity would have been the least of their concerns if a New York policeman were to stop them on the street. All of them, Shadak expected, were packing guns.

"Hey," said one of them as Shadak set his bag down. "We're closed for business, buddy. New fuckin' management—you got it?"

"I am here to see my friend Gepetto," said Shadak pleasantly. "I have an appointment."

"Do you now?"

"I am Amar," said Shadak. "I called ahead last night."

"Amar," said another one of the guys. "From Istanbul, right?"

"That's right." This one was taller than his friends, with greying hair. He looked Shadak in the eye. "They said a guy from Istanbul would be showing up here this morning. Guess you're him."

"That's right." Shadak smiled.

"You just fly in? Shoulda called from the airport. We woulda sent a car."

"Under the circumstances," said Shadak, "it was better I take a taxicab."

The grey-haired guy nodded. He didn't take his eyes off Shadak. "Sometimes that's better," he said.

"Don't know who you can trust these days," said the smaller man. He looked over to grey-hair. "Isn't that right, Jack?"

Grey-haired Jack nodded. But he didn't take his eyes off Shadak. His eyes scanned down his torso—probably, Shadak thought, checking him out for weapons. He didn't blame him. Jack was one of Gepetto Bucci's boys—and the whole gang of them had just discovered the biggest mystery of their lives here: a ghost hotel. Lights on, sheets turned. But empty. Whole staff gone AWOL. Not a guest in the place.

Shadak remembered the argument he'd had with old Bucci, when he'd first asked him to send someone over to the Emissary Hotel on Broadway:

"What the fuck you want to go to a fuckin' dry cleaner's for?"

"It's not a dry cleaner's. I need you to go to the 14th floor of the Emissary and find an old Russian named Kolyokov. I think maybe he is gone. If he is—I want you to bring some people to me."

"There ain't no 14th floor there. If it's the address I'm thinkin' of, it's a fuckin' dry cleaner's. Not even Russian. I think it's maybe Korean. Japa-fuckin'-ese. Fuck do I know? Does a shitty job and there's no more than four fuckin' floors in the whole building. Maybe you got the address wrong."

"It's the right address."

"I'm telling you: you're wasting a favour."

"A favour is mine to waste."

"Up to you."

"A *favour*. You owe me."

"Fuck. All right, but you're a fuckin' idiot."

"It's important."

"I get that sense, Amar. We'll take care of it. I'll send Montassini this afternoon."

The telephone conversation he had just before he got on the trans-Atlantic flight to New York, not two days after the first, had a remarkably different tone to it:

"You weren't fuckin' kidding." Bucci was giggling, like a kid who'd just found pirate treasure. "It's there all right. It's a fuckin' ghost hotel. Never fuckin' heard of it before you called me. Must have driven past it a million fuckin' times—never saw it."

"I'm coming out. Where shall we meet?"

"You're comin' out? Well fuck—I'm at the hotel right now. Trying to figure out what the fuck's going on."

"We have something in common then."

"Fuckin' right."

Jack got into the small elevator with Shadak. Pressed *18*. "Mr. Bucci's stayin' in the bridal suite," said Jack. Shadak took a step back—the old gangster was standing a bit too close, even for the tight elevator.

"You wear a lot of cologne," said Shadak.

"You like it?" Jack gave Shadak a funny look.

"No," said Shadak. He smiled, exuding all the good will and warmth that he could muster after seven hours in an airplane seat. "It makes me want to cut your fucking throat you piece of shit funnyboy."

Jack took a step back and looked at his feet. Maybe, thought Shadak, he was thinking about the stories they told about him. The things he'd done to some of the others. That would be good.

The elevator lurched to a stop. Somewhere in its guts, a bell chimed. Then the door opened to the corridor of the 18th floor. A brass plaque announcing the bridal suite was fitted on the wall opposite them.

"I can find the rest of my way without you," said Shadak. Jack didn't argue. The door slid shut, and Amar Shadak set off to meet his nominal partner Gepetto Bucci on his own.

"You okay? You don't look so fuckin' good."

"I swallowed the wrong way," said Shadak. He set his bag down by a pressed-board wardrobe, and smiled at Bucci. The Italian looked older today, and smaller. His white hair, normally plastered back over his skull, was a bird's nest. His cheeks were sunken and his eyes floated in the middle of raccoon-dark pits. The spot on the left side of his skull where the hair wouldn't grow anymore was white as bone. He didn't smile back.

"Sit down," he said.

The old man was not alone in the bridal suite of the Emissary Hotel. There were three other guys there—two of them playing cards, another one back in the kitchenette, a cell phone at his ear. He was wearing a bright red Trekker's Outfitting Co-op T-shirt. Shadak didn't like it. He didn't stop smiling, though.

"Can we talk alone?"

"Sit *down*," said Bucci. "No. Ordinarily fine. But not today. This place is too fucked up. It's like a fuckin' horror movie this hotel. You gotta observe the rules. Send a guy off into the crapper by himself, he's likely to get his nuts ripped off with a fuckin' weedwhacker, you know what I mean."

Shadak didn't, exactly. But he was used to that with Gepetto Bucci. He sat down. The two guys playing cards ignored him. The idiot in the TOC shirt turned away and whispered into his cell phone. Shadak decided he would keep his eye on that one.

"This is not a haunted hotel," said Shadak. "But it's good to be careful. How long have you been here?"

"A day and a night. When I heard back about how things went with your job—couldn't believe it. So I sent some of my guys out here. Take a better look."

"And they found this place deserted."

"Deserted." Bucci snorted. "Ali fuckin' Baba's cave, that's what they found. Yeah—no one was here. But we got into the safe—took a look at what they got goin' on in the basement. Fuck, Amar. Who is this Fyodor Kolyokov guy anyway? How long did you know about this place?"

Shadak didn't answer. The guy at the phone was writing something down now. He was shaking his head.

"No fuckin' guests—no fuckin' staff. But cash—cash by the fuckin' boatload."

"Did you find the isolation tank?" said Shadak.

"You mean that UFO. Roswell thing on the 14th floor? Yeah. It was in the room with the two people we got for you."

"And Fyodor Kolyokov was nowhere to be seen."

Bucci made a face. "No. Not exactly. But what with everything in that basement—it'd be easy to make him go away."

Shadak looked at him.

"Acid baths," said Bucci. "There's this room next to the laundry—with big bathtubs like in hospitals. Whole wall covered in brown fuckin' jugs of hydrochloric acid. Place stank, too. Easiest fuckin' thing, to take your pal Fyodor Kolyokov down there and make him disappear."

"Yeah—like almost happened with fuckin' Leo," said one of the card players.

Shadak ignored him for now. "So you think Kolyokov is dead then," he said.

"Don't you?"

"I do think that. But I value your opinion."

Bucci steepled his hands and frowned. "Yeah," he said. "Yeah, I think he's dead."

"What about Kilodovich?"

"Kilodovich?"

"Alexei Kilodovich." Shadak fished into his pocket and pulled out the old Polaroid—taken in better days, in the back of a Soviet jeep outside Kabul. They were both grinning like schoolboys, and they weren't much older than that either. Bucci finally cracked a grin when he took the picture.

"Look at you," he said. "Little fuckin' Amar. That is you, right?"

"It was some time ago," said Shadak. "Kilodovich is the one beside me."

"Figured that out." Bucci handed it back. "Never seen him. 'Course, judging from the time that picture must have been taken, he could have grown himself a new face by now. But I told you—" the smile slid off his own face, like a sheet of ice from a sharp awning "—nobody was here when we came."

The TOC man put down the phone. "Hey," he said, to Bucci. "We got another message."

"Yeah? Excuse me for a second, Amar." Bucci shifted around in his chair. "Montassini?"

"Montassini."

"Where is he now? He get to fuckin' Halifax yet?"

"Didn't say where exactly. But I don't think he's in Halifax. Said he was on some kind of satellite phone."

"Satellite phone? Fuckin' Montassini! On a fuckin' satellite phone! So anybody could be listening! Where the fuck is he?"

Shadak leaned forward with interest. "Halifax," he said. "Satellite phone . . . *Montassini* . . ." He snapped his fingers. "Ah! Wasn't Montassini one of your Capos—one of the people we agreed you should send here for my favour? What has this to do with a satellite phone and the city of Halifax? Tell me what is going on here, Gepetto."

Bucci turned to look at Shadak. He lips curled to say something—then he saw Shadak's smile, the implicit menace of his Turkish associate's chillingly accommodating demeanour.

"Take it easy," said Bucci. "Don't go fucked up on me, Amar. We're talkin', all right?"

"I'm not getting fucked up," said Shadak. "Tell me about Montassini."

"Yeah. Montassini. Complicated story. But I was gonna tell you about it. 'Cause I value *your* opinion on the tapes."

Shadak raised his eyebrow in a question.

"Leo Montassini's a solid guy. Not too much up here, you know what I mean. But yeah—he led the team in to bring you your people. Took 'em to the landing strip—put 'em on the plane. Just like he agreed. Only thing was, when that was done, he tells Jack and Nino—the boys what were with him—he's going to take a leak. Fine. Happens to the best of us. While they're waiting, he fucks off in the van. Leaves 'em at the airfield, nowhere to go. I gotta send out a fuckin' car to pick them up, same time as I'm sendin' more people out to this place. All the time, I'm wondering what the fuck's with Leo? I'm getting concerned, you understand—that Leo's workin' some kind of racket. Tryin' to fuck me over. I don't take kindly to that kind of thing."

"Understandable," said Shadak. "I don't take *kindly* to that sort of thing either."

"Fuckin' right. So I put out the word that Leo Montassini should be brought straight to me should he turn up. Word comes to me just about right away, from a business associate of my son's who runs a sandwich thing in the Port

Authority Bus Terminal. That he sold Leo a pastrami eggplant deal just an hour ago. That Leo looked kind of messed up. And that he looked like he was on his way somewhere. Fuck, I think. Bastard's leavin' town on me. I'm just about ready to put out the word on him—when I get another call, from the Co-op—about a message on the Complaints Line."

"The Complaints Line?"

"It's a line we got in there in the, what do you call it?"

"The Collective Office," said the guy in the red Trekker's Outfitting Co-Op T-shirt.

"Fuckin' Commies," said Bucci. "Couldn't just call it the Assistant Manager's office, like every other camping store."

"You were saying about the Complaints Line? What exactly is it?"

"Just what it sounds like," continued Bucci. "Whenever a customer gets pissed that the Pel-flex on his coat leaks in rainwater or his Maglite let him down in a fuckin' spelunkin' trip, he calls that line. Gets a message where he leaves a number and says why he's so pissed about our products. We got a guy who checks out those complaints regularly—makes 'em go away. He also checks for other messages, which me or one of mine sometimes leave. Who's gonna tap a fuckin' complaint line, right? It's like that old rule—what is it?"

"Hide in plain sight," said a card-player.

"Right. *Hide in plain sight*. Get it?"

"Sure," said Shadak.

"All the same, messages on that line intended for me or my associates shouldn't go into too much detail. Short and vague. That's supposed to be the rule."

"And Leo Montassini, I take it, left you a message that was neither."

"Fuckin' mind reader," said Bucci, looking levelly at Shadak.

"No." Shadak folded his hands. "No mind reading."

"Whatever. Yeah, he left me a message. A whole series of messages, all of them way too specific—went on for the length of the tape. I tell you something, if I didn't see this place—" Bucci waved his hand over his head to indicate the hotel "—I'd have thought Leo just went off the deep end."

"Do you have the tapes?"

Bucci nodded. "Yeah, we got some of the tapes here—the first tape. There's more at the store."

"What is on the tapes, please?"

Bucci made a small smile. "Nothing about that guy in the picture, that Alexei Kilodo-fuck, if that's what you're wondering."

"I assumed that," said Shadak, "because you would have said something earlier. But what was so strange on these tapes, that you think your trusted

Captain went off, as you say, 'the deep end'?"

Bucci snorted. "What wasn't strange about them?"

One of the card players looked up. "Like a fuckin' horror movie," he said.

"What the fuck do you know?" said his opponent. "Deal."

Bucci shrugged.

"I'd like to hear the tapes, please," said Shadak.

"Yeah," said Bucci, "I thought you might." He turned back to the card players. "Hey! Get the fuckin' tape deck out here. You heard our friend here! He wants the show!"

"I am calling," said the disembodied voice of Leo Montassini, "to complain about these fuckin' boots you sold me. They leak and shit, and they aren't warm like you said they would be, and they don't fit like they did in the store. You send this complaint straight to the fuckin' top. You got that? Straight to the fuckin' *top*. *Top*. You know what I mean, right?

"Okay. Now you listening, Mr. B? It's Leo here. First off, let me say I'm sorry I had to leave Nino and Jack like that at the plane. Can't fuckin' explain it. Hope they got home okay. I couldn't stay with those guys any longer. Like something's callin' me. Someone's callin' me. From the sea . . .

"Look. Main thing is, I think I'm on to something. I think I know where Kolyokov is. You want to pay attention to this, boss. Those guys—Nino and Jack—even you, B.—I don't think any of you would understand. It comes from listening to the sea—inside that tank they got at the hotel, in that Russian fuck's room. I stuck my head inside that tank, and it was like sticking my head outside the tank. Like it went on forever . . . And I heard him, boss. I *heard* him.

"I'm usin' up space on your tape. I'm callin' you from the Port Authority Bus Terminal. Just want to let you know where I am. Now I'm gonna tell you how I got here.

"Like I was telling you, I went back to the Emissary. It was dark by the time I got back there. Lights were still on in the hotel. Nobody was at the desk when I looked in, but you never know, right? So I took the truck around to the loading dock at the back. Tried to get in through there. Door was locked. So you know . . . I do this and that . . . And I'm inside. Fuckin' scary place, Mr. B. Like it's got an echo in it, only the echo's not in your ears it's in your fuckin' head. I can't explain it. Just take my word. Fuckin' *scary* place. So I make my way through the back, checkin' things out. And everything's, like, neat and tidy. But it's like that movie your kid keeps watchin': *Marathon Man*, right? *Omega Man*. I don't fuckin' know. Somethin' like that. It's the one with Charlton Heston, where the whole world's like normal—but nobody's there. . . . Well, it makes me feel like I'm Chuck in there, and it's night, and the place is empty and nothin's getting' any better, so what the fuck? I pull out my piece.

"I make my way out through the back office. And there I am in the lobby, standin' behind the fuckin' front desk. The place is fuckin' huge or that's what it looks like. So I make my way into the lobby itself. Then I went back up to the fifth floor, where that guy Alexei Kilodovich slept.

"Didn't feel right—just leavin' that alone. Kilodovich was an important one, right? Right. So I went into his room and sat down on the bed. Closed my fuckin' eyes and thought—where'd I hide shit. Under the mattress? So I pull up the mattress—start searchin'. Nothin' there. So I think—if I was Alexei Kilodovich, what would I do?

"Right about then, there's footsteps in the hall. So I get down behind the bed, hold my gun up—wait for the door to open—which it does. And just for a second, I'm feelin' like an asshole. Because there I am, waitin' to shoot this little cleaner, comin' into the room. She's got her cart with the laundry bag and a big fuckin' mop handle stickin' out. She can't weigh more than a hundred pounds soakin' wet. Stupid fuckin' Leo, right? Jumpin' at shadows.

"Well I should have done a bit more jumpin'—because before I can do anything, bitch is on top of me. She's knocked my fuckin' piece out of my hand, straddlin' me like a whore and jammin' the handle of her mop into my mouth. Make a long story short I manage to get it away from my mouth, but she gives it a little twist or somethin' and clocks me on the side of the head. Knocks me cold, no shit.

"Must have figured me for dead, 'cause next thing you know, I'm awake—in what I first think is maybe some kind of fuckin' bathtub. And I'm thinkin', fuck Leo, what'd I do, fall asleep and have a dream? I don't think that for long though, because I look over the edge of this bathtub thing, and I see there's that bitch cleanin' woman haulin' a big brown jug off a rack of big brown jugs. And I put it together: this ain't no bathtub. It's tiled and shit, and the drain's pretty big, and it's got marks on the tile that are all brown and smell like old fuckin' batteries. And all of a sudden, Mr. B., I got a pretty good idea what happened to that Mr. Kolyokov we were supposed to be lookin' for. Do I have to fuckin' spell it out? He got *liquidated*, Mr. B. *Liquidated*. Those jugs were filled with acid—an' the cleanin' woman was gonna fuckin' liquidate me with one of 'em now.

"She hadn't noticed I was movin' yet. She turns around with a big fuckin' jug in her arms, and her eyes—they were dead, Boss. Like startin' to fog over dead. She was like a fuckin' zombie.

"So now it's my turn to get the jump on her, and that's what I do. I'm up and it's like, *bam!* Take that you fuckin' bitch! *Bam!* And she's like, nothing—kicks me near the nuts but misses, so I'm like—*Bam!* An' finally, she drops the fuckin' jug in the bathtub an' it cracks, an' I'm like, pushin' her, and then she's the one in the bathtub, Mr. B., an' I'm the one with the acid. Oh yeah. And that's kinda how that went down. I cleaned up, you know what I mean, and on my way out from the basement, I find a couple of suitcases. They're filled with, you know, lady shit. But one of the things I find there, is this bus ticket. Fuckin' Greyhound ticket out of Port Authority, up to Halifax. It's a special ticket—on this charter, it says. Weird name of the company. Here, I got it here: I'll read it: *Manka. Vasilissa. Baba Yaga. One Way*, it says. Leaves in a couple hours.

"So that's how I get here, and how come I'm callin' you from here. I figure, you know, maybe I go check out this bus shit, see what's goin' on. 'Cause I just couldn't get that woman's dead fuckin' eyes out of my head. I'm thinkin', it's a mystery. Just go take a look right?

"So I get to the platform—we're talkin' just half an hour ago now. And it's *crowded*—with all kinds of people. People I recognize. That I'm sure I seen when we went to the Emissary this afternoon.

"Here's what I'm gonna do. I'm gonna get on that bus, and see where it goes. No one's name's on this ticket, you know what I mean? I got a piece if I need it. So I'll call you again once I'm at Halifax—let you know what the fuck's goin' on with the Emissary and all 'at. 'Cause I gotta know, Mr. B.

"First, though, I gotta get a sandwich. I'm starvin'. Hey, does Vinnie still run that stall down here? Makes a mean Pastrami. I'm gonna go check. Seeya."

A duvet of cloud had spread itself over Manhattan, and as the tape beeped to the new message, thick splatters of rain crossed the Bridal Suite's window. Gepetto Bucci clicked off the tape machine. He massaged his hands together and looked across the table to Shadak.

"That's *Omega Man*," said Shadak.

"What?"

"He's referring to *The Omega Man* with the ridiculous vampires with 'fros. *The Marathon Man* is the film with the dentist. Charlton Heston is not in that one."

Bucci squinted at Shadak. "You sure you want to go on with this?"

"Of course. Why?"

"You appear agitated."

"I am not agitated."

Bucci shrugged. "Up to you," he said, and pressed the play button.

"Your kayak is a piece of shit. I take the fuckin' thing onto the water, and whattaya know? Dip my fuckin' paddle in the water and the fuckin' thing turns upside down—and I'm halfway drowned. My kid has to fish me out of the fuckin' lake. I want you to take this complaint to the top. The *top*. I'll wait here.

"Okay. Mr. B.? You listening? Good. I am calling you from just past the border in New Brunswick, Canada. I'm at this little diner we pulled into outside a shitheel little town called Edmunston. I'm out back. Using a fuckin' pay phone—my cell won't work here. We just ate this fuckin' great meal. It's a Canadian thing—french fries and cheese and gravy, all mixed up in like a paste.

"I'm over the fuckin' border. Got through without any shit from the customs guy—but I tucked my number under the seat anyway, because you never know. I got it out again now. These fuckin' people, I don't want to be walkin' without some protection, you know what I mean?

"Fuck—these people I'm on the bus with. I can't figure them out. It's like the fuckin' Peace Corps with piano wire. They all know each other. Like, from the start. I get onto the bus platform and join the line, and there's five of 'em, hugging and crying like they were long-lost family. Me, I just get in line. Mind my own business. After a couple minutes, this old lady steps in line. Looks me up and down. So I look back at her, ask her 'What the fuck you lookin' at?' Not like that—she's an old lady, and I'm not disrespectful. More like: 'Can I help you, ma'am?'

"'Sergei?' she says to me. And I'm all, 'What the fuck?' And she's all, 'Sergei, it is you!' And then before you know it Grandma is givin' me a big hug right around the middle. 'I haven't seen you since you were this high. Don't you remember? We were together a year in Berlin! You were just a little boy and I was a young girl.'

"I gotta be honest with you, Mr. B., I almost blew it right there. I mean, what am I supposed to think? Some old whore who sleeps with little boys in Berlin gets me mixed up with some other guy she diddled while he was in short pants? Fuckin' pervert, I'm thinking. But before I say anything, I start thinking some more. That maybe I have a better chance lasting it out with these freaks if Grandma Walton here thinks I'm her little boy toy Sergei, than if they work out I'm Leo Montassini. I'm thinking, one of them already tried to waste me knowing who I was. Maybe being Sergei from Berlin isn't such a bad idea. So I say, 'I remember it like it was yesterday. Mrs. . . .'

"'Kronstein,' she says. 'That's what I call myself these days. It used to be Olga. That's how you remember me. But when we went into deep cover, I became Mrs. Kronstein. I know that I'm Olga Vilanova. But Kronstein's the name I'm most comfortable with.'

"*What the fuck?* is what I'm thinking. What's this shit about deep cover? And she's looking all . . . intense. Common sense says I should just get the fuck out of there. But curiosity killed the cat, right? I just let her talk.

"Well it turns out that Mrs. Kronstein used to work in publishing. Oh fuck, Mr. B., she knows everybody to hear her tell it. Stephen Fucking King babysits for her when she and the husband go out for brunch. John Irving's her tennis partner. She got to know everybody. She says she was part of some 'cultural operation.' She says she and some others were there to feed the decadence of the West. All the time she's telling me this, she's giggling.

"And then, I can't take it no more. 'You're a spy, is what you're saying,' I say. 'For the Russians.'

"Well that just sets her off. A couple of other people, this bald guy in a leather jacket and his girl, say, 'What's so funny?' And Mrs. Kronstein wipes her eyes.

"'I'm a spy!' she goes, still laughing. 'Sergei here thinks I'm a spy!'

"They all get a really good laugh at that. Big fuckin' joke as Sergei's expense. Fine. I laugh too. I mean, if I'm going to find out what the fuck's going on here, I can't go doing the first guy who pissed me off. And I'm thinking, we found ourselves a whole new arm of the Russians here. Bunch of crazy ex-fuckin'-KGB agents, right? Smart enough to hide a fuckin' eighteen floor hotel in Manhattan. Maybe I should have run then. Just gotten the fuck out of there. But I'll tell you something, Mr. B.—you stick your head into that fuckin' UFO on the 14th floor of the Emissary, catch a whiff of that weird—fuckin' *alien* sea. Hear the voice. The voice . . .

"See if you can give up the scent after that.

"So the bus comes. It's a Greyhound. Got Halifax written on the sign. Door opens up, driver steps down. Creepy fucking guy. Thin as a rail. Looks about a hundred. Name's Orlovsky. Found that out later. Looks me in the eye, takes my ticket—and there I am. On the bus. I went to sit by Mrs. Kronstein, but she picked a seat by this other old bat. Doesn't even meet my eye when I say hey. Fuck that, I take a seat at the back by the can. Everybody else sits further up near the front, so I got a few seats between me and the rest. Suits me fine. I got my piece. They should leave me in peace. Heh heh.

"So we get going. Takes a while to get out of the city—you know how it is. And before we're out of the Lincoln Tunnel, the bald guy's got a blaster with some tapes. Starts playing this Russian singer, some guy with a deep voice. He's singing about some broad called Natascha. In Russian. And fuck if everybody doesn't join in. Laughing and singing along like they grew up on this shit. Orlovsky the driver yells for them to shut up but they don't hardly hear him. They're singing too loud. And pretty good, too. All in tune. Like they been practising—which of course is impossible, right? Finally, we get to the toll gate. And the driver stops the bus and gets up. Turns around like fuckin' Count Dracula, and fixes his eyes on the sleepers.

"'Manka!' he says. "'Vasilissa! Baba Yaga!' And they all stop singing.

"'The song,' he says, 'that kind of thing, is one of the things that will put you all back to sleep. You cannot go to sleep again. We are paying a toll. We will be crossing the border in a few hours. Now is not the time to retreat to your Safe

Place.'

"Whatever, I think. And then—that's when I learn Orlovsky's name. Because he fixes me with this look—and squints—and comes back, hand over hand over the seat backs like some fuckin' spider. And stands over me.

"'I am Pavel Orlovsky,' he says. 'Who are you, who does not sing?'

"'Sergei,' I tell him. 'I'm Sergei.'

"'Well, Sergei,' he says, 'you are a strong one, then.'

"He might have said something else, but traffic was moving and the cars behind us started honking. So Pavel Orlovsky the bus driver turned around and went back to take us through the toll. Tell you what, I kept to myself after that. Hardly slept through the night or rest of the day. Kept my fuckin' hand on my gun.

"So here I am, outside Edmunston, New Brunswick. We're gonna drive through the night and then some to Halifax. But I hear there's a couple stops along the way. I'll try and call you with more then. Maybe I'll see if I can talk to Mrs. Kronstein more—find out about where we're going. What's with the ocean in the tank. The fucking ghosts in the hotel.

"Okay. That's all for now. Gotta run. I'll call."

"What does he mean," said Shadak, "about the ocean in the tank? That's the second time he's mentioned that."

Bucci shrugged. "Tank's filled up halfway with salt water. Maybe it reminded him. How should I know?"

"He doesn't seem right in the head."

"Tell me about it. Listen to this next one."

"What the fuck is Pel-flex anyway? Feels like fuckin' nylon, what it feels like. I bought a fuckin' Pel-flex jacket, and my fuckin' loser nephew turns the garden hose on me, and I'm fuckin' soaked to the skin, everybody's laughing like I'm some kind of joke. Lemme tell you somethin'. Pel-flex is the fuckin' joke. Why don't you call it Kleenex? Extra-fuckin' absorbent? In fact, that's what I'm gonna call it. I wipe my ass with your Pel-flex. Send this to the top. *Top*. I'm fuckin' pissed.

"Mr. B? Fuck, Mr. B., I can't talk long. They're scratchin' around my ears, trying to get into my fuckin' brain. Fuck. Fuck. *I'm a little teapot short and stout. This is my handle and this is my—*

"Okay. I think it's okay now. We are clear. Mr. B.? All right. It's like nine o'clock now. I'm calling you from outside a place called Rimouski, at a truck stop called—Huskie. Like the dog. Fuckin' Canadians. They like their fuckin' dogsleds and cheesy french fries and come to think of it half of them speak French.

"Half the ones you can find that is. This place is barren. Nothing but crappy little trees and big wide rocks. The highway's the shits. I can't fuckin' believe that this is the road to Halifax.

"Anyway that's where I am. I don't know how long it's going to take—but I got to tell you, this is feeling like forever. I'm half tempted to just jump here, make my way back however. Because weird shit's been happening. You wouldn't believe it.

"People are crying. They're crying and talking in weird languages and sometimes fallin' over like they're getting seizures. And they stare at me, Mr. B. They're staring at me like they *know*. So what the fuck? I'm cryin' too.

"Okay. Look. I gotta go. They're in my ears, man. Fuck. I'll call again when we get to Halifax. Fuck."

"He never got to Halifax," explained Bucci. "We started checking maps after this call. Turns out there was a reason half the people spoke French. The stupid fuck went up into Quebec. Didn't even fuckin' know it. Halifax is the other way. Rimouski's a little town on the Gaspé Peninsula."

"The Gaspé," said Shadak. "Is that significant?"

"*In*-significant," said Bucci. "Like my boy said. Nothing but shitty little trees and rocks. Not too many people. The whole thing runs up the south side of the St. Lawrence River and then out into the Atlantic."

"So why—" Shadak paused as the room was illuminated by a nearby flash of lightning, and a deafening thunderclap. "Why do you suppose they were going there?"

"You'd think my boy Leo would be able to figure that out, wouldn't you? Instead of giving me shit like this."

Bucci pressed "play."

"One of your people on the floor of your stupid fuckin' store was rude to my mother, all right? She comes in to buy one of your fleece ponchos because you know she ain't getting any younger and she likes the way fleece feels on a cold day—and your little fuckin' miss mountain-biker makes her feel like a fuckin' Grandmother, which she is not, for complainin' about the fact that the fleece poncho is goin' for a hundred and eighty nine dollars, which it should not. Mom cried an' cried after what that fuckin' bitch said to her, and lemme tell you, if you guys don't take care of it then I may just have to. I want you to send this to the top. The *top*.

"Okay, Mr. B. This is probably going to be the last call you get from me for a while. The road's running along the fuckin' ocean right now and there's nothing along here but grass and darkness. Nothing. It's like we're goin' into the fuckin' sea, into the sea in the space capsule. . . . It smells like that.

"We're stopped at a gas station right now, and the driver says—he says we're not going to be stopping again. Until we get there. Halifax. Fuck. Sorry. I'm scared out of my fuckin' mind I don't mind telling you.

"Everybody's gone like the fuckin' maid now. Like zombies. I can see 'em from here—all sittin' up straight in their bus seats waitin' for the driver to finish pumping. Someone's put on the fuckin' tape recorder again. That same guy. Deep voice singing in Russian about some woman called Natascha. Probably a fuckin' stripper, right, Mr. B?

"Fuck, Mr. B.—they're getting just like that bitch in the hotel—you know the one of whom I'm speaking. Like anything inside them is gone, you know? Think they're goin' to try and do me? I don't—

"—Fuck. That fuckin' driver Orlovsky is coming over here. He's got a look in his eye—like—fuck. I gotta go."

A scuffing noise, as if the telephone receiver was rattling on the side of a phone—

—a deep voice, mumbling in Russian: "Sergei," was the only word that came through.

Leo spoke at a great distance. "What the fuck?" he said. And the line beeped again.

"That's all on the tape," said Bucci. "Assistant manager picked up the messages when he came in to work this morning. We figured maybe Leo was dead by now, being as we had not heard from anyone. But now it turns out he's not dead—right?" He turned to the red-shirted TOC-er.

"He said he was on a boat," said the TOC-er.

"That's right," said Bucci, "using someone's satellite phone."

"Your man," said Shadak, "is incompetent. He allowed himself to be captured. Gave himself away. Incompetent."

Bucci stood up and went over to the window. Water streamed down the glass as black clouds blotted out what remained of the sunlight. Bucci tapped on the glass. "Hmm. Stupid. On some weird fuckin' midlife crisis jag that I don't understand. But he's not dead. Now he's on a boat. And he's using someone's satellite phone. Flavio?"

"Yeah?" said the red-shirted Flavio.

"You got a tape of the guy?"

"Nuh-uh. No tape. He talked with Neil direct."

"Neil?"

"Neil Walberg," said Flavio. "Your new Assistant Manager. Skinny fuckin' kid. Got a big metal stud on his nose. Tattoo of a whale or some fuckin' thing on his back. Hair like a fuckin' fetus, which is to say none."

"Right. Fuckin' little Commie."

"So Leo made Neil write down what he said. Word for word. Neil read it to me over the phone. Said he was going to fax it."

Shadak gave Bucci a look.

"Go get it," said Bucci.

> *Dear Mister B,*
>
> *I am in a boat out in the ocean, It is a freight boat. Its carrying me and the other people on the bus, and boxes of expensive food. We got on the boat in a town called ~~Cloriform~~ Cloridorme. They have docks and a post office and shitty little houses but no where to eat and no people at least not out at night, The guys on the boat speak Russian. We are not going to Halifax I found out. We are going to a place called New Pokrovskoye. It is where everybody's Grandmother lives. That is all that they say when they talk in English which they hardly ever do now.*
>
> *I kind of got into trouble with Orlovsky, but it is okay now. I am just doing the zombie thing all the time and that seems to be good enough for the rest of them. Orlovsky thinks I am just more messed up than usual. He keeps saying these words to me: "Mango Vasaline Bubba yaya." I do not know what they mean but his eyes go all wide like he expects something from me so I just make my eyes go all blank and mumble like the rest of them. It seems to be working so I am sticking with it.*
>
> *I am calling you now from a satellite phone that I found down below. The battery is no good though so I do not know how long I can talk. But I'll call you again when no one's*

Shadak put down the paper.

"All right," he said, "where is this New Pokrovskoye? This Cloridorme? Do you have a map?"

"Just use the Internet," said Flavio.

"Fuck off with your fuckin' Internet," said Bucci. "That's for porn and gambling. This is serious shit. Get our guest a road map. This is a fuckin' hotel, there's got to be a road map in here somewhere."

Flavio nodded, and turned to a card player. "You!" he said. "You heard 'im. Go!"

Lightning flickered like a short circuit through the blinds. Bucci steeple his hands and peered over his tall middle fingers at his thick pinkies, like they held some clue. The card players put their cards down and stared under the table at their feet the same way. Amar Shadak stood by the window and stared out into what was turning into a very angry day.

Shadak felt himself, his own anger, growing ever closer to the surface. He looked out the window, at his faint reflection in the glass. His eyes were blazing—his mouth, thin and quivering. He rolled his shoulders—straightened his back—and tried to force his lips into a pleasant smile. He looked like one of those vampires from *The Omega Man*, all crazy and hungry for blood. Shadak much preferred the look of the old Nazi dentist—calm and pleasant, a consummate professional who applied his craft at the diamond-tipped end of a drill. But that wasn't coming. Not today. Shadak stopped smiling and tried to relax.

The door opened and the map guy came back. He had a little blue American Automobile Association book called *Drive North America*. Gepetto beckoned the map guy and Shadak to join him at the table, and they spent a while flipping through the road Atlas. They found Cloridorme quickly enough—the Gaspé Peninsula was indeed like a tongue, and all the towns on it were cankered along its outer edges. Cloridorme was out near the end, on the north coast.

New Pokrovskoye was another matter. It didn't show up in any indices, and wasn't marked anywhere they can see. Finally, throwing up his hands, Bucci said, "Fine! Try the fuckin' Internet!"

They had to go downstairs to the front desk for that. The little office in back of it had a big old computer with a tiny little monitor, and a screeching little modem hooked up to the telephone jack. Flavio seemed to be the only one who knew what he was doing, so they all waited while he started going.

"There ain't no New Pokrovskoye anywhere that I can see," he said finally. "All the references are Russian."

"So is there a New Pokrovskoye in Russia?" said Shadak.

"Just a Pokrovskoye." Flavio tapped the screen, which showed a list of names next to advertisements for casinos and cars and cellular telephones. Shadak squinted at them.

"Those are web sites," said Flavio.

"Shut the fuck up—he knows that," said Bucci.

"Most of them," said Shadak, "reference 'Rasputin,' I notice."

"Yeah," said Flavio. He moved the arrow to the first of them. "Let's see why."

The screen went white for a moment, then after a certain amount of waiting started to fill up with words and pictures.

"*Rasputin's Lair*," read Shadak, then scanned down. The web page appeared to be concerned with an elaborate fiction about the mad monk Rasputin, and his adventures in the boudoir of a Russian noblewoman called Tanya. The picture, as it loaded, showed a crudely manipulated photograph of a black-bearded man in monk's robes, mounting a plump young woman from behind.

"What I tell you—gambling and porn," Bucci snorted. "Fuckin' Internet."

"Where is Pokrovskoye in all of this?"

Flavio typed quickly. "There," he said.

The computer had highlighted a single sentence:

"*Ah, my lovely vixen, if you are very good, I shall return you to my harem, in the town of my birth Pokrovskoye,' said the amply endowed monk as Lady Tanya squeeled in extatic delight*."

"*Ecstatic delight*?" Flavio shook his head. "Who writes this shit?"

But Shadak moved away. For the first time in days, he felt a genuine smile creeping across his lips.

"Rasputin's birthplace," he said, and reached into his jacket pocket—where the photograph of the bastard Alexei Kilodovich rested. "New Pokrovskoye." He turned to Bucci. "Who do you think was born there?"

Bucci shrugged.

"I need to go upstairs," said Shadak.

"Back to the bridal suite?"

"No. The 14th floor. I need to see the tank. And then—"

"Then?"

"Then," said Shadak, "we need to go north, I think."

Bucci looked at him quietly for a moment. "You know about this shit, don't you?"

"I know about this shit," said Shadak gravely and Gepetto Bucci nodded. "So north," he said, "it is."

THE IDIOT

Идиот

Alexei stood in front of the lighthouse door and wiped his mouth. The sun was low in the sky now, and it etched his shadow on the rough stone of the building. At his feet, poor young James was barely able to move he was so intoxicated. The stink of puke and sweat and alcohol drifted out of his pores like a mist. Alexei allowed himself a cold little smile: let Holden Gibson try and dream-walk this young wretch now. James' inability to hold his liquor had proven Alexei's salvation.

"James," said Alexei. "Can you walk?"

James looked up at him with red, stupid eyes. Alexei nudged him with his toe.

"Up," he said, and scooped his hand under the boy's arm. He hauled him to his feet. "We're going back inside."

James got up with considerable difficulty, and Alexei walked him back into the lighthouse. He sat him down in a chair, then gathered some rope he'd found in a box underneath the bed, and wrapped it in tight coils first around the boy's legs, and then his arms. He tied it firmly, but not too tight. He didn't want to hurt the kid. He pushed a bucket up to James' feet.

"You need to sick up," said Alexei, "use that. You need to piss? I'm afraid there's no easy way."

James looked at Alexei.

Alexei nodded. "It's an indignity, I know," he said. "But nothing really, compared to the things that Holden Gibson has put you through. That Fyodor Kolyokov has put *me* through."

"Goo' poin'," said James, language returning to him at last.

"Now I'm going to go away," said Alexei.

"To ki—to kill Hol'en?"

Alexei snorted and waved at him dismissively. He brushed the handle of the gun tucked into his trousers, and stepped back outside.

Was he going to kill Holden Gibson? It was an idea, Alexei admitted. Probably he would have to kill someone before this thing played itself out. But Gibson, necessarily?

Alexei hurried back to the long staircase where the Koldun had left him earlier that day.

Now there was someone who was a candidate for killing. When they first met, the old man Vasili Borovich had seemed like an ally. Alexei was sorely tempted to reassess that, and cast the Koldun in Holden Gibson's camp. After all, it was the Koldun who sent Alexei alone to the lighthouse. Where Holden Gibson had sent an agent—a puppet, really—to interrogate and kill Alexei.

It was a tempting theory. But truly, if the Koldun and Gibson were working together, and killing Alexei was their shared objective, it would have been simpler to murder Alexei as he slept. No—there was more to this place and the people here than simple murder.

And, he began to think, there was perhaps more to himself than simple murder too. Would the day end in killing at all? In the sobering summer air, Alexei began to wonder about that. Heather had set him up early to murder Holden Gibson. But how many times had he hesitated? Lost his nerve? Rationalized it away?

Alexei fingered the butt of the Glock. Was he really made for these things? If not these—then what? As he climbed down the stairs, Alexei came upon the thought that this place would, in its way, be just as useful in deciphering his present as was his metaphorical idyll into a childhood in assessing his history.

Alexei looked out over the harbour. There were more boats in it than before—which made a certain amount of sense. The sun was going down, casting a long, blue shadow over the breadth of the village. Lights were coming on in the buildings already. The fishing boats would be coming in for the night.

But he began to count. There were more boats there, really, than a prodigal fishing run could account for: more boats than there were moorings.

The stairs bottomed out in a yard, behind a two-storey wooden building that looked as though it might be a store. The back door stood ajar, and as Alexei listened, soft music drifted out. He approached the back of the building through the tall grass of the rear yard. The music was familiar—a Russian singer, bass. Singing to someone called Natascha.

"Rebroff," said Alexei, as the recognition dawned. "Ivan Rebroff."

Alexei remembered. Ivan Rebroff was an old Russian singer from the 1970s; a big round-faced Cossack, with an incredible vocal range who lived in a chateau in Austria with a couple of Siberian tigers for pets. Alexei had apparently listened to him quite a lot at one point, because he found himself humming along with the ballsy lament.

Alexei cracked open the door. It was a grocery—the sort of grocery you get in isolated little towns like this: a long room with sparsely filled shelves, with rows of old fluorescent tubes lighting everything a grey that flickered. A young woman sat behind a countertop, staring vacantly out the window. She was slight, long dark hair dangling in braids from the back of her skull. She reminded Alexei of something. Like the song, it was a memory unplaced.

"Hello," he said.

The woman shook her head, dislodging a daydream.

"Oh. Hello. I did not see you come in."

"Quite all right," he said. "Sorry for sneaking up on you. Nice music."

"Yes. It's good. Can I help you with something?"

Alexei sidled up to the counter. There was a row of chocolate bars. Packages of cigarettes lined the wall behind her.

"I'm afraid I don't have any cash on me," he said.

The woman shrugged. "I'm afraid I don't have a cash register. You want something to eat? You've been drinking—I can smell it. Food will take the edge off the headache."

Alexei reddened. He'd hoped the little binge had been long enough past that no one would notice. The girl had a point, though.

"For free?"

She smiled. "We're all family here," she said.

"Maybe some cashews," he said.

"Help yourself."

Alexei munched on the cashews and listened to the rest of the song, and looked around. As he did, it became clear that the absence of a cash register was far from the strangest thing in this store.

For one thing, the shelves weren't stocked with the hair combs and the cans of creamed corn and the salsa dips for the real Mexican tortillas in the salty snack section that you'd expect to see in an outpost grocery. In their place were little tins of Russian caviar and jars of truffle oil that sold in New York for $50 a bottle. A small open refrigerator was stuffed with fresh-looking roasts and exotic fowl wrapped tight in plastic. Through the cereal aisle, Alexei could make out a wine rack. There were no cheap wine boxes in sight, and he suspected he wouldn't find many screw-top bottles there either.

"We're family, are we?" he said, lifting a duck and letting it fall back into the ice. In the air, old Rebroff was starting on the Natascha song again, from the beginning.

The girl came around the counter. She was wearing a dark, patterned skirt to her ankles.

"You have just arrived? No. You've been here long enough to know better than to ask that."

Alexei nodded. "Right," he said. He looked to the ceiling and behind the counter.

"Where is your stereo?" he said as Rebroff sang on.

The girl smiled. "Same place as the cash register," she said. "We don't need one."

"Ah."

"Now let me ask a question," she said. "Two questions."

"All right."

"What is your name, sir?"

Alexei smiled. "Alexei," he said.

"Hello Alexei. I am Darya." She extended her hand. He shook it.

"And your second question?"

"Were you a killer?"

Alexei let her fingers slip from his. "A—"

"I only say, because you don't look like a university professor or a lawyer, or much of a politician. Did you kill for them?"

Darya was flushed as she spoke. Alexei looked back at her levelly.

"I have my suspicions," he said.

She nodded and smiled. "I thought so. It's good. It's good. I'm told that I'm getting an eye for this kind of thing. Maybe one day, you think I can become one with the dream-walkers? Babushka used to tell me I'd make a good dream-walker."

Alexei went to the front door of the shop. He looked out into the street. A small group of tourists walked along the road. "Dream-walkers," he said. "I don't know about that." Then Alexei remembered something the Koldun said earlier: he was going to prepare for the "dance" tonight.

"Are you going to the dance?" he asked.

Darya's smile widened and she turned her ankle in an awkward flirt. "Is that an invitation?" she asked. "Because you know that it's not that kind of dance. But—"

Alexei looked at her. She looked back at him with an unmistakable expression.

"—we do have a bit of time before it begins."

Comfort is the torturer's first tool, thought Alexei.

"No," he said.

She was visibly annoyed when he turned down her proposition—but Alexei felt he had no choice. Comfort was indeed the torturer's first tool. After having spent the afternoon comfortably drinking and eating and kibitzing in the lighthouse, Alexei would have been a fool to fall back into the trap again.

"You are heartless," she said, eyes narrow. "Makes it easy to kill, I suppose, being so heartless."

"I am sorry," he said. "Look—I have to look around this place. Find my bearings. I have to find the children. Gibson. I—" he dropped his gaze to the floor "—I don't have time for that kind of thing."

"None of us have more than a little time," she said. Then her smile returned. "But if you don't want to play around—I could show you around. Help you get your bearings, like you said."

Alexei smiled and shook his head. "I'll be going. Thank you for the nuts."

"No," the girl said, following him as he headed towards the front door. "Wait. You want to see things, I can show you things: the fishery. The greenhouse. The museum."

Alexei stopped.

"Museum?" He turned to look at her. "What kind of a museum does a town like this have?"

The girl grinned. "The New Pokrovskoye Museum of Family History," she said. "It tells our whole story. It is very complete. You should go there before the dance, certainly. It helps—well it helps. All the new people must go there—or however will they learn to dance?"

Alexei thought about that. He was, after all, trying to tell his own story. He'd spent what had seemed like months in a metaphor looking for clues. And clues he found—but only enough to confound him more.

He could try to find the children—blunder in—maybe run in to more of Holden Gibson's people. Maybe run into the mysterious Koldun again. That would be how Alexei the KGB agent would handle things.

But there was more to him than that. Simply stumbling in, pounding against a locker—fighting Czernochov in a math class—or killing Holden Gibson—that wouldn't do it. He needed to find out more about himself—about this place—about what he was up against.

The skills he learned decoding his memory—perhaps, thought Alexei, he needed to apply them in the present as well.

He made up his mind.

"All right," he said and held out his hand. "Take me to the museum."

"So it will be like a date?"

"Sure," he'd replied. "A big date."

She followed him outside, turned the CLOSED sign into place and pulled the door closed.

"Come on," she said. "It's not far."

They were perched on top of a rocky slope, that rode down to make a bowl around the harbour. Red and green-painted houses clung to the slope, like Day-Glo barnacles. A single road wound between them. The only noise that Alexei heard was the crying of gulls, the sputtering of boat engines in the harbour. And

Ivan Rebroff, selling the chorus of "Ach, Natascha" one more time.

"Nothing's far here, is it?" he said.

"True enough," she said. "That is the beauty of New Pokrovskoye. Everything at hand. Now do you want to go to the museum? We've got a marvellous collection of Fabergé eggs. The best in the world, Papa says."

The Imperial New Pokrovskoye Museum of Family History was a rambling thing of wood and iron and shingle—a long A-frame that suggested an ancient longhouse, more of a shelter for Norwegians and their livestock than a repository of Russian antiquities. It huddled in the crook of an elbow of rock at the southern edge of the village, at the end of a short gravel road. It had been painted bright red a couple of seasons ago. Now the paint was beginning to peel. The sign was in Cyrillic, hand-painted above a small door, which was marked CLOSED, just like Darya's grocery. She pushed the door open. A smell like cloves wafted out. Darya inhaled deeply.

"Are there speakers everywhere in town?" asked Alexei.

Darya looked at him.

"That song," said Alexei. "I hear it everywhere I go."

"It's a song," said Darya, as though that answered everything. Then she took him by the hand. "Inside!" she said.

In the guise of adjusting his belt, Alexei fingered the handle of the Glock in his waistband. Darya leaned to one side of the door, and there was the sound of a light-switch flipping—and Alexei gasped. His hand fell away from the gun. And he stared.

The inside of the museum was huge—a vast chamber held up by thick tree trunks in the middle that had not even been squared. Lights hung on cords from the ceiling in conical shades, casting round pools onto tables and cases filled with objects that glittered with gold and precious stones. Further back, the pools illuminated other things: machinery that might have been military; a case with a great skeleton mounted from a contraption that looked like a gallows; and something else—a thing that Alexei couldn't quite place—that looked like a great, jewel-encrusted egg.

They had to walk down a short flight of stairs—the floor had been cut deep into the rock, so the first six feet of wall was carved stone before the barn board took over. The sight abruptly reminded Alexei of something he had seen once before—in a strange cavern, in Afghanistan, before he had—had—

No good. He lost the thread of it.

Alexei smiled around the lump in his throat. This place, he thought, might just be as useful as that school days metaphor, in helping him sort the puzzle of his life. He squeezed Darya's hand. "Let's have a look," he said. And together they descended, humming along with the chorus as they went.

"My Papa was a killer," said Darya as they paused over a display case of Imperial Russian china.

"Really," said Alexei. "A killer."

Darya slapped him on the shoulder. "Don't make fun! He was!"

"All right. Papa was a killer. You must be very proud. Who did he kill? How many?"

"We are not certain. He definitely killed an American. Name was Timothy Elkhorn. In Honduras. He used a shovel. And some Italians. Seven of those. That happened just after I was born. He used a machinegun and a boat. And there were the Africans . . ."

"He did this under orders?"

"In a manner of speaking."

Alexei moved past the china, to a display of silver cutlery. "Tell me," he said, "how did these wonderful objects manage to find their way to New Pokrovskoye?"

"The Koldun," she said.

"Vasili Borovich, you mean?"

"The Koldun," she repeated, more firmly. "He brought them with him in a dozen boats, when he came to New Pokrovskoye to rejoin Babushka."

Alexei looked around. A case of three scimitars, their hilts forged of gold and silver, rested next to a fine chain mail hauberk draped over a dressmaker's dummy, bosom jutting absurdly through the woven steel. Alexei counted a dozen gleaming samovars on a long oak shelf behind them. The Fabergé eggs were a little farther off, in a tall-glassed in shelf. Alexei counted a dozen of them. Other than the unlikeliness of their context—here in a barn of a museum in a little coastal fishing village in Canada—Alexei had no reason to doubt their authenticity.

"All of this?"

"Not on the same trip—but yes," she said. "It was a gift. When we made this village, the Koldun was simply a traveller. An old friend of Babushka's."

"Vasili," said Alexei, "Borovich."

Darya nodded. "That was his name. Then. The gift allowed him to change, by grace of Babushka. To become the Koldun."

"Well—Vasili or Koldun, by whatever name he is very generous." Alexei stepped away from the case. He pointed to the giant egg-thing towards the far end of the room.

"That would have required a second trip all by itself, I'd think," he said.

Darya smiled. "Oh. That one, I don't think the Koldun brought."

Alexei approached the thing. It sat on a platform three feet off the ground—circled with deep ochre curtain. It wasn't truly an egg. It was more shaped like a lozenge . . . a fat man's coffin. Where the stones had not been fixed, it was the colour of robin's egg.

It reminded Alexei of something that caught in the corner of his mind.

"That was Babushka's. It was where she slept."

"Is she sleeping there still?" Alexei had a vision of Lenin's Tomb—but with a desiccated old woman in the place of the perfectly preserved corpse of Vladimir Lenin.

"Really now." Alexei circled the strange container, looking for a way in. It didn't take long. On the opposite side, he saw a round hatch—like a submarine hatch, complete with a small iron wheel in its centre. The wheel had been painted a deep violet. It sparkled with tiny foil stars—the kind teachers used to congratulate a student for work well done.

"What an interesting—museum—you have here," he said, and gave the wheel a spin. It turned easily, with the tick-tock sound of a clock. As it slowed, it became more like a roulette wheel. When it stopped, the hatch swung open a hair's breadth.

Darya stood open-mouthed—genuinely alarmed.

"Wha—" she began.

Alexei looked at her.

"What is that smell?"

What smell? thought Alexei. He was about to say it. Dismiss little Darya's observation. But something was changed. He cocked his head—listening.

"I don't know about the smell," he said. "But do you hear?"

"Hear what?"

"Nothing. That's the thing," said Alexei. "No music. Mr. Rebroff has left us."

The opening to the Babushka's vessel yawned at them. Alexei tentatively leaned toward it and sniffed. He looked back at Darya, who was holding her nose now. He sniffed again. The air was cool, and stale as you might expect from a sarcophagus that had apparently been sealed up for a decade or so. But whatever odour had Darya clutching her face was undetectable to Alexei. He squinted to look inside.

"Why—why did you do that?" Darya's voice had taken a pleading, whining tone.

"I don't know," said Alexei shortly. "I don't know why I do a lot of things." He stuck his head into the opening, tried to see around in the darkness. "Who is Babushka?" The question echoed, edging the words with iron. "She is the lady of scents, hmm? Now tell me: what was she doing with this—thing? Out with it, Darya."

"Lena."

"What?" The vessel was making Darya's voice sound strange too. It sounded tinny, as though travelling through a cheap radio speaker. At least she'd stopped whining.

"Babushka is Lena."

"I see. And who is Lena?"

"Dead."

Alexei reached inside, ran his hand over the interior surface. It wasn't metal in here. It felt like ceramic. It was cold as a sheet of ice. "That's not an answer," he said.

"It will have to do."

Alexei frowned. The voice really didn't sound like young Darya's. It was, he realized, too deep. Not mannishly deep. But old. Very old.

Alexei took a breath, and looked behind him. Darya had stepped away—she was back behind the dressmaker's dummy, arms crossed, fingers tapping on her elbows—looking anywhere but back at Alexei.

He turned back into the chamber.

"All right," he said. "You didn't answer my second question: What's this thing for?"

"Butterflies."

"Butterflies." Alexei frowned. "Caterpillars into butterflies?" he ventured. "A cocoon? Like that?"

"It will have to do."

Ah. That was why the voice sounded so strange. He wasn't hearing it with his ears; it was as when Vladimir spoke to him. He heard it in his head.

"You are no fool, Alexei Kilodovich."

I don't know about that, thought Alexei.

"No, it is true. There is something about you, little man."

Ha.

"Your mockery is insincere. Because you know it to be true. You know your true nature is other than it seems. What, I wonder, is it?"

I have been puzzling this for months. So don't ask me.

"You have certainly had a difficult day. Someone tried to kill you."

Are you watching me all the time?

"No. No. Not yet. But do you wonder—why would anyone want to kill you? What is in you?"

I don't know.

"I think you know. Something in you is refusing to accept, hmm?"

If you say.

"Well. Whatever it is—I am sure old Fyodor buried it there for a reason. Best not pry—hmm?"

Why would Fyodor bury anything?

"You tell me. Or maybe—maybe Fyodor could tell me himself. Are you in there, my love?"

The Babushka's tone was making Alexei uncomfortable. It was time to change the subject.

Why do they call you Babushka?

"Because I am an ugly old woman. I am the elder. I am sorry—I *was* the elder. The one who made this place. But Babushka is gone now too. I am just I."

The elder? Elder what?

Alexei waited.

"The elder what?" he repeated, aloud.

"What?"

"What?" Alexei turned around.

Darya was back. She looked at him strangely. "You should take your head out of there," she said. "It's Babushka's."

"My head?"

Darya laughed. "The tank," she said. "But also your head—soon enough."

Alexei turned and leaned against the tank. "What do you mean by that?"

"At the dance," said Darya. "We'll all lose our heads to Babushka."

"I think," said Alexei slowly, "I may have just been speaking with her."

"How fortunate for you." Darya gave him a sceptical look. "Maybe you will lose your head to her sooner. That is why I thought you might like to—"

Alexei raised his hand. "Right. I am flattered, Darya. But no thank you. It would be a distraction."

"You're the sort of fellow who never does anything, aren't you? You never take any risks—and you *hate* distractions." She looked at him, and Alexei shrugged. "I'm right about that. Like Papa says—I'm getting the sight. Well, Mr. Killer—that kind of thinking can't get you very far in your line of work—now can it?"

Alexei opened his mouth. He didn't know what to say to that, and was rescued by the sound of the door opening. He closed his mouth and put his hand on the butt of his gun.

"Oh shit," breathed Darya as a tall, balding man in an overcoat stepped in. He looked around with small, hard eyes. Three others—a man, and two women—jostled in behind him. By the sounds of things, more were waiting to come through outside. "Papa."

"Papa?" said Alexei.

"Hide!" she hissed. "We're not supposed to be here. He'll kill us!"

"Pilgrims!" shouted Darya's killer father, when the crowd of them had come in. "Welcome to the New Pokrovskoye Museum of Family History! This place has been here as long as we have—and yet like our family here, it grows month by month." He repeated himself in French, and once more in Russian.

The crowd nodded at various times. By the time they were all inside, Alexei counted at least thirty. They shuffled down the steps and gawked at the treasure like retirees on a bus tour. But it wasn't just retirees. Old men and women tottered alongside athletes who couldn't have been older than twenty. A fat man with greased-back blond hair and a sweaty blue T-shirt was pointing out the intricacies of a glass-domed clock to a young red-haired beauty in a dark blue denim jacket. Two angular black-haired men, so similar to one another they might have been twins, wandered toward the eggs. One of them wore the black and white collar of a clergyman. His brother just wore shorts and a T-shirt, and a dumb, happy grin. Of them all, just one—a short, swarthy man who lingered near the door, glancing over his shoulder like he was expecting someone to check for his ticket—didn't appear to be having the time of his life.

Alexei pulled back behind the curtain, and whispered to Darya: "We can't stay here. We'll turn up."

"Papa will kill us!"

"Really? Like—" Alexei drew his finger across his throat and raised his eyebrows in a question. Darya shrugged.

"That's what he used to do," she said matter-of-factly.

Alexei looked back—this time paying closer attention to Darya's dad. He had to admit, it was possible. The old man moved in and around the displays with the ease of a jungle cat, his tiny cool eyes unblinking. He wasn't a young man—what was left of his hair was bone white, and his face was a map of wrinkles—but Alexei didn't think there was anything but bone and muscle underneath that coat. He appended the thought: bone, muscle, and a small arsenal of assassin's tools.

Alexei shook his head. That was silly. He was just an old guy who owned a general store, and was right now explaining about the significance of the samovars—which nobleman had made his tea in which of the little tanks, at around about what time period.

"I look at you and I can see—now you wonder," said Darya's father, "how this is Family history and not merely a store of antiquities? Tell us, Orlovsky. Are we all descended from the Czars? The cousins of little Anastasia, who fled the Bolsheviks' bullets? Is this our heritage?"

Darya's father smiled sadly. He shook his head. "No," he said. "We are ordinary folk in this room. Our grandparents were more likely to be peasants than kings. They did not, in all likelihood, even know one another in their times. And yet—this is your heritage. It will become your heritage."

As he spoke, Darya's father walked over to the case of eggs. Alexei pulled back from the curtain, crawled around to the other side of the space there, and peered out through another crack.

"Your treasure," he said. "For there are others, who dream us. These ones—these ones are the true Family. Descended from the Holy Man Grigor Rasputin, yes?" Darya's father's laugh was a cold razor in his throat. "He who healed the Romanovs and foretold the future—who dreamed and saw the world through God's eye. And yes—He who spread his seed through the country, to make the Family.

"Rasputin's bastards, they called them! They have dwelt in our dreams and guided our lives. They are as angels to us. And tonight—"

His grin was wide as he spread his arms.

"—tonight, they give you this!"

Alexei scanned across the faces of the old man's audience. There was not a hint of skepticism in the room; not even rolling eyes at the rich, carnival barker's hyperbole that Darya's father was spewing. They just watched him, nodding, and followed the sweep of his hands as he guided them to look upon the scimitars and the clocks and the china, that according to Darya the Koldun Vasili Borovich had brought here on ships many years ago.

"It will begin very soon," said Darya's father quietly. "You will hear the song, and then there are the smells, and in a joyful exodus, you will visit Paradise."

Members of the group looked at one another with broad grins, nodding in agreement. The uncomfortable little man by the door joined in—nodding and grinning even more forcefully than the rest as he moved down the steps, and around a display case outside Alexei's field of view.

"Soon," said Darya's father. "For now—marvel at the treasures of the New Pokrovskoye Museum of Family History. Marvel, children. And savour. For you will remember them, yes? And with them—construct your paradise together. Savour."

Alexei felt a hand on his thigh. Darya leaned close and whispered in his ear: "Savour me."

Alexei looked at her, and glanced above—where the Babushka's great egg loomed, like a terrible cloud. He thought he could hear a clicking sound—a bonging, as if a great thing shifted in there.

"I don't think—" he whispered, but she interrupted him:

"Savour me, or I'll scream."

Alexei looked at her.

"You won't scream. Your Papa would kill us both."

She sighed. "I thought we had a date," she whispered.

"Pretty exciting date already."

"Alexei." Darya shifted so her flank pressed against his. He felt her hip against him. "Please. Just hold me if you don't want me. I want to feel a touch. Before—"

Alexei put his hand on her shoulder. It was clammy with fear sweat. "Before what? Rapture?" he whispered.

"*Rapture.*" She uttered it as a curse. "Yes. Before *that* particular wonder." She looked at him pleadingly. "I am young, Alexei. I don't want to vanish like the others."

Alexei nodded. "All right," he said, stroking her hair. "All right."

Мастер MASTER AND MAN и человек

The lighthouse's aerie was day's last refuge in New Pokrovskoye. Golden sunlight would catch there before nightfall—and thus trapped, would flit like a moth about the complicated rigging of reflectors and lamps to send phantoms of illumination cascading down to the dark pit of the lighthouse's base. To the eyes of Holden Gibson, it made the great round room look a bit like a disco.

There were all of ten eyes of his inside the lighthouse. Eight of them were able to focus well enough to be of use. The remaining two were blurry and bloodshot and sore, set into a skull still hammering from the effects of a half a bottle of mid-priced vodka, poured down the attached throat and absorbed through the walls of the acid-drenched stomach a foot and a half below.

The other eight eyes were in much better shape. They were able to assess the situation of eyes nine and ten promptly—drunk, crusted in puke and wallowing in piss, and tied rather too efficiently to a wooden chair in the middle of the room.

Holden Gibson had ten eyes, and those ten eyes had ten hands. Eight of them were useful. He set hands one and two to work undoing the knots around the ankles—then made sure hands three and four held the chair in place. Five and six he set to work on the wrist restraints. And with all the other work taken care of, hands seven and eight he sent to the door, to keep watch—just in case that Russian secret agent fucker Alexei had not in fact run off with Holden Gibson's gun, but was waiting in the shadows, for Holden Gibson to drop his guard again.

Hands seven and eight paced back and forth angrily under the whirling light of the setting sun. They spasmed from fists to open palms and back again, slamming themselves into each other with butcher-shop smacks. They pulled on fingers and cracked knuckles, worried at a hangnail and finally yanked it to the quick.

Fucking Russian. He'd been the start of this. Insinuating himself into Holden Gibson's crew with that amnesia act. Until he'd shown up, things were going according to the order. Holden Gibson and his crew sailing off to meet a submarine—get those kids he'd been told about. He'd needed those kids. With the Internet, the magazine subscription business was taking a beating. He needed to boost the organization—give it some new blood—some—

—some *talented* blood.

He hadn't known what that meant, precisely, when the old woman had made him the pitch. The old woman he'd what—met?

He didn't recall seeing her. Just remembered a funny smell. A voice.

It had been on the telephone. It must have been a phone call.

It did all start with the fucking Russian Alexei. He'd played at amnesiac—and now the opposite was happening to Holden Gibson.

Holden Gibson. That was his name. It was not, as the voices kept insisting, John Kaye. Who the fuck was John Kaye? Someone who looked like Holden Gibson—that was for sure. Because Holden Gibson had spent his entire lifetime in the United States. He'd spent some time in Mexico, okay—and he did a lot of business in Canada—but that was practically the United States. He'd sure as shit never been to Prague—or Budapest—or a farmhouse in East Germany, and then a cellar, a deep cellar, somewhere in the Urals where the firmament of his talent was cracked and brutalized by his nation's sworn enemy . . .

Hand seven slammed down on the little card table, knocking over a jug of water. Hand eight twirled a tightly coiled lock of Rasta hair, and pulled it hard.

The firmament of his talent. That was, Holden Gibson admitted to himself, a serious flaw in his John-Kaye-is-someone-else theory. He undeniably possessed this—this *talent*. His crew had become more than loyal since he'd had the memories flood back. He wondered, in retrospect, how much his talent had had to do with his crew's loyalty over the years. He'd always thought it was just his way with kids—which would certainly explain how the younger ones always seemed more obedient than the older ones, who as Holden Gibson had recently learned, were hatching a conspiracy to murder him. As he sifted through their brains, he found thoughts of murder connected to Holden Gibson in an alarming abundance. Stabbing him—poisoning him—tossing him over the side of the yacht.

And all too often—there was the fucking Russian again.

They attached themselves to Alexei Kilodovich. Wanted Alexei to murder him. Like some kind of fucking saviour. And Alexei wanted to murder him too. He'd tried to two times at least. Possibly more in the past. And now he'd taken Holden Gibson's gun and gotten Hands Nine and Ten blind drunk, and tied them up—and could be lurking anywhere. With his gun. Waiting to shoot them.

Hands Seven and Eight opened the door. Looked outside. The stars were starting to come out. Out here, they appeared in truly alarming numbers, spread over the sky in a smear of infinity. The lungs belonging to Hands Seven and Eight took a deep breath. It smelled of the sea tonight—and not much more; none of that perfume box of stinks that moved its way around this place. It was also very quiet. All that ears seven and eight could hear was a faint singing—more of that fucking Russian music—coming from the harbour, probably.

Foot seven began to idly tap on the flagstones. Holden Gibson put a stop to it as soon as he noticed. *Fuck*. That wasn't supposed to happen. *Who's driving this bitch?* he thought. Holden backed up, and steered Hands Seven and Eight back into the room.

He couldn't see a thing. The disco ball at the top of the aerie had gone dark, and that did it for the rest of the lighthouse. He reached out to the rest of his eyes, the rest of his hands—and groped in empty darkness.

Where the fuck was everybody?

Holden Gibson took a breath. He was still rusty with his talent—sometimes, he'd lose a crewmember if he wasn't concentrating; that had happened earlier today, when Alexei the Russian had gotten the jump on him. He groped around now, in a sudden panic over the idea that this was in fact what Alexei had done. Russian bastard.

"Russian fuckin' bastard!" hollered Holden. He opened the door again, to let some of the starlight in. It did no good. He could see nothing in the room—nothing but the empty chair, and the ropes on the floor. "You fucker! I know you're in here somewhere!"

Really?

Holden Gibson stopped. Listened—tried to place the location of the voice. It was male, and sounded Russian.

Somewhere? Do you think you can be more specific, Mr. Kaye?

Holden Gibson turned quickly. The voice had seemed to come from right behind him. Definitely Russian. "Fuck you, Alexei," he said. "I'm not lettin' you fuck me twice."

The voice chuckled—still behind him. It was joined by another voice—a little girl sound, that Holden Gibson recognized somehow. She laughed. And she started to say something. Something that Holden also recognized.

Mi, she said. *Mi mi mi mi*.

Now, said the Russian voice. *Out, old man. Heather wants her body back*.

And Holden Gibson felt a sharp pain on the back of his head that felt remarkably like the flat of a shovel-blade. The last thing he heard before consciousness returned and Hands Seven and Eight drifted further from his reach, was the unmistakable sound of a chainsaw starting up—and the giggling of the little girl—of Heather—as she struggled to maintain the mantra.

Mi. Mi mi mi mi, she sang, as the chainsaw bit into bone.

THE IDIOT
ИДИОТ

Darya didn't make love to him, so much as she mapped him. Whispering repeated thanks, she ran her hands through Alexei's hair, over the stubble on his chin; across this lips and around the mysterious whorls and turns of his ears. She traced the tendons in his neck—up one side, down the other—and paused when she reached the scar that ran a jagged line over his back.

As her hands moved down his torso to his belt Alexei gently pulled out the gun from his waistband and set it aside. He thought he apprehended what it was she was doing.

Soon, she would be in a place like he had been—possibly, reduced to her childhood memories of herself. Flesh and touch there would be a construct—a powerful but still incomplete simulacrum. Memory, distinct, sensual memory, might make it better.

Like the others who were drinking in their true heritage here in the museum—Darya was drinking in those sensations of flesh that she might ever be denied. When she propositioned him, she might have thought it was only about sex. But as her explorations continued—even as she pulled back the band of his underwear, and took his member in her fingers—Alexei understood that her needs were more encompassing than that.

Alexei, however, was on the other side of Rapture. And like the vodka and talk that had seduced him in the lighthouse, Darya's soft touch moved him now. For Alexei, it was not about map-making, as his hand fluttered aside Darya's skirt, and ran up the smoothness of her thigh. He swallowed, and shut his eyes, and only a part of him remembered where he was—the potential peril he found himself in.

"Nuh," said Darya at once. She withdrew her fingers.

Alexei opened his eyes.

He withdrew his own hand.

He felt her hands at his shoulders, pushing him back.

He let go entirely, acquiescent and guilty and pissed off all at once. He had never felt more like an awkward, oafish teenager than this day—even, he reflected ruefully, during his adventures in his own history.

"What is it?"

Her eyes were open—in the dim light underneath Babushka's sarcophagus, they seemed to dance with energy. She looked at Alexei—but she didn't seem to see him.

"The dance?" he asked. "*Rapture*?"

As if in answer, she rose on her legs and hands, arching her back—and crab-like, scuttled to the edge of the podium. She shifted and bent, her long skirt sweeping across the ground, and like that—she was through.

Shit. She was through. Alexei felt a peculiar sense of defeat. She would go out, and her papa would find her, and then the old man would come after him, an angry parent hunting down the boy who felt up his daughter.

Except that this was not an ordinary father. This was a man who had murdered dozens, in Latin America and Europe and Africa.

Alexei lifted Holden Gibson's Glock from the floor and held it ready. Well. Darya's papa the leading citizen of New Pokrovskoye, was not the only one who knew a thing or two about killing.

Ivan Rebroff sang on as Alexei crawled to the edge of the curtain and lifted it. From the sounds of thumping feet, it seemed like there was quite a bit of commotion. But as he lifted it, the last board creaked, and the room fell quiet. He blinked, and moved to another side, and there too—the room seemed empty. At the far end of the hall, he heard the sound of the door shutting.

Alexei waited. He listened. He did this until he felt his legs cramp up. So cautiously, he moved the curtain aside, and crawled out into the empty museum. He felt his knees crack as he climbed to his feet. He held the Glock close to his hip and pressed back against the cool eggshell surface of Babushka's tank.

Hey, he thought, scanning his gaze beyond the puddles of light from the ceiling—looking for any sign of movement; any sign that anyone might be waiting for him. Darya's father—one of Holden Gibson's people. Anybody.

Hey, he thought again. *Babushka*.

There came no answer.

If there is to be a dance, and everyone is going to Paradise, how is it that poor Alexei is left without a partner?

Alexei moved around the tank. The fake gemstones glued onto its surface seemed to shimmer under the light. The song dopplered down a half-tone, as though old Rebroff was driving away on the back of a truck. Alexei drew a breath. Even the old killer Darya's father seemed to have gone. He was alone in this museum. He stuffed the gun back into his waistband.

Alexei stopped at the hatch to the tank. It was still slightly ajar. He pulled it open all the way, and stuck his head into the darkness.

"Babushka!" he spoke into the tank. "Why am I alone here?"

He was met with the barrel of a gun, a touch of ice against the middle of his forehead. The voice that answered him was deep, and it echoed—but not in his head. And not deep like the Babushka voice.

"*Don' fuckin' move,*" it said in English. "*You got that*?"

"I got that."

Alexei did not move.

"*This is a gun that I am pointing at you. You know the word for* gun, *you fuckin' Commie?*"

All Alexei's attention bent and focussed through the lens of the gun pressed against his forehead.

"I do," said Alexei. "Don't worry. I am not moving."

"*Fuckin' right you're not. Now you stand right there, and you think very carefully about how you're going to answer my questions.*"

Alexei thought about a lot of things. Mostly, the gun barrel pressed to his forehead, and how the gun and its owner came to be inside the Babushka's sarcophagus in the New Pokrovskoye Museum of Family History.

"*First question,*" said the gunman. "*Where's the fuckin' sea?*"

Alexei swore to himself. *Where is the sea*? What kind of question was that? The gunman was obviously out of his mind. He tried the best answer he could think of: "Down the hill. Past the harbour. That's the ocean." He shut his eyes, waiting for the bullet. But the gun barrel wavered, drawing a little circle in the sweating skin of his forehead.

"*Fuck. All right. Listen. I'm not talking about that sea. I'm talking about* the sea—*the sea in the fuckin' U.F.O.*"

"I cannot help you," said Alexei. "I don't know where the sea there has gotten to."

"*Fuck.*" The cold circle of gunmetal pulled away from Alexei's forehead. Alexei let out a long and ragged breath, that apparently he had been holding all this time. Alexei blinked, and watched as a face joined the gun in the little circular hatchway. He recognized it immediately: it was the face of the one man who'd seemed uncomfortable in the tour group.

He looked up at Alexei appraisingly. Alexei looked back at him. They didn't speak for what felt like a full minute.

"I give up," he finally said. "No more act. I'm not fuckin' Sergei."

"I didn't think you were," said Alexei.

"I'm Leo Montassini."

"All right. I'm Alexei," said Alexei.

"Alex . . . Alexei Kilodovich?"

Alexei frowned. The little guy grinned.

"Alexei *Kilodovich*. No shit. From New York?"

"Do we know each other?"

"Nah. Well. Kind of. I know you. Mr. Bucci said to bring you if we found you, along with the old guy, whatsisname? Fyodor Kolyokov." Leo Montassini was quiet a moment, like he was doing math in his head. "Well fuck me. I was right to come here! It wasn't just a bullshit midlife fuckin' spiritual crisis thing. That's what I was startin' to think. Montassini, you're goin' all soft and spiritual. Next thing you know, you'll be carryin' a fuckin' crystal around in your shorts and meditatin' all the time and stoppin' eatin' meat. Go to fuckin' confession, forget about this shit with the sea and the smell and the little fuckin' voices in your fucked up head. Well fuck me! I was *right*!"

Montassini was grinning. His gun was dangling. Alexei made no attempt to piece together what this armed lunatic was saying. Instead, he made a couple of quick calculations in his head.

"Shit," continued Montassini. "Everything makes so much fuckin' sense. We are fuckin' soulmates, pal. Fuckin' soul—"

But he didn't have opportunity to finish, before Alexei reached around and swung the hatch cover closed on Leo Montassini's gun hand. The handgun clattered to the floor, and Alexei Kilodovich's soulmate howled like a dog.

RESURRECTION
Воскресение

The Rapture was beginning.

New Pokrovskoye had been building to it for weeks—its children flowing to it from the corners of the continent, in buses and trains and cars and finally boats. Welders, bankers, professors at universities; or as often, quiet and solitary men and women who slept in basement apartments and worked their days in strategically placed gas stations or convenience stores. Men who knew how to fix aircraft, or fly them. Women who bore the children of politicians and businessmen and bureaucrats. An astronaut. Three chefs. Dozens, who had fallen on hard times and lived on the streets.

Fifteen were too ill to properly travel. But when the Babushka's call went out and entered their minds—when it tickled the tiny parts of their brains that registered smells, and pleasure, and comfort—the sick ones climbed out of their beds and made their way to the rendezvous points, along with the rest. They basked in the immediate community of family as they sat in the backs of buses, humming along with the old songs, reintegrating their memories of truth with the lies that their lives had become.

At Cloridorme, they had loaded onto the boats that were gathered for this purpose. They stood at the gunwales, holding the hands of the ones next to them like old lovers, watching as the land receded—the mists of the sea enveloped them. They hummed and sang and sniffed at their memories—at the tantalizing hope of truth, once and for all—until the coastline reappeared, and the anomaly of this place—of New Pokrovskoye—surrounded them with the unfamiliar comfort of its harbour. The sleepers gathered there in rooms and beds—doing good work in the fishery and the greenhouse during the day, humming and thinking and waiting, for the moment they might truly awaken.

It was not only sleepers that came to New Pokrovskoye for the Rapture. The call went out to all of the family, twisting in a great, expanding mist. To the more senior members—the ones who dreamed—there was no need for the crude manipulation of smell. It was a simple shout: *Join in me*.

Join in me. It did not, precisely, appeal to reason—but perhaps reason's near cousin. To those who had hidden fearful as witches these many years in the darker corners of the world, alone but for their own small network of sleepers, the call offered a kind of hope that they had never allowed themselves to feel. Though they might not have known the voice of the caller by name, they knew her in their hearts. For she was their Babushka—one of the elders who had made them.

And she was something else too. Something that they all intuited was greater. For waiting as they did in dark places, feeding off the wealth of their networks, these ones all were haunted by the sense that perhaps something greater might come of them; that such abilities as they had could not simply be a mutation, a trick of the brain. The light they saw at seven thousand feet could not just be the sun. It had to be more. It had to be heaven.

Or else their life is meaningless, said Fyodor Kolyokov. *Who can bear that*?

Heather clutched her torn fingernail in her fist, as though pressing it back down could reunite it with the quick. She stood in the lighthouse's aerie, looking down at the village of New Pokrovskoye. It was lit up like a carnival tonight; strings of white lights drew along its laneways like a spiderweb after a rainfall, winding and radiating out from the middle of the harbour. That fucking song was back again. But this time, it wasn't the scratchy old recording—it was a chorus sung by a thousand voices, as they moved through the brightly lit streets to their convergence.

"Meaning is overrated," she said—subvocalizing like he'd told her to when she spoke.

Her zombie pal laughed. *I* do *like you*, he said, in that freaky in-your-head way he had of talking. Back at the Transcendental Meditation Camp, as they stood over the array of steaming body parts that had been Hippie Pete and watched the world there begin to fade, he had warned her it would be a little strange at first, the two of them sharing one skull. She would hear him as an echo through her bones.

It was a creepy feeling. But creepy as it was, it was not half as bad as losing herself to Holden Gibson or John Kaye or whoever the fuck the old man she'd spent her life with was. She thought it might even be less creepy than taking part in this dance—this Rapture thing—that all these other loser sleepers were falling into now. It was also, she admitted, nice to be able to stay in her body without concentrating on her old Hippie Pete mantra.

"So was Holden Gibson—John Kaye—whoever. Was he coming *here* for meaning?"

As for him, said the zombie Kolyokov, *I don't know. The last time I saw him was more than forty years ago. At City 512—at the place where we used to work. I wouldn't have thought there was enough left of him to walk a straight line. We did quite a job.*

"You sound proud of yourself."

Not proud. She felt the zombie move behind her eyes, a restless foetus. *Merely puzzled. We have to find out more about John Kaye. Maybe when we find Alexei, he will be able to help. Hey. What is that music?*

"What?" Heather listened. She made a face. "Fuck if I know. Something about Natascha?"

I recognize it. Hum.

Heather leaned against the thick glass of the aerie. She squinted, at what she was sure was an optical illusion. The lights below seemed to be swirling—rising, as though they were attached to a great net that something high and huge was pulling out of water.

"I don't know what help *Alexei's* going to be," said Heather, subvocalizing through gritted teeth. "Stupid bastard couldn't even manage a clean killing."

Ivan Rebroff.

"What?"

Ivan Rebroff. The guy singing. Hah. Trite folk songs. She would *be a fan of his.*

"Who would be?"

Kolyokov didn't answer. So Heather stood there with her quiet zombie—watching the lights of the village rise up past her, and illuminate the belly of a great, dark cloud that she could have sworn had not been there a moment ago.

"What the fuck is that thing?" she said. Little flashes of lightning illuminated the cloud's broad underside. Thunder rumbled like laughter.

It is a metaphor, said Fyodor, *of Her*.

THE HONEST THIEF
Честный вор

When the hatch opened again, and his eyes adjusted to the bright light, Leo Montassini found he was looking down the barrel of a Glock semiautomatic handgun. It was accompanied by an open hand, fingers wiggling impatiently.

"You have another weapon?"

Montassini reached into his boot and pulled out a knife. The hand took it, and flung it away. It clattered on the floorboards somewhere near the samovars.

"You may come out." The gun backed away. Montassini blinked and let his eyes focus on the man who held them:

Alex Kilodovich. Well fuck me blue.

He was a big guy—bigger than Montassini had been led to expect. And fuck but he looked like he could take care of himself. He had that kind of hardness about him that all guys in the profession had at one time. And he had the stare. The one that said he'd taken stock of all of the goodness and mercy in his soul—everything that was right—and locked it up somewhere safe. Leo wasn't exactly afraid of him—but he was wise enough to respect him, and respect the fact that he had a gun pointed at Leo's chest. Leo kept eye contact and started to crawl out of the hatch. He winced.

"Your hand okay?" said Kilodovich.

"Nothing broken," said Montassini. "Little sore though."

"Sorry."

"Hey—I was pointin' a gun at you then I let my guard down. I'd have done the same thing in your shoes."

"You are a forgiving soul." Kilodovich reached into his waistband and pulled Montassini's gun out. He pointed it at Montassini's chest too.

"Yeah, whatever." Montassini stretched in front of the UFO. He felt his joints cracking. Kilodovich backed away, holding both guns up.

He frowned. "Mr. Bucci . . . You said he was the man who sent you?"

"Yeah."

"Bucci. Hah. Where have I heard that name before? Wait. *Gepetto* Bucci?"

"Yeah," said Montassini, "*that* Bucci."

Kilodovich raised his eyebrows and tilted his head. "Hmm." He backed up, and motioned Montassini over to the steps. "Why would the Italian Mafia be looking for me, now?"

Montassini shrugged. "A favour," he said.

Kilodovich put Montassini's gun into his waistband and scratched his stomach with his free hand. His own gun he kept trained on Montassini's stomach. "A favour for who?"

"Some fuckin' Turk he does business with. Amar he calls him."

Now Kilodovich lowered the second gun. If Montassini had wanted to, he probably could have jumped him—grabbed the gun back—and had him face down on the floor. Kilodovich's mouth opened and closed, and he stared at the floor. That look in his eye dissolved, and for a moment his face held the innocence of a child. Montassini knew he could have taken him now—but fuck. They were soulmates, he and Alexei Kilodovich. You don't fuck with your soulmate.

"Amar . . ." Alexei snapped his fingers. "Amar Shadak!"

"Yeah—that sounds right. Amar Shadak. Turkish guy. Part owner of a camping store that the boss bought off two old Russians back in—"

But Kilodovich wasn't listening. He was getting that faraway look that had become very familiar to Montassini, since he'd come back to the Emissary Hotel, met that killer maid and started on this insane road trip to hell. Kilodovich was in—what was the word the tour guide had used?

He was in—

Rope?

Rupture?

Montassini snapped his fingers. Oh yeah. That was it.

"Rapture."

Montassini took Alexei by the arm and led him to the door. "It's going to be all right, pal," he said, and reached for the gun in Alexei's hand. "Just give me that."

Alexei looked at him for a moment—and for just a moment, it seemed as though Montassini could see eternity in Alexei's eyes. Like he'd opened up that safe place he put himself, and something older—bigger—had come up.

And then the look passed, and Alexei blinked—and grinned for an instant like a newborn.

"Give me that," said Montassini.

Slowly, as though in a dream, Alexei shook his head. "I keep the gun," he whispered in another voice, one still not his own. "And Alexei is all right now. No Rapture for him."

Montassini cracked open the door and peered outside. The tour group was long gone—but he could hear them. He could hear a thousand of them, humming some song down by the harbour.

"So all right," said Montassini, "what do we do now?"

"Rescue me."

RESURRECTION
Воскресение

Darya Orlovsky spun and reeled in the perfect winter's light, long braids of dark hair trailing over her shoulders like lariats. Her eyes were fixed on a place in her dreams: the City of New Pokrovskoye, the greatest port in the Empire. Snow fell like flakes of gold in a winter afternoon. Godly white horses that pranced in front of a sledge bearing lovers snuggled in thick grey furs. The girl laughed, and spun, and thought to herself with desperate joy:

Bullshit. Bullshit metaphor.

She whirled then, prancing down a long flight of stone steps to the Square. Her father was there—playing an accordion festooned with jewels, in the midst of a circle of girls who danced as though with one mind. His teeth flashed beneath his thick moustache. His eye twinkled. "Darya!" He called. "My little petrushka! Join the dance!"

"Papa," she called happily. But that is not what she thought.

She thought: *Killer*.

A cold, soul-dead killer who came north with a baby daughter and wife in tow; who took hands that had stabbed and strangled and squeezed triggers and brought them to a fishing village—washed them clean in brine of ocean and blood of cod. And now whose hands played over the *keyboard* of the accordion, making it sing a song that no one could resist.

Darya lifted her skirts and spun back the way she'd come, up the stairs and away from the square. As she turned, she looked over the rooftops of this place. They were high-peaked, shingled in fine slate pulled from quarries at the Empire's southern mountains. They overhung houses and apartments and in the distance, a long low palace surrounded by gardens where the *Tsarina*, the Babushka held court in the summertime but now—

Now is summertime, she thought.

And then she thought: *How did I know this*?

And then she whirled again along a broad platform on the edge of the cliffs that surrounded New Pokrovskoye—and she beheld the fountains and the Parliament House and the port, and the great curtain wall where in direr ages there patrolled the Tsar's guard. Now, the people of New Pokrovskoye danced along it, moving in a great human wave in the afternoon light—praising—

—praising—

Darya spun and turned and felt her knees buckle. And for a moment, she stopped dancing.

The world grew dimmer then and the snow faded, and for a moment she blinked, for the light had vanished. And she thought about the man who'd taken her in the Museum of Family History. She remembered the touch of his hand on her bare thigh and the feeling of his lips as they brushed her mouth, the scraping of his tongue against her teeth, and as she did she blinked again.

She was standing in a crowd, in the darkness of the true New Pokrovskoye, near the pier where her father tied up his boat. The crowd was swaying back and forth and humming, and she felt a touch at her shoulder and she turned—in time to see two figures, the only two who did not seem to be keeping a rhythm. Darya took a breath. For one of them—

—one of them was he. He moved with a hunter's ease. The other, a small man with slicked back hair, followed nervously. "These fuckin' zombies give me the creeps," he whispered. And the big man, Darya's hero, muttered something low. Darya spun closer to hear the end of the sentence.

"—no waste," he said. "We die soon."

Darya didn't care about dying soon. She wanted to follow him. Ignoring the call of the song, she elbowed her way through their fast-closing wake.

He was a hero—one who would not succumb. That was why she'd picked him. She had a sense of these things.

"There you fuckin' go, 'we die soon.' We're not goin' to die soon. This is some fuckin' kind of dance."

"Not we. *We*."

"What the fuck?"

The two were heading back toward the store that she'd managed all these years. They were moving quickly—quicker than Darya herself could. She stumbled through the crowd of strangers here in New Pokrovskoye—the people who had come heeding the call. There were so many of them—people who had come like invaders—eating their food and drinking their tea and sleeping in their homes.

The man and his friend were gone and she stood amid a forest of strangers. They moved and swayed rhythmically under the sky—and in spite of herself, she found that she was doing the same. It was a tempting thing to do—to fall back into the magnificent dream that they'd concocted for themselves, an amplification of the game that had played itself out in her dreams when she was just a little girl. She remembered those dreams fondly—sitting at Babushka's feet in the school house, the old woman beaming down at them and beginning: "Have I told you the story of the two stallions, my Children?" and then beginning with a whistling of wind, and transporting them all to such a wonderful place—a place like the Empire.

Babushka died too soon, she thought, and let a hint of sadness creep into her.

But she quickly disciplined herself. Babushka had died. Her stories ought to be finished.

Grimly, Darya set off for the store.

The only narrative that she would inhabit would be the one that she had made for herself today. The one with the man from Russia.

She moved more quickly once she made it past Harbour Street. There were only pockets of people here—heads upturned, swaying back and forth. She elbowed between a thin balding man and a woman with flowing mascara who seemed to be in her sixties. Her shop was in sight.

She fished in her skirts for the key, and rushed up to the door to turn the lock. Her man had made it to the store—she was sure of it. The first place they'd met. In New Pokrovskoye. There was no Empire here and it was summer and—

She opened the lock and stepped inside.

"Hello, my child."

She frowned. The voice was coming from everywhere.

"Who is it?"

"You should have to ask. Tell me—why are you not dancing?"

"What?"

"Why are you not dancing?"

She froze, and whispered:

"Koldun?"

The Koldun stepped out from behind a rack of liquor. He was carrying something in his hand.

"Everyone dances," he said. "That is why we went to such trouble—to create a world for you, one you might all share. A world of treasure and gold and magic."

"P-programming," said Darya. Her hands scurried across the counter behind her—seeking some kind of a weapon. "There's no world."

The Koldun shrugged. "All right," he said. "Programming then. And you, little Darya, have managed to figure a way around the programming."

He looked at her more closely. "But you're not that clever." He sniffed the air. "Kilodovich," he said. "Alexei Kilodovich has touched you."

Darya backed away. The Koldun moved closer.

"What a thing he is, this thing our Babushka has found. The power to free a girl. Hah. Where is he now? He cannot be far."

"I—I don't know who Alexei Kilodovich is," said Darya—although she thought she might know who the Koldun was talking about. She felt a sliver of fear through her—and suddenly, she wanted nothing more than to return to the Empire—to the beautiful dream her beloved Babushka had crafted in her, with stories and the museum and a lifetime of programming.

The Koldun smiled sadly and shook his head. He raised the thing in his hand—Darya's eyes widened as she recognized it for what it was.

"You can never go back, my little puppet," he said softly, aiming the machine pistol at her middle. "Babushka would know everything then."

THE IDIOT
ИДИОТ

There was a great oppressive darkness all around him and everywhere. Alexei Kilodovich screamed into it.

He screamed a lot of things. He screamed his rage at Babushka—at Holden Gibson—at Vladimir. He struggled too—trying to move and tear a hole for himself in this dark place where he'd fallen There was nothing to tear, though. For a long time—days or weeks or hours or minutes—Alexei grasped at unyielding dark—at absence. Then, for a time, he could hear things: music—laughter—dance.

Dance.

Was this the thing that Orlovsky, the Koldun had promised? A dance in the village?

After everything he'd learned, Alexei wasn't sure he wanted to go near this dance. No. He was sure, in fact, that he didn't want to go there.

Not, at any rate, to fulfill Babushka's plans for him.

If he were to be trapped in a void—well so be it.

So Alexei settled back. And as he did, he detected substance in the firmament beneath him—cold rock. There was a faint glow too—a pinkish glow that surrounded him, filled his vision.

Or not precisely his vision. Alexei did a thing with his eyelids, and suddenly he saw—

Rising sun.

Pink over distant mountain peaks.

Alexei blinked, and stared up at the vanishing starscape. The distant peaks.

"More memory," he spat.

Just what he needed. Alexei got up and started walking.

Маленький THE LITTLE HERO герой

If any man on the Romanian crew ever sang, or had conversations, or just coughed and belched, that man saved it for times when Stephen was not around. The bridge of their submarine was quiet as a monastery.

That was fine with Stephen. He found, as the submarine dove deeper and further, that he was happiest free of the burden of conversation. His bunkmate Uzimeri was becoming more snide and contemptuous of him by the hour. Chenko and Pitovovich had launched into a full-bore campaign to get Mrs. Kontos-Wu to open up and really *talk* about the traumas Fyodor Kolyokov and City 512 had inflicted on her. Conversations with the three of them offered up all the subtle pleasures of a Scientology breakfast seminar. As for Zhanna? Happily, she was busy sleeping most of the time. And when they were awake, they avoided one another—both, no doubt, horrified at the potential for wrenching embarrassment that even a chance encounter in the submarine's narrow spinal corridor held for them.

The Romanian "monks" were better. There were always eight of them who manned the bridge. They looked at one another rarely, spending their energy hunched over banks of coloured lights and switches and valves labelled in Cyrillic. They moved the controls with a kind of rhythm that suggested either knowledge or instinct. At some point, Stephen reflected as he came in to watch the morning shift, the two become the same.

A chart was laid out on a light table in the middle of the bridge, just to the fore of the periscope. No one stopped Stephen from looking at it, or the grease pencil marks on the surface of the plexiglass cover that held it in place.

Stephen munched on a stub of bread that would do as his breakfast, as he checked on their progress. From the looks of things, they had somehow made it past the southern tip of the British Isles overnight, and were heading now in a straight southwesterly direction. He took a ruler and set it against the line. The first significant land mass that it would intercept was Cuba. It could also hit southern Florida, or Haiti, or any of the smaller Islands surrounding it with just a small change in course.

But Stephen would put money on Cuba.

It seemed like an obvious place for it to be, whatever it was. Stephen could well imagine that the KGB or the Politburo or whoever it was that gave the okay for City 512 and Kolyokov's dream-walking work would have connections with Castro's bunch in the Caribbean. Still Soviet—but distant from the main apparatus.

Stephen imagined a huge plantation, covered in sugarcane wafting in the tropical breeze, with a bunch of old men and women—the mysterious Mystics—sipping cooling tea and reading each other's auras to the songs of the cicadas; only occasionally descending into their brightly-painted sensory deprivation tanks to commune with the Universe.

It made a hell of a lot more sense than what Zhanna had said: "We have to go deep to find the Mystics."

Perhaps when she said deep, she meant, deep into enemy territory. Deep into Cuba. Not deep underwater. Stephen leaned against a bulkhead. They were deep enough underwater as matters stood. The deck had maintained a notable, discomfiting pitch to forward for far too long during the night—and although he'd been paying attention, Stephen did not once detect a comforting, compensating pitch to the aft. Occasionally, he'd hear the sound of groaning metal—the sound of the ocean crushing in on them. It was not a comforting noise. Not at all.

Stephen wasn't alone in his feelings. As quiet as the Romanians were, they were clearly more and more uneasy the deeper they went. This morning for instance. They still moved through their paces like robots. But every so often, Stephen would see a sign: a nervous tic under the eye of the navigator; or the radar operator run his fingers through his oily hair, and look up with just a flash of terror in his eyes. When he came in this morning, Stephen was sure he heard sobbing, echoing through the submarine's narrow bridge.

Stephen gulped down the rest of his coffee and set the nearly empty cup down on the map table. The waves in brown liquid near the base vibrated in tidy little concentric waves. He put the last of the bread in his mouth and gnawed at the crust. The coffee at the bottom of his cup, he noticed, was pooling to forward.

They were diving again.

"Aren't you supposed to sound a horn or something when you dive?" said Stephen. The bridge crew didn't look up. The hull metal groaned. The engines thudded.

"*Help us*," whispered a voice at Stephen's back.

Stephen turned fast enough to set the cup tumbling. It splashed coffee over the top of the map board, pooling and beading on the grease pencil delineation of their course—running in thick streams toward the American coastline at the fore end of the map table. He grabbed the cup and, seeing no towels about, daubed up the coffee with his sleeve. It still smeared the grease pencil, but not to the point of illegibility. Some did make it underneath the plexiglass, and it spread underneath to make new contours on the sea bottom off Key West.

By the time Stephen looked back, whoever it was that had asked for his help was long gone.

Help us.

Stephen hurried to aft through the spinal corridor—ostensibly to take his coffee mug back to the galley and wash up—but really, because the whole *Help us* thing had creeped him out. The voice had sounded plaintive—beaten. It made it sound like the best way you could help was to find a brick or a rock, and bring it down on the whole miserable bunch of them.

Stephen stopped in the galley. Chenko was sipping coffee there; Uzimeri was fooling around with something at the stove. Boiling water spilled over the forward edge of his pot and made a devilish hissing sound on the element.

Chenko spotted Stephen and smiled at him.

"We are diving again," he said amiably. "How deep do you believe we can go, before the sea crushes us?"

"Hopefully," said Stephen, "a little deeper than this."

"Trust in Zhanna," said Uzimeri from the kitchen.

Chenko rolled his eyes.

"Refill your cup," he said.

"Later." Stephen sat down at the galley table. "So what do you think Petroska Station is?"

"Back to that, are we?" Chenko laughed. It was a little game they'd started at dinner the night before—before Mrs. Kontos-Wu had showed up, and the conversation had defaulted back to group therapy mode.

What on earth could Petroska Station be?

"Okay—here is one. It's a weather station in the Antarctic. Tunnels run deep into the mantle—miles deep—and intersect with the massive tombs of an ancient civilization. The Mystics are using pyramid power derived from complicated crystalline structures that rested there untapped for cold millennia, to commune with the Universe."

"Blasphemy!" shouted Uzimeri and made a face. Stephen laughed in spite of himself.

"What do you think, then, Konstantine?" said Chenko.

"A blessed place where all prayers are answered and Paradise is laid out for all to see." Uzimeri gave a quick curt nod.

"That's what you said last night."

"Well that is what I think." Uzimeri looked at Stephen. "It might have been revealed to me in a Vision, for all that you would know—hey boy?"

"Leave him be," said Chenko. "Look to your water—it's making a terrible mess in here."

Uzimeri shook his head and turned back to the stove.

"So what do you think?" said Chenko, turning to Stephen. "Any clues?"

For an instant, Stephen debated telling Chenko about the strange voice he'd heard, begging him for help; the discomfort he'd seen in the Romanians who crewed this boat; and the dreams of great flowering squid, that kept a pace with the submarine as it sank deeper into the Atlantic murk.

He would, of course, say none of those things.

"Cuba," he said cheerily. "Petroska Station is a little plantation outside Havana. The tourists don't go there much, but it's big with the locals."

Chenko smiled—turned his coffee mug around as he peered into it, perhaps trying to read something in the grinds. He licked his lips, and opened his mouth to reply. Then he frowned, and looked up.

"What is it?" said Stephen.

"Listen," said Chenko. His eyes scanned the bulkhead over them, and he squinted.

"What?"

"Nothing."

"*What*?"

"Nothing," repeated Chenko, and gestured all around them. "Do you not hear it? *Silence*."

Silence.

Now that, thought Stephen, was not entirely correct. You could still hear the rattle of the electric fan as it pumped air from one end of the boat to the other. There was the occasional *ba-bong* from the submarine's hull as it adjusted to the increasing pressure. And there was the hissing sound of superheating water on Uzimeri's stove element.

But much of the din that made the submarine such a joy to ride in was gone. The engines had shut down.

And as Stephen listened, the other noises diminished too: the hissing of steam stopped, and the hull went quiet.

The submarine, Stephen realized with a shiver, was finally levelling off.

Uzimeri looked up—first at Stephen, then to Chenko. He cleared his throat. "Think this is Cuba now?"

Help us.

Mrs. Kontos-Wu staggered into the galley next, accompanied by Pitovovich. Stephen sniffed the air. They had both been drinking.

"What's going on?" said Mrs. Kontos-Wu, clutching her forehead as she sat down. "Why's everybody so quiet?"

"Zhanna will explain," said Pitovovich. Chenko nodded in agreement.

"Do you hear her?"

"Oh yes." Mrs. Kontos-Wu's eyes fluttered shut along with the others'. Zhanna, no doubt, was explaining things to them right now.

Stephen took it as his cue. He got up and headed toward the bridge.

The crew were like statues when he got there. They stood or sat at their posts, staring at nothing—like they had been shut down. Stephen ran his fingers in front of the eyes of one, standing by the periscope. The man didn't blink.

Stephen went over to the map table. The coffee stain had obliterated the southern tip of Florida. Global warming couldn't have done it better. He looked up the map. The grease pencil line hadn't extended any further—although someone had obviously fixed it up after Stephen had left. And they had made a change. Stephen leaned closer to look. Now, at the end of the line, rather than just a dash of red, someone had drawn a tiny circle. Was this their destination? It was far short of the Caribbean—it was a point in the mid-Atlantic. There were no land masses here but Stephen noted that the contours of the chart connoting the topography of the sea bottom were nearly converged. Something was going on, on the sea bottom.

"Who," he said quietly, "needs help?"

The men sat in place. They had not even heard him.

The submarine heard fine. It answered with a lurch, and a *pok-pok-pok* sound that seemed to come from everywhere at once. Stephen grabbed the edge of the map table with both hands. Sweat gleamed a white aura around his fingers where they pressed against the glowing plastic. The *pok-pok-pok* continued a few seconds more—and then there was a grinding noise that Stephen felt through his bones: metal against metal; a *crack!* sound.

A low rasping, like a screw-top turning on an ancient jar.

And then: quiet.

The deck became still as a cellar floor.

Stephen swallowed, as the truth of what was happening settled in on him.

The submarine had arrived. They were at the circle, on a great ridge in the middle of the Atlantic Ocean.

They were at Petroska Station.

Somewhere nearby, the Mystics were waiting.

There was a little room at the bow end of the submarine, just past the torpedo room, that Stephen had chanced upon during his early explorations. It was not wide enough for more than two men to stand side by side. There was a narrow ladder that climbed to the ceiling, where there was a small hatch. He'd asked Uzimeri about it when he first saw it. "Ah yes," said the old man. "That is the docking hatch. For underwater rescue. I don't have to tell you not to open it. On second thought, it's you I'm talking to. Don't open it."

One of the Romanians was on the ladder when Stephen pushed his way into the room—turning the wheel on the hatch. Icy water splashed down over his arms, his squinting eyes. Stephen felt his throat clench at the sight of it. Even when the water flow subsided, just seconds after it had begun, Stephen felt himself shaking.

"What the fuck are you doing?" he shouted over the shoulders of the other Romanians. The one on the ladder—thin and balding, he was not much older than Stephen—gave Stephen a quick, sad look then leaned aside as the hatch swung down.

"Hey!" said Stephen. But the Romanian was already climbing up—through the open hatch. A second crewman mounted the steps at the bottom of the ladder. Others prepared to follow.

Stephen was tempted to bolt for the back of the submarine—back to the galley, where he presumed everyone else was waiting; maybe even past that, to his cabin, where he could curl up on his bunk and pretend this wasn't happening.

Instead, he grabbed the shoulder of one of the Romanians—this one, a squat brown-haired man with wide eyes. The man tried to shake him off, but Stephen made him turn and face him.

"What the fuck is going on?" he said. And instinctively, he tried to push it out of him: imagined himself walking down his fingers, through the man's shoulders, and straight into his brain. "What is up there? Tell me what is up there," Stephen demanded.

The man grabbed Stephen's hand and flung it down. He gave Stephen that same, sad *should-have-helped-us-the-first-time* look that the first one had. Then he turned, and got back in line to climb the ladder.

Stephen stamped his foot—shamefacedly aware he was behaving like a three-year-old, but unable to do anything about it. Where the hell was everybody, anyway? Still hiding back there? Stephen slammed his fist against a bulkhead, shut his eyes and winced at the pain.

When he opened them again, he saw he was alone in the docking room. The last crewman was climbing through the hatch.

Stephen looked up the ladder. A weak reddish light wafted down. He tried to see what was in the chamber above. It smelled like a locker room. The light was very dim, but he thought he could make out spars of metal several metres above the hatch.

What the fuck was up there? Stephen swallowed. There was only one way to find out. He put his foot on the bottom rung of the ladder.

He was about halfway up, when the figure appeared in the hatchway. Flesh white as snow, mottled around the cheeks like a bath-wrinkled thumbprint—and naked so far as Stephen could see. He couldn't tell a gender. The thing had no beard, and hair that was a wispy black and shoulder-length. But if there were breasts up there, they were hidden by the lip of the hatch.

Stephen stared up at the thing with a kind of disbelieving calm.

"Ah, hello," said Stephen, looking into the creature's eye. He struggled to keep his voice sounding casual. "This is Petroska Station, I'm guessing?"

It bleated something Stephen couldn't understand.

"I mean—"

Before Stephen could finish, the thing in the hatch reached across the opening with a long, pale arm and lowered a black metal cover over the opening. It clanged shut with such finality that it did not even occur to Stephen to push it back open to get another look at the thing.

In total, nine Romanians had left the submarine through the rescue hatch. That left maybe a dozen on board. Stephen wondered if that was enough to crew and operate a 641 Attack Submarine.

"No," said Chenko. "We'll need those who went away back with us if we're ever to leave here."

"Aren't you the least bit worried about that?"

"I am not the least bit worried about that." Chenko leaned back on the bench of the galley and stared idly at the back of his hand.

"It really is all right, Stephen."

Stephen gave an involuntary flinch as Mrs. Kontos-Wu patted his forearm.

"You didn't see that fucking thing. Don't tell me it's all right."

"Well," sneered Uzimeri from across the table, "you didn't have the benefit of understanding that Zhanna has bestowed on the rest of us, who are not deaf to the voice of God. So stop trying to panic us with your five senses bullshit misinterpretation."

"It was a fucking *Morlock*," said Stephen. "A zombie. A vampire. Right out of a fucking horror movie. Whatever they're doing up there—the guys didn't want to go."

Konstantine Uzimeri regarded him smugly. "Bullshit," he said.

Tanya Pitovovich smiled in a way that was meant to be reassuring. "They are only borrowing them," she said. "It is a part of the transaction. Apparently, something similar happened the last time."

"Last time. Which none of you were here for."

Pitovovich shrugged.

"We can only be so many places at once," said Mrs. Kontos-Wu.

"For now," added Chenko.

Pok-pok-pok, said the bulkhead. Stephen looked up.

"What the fuck is that noise, anyway?"

"Nothing—"

Stephen interrupted Chenko with a hand. "Nothing to be frightened, of, I know." He sighed. "What else did Zhanna tell you?"

"Ah," said Uzimeri, smiling beatifically, "how to put it into words?"

Mrs. Kontos-Wu gave him a look. "Don't be such a prick, Konstantine." She turned to Stephen. "She told us that we've docked with Petroska Station. It's deep underwater, as we've all guessed. Some kind of an old—habitat. For the next few hours, she and the others are in communication with the Mystics."

"So Zhanna and the rest are in Petroska Station?"

"No. They're still in their bunks."

Stephen was confused. "If they don't have to be on board Petroska Station to communicate with the Mystics, then why did we come all this way in the first place?"

The three looked at one another.

"Good question," said Chenko finally. "We didn't think to ask."

"Of course you didn't."

And why would they? If you live your life based on the premise that the horny teenage girl asleep in an officer's stateroom on a decommissioned submarine is about as fallible as the Pope—then what questions would you possibly have when she was done talking? If Zhanna says you're safe in your submarine while rejects from *Night of the Living Dead* have their way with your zombified crew in some hidden undersea warren in the middle of the Atlantic Ocean—you must be safe.

Stephen was beginning to see the advantage to being a psychic deaf-mute. Around here at least, it let him think for himself.

The man watching the hatch to the officers' section was a different one than the last time. This one was small and thin, with wire-rimmed glasses and light brown hair shaved to a peach fuzz on his scalp. He regarded Stephen with open hostility.

"Go back," he hissed when Stephen stepped up to him.

"I have to see Zhanna," Stephen said. The little man shook his head and told him to fuck off. To emphasize his point, he pulled out a small knife and waved it in Stephen's face.

Stephen took a step backwards. He had been expecting something like this—if Zhanna and the rest of them were busy dreaming, even with a reduced complement of monks they'd make sure to pick an intimidating one to guard them. And if the big stoic ones were all gone—well, a crazy little bastard with a knife could still get the job done. At least Zhanna didn't have them waving around guns anymore.

That had been something else Stephen had counted on.

Stephen muttered an apology as he feinted and ducked, drawing a slash of the blade into the air where his left shoulder had been. He carried the motion forward in a roll, grabbing the Romanian's scrawny forearm and twisting it. The knife clattered to the decking. The Romanian grunted—he obviously didn't want to wake the dreamers with a shout—and tried to grab at Stephen's hair. Stephen let him and in the same spirit as the Romanian, ignored the ripping pain as a hundred or so hairs left his scalp in the Romanian's fist. Stephen plunged his elbow into the Romanian's solar plexus, then when he was doubled over, twisted once more and brought his knee up into the man's face. There was a crunch as his glasses shattered, and a certain amount of blood that stained Stephen's pant-leg. Stephen hoped he hadn't damaged the man's eyes. The man whimpered, and made a desultory and ineffective jab at Stephen's privates with a half-open hand. Stephen hit him twice more in the side of the head, then pushed him to the ground and kicked him twice more. When it was clear the monk wasn't going to get up again, he found his knife, pocketed it, and walked on through.

At least, thought Stephen as he stepped into Zhanna's cabin and heard her quiet snores, they'd kept it quiet.

"Zhanna. Wake up."

"What—who? Who is there?"

"It's me. Stephen."

"Mm. Might have known. You're the only one I can't tell coming. Did you do that to our watcher?"

"The guard? Yeah. Wake up."

"Nuh-uh. Back to sleep. In council."

"Fuck off. Wake up."

Zhanna blinked, sat up, and glared at Stephen through the shadows of her cabin. She wrapped herself in a sheet. Her hair was dishevelled. And the quarters were close enough that Stephen recoiled a little at the sourness of her breath.

"You are fucking everything up," she said.

"I wouldn't know," said Stephen. He was surprised at the petulance in his tone. "Maybe you can expect your monks to respect your 'council.' Maybe you can give the others enough of a show to keep them quiet. But me—" he shook his head. "You can't expect me to buy into any of this crap. Not without some explanation first."

"Because you're dead inside, and you resent it." Zhanna shook her head, wrapped the sheet around her like a sari and got out of her bunk. "All right," she whispered. "We can't talk here. We're already waking the others. The Council has to continue. Come on. We'll go to the engine room."

They stepped out into the hall. Sure enough, it was getting crowded. The low drone of snores was gone—in its place, beds creaked and shadows in robes hovered at the edge of the corridors. They glared at Stephen and Zhanna as they moved past, to aft and the engine rooms.

"Go back to sleep," said Zhanna as they passed one heavyset boy who looked about sixteen. The kid muttered something in Russian that Stephen didn't quite pick up and stayed where he was, watching them as they climbed down the steps into the quiet room. The lights in here were low—conserving batteries, no doubt. A couple of Romanian monks sat slumped next to a bank of valves. It was as though their strings were cut. They might have been dead.

"Now," said Zhanna, looking at him with exaggerated attentiveness. "What do you want to know?"

"All right. First question. What is Petroska Station?"

"It is where the Mystics are," said Zhanna.

"Right. And who are the Mystics?"

"The ones in Petroska Station." She gave a half-grin that was not altogether kindly.

"And why did you consign your crew to living death among a bunch of fucking pod people in a watery hell a thousand metres under the sea?"

Zhanna opened her mouth and closed it again.

"It's pretty tough to fuck with someone's mind if you can't read it," said Stephen nastily. "Now. Answer my question. Those men are scared shitless of the things up there and I don't blame them. Why did you send them there?"

"It was—requested," said Zhanna. She looked at the floor. "Part of the price that the Mystics demand, for dealing with us."

"What are they doing with them?"

"I don't know. They are as lost to me now as you."

"Really." Stephen stepped back and turned to look at the two men huddled in the back of the engine room. "Like them?"

"These men? No. They're resting now. There's no work for them to do—so I leave them to themselves. If I need them—"

"You know where to find them." Stephen looked at her. "Do you think this is what your son Vladimir had in mind when he set this whole thing in motion? I seem to recall you said that he wanted to liberate these sleepers. Didn't he apologize to poor Chenko?"

Zhanna glared at him. "Don't throw that in my face. Your old master Fyodor Kolyokov was far worse to his sleepers than anything we have done. The great leech Fyodor Kolyokov—living rich off the backs of the sleeping army!"

"No one," he said, "who worked for Fyodor Kolyokov begged me for help."

Zhanna's hands made fists. "You—you are a bastard," she said quietly. "You don't know what you are talking about and you don't know what is at stake. Living in America with the stolen wealth of the family. How could you? You are not even one of us. I don't know how I could ever—" she stopped herself. Her face was red, and her eyes were wet.

Whatever, thought Stephen.

"What," he said, "are they doing to your people up there?"

Zhanna didn't say anything for a moment. Finally, she closed her eyes. Behind him, the two men who had been sleeping jerked to their feet like the marionettes that they were.

"Why don't you go look for yourself?" said one.

"They've been asking after you since we came," said the other. "I thought I'd protect you. I'd thought you were worth protecting. But why don't you just go look out for your fucking self?"

Then they fell back to the floor, strings cut. Zhanna had left the room.

Pok-pok-pok, pok.

The noise on the hull seemed to follow Stephen as he made his way to the fore of the submarine, and the hatchway to Petroska Station. The sounds were not, he decided, musical. There was a definite cadence—but it was perhaps the cadence of speech. Sometimes it repeated itself. As though the thing outside the hull was trying to communicate. Stephen narrowed his eyes, so the corridor of the submarine became a dim blur—and tried to imagine himself beyond its confines—perhaps in the body of a huge squid, its alien thoughts rushing past him and through him—its tentacles caressing the hull of the submarine like a lover—its suckers, clicking out the simple message, again and again.

Help us.

Stephen climbed the ladder. The hatch at the top was still closed, and when he reached it, he raised his fist to pound on it. Before he could touch the metal, though, it moved aside. Creaked open. Slammed against a metal stop on the floor over his head. And he was staring into dim red light. There was no Morlock there this time.

Stephen drew a breath, and climbed the rest of the way. He pulled himself over the damp, slimy lip of the hatch, climbed to his feet, and drawing a breath of the stale, metallic air that was somehow even worse than the air in the submarine, Stephen got a look.

He came up in a long room—maybe as long as the whole submarine, and like the submarine, somewhat cylindrical. Lights were positioned regularly near the ceiling—little red globes beneath wire encasements. Some of the lights were dark, and beneath them, the pools of night were absolute.

The Morlock—or vampire or pod person or sea hag—hovered naked at the edge of one of those pools. Stephen called out to it. But it didn't answer with even a bleat this time. It simply motioned to Stephen to follow it to the end of the cylinder, where even at this distance Stephen could see a hatch.

He hurried to catch up—to get a better look at the thing. But it was faster than he, and opened the door and vanished through it before Stephen could see much more than a naked ass and hair that fell below its pale shoulder blades. Stephen found himself panting the stale air, as he stumbled into the new corridor. He called out again—but no one answered. No echoing hellos; no whispers of "Help us." No *pok-pok-pok* on the hull.

Even the Morlock was gone by now.

Stephen realized with a sinking feeling that he was, for all intents and purposes, alone in Petroska Station. The corridor he was in was narrow, and went in three directions: left, right, and in a narrow tube with ladder rungs cut into it, straight up.

It was a long way from his Cuban plantation. It was nearer to the strangeness of Chenko's ancient Antarctic city.

But as Stephen began to think about the implications of a giant station built by Russians, this close to the United States—the reality of this place was stranger than anything any of them could imagine.

Stephen spent what seemed like hours wandering the halls. The further he went, the more it seemed like a bizarre dream. He walked through four huge chambers with great rectangles of greenish water underneath bright white lamps; an infirmary with a dozen beds, attached to two operating rooms; another room with another pool—the water's surface clear, and only somewhat green—with things that could only have been hard-shell diving suits hanging from the ceiling like sides of beef. On a second level, a great domed room filled with blinding white light and rows and rows of hydroponically grown plants: carrots that dangled in murky water like foetuses, and twisting vines of tomatoes the size of a boy's head, and huge zucchinis and stalks of beans. There was a control room with banks and banks of old monochrome computer monitors that flickered with amber and green firelight. And there was a great kitchen, with pots that dangled from hooks and a huge walk-in freezer.

Here, he finally found some of the missing Romanians. They had the freezer door off its hinges, and were working with glue and staples on the seal around it. None of them would have given Stephen any notice on the submarine. Here, they stopped what they were doing, looked up and smiled at him.

"Stephen Haber," said one.

"Old Fyodor," said another.

"Kolyokov's apprentice," said another.

"It is good to see you here finally," said a third. "We thought Fyodor was lost to us for good."

Stephen was fascinated. The three men were speaking perfect English—without a trace of the heavy accent that had scarred their speech on board the submarine. And when they moved—it was without the peculiar rhythm that Zhanna and her brood forced them into.

Stephen snapped his fingers and pointed.

"You," he said, "are the Mystics."

The three Romanians nodded as one. Two others continued to work inside the freezer, pulling apart a complicated tangle of coils. Stephen caught a movement out of the corner of his eye—and saw two figures similar to the pale thing that had greeted him below. They stooped over, hauling an oblong green crate between them towards the freezer.

"Forgive us," said one of the Romanians.

"The freezer hasn't been working," said another.

". . . properly for years," said a third.

"That and a hundred other systems around here," said the first.

"Our People accomplished a great many things in the Great Experiment—but they did not, I fear, build things to last," came a voice from behind him—a fourth Romanian.

"So," said Stephen slowly, working it out as he spoke, "when you took the nine men from the submarine, it was . . . to fix your refrigerator."

"Freezer," said one of the two Romanians working on the coil. "And . . ."

". . . some other things," said his partner. "It is a good thing this place was never tested by nuclear war. It wouldn't have lasted."

The Romanians all turned back to their task. Stephen stood there for a moment, watched as the Morlocks dropped the box at the door. It made a clang. The Morlocks bleated at each other, and shuffled out of the kitchen.

"You see," said a Romanian, "the ones who've been here a while just aren't up to it anymore."

"Like old tractors," said another.

"They have lost their *pull*."

Stephen nodded. "So you press-ganged our crew," he said, "because they are up to it. For now."

"Close enough," said a Romanian, and gave him a look. "You look like a strong boy yourself," he said. "Care to lend a hand?"

Stephen dragged over the box—which was filled with spare canisters and parts for reassembling a fan. He had never repaired a large industrial freezer before—but he found himself catching on to the muttered instructions. As they were putting the huge vault-like door back in place, he wondered aloud why it was they even needed a freezer down here.

"I'd think it was just about cold enough outside to preserve anything, this deep," he said.

One of the Romanians laughed. "Listen to the oceanographer," he said. "*It is cold enough to preserve anything, we are so deep!*"

"Yes, well he makes a good point. Isn't that why we came here? To preserve *us*?"

"And what a good job we're doing."

One of the Romanians turned to him. "It's true," he said, "that it's cool outside. But the freezer is better run by electricity. That is something we have no shortage of here."

Stephen nodded. He described the power plant that he saw, and the Romanians all nodded.

"See? Smart boy. It's a geothermal plant. Very high tech in 1977."

"Would have been a Nobel Prize in it, if it were made by an American."

"Would have never been made by an American."

"So clever, they think they are."

"1977?" said Stephen. "Is that how long this thing has been down here?"

"No. That was when it was planned. I don't think they sank the spike until—when was it?"

"1982. That was when Reagan was making all those threats. Remember?"

"Oh, like it was yesterday."

"We were the 'evil empire.'"

"And they had no idea how far it went."

"So true."

"This thing," said Stephen slowly—working it out as he went, "has been underwater—off the coast of the United States—undetected—for seventeen *years*?"

"Oh yes."

"And you've been down here—"

"Seventeen years."

Stephen leaned back against the wall of the galley.

"And how the fuck," he asked, "did you manage that?"

"Well at first—it was a big secret project. Approved by Brezhnev himself. We thought we could inhabit the ocean's floor. It would be better than the space program. Build a secret city—a secret country—under the sea."

"It was fantastically expensive—but those were the good days for the 'evil empire.' We had lots of rubles to spend on big things."

"At first we were going to put it in the Black Sea. Wasn't too deep, and we could send ships to it from Odessa. It wouldn't be a threat to anyone. Then some of us started thinking: why not be more ambitious? We had already managed to cloak whole installations, using our talents. Why not build it under the Americans' noses?"

"So we sent over some people to Cuba. We set up a special account. We set our operatives to work—in the United States, in South America—and most of all, in the Kremlin."

Ha! thought Stephen. *He was right about Cuba. Sort of*.

"And by the time it was finished—"

"Even Leonid Brezhnev had forgotten it ever existed."

"He forgot first."

"And those of us with the foresight to see the great purge coming—"

"—to foresee the end of City 512, and the scattering of our children—"

"—we moved down here."

Stephen thought about that.

"Kolyokov always said that the sea was a dangerous place for a dream-walker. He never went near it without his bathyscaphe."

"Bathyscaphe!"

"Ha!"

"Kolyokov was a big coward."

"It's dangerous all right. Like the Face of God."

"There you go with God again."

"Look. Stephen. It's dangerous because it's rich. A dream-walker can explore the soul of the ocean for a lifetime."

"A dreamer can lose himself in it."

"And find himself."

"That's deep," said Stephen. "So you remained undetected—how exactly?"

"Well you know—a bit of this," a Romanian tapped his forehead. "Same way your master Kolyokov kept his operations secret all those years. You make the right people forget—"

"And you make sure no one looks."

"And," said another, "this place is well-located to avoid detection. This part of the Atlantic Shelf is in a dead zone—no currents move here. We can be quiet."

"But you know that's not all of it."

"Right."

"We could not have done this without—" another Romanian tapped the wall "—a bit of help from them."

"Them?" Stephen was completely confused.

"You know," said a fifth Romanian as he came out of the cooling freezer. "Fish."

"All the big squids outside."

"They were great from the start."

"Do you know how big their brains are?

"Huge."

"Not much going on in them."

"But that's fine."

"More room for us."

"Squid." said Stephen. He felt his shoulders trembling, as he thought back to his daydreams. His supposed daydreams—the things that could not have been the result of dream-walking . . .

"Don't look so surprised. It's not like you haven't seen them already."

"It's not like you can't see them again, if you want."

Stephen felt tears brimming around the edges of his eyes.

"Look at the crybaby."

"That is sweet."

"You are such a sentimentalist, Yorgi."

THERE ARE NO GUILTY PEOPLE

"So do you not think," said Ilyich, "that perhaps all that vodka might not have been a way to substitute for your true addiction?"

Well you certainly seem to think that, thought Mrs. Kontos-Wu. *So it must be true, I suppose*.

She thought it, but she kept her mouth shut. She had been sitting in a circle with Ilyich and Tanya and Konstantine for what seemed like hours now. And she had learned in those hours—any sign of hostility could send their little encounter session off on a turn of conversation that could take hours.

"She wasn't the only one drinking, Comrade," said Tanya. "I too fell into the weakness."

"See how the *humanist* defends her," said Konstantine.

Tanya stopped, and looked at Konstantine with arch amusement. "I'm a *humanist* now?"

"You deny the divine," said Konstantine. "It makes you susceptible."

"Stop right there," said Tanya. "I fell into the weakness with her, because I've got the addiction same as her. I'm a little further in my recovery—but I'll tell you, there's not a day goes by that I don't dream of the wonder of my old metaphor. You see, Konstantine, that's something that you cannot even begin to relate to."

"Oh?"

"You were never programmed," said Tanya. "You came to this late in your life—with nothing but the benevolent touch of Zhanna and the children to guide you."

"It is true," said Chenko. "Zhanna enters our mind with only love and compassion in her heart. She does not force us into wickedness. She is not like the old masters of City 512."

"I don't know about that," said Mrs. Kontos-Wu—and immediately kicked herself for speaking up. All eyes turned to her.

"How can you say that?" gasped Konstantine.

Mrs. Kontos-Wu drew a breath. "Well," she said, "back in New York, Zhanna dream-walked me on a mission to murder Fyodor Kolyokov. I would have done it, too, were he not already dead when I arrived."

Chenko looked at her. "I cannot believe that," he said. "How do you know?"

Mrs. Kontos-Wu thought back—to her metaphor of Bishop's Hall, and to her "friend" there Lois, who, she now understood, took over her body and kept her locked in the library.

"I know," she said simply.

The submarine went quiet.

"Why," Chenko said finally, "do you feel it necessary to channel your self-loathing toward our saviour?"

"Yes," said Tanya. "It is time to speak now, Jean."

Mrs. Kontos-Wu glared at Tanya. "My name's not Jean," she said. "And I think," she said, "I'm about done for today. If you'll excuse me, I'm going to go get some sleep."

"I'll walk back with you." Tanya started to get up.

"It's okay," said Mrs. Kontos-Wu. "You have things to discuss."

Mrs. Kontos-Wu hurried out of the mess before anyone could follow, and wiped the tears from her with her sleeve. Was she addicted to her metaphor? It was possible. One thing she knew for sure—these makeshift group therapy sessions in the submarine were unpleasant enough to make her yearn for the metaphor of Bishop's Hall. It was an insulation for her—really, her only insulation—from a world that offered her up more than her fair share of harshness.

So if she decided to take a drink or five to compensate—who should care? Mrs. Kontos-Wu ducked into the cabin that she shared with Tanya. The children here, their psychic ministrations, weren't truly the same as her metaphor. It was communication, pure and simple. Uzimeri, and to a lesser degree, Ilyich Chenko, were able to apply religion to that.

But Mrs. Kontos-Wu was a long way from religion.

She shut her eyes, and felt the sea around her—listened to the strange tapping on the submarine—and thought: *I am a long way from everywhere.*

And then she smiled—and let herself slip into the dreaming place, that was still her only real comfort.

The dream, Mrs. Kontos-Wu thought to herself, seemed pretty safe. It didn't involve Bishop's Hall. It didn't involve secret instructions telling her to go out and kill someone. It did involve *Becky Barker and the Adventure of the Scarlet Arrow*—which might be a worry. But that, really, was a side issue to her metaphor. She was reading the final chapters of the book, but she wasn't in the library at Bishop's Hall. In that surrealistically interconnected way that dreams sometimes carry themselves, she was reading it about in a dark underground tunnel, the pages illuminated by a heavy old-fashioned flashlight—very much like the one that young Becky was carrying as she stepped into her own labyrinth, at the end of Chapter Twenty.

In her dream, Mrs. Kontos-Wu turned the page eagerly, and read on:

CHAPTER TWENTY-ONE

(read Mrs. Kontos-Wu)

"A DREADFUL SURPRISE"

Becky held her nose. She had to remind herself that this was a sewer. And not just any sewer—but an ancient one, as old as the Romans. Why, it had seen two thousand years of chamber pots and refuse and Lord knew what else dumped through its tunnels. So if the sewers here had the worst smell Becky could ever imagine, then at least they had an excuse.

That was more than she could say for Jim—running off after the Society of the Scarlet Arrow through the back-alleys of Istanbul, without telling anyone. He had no excuse. And she was going to tell him that, as soon as she found him.

She only hoped she found him soon enough that the doctors could re-attach his right hand. Otherwise, Jim might never throw one of his patented fastballs again.

"*Mon Dieu*," said a voice behind her. "C'*est mal ici*."

Becky turned around. "Antoine!" she said. The irritating Parisian brat that had kicked off the whole wretched adventure just a week ago when the Scarlet Arrow had him kidnapped by mistake, was standing right behind her. "You," she scolded, "are supposed to be at home with your *maman*, not here in the sewers following me into what may turn out to be a very dangerous encounter indeed."

"Nonezeeless," said Antoine, "'Ere I am!"

"Well this is a dreadful surprise," Becky said.

"An' zat," said Antoine, "is not ze only surprise in store for you, *Mademoiselle* Barker."

With that, the terrible twelve-year-old reached into his knapsack. He pulled out a very big revolver, and with both hands aimed it straight at Becky.

"You have fallen into my trap," said another voice—from the shadows, behind little Antoine.

"You may shoot, my child," said the voice.

There was a loud bang, and a very bright light. Becky gasped. It felt *awful*: like the time that her pony had gotten upset and kicked her in the chest. Only part of her knew that this was much, much worse. She put her hand up to her stomach, and when she pulled it away it was wet. The flashlight fell from her other hand. And soon she fell too.

"Was I very good?" asked Antoine.

"Very good, my child. Now, you know what you must do."

Antoine sniffled. He took the gun and walked off into the darkness, beyond the beam of Becky's fallen flashlight.

A mysterious hand reached down and picked up the flashlight. It flicked the light off. When it flicked it on again, the beam was focused on a familiar face.

"You can't believe I killed Becky Barker—can you?" said Lois. She was wearing her old Bishop's Hall uniform. The light under her chin made her scarier than a Halloween mask. But Mrs. Kontos-Wu knew she had nothing to be afraid of. Lois, after all, was her friend; even if she had just murdered Becky Barker—or ordered her death, which was just as wicked as doing it by Mrs. Kontos-Wu's books.

"Well, after having read through this sorry narrative, I have to say it's high time someone murdered that little dolt. I can't believe that Kolyokov was able to keep you tame with this metaphor all these years. So infantile. So far beneath you. We will have no more of this. You have important work to do. And it seems as though I cannot speak with you directly, so the pages of this children's fantasy will have to do."

Deep in the tunnels, Antoine's revolver went off once more. There was a small splash as the gun fell into the filthy waters. And then there was a larger splash. And that was the last anyone would see of irritating little

Antoine.

"Let's go find Jim," said Lois. "We can talk as we walk."

Mrs. Kontos-Wu followed along behind her. She puzzled at her new predicament—it seemed now, as though she had completely submerged herself in the book—to the point where her thoughts and actions were in fact being described by the unnamed novelist.

"We are doing this," said Lois, "because that bastard Fyodor Kolyokov has so effectively demolished the metaphor of Bishop's Hall."

"Bishop's Hall is bullshit," said Mrs. Kontos-Wu.

"Yes," said Lois, "it is. But it was a convenient way for us to speak. And now it's fragmented. You've still got this novel, though. You still believe in that. So I've had to make do."

Mrs. Kontos-Wu shrieked as something scurried over her foot.

"Now. Step carefully. And be quiet. We're almost in the Cistern of Blood—which is where, I believe, the Scarlet Arrow is keeping Jim. We shall have to turn off the lamp, or they're bound to find us. And no more shrieking. Just listen."

Mrs. Kontos-Wu was quiet. Lois whispered as they climbed down a long, slippery set of stairs.

"You are among the enemy," said Lois. "You are in a very dangerous place—probably, I'd wager, near the Society of the Scarlet Arrow by now. They are unconscionable. Wicked men. They must be stopped. You must kill them—and if that little bitch Zhanna tries to stop you . . ." Lois looked at her significantly.

Mrs. Kontos-Wu stopped. "Wait a second," she whispered. "Lois—I thought *you* were Zhanna. Are you saying that you're not Zhanna? Or do you want me to kill you? I'm confused."

"Shhh! Someone's coming!"

Mrs. Kontos-Wu and Lois pressed themselves against the sweating stones of the ancient sewer's walls. Sure enough, there were footsteps in the distance. From around a corner, Mrs. Kontos-Wu could see the flickering yellow of torchlight—and the guttural mutterings of the secret language of the Scarlet Arrow.

As the torchlight grew brighter, the voices grew louder, and their peril became more imminent, Mrs. Kontos-Wu could not avoid the suspicion that Lois—whoever she was, whatever her agenda—had simply avoided answering a sticky question with a conveniently placed cliffhanger.

Маленький THE LITTLE HERO герой

Pok-pok-pok.

It sounded, Stephen thought, very different from the outside than the inside. Echoing through the cold, still waters outside the submarine, it sounded like a deep, rich drum. It reverberated through the sea with a tribal intensity.

Stephen took control of the cadence—tapping along the outside of the submarine, and then stretching great tentacles as far as he could reach—tasting the strange flavours of the ocean. Soon, he felt confident enough to launch himself through the dark waters, climb from the shelf. He spared a glance back at a black sprawling thing, an artefact hammered into the shelf itself, on thick concrete and steel columns; a structure made of spheres and cylinders and boxes, illuminated here and there by flickering lights like Christmas strings; exuding strange limbs like tentacles that moved arthritically around their ancient, rusting joints; occasionally, farting a bit of air skyward in a string of silver that glowed brighter, and grew finer, the higher it climbed. Latching to this assembly was a long squid-shape of a kind that was becoming altogether too common in the deep complacency of the shelf.

But it wasn't enough to worry a mind. Quick enough, it was away—in a great jet of seawater, away to the surface.

The surface, and dinner . . .

Whoa.

Stephen shook his head and propped himself up on his elbow.

"You see, Stephen," said a Romanian, sitting over him, "why we like it down here so much?"

They were in a stateroom in the upper levels of Petroska Station—just one deck below what the Mystics called their Aerie. The walls were a light cream colour. Light came from soft semi opaque globes that hung from a high ceiling.

The air seemed cleaner here. The Romanian lurched, and said in a slightly different voice:

"So there. Now you are a big psychic. Feel better?"

The second voice, Stephen could tell, belonged to the mystic called Yorgi. The first one was Dmitri. There were maybe five other distinct voices that inhabited the Romanians at different times. Those voices had not introduced themselves, but Stephen could tell the difference. The trick was in not paying attention to which mouth was speaking. The Mystics tended to jump from one mouth to another—often while in mid-sentence. Sometimes, there would be overlap, and all the voices in the room would utter the same word at the same time, in a terrible kind of harmony.

It was an order of magnitude more difficult than talking with Zhanna, who could be one voice across many mouths if she chose. This was a crowd of Zhanna's, leaping between a crowd of mouths.

"He's speechless," said the Romanian.

And then, in a woman's voice: "It reminds me of Kiev, you know."

"Reminds you of starvation and cannibalism?"

"No no. *You* remind me of that, Yorgi. Every chance you get. No. I'm talking about the awakening. The first taste of Discourse."

"Oh yes. It's quite a time for everyone. Exhilarating."

"It can also be pretty frightening, if you are not prepared."

"Yes. But our young Stephen here is well enough prepared."

Stephen sat up and looked at the Romanian. It was as though he were looking at five different faces at once—none of them, the narrow-chinned bald man to whom the face properly belonged.

"Why," he asked, "am I awakening now?"

"Oh. He can talk now."

"The magic of the moment has worn off."

"So sad."

"Why now?" Stephen repeated.

"Simple."

"You are far enough away from Kolyokov's influence. So the lock's off."

Stephen thought about that. "Are you saying," he said, "that Kolyokov had locked up my natural dream-walking talent?"

It was something—to see one poor man laugh for five. The Romanian jerked and spasmed and gasped until the Mystics were finished.

"Sorry, Stephen. It's not as though you're a great big talent to begin with. That thing we showed you with the squid? Wouldn't have even gotten you an interview at City 512."

"If they did interviews."

"Notice how we're using the flesh here to talk to you."

"That's right. You're not quite up to Discourse."

"But yes. Fyodor Kolyokov did his very best to hide your limited talent from you."

"It's not all bad, though."

"Yes. It prevented anyone else from dream-walking you."

"Kept secrets safe."

"You were your own man. Look at it that way."

"Don't be too angry about it."

"He's angry. Look."

"Oh come on, Stephen. It's not like you were the only one."

"There was that kid—that Kilodovich."

"Oh yes. That was a good thing. No one would have argued there."

"Would have gotten us all shot if they'd found out about that boy."

Stephen cleared his throat. They all focused the Romanian's eyes on them.

"If I'm not talented," he said, "why did you want to see me?"

"We need you." The Romanian spoke weirdly—his throat stretching and echoing, to accommodate more than one voice. He coughed, and someone held up his hand to wait.

"Swallowed the wrong way," said someone.

"Why?" asked Stephen.

The Romanian leaned close to him. "We need you," he whispered. "There's trouble brewing. We can smell it."

"You've got the children," said Stephen. "Mrs. Kontos-Wu. The others."

"They are here. It's not the same thing as having them."

"You see, Stephen, it's become obvious to us that someone else already has a foothold in their minds. Even in the most powerful ones."

"Really. Who would that be? *Babushka*?"

The Romanian nodded.

"Lena."

"Always was an evil little bitch."

"Don't use that word."

"Evil?"

"You know what word."

"Yes. Sorry. The point is—it's a problem."

"A big problem."

"It appears as though she is *everywhere*."

CHAPTER TWENTY-TWO
"THE CISTERN OF BLOOD"

Two hateful fez-sporting villains emerged from around the corner. One of them carried a torch, the pitch at its tip wrapped in an orange tongue of flame. Another carried an immense curved axe. Mrs. Kontos-Wu held her breath—even though she knew that would make no difference as to how well she was hidden, she was sure it was something Becky would do. Becky would also wonder about whether the axe was the same one that the Scarlet Arrow had used to sever the hand that he'd sent to Becky in the post. And she would wonder how it was that the Scarlet Arrow villains could get away with carrying a flaming torch in a sewer without igniting the gasses there and blowing the foundations out from under Istanbul.

That alone might well have been clue enough to allow Becky to credibly rescue her maimed chum Jim from hordes of fanatical be-fezzed Turks and their evil leader.

But Becky was dead. And Mrs. Kontos-Wu frankly didn't care whether Jim lived or died. She had other things to wonder about.

For instance: just exactly who was the persona behind this Lois character—her old school friend who had steered her so murderously wrong back in New York? It could still be Zhanna—she was unwilling to completely rule that out. She supposed it could also be some remnant of Fyodor Kolyokov. He had left a hidden message in her, after he'd apparently vanquished Lois in the metaphor of the Bishop's Hall library.

Where, Mrs. Kontos-Wu reminded herself, she'd been reading this very book.

"Come on," whispered Lois after the two men had passed them. "We must follow them to the Cistern."

Mrs. Kontos-Wu shrugged. "Whatever," she said.

"Shh!"

The men turned down another corridor off the main sewer. The girls followed as close as they dared. The tunnel became narrower, its ancient brickwork less coated with slime. The rats were replaced by immense spiders and centipedes and other horrid things that Mrs. Kontos-Wu made a point of not squealing at.

Finally, the light of the villains' torch was joined by a brighter light, as the tunnel opened up onto a much larger space.

"Now here," said Lois, "is where we find out what's happened to Jim. I *do* hope he's come to no harm."

"His fucking hand's been cut off," said Mrs. Kontos-Wu. "I think Jim's come to harm."

Lois gave her a stern look. "Language," she warned.

Slowly, the two girls crept up to the light. Lois gasped. In spite of herself, Mrs. Kontos-Wu looked upon the sight before her with interest approaching awe. It could only have been one thing:

The fabled Cistern of Blood . . .

⁂

The tunnel opened out onto a stone ledge exactly halfway up the wall of a great, circular room. Its ceiling was a dome—painted with unrecognizable signs and odd geometries. The centre of the dome was a long tube open to the sky. Water dribbled down lit by the noon-hour sun, and in the distance, Mrs. Kontos-Wu could make out the hubbub of lunchtime traffic in downtown Istanbul.

Halfway round the room, the ledge became stairs that climbed down the other half of the wall, to thing that gave the Cistern its name. The pool was also circular—maybe fifty feet in diameter. It was filled with a thick red liquid that looked like nothing so much as blood.

"The blood of the twentieth century," said Lois. "Of two world wars—hundreds of civil wars. Blood spilled by the Nazis and their genocidal Holocaust of the Jews, and the gypsies, and the homosexuals, and the mentally challenged . . . the half-breed "mongrels" . . . and the sixteen million corpses; our own Josef Stalin, and his *twenty* million victims. The Balkans. Vietnam."

Mrs. Kontos-Wu sniffed. "It's probably just mineral deposits," she said. She couldn't be sure about that—it might well have been an actual cistern of blood—but she wasn't about to let Lois use this stupid image to make her point.

Lois shrugged and pointed. "Look—down there. I think we have found our little friend Jim."

Mrs. Kontos-Wu squinted.

Sure enough, where the stairs entered the water someone had constructed a broad wooden platform. It was tied to the side of the cistern with chains that certainly didn't look as old as the lumber.

And sitting in the middle of it, tied with mere ropes to a metal chair, was a small, trembling figure with a bag over his head. If Becky had been here, she would have gasped in recognition.

It was Jim!

A tall, blond man that Mrs. Kontos-Wu thought she recognized, stood there with a sickle-shaped knife held at poor Jim's throat.

"That," said Lois, "in case you didn't recognize him from Chapter Two, is kindly Monsieur DuBois."

"Antoine's *papa*?" Mrs. Kontos-Wu admitted she hadn't seen that coming.

"It's true," said Lois. "Turns out that the *Famille DuBois* have been members of the Society of the Scarlet Arrow since the Crusade against the Cathars. It's all tied up with the Holy Grail and the Templars and the highest levels of the Vatican, but don't ask me how. The important thing is, Monsieur DuBois is going to slash Jim's throat and drain his blood into a ceremonial chalice unless you do something immediately. Ordinarily, this would be where Becky would step in but—"

"—you killed her." Mrs. Kontos-Wu took a step back into the corridor.

"That's right," said Lois. "Now follow the plot."

Mrs. Kontos-Wu pressed herself against the stone. She was inclined now to creep down the stairs—snap the neck of the villain carrying the axe and behead the villain with the torch—make her way onto the platform, cutting her way through the five others who stood between Monsieur DuBois and her—then finally deliver the *coup de grâce* to the mild-mannered Parisian civil servant that had, in Chapter Two, met Becky, Bunny and Jim at the *Aéroport Paris-Charles de Gaulle* and shown them the *Tour Eiffel* on their way back to the townhouse.

But if Mrs. Kontos-Wu had learned anything, it was that following her inclinations in these kinds of places wasn't what was best.

So instead, Mrs. Kontos-Wu spun around, and took hold of Lois by the hair.

Her former best friend shrieked in spite of herself.

"What are you *doing*?" she demanded.

Mrs. Kontos-Wu yanked on Lois' hair and pulled her face around to meet her eye.

"Not finishing the book," she said, and—as the army of fez-sporting cultists looked up—Mrs. Kontos-Wu spun around and flung Lois off the precipice, and into the Cistern of Blood.

Lois looked up at her—with tears of horror and rage in her eyes—and a moment before the impact of death came upon her—

She vanished.

"Manka. Vasilissa. Baba Yaga."

And just like that—under nobody's direction but her own—Jean Kontos-Wu closed the book.

Mrs. Kontos-Wu blinked. She was standing in another large room—not as tall as the Cistern of Blood, with no afternoon light coming down from the ceiling. There was a pool—this one like a swimming pool, a sad old movie star's swimming pool, filled with water green with algae. The light came from long banks of fluorescents, hanging from a ceiling that was barely twelve feet from the surface of the water.

Mrs. Kontos-Wu looked down at her hands. She was carrying an axe. She lifted it, and examined the blade. Good. No blood. Wherever she was now, with any luck she'd managed to get there without fulfilling Lois' instructions—of destroying Petroska Station, and killing the children.

Mrs. Kontos-Wu lowered herself to her haunches, and held the axe close to her chest. She would have to be very careful. As irritating as they had been, Ilyich and Konstantine and Tanya had obviously been on to something. She was addicted to this thing, this metaphor. That was fine as long as Kolyokov was around to mind her. But now that he was gone? The addiction left her open—open to suggestion. And that made her a danger to everyone around her.

Mrs. Kontos-Wu sat like that, stewing, until a sense at the back of her head tightened, a drawn thread.

There had been a noise. A wet slosh; a slap; a bleating sound, like a goat.

Echoing across the chamber. She squinted toward its source—and saw a lone figure, horribly pale, with long hair and rags for clothing, standing on the far side of the pool—shuffling tentatively, grasping its hands and tugging at stray locks of hair like a nervous child.

"Help," it croaked.

"Why should I?" demanded Mrs. Kontos-Wu.

"We are being invaded," it said.

THE INSULTED AND THE INJURED

Оскорбленные и униженные

"We held off Comrade General Rodionov," said Fyodor Kolyokov, "for years with all sorts of tricks."

"That so?" said Heather. She was sitting in a small kitchen that reminded her of her parents' kitchen back when she had parents and wasn't a runaway slave in Holden Gibson's magazine subscription crew. It was small and simple. Along one wall, there was a stove and a refrigerator and a little bit of counter space. The cabinets above and below were dark wood laminate; to the right of the sink, there was a lousy little under-the-counter dishwasher. Comrade Zombie Kolyokov positively glowed under the light, propped up as he was at the little kitchen table in a tattered grey bathrobe with a tiny cup of tea.

"That is so," said Kolyokov. "Rodionov had us in his sights for seven years before he was able to take any action. At first, his problem was that he did not truly apprehend the nature of City 512. He thought we were simply managing sleepers. He made the fatal error that so many of his Comrades had also made—in assuming that the research we conducted there was but a fraud."

"The fool," said Heather.

"He was a fool. But not so complete a fool as some of my comrades. They deluded themselves—believing that in time, Rodionov would be replaced by a more sympathetic administration. When Gorbachev moved into the Kremlin, they were certain Rodionov would be held in better check."

"You knew better of course."

"I took steps," he said.

"Like Babushka did?"

Kolyokov winced, and sipped at his tea. "No," he said. "Babushka, as you call her, was smarter than us all."

They fell quiet for the moment. Heather smoothed over her skirt and leaned on the Formica of the kitchen table. They'd been here for hours now; since seeing that cloud over New Pokrovskoye. Heather had felt her vision fade and before she could think to do the mantra trick again, here she was in her childhood home. Sitting next to Fyodor Kolyokov while the T.V. played a hockey game in the living room.

At first she was angry:

"You fucking lying piece of shit zombie!" she'd yelled, lunging at Kolyokov with a steak knife she'd pulled from a wooden block beside the coffee maker. The old man had moved quickly and the knife embedded itself in the kitchen chair behind him. By the time she could yank it out, he was able to explain:

"You are not trapped. You are hiding here. If you had stayed near the top of your mind—the thing that Lena—that Babushka had made of herself—would have found us instantly. She is living within minds—many minds. And she has the key to yours."

Heather was still pissed. She stalked off to the living room and kicked in the tube of the television. Kolyokov followed patiently.

"We have to make it through the night," he said. "That is all. By morning—we should be able to venture out again. Learn some things and maybe start to undo this."

"We had a deal," said Heather, tears of rage streaming down her cheeks. But she sat down on the couch facing the sparking television and crossed her ankles. "What do we do until the morning?"

"Watching television is out of the question now," said Kolyokov. "We'll drink tea and tell stories. How about that?"

Over the ensuing hours, Kolyokov made good on his promise. He told her about the Russian military city called 512—about how he came to be there, snatched from his parents' home in the 1940s, after taking a test that showed he had certain abilities beyond those of his neighbours. She learned about Lena and the Koldun, Vasili Borovich, and the others who had trained there and spread out to use their talents in the world. He told her about the network of spies and sleepers that they created in that city and eventually beyond.

"So why," she asked, "don't you Russians rule the world? Couldn't you just get into the head of the President of the United States and fuck him up? Why not just use your big psychic network to take over."

Fyodor laughed out loud. "Because," he said, "the psychic network functioned. Because we could leave our bodies and view anything we chose. We could step into the minds of anyone we'd prepared, and operate them like puppets. We could move invisibly if we just concentrated a bit.

"Why not take over the world? Because, my dear, we were too powerful."

"I don't get it."

"Let me explain with a question," he said. "What is the first thing you would do if you found you had won a fabulous sum of money in a lottery?"

Heather shrugged. "I don't know. Buy shit."

"*Buy shit.* Yes. You would do that. Would you continue to work at a job you disliked?"

She laughed. "Like for Holden Gibson? Fuck no."

"*Fuck no*. I do adore you, Heather. Quite right. Fuck no. You'd quit right away. Well the way to look at us is that we were all lottery winners—of a much larger sum of money. We didn't need to work for anyone. Some of us came to that conclusion earlier than others—but we all at a point came to understand that we would ever be tools for venal men and women. And to allow that would be foolish. For those men and women—they could become tools for us."

"To do what?" Heather had asked. "You don't want to take over the world—what's left?"

Kolyokov hadn't answered that immediately.

Now, in the early dark of morning, sitting at the old kitchen table, Kolyokov looked around himself pensively. He set down his tea.

"Babushka—Lena—understood early what we took a long time to apprehend. We were not gods. We had it in our grasp—but we were limited. By Physick."

"Stupid word."

"It's what we call it. Lena was the first of us to disappear. She did so early. I think she did so to this place. Very smart of her."

Heather was quiet now. She got up and opened the refrigerator. It was full of condiments, but after some rooting around she found an old piece of cheddar that hadn't been wrapped tightly enough. She yanked off the dried end of it and put it in her mouth. It had the consistency of an eraser. Yeah, she thought, Comrade Zombie Kolyokov had pretty well nailed the old homestead.

"What about Holden Gibson?" she said. "Was he smart?"

"John Kaye?" Fyodor Kolyokov smiled sadly. "No," he said. "He was merely fortunate."

Holden Gibson sat upright in living darkness. He was confused and lost. It was dark and warm and damp, and he was scared shitless because in addition to not knowing *where* he was, he wasn't sure *who* he was. This kind of sudden dislocation in place and identity was becoming more the rule than the exception—but still.

It scared him shitless.

He took a ragged breath. The only thing to do was find his bearings. Work at it. He exhaled then breathed in again, let his own senses work for him.

He made a list.

Smell: like he was in a funeral parlour.

Sound: a papery susurrus, like wind through a forest canopy.

Touch: the soles of his feet touched cool, bare earth.

But then he remembered: not earth. Concrete. He curled his toes, felt the harsh roughness. Concrete. They'd poured concrete to make the foundation of their greenhouse.

Gibson stood up and stretched. He stumbled around for a moment, then found the dark cloth that kept the daylight out of his sleeping space. He pulled it aside and stepped out. The faux-tropical air of the greenhouse washed over him—the sweet smells that now seemed less funereal than they did simply tropical. Hands dangling at his side, he walked naked into the dark, among the shadows of tall ferns and giant tomato plants that climbed nearly a dozen feet along iron runners. Over his head, the flickering of summer lightning cast a grid of shadows through the jungle here, from the facetted glass roof.

He had called for help.

Why the fuck, now, was he calling for help? Gibson worked to reassemble his recent memories. The senses were easier. Recent memories tended to jumble with those long past.

His training, for instance, in the cabins—when he first shut his eyes and flew with the wings of a mayfly; when they sat him down next to the retarded boy from Cleveland—Bobby Turnbull, with eyes narrow as slits and that thick wet smile—and let him step into his mind and walk him all the way to the Arts and Crafts building like a wind-up robot toy—or when, in East Berlin, the KGB had found him in the back bedroom of the librarian's flat, and hauled him to the farmhouse, where he'd been stripped . . .

Gibson smiled bitterly. *Could have used some fuckin' help then.*

The recent memories came more slowly:

The lighthouse.

The Russian, Alexei Kilodovich.

And the push. The push from Heather.

She had pushed him clear from her—like a bug, like a fucking little insect.

Like the night in the farmhouse, where he'd fallen to pieces.

Gibson stopped. His hands formed into fists at his side. He was almost back. Almost in control. Enough within himself to be able to see and feel and react.

Enough to tell—

Someone was moving in the dark.

THE HONEST THIEF
Честный вор

The two of them sat still in the dark. Leo Montassini rubbed his chin and peered over the rocks.

There were two guards on the main gate to town's greenhouse. The gate was high, sheltered under a peak of shingled roof. Underneath, a pool of fluorescent light made everything sick green. The pair of them stood underneath that light. They stared down the slope at the milling town. One was big—he looked like he ran one of the fishing boats that worked out of this place: deeply tanned, with muscle-banded forearms, and a broad red forehead underneath a baseball cap two sizes too small. He wore big black boots that laced up to his calves, which themselves bulged out the top like round river-rocks. The other one was small but only by comparison to the first. He was still respectably put together and looked like he could fight. Montassini pulled back down behind the rock where they were hiding and reported this to Alexei.

"The big one," said Alexei, without looking, "is Makar Trolynka. He's got a scaling knife tucked into his belt. He has never used it on a man and would hesitate to do so with us. He prefers his fists. His brother Oleg—who's standing beside him—is another matter. He's not armed, but if it comes to it, he'll take anything and use it. Oleg won't care if he kills you."

Montassini looked at Alexei, and choked back the questions: like: *How in fuck did this guy know who these people were, how they were related, and how they liked to dust it up*?

Uncomfortable questions that would lead to uncomfortable places. He let Alexei continue:

"Of course, there are two others looking after the west side of the structure. They've got rifles, and they'll come around quickly if there's any commotion."

"Why not just avoid commotion," said Montassini, "and find another way in? What about through the roof? It's a fucking greenhouse."

"This is not the movies. We fall through the roof and cut ourselves to bits."

Alexei shook his head firmly. "Other doors? No. No other way in."

"Smash a window?"

"No."

Alexei was firm as he could be—but Montassini wasn't going to give up. He tried reason one more time.

"Wouldn't attacking these guys just alert her?"

"Her?"

"That Babushka chick."

"Ah." Alexei appeared to consider. "The *chick*. No."

"There has got to be another way in."

"Those," said Alexei, "are not Babushka's guards. They won't alert her."

"Not Babushka's. Who the fuck's are they then?"

"The Koldun's," he said.

"What?"

"Never mind. Pay attention. This is what we're going to do," said Alexei. "This will work."

Montassini sighed.

"Fuck, man. You just know that, don't you?"

"Alexei just knows that."

"Right. *Alexei*."

It was always *Alexei*. Never *me*. Or *I*.

He'd worked with a guy who'd done that back in '92. Vinnie Capelli. Vinnie was working the Port Authority, helping out Gepetto Bucci's capo Milos Spinazzi. Every time Vinnie was seriously pissed at some guy, he'd say, "Vinnie is seriously pissed. What does Vinnie do when he's pissed?" And then he'd start in on the guy, doing what Vinnie did which usually involved a sock full of quarters. Montassini guessed that saying "Vinnie is seriously pissed" was marginally scarier than saying "I am seriously pissed"—but it struck him as phony shit, and phony shit irritated Leo Montassini like nothing else. It didn't surprise him one bit when it turned out that Vinnie was running a heroin deal without Spinazzi's blessing.

But it was different here.

After a few days among these weird Russian fucks he was starting to understand how they worked—how they could one minute be a guy from the South Bronx who worked at the Trump Towers and the next be singing "Ach Natascha" with a bunch of strangers on a bus. Like they had a whole set of personalities in their guts and could just swap them at will.

At someone's will, anyway.

Montassini thought he was getting good at spotting it. He'd spotted it immediately in that weird museum, when the Rapture had taken over, and Alexei Kilodovich had started speaking about himself in the third person.

He thought he might be able to spot it now. He looked back around the rock.

"Are those two—"

"Sleepers?"

"Quit finishing my thoughts for me." Montassini hushed himself. "Yeah."

"Those two are sleepers," said Alexei.

"Like you."

"Once. I am a dream-walker now. Different."

"Whatever. Those two are the zombies like down by the boats."

They had just made their way through a crowd of about a thousand zombies who were milling around New Pokrovskoye harbour. Montassini hadn't been able to shake the feeling that every time he looked in one of their eyes, he was looking at the same person—that every time one of them looked at him, that person was just holding the same stare as the last; through different eyes. Montassini jerked a thumb in the direction of the greenhouse. "First time one of them sees us, they'll tell the rest of them in a second."

Alexei shook his head. "Not now," he said. "These ones are operating on implanted program. The program was not implanted by Babushka. It was implanted by—her lover, who is betraying her and knows her well enough to succeed for a while. The Babushka is concentrating down at the harbour. She is still growing—building herself in the minds of her sleepers. Our worries start if Babushka realizes what is going on here, and has sleepers nearby who are—awake."

Montassini nodded again, more slowly this time, as he worked it out. "So we got to put the sleepers to sleep."

"Right."

"How do we do that?"

"You are the expert."

"The—" Montassini's mouth hung open. No words now for the questions that cascaded from that. This fucking KGB agent who'd probably broken into Cheyenne Mountain in his day—who'd disarmed Montassini like a cat whacking a mouse—who was on the lam from Amar fucking Shadak.

What the fuck did Montassini know to make him an expert? That he could hear voices when he stuck his head into a U.F.O. in Manhattan—that he found another U.F.O. here in fuckin' Russianville Canada?

"I've never done this before." Alexei looked nervous. "Alexei has. But he can't come now."

"You're fuckin' crazy, whoever you are," Montassini muttered, then pushed himself up to take another look at the two of them at the door. They were more like statuary than men—staring out into the dark with unseeing eyes—

—looking across a black ocean.

Montassini shook his head.

"Four guys altogether," he said, thinking as he looked. "Could be worse."

Gibson stood still and listened. It didn't take long before he heard the noise again—the rustling of leaves as someone stepped through. There was a subtle shift in the shadows.

"John," said a voice.

Holden glared into the dark. But he was relaxed now. Back on top.

"Stop calling me that," he said.

A figure stepped out in front of him from behind a row of tomato plants. He wore a long coat. His hair was pulled back in a ponytail. His beard was white. His name was Koldun, and he was as close to a host as Gibson had been able to find in this town.

The Koldun shrugged. "John's your name," he said. "John Kaye. It upsets you to hear it."

"Call me Holden," said Gibson.

"Of course. Bad memories for John Kaye, hmm?"

"If you say so."

"Makes it difficult to sleep."

"I got to piss."

"No you don't."

It was true. Gibson didn't have to piss. He was panicked and dislocated was all. Like a kid with a bad dream. He glared at the Koldun. He wasn't going to say that out loud.

The Koldun looked at him across the darkness. "I've done my best to help you," he said. "Twice now you've messed it up."

Gibson looked away. The Koldun didn't have to say messed up what because now Gibson's short-term memory was working fine and he knew exactly what he'd messed up.

Earlier in the day, the Koldun had told him where Alexei, the traitor Russian, was resting. Told him Alexei had been doing nothing but trying to figure out a way to murder Holden Gibson and fuck Heather. Gibson hadn't been able to get to Alexei for days while he was lying out cold in the bathhouse—he was under some kind of protection as long as he was there. But when he came to?

"Fair game," the Koldun had told him then.

"He was fair game," said the Koldun now. "You didn't manage it though."

Gibson glared at him.

The Koldun shrugged. "I'm not giving you shit, John. It was my mistake in attempting it. Leaving it to you. You're a mess. You can't even remember your own name."

"Holden Gibson." Gibson blinked. "Holden fuckin' Gibson. So here we are. I fucked up. Couldn't kill him. But that Russian—he's more than he seems, isn't he?"

"That's why I needed him dead."

Gibson narrowed his eyes.

"Why didn't you do it yourself?"

"Because—" the Koldun licked his lips. "Because I would have been observed."

"And I wouldn't?"

The Koldun didn't answer and he didn't have to as far as Gibson was concerned.

"You were fuckin' setting me up, weren't you?"

"You know that's wrong," said the Koldun.

"I don't know anything."

The Koldun shrugged. "That's not true. You know who you are, John."

Gibson massaged his knuckles. "I could fuckin' kill you right now. Set me up. Fucker."

The Koldun went on. "You know your name is John Kaye. And being as that is your name—you should have known better than to listen to her."

"Her?"

"When she contacted you. With the children."

"What do you mean?" Gibson bristled. "You talking about the phone call? These kids? I'd have been fucked if I hadn't agreed to it. It was the best fuckin' deal to come along the pipe in a year." *These children—they're talented. They'll make you rich for as long as you're alive. Come get them*. "More than a year. A fuckin' lifetime."

"Yes. It seemed that way for all of us. But we fell into her trap. As we have all in the past."

"What the fuck do you mean?"

The Koldun threw his hands in the air theatrically. "Oh. I forgot. I am not talking to John Kaye. I am talking to Holden Gibson. You have no idea what happened to you that night."

"Fuck you," said Gibson. He turned to walk off. *Brought here by Babushka. Fuck off*. He was here because of a deal that he'd made with a woman on a telephone to bring some very talented young people—that was how she called them—very talented young people—into the fold. The woman was tough—she made a lot of fun of Walt Disney for some reason—and that pissed Gibson off for some reason—

For fuck's sake, it was supposed to be frightening: the Devil; shrieking winged demons, the souls of the dead, lakes of pitch—that big mothering Satan in the middle.

Really, she'd said. Fantasia? *Why don't you just have the mouse send broomsticks after us? That is every bit as terrifying as this scribble of a demon you've made of yourself.*

Was that all it took to bring down John Kaye? Just a little doubt? Mockery?

"Bitch," said Holden Gibson.

"Shh," said the Koldun. "You don't want her to hear."

Gibson turned around. Now he was feeling tears in his eyes. "Bitch," he said again.

The Koldun shook his head sadly. "She had very little to do with why you are the way you are, you know. That responsibility fell to others—afterwards. But without her? John Kaye would still be the man that he was, I think."

"Ball-busting bitch," said Gibson.

The Koldun frowned and looked to a spot behind Gibson.

"Shit," he said. "Someone's coming."

"Who the fuck would be coming?"

"It doesn't matter." The Koldun, Vasili Borovich, reached into his coat. He produced a machine pistol and handed it to Gibson. Then pulled another one out and kept it for himself.

"What the fuck?"

"The children," he said, his voice flat. "We have to take them—before it becomes any worse."

THE INSULTED AND THE INJURED

Оскорблённые и униженные

Fyodor Kolyokov spread two blinds apart with his thumb and peered out the window. Light flickered across his eyes. Heather squirmed in her chair.

"Is it time or what?" she said.

Kolyokov appeared to weigh the question, rocking his head to the left—to the right.

"Well?"

"Ha," he said. "She is dissipating."

"Is that good?"

Kolyokov looked at her. "Not good, not bad," he said. "Just—"

"Just? Just what?"

"Just next. The next thing."

THE IDIOT AND THE HONEST THIEF

Идиот и честный вор

Alexei and Montassini decided to leave Makar and Oleg for last. Montassini didn't care how tough Makar and Oleg were supposed to be; he figured it was better to deal with gunmen first. And so he did—creeping around the side of the building, keeping low. When he saw the two patrolling guards to the west, he motioned to Alexei to follow him—moved forward, keeping down, stopping when one of them seemed to pause. They got inside twenty feet before Montassini did it—just muttered "fuck it" and ran—motioned Alexei to do the same. One of the guards saw him and brought up the rifle, but it was too late for gunplay. Montassini grabbed the gun barrel and twisted, jamming the rifle butt into the guy's gut. Alexei cuffed the gun out of the other guard's hand before it could even fire, then stepped around him and pushed, sending him to the ground. Montassini spun the rifle barrel around, smacked it across his guy's temple. Alexei stomped down on his guy's forearm, then bent and grabbed something out of his hand. Montassini's guy crumpled. There was a click, and a whizzing sound, and Alexei's guy stopped moving. Montassini stood and looked more closely at Alexei. He was holding a little metal rod, with a ball on the end of it. The ball looked like it was vibrating. Montassini stared at it, snapped his fingers, and then it came to him.

"Fuck," he said. "You got an Asp. That's cool shit. Loco keeps one of those in his organizer right next to his laser pointer. Why didn't you say?"

"This guy had it," said Alexei. He held it like a strange treasure, arm's length, looked at it with wonder. "It used to belong to Alexei."

"How'd he get it?"

"From Borovich."

"Boro—"

"The Koldun. He robbed Alexei," said Alexei. "Just as they robbed us all."

"Let's go take care of the other two," said Leo, hefting one of the rifles. He caught a look from Alexei.

"No shooting," said Alexei.

Montassini rolled his shoulders and hefted the rifle. "Just in case."

"You are a clever fighter," said Alexei. "Don't shoot anybody."

They rounded the corner. Makar the giant fisherman and Oleg his vicious little brother were standing there, unarmed and unmoving. Montassini raised the rifle then lowered it as Alexei took off in a charge. Montassini hesitated for a moment—in admiration, watching as the Russian spy seemed to fly through the air, in the same motion clicking his Asp open and bringing it across Makar's skull in a stroke that was almost painterly. Alexei continued past, as Oleg spun away from him and rolled onto the ground.

Montassini was tempted to just shoot Oleg right there but he held himself back. He charged at Oleg—who was far from the psycho that Alexei described. He seemed to be in retreat. He pulled down the handle of the front door and had started to step inside when Montassini caught up with him. He brought the butt of the rifle down on Oleg's forearm, then pulled down on the barrel in a manoeuvre that was supposed to see-saw the butt up into Oleg's chin.

It didn't work out that way. Oleg swung back and turned to deliver a knee to Montassini's unprotected groin. He had been groined three times in his life: once as a kid in some back-alley schoolyard shit; once by his ex-wife's sister when he probably had it coming; and once in a deal with a guy who'd led everyone to believe was an uncle with the NYC Fuk Ching, but in fact was just a faggoty street fighter from San Francisco with a video collection and a death wish.

It never got easier.

Montassini fell back. It felt like his lungs were in seizure. He was able to hold onto the rifle at least. But Oleg had hold of it too, a ways up the barrel. The murderous little Russian fisherman rolled to the ground with Montassini.

Fuck, but it hurt down there. Montassini did his best to put it out of his mind—but it was tough. It was all he could do to dodge out of the way as Oleg jabbed two rigid fingers towards his eyes and suck air back into his spasming chest.

Montassini did his best. He twisted the rifle butt so it wedged in the general vicinity of Oleg's solar plexus, but it wasn't close enough. He shifted to one side, then the other, and then tried to use the momentum to flip Oleg over, but Oleg was doing his own shifting and rolling and it was no good. He finally grabbed Oleg's ear and twisted it, but Oleg didn't seem to mind that as much as another guy might and Montassini was just left twisting the guy's earlobe while Oleg looked at him all "you getting off on this buddy?" and then grabbed Montassini by the hair and hit his head against the ground which hurt like a sonofabitch. Montassini's vision got blurry before he could try anything else.

THE DOUBLE
ДВОЙНИК

"You want to take the children." Holden Gibson looked at his hands—back up at the Koldun. "You want to *kill* the fuckin' children."

"I don't want to," said Borovich. "No. No one but a monster wants to kill children. But these ones—"

They were standing outside a large metal door at the back of the greenhouse, behind Holden Gibson's little bedroom. Vasili Borovich the Koldun was working a latch on the door. Holden Gibson was clutching his nuts with one hand and the knife the Koldun had given him with the other and trying to put it all together.

"What the fuck about these ones?" said Gibson. "They're not anything but little kids—little kids with the power, yeah. But what the fuck do they have to do with this fuckin' Lena?"

The Koldun sighed. He stepped back from the door. "These kids," he said, "are different than you and I. They are more than just dream-walkers. When Babushka gets into their heads—she can use their abilities to extend her reach beyond just the sleepers here that we have made. And that little one—" he pointed at a baby "—he is a key to them all. Because he—his *mind*—is made up from *all of them*."

Holden Gibson was still putting it together. He thought about that. He thought about his time—John Kaye's time—his time back in that City 512 place. Something clicked as he did.

"Those kids," said Gibson. "That little one. They're my fuckin' grandchildren, aren't they?"

The Koldun looked at him appraisingly. "You've been thinking," he said.

"My *grandchildren*." Gibson shook his head. "It's just starting to make sense now."

"Not necessarily," said the Koldun. "But maybe. What do you remember?"

Gibson ran a hand across the stubble of his chin. "I remember—the sex was good."

Gibson remembered a lot of other things. He remembered the rooms he lived in—a comfortable bed, a sofa, and a hi-fi unit in the corner of a room panelled in wood like a basement recreation room. Although the room had no doors that he could see, he had plenty of visitors: young women, for the most part. Almost all of them spoke Russian—although there were other languages there too. Only three or four ever spoke English to him. They'd bring him meals and spend the night and he would fuck them and they would disappear when he woke, never to return. He didn't miss any one of them—they all seemed to be about as drugged up as him.

"So are they my grandchildren?"

The Koldun shrugged. "Hard to say," he said. "I was not there for most of your stay. I know there were many that . . . contributed."

"You want me to kill my grandchildren?"

The Koldun sighed and looked at him sadly. "*Da*," he said. "I would have my sleepers do so . . . But they are vulnerable. You must do it."

"Then why—" Gibson glared at him. "Why the fuck did you tell me this?"

"I did not," said the Koldun, "tell you anything. You came to this place yourself, Holden."

Gibson half-smiled. "You're callin' me Holden all of a sudden."

"That is what you prefer to be called, is it not?"

Gibson didn't answer that. The Koldun shrugged, and turned back to the door.

"I have to kill my grandchildren?" said Gibson. It was a question and a statement all at once.

There was a click, and the door swung open. Dim light—like Christmas lights, or the glow from a dozen nightlights spilled out. The Koldun put a finger to his lips and stepped through.

Gibson followed. He had been near this room during his entire stay here—literally just a few steps away—but he'd never caught more than a glimpse of what was inside, a tantalizing view of pine board, stacks of linen and that low, diffuse light. He stepped through and looked around.

The room was long and low—with a carpeted floor and walls and ceilings made out of slats of stained pine. There was nothing adorning the walls—but along them were lined bunk beds—not dissimilar to the bunks that Gibson kept on his yacht, in the hidden room. Except these were larger—an adult could comfortably sleep in them and they were sealed.

On the side of each bed, there was bolted a sheet of what looked like glass, reinforced with a grid of black wire. The light in this room, Gibson saw, came from inside the bunks, one in each, no brighter than a few watts. Each illuminated a sleeping child. Gibson moved quietly to one and then another. The children looked innocent—like tiny angels—or premature babies who'd been kept a year or ten too long in the incubator.

"Fuck," he murmured as he stepped back.

"The glass," whispered the Koldun, "is a two-way mirror. The room itself is soundproofed, and the bunks are soundproofed too. They are not, however, entirely bulletproof." The Koldun lifted his machine pistol.

"Fuck." Gibson's gut was churning at the thought of this thing. He looked at the gun in his hand. He looked at the Koldun, who looked back at him and said levelly, "Come on now, John. They were only ever tools to you. Do you want them to be tools to the Babushka now?"

Gibson looked at the gun in his hand—and back at the Koldun—and then, as a dark blur flew in through the doorway and spun behind the Koldun, his mind was made up for him.

He fired, even as Alexei Kilodovich's asp came screaming down at the back of the Koldun's skull.

Bullets tore white pine scars through the ceilings and walls as the machine pistol bucked in Gibson's grip. It made a half-dozen stars in the soundproofed glass. A light shattered on the far side of the room and a child screamed. Gibson gasped and let go of the trigger. He dropped the gun. The room was still around him—the only sound now the ringing in his ears, and the panicked wail of children.

"Oh fuck I'm sorry," said Holden Gibson as he stumbled up to the glass nearest him—glass that had three snowflake-shaped bullet holes in it. A child, black-haired and not more than five years old, huddled in the far corner, eyes wide and knees drawn to her chin—staring not at him but at her reflection in the glass. "I'm sorry," said Gibson as he moved to the next—a bunk where an older child lay still, maybe dead, beneath sheets. The kid wasn't dead—when Gibson tapped on the glass with a trembling knuckle the kid twitched, and started shaking himself. Just playing possum, thought Gibson. Smart fuckin' kid.

He made the rounds with similarly cheering results. There were six bunks he'd hit—and none of them had done worse than break glass. It looked as though the worst he'd done to the children was wake them up and scare the living shit out of them. "Thank fuckin' God," said Gibson. "Thank fuckin' God."

He turned to the centre of the room—to the doorway—and saw that he had something else to be thankful for. The Koldun was gone. The only thing that was left was his machine pistol, which he must have dropped fleeing for cover. The gun, and Alexei Kilodovich, the fucking traitor Russian, who lay now in a tangle. Blood stained the carpet underneath his right shoulder like a spill of cheap wine. Gibson worked his face into a smile.

"Fuckin' Russkie," he said. "Now who's killin' who? Now—"

Gibson stopped. Against all reason, the Russian was starting to move.

His face was pale with the loss of blood. His shoulder was soaked in that blood. Nevertheless, Alexei the traitor sat up, and pulled himself to his feet. Gibson held the machine pistol in front of him. He pulled the trigger. But it clicked empty.

Gibson tried to bring back that smile. "Jesus, pal, you don't look so good."

Alexei stooped to pick up the asp. He jiggled it in his hand. At first, he was trembling—but as the asp tip oscillated faster, he got that under control. He looked at Gibson with hollow, unfeeling eyes.

Gibson raised the machine pistol. It clicked empty again. Kilodovich stepped over the unconscious form of the Koldun. He held the asp to his side, bobbing up and down. The ball on the end of it gleamed in the low light. Blood continued to seep from his shoulder. His lips pulled back from teeth. He seemed almost feral. His feet scraped across the carpet.

Christ. The fucking Russian had wanted to kill him from the get-go. Now it looked like he was going to get his wish. Gibson backed away.

The Russian continued forward. The pain from the wound in his shoulder must have been ferocious. It should have knocked him unconscious. It probably, Gibson realized with a chill, very probably had.

"You're not Alexei," he said cagily, "are you?"

Gibson felt the cool smoothness of glass behind him. He glanced over his shoulder. A little kid of no more than three looked back at him with wide eyes.

"Is it you?" he asked. "Nah. Couldn't be. You're awake."

The kid looked away, and Gibson took the cue. The asp made a star in the glass behind where Gibson's head had been a moment before. When it struck again, Gibson was on the ground and had rolled away. He wasn't fast—but like many big men, he was faster than his opponents would give him credit for.

He crawled like a panicked crab across the floor to the Koldun' s machine pistol. Gibson grabbed it, rolled onto his back and aimed it at Alexei.

Or rather, where Alexei had been.

Gibson pulled up the barrel. He would have shot straight into the bunk-bed. Killed the three-year-old, who was staring at him now with wide, knowing eyes.

John, said a voice in his head.

"Who the fuck is that? Is that you, kid?"

No. It is I.

"You?"

I.

Gibson put down the machine pistol because with the way he was shaking, he was afraid the thing would just go off. He knew who *I* was, and he knew it wasn't the kid behind the glass.

No. I *was the one who decades ago, invaded the mind of John Kaye—tore its defences to shreds—broke down his identity—and laid the groundwork for the construction of Holden Gibson.*

I *was John Kaye's murderer.*

"You b-ball-bustin' fuckin' bitch," said Gibson. "Wh-where did you put the fuckin' Russian?"

Gibson felt his chest hitch—felt himself chuckle. Even though he had nothing to chuckle about. It was her chuckling. She continued.

I wish you could tell me, said Lena.

"Well he was just fuckin' here."

No, she said, *he was not. Alexei Kilodovich has been hiding from me since the dance began. He and—and several others. It does not please me.*

For a moment—just a moment—Gibson felt the world shrink underneath him, the lands crumble, and he felt as though he were sitting on a great desert under scorching sun. A cloud loomed and rolled in the distance—like some cartoon version of Yahweh. Beneath the cloud, a great city of golden towers and spires grew, like the Kingdom of Heaven.

If he had more wit, he'd have found words to mock it—tear it down. But as he looked upon it, he saw that the vision the Babushka had constructed simply dwarfed his own conceits. There was no mocking the divine. Not, he shivered, when it was real.

Gibson shook his head, and the vision disappeared. He was back in the room inside the greenhouse. The Koldun lay beside him. Blood soaked the carpet underneath Gibson's bare ass.

You should not have awoken, said Lena. *With that one's betrayal—I had need of you dreaming, John Kaye. I had need of your dreams.*

"B-ball-bustin'—"

Bitch. This is tiresome. This construct of yours—Holden Gibson. How did you come by it? Thumbing through old Mickey Spillane novels?

Gibson picked up the machine pistol again. "Hey fuck you—"

Bitch. That is how you deal with the world now. I must say, John, it is scarcely more convincing than your red devil costume. Do you remember that?

Gibson raised the pistol. "I'm fuckin' warning you—"

You'll shoot. No you won't. These children are your flesh and blood. You won't kill them because you haven't the stomach for that sort of thing. I remember when we finished with you, you were nothing more than a little puddle of flesh. We destroyed you, Fyodor Kolyokov and I. It was very easy. Do you know why?

He could feel the spring pushing back as his finger rode the trigger like a clutch.

You are, said Lena, the Babushka, *a fake. Then and now, John. Then and now.*

He let go of the trigger. He put down the gun. He stared down at his bare, pimpled thighs—the blood underneath him. He felt tears well in his eyes and snot thicken in his nose.

Now, said Lena, the Babushka, *there is nothing for you. Nothing for you but to be absorbed. It is time for you to join me as I spread across the world—and consume it, yes?*

"I don't think," said Holden aloud, "that my joining you would be an equal partnership."

Shh, said Babushka. *It is never an equal partnership in love.*

What the fuck? thought Holden.

Vasili Borovich could never accept that. He was too hungry in the beginning—and that hunger made a weakling of him. It put him in my thrall. That made him a useful ally for many years. But that, I know now, is also why he betrayed me.

Ah. Holden nodded. *So this whole fuckin' thing is what—a lover's quarrel*?

We were not lovers for a very long time—not, truly, since before you and I met.

Holden was about to say—to think—something else. But something was happening in the air in front of him. A figure was forming—a young woman, wearing a hooded cloak covering all but her cheeks, her red, red lips. She wore dark, form-fitting pants. Holden Gibson whistled—remembering now, seeing the figure a lifetime ago on a blasted plain of ice.

He could see how this Babushka could keep a guy like Vasili Borovich on a string all these years. It wouldn't be that difficult.

Babushka's mouth spread in a small, teasing grin.

Join with me, she said. *Spread with me. Come with me across the ocean and beneath the waves. We shall wipe the world clean of the Vasili Boroviches, and make all of the minds of men and women minds of ours. Sit at my knee, John Kaye. It need not be equal to be a joyous thing.*

Gibson thought about an answer, thought about the prospect of doing this, at the knee of this magnificent creature. Thought about spreading across the world.

Sure, he said, *on one condition*.

Yes?

But he hadn't the chance to name it. The asp tore down on the back of his neck and in a brief flowering of light he was unconscious.

RESURRECTION
Воскресение

The Empire of New Pokrovskoye danced in frenetic celebration for hours, reeling and pumping at the old songs—marvelling at the beauty of this land. They had arrived in this place, this grand consensus at last. Had it once been a fishing village? Well hadn't Rome once been a swamp—London an old provincial outpost of that—New York City, a clutch of tribes conquered by London? New Pokrovskoye was no more a fishing village now than any of those places were a picture of their humble beginnings.

New Pokrovskoye was a beginning of a new empire that would erase the rest more thoroughly than before. The sky was a great pink canvas, bejewelled by strange constellations now visible through Babushka's stretching mantle. It stretched as she expanded—over the sea, across the lands, and south along the jagged coastline. Easy to imagine her overtaking the world in this way. She had everything she needed to do so, surely.

Almost everything she needed. There was still rage in her belly—for while she inhabited ten thousand minds, and was prodigious at that—there were six billion others in the world that she could not touch. Six billion whose dreams were their own and whose minds were closed.

It must be driving her mad, thought Fyodor Kolyokov as he let the blinds close and turned back to Heather; mad to be denied the key to those minds, while its vessel lay so near.

"Now?" said the girl, and Kolyokov smiled. "Now," he said.

THE HONEST THIEF

Честный вор

Leo Montassini hurt all over. His stomach hurt—his ribs hurt—his balls ached. He hurt enough that it caused him to wonder just what he was doing alive. The last he'd remembered, he was on the receiving end of a beating from that little fucking fisherman—and he wasn't doing too well. He'd blacked out. He should have been dead.

He blinked and sat up. He was lying some distance from the entrance to the greenhouse where all this had happened—but not that far. He could see the flickering greenish light behind the girl who was leaning over him.

The girl who was leaning over him. Leo blinked.

"Who the fuck are you?" The girl was kind of a looker, Leo had to admit. She was blonde, which was how Leo liked them, and tight. She probably worked out. Leo liked that too. He smiled at her.

The girl smiled back and extended a hand.

"I am Fyodor Kolyokov," she said in a thick Russian accent, and brushed aside a lock of rasta hair from her eye to look more closely at him. "I recognize you. Are you not one of Gepetto Bucci's *capos*? Not the funny one, surely?"

THE GRAND INQUISITOR

Великий инквизитор

"I am quartermaster of the Imperial New Pokrovskoye Tea Company," explained the little man one more time. "Now let me go or there will be trouble."

Amar Shadak looked over to Gepetto Bucci, who shrugged and twiddled his forefinger around his ear. He looked back at their prisoner. Shadak didn't even bother making a nice face for this one.

"Where," said Bucci, leaning forward, "is New Pokrovskoye?"

"Everywhere," said the prisoner. "It will come upon you soon. Then you will be in trouble. Trust me. Better to let me go. I will put in a good word for you with the Imperial Guard."

Bucci nodded. He reached into his pocket and pulled out a cigarette lighter, flicked it to life. "I got this from my old man. He used to run an empire up this way too."

"Is that so?"

"Yeah. That's so. Not fuckin' tea, though."

The Quartermaster looked up at the bluish flame. "Vodka," he said and nodded.

Bucci shook his head no. "Screech," he said. "Used to run it down through St. John's. Newfoundland. Big empire. *Roman* empire, you could say." He looked at the quartermaster. "Don't fuckin' threaten me," he said. "Answer questions."

Their prisoner rattled the handcuffs they'd used to affix him to the chair at the Cloridorme Marina office. Outside, the harbour stood empty, but for the motor launch that Bucci had arranged to meet them there. It was nearly dawn. The prisoner was the only living soul they had seen since pulling into town.

Shadak rolled his shoulders and stepped back from the interrogation. He had suddenly lost his stomach for it, and as he stepped back leaned against the flimsy screen door that led outside. Just like that, he was standing on a cracked cement pad in the pale illumination of a Coke machine, listening to the surf crash rhythmically against the pier. Another sea—of car and truck hoods—gleamed nearer in the pre-dawn light.

He scraped his foot along the cement. It was sandy. The way the sand rasped between the toe of his shoe and the cement made him think about the way the sand flowed like a river through the caves where he had lost himself in the Black Villa which made him think about the townspeople who even if they were in their beds might be in a place far off now. Rapture had come to this place; there was no mistaking it.

Rapture had taken the men in the caves. It had taken his caravansary—and it had assuredly taken everyone in the Emissary Hotel, prior to the arrival of Gepetto Bucci and his crew.

"Everything okay in there?"

Shadak shuddered and turned. Jack Devisi stepped into the pool of light outside the Cloridorme marina. Devisi dropped his spent cigarette and mashed it under his toe.

"Mind your business," Shadak said.

"Right." Devisi shrugged, moved his toe off the squashed butt. Smoke curled across the top of his shoe then vanished in the maritime breeze. Devisi reached into his jacket, pulled out a package of cigarettes and offered Shadak one. Shadak made a swatting motion. Devisi shrugged, pulled one out between his lips and lit it.

"I been at the diner here in town," said Devisi finally. "Supposed to open at six a.m. It's five-twenty now. You think someone'd be in there—getting' ready. Fuck, with all the cars in town . . ." he gestured to the cars—they were double-parked along the road to the edge of town. Volkswagens and Chryslers, Hondas and Toyotas . . .

There was a muffled cry inside the marina. Devisi looked back over his shoulder. "Workin' him over, huh?"

Shadak looked out at the ocean. Dawn was creeping up in the east, painting a thin pink line at horizon's edge. The moon and a couple of stars perched a little higher in the part that was still night.

Devisi laughed nervously. "Surprised you ain't in there," he said.

Shadak took his hands from his jacket pocket. He looked at Devisi. "Why would you say that?"

"I only mean, it seems you like that kind of thing."

Shadak raised his eyebrows. Devisi stepped a little closer.

"You know," he said. His voice was like gravel in Shadak's ear. Stale cigarette smoke enveloped Shadak. "Rough shit."

Shadak turned to look at Devisi, calculating as he did so. He thought about killing him. For no reason better than the exercise, and he was in reach. It would be misplaced, such an act. *But*, thought Shadak, *it would be satisfying.*

"Hey!"

Devisi and Shadak both looked back. Bucci was standing in the door, his sleeves rolled up, his cheeks pink with the exertion. He looked at Devisi and jerked his thumb back. "Get inside. We gotta talk."

Devisi nodded and stepped away. Shadak's thoughts moved elsewhere.

Bucci ambled up beside Shadak.

"You all right?" he asked.

"Fine," said Shadak, and Bucci shook his head.

"That fuckin' guy in there," he said. "Don't blame you for getting air. He's whacked."

"Does he know?"

Bucci looked out at the sea. "He knows. Fat lot of good it'll do us. I ask him where New Pokrovskoye is. He won't say at first. Then he tells me it's on the—get this—the Iliana Peninsula. Through the Petroska Straits. He gave us directions, but he may as well have told us to follow the fuckin' Yellow Brick Road."

"The sea," said Shadak. "How fast can we get your boat here? You said later this morning."

"My guy says about eleven, depending."

Shadak nodded. The crew of them had flown in overnight and driven here in a rental, to get a fast lay of things in Cloridorme. But it didn't sound like you could fly to New Pokrovskoye that easily—and anyway, Shadak wanted to go in with some firepower. Bucci had a boat he kept in Newfoundland—a big fast boat that Shadak was familiar with. There were guns there too—cached underneath the new Trekkers Outfitting Co-op that was slated to open there in the fall. That was the plan: load up the boat, send it to Cloridorme, and then the crew of them could follow the trail across the water to New Pokrovskoye.

Where, he was sure, he would find Kilodovich.

"How close are we?" he said.

"To leaving?" Bucci smiled. "I told you."

"No. You know. To finding Kilodovich. You have been asking the Quartermaster there about Alexei Kilodovich, haven't you?"

The smile vanished. Bucci leaned in close to Shadak. He put a hand on Shadak's shoulder.

"Fucker did a real number on you," said Bucci softly. "Didn't he? Well don't worry, Amar. We'll make things right.

"You know what this place reminds me of?" said Bucci. "Marcia."

"It reminds you of Marcia? Who is Marcia?"

"An old girlfriend," said Bucci. "Great in the sack. But she had one problem."

"What was that?"

"Thought she had psychic powers. *The Sight*."

"Did she? Have the Sight, I mean?"

"Who knows?" said Bucci. "She said a lot of things that were true. But they were also things you could figure out by looking at a guy." He thought about it. "So could go either way. Probably she wasn't no psychic. But you couldn't tell her that. She spent all her money on books and crystals and fuckin' tapes—most months it was me that paid her fuckin' rent and not her."

"It sounds like a waste."

"It was a waste I guess," said Bucci. "But I think she used it. To keep out of serious shit. See, one day I finally got sick of her. Told her that was it—she was on her own, no more gifts no more nothing."

"Hmm. What did she do?"

Bucci laughed. "She told me I had bad energy or some fuckin' thing. She told me I didn't know what I was saying and she knew because she could see the energy all around me." Bucci fanned his fingers around his head and wiggled them. "All jaggly. She said I should fuckin' meditate and I'd feel better about things."

"Did you?"

"Fuck no. I left."

Shadak looked at him sidelong. "She was not psychic," he said. "If she was—"

Bucci looked back. "If she was," he said, "I still would have left. Wouldn't have changed a fuckin' thing."

Shadak didn't finish what he was going to say: *If she was psychic, you would have been her fucking hand-puppet until she was finished with you, and when you left you would have taken away less than half of yourself. The rest would have stayed in her clutches until you died.* Instead, he asked: "Do you think that Cloridorme is pretending to be psychic?"

Bucci leaned back and crossed his arms. "You know," he said, "with the shit I've seen the past couple of days, I don't think Cloridorme is pretending anything. I sure as shit don't think New Pokrovskoye is playin' a game here. I'm goin' there because I said I would and I owe you from way back and I do what I say and I pay my fuckin' tab. But you know something? In the end, I don't think it means shit."

"You have not met Alexei Kilodovich," said Shadak.

"No," said Bucci, "I have not. But we'll see about meeting him soon. That fucker did a real number on you. I can tell. Soon as the boat comes. We'll get on that fucker's ass."

And with that, Bucci stepped back inside.

Shadak peeked into his breast pocket—at the photograph there, of himself and Kilodovich—on the back of a jeep, grinning like fools. Shadak's girlfriend had taken it—Ming Lei, with her long black hair and thighs smooth as silk. She was the kind of girl that a resourceful young hero like Amar Shadak ought to have three of. But Shadak, at just twenty-two still reeling at the responsibility of the shipment of small arms and mortar bombs that the Americans had dropped for him across the Pakistani border, one girl like her was enough.

Closer she'd said. *Don't worry—no one call you faggot, Amar. Cuddle up*. And they'd laughed, and Alexei had thrown his arm over Amar Shadak's shoulder like they were brothers—and she had taken the picture and handed it to him. He sat there, as the convoy started moving, watching the picture turn from creamy nothing into the instant of history, where Alexei Kilodovich embraced Amar Shadak as a brother.

He hoped that Bucci's boat would do the trick. Shadak had acquired it for Bucci a couple of years ago from a cartel of Filipino pirates. It was one of a fleet of very useful little boats; it could pass muster in an only slightly well-oiled harbour. But given a half-hour's notice, the deck gun could be up and assembled on the prow and the boat would be ready for combat. It was a good choice. Shadak thought that they might well have need of it.

Particularly, if Kilodovich was in charge of the force of men and women that were awaiting them.

He was sly enough to be. Particularly now that Fyodor Kolyokov was out of the picture.

They had first met in Quetta—during Shadak's second and last meeting with Jim Saunders, his C.I.A. contact—the man who, at the time, Shadak saw as nothing less than his gatekeeper, to greatness. Kilodovich was lolling under a Banyan tree across from the café, sipping on a frosted bottle of beer and drumming his fingers impatiently on the wood of the bench. He was barely a man—skinny and pale, with close-cropped black hair and that unibrow, a little dusting of beard. He wore acid-washed blue jeans that did not fit him and a wine-coloured shirt with lapels wider than his chest. Shadak was not happy when Saunders had insisted that Kilodovich go along.

"The kid has contacts," said Saunders.

"I have contacts," said Shadak. "That's why you hired me."

Saunders had smiled that apologetic little half-smile of his. "We move in Soviet Afghanistan, we go with the Russian kid. Otherwise—"

He left it unspoken.

"Fine," said Shadak. He had not yet worked with the Americans—and in 1985, if you worked with the Americans it was either Central America or Afghanistan. At that point Nicaragua was just a set of possible locations on young Amar's mental map of the world. But Shadak had been doing heroin deals with certain Afghani parties since long before the Soviets had marched in. At that stage in his career where he could not afford to stand still, he could not afford to leave the American opportunity untapped.

At the time, Amar assumed that Saunders had given Alexei Kilodovich some kind of secret signal. The kid downed his beer and started immediately across the street. He was gawky and thin, but he moved even then with an easy confidence. He stepped around the low fence of the café's patio and pulled up one of the plastic resin chairs.

He nodded hello at Shadak, who gave him a little smile in return.

"So we are going to be travelling together, *da*?"

Shadak nodded. "So it seems. You know Afghanistan pretty well, I hear."

"Not really," said Alexei.

Shadak laughed. He had no idea, of course, that Alexei was telling pretty much the truth. He had never set foot on the lunar landscape of Afghanistan. He was along for another purpose.

Amar Shadak killed the next couple of hours wandering around the little town. The dawn light flattered it. If you squinted, and thought back to happier times, you might have imagined you were in a little French fishing village in the south—where you could while away the morning with a bottle of wine and some fresh-baked bread, before you climbed back into your Peugeot for the drive back to Paris and a night in the clubs.

Except of course you would never find a parking spot for your Peugeot here. The roads were all lined with cars. The town could probably build a hospital with the money it collected from parking tags this morning. . . .

Shadak wandered up the gentle slope from the harbour to the main streets. He walked past a gas station—still closed—a grocery store, a dark structure of corrugated steel and cinderblock filled with empty shelves and a couple of old video games. There were houses that crawled back further from the water, simple wooden buildings roofed in tar paper. Everyone in town seemed to have a truck, parked next to sleek, bullet-shaped little vehicles that Shadak understood to be snowmobiles. The houses were all dark, and as he walked he began to wonder whether the town was deserted. He thought back to *The Omega Man*, which made him think about the caves again, which made him wonder how well he'd do if the town rose up before him now—one terrible mind.

Shadak was saved from his own thoughts by the OPEN sign in the town's little restaurant. He stuck his head inside, and saw a thickset woman behind the counter. A coffee machine was sputtering in the corner. The woman looked up at him and said *bonjour*, and Shadak said *bonjour* back, but when he tried to order a light breakfast it developed that there was no cook; he had left with the others. Shadak could have coffee and some cereal, but there was no bread for toast. "Les pilgrims" had cleaned them out. On a hunch, Shadak asked her where they'd gone and the woman shrugged. "Away, thank God," she said. Shadak thought about working her over—but truly, if he'd been in a frame of mind for working people over there was honest work for him in the marina. She poured him a cup of weak, strange-tasting coffee and he sat there at the counter in silence and thought about Afghanistan.

They were almost equals at first. In the two weeks it took for Shadak's and Saunders' people to coordinate the shipment of munitions and guards for it at the border rendezvous, Amar and Alexei got to know one another very well. They spent time in clubs—partied with the Mujahedeen staffers at Captain Musa's villa outside Quetta. After only a little hesitation, Amar introduced Alexei to his girlfriend. Her name was Ming Lei. She was twenty-one years old and Shadak had met her at a club in Hong Kong, where she had been working as a dancer. She had implied several times that she was trying to gather enough money to smuggle her family out of the People's Republic and this was the best way of earning it quickly. He trusted her, the way only a twenty-two year old can trust a beautiful woman who doesn't answer questions directly.

"I want to bring her with us," said Shadak at their favourite club, while Ming was off for a pee.

"To Kandahar?" Alexei appeared to consider it. Amar had expected him to do the sensible thing and tell him to fuck off. But then Alexei surprised him.

"Why not? She is good luck, yes?"

Amar blinked. "She is good luck."

"Can she handle a gun?"

Amar laughed and stubbed out his cigarette in the little bronze ashtray at their table. "She doesn't know about guns," he said.

"That's good," said Alexei. "It never pays to love a woman who knows about guns."

And they'd laughed. And Ming had come back, straightening her short skirt, and looked at them both. "What you laughing about? Crazy bastard?" She punched Amar hard in the arm. "What?"

Alexei propped his own cigarette in the crook of his smiling lips, and extended a hand across the table to Ming. She took it. "Congratulations, darling," he shouted over the club's booming techno-pop soundtrack. "Amar and I have voted on it."

"What?"

"We've decided," shouted Alexei.

Amar slid his arm around Ming's ass.

"You're coming to Kandahar!" he hollered. "With us!"

Ming laughed and nodded, and rubbed her hip deliciously against Amar's shoulder. She seemed pleased enough at the time. Although later, Amar would learn that was because she hadn't understood a word either of them had said over the din of the nightclub.

"You crazy?" she demanded later that night as they lay in bed. "Take a Chinese woman to Afghanistan? With luck I would be raped by Russian soldiers. No luck, and we meet Mujahideen? Who knows what would happen?"

"If you don't—want to go, you don't have to," Amar stammered.

"Who is that kid you working with, anyway? This his idea?"

"No. It was mine."

Ming faced him, hands on both his shoulders. She pretended to study his face. "You look all hurt. Aw. Don't look hurt. Stupid idea, that's all."

They hadn't spoken about it the rest of the night. But the next morning, when they met Alexei, Ming just nodded when he went over their travel itinerary. When Alexei left them, Amar asked her about it.

"So you've changed your mind? Do you want to come?"

Ming grinned and nodded. "Sure," she said, infiltrating his fingers with her own and squeezing hard. "Big desert trip. Sound like fun."

And that was all she would say about it, until they were at the border and pulling the tarps off the Red Cross trucks that his Calcutta contacts had moved in for him.

"Well well," said a voice from the back of the restaurant, "another tourist. I thought we were done with them, eh, Marie?"

Shadak looked up. The man who'd come in was skinny as a rail, with cropped hair and a face rouged with exploded capillaries. As he worked his way closer to the counter, Shadak could smell liquor coming off him. Liquor and bile. He went past Shadak and set himself down at the end of the counter. The waitress, Marie, poured coffee into a cup and saucer and brought it to him.

"Good morning, Bill," she said.

"You have had a lot of tourists?" asked Shadak.

Bill shook his head and belched. "Oh, a few," he said.

"Where did they go?"

Bill looked at him wearily. "Jeez-us," he said. "Not so loud. They went away in boats."

Shadak looked at him. He smiled pleasantly. "You," he said mildly, "know more than that."

Bill sipped his coffee noisily, like soup. "I don't know anythin' anymore," he said.

Shadak stood up and took the stool next to Bill.

"Took my boat, what they did," he said. "No gratitude, isn't that right, Marie?"

Marie smiled and shook her head. "They paid you," she said.

"Where," said Shadak, "did they take your boat?"

"No idea."

Shadak picked up his coffee and sipped at it. He smacked his lips and turned to the waitress.

"*What's that I'm tasting*?" he asked in French.

"*Salt*," she said.

"*You are joking*."

"*It is a family secret. Takes away the bitterness*."

Shadak might have asked another question—but there was a jangling at the front door. Jack Devisi stepped in. "Fuck," he said, "there you are. We been lookin' all over for you. Fuckin' harbourmaster lost—" Devisi stopped himself, seeing the two others in the diner "—lost his train of thought," he finished.

Shadak nodded. He looked at the drunk. Studied his bleary eyes.

The drunk blinked and stared at him, suddenly alert. His eyes had a hungry glitter to them.

"*You aren't a grandchild*," he said. In Russian. "*You are close. But you are missing*."

"What the fuck," gasped Devisi.

Shadak stepped back from the counter. Marie stepped back into the kitchen.

"Oh *merde*," she said.

Shadak smiled. Russian. This wasn't old Bill talking. This was—who?

"Babushka?" said Shadak.

Bill's face broke into a grin.

"*Where*," said Shadak carefully in Russian, "*is Alexei Kilodovich*?"

"*I was hoping*," said Bill, "*you could tell me*."

Then he faltered and grabbed the back of his chair. He settled himself into it.

"Wow," Bill said, shaking his head.

"What the fuck?" said Devisi. "A Russian?"

Shadak looked around him. Devisi bent over the guy and slapped him. "Hey!" he said. "Fuckwit! What the fuck do you mean you could tell me? Where the fuck do we go! Answer me!"

Shadak was about to grab Devisi's shoulder to make him stop when Marie appeared at the door to the kitchen.

"*We both want the same thing*," she said in Russian.

"Ah, shit," whispered Shadak. Then to Devisi: "Leave the old man alone. He has nothing to say to us."

Bill was sobbing now. Marie, the waitress, touched her forehead and stumbled against the counter. She gasped. "I'm—sorry," she said. "I didn't say anything, did I?"

Rapture. Shadak swore. It was the same as at the caravansary—the whole world might turn against him. The same as—as the caves.

Except this time, he was unarmed.

Shadak turned to Devisi. "Give me your gun," he said.

Devisi's eyes widened and he made shushing motions with his hands. "Fuck," he whispered, "don't talk—"

He didn't get a chance to finish. Bill was on top of him like a bouncer at a Belarus nightclub. "Fuck!" said Devisi, as Bill pushed him from the stool and onto the floor. Shadak slid back off his chair and tried to grab Bill, but the old man was quick, and rolled away. Shadak turned around and picked up a stool, as Bill fumbled in Devisi's coat while Devisi hung onto the old man's throat. Shadak held the stool over his head, when he heard the unmistakable *click!* of a firearm cocking.

"*Put down the stool*," said Marie in Russian.

She was holding a double-barrelled shotgun levelled at Shadak's chest.

Fuck, he thought. He put down the stool, as Bill pulled Devisi's gun from underneath his jacket.

Bill got up, coughed, and motioned for Devisi to do the same.

"In the back," said Marie, motioning with the gun.

After listening to Leo Montassini talk about his travels, locating this place, Shadak had made his way to the 14th floor where old Fyodor Kolyokov had kept that tank of his. More than anywhere in the hotel, this place seemed haunted. It smelled like salt and rot, making Shadak wonder if that sea that Montassini described wasn't just beyond the closed bathroom door. He felt, almost, as though he were walking into another world as he crossed that threshold.

You don't mind if we wait outside, Bucci had said, and Shadak had said he didn't. He stepped into the bathroom, flicked on the light, and beheld the "fucking UFO thing."

It was a marvel, he supposed. But it was a marvel in the manner that seeing a mysterious thing you've only ever imagined is marvellous: it brings the fancy of imagination down to earth. Shadak had once imagined this sort of thing as a great gleaming pod—mirrored surface distorting the world around it like the eye of a huge fish; powered by crackling Van de Graaff generators and operated by monsters with strange appendages and wicked intent. Seeing this thing—a dark lozenge with rust streaks around the welds where pipes and hoses emerged; a simple steel-wrapped conduit providing it with power from a converted wall socket, Cyrillic notations stamped into its skin—made him wonder at its simple reality. Shadak had opened up the hatch—stuck his head inside and sniffed around for the ocean that Leo Montassini had fantasized. He'd chuckled. The tank smelled as much like an ocean as a toilet did, which was to say quite a bit—but Amar Shadak would never confuse the two.

Now, he, Devisi and their two captors marched through the door into the kitchen, and then down stairs to a rough-hewn cellar that had been cut into bedrock some time ago. It also, Shadak noted with a chill, contained four more tanks.

"What the fuck?" said Devisi.

Bill jabbed Devisi in the small of the back. "Open the hatch," he commanded. Devisi did as he was told. "Inside," said Bill. Devisi gave Shadak a horrified look—but looked back at the gun, and climbed in.

"D-don' fuckin' close—"

But that was all he could say. Bill swung the hatch shut and twirled the handle.

"What are you doing?" demanded Shadak. "Don't think I'm getting into that fucking thing."

Marie shook her head. "*No,*" she said. "*There is no point. I could not reach you through there. You are broken.*"

"*Him, though,*" said Bill. "*He will open his soul to me. In a week, he will become one of us.*"

Shadak sneered. "In a tank? Those are not for sleepers. Those are dream-walkers'."

"*These are not dream-walker tanks. It is an improvisation of mine. There are drugs and gas and media in there. He will break down in a matter of days. It is practically automated. Listen.*" Marie motioned to the tank with her shotgun. Shadak went over, and pressed his ear against it. Faintly, he could hear the sound of music—some Russian folk song—something about a girl called Natascha—overlaid with shouting and pounding.

"But not for me," said Shadak.

"*No,*" she said. "*You do not know where Alexei Kilodovich truly is. You are a dangerous mistake. You must be—*"

She held the gun. Shadak stared at her. She did not fire.

"*Where is he!*" she shouted at him. "*Let me into the Villa to see!*"

Shadak looked at her levelly. "If I knew how to get into the Black Villa," he said, a smile creeping into his voice, "don't you think I would have gone there myself by now?"

"*I—*" said Marie, and Bill finished for her: "*I am tired of this. I have a battle to fight elsewhere.*"

And with that, Marie let the shotgun fall to her side—and Devisi's nine millimetre fell to the cut-stone floor from Bill's limp hands. The two looked at each other in confusion as Shadak let his breath out and prepared himself for beating the living crap out of both of them.

Gepetto Bucci was not happy when Devisi told him what had happened in the café. Shadak could hear him from outside. He swore and paced and hit things in the little marina office. Shadak couldn't really blame him. Shadak felt his face flush with the stupidity of the act. They needed to make a clean exit from this place. Who knew how far it would be to New Pokrovskoye? Who knew?

Shadak sat against the cinderblock wall of the marina and rubbed his face in his hands. The knuckles of his right hand were bloody where they'd come into contact with Bill's belt-buckle.

He should never, he knew, have engaged in this chase. When Fyodor Kolyokov had told him he could provide him with Alexei Kilodovich—Shadak should simply have left. Kilodovich was not good for him. The last time he had seen him . . .

The last time, he had been in a place like this. He ran his hand over the rough cement of the wall. Did it remind him of the caves? The concrete wall here was not of a piece with the fantastic natural chimneys that twisted and curved to admit dusty light from a distant sky, the layered sediment that measured height and years in the walls like rings on a tree. The poured cement pad here had nothing in common with the fine sand that flowed in solid rivers through the base of the caves.

And yet—the mind draws connections.

He could lose this thing—lose what little of himself that he had retained since Afghanistan. Kilodovich could see to that, if Shadak weren't clever.

"Hey."

Shadak looked up. Bucci stood, his hands jammed into his coat pocket, looking down at him.

"You cryin' now, Amar?"

Shadak wiped his eye and looked at his fingertip. Sure enough: tears.

Bucci knelt down beside Shadak. "You know," he said, "you once upon a time were a pretty formidable fuckin' guy."

"I am," said Shadak, pushing himself to his feet, "still a pretty formidable fucking guy."

"Well I hope so," said Bucci. "I owe you a lot. And I'm pretty fuckin' curious about all this shit. But fuck."

Shadak nodded. He thought briefly about taking on Bucci—about slamming his fingers into the soft space underneath his ribcage, pushing up through the muscle and flesh and crushing the breath out of his bare lungs. But he didn't think he could do that now. So he looked at Bucci and just nodded.

"Now we got a plan," said Bucci. "We managed to wake up the fuckin' harbour master, and he's given us a map."

"To New Pokrovskoye?"

"Yeah. It's a chart that he had under his desk. All of a sudden, the fucker broke. He just blinked and started beggin'—like he'd lost his nerve all at once. So we asked him again and he spilled. Said the maps were there. Map of the eastern fuckin' seaboard, but the names are all different. They're written in Russian, so we can't read them. He showed me where New Pokrovskoye is. It's in fuckin' Labrador. Way fuckin' north. It's gonna take some time to get there, but we can do it."

"Good."

"Now I don't think he's lying—but he's not all there either you know what I mean?"

"I do."

"So we're going to take him with us. I'm thinkin'."

Shadak thought about that. The sea voyage, on a boat filled with guns—in a convoy filled with guns. To New Pokrovskoye. The Black Villa. Where he slept. Where even Babushka could not enter.

"Hey!"

Shadak looked up.

"Fuck, Amar, pay attention."

Shadak blinked. "The caves," he said. "The Black Villa."

"What?"

Shadak shook his head. He didn't know what. He leaned back against the wall and lowered his hands into his face.

"He's not the only one we should take," said Shadak.

"That so? Who else?"

"New friends," said Shadak. "We should wrap their eyes in bandages and plug up their ears—and if Babushka comes back . . . she can fucking well talk to me."

"Ah fuck." Bucci gave Shadak a despairing look. "I'll go back inside—I've got to—"

Bucci's voice trailed off. There was the sound of a car engine coming up the road. Shadak looked up.

A Ford minivan with California plates on it, its sides covered in mud, jostled along the road and pulled to a stop. It seemed to shimmer with the heat from its engine. Shapes moved inside, seat-lights flashed on and off, beyond the grime of the tinted windows.

Bucci sniffed. "Fuck," he said, "What's that smell?"

Shadak sniffed. It smelled like the Black Villa—inviting, comfortable . . .

And poison.

The side door slid open, and a young man stepped out. He looked like a surfer—all suntan and streaked blond hair. Behind him, Shadak could see others: a young woman who might have been the surfer's girlfriend; an older guy with swept-back hair and tinted glasses that might have been the surfer's girlfriend's father.

"Hey," said the surfer. "Are we too late to go to New Pokrovskoye? Man, we been driving through the night and then some."

"We'd hate to miss out," said the girl.

Shadak smiled his warmest come-hither smile.

"You have been talking with Babushka?"

"Whoa," said the surfer. "How'd you know that?"

Shadak smiled again.

"I've been talking with her too," he said. "I would like to talk with her again."

The older man stepped down. "Well good luck," he said. "We haven't been in touch for hours."

"She said we would see her again in New Pokrovskoye."

"But we think we've missed the boat," said the older man.

"Yeah," said the surfer. "We're bummed."

"Bummed." Shadak made a sympathetic face. "Well not to worry. It so happens that the last boat to New Pokrovskoye is due to arrive—" he looked at his watch "—in an hour or so."

"And there's room?" said the girl.

"Plenty," said Shadak—and he didn't add that if there wasn't, well they'd make some room in the harbour. He wasn't going to leave anybody behind in this place. And if he had his way, he wasn't going to leave anyone in New Pokrovskoye either.

THE IDIOT IN YOUTH

Идиотство в юных

Alexei spotted the baby carriage wedged between two tall rocks on the steep slope of a valley. The carriage was a geometric marvel of dark blue steel tubes, plastic armatures and soft foam cushions, riding on four big, knobbly tires that looked purpose-built for the tricky off-road conditions of southeastern Afghanistan. The timing was wrong though—this thing had probably been manufactured in the late 1990s. Afghanistan, on the other hand, was vintage 1987. A rich black puff of oil smoke drifted across the blue sky. Small-arms fire chuffed in the distance, softening to pops and fizzes in the echoes of the rocky hills. Russians or Mujahedeen—one or the other or more likely both—were not far off.

Alexei wiped sweat off his brow as Vladimir glared up at him.

"Alexei Kilodovich! You are an idiot!" Vladimir was wearing a little blue terrycloth jumper, which offset the girlish bonnet tied over his head to keep the sun off. He clenched two tiny fists and kicked his blue-clothed feet in little circles. Alexei struggled with the carriage, and finally pulled it loose. Vladimir, faced scrunched in rage, continued talking as he went.

"I show you your history—give you a door to make it—to discover yourself. And what do you do? You walk through the fence—just as you were about to discover yourself."

"It's all bullshit," said Alexei glumly. He righted the carriage, and walking backwards, pulled it jostling down to the little creek-bed at the valley's base.

"Why do you use that term?" said Vladimir. He was in full sunlight, and tried vainly to turn away from it. "*Bull-shit*. Cattle feces. Fertilizer. It means nothing."

"That," said Alexei, "is a good read on *my* meaning. This metaphor you put me in. Where's the meaning? You can create anything with your mind—so can I—make it as convincing as flesh—and before you know it the memory and the truth and the shit start to mix."

"How *deep*," sneered Vladimir. "Are you a philosopher, Kilodovich? Pah. I think you just have no stomach for this."

The carriage wobbled over the jagged edge of a rock.

"It's mental masturbation."

"The way *you* approach it maybe."

"Tell me how I should approach it then?"

"Oh, I don't know . . . How about like the mystery that our lives are? A tapestry of a lie, that by unravelling you can discern the truth about yourself?"

"What a good idea," said Alexei. As the ground grew more level, he turned the carriage around so he was pushing it. All Alexei could see was Vladimir's tiny gesticulating hands over the carriage's sun-shade. The diabolical baby was prattling on now about taking responsibility for life and facing up to one's past with courage—and something about a present threat that would undo them all unless Alexei got to it, but Alexei paid him scant attention.

He found himself looking beyond the carriage, at the terrible splendour of Soviet Afghanistan. The valley they moved through was wide, and like the surface of the moon. Bomb craters had drawn radial pictures on the earth, marking trajectories of ash and sand and bone. On the far side, high cliffs thrust up in great spires like dribbling mud-crusted candles that blotted the sun. In the distance, there was a woofing sound that Alexei knew to be the noise of mortar fire. More craters on the way. He found himself smiling slightly, an unfamiliar feeling moving like feather through his middle.

He knew this valley.

He had been here before.

There had been, he started to recall, some good times here.

"You're feeling nostalgic," said Vladimir. "That's what that is. It feels like you're going to be sick. Like you've eaten too much ice cream. Like you've forgotten to bathe."

"It's pretty here," said Alexei.

"It is *not* pretty here," said Vladimir. "This is a great shame—a great evil."

"You weren't even alive," said Alexei.

"It was a great evil."

Alexei shrugged. He wasn't going to get into a debate about Brezhnev-era Soviet foreign policy with a five-month-old in a baby carriage. "What are we doing here?" he asked.

"We are here for a look," said Vladimir.

"At?"

Vladimir raised a tiny hand and pointed. "You."

Alexei squinted and looked. "Ah. I see."

The valley was near the Khojak Pass, just across the border in southern Afghanistan—on a route to Kandahar that was only nominally roundabout. The convoy that crossed it was a mix of trucks and camels. It moved under the shadow of the cliffs like a nervous snake.

The convoy was carrying a large load of weapons: old Soviet weapons, brought in by way of Egypt. There were a lot of them—RPGs and rifles; rockets and grenades and landmines. Some of them—the ones that Amar Shadak had arranged, through a Chinese contact of his—were serviceable. The bulk of the shipment was no more than dangerous junk.

There were four trucks all told and maybe thirty men accompanying them. They wore cowls and carried rifles. Alexei leaned forward and squinted. "I remember those guys," he said.

"Really?"

"Yes." One of the guys riding a camel alongside the lead truck held his rifle up, made chuffing noises as he pretended to shoot it in the air. From inside the cabin, girlish laughter echoed through the valley. The guy rested his rifle on his lap. "There is Wali Beg. What a clown."

"This is like a holiday," said Vladimir. "You even brought a girl."

"It *is* like a holiday." That morning, Alexei remembered meeting the trucks at the border rendezvous. It was still dark and would be for hours. His pal Amar Shadak had pulled himself out of bed just an hour before and he was bleary-eyed. Shadak's pretty girlfriend Ming had handled the odd hour better. She'd put on a pair of loose coveralls that didn't quite disguise her sex but appeared to quiet any last-minute objections Shadak might have had. Alexei had brought some thin pastries for breakfast and given the best to Ming.

"You even brought a girl," repeated Vladimir. "Into Afghanistan."

"Yes," said Alexei. "I would be sitting beside her in the back of the truck right about now. Ming Lei. Ha. I have not thought about her in years."

"Good for you," said Vladimir. "What happens next?"

Alexei thought about that. "Next, I—" and he thought about spy school "—we—" and he thought about Czernochov and trigonometry "—soon—" and he looked down at Vladimir, who had twisted around in his seat to peer back up at Alexei.

"You can't remember, can you?"

"It was a good time," said Alexei—even as he began to suspect this was not the case.

Vladimir sighed. "Pay attention," he said. "You're not in yourself anymore; you're watching yourself. Maybe this way you will learn something."

The convoy proceeded through the valley. In the rear cab of the truck, Ming Lei was sitting quietly—peering out the small, dust-crusted windows with only a little worry in her eye. Shadak sat up front with the driver. Young Alexei sat back with Ming Lei. The flirtatious Wali Beg had ridden ahead for a moment. Shadak was talking to the driver. Alexei was staring at Ming's right hand, which had begun twitching in her lap.

She had not apparently noticed this—nor had anyone else. Alexei was smiling.

"Hey. What you got to be happy about?" Shadak turned around to look at Alexei. Ming's hand stilled, and Alexei looked at Shadak.

"Things are going well," said Alexei.

"Are they? That's mortar fire in the distance." Shadak appeared pissed off. "I thought you knew this pass."

"I have never been here before in my life," said Alexei.

"Funny."

Alexei looked back at Ming. He smiled. She smiled.

"Just relax," said Alexei.

Ming repeated it on his heels: "Just relax."

Shadak sighed and faced forward. He would be thinking about the rendezvous—fifteen kilometres or so north from here, a squad of Mujahedeen and their captain should be waiting. If everything went according to plan, they would escort the convoy to a hidden camp somewhere east of Kandahar. But Shadak would be uneasy with the whomping of artillery so close. He would be uneasy about the small-arms fire chatter that echoed through the hills. He would not admit it, but he would be very uneasy about Alexei Kilodovich, sitting in the back of the truck next to Ming.

Alexei appeared uneasy too. He looked at the back of Shadak's head as they jostled along, frowning slightly. He looked at Ming. Her hand came up to her face, and she drew a finger across her chin. He nodded to himself and looked at the back of Shadak's head. Shadak sat still.

A hillside not far ahead of them exploded in a shower of dirt and stone.

Shadak jolted upright in his seat. So did Alexei. Ming remained calm. Outside the cab, the camels' eyes showed white and their masters struggled to keep control of them.

The convoy stopped.

"What is this? What is this?"

Shadak appeared panicked. Alexei said nothing—just stared at him.

The driver did a better job of calming Shadak. He put his hand on the young man's shoulder and spoke calmly: "That would not be for us," he said. "It is stray fire." But he did not appear to believe his own words.

The convoy sat still in a settling cloud of dust. Finally, Ahmed Jamal—one of Shadak's original Mujahedeen contacts—rode up to the truck. He leaned into the cab.

"I will send scouts ahead," he said. "To see what is going on."

"Fine." Shadak was pissed. They sat still in the cab, as Ahmed rode over to a clutch of his fellows. Two of them took off on foot, up the slope of the valley—with binoculars and rifles.

The caravan sat still. Shadak fidgeted. Alexei tapped his thighs with his fingertips. The shadows lengthened. And finally, Ahmed came back.

"We don't go farther today," he said. "We don't go back, either. We're trapped. There are caves to the east of here. We go there for now. "

"What of the exchange?" said Shadak irritably. "We're expected."

Ahmed nodded. "Maybe by more than just my brothers," he said. "There is evidence of a large battalion ahead of us. A large engagement. We think that firefight might be one with our brothers. We go to the caves. When the battle finishes, they will meet us there maybe."

Alexei mumbled something inaudible as Shadak threw up his hands and swore.

"Why can't I hear what I'm saying?" Alexei asked Vladimir as they watched the drama unfold from the back of the truck. "For that matter—why can't I tell what I'm thinking? This is my memory, is it not?"

Vladimir was perched in Alexei's lap. He pulled his foot out of his mouth and looked up. "Good question, Kilodovich. It's true, isn't it? Every other memory you've seen, you've been able to watch from inside your own head. But here—we're stuck on the outside, yes? Like ghosts." He waggled his little fingers. "How *terrifying*."

It wasn't terrifying, precisely. But it was unsettling—like listening to a tape made of one's self made twenty years ago, too late on a night after consuming far too much liquor. From the inside, even the worst of memories are seen through the reassuring filter of self-delusion. From the outside, this day in Afghanistan, there was no such filter. Alexei took an instant dislike to himself.

"Hey," he said, leaning forward. "What am I doing now?"

Amar Shadak's head was down. He was staring at his hands. Alexei raised his own hand then, extended his forefinger—and held it, less than an inch from the nape of Shadak's neck. His lips moved as though he were mumbling something. The finger hovered there for a few seconds, until Shadak started, looked up, and turned around. Alexei snatched his hand back.

"What in fuck are you doing, Kilodovich?"

Alexei blinked. Ming blinked.

"What in fuck are you doing?"

"I saw a scorpion," whispered Ming.

Alexei cleared his throat. "She thought she did," he said. Ming's hands folded on her lap. "You're fine. Don't worry."

Beside Shadak, the driver waved out the window—returning a signal that neither of them had seen. He started the truck's motor, threw it into gear—and the little caravan began a long circle across the valley—to the east, and the caves.

"This is a fuckup," said Shadak angrily as the reddish dust rose into shafts of late-day sun in their wake, and the mortar-fire continued. "A complete fuckup."

Three kilometres out, Alexei finally convinced Vladimir to leave the cab of the truck and follow at a distance. The conversation had pretty well died, and Alexei had been reduced to regarding his twitchy, gawky former self try and make it through the afternoon. *What is it about youth*, he wondered, *that fits so poorly in its own skin*? Then he'd started to wonder whether he fit into his own skin any better now—and how it would be if he were to review his thirty-sixth year two decades hence. Would he seem the same slouching creep of a boy that he did to himself now? Every venality pasted to his forehead like a sign?

It hadn't taken long before Vladimir announced he'd had enough of this recursive morosity. They stepped out of the cab—Alexei lowered Vladimir back into the pram—and they walked among the camels and transports as the convoy made its way through a narrow pass that twisted like a serpent, as it climbed higher into the eastern foothills.

"I don't remember this part," said Alexei.

"Really?" said Vladimir. "Here you are. Maybe you fell asleep and woke up in the nice cozy cave."

Alexei shook his head. "I don't remember waking up in a nice cozy cave," he said. "You want to know what I remember?"

"Please," said Vladimir.

"I remember this assignment. They sent me in to infiltrate the C.I.A. arms pipeline into Afghanistan. I established myself as a deserter from the Red Army in Pakistan, arranged it to be contacted by the CIA. Saunders was easy to trick. He set me up with that character Shadak. What a character he was!"

Alexei smiled to himself, as he thought about the weeks spent nightclubbing with Shadak, meeting up with his girlfriend Ming—insinuating himself in with them both—as the CIA stalled, running checks against his background and so forth. It was a good time: it was one of his first missions out of school. And in spite of the deception, he liked Shadak. Vladimir glared up at him. Alexei cleared his throat and went on.

"So we made the contact with the arms supplier, established the border crossing, arranged the drop-off. All the time, I sent back reports to the headquarters in Kabul. Things went very smoothly. Then—"

"Yes?"

"Then . . ." Alexei frowned. "Well, I couldn't very well contact anyone once we were underway. But that was fine. The run into Afghanistan didn't take very long. Although—"

"Yes, Kilodovich?"

"Although," said Alexei finally, "it took longer than expected. I remember that. There were some complaints from Kabul. Oh, that was a bad month afterwards. I spent—how long in debriefing? A long time." He shook his head. "So you see, there was none of this ambush and trek to the caves. I think that perhaps we are watching another fiction."

"I see." Vladimir clapped his hands over his head. "Another fiction. Let me ask you this, Kilodovich. How late were you in finally delivering the arms and reporting in?"

"It hardly matters—"

"How late?" Vladimir glared.

"I don't see—" Alexei bent forward suddenly, a terrible pain lancing through his skull. "Ah! What the fuck was that for?"

"How late?" said Vladimir with real menace. "Tell, or I send another one your way."

Alexei straightened and rubbed his temples, worked his jaw.

"Three weeks." He frowned. "Three weeks?"

"No wonder they locked you up for a while when you finally reported in," said Vladimir. "They must have thought you'd deserted."

"What did I do," said Alexei, standing still for a moment as a pair of camels insubstantial as a desert mirage passed around and through him, "for three weeks?"

The cave's mouth was shaped like a scream. It was a wide scream—wide enough to admit the trucks and the camels into the shadows beneath its yellowish upper lip, the blunted teeth of rocks that littered its lower jaw. Beyond, the cave's floor was flat enough that they could all stop there, safe in shadow but still near enough the entrance to make a hasty escape if need be.

Higher on the cliff-face there were various perches, good for sentries. Wali Beg handed his camel over to one of his brothers and, AK-47 in hand, clambered up to the lowest of these—an outcropping of red stone with a small, skeletal bush growing from the cracks. He vanished for a moment behind the rock, only emerging briefly to wave curtly to those below that he was safe. Then he was gone again.

Inside, the four trucks lined up behind one another. The men threw what camouflage they could over the truck nearest the cave mouth, and then began to unload the cargo. Shadak ordered the munitions taken deeper into the cave—the larger ones to a level plateau some forty metres inside; some of the smaller cases—which were in some circumstances more valuable—into what turned out to be a network of side tunnels, some of which were no wider than a thin man's shoulders.

"We will reload the trucks," he said, "when it is safe."

Ahmed nodded. "It may be," he said, "that we won't reload the trucks at all. Tonight, I will send two men to the contact point. See what has become of our friends. If things have not gone well—this cargo may have to stay here for some time, until we can arrange another party."

Shadak looked at him. "I don't want to leave this untended," he said.

"No need to," said Ahmed. "This place is not unknown to us. We call it the Cistern. We have used it in the past as a—staging ground. We shall use it again perhaps. So there are provisions."

Ahmed Jamal led Amar and Alexei and Ming Lei down one of the side tunnels they'd ignored—a narrow fold in the rock that seemed almost not to be there, unless one's lamp were held just so, and one knew where to look. They had to bend forward and backward, and sharp stone scraped painfully across their backs and shoulders. But quickly, they emerged into what seemed like daylight.

Shadak laughed out loud at the sight of it. They weren't outdoors precisely—but at the bottom of a twisting channel through the rock that dribbled sun through a high opening. The cave at the bottom was large—shaped like a letter "E" that had been tilted on its back to make three smaller cubbyholes.

In here were tidy stacks of crates—each one too large to move through the passage by which they entered.

"How—" began Shadak, looking at the crates.

Ahmed pointed to the sky. "We lowered them," he said. "On a great winch that we then tossed down the hole and buried in the sand—" he pointed at a small mound toward the top left corner of the E "—there. They are not intended to be carried out again. They are to be consumed in this place. By men who need to hide."

Ming Lei bent down and ran the sand on the cave's floor through her fingers. "Like beach," she said. "But no water."

"There is enough water," said Wali Beg. "You will be able to live here comfortably for weeks."

"Only us?" said Shadak. "You are not staying here then?"

Ahmed shrugged. "I will leave you some men. I must go and see to our brothers."

He pulled loose his cowl then, shaking loose long black curls down to his shoulders, and strode across the cave-floor to the first of the three cubby-holes. "You will find blankets here, and rations of food in tins, as well as lamps and a stove for heat in the night. Here—" he stepped to the next hole— "is ammunition and some small arms. Better to use these than the merchandise." He stepped out and with a flourish to the next one—with the same little crates. "Here is your water," he said. "It seems plenty, but that's all there is. Don't use too much."

And then, with the same flamboyant stride, Ahmed crossed the cave to the space in the rock, and vanished into it.

"Well," said Alexei. "It is us three for now. Others, no doubt, will join us soon. Let's see what the Mujahedeen have left for us."

"I would like some water please," said Ming. "Not too much . . ." she added with a little grin.

"We brought a woman," said Alexei. "Into Afghanistan. That's crazy. What a risk!"

"You are just figuring that out," said Vladimir. His eyelids fluttered.

"No, I'm not. But I'm just looking at it. Why didn't we figure something else out? Why didn't someone else object? Wali Beg, for instance?"

Vladimir closed his eyes and curled his chin into his shoulder.

"Unless," said Alexei, "none of them had the capacity to object. It is puzzling—wake up!"

Vladimir shook his head and blinked sleepily. "I am listening."

Alexei was quiet for a moment. He shook his finger in the air, opened and shut his mouth. Looked at the sand at his feet as he thought it through.

"I think I know why I am not in my body—why I cannot know my own thoughts."

"Tell."

Alexei took a breath. He felt the excitement of revelation coursing through his blood. "In our own memories, we change history. We delude ourselves half the time anyway. And then as the days and weeks and years pass, we change them. We forget the things we don't want to have as a part of ourselves, and we edit and amplify those things that bolster us. So any memory, unchecked, is a lie." He looked at Vladimir expectantly. Vladimir said nothing.

Alexei continued. "I have failed to find truth in memory. So you have taken, somehow, a film of the past—in the manner of tape-recording a drunken man at a party—to show me the true scope of my history. It is true, isn't it?" Alexei pointed at his younger self—awkwardly stepping over the sand to lift a crate from the bottom tine of the *E*. He struggled and swore as the older Alexei stood behind him. "Look at him! Thin and weak and lecherous. Stupid enough to go along with a scheme to bring a pretty girl on a KGB operation. This is not how I care to remember myself. An indication that it is true—yes?"

Vladimir grabbed his foot and sucked on the toes. Alexei suspected it was unsanitary, but he didn't stop him.

"Why don't you answer me?" he said. "I am coming closer to understanding my history! This is what you wished, is it not?"

Around them, the phantoms of Alexei's past were busying themselves setting up a camp. Shadak stepped back out with Ahmed, to supervise the camouflaging of the trucks, and study the routes to the sentry points that the guards would use to watch the pass over the coming days. Young Alexei dragged the crate a few steps further, but dropped it in the sand and swore. He turned around and sat on it. And as he did, his face slackened and his eyes went blank.

Ming, meanwhile, stopped what she was doing and walked gracefully into the shaft of light that was coming down through the chimney. She stood straight for a moment, then lifted a hand to the coveralls she wore, and undid the top button. Her eyes were on thin young Alexei but they were focused elsewhere.

Alexei stopped talking. He walked over to himself, and studied his face. It was as a statue. He turned back to Ming. She had removed the top of her coverall and was pulling off the T-shirt underneath. Her small, dark-nippled breasts gleamed in relief from the sun. Her eyes held the same stillness as those of Alexei's younger self.

"What is this?" he asked.

Vladimir said nothing.

"Is she—"

Ming dropped the top and bent to pull off her boots. She slipped off the rest of the coveralls and stood naked before Alexei.

"Did we—" Alexei blinked. "Did we . . . make love?" He would, he hoped, have remembered that.

"I don't think so," said Vladimir. "If I remember the file—about now—look to there."

Alexei turned. There were noises in the tunnel.

Wali Beg stepped into the chamber. He too had removed his cowl, to reveal a half-bald head and eyes that on another occasion would have been laughing. Now they were dead as Ming's.

Ming turned to him. Young Alexei sat perfectly still, his eyelids fluttering. Wali Beg stepped into the light. He extended a hand to touch Ming's shoulder. Ming did not flinch away. Wali Beg moved his fingers down her collarbone and took hold of a breast in the calloused palm of his hand. Ming pressed herself into it. Young Alexei's eyes opened to behold the scene.

Alexei sat stunned. He looked to himself—the couple—awkwardly up into the shaft of light through the cave—and finally, back at Vladimir.

"I'm dream-walking them. Aren't I?" Alexei paced off to the far end of the cave and came back again, hands excitedly grasping one another behind his back. "That is it! Of course! All the times that Kolyokov and the rest told me that I had no talents—that is the lie of my life!" Alexei thought back to the tiny memories he had of his mother and what she used to say: *You are a little Koldun—a little lodge wizard*. He looked back at the strange couple, clasped in a passionless embrace. "I am dream-walking them! I have been a dream-walker all along! A wicked dream-walker like Fyodor Kolyokov!"

"What a clever man you are," said Vladimir drolly. "Good thinking. But no. Completely wrong."

Alexei's face fell. "No?"

Vladimir shook his head. "You talk too much, Kilodovich. Too much talking is dangerous. You should listen more."

Alexei opened his mouth. Vladimir made a hushing motion with his little hands. Alexei closed his mouth again and frowned—and listened.

Alexei blinked in astonishment. There were voices. Other voices. Russian voices—which he vaguely recognized.

Stop playing. This is serious business.

What is serious business? This? It is done?

Not done.

Not done?

All.

All but—

All but one.

Soon.

Why?

Remember Rodionov.

GeneralRodionovsaidhewouldreturninforceandfinishthisobsceneexperimentwithgunsandtechnology"YouarefinishedKolyokovwehaveawartofight'""thenletmefightthewarwithyou'""onelastchanceonelastchance"

Your problem.

Our problem.

Problem?

Letrodionovdohisworstweshallbebeyondhisreachinthestationinthestationwher-etheseasingsandthedevilcannotreachus

Problem if he discovers our boy here.

Point.

Point.

Agreed.

Pay attention.

Over

By

Shipment—

Who?

Thedeafonetheonethatwillnotmaketheonewiththecontactsinpakistantheonewho-broughtthegirlwelovethegirlthegirltheonewhobroughthimtheonewiththesolidskull-solidskullsolidskull

Amar Shadak.

"What is that?" whispered Alexei. "It is incomprehensible."

Vladimir's smile was all gums. "Discourse," he said. "That which you are hearing is what we call Discourse. When we speak to one another without words. It is like the conversation we are having now. But broader."

"Broader?" Alexei frowned. "It sounds insane. Who is it that is speaking?"

"Many," said Vladimir. "You really have no inkling about Discourse, do you?"

"I've heard the word. Many who? Is Fyodor Kolyokov among them?"

"Oh yes." As they spoke, Ming and Wali Beg separated and turned on a foot to face away

from one another—like dancers in a music box. Young Alexei stood with his hands dangling at his side, his head back and jaw slack.

"Am I—was I among them?"

Vladimir rubbed his face and his smile vanished.

"You are getting close," he said, "to the nub of things."

"You say that like it's a bad thing," said Alexei.

"Listen," whispered Vladimir.

The caves fell silent: only the faint whistling of wind through unseen fissures; the distant thunder, more sporadic now, of artillery fire. Ming and Wali Beg had sat down, backs to one another and cross-legged in the sand. Young Alexei's eyes were open, and seemed alert, but he sat still, leaning laconically against a crate in the top tine of the *E*. The sky was a disc of gold and azure at the top of the chimney. It mingled with the dark blue of the top of the carriage to make purple. Nothing moved—it was as if nothing lived. Idly, Alexei rocked the carriage.

"What is to happen next?" asked Alexei.

The carriage creaked.

"Vladimir?"

Alexei stepped around the carriage. His breath caught in his throat.

"Vladimir!" The seat was empty. Vladimir was gone.

Alexei bunched his fists. And looked around the cave. He swore. The little bastard had abandoned him! Left him at the cusp of understanding. In a great, silent cave, where even the whistling of the wind was muted.

"Talk to me!" He hollered it to the sky. To the others. The wind whistled.

And after a moment, he could hear:

RodionovRodionov

Discourse.

The Discourse was still going strong—but the more Alexei listened, the more he could hear of it. And hearing more of it turned the entire thing into a cacophony; it was like trying to tell the data from a telephone modem by listening to the connection screech:

Iyouitwillnotbeinthehellofyourmakingwewilltransformyouwalkwalkrunrunmoverunredorangeyellowgreenblueindigovioletranoverrodionovcaseykandaharasey . . .

Was this Vladimir's idea, Alexei wondered? To leave him alone with this indecipherable rant, to let him figure out his history with this? He couldn't believe that. He got up off the crate, and strode across the sand. He turned sideways and folded himself through the crack in the cave wall. And then, as he bent back and forward around the difficult rocks in the tunnel, Alexei lost track of the Discourse. And the silence of the caves was broken by another sound—of angry whispering—just two voices; and just ahead.

Alexei continued forward—creeping, trying to be stealthy, in spite of the fact that he could move unseen and unheard. Finally, he made it to the end of the tunnel—and stepped out into the small antechamber. There was Shadak—and another man: one of the Mujahedeen. A thin-bodied, thin-bearded young man who Alexei vaguely remembered from the trip out.

"This is complete shit," Shadak was saying. "You are not even attempting to hide the shipment. Why are there no guards on the hillside? This is a fucking set-up, isn't it?"

The man was didn't answer. He stared at Shadak and through him. Shadak ran a hand through his hair. He glared at the man.

"You fucker," he said. "If this were a fucking drug run, I'd have shot you by now.

This is fucking intolerable."

The man ran his own hand through his hair.

"Why don't you fucking answer me?" he demanded. "Why don't you fucking—"

Shadak stopped. He looked up. Directly at Alexei.

"You!" he said, eyes wide. Alexei's own eyes went wide too. Then he felt a chill at his back—moving forward through him, like a storm through his flesh.

"What do you know of this?" said Shadak darkly.

"I—I don't," said Alexei.

"More than you," came a voice from Alexei's throat. "But not for long." At the same time, he heard:

Redorangeyellowgreenbluepreparetheagentonetwothreereadysetgowemust-finishthisoneorallmaybelostthenRodionovRodionovRodionovonovovovovovfocus-focusonlyonechancetodothisrigh—

And then, Alexei found himself looking at the back of his own head. His own younger head. As the head receded, Alexei pieced together what had happened: his younger self had just passed through him—an intersection of his ghosts.

Of many ghosts. Locked in Discourse.

Alexei stepped back and watched his younger self step up to Shadak.

"What the fuck," said Shadak darkly, "is going on?" He thrust his thumb back over his shoulder. "Nobody out there is doing a fucking thing! They're standing still like fucking zombies and there's work to be done! Those fucking Russian guns aren't going away—they're—they're—they—"

"On your knees," said young Alexei.

"What?" Shadak blinked, and looked down at Alexei's right hand. It was holding an old Tokarev automatic pistol. Pointed at Shadak.

"On your knees," he repeated.

Shadak's face reddened. "What the fuck is this?"

OhhesgoodgoodskullthickasleadnothingthroughtheregoodgoodbadRodionovhere-soonohey

heresoon

Alexei bent—stepped forward—

And stepped into himself.

He sat there a moment—crouched with his head sticking out of his younger chest, his ass poked out of the back of his younger knees. Shadak was staring up at him in a mix of outrage and terror. The gun was indisputable betrayal—Alexei didn't need to read Shadak's mind to know his mind. Shadak was saying something else—but intersecting as he was with himself, Alexei couldn't make it out.

All he could hear, this close, was the chaotic scramble of Discourse.

Fyodorconcentrateonmetaphoryoudmitritakeinthroughidtherestofyouhelpkilodovich-vesseltoestablishthespacialstimulusstimulusstimRodionovRodionov

And then

—a fugue—

"Rodionov could kill us in a second. This is folly."

Alexei blinked. The caves of Afghanistan were gone, replaced by a great darkness—a deep void where the voices of the Discourse slowed. Alexei floated in this void, rolling head over heels like a cosmonaut. In the darkness, he could make out shapes—huge shapes of men and women, ass-end toward him. They were big as skyscrapers, as submarines. They spoke with voices as deep as a thunderclap and as affecting as an earthquake.

"Rodionov," said another of the giants, floating beyond his reach, "will not kill us. He does not even know where we are."

"Still—he has it in him. He's got the will."

"We should turn him."

"Set your Alexei on him, Fyodor—and see."

"Yes. Make him sleeper."

Alexei swam toward the giants. He felt as though he were rising, and for a time imagined this place not a void at all, but water: a huge lake on which these bickering creatures floated. But that metaphor strained quickly; for as he looked up at them, he saw that they couldn't be apprehended as floating in a particular order. They overlapped one another as they floated.

"No need to worry about Rodionov," repeated the first one. "We make these sleepers here—he will never know. And we—we will control the arms pipeline through Afghanistan. Now, and forever."

The giants continued to bicker, but Alexei couldn't hear it. With a popping sensation, he broke through the surface of the medium of this new place—

—and looked on lights. Like a night sky in wilderness, there were so many.

Not stars, though. They were paired—like eyes, staring down on him—across at him—from a wall of black, roiling cloud. Some were bright, some were dim, and occasionally they winked on and off—as though they were blinking.

Behind him—below him—at the surface of the liquid medium from which he'd emerged—giants conferred.

"Comrade Vostovitch. Stop playing sex games with the girl. Assemble the Mujahedeen. Make the ready the Cistern."

"They are on their way."

"And Tokovsky. Bring one more along to watch Shadak. Kilodovich has other work to do."

"This one?"

"No. Too small. The one by the truck."

"Where?"

As Alexei watched, a great arm reached out—up—possibly down—from the surface of the liquid, and touched upon the wall—ceiling—floor?—where two points flashed on and off. "There," rumbled the giant.

Curious, Alexei approached those two, climbing/crossing/falling the expanse in a heartbeat.

It was as though he put his eyes to the lenses of binoculars. But rather than seeing a distant peak through them, he now looked upon the side of a truck. The picture turned sickeningly and was replaced by the darkness of the cave mouth. Men were moving away from him—heading deeper into the cave with boxes and weapons. Then the view shifted again, and approached the fold in the cave wall that Alexei knew led to the chimney room. If he concentrated, he could hear conversation coming through the fold. Then the view was through it, and all was dark for a time.

Alexei pulled back from the lights, and pushed away from the wall, drifting back toward the giants. He felt himself smile as the understanding dawned on him.

This, he realized, was a catalogue of City 512's sleepers. Two points of light for all of them. He tried to count, but stopped: it seemed there were as many on this wall as there were stars in the sky. He flitted over to another set of eyes—looking down at a sheet of typewritten French—and another, that were sitting on a train, inches from the glass, watching the industrialized outskirts of some city or another drift by in the rising, or possibly setting, sun—and others, in meetings and driving automobiles and masturbating at pornography and actually making love . . .

Alexei laughed, and did a little cosmonaut tumble. He turned around in so doing, to face the giants. His eyes had grown accustomed to the peculiar non-light in here. The giants were floating on the odd surface, all in the same place—overlapping—like a great Shiva, a multi-armed, multipeded god-goddess. Arms would flash out, touching these lights or those lights, or one of them, to reach below the water to pluck at something, or rest folded on the shared stomach.

Where in all that, wondered Alexei, in all that great collective of being, was Fyodor Kolyokov?

Where, he wondered, was Alexei?

"Where is Kilodovich?" said one of the giants as the hand came back above the water.

"There!" And before Alexei could move, one of the great arms shot forward and wrapped around his waist. "Gotten loose! Nearly escaped!"

"I told you this was dangerous, Fyodor."

"Many tools are dangerous in untrained hands."

Alexei twisted in the grip of the giant. As he did, he saw the star field had increased: as though the contact with the giant had expanded his vision.

For now he saw not just the brightest points, but dimmer ones too. The hand drew him along the wall, and he caught more glimpses through these: a forest, with high coniferous trees, and a large bearded man muttering something about a "mantra" to a group of attentive children while armed guards hovered conspicuously near the tree line; a woman, legs crossed, bouncing up and down on a mat (the unseen sleeper was bouncing too, making the whole thing as nauseating as a roller coaster); another bouncing view, this time looking at a man—heavyset, with a drooping handlebar moustache and receding hairline, that Alexei thought he recognized before he sped past. Then views of Moscow and the sky and a city that looked like London and other places that were but blurs of colour. What were these, wondered Alexei? Were they sleepers less accessible to these huge dreamers? Sleepers belonging to Americans, perhaps? Who was the bouncing man that he thought he'd recognized?

And what, he wondered, was that dimmest light?

It flickered in the distance—barely visible at all, like the last dying ember of a candlewick.

"There," said a dreamer.

Alexei found himself propelled toward the two eyes. They held a view that blurred and faded in the dark cave . Of a gun barrel. Of a figure that through this filter Alexei took a moment to recognize.

It was himself—young Alexei Kilodovich—woven of strands of understanding and perception that were alien to him. The eyes, Alexei realized now, belonged to Amar Shadak.

"Inside," said another dreamer.

"Alexei," whispered a dreamer's voice that was this time unmistakable: Kolyokov. "Do that which we have made you to do. Disassemble Amar Shadak. Make him ready for us."

And then, the light faded altogether, and the grip around his middle loosened, and Alexei found himself on the ground—held only in the grip of gravity, outside a low house before mountaintops. The sky over its red clay shingles was dark, the trees growing around its cut stone foundations were bare. The house itself was made like a Roman villa. There was a stone archway at one end that led into a weed-choked plaza. Alexei stood up and headed for the villa, a purpose in his stride. He didn't know what that purpose specifically would be: but if he could trust Fyodor Kolyokov's words this one time, it would be the thing that they had made him for.

It was a strange and tricky villa. When Alexei stepped into the courtyard, the stones were white with snow and the pond in its centre was covered in a thin veneer of ice. The sky overhead had turned a terrible white and where the light from it struck it made a flickering, washed-out glare. Alexei retreated for the shade of the overhanging roof. In spite of the ice and the snow, Alexei found himself sweating. He heard the sound of sloshing water through another archway, and he followed it through the arch, into a narrow corridor that seemed to run the circumference of the courtyard, and then to what must have been a kitchen. Embers burned at the bottom of a great hearth at one end; the middle was dominated by a long wooden table covered in a brown canvas cloth. The cloth was stained a deep purple here and there—maybe wine, from the tipped-over jug that rocked through a twenty-degree arc in a divot at the far end of the table. Or maybe blood; at the far end, the skinned carcass of an animal—a sheep, or perhaps a goat—hung from an iron hook over an open wooden barrel. The sloshing came from inside the barrel.

Alexei crept over and looked inside. The barrel was dry. The sloshing sound continued.

Alexei rubbed his chin, and looked up at the animal. He took a finger and touched the bare muscle at its shoulder. It was cool, and although it glistened in the dim light, it was dry. It felt a bit like plastic. Maybe, thought Alexei, that was how flayed muscle feels after it's been draining for a day. *Maybe*.

Alexei went over to the embers in the fire. He licked a finger and touched it to one. There was a convincing hissing sound, as the spittle boiled against his skin. There was the barest hint of pain. He nodded, scrunched his mouth. *Not bad*.

Alexei pushed himself up off his haunches, and next regarded the rocking jug. He touched it lightly. It stopped rocking, and settled into the divot in the old table. He took his hand away—and the jug rolled to its left. By the time he stepped away, shoved his hands into his pockets, the jug was rocking back and forth again like nothing had happened.

He was tempted to go back outside—test the ice on the pond—test the snow on the flagstones—maybe go outside altogether, run to the nearest of the mountain-peaks, reach into the rock and see if it weren't just as soft as wet clay, as insubstantial as gauze, and see if he could just step out of this place.

Alexei resisted the temptation. If he'd learned nothing over his time stewing in his own history, he'd learned to recognize this place for what it was:

A metaphor.

And not a particularly good one.

Alexei stepped back to the hallway. He ran his finger along the stone of the wall, felt for the coolness, the fractal roughness of chipped, ancient stone. It was there, he thought. Or it was coming.

Alexei leaned against that stone, so he had a view of the courtyard and the entryway, and he waited there—for whatever it was coming to complete its arrival.

He didn't wait long.

Amar Shadak stumbled through the archway, flinching at the lash of a great, devilish whip. He was smaller than he had been for a long time—as small and soft and weak as he had been when he was just fourteen; when his mother still lived; when his father was still in Romania, building the beginnings of his empire. He stumbled through and fell to his knees, felt the lash, and climbed again to his feet. The whip withdrew through the arch like the tail of an immense rat. Shadak stumbled to the edge of the pond, reached into its icy waters and splashed some on the reddening fabric of his shirt.

"Fuck you!" he screamed. His voice was high, but it was tinged with violence.

"Manners, boy."

"What? Who the fuck—"

A shadow grew over the stonework of the little plaza.

"You know who the fuck."

Shadak forced himself to look into the archway—to the figure that drifted from beneath it. It was all greys and blacks—a pale creature wearing a long dark coat, black hair that seemed to drift around its skull as though suspended in water. The eyes reflected glints of fire. It smelled of river mud. It carried its whip like a great phallus or maybe a severed umbilical cord, dangling out its middle while both arms twitched and gestured. Clearly, it scared the crap out of Amar Shadak. But he didn't look away.

"What is this place? Where the fuck are we? Where is fucking Kilodovich?"

The thing was twice as tall as Amar Shadak. In the pale light of the courtyard it stood like a hangman's tree, like the Crucifix. It wore a beard on its chin, thin and scraggly and long. When it spoke, it spoke with wind that stank.

"You are home. In your safe place. A place where I shall not trouble you, so long as you remain. It is a place that reminds you what you are."

"And what is that?"

"A rich man. Who collects. Weapons and vehicles and money. Collects it for us."

The Shadak boy stood up. He clenched his fists defiantly. "Fuck off," he said.

"Manners." *The thing lifted a narrow arm, and bent a finger chidingly as the whip twitched. The kid Shadak flinched at the sight of it. He still didn't look away, though. His eyes narrowed thoughtfully.*

"My safe place?" he said. "What is safe about here?"

Leaning against a pillar, Alexei found himself shaking. A *safe place*. That's what this metaphor was—just like the spy school that Alexei had believed was a part of his childhood. This place was the equivalent for Amar Shadak: a Roman-esque villa, with food and wine and a view of mountains. In the courtyard, Shadak was working it out too—with considerably less success. He wouldn't, of course, stand a chance. Alexei had been mired within his own safe place, his own metaphor, for what seemed like months before he'd broken loose—and that had been on its revisitation, with more than a few hints from Vladimir that escape was necessary. For Amar Shadak, this place was real.

Alexei pushed himself away from the pillar and strode out from beneath the overhanging roof. Neither Shadak nor the tall thing noted his presence as they continued to spar with one another, and there was no reason that they should. For although this thing had no doubt happened in Afghanistan in the 1980s, it had not happened with a middle-aged Alexei Kilodovich bursting in and interrupting the session. Alexei was tempted to do so—but he knew it would be about as effective as shouting a warning at a movie hero from the balcony.

But still—right now, he intuited that watching was not enough. If Vladimir were here, he'd ask him questions—make him explain the goings-on in this strange villa. But Vladimir was gone now. The guided tour was over.

He sat down next to the trembling little metaphorical body that Amar Shadak inhabited. Shadak was listening now, his eyes locked on those of the spectral thing, who was engaged in some kind of recitation. Telephone numbers; addresses; symbols and images; a sequence of colours, each of which might be associated with a different animal, which in turn might be associated with a string of numbers or an address in a strange city, or the face of a stranger. They all combined into a chaotic modem-squawk of imagery and words and numbers. Alexei watched little Amar Shadak's lips move as he silently repeated back certain things, and drew up new associations. Then he looked around the courtyard. It seemed to be saturating the tiles deepening their reds, the ice on the water gaining depths and imperfections, the sky overhead shifting from a pale white to a deep alpine blue. Alexei nodded to himself. The more that Shadak heard, the firmer his metaphor became.

Alexei looked at the thing's eyes. He knew, of course, who those eyes truly belonged to. Hadn't those been Kolyokov's instructions to him? Disassemble Amar Shadak. Make him ready for us.

Somewhere inside that preposterous masquerade, thought Alexei, lurked young Kilodovich, hell-bent on a mission from Fyodor Kolyokov to break the spirit of Amar Shadak. For himself, Alexei began to feel dizzy. He was inhabiting a metaphor within a metaphor, watching a metaphorical version of himself operating with an assassin's assurance within the second of those metaphors.

Alexei leaned close to Shadak. "I am sorry," he said.

At that, Shadak's eyes flashed—and he looked up at the apparition with new understanding.

"Kilodovich," said Shadak.

The thing reeled back at that, and looked about in confusion. Shadak grinned at that.

"Alexei Kilodovich," he said, his adult sneer creeping back into his voice. "You miserable fucker. You fucking steal my woman and usurp my contract. You are KGB aren't you? Setting us all up for a big bust."

The apparition grew, and the whip pulled back from its middle, twitching in the air over Shadak like a huge tentacle.

"Oh fuck off. You've hypnotized me. This is complete bullshit."

"Manka. Vasilissa. Baba Yaga."

"What the fuck is that supposed to mean?"

The whip cracked in the air like a pistol shot, and Shadak shrieked as it lashed down on him.

"You fucker!" he howled. "You fucker!"

Shadak bent over himself and shut his eyes. He began to weep.

The metaphor, meanwhile, continued to flower. Cracks appeared in stone that had been smooth; Latin scripts appeared on stones; in the pond, the ice began to melt and crack. The wind from the mountains smelled of flowers. The apparition looked into the blue perfect sky—as if for advice—and at that moment, little Amar Shadak rolled across the ground and fled behind the giant. It flipped its whip at Shadak, but the kid was too quick. He vanished through the archway. The apparition began to follow it, but stopped again—listening to the cascade of words and ideas and pictures that inhabited the substance of this place:

RodionovRodionovtoolateabandonthisoneabandonabandontoolatetoolate . . .

Alexei left the rumbling Discourse behind to follow little Shadak. He felt tears in his eyes, in a sudden burst of empathy for Amar Shadak. Hadn't he, just days ago, undergone the same revelation? Hadn't he too fled his metaphor—torn a rip in the side of it and crawled out, back into himself? He had an unreasoning desire, then, to see Amar do the same thing: tear his way from the metaphor, return to his body, and begin the process of reassembling himself.

Alexei stumbled out the gate. The stones outside the villa were sharp on his feet, and the wind whipped off a glacier that hadn't been there before. He turned back to the villa. The building was twisting and reorienting too. A slim tower that Alexei was certain had not been there before had thrust itself up from the rear of the building. A murder of crows competed for perch on its steep, tiny roof, cursing each other as they flapped and scrambled. Clouds now gathered to the east. The air felt electric with the coming storm. The world of this villa—this safe place—was becoming real.

So quickly. When Alexei was in City 512, it had taken months to make him believe his place. It had taken all of Fyodor Kolyokov's strength and will; all of Alexei's time; for months, to create a world that was only a skeleton compared to this one. Alexei waded into the grasses and peered down the hill. Where, in this blossoming metaphor, had Shadak lost himself? Unthinking, he put his hands to his mouth and called out: Amar! Show yourself! He smirked as he did so. He was not, of course, really here. He was observing—a ghost. He could no more make himself felt here than he could—

A whistling came across the grasses then, and a sharp pain in the side of Alexei's head—and thought incomplete, Alexei fell.

The dark was silent and empty this time—a void like death. Alexei spun in it—or maybe he didn't move at all and simply imagined himself spinning. Or maybe he was dead and this was how death was.

The silence fell away.

"Kilodovich."

Vladimir?

"Apologies, Kilodovich. Things are taking place in the world of Physick that required my attention. Urgently."

So urgently you disappear without a word?

"Stop whining. I see that you have learned some things."

Oh fuck off. What's going on in the world of Physick that's so urgent?

Vladimir sighed. "I must apologize, Kilodovich. I have used you once more."

What do you mean, used me?

"It was important," said Vladimir, "that my siblings and I escape from the school house in New Pokrovskoye. There has been a fight. You are injured. You need to come back or you will die."

So you have been using me. Alexei spat into the void. *Just as Kolyokov used me here—as a vessel for his own designs.*

"Hmm. Good. So you are working through your history."

Do not change the subject. You're using me what—to engineer an escape?

"And I am paying you for the privilege. Unlike what Fyodor Kolyokov did."

Paying.

"Alexei. Fyodor Kolyokov used you for more than a vessel to engineer an escape."

Did he now?

"He used you like a sleeper agent. But instead of sending you into a foreign city or an embassy, he sent you straight into his enemy's mind."

This I have guessed. He used me there, to break down his enemy—to turn him into a sleeper agent too. But to do so quickly—in the field—without having him forced to visit City 512. He used me—Alexei felt a rush of understanding sluice through him, like half-frozen runoff—he used me to make all of them into sleepers, didn't he?

"There. Good. Now you can come back. We have work to do in New Pokrovskoye. You do not have much time."

Alexei thought about that. He thought about returning to his body, doing more work that Vladimir bade him to do for him. Metaphorical bile rose in his metaphorical throat.

Fuck off, he said.

"What?"

Babies aren't used to being told to fuck off, said Alexei. But I'm saying it. I'm done with you, Vladimir.

Suddenly, the weightless void felt more like the sky—and Alexei felt as though he were falling, his stomach catching in his throat. He could see shapes in the darkness, whirling past him. He grasped at the darkness, reaching for something—Vladimir, the pram—

"Kilodovich."

Now Alexei was lying on flagstones in the courtyard of Amar Shadak's metaphorical villa. His head hurt. The kid—Amar Shadak—was crouched over him. He looked, Alexei thought, kind of like Ivan, who'd struck him in the head with a rock back in his imaginary spy school, when he'd started asking uncomfortable questions about reality. Little Shadak had probably used the same trick on him now—a rock to the head—to knock him unconscious and bring him here to this much better-made metaphor of a plaza.

"You are a lying fuck," he spat. "You've been working for the fucking KGB all along, haven't you? This whole plan is fucking compromised."

Alexei tried to sit up. As he did, ropes bit into his arms and ankles. Shadak had tied him up with metaphorical rope. Shadak slapped him backhanded across the face.

"This is some kind of brainwashing shit, isn't it? That's why everybody was acting so fucking strange in the caves, wasn't it? You slipped some drugs into the food or the air or something—and fucked us all up."

"N-no drugs," Alexei heard himself saying. "You are the one who knows about drugs."

Shadak stood up and kicked Alexei in the stomach. The pain was excruciating. Alexei shut his eyes.

"How far does this—this thing of yours go? The Mujahedeen? Jim Saunders?" Shadak sat down against the wall of the pond. His eyes were narrow with rage. "Ming Lei?"

Alexei tried to distance himself from the conversation, so he could put things together. But it was difficult—while he still didn't seem to have direct control over his actions, he was so wrapped in this metaphor of flesh that the pain and the twist and the smell of things overwhelmed him. It was a bit like being drunk—his mind was fine, but his body acted as if with a will of its own.

"Untie me," he heard himself say. "I can explain."

Shadak looked at him. "You can fucking well explain tied like a fucking ape on the ground," he said.

Alexei felt himself struggling. The ropes tore at the flesh of his wrists and ankles. Which was puzzling; hadn't he, just a moment ago, been in complete control of this metaphor? Alexei heard himself sob, his breath rasping inside his skull. He listened then—for something else, a sound that had been at the core of this matter since the beginning:

The rumbling sound of Discourse.

And he realized with a chill that it was gone.

Alexei was alone in this metaphor. Fyodor Kolyokov and the others had grown silent.

Or, he thought, been made silent. What had been the name he'd heard most in Discourse? Rodionov?

Alexei thought back—to the general in City 512, who'd played at executing the poet, to discredit Kolyokov.

Rodionov was coming. They had seemed worried about that. Alexei thought he could understand why they might be worried about that.

Perhaps, thought Alexei, General Rodionov had finally arrived.

"This isn't supposed to be happening like this," said Alexei miserably. "This has gone bad."

"Ha. Bad for you maybe."

"No. Bad for you too."

"What do you mean?"

"It's not finished," said Alexei. "And I don't know how to do it on my own."

"Do what?"

"Make you," he said. "I don't know how to finish making you."

"What?"

"I didn't know," said Alexei. "I didn't know anything."

Shadak came at him. He punched him and kicked him and tore at his shirt. He picked up a stone from the ground lifted it over his head. He glared down at Alexei.

"You don't know how?" he said. "Then learn."

And with that, he smashed the stone down—into Alexei's skull.

The void again. Alexei spun in it. It was like being dead. He opened his mouth to cry out for Vladimir, then shut it again. He'd told the baby to fuck off. He couldn't go crawling back to him now.

No. Alexei thought about what little Shadak had told him to do:

Learn.

Alexei would have to take charge of this realm of memory on his own. He had done something awful—become the agent of Fyodor Kolyokov and those others—to create something in Afghanistan.

But they—the dream-walkers—they weren't in Afghanistan. They hadn't set foot there.

They were in City 512.

The place where they all were born.

Where Kilodovich had come from.

That, he knew, was where he would have to go.

And it wouldn't do to have Vladimir take him there.

Alexei breathed and turned and willed himself to leave Afghanistan for the moment. He blinked, and imagined, and used what force of will he had—

—and the void faded. Alexei Kilodovich steered himself north, and into the heart of old Soviet Russia.

It was a thin, dry snow that fell outside City 512. Comrade General Rodionov was wearing a heavy woollen overcoat and a fur cap but it wasn't good enough. He was still freezing cold as he got out of the car. He rubbed his hands together and watched his breath cloud in front of him. The dozen KGB men alongside him were better off—they were wearing body armour and heavy gloves and helmets. Some of the men wore crucifixes and charms around their necks. Others lined their helmets with tinfoil, or carried garlic bulbs in their pockets. Some of them etched crosses in the tips of their bullets. Still others muttered little prayers and hexes that their grandmothers had taught them.

Rodionov simply hummed as he got out of the car and started toward the low buildings that hid the top of the shafts. It was a tune that his own Babushka had sung to him when he was tiny—one so old he could not even remember the words or where it had come from. But it had helped him sleep. Now—perhaps it would keep Rasputin's devilish progeny out of his mind.

It was probably the most effective thing. Alexei Kilodovich found the old bastard's brain completely impenetrable. He stood beside Rodionov, still a spectre.

Rodionov strode toward the huge open doorway in the nearest warehouse. There were perhaps a dozen men and women lying naked, face-down on the cold concrete, while Rodionov's men held rifles on them.

"The assault has gone well, Comrade General," said one of the men—a Colonel by his insignia. He gestured with his rifle to the prisoners. "We have rounded up these ones from the coffins. There are others still—"

Rodionov held his hand up. His eyes narrowed.

"I do not recognize these," he said.

"Comrade General?"

"These," said Rodionov, "are not the dream-walkers."

"We found them in the coffins," said the Colonel, but he said it like a question. "Surely—"

Rodionov hummed out loud. He stepped into the warehouse building, past the prisoners. The building was lined with his men, several of whom he obviously did recognize. He nodded at one or another, as they clutched their assault rifles to their flak-jacketed chests. The space in here was as big as an airplane hangar and all but empty. Alexei trotted along behind him. This following along wasn't very illuminating, and as they stepped through a metal cage-work structure in the middle, Alexei decided to take another step.

He had, in little Shadak's metaphor, been able to break the wall and hold a conversation. So he would, he decided, do the same thing here.

"Comrade General," said Alexei as they stepped into a stairwell. "Stop that music."

Rodionov blinked.

"Rasputin," he said.

Alexei frowned. "Rasputin?"

Rodionov nodded. He didn't precisely look at Alexei—but he was responding to him.

"You healed the Czar's son and made yourself a place in the court," he said, "and you used that place to do what?"

"Tell me," said Alexei.

"To do nothing," said Rodionov. "Nothing but fuck women and drink vodka and live in nice houses." He sneered. "Mystics. You could have the world, and you just feed off it."

"I am not Rasputin," said Alexei.

"You are Rasputin. You are all Rasputin."

"You sound as though you have been practising this little speech," said Alexei.

"I have," said Rodionov. "Indeed—I have found it useful to practise everything I do beforehand, when I am dealing with you bastards here at City 512. When I do not—well. I become distracted."

"How is that?"

Rodionov stopped and looked around. "I cannot see you," he said. "Can you make yourself visible?"

"I am visible," said Alexei.

"No," said Rodionov, "you are not. How do I become distracted? Well. I start to investigate the odd appropriations moving to Cuba—for an underwater project that had supposedly been cancelled. Before I know it, I have had too much to drink. My memories are foggy, and I remember another appointment. I decide to review intelligence reports coming out of this division—see whether we have made any headway in Central America. And suddenly I am on my way to the airport to meet an old friend, who does not arrive until next week. So—I practise. I write things down. I leave little tape recordings for myself. Clues. I have done enough of that—and lo! Here we are! Bringing this pestilent time of our history to an end."

"I see," said Alexei.

"Except I must ask myself," said Rodionov, "what distractions might come before me now? Perhaps a ghost walking beside me to keep my eye off the mark?" He shook his head. "Appear—so I may deal with you in flesh. Or walk behind me if it is your wish to view your destruction. Or better, return to your little water tank. Take time to make peace with yourself."

And at that, Rodionov hurried down the stairs, shouting ahead to his men who had secured the second level. He stepped deftly around the carriage on the landing. Alexei paused and crouched down in front of it. Vladimir glared back at him.

"You," said Vladimir, "are not being helpful."

"I am sorry I told you to fuck off," said Alexei. "That was rude of me."

"You are forgiven," said Vladimir. "Now come back."

"To my body?"

"Yes. Your body is injured. I am spending all my time tending it. We also have a prisoner." He leaned forward and regarded Alexei slyly. "Holden Gibson."

"You have Holden Gibson," said Alexei. "I see."

"You wanted to kill him, yes?"

"You put me here to stop that as I recall."

"Things have changed, Kilodovich."

Alexei looked at little Vladimir levelly. "Now you want me to come back to kill him?"

"I did not say anything. Only it is time to come back. You understand your true self now."

"I understand," said Alexei, "that I have been used and manipulated."

Vladimir sneered. "You have been used—but as you have seen, you did not protest too greatly. We saw the games you played with Amar Shadak's poor girl. That was not only Fyodor Kolyokov playing that game, Alexei."

Alexei nodded. That was true. He could come up with any rationalizations: *I was a young man, whose ethical compass was not exactly well-configured at that time; it was a fleeting lapse; I may well have been deceived by a false metaphor such as my dreams of an early childhood.*

But the fact was that whatever the excuse, Alexei had done the thing. He had torn Amar Shadak in two and made puppets of the rest. From the lower levels of City 512, he could hear shouting as Rodionov's men found the empty isolation tanks, and realized that their quarry had left. Then the small-arms fire, as some of those men turned on one another—obscuring once again the KGB's trail to the dream-walkers of City 512.

Those puppets would never be right, Alexei knew. He had made them badly for his masters, and his masters had dropped the strings. He looked at Vladimir.

"Now," he said, "you have work for me—to make things right."

"Come," said Vladimir.

Alexei looked at him. "I apologize," he said. "This is very rude. But once again: fuck off."

And Alexei floated again—this time not in a void, but in the air over the world. He was flying over mountaintops—high over the red-brown hills of Afghanistan. Clouds obscured things here and there, but he could see men and machinery moving below in what looked like a mountain pass. He could see the flash of explosions, the drifting of white smoke. People scurried beneath that smoke like frightened insects. Some fell and stopped moving. He could see smaller groups of men, moving around a more remote hilltop. Near the top of that hill, an opening in the stone. When he peered into it, he saw others—these ones moving through the tunnels of a cave, like ants or termites, with a common seeming purpose. He let himself float down to see inside. To return.

He fell down the chimney and drifted through the supply chamber—where an exhausted Ming Lei sat with Wali Beg, munching on biscuits that they'd liberated from the supplies. They looked at each other warily—they smelled of each other and couldn't, either of them, recall what had happened to make that so. Alexei slipped through the crack in the wall, until he was in the chamber where he had last encountered Amar Shadak. It was empty now, so he followed the fissure into the main chamber of the cave. There, he found Shadak—and himself. Young Alexei sat cross-legged in the sand, barely a metre from Shadak—who was curled in the dirt, his fists pressed against his forehead. The Mujahedeen that were with them stood a respectful distance away—their heads lowered, as though in prayer, their shoulders trembling as though with grief. Young Alexei was mumbling something in Russian—Amar Shadak was sobbing in no language at all. Older Alexei settled down on the sand, and leaned into the space between them—as though by so doing, he could intercept the communications that moved between the two like radio waves. It was no good. There was no Discourse for Alexei to hear. The lines had been cut.

He pushed off with his toes, and drifted out the front of the cave to the sentry point halfway up the hillside. A man sat there alone, arms wrapped around an old AK-47 and chin resting on its barrel-tip. His thumb caressed the trigger as tears welled up in his eyes.

He sat there with the man—fascinated and repelled—and watched as his thumb moved away from the gun, and he sat back as the shadows grew long and the sun began to set. Just before the sun disappeared completely over the ridges of the near horizon, Alexei spied a lone figure making its way out of the mouth of the cave. The sentry saw him too. Sobbing, he sat up and levelled the rifle—lining up the lone figure in his sights. His hand wasn't steady, though, and he soon lost his aim. He returned to his perch, shaking his head and sobbing, while young Alexei Kilodovich made his way out of the cave and set off towards the Red Army division, in the newly silenced war zone of southern Afghanistan .

"You should pull the trigger," said Alexei. "There I am. The agent of *your* misery. Getting away." Young Alexei stepped down a slope, and soon disappeared from view behind a tumble of rocks. "Got away." He made to slap the sentry across the back of his head.

To Comrade General Rodionov, Alexei was a haunting, a ghost at the back of his head. Not so here. The poor man didn't so much as flinch. He simply sat there—and waited, for a command that apparently no one would give.

Alexei had taken this man—a gangster from Turkey—an innocent little stripper from Hong Kong—fifty others, maybe more—and he'd mind-raped them. Turned them away from their own wills, their lives, their religions. Made them into puppets.

Or half-made them. Alexei sat down on the rock beside the sentry. He leaned over to look into the man's eyes. There was a spark there—something that was left of him. So he had not completely destroyed him.

But in a way, that was a worse thing. The part of this man that dreamed—that felt—that part was ensconced in some place not so dissimilar to the villa where Alexei had left Amar Shadak. Small and helpless and alone—while his body, his venal body, flopped and turned and marked the years, without motivating force any greater than flesh.

Beside him, the Mujahedeen guard reached into his trousers and scratched an ass-cheek. Alexei looked at him—and then across the little valley here. His younger self had emerged from the rocks again, some distance off. Scurrying like a rabbit back to his Soviet masters. Alexei pointed at him, sighting along his forefinger with one eye closed. "Pow," he said, raising his fingertip like it was a pistol.

As Alexei lowered his finger, the sad Mujahedeen sentry faded like a ghost—the shrub behind which he hid grew and withered and fell away. Alexei kicked his feet. He found that he was suspended now, above the rock—as though he were flying.

"Ha," he said to no one. He really, as he thought about it, couldn't care less what happened to his body in New Pokrovskoye. He kicked higher still, watching as years etched changes over the rough Afghani landscape.

Alexei rose above an Afghanistan finally purged of the Red Army and its shadowy agents. Time passed in a breath, and he rose higher still.

Who needed a body anyway? The only thing his body was good for, Alexei realized, was spreading more torment—tearing men in two, and turning themselves into slaves.

Here—here, was like an afterlife.

Devoid of responsibility.

Alexei spread himself across the sky, to a point where his mind was as insubstantial as a high cloud—then he congealed himself again, and spread his arms like wings.

"Whee," he said softly, as he drifted and swooped free at last of the shackles of his life—of memory. He flew on toward the water's edge. And from there, he dipped into the surface—and *spread.*

Маленький герой
THE LITTLE HERO

Water was before him and around him, above and below—a great amniotic all. Floating in it, he could imagine drawing his thumb to his face, shutting his eyes, and letting the fine, fine mother's food flow in through his belly button. Forgetting about his troubles in a great big womb . . .

He could imagine it, but of course that was wrong. The ocean was no mother. It didn't, for instance, turn around one night, kill your father and try to smother you and your first true love because its piece of shit KGB operator had decided it was time to clean house.

And mothers had nothing like the giant squid. Which Stephen Haber decidedly did: sixty-or-so feet long from ass to tentacle-tip, with eyes the size of soccer balls, two tentacles and eight arms and a nervous system that seemed almost faster than light.

Oh yeah.

Stephen guided himself through the murk—jetting the cold ocean through his middle—revelling in the new sensorium. Stephen laughed and sang inside. He was flying a squid! Through the Atlantic Ocean—miles from his body. He was fucking well dream-walking!

Fuck, he thought—*if Uzimeri could see me now*.

Of course, he couldn't. Because Uzimeri was too busy worshipping the fucking Children and Babushka and Zhanna—making a big fucking religious experience out of everything—to go riding a giant Captain fucking Nemo squid along the bottom of the Atlantic Ocean.

No—you had to be running with the Mystics to do that.

They'd explained to him that the giant squid were actually among the most ideally suited organisms on the planet for dream-walking. Not particularly intelligent, they nonetheless were blessed with the largest brains of any invertebrate on Earth. The brain was mostly occupied with working a prodigious nervous system and fiendishly articulate tentacles. But the lack of much conscious thought also made plenty of room for a piggybacked consciousness.

Stephen spread his squid's tentacles in a Mandela and spun in the dark ocean. He understood that some of the squid that formed the firmament of the Mystics were bioluminescent. When he brought this one in, he'd have to see about taking one of those out on the ocean. Maybe take it up near the surface at dusk—put on a show for some lucky cruise ship.

Maybe they'd even let him start doing the exterior maintenance that the Mystics seemed to use the squid for now.

"Hey. Kiddo. That's enough."

"Yeah. Up and at 'em."

"Get out of there already."

"We're not kidding."

"Yeah. Time to work."

Stephen felt his eyes open—and the ocean vanished. In its place, a big Romanian monk—with a greying beard and piercing black eyes—leaned over him.

He was back in Petroska Station—in the bed they'd set him up in.

The monk started to twitch, as the other Mystics chimed in.

"You got to watch that, Stephen."

"You can get addicted."

"Hurt yourself."

"You'll go blind."

"Oh stop it."

Stephen sat up. He guessed from the changing timber of the voices that there were four Mystics inhabiting the poor Romanian right now.

"Fun for you?" asked the Romanian.

"Yeah." Stephen rubbed his eyes. "Thanks," he said, meaning it profoundly. Since he'd come to Petroska Station, the Mystics had been pretty indulgent allowing him to play with their squids. They seemed to think it was useful to have him do this—although he couldn't see how. He wasn't taking them out on maintenance detail for the station—he wasn't engaging in reconnaissance—and his fooling around didn't seem to have anything to do with dealing with the encroaching threat of this Babushka creature that the Mystics seemed so worried about.

"You're welcome," said a Mystic.

"But now it's time to stay awake."

"Hmm. Whatever you say." Stephen threw his legs over the side of the bed—stood up and stretched. "How goes the war?"

The Romanian pursed his lips, nodded.

"Good."

"Yeah. Good."

"You just stay here."

Stephen laughed. "What am I—a prisoner?"

The monk laughed too—on whose behalf, Stephen wasn't sure.

It was hard to chart just how many Mystics actually inhabited this vast underwater station. He'd been here more than a day and he hadn't yet seen one of them in the flesh. He understood now that the Morlocks weren't Mystics at all. They were the Jacques Cousteau version of Richard at the front desk of the Emissary; sleepers who'd come down here years ago to service the structure while the Mystics went about their business—dream-walking through the waters off Cuba while hidden somewhere in their isolation tanks here at the bottom of the sea.

Somewhere.

"You didn't answer my question," said Stephen.

"You've got to stay put."

"That's what's good for you."

"Yes, because."

The Monk looked at Stephen, his lips slowly relaxing.

"Um," said Stephen after a moment, "because what?"

The Monk turned away from Stephen, walked across the room to a little cushioned seat.

"Because?"

"Because."

"Big fight's coming."

"This one's not your fight."

"Stay put."

The Monk sat down, folded his hands in his lap. His eyes focused somewhere far, past the bulkhead.

Stephen got up. He walked over to the Romanian. Snapped his fingers at first one ear, then the other, and then he waved his hand in front of the guy's eye. Nothing.

"Because," said Stephen. "Fine."

He struggled to keep his voice nonchalant, but it was a trick.

Who the hell was inside the Romanian now?

Maybe no one.

He reminded Stephen of the way the Romanians got when they were guarding Zhanna and the others at the back of the submarine, but not performing complex tasks. Zhanna had said something about leaving them like that—going through their chores like automatons.

Like Richard—at the front desk of the Emissary.

Stephen looked at him. He stared back past Stephen impassively.

Stephen walked around the room. It wasn't large by normal standards—but it was a gymnasium compared to the casket-sized chambers of the submarine. And the light was comfortable—warm and incandescent, with none of the flicker or humming that plagued Stephen in the cabin he shared with Uzimeri. There was even a ventilation grate in the ceiling, that pumped cool, fresh air. He sniffed at it.

It smelled antiseptic—and still. The fan was off.

Stephen turned to regard the Romanian again. The Romanian might as well have been dead, but for his chest, slowly rising and falling.

Stephen stared at him hard—regulated his breathing—imagined a descending scale of colour, taking him down through the spectrum. He tried to picture himself travelling through the air—into the ear of the Romanian—behind his eyes. To see himself, standing in a room near the top of an ancient Soviet sea station, trying to read a mind without the scarcest hint of talent or ability to do so.

"Shit," said Stephen aloud. Babushka, Lena, right in front of him—and he couldn't get a hint. Maybe if she was inside a squid . . .

Stephen sighed. What, he wondered as he stood up, walked past the insensate Romanian and pushed the hatch open, would Uzimeri say now?

The hallway outside was narrow, and the painted metal panels along it described a wide curve. Stephen picked a direction and hurried along it. He felt his pulse hammering. Shit. Babushka. The Mystics had named her as a threat—told him that she had already invaded the minds of his comrades down in the submarine and then—for all intents and purposes—disappeared.

Stephen finally stopped what seemed half-way around the circle, when he found a doorway that seemed to lead deeper into the station. He passed through it—found a room with a narrow spiral staircase going up—and followed it. He had to find the Mystics.

Stephen emerged in a large domed room—maybe thirty feet in diameter. The floor was covered in green carpet that smelled faintly of mould. Sconces in the ceiling projected swathes of light from the circle's edges towards the middle, but not quite reaching it. The whole thing created the discomforting aspect of a giant iris over Stephen's head.

But that wasn't the only discomforting thing.

The room was filled with sensory deprivation tanks. There must have been two dozen of them—arranged in concentric circles, from the middle of the room to its edge. They were identical to Fyodor Kolyokov's—huge Soviet sarcophagi, with tubing and conduits coming from them and disappearing into little black boxes set into the floor.

Stephen approached one. He touched the hatch cover, to confirm what he thought.

Sure enough—the hatch swung open, and the stink of eons wafted out.

The old woman was in chains in the bottom of Filtration Room Three. She was like the rest down here—pallid, with wide dark eyes and a mouth that puckered back over too few teeth. She glared up at Mrs. Kontos-Wu from her prison between the two intake pipes. Mrs. Kontos-Wu rested her hands on opposite elbows, drumming her fingers, as she looked into those dark, empty eyes.

"Lois?" she said.

"That," said the hag, "is one of my names. To *you*."

Mrs. Kontos-Wu sighed. *Why don't you just spin your head around now*? she thought. But she said instead:

"Babushka, then?"

The hag didn't answer—just held Mrs. Kontos-Wu's gaze, trying to worm her way inside, until she had to look away. Mrs. Kontos-Wu walked back across the gantry to her two companions—Vanya and Mishka, who looked scarcely more human than the woman below.

The two were trembling—much as Vanya had been, when he'd first hailed Mrs. Kontos-Wu from across the algae pond. *Help us*, he'd said. He'd repeated that over and over again, even after Mrs. Kontos-Wu promised she'd try—if he'd only tell her what the trouble was.

"Minds are going," he'd said. "One by one by one. You can save the minds—stop this, yes?"

Mrs. Kontos-Wu didn't know. But she was looking for a distraction now—anything to keep her awake, and out of the metaphor that had so betrayed her.

"I'll see what I can do," she said.

Vanya took her hand in his own clammy paw and led her further into the depths of this station—yammering on the way. It developed that he was an old submariner who specialized in the nuclear plants. His family came from Belarus, near Minsk. He'd been transferred to Petroska Station after taking an aptitude test, one winter's morning in 1978. Left behind a daughter and his young wife. Mrs. Kontos-Wu politely suggested that he might be missing them but he explained that no, he visited them every chance he got. "They have nice country house now—big A-frame. On lake. I go there every day. Make love to my wife."

Mrs. Kontos-Wu looked into the creature's dark eyes, set back in pale, hairless brows, and tried to convey credulity.

"But now," he said as they climbed a narrow spiral staircase and pushed open a hatch to the machinery decks, "I soon will never go back. She take our minds."

"*She*?"

"Oh yes." he said, nodding quickly. "Then we good for nothing."

He'd taken her up four floors, and into a room that might at one time have been a comfortable barracks room. Now, though, it resembled a ward room in a government-run retirement home. The walls were panelled in wood veneer punctured with thousands of thumb-tacks. It was lit by flickering fluorescent tubes set into the ceiling. It smelled like pee. There were maybe a dozen beds there—all of them occupied, with the same sort of bizarre, pale creatures. They stared vacantly like Alzheimer's patients.

One other—who Mrs. Kontos-Wu later learned was Mishka—looked after these ones, shuffling about with bed pans and trays of food.

"She take our minds," repeated Vanya. "We good for nothing."

Mrs. Kontos-Wu frowned.

"Are these," she guessed, "the Mystics?"

It was certainly possible that they might be. She could in fact imagine Fyodor Kolyokov like this, if he'd managed to a few more years in that isolation tank of his.

Vanya, however, seemed to think that idea was hysterically funny. He laughed and laughed. "Mystics? No, no. Not Mystics."

"Not Mystics."

He nodded. "Tools of the Mystics," he said. "Tools."

"Puppets."

"Puppets. With—" he made a snipping motion with his fingers.

"The strings cut," said Mrs. Kontos-Wu wryly. "Yes."

He nodded. "You here to save us. Like the other one. The baby."

"Like the baby?" Mrs. Kontos-Wu frowned.

"You," he said. "Like the baby."

"Vladimir? No. I'm not like Vladimir."

The old man looked disappointed for a moment, then brightened. "We begged for new saviour. Boy came through—just ignored us. Went fooling around in the sea. But now—here you are. Saviour."

"I'm no saviour," said Mrs. Kontos-Wu.

"Perhaps," he said, "you simply do not know it yet."

Mrs. Kontos-Wu shook her head. "I think," she said, "I'm just a puppet with its strings cut. Let's leave it at that, shall we?"

Now, she was facing down a puppet with its strings very much intact. They had led her here—to a place where they'd tied the puppet up, after she'd become quite violent just a day ago. The creature would not talk with Mishka and Vanya—tell them what's going on—but they told them to bring Mrs. Kontos-Wu there, and she'd talk to her.

Of course, when they met it was clear what the creature's agenda was.

She called out to Mrs. Kontos-Wu now.

"Hey! Don't you want to know how the book ends?"

Mrs. Kontos-Wu went back to the railing. She leaned on it.

"It's not a real book," she said.

"Oh," said the hag. Lois. Babushka. "You know what is real, do you my child?"

"I'm not your child." Mrs. Kontos-Wu stepped over to the stairs going down to the floor of the pumping station. "And I think I do know what is real. At least, I know the real that I choose."

"Ha. Wise answer. Are you sure you want to come down here?"

Mrs. Kontos-Wu swung around and stepped onto an access ladder. "Why wouldn't I?"

"Doesn't it remind you of someplace?"

Mrs. Kontos-Wu stopped. "What place?"

"Why, that book," said the hag. "The one that wasn't real."

Mrs. Kontos-Wu looked down at the woman. Her hair was black and frizzy—it trailed down her shoulders and ended in twisted, greasy knots.

"The Cistern of Blood, child."

Mrs. Kontos-Wu looked around. Certainly there was a superficial resemblance—the pumping room was entered through a space high above its floor, and it took the form of a deep cylinder. Overhead, there was a grate that led to some other chamber. It wouldn't take much to imagine the steel walls replaced with stone—and the light of an Istanbul marketplace filtering in through the grate above her. The hag continued. "You might find yourself rescuing Jim. Or," she added, "doing as I said and returning to your berth—taking care of the bastard children there—and joining me."

Mrs. Kontos-Wu stopped on the ladder. Above her, Vanya and Mishka watched expectantly.

"How are you doing?" called Vanya. "Almost got it?"

"Doing fine," said Mrs. Kontos-Wu nonchalantly.

She climbed down the stairs.

"Heh heh. Good girl," said the hag. "Now. Do as you are told. Go and kill the children and destroy the Mystics—and join me back at the school."

Mrs. Kontos-Wu stepped over to the old woman who was possessed by Babushka—the woman who'd killed through her. She looked back up—thought briefly of climbing the ladder and heading back to the submarine, along a route that was suddenly clear to her.

But she looked back at the hag, leaned down in front of her.

"It's been a long and sad life here, hasn't it?" she said, and with one hand delicately pinched the clammy nostrils together—put her other hand over the old woman's mouth.

When he'd been outside swimming in the brain of his giant squid, Stephen had treated himself to a tour of Petroska Station from the outside. It was an eccentric structure—a rambling thing that in some places resembled a giant bathyscaphe—others a medieval castle—and others a high-rise apartment building done on the cheap. How tall was it? If you counted some sections that scudded down the slope of the shelf, and the five little towers that poked out of its middle, you could probably put fourteen storeys on it. But those towers were narrow as needles, and you couldn't say whether they were inhabitable. And some of the shapes that crawled down the slope could have housed nothing more than conduits. It was as though the place had been grown rather than built. Stephen had circled it for hours—tapping it with tentacles and sliding one of the squid's immense eyes close to the bulkheads. But it was no good. He couldn't make a useful map of the place.

That was clearer now than ever. He knew he had to get out—he'd checked each of the sarcophagi, and found all but one empty. The one that was locked contained a body—a corpse, bloated and swimming in the brine. Fyodor Kolyokov would have been like that, if he'd stayed in his tank a few weeks longer.

It all raised very interesting questions—questions like: if the Mystics weren't in their tanks—where they should have been, if they were dream-walking Romanians and teaching Stephen how to fly squid and having a big conference with the children on the submarine—if they weren't there . . .

Then first: where were they, and second: were they even the things that Stephen had been talking to in the first place?

What had they said about the ocean? It was dangerous like the face of God? You could lose yourself in it and find yourself in it.

Was it possible that the Mystics had migrated into the ocean itself? Just maybe kept this place operating and alive for old times' sake?

Stephen set it all aside. Bottom line: he had to get out. Talk to the children. Because now more than ever, he was certain that the thing the self-proclaimed Mystics were worried about—Lena, the Babushka—had come upon them. The fact that the Romanian in his stateroom hadn't even bothered to pursue him actually confirmed that: if indeed "she" was "everywhere" as they put it, then there would be no need to stop him from doing anything. Anytime she wanted to, she could just swat him.

Stephen made his way to the edge of the aerie. He reached up and touched the curve of the dome. It was cool. On the other side, he suspected there was nothing but ocean.

Ocean, where squid roamed.

His squid.

Stephen wanted to try the squid out again. Of course, it would be dangerous—before they had vanished, the Mystics had warned Stephen not to go to sleep—to stay put. No doubt, dream-walking into a giant squid right now would put Stephen at risk.

Wouldn't it be worse, though, Stephen rationalized, to remain lost in this giant underwater catacomb? Abandoned here when the submarine detached? Wouldn't that be worse?

Stephen concocted a plan. He'd dream-walk a squid—send it along the bulkhead, tapping it with its tentacles as he went. When Stephen heard the *pok-pok* sound, he'd know where the squid was—and thereby, have an idea how to get back to the submarine.

Plus which, thought Stephen, he'd have another chance for a go-around in a giant squid.

Of course, it was a cheap rationalization. Stephen closed his eyes. He watched the light crawl across the inside of his retina. He did the things that he'd done when the Mystics had sent him there. He was prepared for failure—for waking up, gasping, as he had a hundred times at the Emissary while Fyodor Kolyokov flew the skies.

And yet—

—it worked.

Stephen spun around, sent tentacles reeling out, contracted the chitinous suckers like camera irises—peered into the dark, got his bearings—thought he spotted the peculiar signature of Petroska Station.

"Stephen? Stephen Haber?"

Stephen spun in darkness, looked around for something else—another creature here that might have the gift of language. There was nothing, though. He was alone with his squid. If not alone in his squid.

"Who the fuck's that?" he demanded. It didn't sound as he'd imagined Babushka sounding. The voice was Russian, true enough. But it was deep. Familiar sounding.

"I am surprised you do not remember me."

Stephen glared around in the dark. "Yeah, you know what? I'm sure that in context—"

"Alexei Kilodovich."

"What?"

"I am Alexei Kilodovich."

Stephen thought about that for a moment. He thought about how Alexei

Kilodovich could end up here inside the brain of a giant squid, at the bottom of the ocean and just outside a secret Russian underwater city.

"Here?" he finally said, and—"What?"

"You remember me now? You hired me to look after Mrs. Kontos-Wu."

Stephen's mind raced. "Um, yeah. Right."

"You are aware, I am assuming, that the whole thing was a bullshit ruse by Fyodor Kolyokov."

Stephen took a breath—felt himself slipping away from the squid brain and back into the real world—and put things in order. This was not, in fact, all bad.

"Fyodor Kolyokov," he said. Kolyokov had, Stephen remembered, told Stephen to find Kilodovich. He was to be a "hidden asset" in New York—and yes, he was to understand himself to be a bodyguard. This was before Babushka—before the submarine, and Turkey—before the old man even knew he was dead. Stephen felt a momentary pang of guilt—because instead of searching for Alexei Kilodovich, Stephen had spent his time here goofing around inside the giant brain of a giant squid. He was hardly showing the take-charge attitude that Kolyokov had demanded of him.

Yet here was Alexei Kilodovich—right now. The hidden asset—the dumbass bodyguard—and Shadak's price. Here. In the brains of a behemoth.

Stephen laughed.

"You think this is funny?" said Alexei. "Fyodor Kolyokov fed us a huge bucket of shit and made us like it. Even Wolfe-Jordan." In the dark, Alexei Kilodovich paused significantly. "A lie, Mr. Haber. *A lie.*"

Stephen kept laughing. "Oh fuck off, Alexei. No one was fooled by Wolfe-Jordan—except maybe the I.R.S. And obviously yourself." He felt his composure returning as he talked. "Okay, now you tell me—what are you doing here?"

The squid brain went silent for a moment. Stephen turned his attention outside—watched as the sea reeled past—guided the kraken down, to the tangle of metal and glass that sprawled across the shelf—the submarine that suckled at its belly. He let the tentacles flutter out, scraping along the bulkhead of the thing, tapping on it.

"I flew," said Alexei finally. "I flew across time, and then through the sky. For a long time, I flew over land—I saw Rome, you know, from high—it looks beautiful in the dawn light—then past Gibraltar. Like a bird, but far faster. And not with the cold that would come."

"Dream-walking," said Stephen. "Fine." Kolyokov did that kind of thing all the time.

"And all the time, I am getting nearer to the ocean. I am thinking: fuck New Pokrovskoye."

"Where?"

"New Pokrovskoye. Where I am—I think, fuck Vladimir and his plans for me. He wanted me to figure things out—fine."

"Vladimir?"

"Little kid. Brain like a forty-year-old."

"Vladimir." Stephen caught his breath, and thought about Chenko and Pitovovich's incredible story. "*The* Vladimir."

"Are you listening? I am telling you a story. So I fly along the water, and just for fun I stick my finger in it. Felt okay, so what the hell, I stick my head in. Before you know it, I hear a beautiful song. And then—I'm like an oil slick on that ocean. Everywhere. Including here."

"You didn't use the bathyscaphe, did you?"

"The what?"

Stephen sighed. Kolyokov didn't tell him much about dream-walking. But he had made clear to Stephen for many years about his anxiety coming from deep water—the compelling song of the ocean. The bathyscaphe was Kolyokov's safety metaphor.

"That's what Fyodor Kolyokov used to use, any time he had to dream-walk underwater. A bathyscaphe—a diving bell."

"What are you, crazy? I told you I was flying by myself. No bathyscaphe."

Stephen shook his head. "You have a lot to learn," he said.

"That is what everyone keeps telling me."

"You may not know it, but you're in a lot of trouble."

"Trouble?"

"You're spreading." That was one of the things that Kolyokov had warned Stephen about when it came to dream-walkers playing in the water. The medium was so huge—the salt water so perfect a conductor—that the ocean itself took on a kind of diffuse sentience. It was easy to simply dissolve in it. "Alexei," said Stephen carefully, "stop spreading."

"Ah. What is the point?"

"Imagine a bathyscaphe," said Stephen.

Alexei started humming, some Russian song. Stephen swore. He was dissolving. And he didn't have even sense enough to imagine any kind of protection, let alone a bathyscaphe. Stephen thought hard about what to do.

"Manka," he said, "Vasilissa. Baba Yaga."

Alexei continued humming, and Stephen wasn't really surprised. The mnemonic was designed to wake up sleepers. And if Alexei had been a sleeper at a time in his life, that time was long-past. Alexei was a dream-walker. He was a true psychic.

"Shit shit shit shit," said Stephen. *What the fuck do you do for a real psychic*? Then he said, "Oh," and thought: *New Jersey*.

Just a few weeks ago, he'd snuck away from the Emissary to go to this little psychic fair in Jersey, where he'd in addition to getting his aura red and his chakras reset, he'd picked up the tapes: Lorelei Jones' Ten Steps to Psychic Oneness.

Stephen had listened to them just the once—and he wasn't sure if he could remember any more than eight of them. But what the hell, he thought. Better than nothing.

"Alexei," said Stephen, "I want you to visualize the colour red."

Alexei kept humming, but the cadence slowed a little. So Stephen went on. "Red red red red red. Is that good? Now feel your breathing—" he cut that part short. Alexei after all wasn't necessarily breathing right now. "Okay. Imagine orange. Orange orange orange orange. Got it? Now yellow."

Stephen kept that up until he'd made it down the spectrum to violet, and then he said: "Now look ahead of you and you'll see a door."

On Lorelei Jones' tape, that door led to a green field with butterflies and a perfect clear sky and the scent of flowers wafting through the comfortable spring air. Stephen substituted: "The door is very thick and when you open it, you step into a cramped room where you've got to duck your head. The room has all kinds of controls flashing here and there. The controls say how deep you can go and they flash on and off if you're detected by anyone. And the walls of this room are very thick. They're steel and ceramic and insulation material like asbestos but not so toxic. There are air tanks underneath your seat. And from the top of it, there's a line of woven steel that will pull you up to the surface in a second. And—"

"All right." The humming stopped. "Shut up. I get the idea. A bathyscaphe."

Stephen breathed a long sigh. "So you're back now?"

"Yes. Maybe I shouldn't have told Vladimir to fuck off."

"Maybe you shouldn't have gone swimming without a buddy."

"Well. Thank you for pulling me back. Is this one of Fyodor Kolyokov's tricks?"

"Not exactly."

"Well however you came about it—thank you. This looks to be a very useful vessel."

"Metaphor."

"Right. Well, it's got all kinds of instruments. This scope here—it looks like some kind of a radar. It goes round and round—how does it work?"

"Um," said Stephen, "I think you have to decide."

"Ah. Very good. It—let's see. It tells me where I am. Detects others. There—hah! There you are! Little tiny blip."

"Is there anything else?" he said.

"Let me look. Hah. Yes. There are some others—not so far off in the water.

Maybe they are inside squids too? They are a ways away now so it is impossible to tell."

"The Mystics?" said Stephen.

"Could be the Mystics. Who are they?" Alexei paused. "Ah! The ones who fled City 512!"

"That's them."

"Well okay good. I have to say I prefer this method to Vladimir's."

"What is Vladimir's method?"

"It's like psychiatry. You spend all your time reliving things and come out for the most part ashamed of yourself. It does have its uses, but this is cleaner. Where did you learn of it?"

Stephen was quiet for a moment. He had imagined all kinds of meetings with Kilodovich—but they all involved talking to an unimaginative thug that he had understood to be nothing more than muscle to protect Mrs. Kontos-Wu on an off-shore outing. Not some green dream-walker who he could swap ten-steps-to-power techniques with inside a giant squid.

"What," said Stephen, "are you doing here?"

The squid went silent again. Tentacles rat-a-tat-ted across a ganglia of conduits, then extended momentarily into a deep fissure in Petroska Station's superstructure.

"I am unravelling," said Alexei finally.

"Do you want to do the bathyscaphe thing again?"

"No. Not unravelling that way. It is my life."

"What?"

"I have been on a mission to unravel the lie that is my life. Understand it. Know myself."

"Ah." Stephen knew a lot of people who were on that sort of a mission. The psychic fair in Jersey was filled with them. They drifted from booth to booth—checking out their Kirlian auras, sitting down with psychic gypsy mind-readers; buying crystals and listening to tapes and crouching underneath pyramids—on an inwardly spiralling mission of self-discovery. Stephen had found these people maddening, incomprehensible. Here they were, on the cusp of utter transformation—grasping at a tool that could lead them literally to omnipotence—and all they could think to do with it was try and figure out why their marriage went wrong or their father was mean to them when they were six, or whether they were ever going to finally get laid.

"I feel this way too," said Alexei. "It seems like a lot of bullshit."

Stephen whipped a tentacle across a line of rivets. "What are you, reading my mind?"

"No, no," said Alexei. "I can tell from your tone. You think I am some full of shit neurotic. But this thing—this unravelling thing. It has been useful."

"That so?"

"Da. I have been doing much thinking and remembering. I've worked a few things out. I think I understand what my place in things is."

"Okay," said Stephen, "I'll bite. What is your place in things?"

"Well, before this bathyscaphe trick," said Kilodovich, "I have to admit that I was not sure. But here—look! It is a scope for self-understanding. And I can see it! Right here in front of me!"

"And what does it say?"

"I am the destroyer," read Alexei, "of worlds."

"Ow!"

Stephen felt as though he had been lashed—flung at great speed out of the brain of the squid. And at the same time, he felt as if he had been kicked.

He didn't know about the lashing. But the kicking sensation was obvious. A Romanian was looking down at him, pulling his boot back from Stephen's kidney. The Romanian kicked him again.

"You little fucking traitor," he snarled—in a different voice. "What have you done with the Mystics?"

Stephen swore as he gasped breath into his lungs. "Z-Zhanna," was all he could manage before he blacked out.

After a moment, the hag coughed and spat and rolled over, looking up at Mrs. Kontos-Wu as she climbed the ladder to the gantry. Mishka and Vanya looked down at her, then at Mrs. Kontos-Wu. Then at the old woman again.

"Why did you do that?"

"You asked for my help," said Mrs. Kontos-Wu. "You wanted to get the Babushka out of here—am I not correct?"

They looked at her. Vanya ran a rubbery finger across his chin. Mishka started down the ladder, not saying anything.

"Babushka," said Mrs. Kontos-Wu, "is out of her. She thinks the body is dead. I'm willing to bet she won't be back again for a while."

From below, the hag let out a pitiable wail. Vanya looked away, his shoulders shaking.

"You're welcome." Mrs. Kontos-Wu spun on her heel and headed back out the door. They would thank her later, she thought, as she stepped through the portal—and into a room that was sickeningly familiar. It was filled with tall book-cases, lit by golden sunlight admitted through tall leaded-glass windows.

Mrs. Kontos-Wu looked at her hands. They were young and soft—a girl's hands. They were also shaking.

She was back in the library. Over by the window, she spied a comfortable chair with the tented cover of a novel on its seat. The chair beckoned her. She could at last find out what happened at the end of *Becky Barker and the Mystery of the Scarlet Arrow*.

Mrs. Kontos-Wu balled her young hands into fists and stepped deliberately backwards. She set her mouth in a line and narrowed her eyes—giving the outward impression, she hoped, of determination—but in fact, just fighting back the tears of despair that were battling their way to the surface.

"Bitch," she said under her breath. For it was clear to her what had happened. She'd just given Lena—Babushka—Lois—whoever, the finger. Stood up to her. And now, the bitch was making it clear that *that kind of talk wouldn't do*.

"Well fuck you," said Mrs. Kontos Wu. She backed away from the chair. "I'm not reading the book."

Something rustled, and there was the dull thudding sound of old books falling on older carpet. Something grunted, and Mrs. Kontos-Wu saw a flash of movement at the edge of the K-L aisle. She backed into the X-Z aisle.

"I'll burn the place down again," she said in a voice that sounded firm. Like arson was easy here.

It was a different matter in the real world. In Physick. All you had to do was pinch the nostrils, cover the mouth—and if it gets too bad, retreat. Retreat to Bishop's Hall.

Here, though, in Bishop's Hall . . .

There was, really, no retreat.

You could close the book—but the book was always there—tented on the plush seat by the windowsill, tempting you into it with questions. What happens to Jim now that he's down to one hand? Football's out of the question. And Bunny? Poor, poor Bunny. . . What's to become of her?

Mrs. Kontos-Wu shut her eyes—felt the tears come. And then she heard a voice:

"At the end of the book, Becky calls in *Les Gendarmes*, and they break up the order of the Scarlet Arrow once and for all. Antoine's father—or *père* as the French put it—is sent to prison, and Antoine goes to live with Bunny and her family back in America. Jim is fitted for a hook which in the last line he pretends is a pirate hook and everyone laughs."

"That's a lie," said Mrs. Kontos-Wu. But she opened her eyes and gasped.

In front of her, a tall black-haired man stepped out of the sunlight and shut the book. He bent down and peered at her.

"Mrs. Kontos-Wu?" He looked relieved as he extended a huge hand to shake her small one. "You are well. I am relieved—I thought for certain I had lost you when the children torpedoed your boat."

"What have you done with the Mystics?"

Stephen blinked and coughed. He didn't have to look around to know he was back on the submarine—the old-socks stink and the endless tick-ticking of the lights were enough to tell him that he was here, in the old engine room, handcuffed to a chair. He didn't need to look around to see that.

But look around he did. Three Romanians were surrounding him—one, the little guy with glasses he'd pummelled a day ago outside the sleeping chambers.

It was he who was talking. But Stephen knew it wasn't him.

"Zhanna," said Stephen, "I've—I've been in contact with someone you need to talk to."

The little Romanian sneered. "Answer the question," Zhanna said through him. "Where are the Mystics?"

"I don't know about the Mystics," said Stephen. "They're gone. You need to talk to this guy. Alexei Kilodovich."

"Alexei Kilodovich." This time it was the tall bearded Romanian who brought him here. "A trick. The Mystics are dead and you have killed them. Somehow, through you, Fyodor Kolyokov has destroyed the Mystics. Tell me how and it will be quick."

"Zhanna," said Stephen, "please. This is important. I've been in contact with—"

"You've been in contact with no one! You are a fucking little deaf boy who moved at Fyodor Kolyokov's beck and call! We were warned about you!"

"Warned?"

"Yes. We were warned that—that someone on our ship had been given instructions to kill the Mystics and then murder us!"

"And you think it was me."

"What else am I to think?" The third Romanian who was bald and fat stepped around. "We find you with the empty isolation tanks. The Mystics were old—they had not the capacity to dream-walk without the necessary equipment—that being their tanks. What did you do with them?"

"The Mystics," said Stephen, "have been out of those tanks for a long time. Maybe there's another place on board the station. Why don't you ask the Mystics?"

"They are gone," she said. "You know this. I should never have trusted you."

"You never did trust me," said Stephen.

"That is not true."

"That's why you won't meet face to face."

"I can see your face," said Zhanna. "And it's lying."

"You don't have a clue." Stephen sighed. "Look. Something's happened. We can agree on that. The Mystics—they've disappeared. That's a puzzle—but that's not the problem."

"To hell with you!" One of the Romanians kicked at Stephen, but Zhanna obviously didn't mean it—Stephen dodged it too easily.

"The problem," said Stephen, "is Alexei Kilodovich."

The short Romanian snorted, shook his head and looked up at the low ceiling.

"Alexei Kilodovich. You're fixated on him. Just like Vladimir."

"You don't think there's a reason for that?"

"Yes, yes. Alexei Kilodovich. Vladimir thought he was some sort of progenitor. A powerhouse—a key for what he wanted to achieve. Maybe he was right and that's what Kilodovich was. But—"

"But?"

"So," said Zhanna through a tall dark-bearded Romanian, "were the Mystics. And they, at least, were not fucked over by Fyodor Kolyokov."

THE IDIOT
Идиот

Alexei looked around. "This is impressive work. Kolyokov's?"

"Yes. No. I don't know."

Alexei was pacing through the reading area of the library—thumbing through volumes that had been left on the study desks—peering out the window. He was different than Mrs. Kontos-Wu remembered—there was a spark in his eye, of intelligence or self-knowledge or simply excitement she couldn't say, but it was a marked change from his usual indifference. And the long black robe he wore with the hood pulled back—that was a definite change from his usual wardrobe.

Mrs. Kontos-Wu had just gotten finished explaining that she couldn't remember how she'd escaped the torpedo on the yacht—that she couldn't even remember the yacht. The story had sounded lame but Alexei hadn't seemed to mind. He'd just nodded and listened.

"You would not know," he said. "Kolyokov wouldn't have ever signed this."

"He was here though."

Alexei looked over and down at Mrs. Kontos-Wu. "Was he?"

"He destroyed it." Mrs. Kontos-Wu shivered, as she recalled the flames crawling up the tapestries and the glass exploding in glowing red shards.

"Well he did a very poor job, now did he not?" Alexei knocked on the oak table-top, turned one of the green-shaded banker's reading lamps on and off again. "This appears very solid."

Mrs. Kontos-Wu shook her head. "It—comes back. Someone keeps rebuilding it."

"Someone?" Alexei frowned.

Mrs. Kontos-Wu looked at her hands. She balled them into fists and opened them up again.

"Babushka," she said.

Alexei shook his head.

"You have been ill-used," he said. "Babushka, Kolyokov . . . these Mystics here. All the same. They use us like puppets for sickening games. But tell me—do you truly think it is Babushka who keeps remaking this comfortable place for you?"

Mrs. Kontos-Wu looked at Alexei. Squinted. "What are you doing here anyway?" she said. "You're not supposed to be able to do anything like this. You're a sleeper—lower level even than I."

"Such a humble creature." Alexei smiled. "Is that so, do you think? Then how can I be here?"

Mrs. Kontos-Wu frowned.

"You failed to answer my question," said Alexei. "Do you truly think it is Babushka who keeps remaking this place?"

"I—"

"Yes?"

Mrs. Kontos-Wu balled her fists. Opened them again. Looked up at Alexei. "No," she said.

"Ah," said Alexei. "Then who?"

Me.

Mrs. Kontos-Wu couldn't say it—but she knew it. Lena—Lois—Babushka may have come here, may have made use of this place. But ultimately, it was Mrs. Kontos-Wu—Jean Kontos-Wu—who came here for comfort and in terror, and put it back together when other, wiser people tore it down. This place was a prison—but not one administered by City 512 any longer. It was one of her own making.

Alexei leaned down in front of her. He spoke softly.

"Mrs. Kontos-Wu," he said. "I have been on a very long journey since we parted. I have gone to see my history and my past and seen the things I have done and might have done. And I will tell you something."

"Yes?"

"There is nothing that is a greater comfort than living in a convincing lie about oneself."

Mrs. Kontos-Wu stood and stalked over to the U-V aisle.

"Particularly," said Alexei, "when the truth entails so much wickedness."

Mrs. Kontos-Wu turned. Her gut was churning—she felt as though she might puke. The world—the library here—was shifting and bending slightly, fading at the edges. But those shifts were nothing compared to the change that was coming forward in Alexei. He seemed to be growing taller—his skin darker—and from his middle—

"Let me see if I can do this right."

She gasped. "K-Kilodovich," she said, "zip up your fly."

But that wasn't what it was. The long black thing was emerging from his stomach—where his navel should be—snaking out from behind his shirt, lashing across the room towards her.

"It is painful," said Alexei. "But it will be quick. It *should* be quick."

As the whip lashed her face, Mrs. Kontos-Wu fell backward—

—backward into the lie that was her life.

THERE ARE NO GUILTY PEOPLE

Виноватых людей нет

Tom Wu was fifty-three. Jean was twenty-two. Standing amid the lilies on the roof of his penthouse, thirty-seven storeys above Hong Kong harbour, Tom Wu stared at her, tears running down cheeks beneath eyes weakened with injury, waiting for an explanation. Jean Kontos-Wu shrugged: what could she say? He had the goods—photographs of her and Amar Shadak, "the filthy Turk"—both naked, her legs wrapped around his torso, smiling into his eyes as he rammed himself into her. He had the bank records, which showed the withdrawals she'd made over the past month and a half—the massive transfers of cash from Hong Kong to New York to Switzerland. He didn't have the shipping manifests yet, that showed the unidentified materials that were moving from Kowloon through the China Sea and the Indian Ocean, up through the Suez and into Turkey. He also didn't have time.

So Mrs. Kontos-Wu shrugged.

"You have betrayed us," said Tom Wu and that was all. The chemical she'd insinuated into his drink took effect, and his eyes went wide and his heart stopped and he died.

John Tournier was the head of a consortium in New York that owned the Emissary Hotel. He was sixty-eight. Mrs. Kontos-Wu was twenty-five. He didn't look at Mrs. Kontos-Wu with anything like surprise when his time came and title to the hotel went.

Ian Forrester was forty-one. Mrs. Kontos-Wu was twenty-six. His eyes met hers through four inches of churning water in a hot tub as his lungs filled up with water and the files on his computer shuffled from hard drive to diskette.

Lisa Churley was twenty-nine. Mrs. Kontos-Wu was twenty-seven. It took two jugs of acid to get rid of her remains. In addition to her notebook and tape recorder, her purse held a picture of a heavy-set balding man and a little boy grinning like idiots in front of what looked like the Grand Canyon. Mrs.

Kontos-Wu threw it into the bath with everything else. The man stepping off the turboprop could have been anywhere from twenty-five to forty. Mrs. Kontos-Wu was twenty-eight. Brain and bone spread across the adobe mural in the little airport and Mrs. Kontos-Wu unscrewed the barrel of the rifle, pulled off the stock and folded it into her carry-on bag.

Elmer Bergensen was in his thirties. Jerri Bergensen was a little younger but not much. Mrs. Kontos-Wu was thirty-four. They had rescued her from the ocean and asked a few too many questions. And they were dead.

Mrs. Kontos-Wu blinked. She was sitting in the mess of the submarine. Ilyich Chenko and Tanya Pitovovich were there too. Chenko touched her hand compassionately. Mrs. Kontos-Wu shook her head. Twitched. Her eyes were damp with tears. Her face was hot. She inhaled a mouthful of salty snot. She'd been bawling.

"How long have I been here?" she asked.

"Not long," said Tanya.

"Perhaps a quarter hour," said Chenko.

Uzimeri stepped into her field of view. "Has the Babushka finally blessed you?" he asked.

Mrs. Kontos-Wu laughed weakly. "No," she said. "No more Babushka."

"Well however you've come to it," said Tanya, "you are back to yourself."

"It's not about me," said Mrs. Kontos-Wu.

"Hmm," said Chenko. "Sounds as though you're reaching an *epiphany*."

"Be quiet a moment. She's working it through."

Mrs. Kontos-Wu frowned. It wasn't about her. At least not her victimization. It was true that Fyodor Kolyokov had lied to her and imprisoned her. But the truth was that it was her hands that drove a beer bottle down the throat of a kind and innocent woman—whose only sin was helping a stranger lost at sea. Kolyokov's programming might let her rationalize away responsibility. But it was an escape hatch.

"Where is Stephen?" she said finally.

"He is back," said Uzimeri.

"Where?"

"Where the Children sleep," said Chenko. "They found him in the station. Now they are finding out how it is he betrayed them."

"How he betrayed them." Mrs. Kontos-Wu stood up. "Excuse me," she said.

"Where are you going?"

Mrs. Kontos-Wu didn't answer. She gingerly stepped around the passengers, ducked her head, and half-ran down the narrow spinal corridor to aft.

She met a guard along the way. He smiled at her.

"Mrs. Kontos-Wu," he said.

"Alexei?" Mrs. Kontos-Wu couldn't say how she knew. Maybe something in the eye. "Are you dream-walking here now too?"

The Romanian made a face. "You too?" he said, and reached around to restrain Mrs. Kontos-Wu. "Sorry," she said, and lashed out with her elbow. The guard made a chuffing sound and collapsed, and Mrs. Kontos-Wu gave herself mild shit. The only dream-walkers in here that she knew about for certain were the Children, and they were also the only ones with reliable instincts that way. Jean Kontos-Wu was a person of this earth. She had to rely on other advantages.

She used those advantages to take down two more Romanians and lock a third in an empty stateroom before she made it halfway back. By the time she'd reached the officers' quarters, they were waving guns around. Unconvincingly: the Children knew better than to start firing handguns in a submarine.

"Why are you doing this?" said one, who appeared with a short-barrelled shotgun levelled at her midriff. "What is this Kilodovich thing?"

Mrs. Kontos-Wu sighed. "You need to talk to Alexei Kilodovich," she said. "I can't do it for you. But he's—"

The Romanian gasped, and his eyes sprang open. As though he were a computer, and someone had just rebooted him.

The gun lowered, and Mrs. Kontos-Wu gingerly took hold of the barrel. The Romanian let go of the gun.

He muttered a long, incomprehensible string of Romanian.

And then, he began to cry.

Mrs. Kontos-Wu hefted the shotgun and wondered idly if it were loaded with buckshot—and if it were, just how safe it would have been to have fired it. She shivered: she might actually have been at risk.

Mrs. Kontos-Wu shrugged it off. She elbowed past the Romanian and into the wood-panelled corridor.

There were no more Romanians here—just a narrow, dim corridor. The submarine bonged and creaked around her. Partway down, she stopped as a shape emerged from one of the doors.

It was a kid. He looked about fourteen years old. He was fat—as Mrs. Kontos-Wu looked at him, she was amazed to think: *This kid looks like Fyodor Kolyokov must have*; even more amazed about what that observation implied.

The kid looked at Mrs. Kontos-Wu with wide, nervous eyes. He mumbled something incoherent. Then he hurried across the hallway to another stateroom. Mrs. Kontos-Wu shrugged and continued on. She glanced into that door, saw the fat kid and another boy, same dark hair, same wide eyes, staring out at her.

So that's what they look like.

For everything that had happened, Mrs. Kontos-Wu thought this might be the first time that she'd gotten a good look at the Children of City 512.

Маленький герой
THE LITTLE HERO

"Stephen," said Alexei Kilodovich. "It is okay to open your eyes."

Stephen had been huddled in a fetal position around his middle, while the Romanians took turns kicking him and lashing him. The beatings had stopped for what Stephen has assumed was just a moment. But in fact, when he opened his eyes he saw that he was alone in the room.

"What's going on?" said Stephen.

Alexei's voice filled his mind. "We are having a conference," he said. "Would you care to listen?"

Stephen trembled. He nodded.

"Then shut your eyes again," said Alexei.

Stephen did.

And for the first time in his life, he stepped into Discourse.

Fyodor Kolyokov had explained, once, how he dealt with Discourse. They were sitting in the Emissary's lounge downstairs. Kolyokov was sipping at his fourth bottle of beer, and was a little drunk. Stephen was smoking and paying close attention. Kolyokov was sometimes more forthcoming after drinking and today was not an exception.

It is like, he said, *stenography.*

Yeah, Kolyokov was forthcoming sometimes, but he wasn't always clear. *What does one have to do with the other*? Stephen wondered.

Ha. You must take notes of what you hear in Discourse. You must then separate the notes into columns—words for each speaker. It is laborious work. The younger ones are better with it and they can just listen. But for us—for me, rather—Discourse requires some concentration.

Stephen had asked a few more questions but Kolyokov was done explaining. *You would not understand*, he said, not without a hint of cruelty, then winked. *Stenography*, he repeated and Stephen had left pissed off and confused.

Now, immersed in what was presumably a vigorous round of Discourse,

Stephen thought he understood what Kolyokov had meant.

He seemed to be half out of his body this time. He could feel the floor underneath his ass, his ribs still hurt. But there was a sense of dimension around him—a feeling that this tiny room and submarine had been supplanted by a great, dark hall, as though he might be sitting on the edge of a high gallery overlooking this hall; as though the hall below and above him was filled with politicians and supplicants who all spoke at once. Stephen opened his eyes, and he was back in the submarine. But he still had that sense—that maybe these walls were illusory. That the voices that still filled his thoughts were the reality. They talked and shouted and sang; they protested and justified and spun the facts to their advantage; they offered knowledgeable advice and countered it with bland truisms; all at the same time. Just listening, it was impossible to follow.

But stenography. Stephen slapped the floor around him, as though doing so would cause a pen or paper to roll out. But of course the room was bare.

Then he thought about the way that Kolyokov had worked—the way Mrs. Kontos-Wu had worked.

He thought about metaphor.

Stephen closed his eyes again. He thought about a steno pad—a Hilroy, 200-page pad bound with a spiral of silver wire, little quarter-inch-spaced blue lines on each page. He imagined a pencil—a yellow number two with a little pink nipple of an eraser on the back, and lead sharpened to a point on the front. He imagined it. And he saw it. And carefully, listening to what he could, he began to write.

NOTES ON DISCOURSE, wrote Stephen, then he listened. He thought he could make out a number of different voices, so he made columns for each of them:

ALEXEI; ZHANNA; TEENAGE BOY; PREPUBESC GIRL; BOY WITH SPCH IMPED; YOUNG BOY. STRANGE OLD WOMAN.

Then he listened some more—and wrote what he heard.

He found that as he wrote down one voice, another became clearer, and he wrote down that one too—while continuing to inscribe the first. And then he went to the third and the fourth and so on. Before long, he had the metaphorical equivalent of meeting minutes. As it came together, Stephen found himself becoming very impressed—even as he grew more and more disturbed at the implications.

At the end of it, Stephen nodded sadly. Kolyokov had been right about stenography—but he had been wrong about so very much else. When the Discourse ended and the dreamers went off to do what they had to do, Stephen read over his notes despairingly.

ALEXEI:

MY LIFE HAS BEEN A LIE AND NOW I KNOW THE TRUTH. I AM YOUR SIBLING. I AM YOUR FATHER. I CAN MAKE YOU AND I CAN DESTROY YOU. YOU NEED TO BE DESTROYED BECAUSE THE ONE YOU CALL BABUSHKA IS AIMING TO TAKE YOU OVER. SHE HAS ALREADY TAKEN OVER THE ENTIRETY OF THE SLEEPER NETWORK IN AMERICA AND IS WORKING ON EUROPE AND ASIA AS WE SPEAK. SHE HAS COME INTO THE SEA AND USED HER POWER TO DESTROY THE ONES YOU CALL THE MYSTICS. I AM THE KEY TO DESTROYING THIS. YOU ARE FOOLISH TO THINK THAT THE NETWORK CAN BE PRESERVED. HEY—WHICH ARE YOU? DAMN IT THE OLD WOMAN!

ZHANNA:

BABUSHKA IS A KNOWN THREAT AND WE WILL DEAL WITH HER. WE HOPED TO MAKE A HEAVEN IN WHICH THE SLEEPERS WHO HAD BEEN SO ILL-USED BY OUR MASTERS COULD BE SHOWN THE WAY TO FREEDOM AND PEACE. WE HAD HOPED TO RETURN THE CONTROLS OF EVERYONE TO THEMSELVES. THIS WAS VLADIMIR'S DREAM. IT IS A GOOD DREAM. WE DO NOT NEED TO DESTROY THE NETWORK. WE NEED TO PRESERVE THE NETWORK. NOT TO HAVE SLEEPERS. THAT IS NOT AS MUCH FUN AS YOU THINK, PETRA. DO NOT CALL ANYONE A BITCH, PAVEL. BLOWING UP NEW POKROVSKOYE SOLVES NOTHING. SHIT! HOW DID SHE—

TEENAGE BOY (PAVEL?):

BABUSHKA IS A BITCH. VLADIMIR IS A BABY. SLEEPERS HAVE NO USE NOW. MAY AS WELL DO AS ALEXEI SAYS. SEEMS TRUSTWORTHY TO ME. LEAVE ZHANNA ALONE. SHE IS ALL RIGHT. BAD GUYS? THAT IS SO LAME. AHH!

PREPUBESC GIRL (PETRA?):

WHY TRUST YOU ALEXEI? YOU WORKED FOR FYODOR KOLYOKOV WHO IS A BIG BASTARD. YOU SAY YOU CAN DESTROY THINGS HOW DO WE KNOW YOU WILL NOT JUST TAKE OVER FROM US AND BABUSHKA AND RUN THE SLEEPERS YOURSELF? I WANT TO HAVE SLEEPERS LIKE ZHANNA DOES.

ZHANNA THINKS SHE IS SO SMART. SHE IS JUST SCARED TO BLOW UP NEW POKROVSKOYE. IS THAT WHO I THINK?

BOY WITH SPEECH IMPED:

I FINK WE SHOULD TAKE SUBMARINE TO NEW POK'OVSKOE AND B'OW UP BABUSHKA AND HER F'EINDS RIGHT NOW. ZHANNA DOES NO' GED TO SAY WHAT WE DO. VLADIMIR THOU' ALEXEI SHOUL' BE WIFF US AN' THAT'S GOOD ENOUGH FOR ME. CITY 512 GONE NOW NO GOING BACK. I WORRY ABOU' OUR OWN SLEEPERS HERE TOO. HEY!

YOUNG BOY:

LET OUR SLEEPERS GO. THEY CAN RUN THE SUBMARINE RIGHT? THAT IS WHAT THEY ARE TRAINED TO DO. TELL UZIMERI TO TELL THEM TO TAKE US TO THE SURFACE. THEN GO TO NEW POKROVSKOYE AND DO NOT BLOW IT UP BUT SHOOT THE BAD GUYS. THEN GO HOME TO CITY 512. DOCTORS THERE WERE NICE. BABUSHKA IS THAT YOU?

STRANGE OLD WOMAN:

IT IS I MY CHILD. YOU ARE A BEAUTIFUL CHILD AND YOU SHOULD JOIN YOUR BROTHERS AND SISTERS UP TOP. I HAVE DEFEATED THE MYSTICS AND I WILL DEFEAT YOU IF YOU PERSIST. SEE HOW I TAKE CONTROL OF YOUR SLEEPERS. SEE HOW I USE THEM AGAINST YOU. SEE NOW HOW HELPLESS YOU ARE, AS I, LENA, BECOME THE TSARINA OF IMPERIAL NEW POKROVSKOYE FOR NOW AND FOREVER! BOW DOWN BEFORE ME! YOU—

WH—KILODOVICH?

Mrs. Kontos-Wu was about to step through the rear hatch to the officers' quarters corridor and back into the machine shops when she froze, listening to the sound of a rifle bolt being drawn behind her. She spun and ducked—expecting to return fire.

But she didn't have to. Two Romanians were standing at a doorway—the one she'd seen a Child enter a moment ago. One of the Romanians was holding an old rifle, and aiming inside.

At the Children.

Mrs. Kontos-Wu drew a breath and raised her shotgun.

Shit, she thought. *Babushka is inside him.*

She had tried to order Mrs. Kontos-Wu to kill for her, and now that Mrs. Kontos-Wu had shaken her off, Babushka had gotten inside the Romanians.

She sighted—but stopped, when she saw the second Romanian reach around the gunman's neck. He caught him in the Adam's apple with his thumb. The rifle went off with a thunder and a clang, as the first fell to the ground. The Romanian looked at Mrs. Kontos-Wu and motioned for her to put the gun down and come over.

"Alexei?"

The Romanian nodded. "For a moment. There is a fight on now. You must protect the children against anyone," he said. "Babushka is invading. Come here."

Mrs. Kontos-Wu did as she was told. The first Romanian lay gasping for air. Alexei's Romanian kicked him. When Mrs. Kontos-Wu was beside him, he tapped at the side of his skull.

"When I say," he said, "do you think you can knock me out?"

Mrs. Kontos-Wu thought she could.

"Good. Now," he said, "guard the Children."

The Romanian's eyes went blank, and Mrs. Kontos-Wu drove her elbow into his temple. He crumpled to the floor beside his comrade, who glared up at her.

"What—" he coughed. "What are you going to do? Suffocate this one? Like the old woman?"

Mrs. Kontos-Wu looked down at him and told Babushka to fuck off. She was about to make the Romanian say something else, but didn't get far before Mrs. Kontos-Wu's foot connected with the side of his skull.

She peered in the room. The Babushka's targets were curled up on the bunk beds, staring out.

She stepped inside a moment.

"What is going on?" she demanded.

"War," they both said in unison. "We are under attack."

THERE ARE NO GUILTY PEOPLE

Stephen looked up from his metaphorical notepad. The darkness around him was becoming brighter. For a moment, he saw himself on a great plain. A huge rolling cloud boiled overhead—a deep yellow cloud the colour of an old bruise. Stephen stood and stretched, his toes splaying across the dry, stony soil. He felt a hot wind on his face—and heard a humming, like a thousand voices—and then he saw things fly past him: a great axe and a ballpoint pen and a flurry of paper and clocks and at some point he realized that the cloud had dropped a vortex on top of him and around him, as the noise grew louder and the dust whipped around him and he felt his life strip away for a moment and a great bubble well up inside him and he felt as though he could reach out and make the world of wind and artifice dissolve with but a touch and then—

And then the metaphor of the battleground congealed once more. It was no longer a dry plain—now, it was a sea bed. And it was crowded with combatants.

Some were small—he saw Zhanna, a great bolt of silver that arched up from the ocean floor; other children whose names he couldn't tell, the same silvery energy. And in their midst, he saw what could only have been Alexei—a huge, black-robed creature with an enormous phallus sticking out of its middle. Except it wasn't a phallus at all—it was too high, and it was prehensile. It lashed up to the cloud, tearing long, rippling gashes in it. The cloud, meanwhile, twitched in other spots and sent tendrils down like the tips of whirlwinds.

Those tendrils snatched at the various children, infecting their silvery perfection with a kind of ink. The infection didn't stay—Stephen could see some of them slaking it off, stepping out of it like a casing, leaving it to dissolve over the ocean—but it slowed them.

Only the thing in robes—a twisted, Freudian death figure—seemed immune. It lashed up and up, cutting gash after gash as the metaphorical sea rumbled and shook with a great screaming. A great many rents appeared in the cloud—more than could be accounted for by the single creature's lashing. But the thing had its own defences, and sent tendrils up to lay hold of those others. They writhed and screamed in its grip.

The thing that was Kilodovich turned back then, to the smaller sparks that were the children. He waved them back. He fixed on Stephen.

RETREAT! He shrieked. AWAKEN!

THE IDIOT
ИДИОТ

—a roar of a gunshot—and that had finished it for Stephen.

Now he lay shaking on the floor of the machine shop, staring up at the buzzing lights. Discourse was finished—and he was out—out of the loop and out of tricks. Even when drunk, Fyodor Kolyokov hadn't given him any useful advice on dream-walking, and nothing—not a word—about what he presumed now to be the art of dream-fighting.

Stephen opened his eyes. Fuck it. He was imagining things. That was no better than his plain. He wondered if he might not just be going crazy in this place at the bottom of the Atlantic Ocean.

Well, fine. He got up. It hurt to move, but that was fine too. He didn't think he was imagining that. Stephen stood up and stepped around a device. He climbed up a short set of metal steps and plodded forward into a machine shop. There, one of the Romanians sat huddled, his knees clasped to his chest. He rocked slightly, humming something with easy, comforting cadences that sounded like a nursery song. Stephen bent beside him.

"Babushka?" said Stephen. "Alexei? Zhanna? Petra?"

The Romanian looked back at him with fresh, wet eyes, and Stephen thought: No one. No one but you.

He patted the Romanian on the shoulder, and went on forward.

As he climbed the steps into the officer's corridor, he wondered: what did the poor Romanian signify? Territory gained—territory lost? Or maybe just that ambiguous, volatile state of a territory that had simply been liberated?

Stephen froze at the top of the stairs. Halfway down the corridor, Mrs. Kontos-Wu crouched. She was aiming a gun at him.

"Stephen?"

"It's me," he said carefully, thinking back to the Emissary Hotel when she'd twisted his nuts and really damn near killed him. "Who are you? Babushka? Lois? Zhanna?"

To his relief, Mrs. Kontos-Wu lowered the gun. "Jean," she said. "It's just Jean now."

"Ah." Stephen still proceeded carefully. The fact that Mrs. Kontos-Wu was standing over what appeared to be two bodies did not escape him. "What are you—"

"Guarding," said Mrs. Kontos-Wu. "Alexei told me to guard the Children."

Stephen looked at the Romanians then up at Mrs. Kontos-Wu. He slowly started forward in the corridor. "All right," he said. "Then I'll help you."

Mrs. Kontos-Wu shrugged. Stephen opened his mouth to say something else, but he stopped when Mrs. Kontos-Wu put her finger to her mouth.

Right. The Children were sleeping.

Stephen stepped to the opposite side of the corridor and crouched against the wall. Mrs. Kontos-Wu smiled wearily, and Stephen smiled back.

And in this way they sat in the quiet hallway while the dreaming war waged silently around them.

Stephen awoke with a start. He had dozed off at some point, and everything had changed. Mrs. Kontos-Wu was gone—and in her place was Zhanna. She bent over him—looking at him with a sweet tenderness. Stephen blinked and looked around. Mrs. Kontos-Wu was gone! Why hadn't she wakened him?

"Where is Jean?"

"She went ahead," said Zhanna. "I said she should. I wanted to bring you along myself."

"Along? Along where?"

"Come," she said, pulling him to his feet. "We are to have a meeting."

"Is the war—"

"Over? Is the war over? That was your question, was it not? Well. No. A battle has happened and we are still here. But the war is not over. We are to meet. All of us. There is nowhere large enough on the submarine, so we go into Petroska Station."

Stephen stretched. He was ferociously sore—the combination of sleeping on the decking and the beating he'd received, at the hands of—Zhanna. He pulled his arm away from her.

Zhanna merely nodded.

"I understand," she said. "Will it help if I say I am sorry? That I was wrong—mistaken about you?"

Stephen rolled his shoulder—felt the joint crack.

Zhanna hurried beside him. "That is why I sent Kontos-Wu and the rest ahead. I wished to apologize to you. I—I told you I am no good at this."

"When you can't read somebody."

Zhanna stopped for a moment and looked at her feet. She was wearing scuffed Soviet army boots. She kicked at the bulkhead with them.

"I am no good at this," she said.

There came then another of those awkward silences between them. Stephen, who had been over the past few days subjected to belittlement, torture and open assault, now felt an odd guilt come over him—as though he were being insensitive.

He coughed.

"Why," he said, "do we have to go to a meeting?"

"Much to discuss," said Zhanna.

"Yes—but why not just use your dream-walking? Discourse?"

She smiled sadly, and picked up their pace.

"No more dream-walking," she said. "No more Discourse. It is too dangerous by far. You were there for a little while. You saw how it was. Discourse could destroy us. Certainly it would destroy Vladimir, if we were to continue waging the war on that front."

"Why would it destroy him?"

"Because of the way he's made."

Stephen shook his head. Vladimir—this baby with the brain of a forty-year-old—was a mystery to him.

"How," he said slowly, "did someone young as you give birth to someone like Vladimir? A virgin birth."

"Are you making fun?"

"I'm asking."

"Well," she said, "these things happen at City 512. It is an immense place, with many quiet men and women tending us. For the most part, we have controlled them. But not always. It is tiring work. You need to be asleep all the time.

"Sometimes—"

"Yes?"

"Sometimes, they act on their own. And so it was a year ago—when I awoke, in a small operating theatre. One of the sleepers there—her name is Doctor Turov, and she is our obstetrician—was preparing an injection. She said to me: 'You are to be blessed, Zhanna.' And that is all I remember before waking up pregnant. The sleepers were very agitated—paying unseemly attention to me. It was then that we decided it was time to leave the place of our birth."

"And give birth to Vladimir in a flat in Odessa."

"By that time, things had changed," said Zhanna. "I had come to understand my son. My brother."

"And what exactly did you come to understand? Why Vladimir?"

Zhanna thought for a moment.

"*Why Vladimir,*" she said. "What a question."

"I'm waiting," said Stephen. "Why did you give birth to your brother?"

"There are theories. One is that we decided to create him ourselves. Or that he was made by God. Or the spirit of Rasputin himself."

"Right. But those are theories. Why Vladimir?"

"Well," said Zhanna, "Uzimeri is closest to the truth."

Stephen frowned. "Vladimir's a God?" Zhanna looked at him. "Jesus?" he said.

"Like that," she said. "But he is not the son of God. Do you know how Vladimir works? I mean, how it is that he can think like an adult—talk to you—summon all this power?"

"I assumed that he was just a very evolved baby."

"Very evolved. No. Vladimir does not have a brain much better developed than anyone other baby. He's bright, and wilful—and will one day become very clever indeed. But he thinks, and acts, by occupying a portion of the minds of all the sleepers. He makes use of them—much as Babushka hopes to, in death."

Stephen thought about that. "Like a big computer network," he said.

"Yes," said Zhanna. "A big computer network—without, however, a hard drive. A means to store and back up. It lives in the living minds of the sleepers—and dies with them too. You see—if we continued the war, across what is really the collective minds of the sleepers . . ."

"You'd risk destroying Vladimir too."

"Right."

"So why—" Stephen paused to think—"why then does Vladimir want to free the sleepers?"

Zhanna smirked. "It is a two-way street for Vladimir. And for all of us."

"What is that supposed to mean?"

"You figure it out," she said. "I am tired of being the one to be puzzling things in this relationship."

"Zhanna—"

"Shh. Come. We have to meet with the others."

In a vast chamber overlooking a deep pool, the crews of Petroska Station and the submarine mingled under the flickering reddish lights, on catwalks and staircases and at the greenish water's edge. Zhanna stood with a crowd of pale, nervous children on a platform that was raised up on hydraulics. When she spoke, she stammered and her voice cracked.

"We are at war," said Zhanna. "Babushka, the entity that many of you worship as a Goddess—is—is a Devil. She has come to this place, Petroska Station. She has driven out the Mystics who lived here. And she has tried to steal your minds. The way she is stealing the minds of the world.

"Last night, we fought her. She is—she is weak here because of the sea. When Babushka was . . . er . . . was awakened, dreamers did not do well in the sea. It ate them up. She only learned how to swim in it a short time ago. And she is old. So we could defeat her. But—not forever. She will be back. She controls the surface and she learns quickly."

There was a murmuring now—particularly among the Morlocks who huddled, Stephen noticed, far from him and Mrs. Kontos-Wu.

"We have to leave here. Go up to the surface. Only there—"

Shouting broke out at this point among the Romanians—clearly unimpressed with the plan. Zhanna stepped back from the guardrail, and Uzimeri stepped forward. He barked a few short syllables at them, then pointed at one or another of them with sharp, angry jabs of his finger.

The crowd quieted almost immediately, and Stephen thought: *Uzimeri must have been a mean fucker when these guys worked for him. Religion hasn't softened those edges any.*

"Only on the surface—in New Pokrovskoye—can we hope to defeat her. There, we can contact Vladimir. There, we can finish the war."

Chenko stood forward then and shouted:

"You are mad. Babushka is the one we all serve."

Tanya Pitovovich touched Chenko's shoulder to pull him back. But Stephen didn't have to be a psychic to tell that she kind of sided with him. Uzimeri turned to face Chenko. There was fire in his eye.

"Zhanna," he said, "will deliver us. When she says we are to hunt Babushka, she is speaking metaphorically."

"Metaphorically! What is metaphorical about this! Why are we even speaking? Has Zhanna turned away from Babushka now? Is this why she will not speak in our minds?"

Zhanna stepped forward. She was clearly uncomfortable on a stage in front of a roomful of sleepers. Her voice cracked and she stammered: "N-n-no. We do not speak with our minds because to do so opens us to more attack."

As if to underscore her words, a low scraping rumble came up through their feet. Somewhere in the depths of Petroska Station, wheels turned.

"We have to have faith," said Zhanna, "in each other."

Pitovovich held her head in her hands. The Romanians milled about uncomfortably. Stephen could see why: it was as though the Pope had just declared a crusade against the Holy Ghost while taking a second look at Secular Humanism.

The group became more angry and chaotic. Words were exchanged. Uzimeri yelled. And then all fell silent, as a burbling came from the waters in the pool.

Stephen stepped over to the pool's edge. Looking down, he could see the floor of the pool opening—leading to a larger chamber, twice as deep, lit by dull beams of light. They cut through a ropy tangle that surrounded a shape like a great shark. It grew in the water. The surface began to rise and churn then, and the thing was momentarily obscured.

And then it broke surface.

Several screamed and choked, as the air filled with the sharp bleach-smell of ammonia. But Stephen held his nose and looked down with wonder.

The giant form of a huge squid bobbed in the water, algae washing down off its silvery back in clotted waves. The eye—a sphere as big as his own head, gleaming in a great singular facet—looked to him, and he looked back into it. A tentacle splashed out of the water and fell onto the metal decking and the bulk of the squid slid back underwater.

The room fell to complete silence.

As they watched, the tentacle slid across the decking—but rather than falling back in the water, it began to make a sound.

Pok-Pok-Pok. Po-pok. Pok.

It was the sound the horned suckers made on bulkhead. It was coming in a particular rhythm: *Pok Pok Pok - po-po-pok. Pok. Pok-po-Pok.*

Chenko frowned, counting the *poks* on his fingers. "Is that—?" and shook his head, but Pitovovich, who was also listening intently, nodded slowly. "It is," she said.

"What?" said Mrs. Kontos-Wu.

"The squid," said Chenko, "is communicating in Morse Code."

The squid waited patiently while they found a pad of paper, then continued. Its first message was simple:

"L-I-S-T-E-N-T-O-S-A-S-H-A."

And then, when the squid had rested and the message had sunk in, a longer one:

"W-E-A-R-E-F-I-N-E-T-H-A-N-K-Y-O-U-F-O-R-A-S-K-I-N-G-N-O-W-G-O-B-A-C-K-T-O-Y-O-U-R-B-O-A-T-A-N-D-G-E-T-A-M-O-V-E-O-N-T-H-E-S-T-A-T-I-O-N-I-S-N-O-L-O-N-G-E-R-S-A-F-E-L-E-N-A-W-I-L-L-B-E-B-A-C-K-W-E-W-I-L-L-G-O-A-H-E-A-D-O-F-Y-O-U-A-N-D-M-A-K-E-S-U-R-E-T-H-E-W-A-Y-I-S-C-L-E-A-R."

After much frantic decoding, Chenko wondered precisely how they would do that.

"W-E-H-A-V-E-B-E-E-N-P-R-A-C-T-I-S-I-N-G-F-O-R-D-E-C-A-D-E-S-A-N-D-B-E-S-I-D-E-S-W-E-H-A-V-E-H-E-L-P-N-O-W"

Help from who?

"Y-O-U-K-N-O-W."

"Alexei," said Stephen.

"B-I-N-G-O."

"So why is the station no longer safe?" asked Mrs. Kontos-Wu.

"W-E-A-R-E-G-O-I-N-G-T-O-D-E-S-T-R-O-Y-I-T."

"Why," she asked, "would you do that?"

"Y-O-U-T-A-U-G-H-T-U-S-Y-O-U-R-S-E-L-F-I-T-I-S-T-H-E-O-N-E-T-H-I-N-G-B-A-B-U-S-H-K-A-F-E-A-R-S."

"Destruction?"

"D-E-A-T-H."

THE HONEST THIEF
Честный вор

The dreaming war between the Soviet Union and the United States of America was hardly a war at all to hear Fyodor Kolyokov tell it.

"It was more," said Kolyokov through the lips of Heather, "a series of skirmishes. We had not our heart in it."

"That so?" said Leo Montassini. He turned back to the view. The two of them—or the three of them, depending on how you looked at it—were holed up at the top of the lighthouse in this fucked-up town. Montassini had managed to hold onto the rifle, and he was using it clock tower style to make sure that the zombies kept clear of the place. It was a pathetic defence—if this Babushka thing wanted to take them out, she had more zombies than Montassini had bullets. But Montassini didn't feel inclined to follow that line of logic very far. He was in a tower with a rifle, next to a very hot babe who was possessed by an old dead Russian hotel owner who'd finally cheered up enough to start telling him stories about the Cold War, and the zombies weren't trying to kill him just yet. All of that was fine by Leo Montassini.

"We were unmotivated you see," said Fyodor Kolyokov. "Why fight at all? Cowardice, for a dream-walker, is a natural state. We live in tanks—in safe cocoons, protected by human puppets. The war required us to actually dream-walk out of body—and attend to other dream-walkers, who had powers the like of which we did not know."

"Fascinatin'," said Leo. Kolyokov had been avoiding the subject for hours now. Leo was fine with that. He peered through the glass at the harbour. Another fishing boat was heading out. "When did it happen, this brain war?"

"The early 1970s," said Kolyokov, then adding—in a voice that, unlike Kolyokov's, was all-American, "mid-1970s. Please. He's making this up, you know."

Leo grinned. "Hey dollface," he said.

"Hey fuckface," said Heather sweetly, "did you really just say dollface?" She stepped over to crouch beside Montassini and peered out. "Another boat's leaving? What's that—five?"

"Six," said Montassini. "And I don't think they're going out fishing."

Heather nodded. She put her hand on Montassini's shoulder, stroking it. "Sorry I called you fuckface," she said. Leo smirked.

"Don' mention it," he said.

"Oh get a room the two of you," Fyodor Kolyokov interjected, and pulled Heather's hand away from Montassini's shoulder. "We don't have time for that."

"Well you know, Mr. Kolyokov," said Leo, "I don't see much else to do here." Kolyokov gave Heather's head a brisk nod and crossed her arms.

"The town is beginning to clear out," he said with a wistful tone. Then, after a pause that seemed forever:

"We should think about going after Alexei again."

"We should wait until Vasili Borovich wakes up," said Heather quickly, and Kolyokov said, "shut up. Vasili's escaped. We have to get Alexei. And of course—" he paused "—the Children."

"Ah," said Leo. "Maybe we should just stay put here, big guy."

"I'm not sure the Children want to be got," said Heather and Kolyokov said, "you are not sure of anything," and then he said he was sorry and Heather said it was all right she understood.

Leo sighed, and turned back to the glass, watching the harbour.

Kolyokov would get them killed if he had his way. They'd barely made it here alive after the first rescue attempt, and it had been a bad time.

There were extenuating circumstances, he supposed: Leo was still groggy from the slap on the head he'd taken from Vasili Borovich's meat-puppet Oleg, and they didn't have enough guns, and they also didn't expect the old bastard and Alexei fucking Kilodovich to turn on them like that—in the middle of a fucking greenhouse. It was a miracle they hadn't all been shot dead.

Of course, it might have gone better if Leo had gotten some help from the babe that seemed to contain two people inside her. They'd crept up through the greenhouse that night, and things had been going pretty well. The babe had gotten herself a little auto pistol from somewhere. Leo had his rifle. Things were good.

And then, when they saw the first guard—and Leo had been about to shoot—fuck if the babe hadn't told him to put it down.

"It is Vasili," she said in that Russian accent of hers.

The guard was not a guard at all. He was an old man—pony-tailed, with a thick beard, and blood caked on the side of his head. He staggered out from behind a row of tomatoes—where from the looks of things he'd been crying.

He looked first at Leo, then at the girl blankly.

She grinned at him.

"Vasili Borovich," she said. "You are old as me."

"Wh—?" The older man frowned, and recognition dawned on him. "You? That cannot be."

The girl laughed. "It is Fyodor," she said. "Yes."

"You are part of this?"

She shook her head. "Lena has cut you loose again—hasn't she? You are pathetic."

"Go to hell."

"I am on my way there."

"My God," said Vasili Borovich. "It is you." He stepped forward—too close to the babe. "You are dream-walking young girls now, hey?"

"It is an agreement we have reached. Unlike what you are doing."

"I am not doing any of this. I am no longer the Koldun here."

Leo interrupted them. "Hey," he said. "Koldun! I heard about—"

They'd looked at him. "Put down the gun," said the babe. "This is unexpected. Give me a moment." Then she turned to Borovich and continued the conversation in Russian.

Leo had a moment to sit back and digest the situation. The Koldun! This old bastard was the Koldun—the guy who was supposedly behind the entire Babushka conspiracy—the old bitch's right-hand man.

And now he was talking in Russian to the woman who was apparently possessed by the ghost of the guy Leo Montassini had, a lifetime ago, been sent to retrieve.

Leo had been around the block a few times—and in the course of circling that block, he'd been in more than one situation where things were closing in on him. If he didn't have a knack for recognizing those points in his life, he wouldn't be alive. So Leo Montassini raised up his rifle, stepped back, and cleared his throat.

"Tell me what the fuck's goin' on," he said, "or I shoot both of you an' get my friend Alexei on my own."

The two stopped talking. They looked at one another. They looked at Leo, and his rifle.

"This one might do it," said the babe—or Fyodor Kolyokov.

"Da," said the Koldun. "He just might."

"All right," said Kolyokov in his weird squeaky girl voice, "don't shoot us. Here's the situation. Vasili here has just crawled out of the room where the Children are being kept. Alexei Kilodovich is in there. So is Holden Gibson."

"Who?"

"Holden Gibson." Now the babe's voice was her own—it sounded American, maybe from the Midwest. "You know—big bastard. Runs the boat? You know—the boat?"

"I'm sorry," said Leo. "I thought we were lookin' for kids."

"Fuck," she said. "Didn't Alexei tell you anything?"

"Heather," said Kolyokov through the girl's mouth, "let me handle this," and she said, "Fuck off," and he said, "Please," and she said, "Fine."

"The Children," said Kolyokov, "and Alexei are to the west end of the greenhouse in a sealed-in room. When Vasili escaped, he saw Alexei knock Holden Gibson unconscious and take away his gun. Vasili made it out the door."

"And he hung around here," said Leo. "Right. And no one came to get him."

"They are not pursuing," said the Koldun. "They are all traumatized—from the great wickedness that I nearly perpetrated upon them."

"Heh?" Leo frowned. "Great wickedness? Wha—"

"Not important," said Kolyokov. "The main thing is we must see them now before it becomes worse."

It had become worse anyway. With Vasili Borovich leading them on, they trod down the central path of the greenhouse and to the thick wooden door that led to the dormitories where the Children were being kept. By the time they were there, Leo was wondering at the difficulty they'd had getting this far—and how it would be if the Babushka actually had set her townspeople upon them.

"Right behind here," whispered the Koldun.

And he'd opened the door—

—and Leo Montassini felt like he'd been kicked in the mouth. His sinuses ached, and his back molars felt like they were going to fly out—and the rifle dropped from his hands, as he was faced with the light, and the words, ringing through his skull:

GET OUT!

The rest of it was the kind of blurry fabrication that recollection becomes when it focuses on a dismal, embarrassing failure. There was a kick, and gunfire, and the stink of an asp that missed Leo's skull and hit his shoulder (this one he focused on—dodging the zombified Alexei Kilodovich's swing may have been Leo Montassini's finest instant in the disastrous melee). Somehow he'd gotten out along with Kolyokov—probably, he was sure, because they'd wanted him to get out. And the three of them had made their way up the hill to the lighthouse.

Kolyokov hadn't spoken through Heather for about ten hours after that. It was left to Heather to explain to him what had happened—what the attack in fact was.

"It's like an ice cream headache," she said. "Vladimir pulled it on us on the boat the first time. It makes you feel like your ears are bleeding, doesn't it?"

"Ice cream headache. Nice." It felt more like a needle in the eye to Leo's way of thinking. "Who's Vladimir anyway?"

Heather frowned. "He's a kid. Like a baby. But he's not a baby at all."

"I think he was runnin' Alexei for a while there."

"He was."

"Like the same way that Fyodor Kolyokov is running you."

She looked at him. "Fyodor Kolyokov," she said, "is not running me."

Leo shrugged. "Okay."

"He's not. We've got an agreement."

"If you say so."

"Like," said Heather, "we take turns. He's not running me right now."

"That's true. Why is that?"

"He's—" she frowned. "He's taking a break."

Leo nodded to Vasili Borovich. They'd tied him to a chair at the tower's base, but it was really a formality. He was hurt and fucked up and not going anywhere. "Taking a break like him?"

"Look," said Heather, jabbing her thumb in Vasili Borovich's direction. "I don't know about him, but Fyodor Kolyokov's been through a lot." She leaned close to Leo. "He's dead you know."

"That's gotta suck."

"And that's not the worst of it."

Leo nodded—encouraging her to talk.

"There's something with Vladimir," she said. "Kolyokov tried to talk to him. And that's when things went to hell. The kid doesn't trust him."

"Why's it important that the kid trust him?"

"Well," said Heather, "this is going to sound weird."

"We're way past weird."

"I get the sense that Kolyokov just wants to make amends."

"You get that sense?"

"Stop making fun of me."

"No. I'm serious. You get that sense? All I know is I step in there and my brain's torn six ways to Sunday," said Leo.

Heather laughed. "What the fuck does that mean—'six ways to Sunday'?"

"Fuck if I know."

And they'd sat there, watching Borovich and waiting for Kolyokov to come back to them. It was cold—so what the fuck—Heather sidled up next to Leo, who put his arm around her. She rested her head on his shoulder and they stared out the aerie.

Borovich looked up at them. "Contact," he said. "That is important, is it not?"

Leo felt himself bristling. "Nothin' goin' on here."

"You like our lighthouse?" he asked.

"It's nice," said Leo. "Don' know what the fuck it's doin' here. No ships come by here do they?"

"It was here when we came," said Borovich. "When Babushka came here. She'd had it built in the early days. Canadian government money."

"Why?"

"Because," he said, "she could."

"Like the Emissary Hotel," said Leo, nodding. "A hotel nobody knows about—a lighthouse nobody can see. What is that—some fuckin' Zen Buddhism thing? Like if a tree falls in a forest and nobody hears it is there, like, a sound? Or are you just fuckin' stupid?"

Vasili laughed. "You've been thinking of things—haven't you?"

Heather stirred against him. "Don't listen to him," she whispered in his ear, in the familiarly dense Russian accent of the old Hotelier. "Fuck," said Leo, and pushed her away, as Kolyokov continued through her: "He is an old fool."

"At least I am not dead like Fyodor Kolyokov apparently is. I am an old fool who still breathes with his own lungs."

"No," said Kolyokov, "those are not your lungs. You gave them up to that witch Lena, hey? Idiot. Now look where you are."

"The foolishness of youth." Vasili wriggled in his bonds. They'd tied him to a wooden chair with a couple of lengths of rope they'd found lying next to it. "You should let me up, Fyodor."

"Not yet." Heather got up. It was amazing how she moved differently depending on who was in the driver's seat. When it was her, she was lithe and fast like she knew what she had. With Kolyokov, she walked—shuffled really—like an old man. She shuffled over to Vasili Borovich. "Tell me now. You tried to kill Alexei Kilodovich, is that not so?"

Borovich blanched. "How can you know this?"

Kolyokov chuckled. "I have been watching. In this very room—you sent our friend John Kaye to murder Alexei, didn't you?"

"No."

"Not directly. But you had him send that puppet James. Is that not so?"

"Alexei Kilodovich," said Vasili, "is the most dangerous thing we made. Babushka has been searching for it—from mind to mind. She asks: *Where is Kilodovich*. Can you blame me for wishing his death?"

"You play both sides," said Kolyokov. "A double agent. Is that what I am to believe?"

"Believe what you want."

"Okay. I believe you are a snake who will do whatever suits you. I leave you tied."

"Wait!" He looked to Leo then. "You! Untie me! Tell him!"

Leo sat up. "You tried to kill Alexei?" He went over to Vasili. He leaned over him. Alexei was, after all, Leo Montassini's soulmate. Or something. "You motherfuck," he said and clocked him. Vasili Borovich went out like a light.

Leo went back and sat beside Heather. He looked at her and she looked at him. Finally, he said: "Is, uh, Heather in there?"

Heather's eyes blinked. "She is watching television," said Kolyokov through her.

"Right." Leo crossed his arms and looked out the window. "Television."

"She is a dear child," said Kolyokov.

"She's a grown woman."

"Inside," said Kolyokov, "she's a child."

"You tryin' to warn me off?"

"It would do no good."

"Fuckin' right."

Kolyokov snorted through Heather's nostrils. He sidled up close to Leo, who shuddered but didn't move away.

"Did I ever tell you," said Kolyokov, "of the time we went to war against the Americans?"

The Imperial Navy of New Pokrovskoye stretched in a line south from the Empire's main port. The Navy was expecting attack. It had been warned of this through its network of spies—that there would be a lethal strike against New Pokrovskoye and that it would come from the water.

From an old enemy who dwelt in a fabulous city at the bottom of the ocean.

It could come at any time. That was the word from the Admiralty. So the Navy prepared itself.

Fishing boats that had dragged nets behind them to feed the Imperial leadership these many years were mounted with harpoons and guns. Crew were given rifles and submachine guns from a cache in the back of the museum. They lined the edges, peering down—on a silent vigil, watching for the attack from beneath.

Miles Shute, who had once captained the guard of a great, black tower—a hotel in Manhattan—and was now a midshipman on the *Aleksandr Shabalin*—a forty-three-foot tuna boat—ran his hand over the stubble of hair on his scalp. The rest of the crew here were doing exactly as they were told—just watching down, watching for the thing from below. That was, he understood, how they were raised—how they were made to work.

Miles took a different view toward his servitude.

He had experience watching for attack—it was trained in him as surely as was his life in New Pokrovskoye, his fealty to the Babushka, when he guarded the

Tower in the South in a different life—a different land.

He had hated his old master there—Fyodor Kolyokov, the devil in brine. But he had taught him some things, particularly when it came to standing guard. Anybody could watch for attacks from the front. Miles should be aware of the side, the rear, above. All directions. Leave the obvious weaknesses for others. You—look in unexpected places.

So Miles did. He looked up, at the grey morning sky, with a threat of rain. He looked to the north, where they were coming from—sighting on the diminishing nub of the lighthouse that guided ships to port in New Pokrovskoye. From there? No.

He walked across the pitching deck of the *Aleksandr Shabalin*, pushing past two of the older hands. One of them—Makar—bore a bandage across his scalp, from a fight last night that he would not speak of in any detail. He stood with Orlovsky, the old man whose daughter had died last night. Both stared to the east, sparing him the barest gaze for not doing likewise.

Miles turned his attention to the west—to the rocky, barren shoreline of this land. They were maybe a half-mile out from a tiny isthmus that pushed into the sea, and it looked deserted, like the virgin country it must have been before the settlers who founded New Pokrovskoye came here, and turned a village into an empire.

It was barren. But as he listened, he could hear echoing from the rocks and the water the hum of a motor. It did not sound like the sort of motor Imperial New Pokrovskoye employed in its navy.

Miles tapped another man he didn't know well on the shoulder and pointed. That one shrugged him off, so Miles moved along—first one, then another, each ignoring Miles as the motor grew louder. Finally he stopped and looked again—for the craft had rounded the rock and he could see it for what it was: a fast-moving little cabin cruiser. At least, someone had built it to look like a cabin cruiser. It was maybe thirty-five feet—but judging from the speed it moved at, it came with a powerful engine. And that wasn't the only modification. On its fore deck, where normally one might find a dinghy, there was something else.

It was a deck-mounted machinegun. It looked to Miles like an M2HB. Fifty calibre. A brown tarpaulin flapped around its base in the wind. Miles snatched a pair of binoculars from a mate standing near him. The man swore, but Miles didn't care. He focussed them on the boat.

"Oh shit," he said to no one—because no one was listening.

The gun was manned.

And it was swivelling in their direction.

Великий
THE GRAND INQUISITOR
инквизитор

"Kill them all."

"Amar," said Gepetto Bucci, "I'm not sure you want to get into this here."

Amar Shadak stood on the bridge. Bucci was beside him. Two of Bucci's guys from St. John's were working the gun. And for now, Bucci was handling the wheel.

"If we don't," said Shadak, "then they'll turn on us. Look at them."

"Fuck." Bucci squinted. "They're fuckin' fishing. We should fuckin' cover up the gun. I got half a mind to turn this boat around on you, Amar."

"You are already in," said Shadak, "for kidnapping. For torture. Arms smuggling. Racketee—"

"I'm in for a lot of shit," agreed Bucci. "But my question is: how much more? This shit is all very interesting—weird fuckin' hotels and ghost towns and shit. But at the end of the day, Amar, you and me are businessmen."

"You owe me," said Shadak.

"We are past even on this thing."

"I will kill your family," said Shadak.

"Promises promises." Bucci sighed. "Gimme the binoculars."

He held them up to his eyes and scanned across the flotilla of boats. Shadak counted eighteen of them. He knew from talking with the prisoners down below that there would be more than that on their way. The prisoners hadn't been much help at first. In addition to Bill and Marie, there were eight others. When they left Cloridorme the previous day, at first it seemed as though they hadn't a clue. But as they rounded the coast of Labrador, and drew nearer to New Pokrovskoye, they became more cogent—uttering their little threats. By the afternoon, Shadak had executed two of them, when it became clear that they were possessed by Babushka. *Amar Shadak*, one would say, *you have no hope. The world will soon be mine and you will be trapped forever in your metaphor and there will be shit you can do.* And Shadak would put his fingers over the sleeper's mouth and pinch the nose, and give Babushka a taste of death. After that, he'd have the sleepers to himself—locked in with their delusions and their understanding based on those delusions as to what lay ahead.

The fleet was something that they kept bringing up.

This, Shadak understood, was the fleet.

Bucci whistled. "Okay," he said, "I'm convinced."

"Did you see—"

"—guns," said Bucci. "Nothin' bigger than an assault rifle. But those fucks aren't fishing. They're looking for something."

Bucci stepped around the wheel, tapped on the glass. The gun crew looked up at him, and Bucci gave the thumbs-up.

Reflexes are a funny thing. Genetics have a lot to do with them, as does early conditioning. But far more important is experience: reinforcement by recent encounters. Miles Shute drew on that experience as the machinegun opened fire on the fleet. He dove for the deck shouting—"Attack! To starboard!" and winced at the sound of limp bodies falling to the deck. There was a cry of pain that first he thought he heard, then knew that he felt. And for a moment, he could sense the agony of Babushka as she lost parts of herself. Then, confusion. It was all Miles could do to avoid running to the edge of the vessel and pitching himself into the ocean.

And for an instant, the barest of instants, Miles Shute was himself: the security chief of the Emissary Hotel, stuck on the deck of a boat while bullets tore at the gunwales and men and women screamed and gurgled away their lifeblood.

And for a moment again he thought:

What the fuck am I doing here on this boat? Who am I fighting for?

Even as another voice that seemed to echo off the back of his skull wailed:

Hurts!

It brought back a memory: of two, three years back, when Miles had found himself in a quarry up in Maine—finishing some work for Kolyokov. He hadn't completely been himself, of course—his Master was with him, in the back of his head.

Miles was taking care of a situation: a private investigator who seemed to have a bit too much resistance to the Master's ministrations—who kept asking questions—who in short wasn't going to go away, until he found out what his client's husband had been doing with a tenth of his income all these years. Miles had taken him out here to shoot him and be done with it. Fyodor Kolyokov had been along to make sure. But when they got out of the car and Miles was getting the crowbar, the detective had pulled his ace: a piece of piano wire taped on the inside of his belt. He contorted around the handcuffs so his hands were in front, pulled the piano wire out, wrapped it around Miles' neck, and damn near killed him.

Fyodor Kolyokov had bolted. He screamed in shock and unexpected pain—and for a moment, Miles was all alone with his executioner. Miles struggled and squirmed, but the detective had the upper hand. Miles blacked out.

But here was the thing. He didn't die. He came to in what must have been a very short time; standing over the detective's body, wiping his hands on an old rag. Fyodor Kolyokov lurked at the back of his mind, returned and rejuvenated, already giving orders for the cleaners to come and dispose of the evidence.

Miles crawled across the deck to the starboard gunwale and propped himself up. He raised his own gun—an MP5 that he'd brought with him in his duffel bag—and waited for Babushka.

He waited longer than he'd have liked, alone in his skull. It was long enough to wonder at how just days ago, he'd come to this place hoping for kinship and liberation—with poor old Richard, who'd been so grateful for his freedom that he couldn't stop weeping. When he'd come here, there had been no Empire of New Pokrovskoye—no Babushka. It had been a community—it had been something to live for. It had—

Better, said a voice in the back of his mind. And Miles stopped thinking of those things. Something squeezed the trigger for him as he emptied his clip along the alien coastline.

Bucci ordered his guys to take a wide berth around the fleet of fishing boats, to keep out of range of their smaller arms—but it was easier said than done. The boats were spreading out now, creating a great net across the water, a line they'd have to cross.

"We won't get around 'em," he said to Shadak, who was bent low behind the wheel. "We're goin' to take some bullets."

On the foredeck, the gun went silent for a second as Devisi reloaded. A bullet careered off aluminum nearby. Shadak swore under his breath.

"We have to get around them," he said. "But we won't take bullets."

Bucci looked at him. "What?"

"Keep your distance and keep them covered," said Shadak. "I am going below."

Keeping down, he ducked into the hatch and the converted cabin below. This was no luxury yacht, so things were tight. There were two men with guns there, guarding the half-dozen hostages that they'd brought with them. Along one wall crouched the old man Bill and Marie, along with the California girl (who was named Andrea). Along the other wall sat the older Californian (Martin Lancaster, according to his driver's license) and the surfer (who was actually a cop with the Los Angeles Police Department, name of Michael Baker), along with the quartermaster of Cloridorme. They were each handcuffed to steel hoops that had been welded into the bulkhead for precisely this purpose.

"Good afternoon," said Shadak. The prisoners looked at him fearfully. He rolled his shoulders and took a breath and smiled his good host smile. "I hope that you are fucking comfortable you pieces of shit," he said in carefully modulated tones.

The quartermaster glared at him through swollen eyelids. "Fuck yourself," he said. "Babushka will come for you soon."

Shadak smiled. "Is that so? Well," he said, "I look forward to meeting Babushka. Is she here among you?"

The prisoners were silent. If Shadak didn't know better, he would say none of them had the faintest clue what he was talking about. Above them, the M2HB began to chatter again.

"Come now," he said. "It is obvious that Babushka has been here for some time." A bullet made a star in one of the cabin's little portholes. Shadak gestured to it. "She is certainly in the region."

"You," said Andrea.

"Me?" said Shadak. "No. I am my own creature today I think. But I will assume that Babushka is in one of you. So here is my bargain. Let me pass, and I will not execute each of you to see where she may rest."

He didn't know if Babushka was in any of them—but he could tell that his threat had had the desired effect. They all regarded him nervously.

"Are," said the cop.

Another bullet whanged off the bulkhead. They were getting closer. Shadak spared a glance out the shattered porthole. The boats were much closer than they should have been—they appeared to be trying to close—suicidally. Shadak wondered if the Babushka might not be trying to call his bluff. There was another sound on the hull—not the sound of a bullet striking precisely, but a hollow impact. It sounded like a pok.

"In," said Martin Lancaster.

"In?" Shadak felt his smile leak away. And for an instant, he felt himself back in the Black Villa—his true self, crouching as a tall, black-robed thing came towards him. Something lashed out of its middle.

"The way," said the quartermaster.

"Oh fuck you," said Shadak, "take me to Alexei Kilodovich. Or I'll fucking kill you."

"Easy," said Martin Lancaster, "enough," said the cop, "to arrange," said Andrea.

And with that, the boat pitched to one side, and Shadak tumbled. He glanced up just in time to see a thing that looked like a pinkish-grey length of intestine flash by the porthole, as a sharp stink of ammonia reached his nostrils.

And then Shadak was gone from there—back on a cold stone plaza—in the place where his true self had been locked and imprisoned for two decades. Ominous clouds scudded across the sky overhead. Things moved in the shadow of the Villa's overhang. Black branches from a dead fig tree rustled in the wind. And in the middle, by the well, the black devil Kilodovich stood over him—a thick length of tentacle whipping from its midsection.

Miles Shute had moved to the top of the wheelhouse of the fishing boat *Aleksandr Shabalin* to get a better shot. He couldn't be sure, however, that instinct didn't have something to do with it as well. Because consciously, Miles had no idea what was going on until the attack had nearly played itself out.

At first there were fifteen men who'd spread across the deck of *The Aleksandr Shabalin*. It took five of them to run the boat, and the other ten were eyes and firepower—nine of whom had been spending the day staring down into the water before the little cruiser had opened fire on them.

Three of those went down under fire—which was not surprising but still distressing. Miles hadn't been here long, but he felt as though he'd made a bond with almost everyone he'd met—they'd all been violated by psychic puppet masters, after all. Even if he couldn't place their names, watching three of them go down was queasy-making.

The other twelve were worse.

The first one disappeared while Miles was making his way to the iron rungs of the ladder that had been pounded into the front of the wheelhouse. There was some shouting, but he didn't pay it much heed until he got to the top, and noticed two others turned away from the gunboat, scratching their heads and peering into the churning water off the portside. Miles yelled at them to pay attention then turned back to the launch, aimed the MP5, and let off a short and ineffectual burst. Two 50-calibre-sized furrows in the wood in front of Miles splintered open.

By the time Miles had summoned the nerve to put his head back up, another three were gone. He saw one of them in the water to starboard, splashing and screaming for help before a slick thing wrapped up around his throat and pulled him under.

Miles sniffed. The fishing boat smelled of diesel fuel and fish gut—but the air was suddenly sharp, with the stink of ammonia. He frowned, and squinted across the water at the cabin cruiser. The machinegun had stopped, and as he noticed, the boat itself was listing in the water, toward the rocky coast. Its motor whined. Miles held up the binoculars. He could see the water frothing at the seaward side. The only two men he could see were manning the gun. They were turning it away from the fleet now, and toward the frothing water.

Something whipped out of the water then, and lashed across the chest of one of the men.

"Shit," said Miles. He lowered the binoculars, caught in that moment of wonder between perception and understanding. He was near to convincing himself that he in fact hadn't seen what he'd just seen, when he looked down to the side of the boat, and watched as a torso-thick tentacle flopped onto the deck and whirled itself around old Orlovsky's ankles. Miles followed the tentacle over the edge of the gunwale—and in the dimness of the twilight, saw the thing it was attached to. The thing had a torpedo-shaped body that gleamed in the dim light where it broke the water. A single, giant eye gleamed up at him with terrible, alien intelligence.

"A giant fucking squid," said Miles, and, "Wow," and without another thought he emptied the MP5 into the thing. The water frothed and a wave of ammonia nearly choked him, and Miles had another thought.

He was pulling the trigger. Him.

Babushka had left the building.

THE IDIOT
Идиот

Kilodovich swept his robes aside—lifted the tentacle away from little Amar Shadak, and knelt on thin, clicking knees. The thick swath of hair still obscured his face, but Shadak could see the faintest outline of cheekbone—two rows of teeth—and a distant blue flicker of corneal reflection. Was it a skull under there? A bare death's-head skull, come to torment him? Frighten him like some superstitious schoolboy?

Fuck it. Amar Shadak rolled his shoulders and forced his mouth into the barest of smiles. He took a breath. Balled his child's hands into fists and stepped back.

"Kilodovich, you fucking bastard," he said. "You cannot frighten me away with these tricks. I am almost upon you now."

The robes rustled, and a voice like a desert wind wafted from behind the folds of the hood:

"*I am sorry,*" said the black thing.

"You are sorry," said Shadak. "Fantastic. We'll see how sorry you are when I stick a nail up your urethra and fill your eyes with acid."

The black thing didn't answer. Shadak stepped away from him. "Why the fuck are you even here?"

"I cannot stay long," said the Devil. "It is a busy time for me now."

Shadak laughed. "Busy? Well it is good of you to stop by! Welcome to this hell you have made for me!"

"I am sorry. I have done terrible things to many people in my lifetime. And I am very sorry."

Shadak crossed his arms and glared at Kilodovich. "You betrayed me," he said.

"I am sorry."

"You destroyed my love, Ming Lei."

"I will apologize to her for that too."

"You locked what was good in me," said Shadak, "away in this place."

"I know," said the Devil. "Although it is not that simple."

"What do you mean?"

"'What is good.' That is not what I did."

"Oh."

"When we put a sleeper into metaphor, we lock away not the good—but their will."

"That makes no sense—"

"—because," said Kilodovich, "you have lived your life wilfully—or so you think."

Shadak stepped forward. "I will kill you and everyone you love!" he shouted. "Restore me!"

"You are," said Kilodovich, "restored already. That is why I am sorry. When I put you here, I was—inept."

"Wh—"

"I would say that I was but a tool, and it was the ineptitude of my masters. But that is not true either. No, I fouled it for you."

"Then fix it!"

"The problem," said the Devil, "was that I did not properly fix you in this place. You straddled the worlds. Your will was in one place, your anima in another, each infecting the other with only cruel and incomplete hints. It meant that you could not be controlled as others were—but that you could never be wholly yourself. You exercised part of your instruction—you made a great arsenal for us, in the caves in northern Turkey. But past that—the only way anyone could control you was the old-fashioned way: through seduction and coercion. Past that, you became a true psychopath and made your way in the world thus. This is something that would not, I think, have been possible had we not intervened."

"I am," said Shadak, "almost upon you. You cannot save yourself with talk. You cannot survive. I will have my revenge—and at the moment of your death, you shall so beg for release that you will restore me."

"I am sorry," said Kilodovich. "No."

"What—why?"

"You will not leave this place," he said.

Shadak thought back—to the tentacle spreading across the window. To the machinegun fire. The boat pitching.

"You are correct," said the Devil. "You will not arrive at New Pokrovskoye. That is why I must apologize now. I hope that bringing you here will at least spare you the suffering."

"Suffering?"

"Of death."

"I am dying?"

"Most likely," said the Devil. "I am as I said, sorry. It is a war. We must make way for the main invasion force. And you, Amar Shadak, are in the way of that. We have all agreed."

"You—you fucking—" Shadak felt his cheeks redden. He felt tears well in his eyes—as his pitiful, sundered life spread before him. The Devil tried to comfort him with a tentacle on his shoulder, but he swatted it away.

"Hey! Alexei!"

The Devil looked up at the sound of the voice—and Shadak did too.

They were not alone in the courtyard. At some point, three other figures—also in robes, although not as dark as the Devil Kilodovich's—had arrived. They were rocking back and forth on invisible feet—impatient, like they had to pee.

"Enough of this," said one. "Leave him."

"I feel responsible."

"You are responsible—but that's not the point," said another.

"We are getting our tuchases whipped," said the third.

"They got guns! And they're shooting at us!"

"What did you expect?" said Kilodovich. "You have spent too much time in the sea, Comrades. You have forgotten what a real fight is."

He turned back to Shadak then. "You should not concern yourself with these things," he said. "Listen—I can restore you. But not in your body."

"Wha—"

And with that, Alexei's tentacle came out and pierced through Amar Shadak's chest. The world flowed back into him, and he grew, and became a man.

"My gift," said Alexei. "And again—my apologies."

Shadak stood alone in the Black Villa.

Or not precisely alone, perhaps. He stared at the place where the creature had been—felt his heart beating in his chest, felt the air in his lungs. He went over to the well, took a wooden bucket that was beside it and lowered it on a thin, hemp-like rope. After lowering it just a dozen feet, there was a hollow-sounding splash. He pulled up the bucket—credibly heavier now. He lifted it to his face, and sniffed at the dark liquid inside, sloshed it around.

In the distance, he could hear another sound water makes—splashing, flowing. Deep in his bones, he felt a twisting. Was he dying? Shadak looked around himself. Was this the gift that Alexei Kilodovich had offered him—to insulate him entirely from death? To remove him, therefore, from play?

"Fuck this," said Shadak. He tossed the bucket back into the well. It bounced credibly against the well's stone walls. "Fuck you, Kilodovich," he said to the scudding grey sky. "I choose death!"

And as he spoke it, the sky seemed to draw apart, like a badly woven cloth, and something like rain fell from it, hitting Shadak's upturned face like ice.

"Fuck you!" he shouted. And the water became a torrent—coming from above and beside him, as the hull of the Filipino cabin cruiser ruptured against a sharp rock. Shadak spun in the water, and kicked against someone, and for a perverse moment laughed as the water filled the cabin. He kicked and he dove and a moment later he came up again, under the dark sky of the Atlantic. Something slipped past his ankle, but missed as a wave lifted him, and carried him on its silvery crest, toward the jagged rocks of the Labrador shore.

Miles Shute fought as best he could—and that was better than most of his less-experienced comrades—but in the end, he too wound up in the water, gripped in the tentacles of a giant squid. He'd emptied his MP5 into the side of one of them, then managed to lay hold of a boat-hook and whack away at another one that had managed to get one of its whiplashing tentacles up top of the wheelhouse. He probably could have held out there indefinitely, if one of his shipmates hadn't tried to climb up to join him. Miles didn't have anything against the kid—far from it, he was one of the few who Miles had gotten to know by name since joining the Imperial Navy: Arkady something-or-other. The kid was a grad student from Boston—not one of Richard's MIT students for once, but a microbiologist from Boston University. Arkady was a bright, fit young man with a thick beard and as far as Miles was concerned a good attitude. He was pissed as anyone to find out he'd been duped into spying for the old Soviet Union, but he said he was going to use this whole thing as an opportunity to expand his horizons.

So when three rungs up, a tentacle whipped around the kid's ankle and started tugging him back, Miles felt obliged to help out. He got on his belly, took hold of Arkady's arms, told him to calm down, and tugged. Over Arkady's struggling shoulders, he could see the huge beast half out of the water itself, wrapping its shorter arms around the still-extended net poles, giving off the wafting stink of bleach. If Arkady weren't screaming, he probably could have explained what that smell was all about. Miles figured he'd ask him when he got him up.

Which is why he was so pissed when Arkady's hands slipped from his, and he tumbled down the ladder and landed with a wet smack on the deck. Before he had thought it through, Miles was down after him.

Which was, Miles realized an instant later as he fell into the water with two tentacles wrapped tight around his middle, a big mistake. He flailed and kicked and tried to pull the thing off from around him—and if it had just been a big rubber thing, he might have been able to. But another question he might have asked little Arkady was about the suckers, which actually seemed to have teeth. He screamed as they cut through his shirt and his trousers and began to bore into his flesh. He skidded across the wet decking—caught up briefly at the gunwale—and fell into the briny ocean along with Arkady, and the rest of his comrades.

The squid pulled him under, into a flurry of darkness. It took all of Miles' will to keep his breath—not simply draw in the ocean and drown. He didn't know why he ought to do that. But as he sank, and death came closer, he felt something leave him.

Goodbye, my child, it said.

And at that moment, Miles felt like he might as well draw water, for it was clear to him: Babushka had left him to die.

As that realization hit him, the tentacles let him go.

And so it was that Miles Shute flew to the ocean's surface, and when he broke it, he gasped air and screamed—in pain and terror and sheer, awful loneliness.

The moon was full over New Pokrovskoye and it painted it silver. From the houses and docks and fields of the town, a great noise arose. "Something is happening," said Leo Montassini.

"No shit," said Heather, and Kolyokov said, with inscrutable satisfaction, "Yesss."

"Can it be?" said Vasili Borovich. "Is she gone?"

Montassini frowned. "Is that—screamin'?"

He pressed his ear to the glass. Well, fuck, he thought. It was screaming. Like everybody was waking up from a bad nightmare, all at once. It broke into a cadence of sobs and shouts. Lights went off and on again in windows. The world was going mad.

"Well," said Kolyokov, "it looks as though our Babushka has faltered," and Heather said, "she's gone?"

"Too soon to tell," said Borovich.

"Now is the time to go back," said Kolyokov. "To find Kilodovich, and finish this thing."

"I don't think you're gonna have to do that," said Montassini, staring out the window.

Heather and Kolyokov joined him, while Borovich struggled and craned to try and get a look. Montassini pointed—to a lone figure: a thick-shouldered, black-haired zombie of a man, carrying a swaddled infant in his arms, coming up the path to the lighthouse.

"Alexei," said Kolyokov, and Heather said, "He doesn't look so good."

Маленький THE LITTLE HERO герой

The Cold War was long finished and the West had new enemies to worry about but still—moving a Russian-built, gangster-crewed submarine up the eastern coast of America and into Canadian territories on nothing but battery power and a wavering sense of communal purpose was not an easy thing. It was, supposed Stephen, a miracle they were moving at all.

The submarine's crew was used to working under the instruction of the dream-walkers. But since they'd departed, Zhanna had rigidly enforced what she termed "cranial silence." So the crew had to find its own motivation.

Motivation was hard to come by when most of those crew were dirt poor, uneducated Romanian thugs who'd been given a taste of Paradise.

Stephen learned early on to stay out of the former monks' way. Where before they ignored Stephen's presence when they went about their duties, they now stalked the submarine in a kind of sullen rage—much of it seeming to be directed at Stephen himself. They met his eye with alpha-male challenges; made sure to elbow him when they passed in the hall; talked in harsh, angry whispers, glancing up with murder in their eyes.

Stephen couldn't blame them—after all, he'd done serious injury to at least two of them over the past few days. He could likewise understand Konstantine Uzimeri's hostility toward him; the two of them had never got along, things were coming to an ugly head in the world of dream-walking messiahs, and Uzimeri was a religious whack-job anyway.

Chenko and Pitovovich, though, he couldn't figure. To them, Stephen Haber had become invisible. They talked in fast bursts of Russian whenever he came into the room, and if he were so craven as to sit down beside them with a plate of food—they would without a word stand up and leave. That pissed him off—only slightly less than the fact that Mrs. Kontos-Wu seemed to be siding with them more than with him.

The Morlocks were more welcoming—they were pathetically welcoming in fact. They'd taken up in the submarine's torpedo room. And visiting them was like visiting aging relatives in cut-rate nursing homes. Stephen had spent less than an hour perched on the port tube while a half-dozen of the ancient creatures had sat on and around the starboard tube, gaping and grinning inarticulately at him.

He'd finally found a place where he could spend time among the children, who spent the days hopping back and forth between staterooms in their section of the submarine. They were at least decent toward him—although Stephen couldn't help but feel that the kindness was partly due to guilt—they had, after all, erroneously tortured him if only by proxy—and partly for the practice. The Children, Zhanna included, together had the all the subtle conversational skills of Appalachian-born Star Trek fans.

"You fuck fellows?" said Petra, a greasy-haired former psychic girl who seemed to be about eleven, as they sat together in the converted map room sipping tea ten hours into their voyage.

"No," said Stephen, "I've got AIDS and I don't fuck—*fool around* with anybody. We've been through this."

"Zhanna likes you," said Petra, pressing onward bravely, and Zhanna, briefly the only one in the room more mortified than Stephen, pushed herself further back into the corner. "She has no hope, right?"

"I think Zhanna's got other things on her mind right now," said Stephen. Petra stuck her finger up her nose, and Stephen reached over and put his hand on her arm. "Don't do that," he said.

"Yes," said Zhanna, "it is gross," and she turned to Dmitri—a fat-assed fourteen year old with acne and wide, goggly eyes. "Stop staring," she said, and he looked away, horrified. Zhanna gave Stephen a pained look. He decided to risk sending another mixed signal and patted her on the hand. Zhanna at least was learning how to deal with people and took it for what it was. She smirked and gestured around her.

"And you wanted to be a psychic," she said. "Having second thoughts now?"

Stephen shook his head and chuckled. "You guys aren't really much worse than the New Jersey Spring Psychic Fair."

"That is bullshit."

"Hey. I'm trying to be nice."

"Yes you are." Zhanna reached over to the little electric samovar and refilled her tea. "You want some?" she asked Stephen.

"Sure."

Petra got up and excused herself to visit the head.

"Sound of that tea makes me want to piss awful," she hollered as she slammed the door.

"I got to shit when you're done in there!" yelled Dmitri with characteristic grace.

They had been drinking a lot of tea since taking off. It was important for the children at least to remain awake for the duration of the trip. Falling asleep would mean the possibility of dream-walking. While it was strictly speaking possible for a Child to sleep and not dream-walk, the temptation was really too great.

And maintaining absolute silence was crucial. That had been the plan—to keep the submarine off-line, and running deep—and distract Babushka and her minions at New Pokrovskoye with the squid attacks that would appear to the dream-walking Babushka as nothing so much as certain and horrific death. Stephen had wanted to go on those. During the briefing before they left, he'd tried again and again to enlist. But Zhanna had made the point that even Stephen's crude, rudimentary squid-enhanced and oddly anomalous dream-walking wasn't safe. The whole point of the exercise, she said, was to keep off the Babushka's radar.

Of course, an equally acute problem was keeping off of real radar—and sonar. And satellites. As long as they stayed mid-Atlantic it was fine—but the final approach to New Pokrovskoye was going to be a bastard. The Canadian Navy patrolled those waters—mostly looking for poachers who were fishing the cod beds. But the submarine would raise questions.

Toward that end, they had enlisted some help—in the form of a school of shrimp that followed in the submarine's wake. And occasionally, they were visited by one of the Mystics in the form of a squid—who would give them Morse Code messages. The first few were, things like "B-U-C-K-U-P-I-N-T-H-E-R-E-D-O-N-O-T-G-O-T-O-S-L-E-E-P" and "W-E-A-R-E-W-A-T-C-H-I-N-G-Y-O-U-R-B-A-C-K." The first one of any note happened about five hours in with: "W-E-L-L-T-H-E-R-E-I-T-G-O-E-S" and "P-E-T-R-O-S-K-A-S-T-A-T-I-O-N-I-S-G-O-N-E."

The last message, which had come just an hour ago, was more encouraging. They'd sat silently, listening to the *pok-pok*-ing on the submarine's hull, while Pitovovich, who'd been working on the key while Chenko slept, took it down.

Finally, she read over the scratchy P.A. system:

"The way to New Pokrovskoye is clear. We think that we have driven Babushka off. Your reunion is imminent. Kilodovich has done his work. Victory is ours."

An hour after that, the toilet in the officers' mess flushed, water clanking its way through the pipes of the old 641, and little Petra stepped out, adjusting her track pants. Dmitri hurried in.

"Are we there yet?" said Petra as she returned to her seat.

"Soon," said Zhanna. "Soon."

THE IDIOT
ИДИОТ

Alexei Kilodovich's body was in awful shape. The back hurt and there was a blinding headache, and it had new injuries all over from what Alexei assumed were particularly vicious fights it had fought on someone else's behalf. The worst of these was his left shoulder. It felt like it was on fire and when he checked it with his good hand he found a thick bandage there. When he poked it, he wanted to scream.

Someone had shot him.

Great.

"I told you to come back, Kilodovich," said Vladimir. "But I guess you had other things to do."

Alexei opened his eyes. He was standing in a low, wide room that he'd never seen before. It was a bunk room, obviously, and the Children such as he remembered them were all here. Vladimir sat in a makeshift crib. Alexei glared at him.

"What did you do to me?" he said.

Do you want another apology, Kilodovich? said Vladimir. *I had hoped to engage your help in rescuing us. But events have taken a turn.*

"Yes," said Alexei. "They have."

As he scanned the room, it became apparent that Alexei's body wasn't the only piece of furniture to take some damage. Bullets had torn ruts in the wood panelling—a couple of lights were dark—there were dark stains on the carpeting here that Alexei assumed was someone's blood . There had at one point been glass doors on the bunk beds. There still were some, but many of them had been smashed, and now the glass was in neat little piles in the corners of the room.

And as Alexei looked over the damage, he saw that he was also not alone as the sole adult in this room.

Holden Gibson was in one of the bunks—one with glass on it—lashed to the mattress with thin cord. He was staring at the top bunk, his mouth working around his rage.

"Gibson is here," said Alexei. "How did that—"

He came here to murder us, said Vladimir. Now he is under the thrall of the Babushka.

"Hah." Alexei strolled over to the bunk and tapped on the glass. "Hello Holden."

Gibson turned to the glass. His face pulled into a rictus of anger.

"I'm in fuckin' communication with the Babushka right now, Russkie. And let me tell you—you're fucked."

Alexei shrugged. "I am fucked maybe." He turned to Vladimir. "Has there been a doctor to see me?"

No. You applied that dressing yourself.

"*You* applied it, you mean."

Yes. Using your hands, however.

"You think you got her beat—but let me tell you from experience. There's no beatin' Babushka. She'll have the whole fuckin' world in the Empire of New Pokrovskoye."

"Is that so? Is she talking to you now?"

"She's been talkin' to me off and on since before you were born," said Gibson. "You can't stop her."

"We did, though."

"Fuck you. You didn't come close. You made her retreat—twice. But you didn't come fuckin' close." Gibson struggled against the bonds, his eyes rolling to look at the Children. The bunk bed rattled under his struggles, but it held. "You're all fucked."

Alexei shook his head. "I was thinking about killing you, you know that?"

Gibson's eyes narrowed. "Yeah. That's what the Koldun told me."

"Which was why you tried to kill me. I guess I cannot blame you for that. It still pissed me off though."

Gibson's lips went thin and petulant. "So kill me now," he said. "Fuck you. I'll just ascend like Babushka." He gave Alexei a look. "And from what she told me, you could ascend too."

Alexei looked around. "Me," he said, "these kids."

"Right."

"To be—what? Fuel for the Babushka's great machine? Amplifiers, so that when she wants to take on more sleepers—or dream-walk—she can do so, without the inconvenience of using her own aging body?"

Gibson was quiet at that.

Alexei felt a welling inside himself—like he wanted to throw up. He thought back to Afghanistan, and the thing he had done to Amar Shadak and Ming Lei and Wali Beg and all the rest—for no better reason than to serve the ambitions of some degenerate dream-walkers who wanted to build an arsenal for themselves, and needed the people to do it.

"You," said Alexei, "are an evil bastard. I feel no guilt for what I am about to do."

"Go ahead," said Gibson. "Like I said—I'll—"

"Ascend?" Alexei let himself smile. "No. You won't. There will be no more of that for you."

"What—" Gibson's eyes narrowed. "What do you mean?"

"I am the destroyer," said Alexei.

He shut his eyes and took a breath.

Holden Gibson started to twist in his bonds. He looked at a space in the air just above Alexei's navel. "Hey!" he said. "Fuck! Do up your fuckin' fly!"

Alexei, eyes still closed, smiled. "That's not what it is," he said.

Gibson screamed. "Babushka!" he yelled. "Deliver me!" and "Fuck! It's got me!"

There was a rustling then—a rustling of the soul. And then he went quiet—sobbing softly. Several of the Children joined him. Alexei withdrew the tentacle from Holden Gibson's middle and opened his eyes.

The only sound in the room was the soft clapping of an infant's hands.

"Why Kilodovich," said Vladimir. "I am impressed. Clearly you have—"

"—unravelled the lie that is my life," said Alexei, knees cracking as he stepped away from Holden Gibson, suddenly alone in his head once more. "I know. Now come—we have work to do."

Alexei bent down and lifted Vladimir from his crib. Vladimir looked at Alexei with wide eyes and held up his little hands as if to fend off a blow. *No*! he shrieked with his mind while he wailed with his little mouth. *Do not undo me! I am not ready!*

Alexei smiled. "No," he said. "You are not."

And with that, he hefted Vladimir against his chest and carried him out of the greenhouse.

"You must show me the others," said Alexei.

The others. What do you mean, Kilodovich?

"You must show me this Koldun who ordered my death so easily."

THE HONEST THIEF
Честный вор

Leo Montassini met Alexei at the main door to the lighthouse. He was holding a rifle, but not like he was seriously going to shoot. Fuck—it was Kilodovich! "How the fuck you doin'?" he demanded.

Alexei looked at him sidelong. "The guy," he said, "from the tank?"

Montassini grinned. "You're back!" he said.

"Yeah," said Alexei. He stepped inside with the rest of them. Heather stepped into the shadow of the door, just out of sight.

That is a good instinct, whispered Kolyokov. *Kilodovich is on a rampage*.

"A—" Heather swallowed, and thought the question: *A rampage? He's got a baby in his arms and looks like he's just about dead.*

No, said Kolyokov. *He's doing what he was made to do. But I don't know that anyone is telling him. This is very dangerous.*

Heather moved back further into the shadow. She wasn't about to question Kolyokov's assessment any more. After all, the last few times that the baby Vladimir and Alexei had hooked up, things hadn't exactly gone swimmingly for Heather or the rest of Holden Gibson's crew.

Alexei and Montassini were talking quietly as they walked into the round room at the base of the tower. The baby Vladimir was peering around with wide, nervous eyes. They passed near them.

So what should we do to ge—

Your mantra, said Kolyokov. *Now*!

Mi, thought Heather at once. *Mi mi mi mi.*

Alexei Kilodovich started up the stairs first, while Montassini continued: "He's upstairs. We got the fucker tied up like nothin' else. You aren't gonna fuckin'—"

And that was all Heather heard. Pushed by Fyodor Kolyokov's hurried urgency, she stepped out the door and into the New Pokrovskoye night.

Маленький THE LITTLE HERO герой

Amar Shadak's antique submarine broke surface two kilometres off from New Pokrovskoye amid a school of kraken and moon-silvered froth. A trio of Romanians emerged on deck immediately, carrying with them the components of a Zodiac. Two more came out with a machinegun, which they set about assembling on the foredeck. Konstantine Uzimeri remained atop the tower, surveying the horizon with light-enhancing binoculars. Stephen took his own binoculars, and focussed them on the coastline, and the faint glow that rose beyond the jagged rocks.

"You should not go ashore," said Uzimeri. "You are too weak."

"Fuck you, Konstantine." Stephen squinted. Aside from the light, the coast looked utterly barren. He played with the focus—for a moment, he thought he could actually see a structure—a tower, maybe a lighthouse—but then it faded. And the light faded too. "Don't talk to me about weak. I'm not the one who fell for Babushka's line."

"You never had the chance," said Konstantine. "You are too weak."

Stephen didn't bother answering. Instead, he slung the Skorpion machine pistol under his arm and swung himself out onto the ladder. The water was calm, but it was still dizzying making his way down the four-metre conning tower. He shivered. If it was possible, the submarine from outside seemed even narrower, less substantial than it was on the inside. It was slippery and narrow on top—every step to the boat's prow was like a step along a tightrope. Finally, Stephen set down on the wet decking, crossed his legs, and squinted at the coastline. He left his binoculars around his neck.

It was like seeing Central Park from the Emissary Hotel, looking at New Pokrovskoye. Stephen began to imagine his way through the rock, through the illusion. He slowed his breathing—tried some of the techniques he'd learned in Jersey. And after a while, sure enough—the glow came back. He could even make out the shape of the tower.

And then, bit by bit, more things became visible: smoke coming from some buildings—great stone ramparts going down to the sea. The masts of tall ships. Flickering oil-flames further out, on top of buoys. A glorious hot-air balloon, tethered to the topmost tower of a fantastical palace that looked like it was out of a fairy story.

And a voice, a deep basso, calling out for someone called Natascha.

Stephen shook his head.

Fuck it, he thought. What the hell did a bunch of fortune tellers in New Jersey know about dream-walking anyway?

"Hey!"

Stephen looked over his shoulder. Mrs. Kontos-Wu was maybe a dozen feet behind him. She had changed into the same getup as had Uzimeri: a black sweater, black jeans and high laced boots. Stephen nodded at her.

"You shouldn't be out here alone," she said. "Easiest thing in the world, to slip off the side and fall into the ocean."

"Okay." Stephen spun on his ass so he was facing her. "Now I'm not alone."

"We got another set of messages," she said, "from the Mystics."

"Which is?"

"We're not as done as we thought we were," she said. "Babushka's still a threat. Soon, Alexei will confront her. Hopefully, he is strong enough. And there is something else . . ."

THE IDIOT
ИДИОТ

Alexei Kilodovich and Vladimir climbed to the top of the aerie and faced the Koldun, Vasili Borovich. He was tied to a chair, and in rough shape. He regarded Alexei levelly.

"Name the smells," said Alexei.

"What?"

"That is what you said to me, just days past," said Alexei. "'Name the smells.' As if by doing so I would be welcomed to this magnificent community that you have built here in Canada. It made me very sentimental and trusting to you. And then you fucking set me up for a killing."

"I had no idea," said Borovich, "who you were."

"That," said Alexei, "is bullshit. You knew me well enough to kill me."

Borovich struggled in his bonds. "Only enough to know that Lena—the Babushka—wanted you alive. That she had a special purpose for you."

"Bullshit," said Alexei.

It is true, said Vladimir. *Babushka asked and asked about you. We did not tell her anything.*

"Borovich tried to kill you too," said Alexei.

"The Children?" Borovich looked back and forth between the two of them—and to Montassini, who was standing behind Kilodovich like a mob enforcer. "Yes—again, only because the Babushka wanted them so."

"This does not cause me to feel better," said Alexei.

"You don't know what the Babushka can do when she has everything she wants."

Alexei shook his head. "Take the world over—live in the backs of the brains of everyone on this planet. Change the names of things to suit her tastes, and live forever."

Borovich glared at him.

"And you," said Alexei, "would have stood for it—if she had loved you properly. Yes?"

"Oh God," said the Koldun.

Alexei felt himself grow before him. His head was scraping the ceiling of this aerie. Robes flowed from him like liquid. And the thing in his belly stirred and reached across the space to Borovich. Vladimir started to snuffle and tear up at the sight of the thing.

"I think," said Alexei, "you shall be unravelled."

"What the fuck is goin' on here?" said Montassini. "You okay, Alex?"

"Oh God," said Borovich.

And Alexei said, "No. The lie."

In 1976, Borovich awoke in Toronto. He had connived an assignment here—and it was a poor one. He worked the University of Toronto—pulling students here and there into a suite of rooms he kept in an old house in Parkdale, near the lake, seeing if he could manage the slow technique of remaking them for City 512. He could not, of course, on his own—the techniques were too difficult in those days for one to do alone. But it was rumoured that Lena, who had been there two decades earlier, had perfected a technique. She was gone, but Borovich had convinced certain others that he might continue the work. So he occupied his flat and whiled away the days.

"You did nothing here, did you?" said Alexei.

Borovich squinted at him. Alexei was sitting on a rattan chair at the back of Borovich's house. Behind him, the skeletal phallus of the half-finished CN Tower rose up. Borovich looked at his hands—still smooth, long fingers with nails bitten to the quick.

"You were desperate," said Alexei, "to find Babushka."

"That was not her name," said Borovich, "then."

"Yes," said Alexei. "You are so disgusted with her—with your choice of her. Because you are such an honourable man."

And Borovich's eyes fluttered shut—as a great black thing pierced his middle—and he remembered finding her; finding, in addition to all those university students, the names on a list of sleepers that Lena had made, and hunting them. Getting angrier and angrier as one after another turned out to have quit their jobs and left their families and abandoned their lives, to disappear from the world. He dreamed and scoured the world looking for their signatures—seeking them out.

Finally, one night in the midst of a July heat wave, he found one. His name was Jack King. He was staying in the Royal York Hotel, just having arrived by train, with nothing but a suitcase containing a change of clothing, a small automatic pistol and a little packet of subway tokens. He was on his way to Parkdale—to murder an upstart who was getting too close.

Borovich had smiled to himself—made a note of his room number, and gotten one of the few sleepers he managed to control: Alice, her name was, an undergraduate political science student at U of T. She was small-boned and slender but for a tiny potbelly and thick, dark brows that accentuated her eyes. He sent her over to the hotel; made her knock on his room door; and when he answered, step inside and say: "Do not be hasty, Lena. I bring this gift."

Lena accepted it graciously—he had not been with her long, but he'd been with her long enough to know her tastes. At the end of the night, her sleeper had said: "All right, Vasili. You may join us. But you must bring gifts."

It was two and a half years before Vasili could assemble gifts rich enough for Lena's tastes. He raided the Hermitage, the treasure vaults of the Kremlin, riding sleepers at the highest level of the party. Where necessary—

"You murdered," said Alexei. "You murdered people who had nothing to do with this. It is fascinating."

"How can—how can you be here?" said Borovich, manipulating a KGB Colonel named Vlochma to wrap his lips around a gun barrel.

Alexei sat beside him, crouched in the younger man's mind.

"Was it worth it?"

Vasili looked at him, tears in his eyes. "Of course not," he said. "What are you doing? How can you be here?"

Alexei was about to answer when another voice came up around them in a great, angry cloud.

"It is obvious, my love," said Babushka. "He is the Destroyer."

Heather stopped at the top of the wooden stairway that led down the cliff, to the main town of New Pokrovskoye. "*Mi mi mi mi mi,*" she said aloud. "*Mi!*"

"All right!" said Kolyokov. "Enough with your mantra! You can stop now."

"Is it safe?"

"Maybe," said Kolyokov. "Who knows? But I need to think and that Goddamn mantra is making it impossible."

"Sorry." Heather sat down on the edge of the stairs and looked out over the village. There were some lights on—and she could see shadows moving in front of those lights—but the town had an eerie quiet to it.

She took a deep breath, and felt an odd squirming in her middle. Was that Fyodor Kolyokov? Like some twisted foetus, making itself at home in her uterus? It felt creepy, but also kind of good. She was getting used to sharing her body with the old zombie. At least with Kolyokov, you knew where you stood. Holden Gibson had done the same thing with her, with the rest of them, on a whim.

Fyodor Kolyokov had enough respect for her to pay for his time.

And really, Heather had to admit that there was something oddly liberating being dream-walked by an old creature like Fyodor Kolyokov. As she sat there thinking, her hands worked in her lap—fingers counting. She heard muttered Russian coming from her lips. It faltered here and there—like a grandparent. Kolyokov was getting on—she didn't know how long he'd be with her.

Her hands fell into her lap then, and she felt her head turning toward the lighthouse.

She blinked at the sight of it: the top surrounded by sparking blue electricity—its very tip connecting with a whirling, silent funnel cloud that drew down from the otherwise clear night sky. Then he turned her head to the port—where now could be heard the high-pitched hum of an outboard motor. A boat was coming in to the harbour.

"Start singing your mantra again," said Kolyokov. "We must go meet that boat."

Alexei Kilodovich and Vasili Borovich stood on the remains of a cracked riverbed. Mountains rimmed the horizon, but the land that led to them was flat and dry and monotonous. The sky was more interesting. It was filled with a great bruise of a cloud; a cloud that bled and pulsated and burned with a terrible fever. It had a kind of face to it—an alien face, that expressed unguessable emotions. Vasili tried to shrink away from it, but Alexei would have none of that. He stared up into it, unapologetically.

"You," said the face, "have been ill-used."

"Do not blame yourself," said Alexei.

"I do not apologize," said the cloud. "It is a statement of fact. I had wondered, when we first met, just what it was you are. And you know—with the potential that you carried, you might have lived a much better time on this earth."

"Like your Vasili?"

The cloud rumbled. "Vasili? Is he here?"

Alexei gestured to his feet, where Vasili Borovich lay huddled.

"Ah," said the cloud. "The traitor. He is of no consequence. He is barely here—thanks to you."

Sure enough, Borovich seemed to be fading from this place. Alexei could see the ground through his insubstantial flesh.

"Of course," said the cloud, "if you wanted to, you could return him here."

"I see no need."

"That is your ability, yes? To make—and break—sleepers. At will. What a thing you are, Kilodovich."

"You are Babushka," said Alexei.

"Had you any doubt?"

"Not truly," he said. "I wished to confirm it. For we had defeated you."

The cloud rumbled. "You tricked me. You drove me out of sleepers by placing them all in such peril. Now we are not in sleepers."

"It does not matter," said Alexei. "For I am—"

Alexei took a breath. He reminded himself: he was not a KGB agent who worked for Wolfe-Jordan and had failed to protect Mrs. Kontos-Wu from gangsters. He was not a low-level sleeper who had failed to perform even rudimentary remote viewing exercises.

"I am the Destroyer."

So without more thought, he set his attention to the world that Babushka had created: the sick, indulgent conception of the Empire of New Pokrovskoye.

"Is that the best that you can do?" demanded Babushka. She had taken on the personification of a beautiful young woman—pale, alabaster skin underneath a dark crimson hood. "It is, I take it, designed to inspire fear of rape, yes? Or perhaps to erase your own sense of inadequacy. Did you play Dungeons and Dragons in college?"

Alexei looked down at his robes—at the twitching tentacle that came out of his middle. He could see what she meant.

"I suppose," he said. "In truth I have not given it much thought."

"Well," said Babushka, "how effective you must think it to be then. It must strike fear into all the metaphorical children that you undo."

"Just as I suppose that little whore you dress yourself up as inspires lust in all the metaphorical boys and girls you seduce, hmm?"

Babushka's metaphor pulled her cloak around her chest. They were standing in a town square underneath golden onion-domed churches. Her lips turned up in a slight smile.

"Perhaps you invoke death, you think—with that cliché of a robe, with those little glowing eyes and the hint of a pecked-clean skull."

"I don't think I made this up myself," said Alexei. "I was trained by wicked men after all. But tell me—was there ever a time you looked like—" he gestured with a bony hand up and down Babushka's slim body "—that?"

Babushka laughed. "I like my metaphor," she said. "It pleases me to no end."

Alexei looked around. "Yes," he said. "You do a great deal to please yourself. This whole place—very nice. The Empire of New Pokrovskoye?"

"It is," she said, "an ancient empire. Ruled by a benevolent Tsarina."

"Ah." Alexei gestured to her. "Yourself." Babushka nodded. "It is very—magical. Tell me—how long has the Tsarina ruled?"

"Ten thousand years," said Babushka with obvious pride.

"And still—she is as beautiful as the day she took the throne. How does she do this?"

Babushka waggled her fingers. "Magic," she said.

"Oh," said Alexei, in a condescending tone. "Magic. Wonderful. Does she have a little wand?"

"No," said Babushka. "It is innate."

"I see." Alexei looked around. " It sounds like a fantasy novel. Or a fairy tale."

"It is," said Babushka, "very real as you can see."

"No," said Alexei and he squinted. "It's not. It is a little girl's fantasy. The sort of fantasy concocted by a little girl born into poverty under Stalin's rule—a girl who had watched her family die and who had rarely known the taste of proper food—who was snatched from her village one day by wicked men and raised in a cave underneath the mountains to dream. Such things are not real for they exclude the grit and dirt of reality. It is all fine pastries and great halls. The poor, if they are seen at all, are rustic and grateful—all craftsmen who make fine leather or lovely dresses. Criminals are mainly dashing young rogues who only steal for the love of their Tsarina. The ones who are wicked—well. They are easily defeated. It is a great lie of a life. Is it not?"

As Alexei spoke, the towers around them began to fade and crumble. The golden light that pervaded this place began to fade, and was replaced by a relentless grey—and then darkness. Alexei could see nothing.

He let the tentacle extend. "You see," he said, "how ridiculous your fantasy is."

Somewhere behind him, he heard a deep chuckling then. "Oh," said Babushka—her voice now an old woman's, "Kilodovich. How you have miscalculated. The metaphor," she continued, "has not been for my own benefit for many years. It is for my children. You don't need to convince me that it's a stupid lie."

And with that, the darkness turned into a night sky. A night sky of perfectly paired stars—a million eyes, maybe more, looking out on vistas that were not fantastical at all: highways and offices and houses, and television screens. "See," said Babushka. "These are just the beginning. Now that you are here."

And to his peril, Alexei looked—and fell into the soft discourse that Babushka had crafted.

Leo Montassini was always pretty fast, and it was a good thing, because if he was any slower the baby could have taken a serious tumble down the stairs of the lighthouse when Alexei's arms went limp and he fell to the floor.

He dropped the rifle, which by a miracle did not go off, and managed to catch the baby under his arms before he'd even touched the floor. The baby didn't cry, which was good because Montassini was no good with crying babies, as his cousin Tina was fast to point out—but the kid sure looked worried.

"I don't blame you," said Leo, jostling him up and down. "Should never have gone to that fuckin' hotel—'scuse my language."

The baby looked at him, frowning. Leo could feel a faint ache at the back of his jaw. He went over to check on Alexei. The guy had a pulse—Leo could feel it at his neck. But he wouldn't move or respond.

"It is too late," said the Koldun from his chair. "She has him. And now—now she can convert the rest of the world."

"Convert," said Montassini. "To what?"

"To one mind," said the Koldun.

And at that, Leo Montassini felt a tickling at the back of his skull—and a scent in his nostrils that made him think of New York, and the strange concoction inside Fyodor Kolyokov's tank.

"Whoa," he said, as much to himself as anyone else, "the sea."

The Empire of New Pokrovskoye reassembled itself as quickly as it had collapsed. It spread like a stain across thin fabric—remaking the lands of Labrador into a great rich agricultural land, the breadbasket—turning New York and Washington into the Dark Provinces; redrawing the maps, stronger than ever. For now the Babushka flew with Alexei Kilodovich. And every set of eyes he peered through now saw others, and turned them instantly. The Empire spread like an oil slick through the world from its birthplace in the north.

Stephen looked at the girl, as the sky swirled and bent overhead. Zhanna hung behind him, eyeing her with suspicion. Mrs. Kontos-Wu didn't lower her gun, but she seemed slightly less suspicious.

The girl had greeted them at the main pier when the Zodiac came up to it. She wore her hair in faux-Rasta beads and looked only a little older than Stephen. She shouted "Hello" in Russian, and called Stephen by name. Stephen thought about that—thought about the squid that now hung still and waiting beneath the water of the harbour—and ventured a guess.

"Fyodor Kolyokov?" he said.

"That is correct," she said in a voice that aside from its pitch sounded remarkably like Kolyokov's. She squinted, regarding the assortment of Romanian thugs still in the Zodiac. "It is good to see you, Stephen. I take it that you did not manage to find Kilodovich."

"A lot has changed," said Stephen. "for one thing—"

"I died," said Kolyokov. "I know this now. You are no doubt surprised to be talking with me here."

Stephen shrugged.

"Not really," he said. "You're just like the Mystics."

"The Mystics?" The girl's eyebrows raised up. "You know about the Mystics. Things have changed."

"I also know," said Stephen, "what you did to me."

"And what was that?"

"You—you cut me off," said Stephen. "You buried what talent I had."

"That is what you think I did?"

"Yes."

"Are you looking for an apology?"

Stephen thought about that. "Yes," he said. "I am."

"All right," said Kolyokov. "I apologize. But not for that."

"For what then?"

"For this," he said, and then he said: "Manka. Vasilissa. Baba Yaga. One three four seven."

Beside him, Zhanna's eyes widened.

"The code," she said.

The blonde girl smiled. "Why else," said Kolyokov through her, "do you think you had such a difficult time reading him? I would not leave such a device in the open."

Stephen felt his eyes widen as a sliver of memory opened to him, and his sense of his life unspooled before him.

"You bastard," he said. "I'm a bomb!"

Stephen Haber, a bomb. He knew as he said it, that wasn't precisely correct. He was not, precisely, a bomb.

In addition to not precisely being a bomb, Stephen was not precisely a great many other things he thought he might be. He was not the natural child of Mr. And Mrs. Haber the sleeper agents. He had lived with them as their child, but he had another origin—another lineage. They were sleepers, true. But he slept more deeply than any of them.

Because he was that most dangerous of things: not a bomb, precisely—but for the purposes of Discourse, the great psychic computer that they all lived in, he was something worse.

He was a switch.

If the KGB'd found him, they'd have destroyed him.

Luckily for him, Fyodor Kolyokov had found him first.

He became for Kolyokov an insurance policy. If the other sleepers ever came too close—if they ever decided to attack Kolyokov, reveal him, or just send too many killers after him, he had one way out.

His switch.

As Stephen's timer counted down, he recalled so many other things. He recalled killing the attaché in New York with a small gun—but for no other reason than Kolyokov needed him out of the way. And he recalled the New Jersey Psychic Fair: the fortune that he'd gotten from Lorelei Jones herself.

"I'm getting a sense that you feel like people use you," she said.

"Amazing."

"I'm not getting a sense that you are angry about that though. More—"

"Yes?"

"More grateful. Gratitude? Does that make sense?"

Stephen wasn't sure that it did. But as he thought about it, he could see how it might. After all, Kolyokov kept him in comfortable living circumstances and didn't make any sex demands on him. As he thought about it—yeah. Sure.

Stephen nodded.

"I'm getting—a woman," said Lorelei. "A woman is using you."

Well no. That wasn't possible. But Stephen didn't say anything—just to see where she went.

"All right. Maybe not a woman. Women. You're a pretty young boy and women like you. But they use you."

Stephen shook his head. The boldest of rationalization couldn't carry that. "No women trouble," he said.

The psychic put her hand on her forehead. "Hmm. It's cloudy right now. Hard to see. Are you resisting? Because it doesn't work if you're resisting."

"I'm not resisting."

"Well I'm definitely getting exploitation," she said. "Maybe not a girl at all."

Getting warmer, thought Stephen.

"Maybe," said the psychic, "your father?"

Stephen felt his ass clench shut. He bunched his hands. He looked past her, over to the table behind her, where a little display of cassettes was propped. "How much are those tapes?"

Later, Stephen listened to the three tapes that outlined Lorelei Jones' Ten Steps to Psychic Oneness. They were comforting in their way. Lorelei had a way of talking that made everything seem all right—and her methodology had a certain dream logic to it that seemed to mirror Fyodor Kolyokov's methods. At least those few methods he would share with Stephen.

Still, a part of Stephen knew that those tapes were as creaky as Jones' ham-fisted attempts at psychic readings. They weren't going to teach him how to dream-walk—they weren't going to help him take control of the minds of the unwilling and bend them to his own will—they weren't going to give him access to the real powers that he knew lay just beyond his grasp.

But they hinted at them—they promised them. And Stephen found that promise, that idea of absolute power so compelling that he couldn't resist.

Then he thought about that power—its true exercise, in lies and deception and cruelty. Was that worth preserving in any way? When people like Babushka and Kolyokov and others exercised it with such evil in their hearts?

One of the clean things about running a giant squid was all that room. Squids had great big brains and high-bandwidth nervous systems. What they didn't have was a complex mind. There was no need to trick a squid into giving up the controls. No need to cajole the squid into lying to itself. It just welcomed you inside, let you along for the ride, and if you wanted to take the controls—there was no problem.

It was a compelling line of thinking—made no less so than by the fact that it might have been as falsely implanted as a scripted part of his end-game. Scene Twenty-Four: Stephen Haber convinces himself of the rightness of this course, just as the countdown reaches zero.

But ultimately, Stephen thought, the choice was his own to make. He wasn't a squid. If Fyodor Kolyokov or someone else had put a bomb inside him—the choice was his own.

"Maybe your father?"

The choice was his own.

Stephen Haber's consciousness, wound tight as a spring for his entire lifetime now, came loose. The light of it was blinding in the consensus metaphor of New Pokrovskoye. The Imperial Palace, built of stones that were quarried by hairy and belligerent dwarves from the provinces of Motavaria, dissolved into dust. The great ramparts surrounding the harbour saturated with the sea and slid and fell and returned to the muck. To the south, the Province of Cloridorme revolted, and when the occupying Imperial Army turned out to be nonexistent, returned to its status as a township in a remote part of Canada with a surfeit of abandoned automobiles. The millions of blinking eyes that saw the empire and moved on its behalf blinked, and fluttered, and extinguished. A million hands reached over to their tape decks and compact disc players and radio stations, and with a huge, simultaneous flick, even the heartfelt rumblings of Ivan Rebroff were ended.

Quiet fell on the land like new snow.

And in the quiet, a baby wailed.

"Shh," said Alexei. "Hush."

Vladimir only wailed more loudly as he flailed in the straps of the carriage, the thick madhouse padding of the little blue snowsuit he was in. It was night, and freezing cold—cold enough to make everything brittle. It seemed as though Vladimir's shrieking would be enough to shatter glass. Alexei rubbed his hands together, and noted ruefully how small they were. He peered across the icy plain in front of him: sure enough, not a quarter-kilometre distant were the low buildings of the Murmansk spy school that never was.

Alexei swore.

He was back. Back at the beginning—enmeshed in the vicious lie that had been his childhood. "This place doesn't exist," he said. "Right, Vladimir? All bullshit."

Vladimir bunched his fists together and turned his wail up a notch.

Alexei turned the carriage around to face him and knelt close to the kid. He met his eye. There was still an intelligence there—the kid knew who he was, there was a spark of that. But only a spark.

"He is spectacular—is he not, my old Comrade?"

Alexei started and turned. Behind him stood an old man in a bathrobe and slippers—his hands jammed into the pockets for warmth. Whips of hair fluttered in the light Barents Sea breeze.

"Kolyokov," said Alexei.

The old man nodded, and knelt down. He tucked a finger under Vladimir's chin. "There, there, little petrushka. Do not mourn. Do not cry. Shhh, shh . . ." He turned to Alexei. "Little Vladimir is losing his mind," he whispered. "He is losing all the connections with all the people he has met with—losing their memories, the computing power of their brains. Now—" Kolyokov patted Vladimir's head "—soon, he will just be a baby again. In a sense, he shall be free of them."

"Kolyokov." Alexei looked around for a rock—something heavy to bash the old bastard's brains in.

"Do not bother," said Kolyokov. "It would not make things any quicker than they are to be anyway."

"I do not want to make things quicker for you necessarily."

Vladimir was inconsolable, so Kolyokov sat back in the snow and looked at Alexei. He didn't say anything, but after a time, he started to smile.

"What?" said Alexei. "What?"

"I am just," said Kolyokov, "looking at you. Cannot a grandfather admire the children?"

Alexei shook his head, as his mouth half-opened to spit some angry rejoinder.

Christ! The old bastard had robbed Alexei of his childhood—of his life, his memory—had coerced him to do terrible things for no cause greater than the persistence of Kolyokov's great spiderweb. He had sold him out, in a deal with Amar Shadak! To purchase Vladimir and his siblings—like chattel, like slaves!

"Why?" said Alexei.

"*Why*." Kolyokov inflated his cheeks. "What a question. I don't know that I can say why—but I will tell you some reasons why not. Not because I wanted to live forever as a parasite in the hindbrain of the human race. Not because I wanted to turn Vladimir and yourself and everyone else into my slaves in some elaborate crime ring to con people out of their retirement money, or a group to aid sceptical secret agents in their quest to win the intelligence war with the United States. Why don't we go indoors?" he said, pushing himself to his feet. "It is Goddamn freezing here."

Alexei stood up too and followed Kolyokov, pushing the carriage over sheets of ice and little drifts of snow, while Northern Lights flickered like ghosts overhead. They came upon the school quickly. Kolyokov fumbled in his bathrobe for a key, opened the large sheet metal-covered door and led the way inside.

They stepped into a large gymnasium. Alexei smiled. He remembered how it was to play floor hockey there—feel the sting of the ball as it touched his fingertips on its way to the goal, the exhilaration of his cheering classmates. The floor was scuffed birch wood, with lines taped and lacquered onto it in red and blue and white. Long banks of fluorescent light hung on chains from a high ceiling. Their footsteps echoed as they crossed the room. Alexei inhaled the scent of sweat and socks. At least it was warmer.

"Was this," asked Kolyokov, "such a wicked lie? Truly?" He peered at Alexei, and Vladimir, and then nodded sadly. "I suppose that it was. And so the question remains. Why?"

Alexei and Vladimir looked at Kolyokov, waiting.

"It was a sick game that we played with you. With our children." Kolyokov smiled sadly. "I cannot blame you, Vladimir, for locking me in the room with that detestable Nazi—after the things that we did to you and the others. Those for whom you are truly an able advocate." Vladimir squirmed in his chair. "Why, then do I do this? Try to bring you here? Well—I had hoped not to die. Not just yet. I had hoped to bring you here—teach you about things that your training might not have prepared you for. Teach you how to make your way in the world of senses—before I passed into death. Make some amends. Is that very foolish?"

Alexei shook his head. "What do you want—a fucking hug?"

Vladimir coughed.

"Kolyokov," said Vladimir, in a clear, high voice, "you are a big bastard and you deserve to be eaten."

Kolyokov shook his head. "My child, do not waste your last words to curse a dying man."

"My last words? I do not think so."

"Ah but they are. You had a fine vision, boy—but unattainable. You cannot free the sleepers and the dream-walkers alike. They cannot in the end coexist. Babushka has shown you that."

"Babushka also deserved to be eaten," said Vladimir. "As she was."

Kolyokov shook his head sadly. "Ah, my beautiful boy," he said. "My greatest regret is that I will never be alive to see you, the day that your own mind grows to a portion of the many minds you occupy now. At least," he said, "you shall have your inheritance."

And with that, the ceiling rumbled, and cracked—and the exploding consciousness of Stephen Haber ripped through the metaphor of Alexei Kilodovich's childhood, and tore it to dust.

He was alone—for the first time in his life. Altogether alone.

He had vague recollections of another dream. A dream in which the world of his siblings and fore-parents was unshackled. Where all could pursue their dreams and their lives according to their wishes. That world was now upon them—and the baby wailed, as their dreams and wishes all receded from him.

But that was fine. For he understood as thought faded from his mind that this had been his purpose—that as much as he used these minds, he was their creation—a manifestation of their collective will. Now, that will dissipated. And Vladimir was left on his own. A mere baby.

The baby looked down at the floor. Two men lay on it—both staring with unseeing eyes ahead of them. They had been unshackled—the baby's face scrunched as understanding came to him and fled again, as the large mind he used dissolved—so badly unshackled that they might never return. The one he could not weep for. The other, Alexei Kilodovich . . .

That was someone worth mourning, from the baby's perspective.

"There there." A big smelly man picked him up and held him. "There. Let's go find your mama," he said. "I bet she's not far."

By the time they got to the bottom of the stairs, the kid had stopped crying. His mother, whom he no longer recognized by name, stood outside the building next to a skinny boy and a pretty blonde lady. He put out his arms and waggled his fingers. The man who carried him was being nice to him, but he still didn't like the way he smelled so he let his mother take him away.

First, she thought:

I die.

Kolyokov's pawn has killed me. Me! Snuffed out like a candle!

And thinking these thoughts, she despaired.

But she need not have. For what she was doing was not dying. She was drifting across and through the salinity of the world, like a sea-dense Medusa trailing her rage in poisonous tentacles beneath her in a way that reminded her of the early days—which she remembered more clearly now in the hyper-conductive medium as they called it at City 512, the place where dreamers would drown, where thought would spin away in the call of whale song, in plankton, shrimp—a rage that she dangled across the insensate few who could hear her pleas as she flew the cold night sky, a rage that motivated armies in her stead, a rage that finally drove her to isolation on the shores of the New World.

Why, she wondered, *do I not die*?

Green shafts of light passed through her as she spread and sighed in the sea, and for a moment, a kind of peace came over her. The peace that comes of warm bathwater, running through nostrils and filling the lungs, stilling a medicated sensorium. Rage was not all she had, in those days. For rage is not born of itself.

It is born of love.

Ah, she thought, *love*.

Memories drifted through her gossamer substance like drowned cruise ship passengers. Stupid Vasili; sanctimonious Fyodor; her children and grandchildren and great-grandchildren, on whom she doted, and who danced for her in death.

And so it was, holding these thoughts near to her—Babushka entered the brine of the sea, and insensate . . .

She began to spread.

Alexei Kilodovich looked up at the face: slim and tired and very sad. He blinked and frowned. "I am sorry," he said to her. "I failed you."

Her frown deepened. "Failed me?"

Alexei nodded and coughed. "I left you to the gangsters," he said. "On that boat. I was stupid. A child hit me on the head." He rubbed his chin, which was thick with a growth of beard. He felt cold and shaky—he had some new injuries. They were probably from being manhandled after they'd knocked him unconscious. "I thought you might be dead. You may have my resignation."

"You—" Mrs. Kontos-Wu sat back. Alexei pushed himself up. He was lying on a rough wooden floor in the middle of a round room, with windows everywhere. "You are resigning?" she said.

"You may have my resignation," he repeated, and then said, "Where did you get those clothes?"

"On the submarine," said Mrs. Kontos-Wu.

Alexei stared at her. "Submarine?"

"Sure," said Mrs. Kontos-Wu. "Don't you remember?"

"No," said Alexei. "I remember nothing."

Mrs. Kontos-Wu looked at him, peering close as though trying to see something he'd caught in his eye. Then she put her arms around his shoulders, and held him. Alexei thought he must have been very glad to see his employer healthy and alive after all. That was the only way he could explain the tears.

EPILOGUE

Эпилог

The beach was long and deep and covered with small, round rocks that dug like fork tines between a man's ribs. Amar Shadak bled onto those rocks from a hundred little cuts, and three or four fairly large ones as sunlight filtered down through an even blanket of cloud. Not that he minded—with the way things had gone the night before, he was amazed he was still alive.

In fact, he was amazed that so many people were still alive. The beach on this northern part of Labrador was crowded as a Baltic resort town in August.

Or the banks of the River Styx.

Shadak lay there, eyes on the sky. He drummed his torn fingers on his chest. He thought about his wounds and wondered idly if his first assumption might have been wrong. *Am I dead after all?* He wondered. *Is this only just an afterlife?*

It was a credible position. When he looked around, he saw all sorts of others move by who ought to have been dead: Gepetto Bucci, his shirt torn, his eyes wide, sat with his arms around his knees rocking back and forth, while his funnyboy Capo Jack Devisi crouched in the surf, letting the froth run around his ankles.

A short time later, the waitress Marie limped over to where Shadak lay and looked down at him. She gave him a kick in the ribs. "Fuck you," she said as he writhed. "I hope you die here." And she stalked off to join Bill and Andrea and the cop and Martin Lancaster, who huddled in a circle beneath a low shelf of rock. They were all in remarkably good shape for a collection of shipwrecked torture victims.

It was all about right for Shadak's afterlife theory—the torturer diminished, his victims restored. It was the sort of irony that God would appreciate.

God. Or the other one. The Devil Kilodovich.

Shadak shut his eyes and listened to the pounding of the surf. It was rhythmic—as rhythmic as the dripping in the Black Villa. Could this place be simply another prison, concocted for him by Kilodovich?

It was unlikely. Shadak had spent enough time with his soul asunder to know when he was all in one place. And right now, if nothing else, Amar Shadak was whole: there was no small piece of his conscience held hostage in some distant and imaginary place. If anything, the whole of him was. And that didn't seem likely.

Shadak felt another poke in his ribs. He opened his eyes, to look up at a face he didn't recognize—a small pug-face with slicked back hair. Looked to be in his forties somewhere.

"Fuck," said the man. "You ain't dead."

"That remains to be seen," said Shadak.

"No," he said sadly. "You ain't dead." The man leaned closer. He put one hand over Shadak's mouth. With his other hand he pinched Shadak's nostrils shut. "Look buddy—I'm sorry about this. But Mr. Bucci says that if I want to get back into his good books, I gotta do this thing."

Shadak felt his lungs burn. He hitched his back and widened his eyes and shook his head desperately—a move intended at once to dislodge the man's fingers and plead his case: *No you do not have to do this thing!* the gesture said. *Arrangements can be made!*

"You must have really pissed Mr. B. off somethin' good," he said. "More than me—which, owing that by my crappy judgement, I caused him to have to come to this place and wreck his boat an' fuck up his St. John's operation, is something."

Shadak frowned and looked up. "Leo Montassini?" he tried to say, but only managed "Mm-Mm MmmMmmMmmMmm?"

Leo Montassini didn't answer. Instead, he started to whistle—a tune that sounded vaguely Russian, like a folk song or an anthem. It reminded Shadak of a song that he'd heard as a kid, by some Russian folk singer. He couldn't remember its name for the life of him.

The main rescue party from New Pokrovskoye arrived by boat later in the afternoon. They'd been alerted by Leo Montassini, who'd found the castaways, he said, while taking a walk along the beach to clear his head. The fact that the walk had taken him twelve miles each way, half of it in the pre-dawn dark . . . well, that was just an indication of how badly in need of clearing his head in fact was.

They loaded the castaways onto one of New Pokrovskoye's few remaining vessels—a motor yacht that had an unusual amount of bunk space hidden away under the foredecks. It was still a tight fit for the thirty-nine survivors that they'd managed to collect—particularly as most of them were injured.

Fortunately, it was a short run up the coast to New Pokrovskoye. The trip was joined mainly in a kind of puzzled silence. The makeshift crew of the motor yacht was not prone to discussion in any case. And the castaways themselves were disoriented enough by the trauma of the previous night's attack—never mind the bizarre quality of their rescuers, which included hard-faced Romanians, children who shouldn't have been out of grade school yet, and odd, grey things who hunched and drooled and capered on the decks.

The boat slid into the protected haven of New Pokrovskoye's harbour just past four in the afternoon. It moved into the slip next to the submarine, where Konstantine Uzimeri was busy drawing up a duty roster and a course back to Turkey. Jean Kontos-Wu watched it from the window of the town's café. She sipped at her tea. It was jasmine, her favourite—which she hadn't expected to find at a distant outpost like this one. She turned back to her table mates. Stephen Haber was poking at the baby Vladimir sitting in Zhanna's lap next to him. Heather—the woman who'd obligingly carried Fyodor Kolyokov's soul the past few days—was still scribbling madly on a napkin.

"There," Heather finally said, and slid the napkin into the centre of the table, "that's all of them."

Mrs. Kontos-Wu turned the napkin around so that she could read them: a list of four ten-digit numbers, topped by the address and telephone number of a bank in Geneva.

"Is he saying anything else?" asked Mrs. Kontos-Wu.

"Well," said Heather, "he's pretty sorry."

"He has cause to be," said Zhanna, "the old bastard."

"Shh," said Heather. Her eyes fluttered closed. "He's dying."

"Dying." Mrs. Kontos-Wu shook her head. "How does that work?"

"We have a metaphor. A living room." Heather let her eyes flutter shut. "Fyodor Kolyokov is lying on the sofa in front of the television."

"What's he watching?"

"The television—doesn't exactly work any more."

Mrs. Kontos-Wu patted Heather's hand, as Heather said, "Oh."

"The old bastard is dead," said Zhanna. "Good."

"He wasn't so bad," said Heather.

Vladimir rolled his eyes in what was an innocuously adult expression of disbelief, and Zhanna snorted. "He was so bad. He tried to purchase us from Amar Shadak—with the life of poor Alexei Kilodovich—to turn us into mind-slaves to further build his wealth. Is that not so, Jean?"

Mrs. Kontos-Wu shrugged. That had been her understanding too.

Stephen reached across to the middle of the table and picked up a salt shaker. He idly sprinkled some on the red-and-white checked tablecloth and blew on it.

"Well," said Heather, her lips pulled tight, "at least he didn't want to take over the world."

"Do not be so sure," said Zhanna. "Who knows what he might have done had things not gone better for him?"

"Things went as they went," said Mrs. Kontos-Wu. "The important thing is that now we all have our wits—and," she tapped the napkin with a fingernail, "this."

The five of them looked at the napkin. If Heather was to be believed, those numbers allowed access to bank accounts containing on the order of a half billion U.S. dollars. It was, she claimed Kolyokov had told her, an inheritance.

Divide this evenly between the sleepers and dream-walkers, who have been so ill-used, he had told her. *This is truly theirs. I should never have taken it to begin with.*

Zhanna snorted. "Deathbed repentance."

"Maybe, maybe not," said Stephen, and all looked to him. Those three words were the most he had spoken since he had detonated the psyche bomb and wiped Discourse from their minds the previous night.

Zhanna put her hand on his arm. "Stephen?" she asked. "Are you well?"

Stephen looked at her and looked away, out the window. He squinted at a point on the rocks, across the harbour. There was a figure there. He got up, pushed his chair away, and stepped outside.

Mrs. Kontos-Wu, Heather and Zhanna followed as Stephen tromped down the narrow roadway to the docks. They followed him as he clomped across the wooden boards, back up some cement steps, and onto another dock that jutted just a few feet from the rocks where the old man danced.

"Hey," said Heather. "I know that guy."

"From where?" said Zhanna.

"From here," said Heather, and Mrs. Kontos-Wu blinked, recognition dawning on her.

"Here?"

Stephen smiled. He stepped closer onto the rocks, and put his hand out. "Richard," he said. "Well fuck me."

Richard spared Stephen a sidelong glance and a wink before returning to his reel. He danced and sang on the ridge, his arms raised up and fingers snapping over his head. His voice trembled, and occasionally he stumbled over the lyric, and he could not hold anything approaching a melody.

Mrs. Kontos-Wu found herself smiling as Stephen climbed onto the rocks to stand a little closer to Richard. *Discordance*, she thought, *has never sounded so good.*

ACKNOWLEDGEMENTS

Rasputin's Bastards was a long haul in the writing, and many people had a hand in encouraging and guiding it along. The members of the Cecil Street Irregulars writing workshop past and present helped me chart the course of the manuscript as it developed. In particular, Peter Watts helped me bring the deep sea to life around Petroska Station and all those squid. Karl Schroeder provided me with basic training for the writing of this kind of gonzo Cold War tale, with our collaboration on our first novel, *The Claus Effect*. He and the rest of the crew at the Cecil workshop helped me know when to ground the book, and when to let it take flight.

Sandra Kasturi, Brett Savory, Erik Mohr, Sam Beiko and the rest of the team at ChiZine Publications took that last task to the final stage. During the editing process, we took to calling the book Fat Bastard—it is, as I write this, the longest book that ChiZine has acquired. Taming the Fat Bastard was a task that took patience, elbow grease and no small amount of mutual faith. I think it's paid off. Erik Mohr's cover art is, as always, a work of art. And as we edited, the help, love and support of Madeline Ashby proved invaluable.

There was no small amount of research involved in putting *Rasputin's Bastards* together, but readers will not be rewarded tracing the location of City 512 or the Emissary Hotel or New Pokrovskoye. Need it be said that I made it all up?

The aesthetic of the novel and its characters is another matter. For that, the Russian side of my family proved foundational. My grandmother came to Canada with her sisters shortly after the Russian Revolution, and they formed an expat community in Canada founded on family, and a deep nostalgia for a magical pre-revolutionary Russia that may or may not have ever existed. It didn't really matter; that Russia lived on in revisionist memories and dreams of my grandmother, who I think took comfort from them as she engaged in the formidable task of surviving as a single mother with no formal education in 1930s Toronto. She was able to convey that nostalgia, through story and song and acrylic paintings that she made later in life, of wide fields of impossible green surrounding golden onion-domed churches lit by a brilliant, pre-Soviet sun. When I thought of the dream-walkers, or at least the mechanics of the dream-walkers' Metaphor, I thought of her.

ABOUT THE AUTHOR

David Nickle is a Toronto-based author and journalist whose fiction has appeared in magazines and anthologies like *Cemetery Dance, The Year's Best Fantasy and Horror*, the *Northern Frights* series and the *Queer Fear* series. Some of it has been collected in his book of stories, *Monstrous Affections*. His first solo novel, *Eutopia: A Novel of Terrible Optimism*, led the *National Post* to call him "a worthy heir to the mantle of Stephen King." He also works as a reporter, covering Toronto municipal politics for a chain of community newspapers.

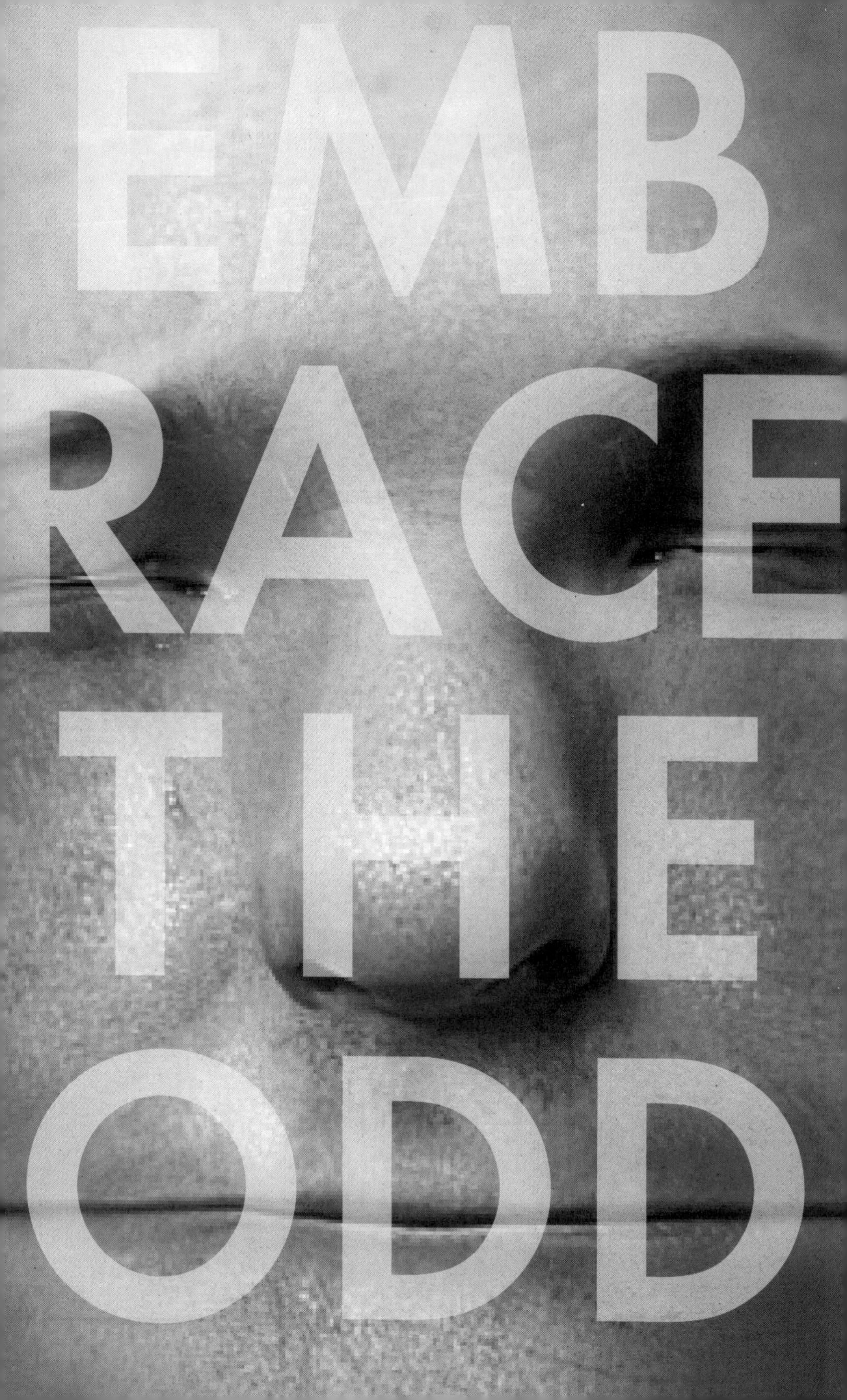

EMB
RACE
THE
ODD

SHOEBOX
TRAIN WRECK
JOHN MANTOOTH

CZP

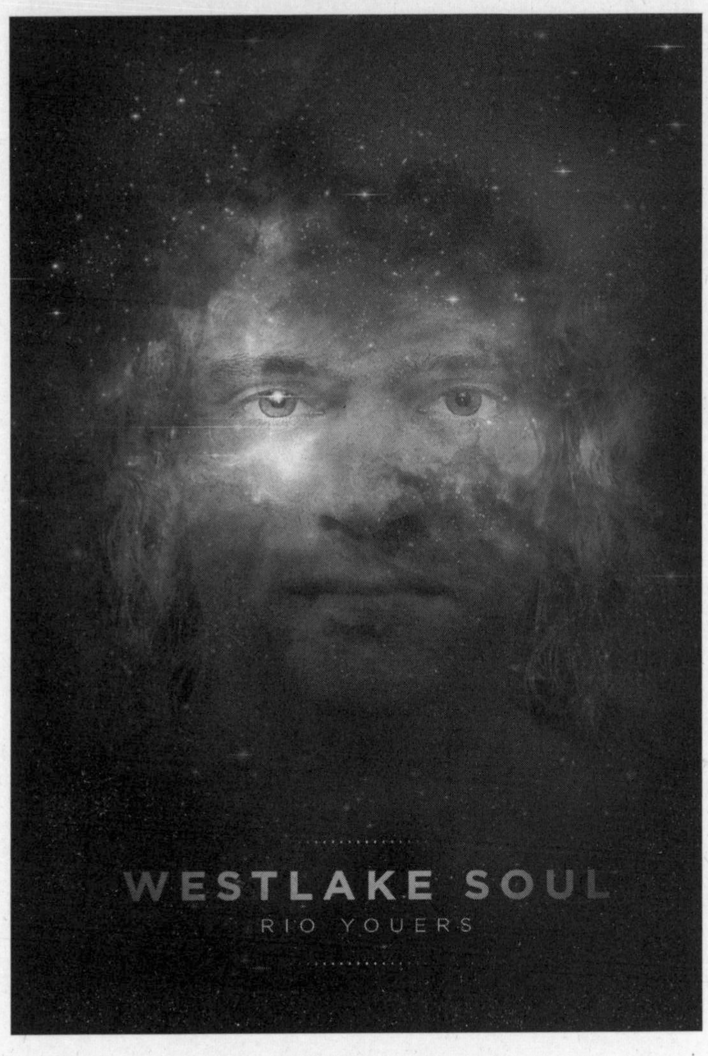
WESTLAKE SOUL
RIO YOUERS

CZP

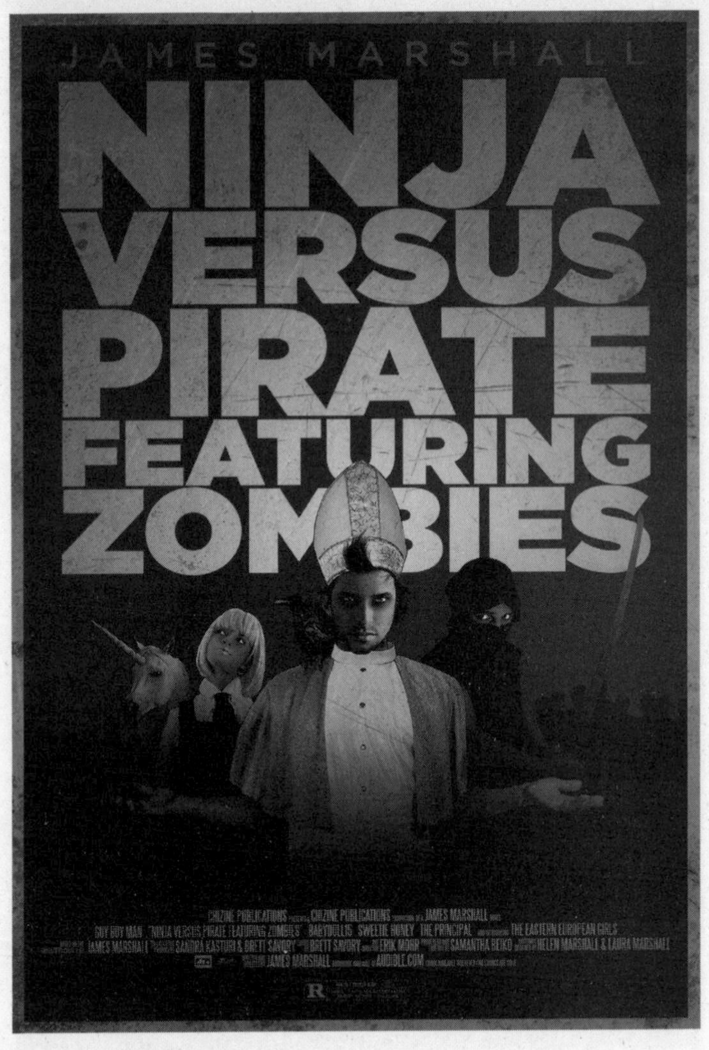

NINJA VERSUS PIRATE FEATURING ZOMBIES

JAMES MARSHALL

AVAILABLE MAY 2012
FROM CHIZINE PUBLICATIONS

978-1-926851-58-7

ALSO AVAILABLE FROM CHIZINE PUBLICATIONS

EDITED BY SANDRA KASTURI & HALLI VILLEGAS

INTRODUCTION BY STEVEN ERIKSON

WITH
KELLEY ARMSTRONG
CORY DOCTOROW
GEMMA FILES
SILVIA MORENO-GARCIA
DAVID NICKLE
GEOFF RYMAN
PETER WATTS
RIO YOUERS
AND MORE

the best canadian
speculative writing

IMAGINARIUM 2012:

THE BEST CANADIAN SPECULATIVE WRITING

EDITED BY SANDRA KASTURI & HALLI VILLEGAS

AVAILABLE JULY 2012
FROM CHIZINE PUBLICATIONS

978-0-926851-67-9

CHIZINEPUB.COM 

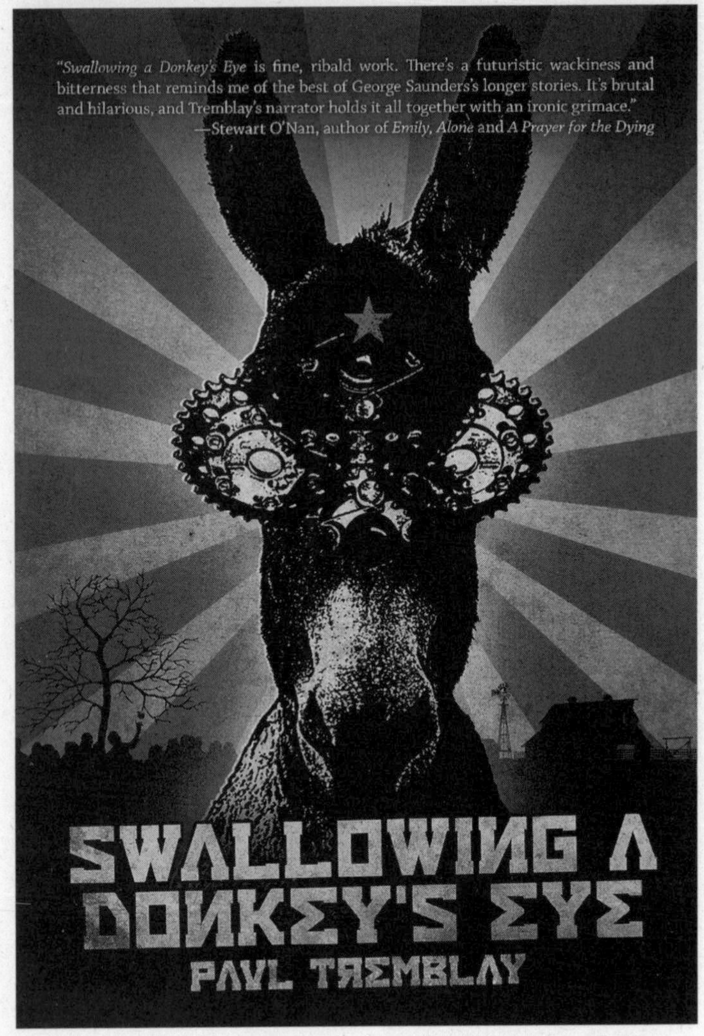

SWALLOWING A DONKEY'S EYE

PAUL TREMBLAY

AVAILABLE AUGUST 2012
FROM CHIZINE PUBLICATIONS

978-1-926851-69-3

CZP

978-1-926851-35-8

TONE MILAZZO

PICKING UP THE GHOST

978-1-926851-43-3

CAROLYN IVES GILMAN

ISLES OF THE FORSAKEN

978-1-926851-44-0

TIM PRATT

BRIARPATCH

978-1-926851-43-3

CAITLIN SWEET

THE PATTERN SCARS

978-1-926851-46-4

TERESA MILBRODT

BEARDED WOMEN

978-1-926851-45-7

MICHAEL ROWE

ENTER, NIGHT

"THE BEST WORK IN DARK FANTASY AND HORROR FICTION THESE DAYS IS BEING PUBLISHED BY SMALL PRESSES, HAUNTED LITERARY BOUTIQUES ESTABLISHED (MOSTLY) IN OUT-OF-THE-WAY PLACES, [INCLUDING] CHIZINE IN TORONTO. THEY'RE ALL DEVOTED TO THE WEIRD, TO THE STRANGE AND—MOST IMPORTANT—TO GOOD WRITING."

—DANA JENNINGS, THE NEW YORK TIMES

ALSO AVAILABLE FROM CHIZINE PUBLICATIONS

978-0-9813746-6-6

GORD ZAJAC

MAJOR KARNAGE

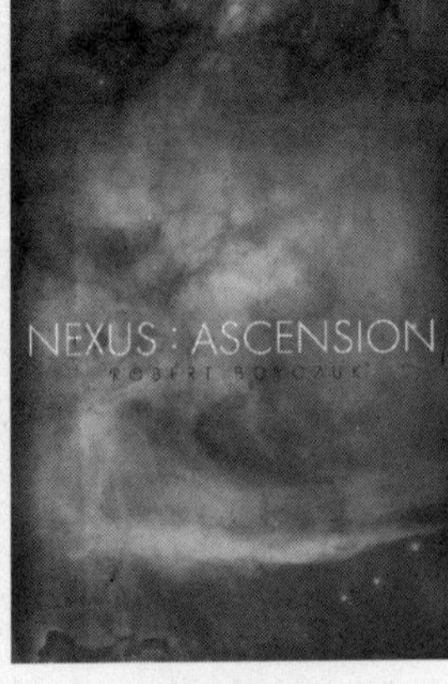

978-0-9813746-8-0

ROBERT BOYCZUK

NEXUS: ASCENSION

978-1-926851-00-6

CRAIG DAVIDSON

SARAH COURT

978-1-926851-06-8

PAUL TREMBLAY

IN THE MEAN TIME

978-1-926851-02-0

HALLI VILLEGAS

THE HAIR WREATH AND OTHER STORIES

978-1-926851-04-4

TONY BURGESS

PEOPLE LIVE STILL IN CASHTOWN CORNERS

"IF I COULD SUBSCRIBE TO A PUBLISHER LIKE A MAGAZINE OR A BOOK CLUB—ONE FLAT ANNUAL FEE TO GET EVERYTHING THEY PUBLISH—I WOULD SUBSCRIBE TO CHIZINE PUBLICATIONS."

—ROSE FOX, *PUBLISHERS WEEKLY*

ALSO AVAILABLE FROM CHIZINE PUBLICATIONS

978-0-9809410-9-8
ROBERT J. WIERSEMA

THE WORLD MORE FULL OF WEEPING

978-0-9812978-2-8
CLAUDE LALUMIÈRE

OBJECTS OF WORSHIP

978-0-9809410-7-4
DANIEL A. RABUZZI

THE CHOIR BOATS

978-0-9809410-5-0
LAVIE TIDHAR AND NIR YANIV

THE TEL AVIV DOSSIER

978-0-9809410-3-6
ROBERT BOYCZUK

HORROR STORY AND OTHER HORROR STORIES

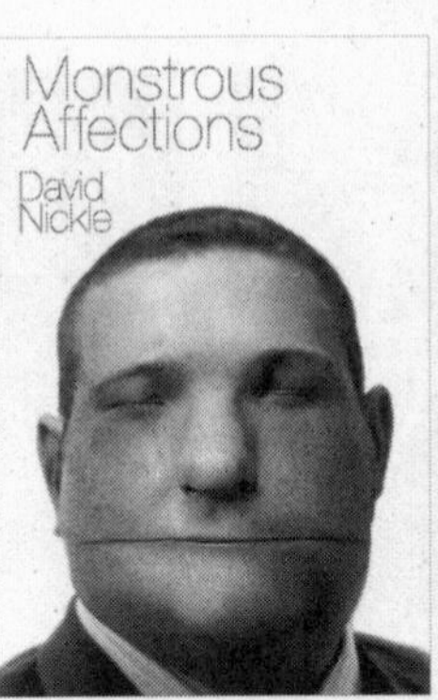

978-0-9812978-3-5
DAVID NICKLE

MONSTROUS AFFECTIONS

978-0-9809410-1-2
BRENT HAYWARD

FILARIA

"CHIZINE PUBLICATIONS REPRESENTS SOMETHING WHICH IS COMMON IN THE MUSIC INDUSTRY BUT SADLY RARER WITHIN THE PUBLISHING INDUSTRY: THAT A CLEVER INDEPENDENT CAN RUN RINGS ROUND THE MAJORS IN TERMS OF STYLE AND CONTENT."

—MARTIN LEWIS, *SF SITE*

ALSO AVAILABLE FROM CHIZINE PUBLICATIONS